MW00452883

VOLUMES

G.M. McGeorge

ISBN:
9781720136385:

I believe in epic love. I believe in happily ever afters. I believe in destiny, and I believe in soul mates. I believe in these things because I am living them.

For 45 years I carried around the first third of this book in my head. Looking back I think I needed to live my life in order to write about Sarah, as she was always a kickass 55 year old. She was always someone I wished I could be. I am working on it.

We all should be lucky enough to have a Sam. I am. I've been married to him for 43 years.

The first 25 chapters are taken from my 45 year old story then I just let Sam and Sarah's story lead me to their conclusion.

To my husband, my knight in shining armor, who ALWAYS believes in me, who ALWAYS loves me, and who ALWAYS makes my heart go pitty pat. Thank you for letting me experience this journey with you. It has been life changing. I love you more than lightning bugs.

To my daughters who encouraged me to start this process called writing. Without your encouragement and belief in me, this would never have happened. I am a lucky mom to have such amazing daughters, who also happen to be my best friends.

Julie ... you rock. A thank you for your sweet words, encouragement and hard work seems so inadequate. I love you.

To my fellow dancers, my co-workers and friends. Thank you all for listening to me talk about this for the last year. I know you all got sick of me.

Thank you to my Advanced Readers. Thank you for your honesty, and love, and good critique.

Finally. For all of you out there who have a head full of stories, don't waste as much time as I did with

PLAYLIST:

Respect: Aretha Franklin

When Love Runs Out: One Republic

Car Wheels on A Gravel Road: Lucinda Williams

Thinking Out Loud: Ed Sheeran

Fly Me to the Moon: Tony Bennett

Wicked Game: Chris Isaak

Howlin' For You: The Black Keys

Riviera Paradise/Lenny: Stevie Ray Vaughan

Fever: Peggy Lee

Have A Little Faith in Me: Jon Hiatt

My Funny Valentine: Linda Ronstadt

Natural Woman: Aretha Franklin

I'd Rather Go Blind: Beth Hart

A Song For: You: Leon Russell

La vie en Rose: Louis Armstrong

'O Sole Mio: Luciano Pavarotti

Bound To You: Christina Aguilera

Feels Like Rain: John Hiatt

Sometimes I Cry: Chris Stapleton

Birds: Neil Young

Baby Its You: Smith

Stardust: Frank Sinatra

The Dance: Garth Brooks

Moondance: Van Morrison

Fanfare for the Common Man: Aaron Copland

Perfect: Ed Sheeran

Need You Tonight: INXS

Cry Me A River: Julie London

Shape of You: Ed Sheeran

Bridge of Sighs: Robin Trower

At Last: Etta James

I Put A Spell On You: Annie Lennox

Feelin' Good: Nina Simone

Unforgettable: Nat King Cole

Reign O'er Me: The Who

January

Chapter 1:

Sarah stood at the window with her coffee cup in her hands, looking out at the creek. She took a sip and wondered what she was going to do with the rest of her day. The holidays were over and all of the decorations put away until next year. All of the children were gone, and the house was quiet. As Sarah wandered through the home that she and David had been so proud to build, she noticed everything that they had picked out together. All of the lighting, the baseboards and hardware. The family mementos and her photographs. It had been a labor of love over a thirty five year marriage. They had both worked hard to achieve that dream. David got to enjoy one Christmas in the farmhouse that they loved. Then he was gone. An aneurysm had been a silent monster.

There was the master bedroom and en suite downstairs, with four bedrooms and two baths upstairs. It was a house big enough for all of their family to stay as long as they wanted. A room just for Sarah to have for her photography. David had insisted. He knew how important it was for her to have her space. Now, it was just hers. Sarah slowly shook her head. David had been gone for four years - and she missed him every day - but she had overcome the mind numbing grief and loneliness that was her life the first year after his death. She had wallowed in self pity for that first year, and then she had started rebuilding her life. Her life without her husband.

Maybe it was just the weather or the letdown after the holidays; it was quiet; she was a mix of melancholy and nerves.

"Snap out of it, Sarah!" she said out loud.

Sarah normally loved the winter. She loved all of the seasons, so she didn't think she suffered from any kind of seasonal disorder. She just suffered from Sarah disorder. It would be good to see the girls this evening at her photography class, and even better to have their monthly get together for cocktails and trash talking. It would do her good. The girls had been her saving grace after David's death. She was the oldest person in the class, and the only widow, but the girls had taken her under their collective wings and enveloped her with love and compassion, all the while plying her with alcohol and laughter. They were filthy, obnoxious, and wonderful. Over the last few years the roles had reversed, and Sarah had become a mother figure and sounding board. She had offered advice through breakups and health scares. Through business ventures and divorces.

She always tended to gravitate toward younger people. Sarah liked their energy and optimism, and they always kept her up to date with new music and apps. It used to drive David crazy when he walked in the house after work to hear Kanye West blaring from the stereo. He was such a rock – and - roll snob. He really hated the modern sound, but he loved her, so he would just sigh with a big grin on his face and watch Sarah dance to One Republic. Sometimes she would surprise him. She would prepare a gourmet meal, filling the house with delicious smells, and meet him at the door with nothing on but an apron. Tony Bennett or Frank Sinatra would be singing and he would drop everything to slowly dance her around the floor. They never made it through the entire song, as the apron would always be untied from around her neck, just to be picked up from the middle of the floor later. They would eat their gourmet meal on paper plates in bed. They had been high school sweethearts, and they proved to everyone that it could work. They had a good marriage. They truly had fun with each other and enjoyed each other's company. They had raised 3 strong, independent and hilarious daughters who were their best friends. Life had been so good. Sarah sighed again and then said "No! No! No! What the hell is wrong with you? Enough of this shit." She turned back to the kitchen to pour another cup of coffee and make a grocery list. She could go into town early for groceries and errands before going on to class.

She sat at the kitchen island and started planning her day.

~~~

Hours later, the girls were sitting around Bev's dining table with stacks of glossy photographs strewn about. Bev Collins was in her late 30's and had the biggest house of the group, thanks to her ex-husband doing the horizontal bop with his secretary. Bev took him to the cleaners. Literally. She picked up his suits and shirts at the cleaners, burned them in the fireplace and promptly got the best divorce attorney in the state. She got the house, the cars and the retirement account. She also got a nice monthly check from her ex. She had never looked back with any sorrow or malice. Bev had a big heart and chose to live life large. Large blonde hair and large boobs. All paid for by her ex-husband, "the attorney." That's what she called him. "The attorney." Bev was similar to Sarah, in that she was a nurturer with a heart of gold. She was a hugger and a kisser. She was what they liked to call "good people."

Ashley Grey was in the kitchen mixing up the cocktails of the evening. The drink of the evening was some kind of hot toddy due to the cold weather. Ashley was a raven- haired, thirty five year old, single nurse practitioner who was great at her job, and even better at mixing alcoholic concoctions. Sarah had always thought that Ashley must have been a bartender or a man in her former life, what with her gift of mixing and swearing. Ashley could make a sailor blush and had no problem with having no filter. Her job was her priority. Not a husband or children. She didn't want a relationship at this point in her life, but she had several "friends with benefits." She liked to tell the girls to "pump 'em, hump 'em, and say goodbye."

Sitting at the table with Sarah was Karen Hall, a thirty–year-old red head who was a happily married mother of three children. Karen had gotten lucky like Sarah had, and was married to a good man. All of the girls in their group loved Jack. He loved that Karen had outside interests because it made her happy. When Karen was happy, she tended to be very creative in the bedroom. They all thought that Karen and Jack should have at least 6 children, because Karen was usually happy. She was listening to a filthy story told by Julie Campbell, laughing loudly, and snorting.

Julie was a thirty-two-year old brunette pursuing her Doctorate in English Studies. Julie was a tall, thin, reed of a woman who looked like a stereotypical librarian. She even had the glasses. Then she would open her mouth. Sarah had never heard anyone who had so many dirty, filthy stories. Julie always kept them in stitches. She had just been dumped by her boyfriend of 7 years. He had told her that they just weren't "progressing" like he thought they should. Instead of heartbreak, Julie was actually quite relieved. She had told them that she would never have to "pick his fucking underwear and socks up off the floor again." She was also content to eat cereal for supper any night of the week she wanted, and to go to bed when she wanted, and to wear her pajamas until noon if she wanted. Julie definitely enjoyed her newfound freedom.

Interrupting Julie's filthy tale with a "What the fuck?" was Liz Stotler. She was a forty six year old curvy, petite brunette, she was the closest to Sarah in age. Liz owned a thriving gift shop in town- and had been divorced for twenty years. Her life and her business were all her own doing. She had worked hard to raise good kids, and to make her shop a success. She was Sarah's go-to person for honest and loving advice.

Sarah sat back in her chair quietly studying the faces that she loved so much. All of them had drunk several cocktails by now, and they were all talking over each other. Sarah was enveloped in a cocoon of thankfulness. Her farmhouse was the farthest from town, and she had been known to pack a bag and stay the night if Ashley's cocktails were particularly yummy and she over- imbibed. Tonight was just what she needed, even though she still felt that restless melancholy. Who better to get her over this hump than the girls?

"Sarah!" Julie yelled. "Are you here tonight or what? You didn't even hear me talking about the cowboy and his wanker. And it was a great story!"

"I'm so sorry, Julie," Sarah said truthfully. "I'm just a little weird tonight. I don't know what's wrong with me. You could always tell it again."

"Nah. I've got plenty where that came from, but are you okay?"

"Is there anything in particular you need from us?" Liz asked with concern.

Sarah smiled contentedly and said "You all are giving me exactly what I need right now."

Julie squealed loudly. "I know what we *all* need! We need naked men! And because we don't have any handy, the next best thing is....pictures!" She picked up a bag off the floor and dumped a huge pile of glossy eight by tens on the table. She said very seriously "Sex and pecs, ladies! Sex and pecs! We *have* been studying the male form with differing shadow and light techniques. So we should just consider this part of our homework."

"Where in the hell did you get all of these naked men... and can I keep some?" asked Bev.

"Google images." Julie replied. "You can find anything on Google images. Did you know that you can even find gigantic plaid dildos? Different strokes for different folks. Did you see what I did there? Different strokes for different folks! Haaaahhhh!" They all just stared at her while trying to keep from laughing. "It's true," she said quietly while pretending to be embarrassed. "You can find anything."

After catching their breath from the laughter, they dove for the pile of glossy nakedness in the middle of the table. They looked like a family of ten going for the last grilled cheese sandwich. The dirty remarks dwindled, as they all took their time looking at the different techniques, and lighting, trying to guess what type of filter and shutter speed the photographer had used. Sarah had picked up a handful of the photos and was studying them quietly. The last one caught her eye. She studied it with her mouth hanging open and blurted "Holy mother of God! He is perfect. I need a cigarette just looking at him. This right here is a righteous panty melter."

The rest of the girls quickly huddled around and the room got eerily quiet. That's how the man's incredible beauty affected everyone. It was like being in church. First they wanted to scream "Hallelujah", but then they wanted to whisper about the work of art that looked like one of Michelangelo's creations.

The model was not an androgynous, wafer- thin stick that the modeling world liked to use. He was definitely all man. Black hair, black stubble, ice blue eyes. That combination by itself was eye catching, but what was even more breathtaking was the fact that he was just so *symmetrical*. The eyes were placed perfectly, as was the nose and, oh my God, that mouth! He was not big, nor was he thin. He wasn't thick. He had a small waist that would look fabulous in a suit. His muscles were sharply defined, as were the angles of his face. The chest was defined with beautiful biceps and triceps. His broad shoulders made Sarah want to cry. A phenomenal six pack leading to the hottest "V" Sarah had ever seen, where his abdominal muscles met his hip flexors. You could melt butter on those obliques. This man had no body fat. He had taken very, very good care of himself. Some men concentrated on their upper body and forgot about their body below the waist. This man had not, His thighs and calves were developed with thick muscles, and even his feet were, well, just perfect. Not forgetting the fact that he was naked, his ass was tight and well rounded and even his manhood was perfect. Not too big, not too small. The dangling participle, too, was perfect.

As beautiful as his body was, Sarah was engrossed in the face. The angles, the light and shadow, and, oh my God, those eyes! It stayed very quiet for a few minutes as all of the girls just stared at this most perfect specimen of manhood.

"My God" Bev whispered. "That's pure perfection right there."

"I've never seen anything like that in my life. Fuck." whispered Liz.

Julie just stood up and said "Boy! Would I love to break that stallion! I'd wear assless chaps and spurs to tap that!"

Sarah slowly lifted her head and said "I know, right? I didn't think there was such a thing as pure perfection, but that right there is pure perfection. Do you mind if I take this Julie?"

Julie shook her head and said "Take it. Enjoy it. He's probably a narcissistic dick and he probably with the brain of a bowl of soup anyway. And if I want to see him again I can just go -"

"We know!" they all said in unison. "Google!

~~~

Sarah had been home for an hour. She had turned off the lights, and locked the doors. As she was making her way to the shower, the picture caught her eye. She had laid it on the bed with her coat and gloves when she got home. She picked it up and stared at it again. All she could say was "Wow." Her stomach did a little flip flop. "Get a grip Sarah," she muttered. It was

beginning to piss her off. She threw the picture back on the bed, and made her way to the shower. As Sarah was washing her hair her mind wandered back to the glossy that was laying on her bed. As Sarah was washing her arms and legs and brushing her teeth, her mind, again, wandered back to that damn picture on her bed. She thought to herself, "Damn! You stupid old woman! Have you turned into a horny, lonely woman who has to look at pictures to get off?" She shook her head and dried off, thinking about the few times she had pleasured herself since David's death. There was something terribly sad about coming and crying. She'd had plenty of men asking for dates, but she kept herself busy with the classes, and her flower and vegetable gardens. The upkeep on an eighty five acre farm was sometimes daunting in the summer months, but it was her therapy. She wasn't interested in dating.

Traveling to see the kids was always a pleasure. She usually drove, as it created so many opportunities for more shots. She was going to start making preparations for a trip to Venice and Italy. It had been her and David's life long dream, and her husband would want her to go. She was a little terrified and excited to go alone, but after David's death, she could do anything. She was woman, hear her roar. They had traveled to Europe, Asia, Mexico and Canada, so Sarah wanted to finish her "bucket list."

David's death had allowed her to retire. She had bitterly laughed about the fact that she was better off financially since his death than she had been when he was alive. She could pretty much do what, where and with whomever she wanted, but she would rather be poor. With her husband. She had discussed dating again with the girls, but the mere word "dating" made her a little sick to her stomach.

She looked in the mirror and saw a fifty- five- year- old woman. Honestly, she wasn't too bad. People would guess her to be in her forties. She was lucky to have been blessed with good skin and good moisturizer. She was tall at five ten. She had stretch marks from pregnancies. Her boobs were good and were still where they were supposed to be. A solid E cup, she couldn't complain. She had laugh lines on her forehead and around her mouth and eyes. They didn't bother her, as she felt as if she had earned every single one of them. And a face that reflected a life of laughter was a gift. On a good day she was a size fourteen. Hey, she had a booty and boobs! But she ate healthy, and was an active person.

She hiked the farm frequently, and she took care of herself. She had striking blue eyes with black eyelashes and short, spiky hair. She kept her hair short because she hated messing with it, and it tended to do whatever it wanted. She had always had long hair, but she never regretted the day she had it all cut off. This month's color of choice was purple. Not a glaring, in-your-face purple, but in the right light it was purple. Sarah most certainly did not have hair vanity.

She was sure she dressed too young for her age, whatever that meant, but she wore what she liked. Leggings, T- shirts and boots were her dress of choice. When she found a good shot, it made it easier to not have to worry about grass stains or mooning someone. She could lay on the ground, or a bench, or a car, to get the right angle, and getting off the ground was much easier than it would be wearing support hose and a girdle. "God!", she thought. "Do they still make girdles? Spanx! Spanx were what the old ladies wore nowadays. She would *never* wear Spanx. But she also loved getting really dolled up for a special event and feeling girly. A fancy dress, dramatic makeup, and stiletto heels. But those days were few and far between. David had enjoyed her in nothing *but* her heels.

Death and aging had a certain way of making her not give a fuck about what she wore or what anyone had to say. Yep. Aging did not bother her at all. As she couldn't change it, she might as well embrace it. And she did. But she was lonely for a man. Not an unknown man, or a perfect man, like the man in the picture, but *her* man. She missed David. She missed his voice, his smell, the feel of his hands on her body, and his stupid, horrible jokes. Just David to have a conversation with and a hug at the end of the day. Just David.

Sarah hung up her coat, and picked up the picture of the perfect man, laying him on her bedside table. She picked up her Kindle, and crawled between the sheets. She always read at least two chapters before calling it a night. But tonight she went to Google images to do a little investigative work on the unknown perfect man. She really wanted to see some different shots of him in different light and different poses, naked or not. Hey! If she couldn't find any more shots of Mr. Perfect, she could always find a giant plaid dildo. It would give her and Julie something to discuss at their next get- together.

She scrolled. Then she scrolled some more. As Sarah was about to give up and call it a night, *he* popped up on the screen. Mr. Perfect. The thumbnail asked if she would like to visit his page. "Hell, yeah!" she muttered excitedly, but she decided to get the laptop open to observe bigger pictures. Rapidly scrolling to get to the right site, Sarah quickly clicked the link and gasped out loud. Hundreds of pictures of Mr. Perfect. Hundreds. And, yeah, he *was* Mr. Perfect. Not a single bad shot. Not a single one. After reading the descriptions, Sarah realized that she had seen this man in an ad campaign on television a few years back. She usually didn't pay much attention to film or ads. Her preference was still shots, not active ones. But this campaign she remembered. Shot after shot, she stared at that face. Any angle. Color. Black and white. Glaring. Intense. A few smiling. The camera made love to him like a dick to a porn star.

Sarah was mesmerized. Picture after picture…. But something began bothering her. There was just something that she couldn't put her finger on. Yes, he was undeniably beautiful. Yes, he was a camera whore. But there was just something. She finally realized what it was. None of his scowls, or his intense stares at the camera could hide the fact that he had some of the saddest eyes she had ever seen. Sarah knew sad eyes. She was looking at her own eyes in his photos.

They were her eyes the year after David died. A foggy, lost kind of look. No one else would notice the sadness, because of the pure beauty of his face. No one would notice if they hadn't experienced pain in their own life. Sarah knew what wanting something you couldn't have looked like. What needing looked like. Sarah and Mr. Perfect were kindred spirits in pain or loneliness. Perhaps both.

"What the hell could he be sad about?" Sarah asked herself. The older photos of him as a fresh faced teen didn't show the pain, but the later ones sure did. It was a given that he had fancy cars, big houses and probably freakin' ponies and a carousel in the back yard. Sarah was sure that he could have a woman anytime and anywhere he wanted. "Hell, all he would have to do is snap his fingers, and any female on the planet would have moist panties. They'd probably do him in the middle of Times Square."

Exotic travel, private jets and freakin' ponies. Sarah was pretty sure that he experienced all of that. How likely could it be that she would ever see him much less meet him? And if she did, Mr. Perfect would think her a love starved crazy person. Sarah continued looking at him and his sad eyes. She thought that a life based on just your looks would be terribly empty. Granted, it would be fine for a while, but beauty fades, and then what? At this stage in Sarah's life, she knew that friends, family and home were life's most precious gifts.

Did Mr. Perfect have family who loved him? Children? A wife? A husband? A special woman or man who adored him for himself, and not just the way he looked? Did he have a quiet place where he could just be? Could he go to the grocery store? Or the movies? Had he lost himself somewhere in the "persona?" Mr. Perfect had evidently been modeling for a while, as there were hundreds of pictures of him as a fresh faced youngster as well. Today's face was much more striking. More angular, with more character. More everything. He had a scar on his chin. How did he get it? Childhood accident? "He probably got cut in a sword fight," Sarah chuckled to herself. Did Mr. Perfect even know how to *not* pose? Did he even know who he was? Or who he used to be? He surely didn't pop out of the uterus looking like that. He had to have been a bed wetter, had pimples and gangly legs (as he looked really tall), and wet dreams at some point in his life. As silly as she knew it sounded, Sarah thought that being that beautiful would have to be a difficult and tiring cross to bear. She said out loud to the computer screen "Okay, Sarah, you have officially become a silent stalker. Say goodnight."

She powered off, turned off the light and dreamt of sad, ice blue eyes.

Chapter 2:

Slumber party! The girls were at Sarah's house this month and had brought their overnight bags. A fire was blazing, and Sarah had homemade chicken and dumplings simmering on the stove, with bread in the oven. It was still cold and overcast, and the weather had put pretty much everyone in a foul mood. Sarah had decided that comfort food and lots of alcohol were just what the doctor ordered. She had even kept Ashley out of the kitchen. No mixology for her tonight. A night like tonight demanded good Scotch. So Lagavulin it would be.

Everyone's mood had lightened when they walked in. The smells were heavenly. How could the smell of baking bread not make your mouth water and put you in a better mood? The girls were stretched out in front of the fire, anticipating the hot bowls of yumminess that would soon arrive. Sarah loved the sleepovers at her house. She missed having someone to cook for, so she usually went a little crazy when the girls were at her place. She filled everyone's glasses with two fingers of the golden, oaky Scotch and settled down next to Bev to enjoy the debauchery and sex talk that usually occurred. Everyone was chatty, and Julie's story about putting duct tape on an ex-boyfriends ass cheeks had them crying with laughter.

Liz spoke up by saying "Speaking of asses, has anyone seen an ass as good as the ass of that perfect hunk of man that Sarah found in the pile of pictures last month? Do you still have that picture, Sarah? Or have you worn it out by rubbing it on your naughty bits?"

"Liz!" Sarah said sharply. "I have *not* rubbed it on my naughty bits, and yes, I still have it. Why? Do you need it for *your* naughty bits?"

Liz laughed and then got serious and said "My naughty bits are just fine, but I have found myself thinking about that hunk of masculinity a few times. He's just so perfect." And then she sighed. " I wonder who he is? Or what he does? Is he a doctor? Does he do house calls? I would love to play doctor with him and my naughty bits could always do with a house call."

Everyone chimed in with the same thoughts. About picturing him in all of his glorious manhood, and wondering who he was. And the numerous comments about the love the camera had for him. Their comments actually made Sarah feel better, as she had been concerned that she was turning into a horny psychopath. She actually knew who he was, but she felt a little embarrassed about letting the rest of the girls know that she had researched Mr. Perfect.

She stood up to go take the bread out of the oven and said quietly "I know who he is and where he's from."

She continued walking into the kitchen. The next thing she heard was all of them squealing and jumping up to follow her. "Shit!" she muttered. "They're going to think I'm nuts."

"Who is he?" they all squealed. "Who is he? Is he married? Is he Italian? He looks Italian or Spanish with that dark hair."

Julie smirked "Oooh I would love for him to say sweet nothings in Italian as he's licking my belly button." They sounded like a bunch of school girls.

And then....Julie asked. "How do you know who he is?"

Sarah sighed as she took the bread out of the oven, and got bowls out of the cabinet. She continued talking as she spooned out their dumplings and set them on the kitchen island. "His name is Sam Ramsay, and he's from London. He's a Brit."

Everyone found a chair to sit in, and pulled their bowls up. Sarah refilled everyone's glasses and started slicing the hot, yeasty bread. "He's been modeling since he was eighteen years old. He's now forty. He's been the number one male model in the world for more than twenty years. He did that ad campaign for Oak Wood a few years ago."

Bev smeared butter on her hot bread, took a huge bite, and said. "I remember that campaign! How do you know this? *Why* do you know this?"

Again, Sarah sighed. This was the hard part. She really didn't know why she had become obsessed with Sam Ramsay. She felt like a twelve-year-old who had experienced lust for the first time over a rock star. Except, it wasn't lust. It should have been, and no doubt, it would be hard to say no to a panty melter like Mr. Ramsay, but, no, it was something more. So, because Sarah didn't know, she told the girls she didn't know. "It's the eyes" Sarah sighed. "He has sad eyes. And I know sadness when I see it."

Everyone grew quiet, as Sarah continued. "They make me sad. They make me want something for him, something that he probably doesn't even know he wants. I certainly don't know. He needs touching and comfort. I feel like he needs someone to take care of him, if even for a little while. I feel like that's what he *needs.* There's just something about..." she trailed off. "... those damn eyes! And it's driving me crazy."

"I'd like to do more than touch him," Ashley said quietly.

Sarah continued "Seriously, it's not so much a lust thing, as he's way too young. And it's not like any of us would ever even meet the man, much less have a chance to jump his bones. But Mr. Perfect has wiggled his way into my brain, and I just can't let it go. Arghhhh! I just don't know!"

Julie jumped and clapped her hands." You should go to London and try to find him!"

Liz excitedly said "Ooooh! That's a really good idea, Sarah!. And if you cann't find him, just think of all the great pictures you could take! The double decker buses, Big Ben, The Tower of London, and those funky red telephone booths. I wonder if they still have those?"

Ashley chimed in. "Oh! You could always take a side trip to Scotland. Hey you might get lucky and bang a Scotsman in a kilt. They don't wear underwear under those things you know."

"I've always wanted to play Snooker with a British man," Julie said, completely deadpan.

They all turned and looked at her for a moment before breaking out in hysterics.

"And then what?" asked Sarah after catching her breath. "Tie him up and bring him home? There is no earthly reason for me to go to London. And there is absolutely no way I could *find* him to even get close enough to him to tell him that he has sad eyes. He would think I was nuts. And I guess I am. Anyway, Liz, let's talk about that wedding that you're in the middle of. Do you need any help?"

The subject changed, the girls moved back to the fireplace, and they all continued with the scotch and fixing the world's problems.

Sarah went to bed and dreamt about her life in London and screwing Mr. Perfect in a red telephone booth.

~~~

Sarah had fixed mimosas and a big breakfast for the girls the next morning before saying goodbye. She turned and started picking up the glasses and bedding. Her day would be busy with cleaning, and she needed to go into town for some errands. She needed wood, and the truck needed an oil change. She was humming as she started her tasks, and suddenly she realized that her restless melancholy was gone. The comfort of good friends had done her a world of good. Comfort from what, she wasn't sure, but it had worked.

Sarah gave her daughters a call, and chatted with each of them for forty-five minutes. They were the only people that Sarah could stay on the phone with that long. She preferred to text, but those girls always had her laughing so hard that she enjoyed the weekly calls. She promised each of them a visit later in the summer and was truly looking forward to it. They were her favorite people.

She changed her clothes, put on some makeup and pulled her boots on before leaving for town. The guys at her local garage got her truck right in for the oil change, so Sarah walked across the street to a coffee shop to kill the thirty minutes. She ordered a large black coffee and opened her Kindle. As she was reading the news items an advertisement caught her eye. They were promoting a street carnival on the riverfront in St. Louis in two weeks. Sarah thought that might be a perfect road trip. St. Louis was just a couple of hours away, and a carnival had immense possibilities for some excellent pictures. She could rent a room and make a weekend of it. She would check that out when she got home. Yeah! She had a plan.

Before picking up her wood, Sarah thought she would stop by Liz's shop to see if she needed any help with the big wedding preparations she'd had been hired for. Sarah wasn't crafty, but she was an excellent gofer. As expected, Liz was up to her ass and elbows in ribbon, colored cellophane and party favors. She was thrilled to see Sarah, and she put her to work immediately filling candy boxes with M&M's. They talked as they worked, passing the time quickly. Out of the blue, Liz stopped and looked at Sarah, asking "Does he have a Facebook page?"

Sarah stopped tying tiny bows and asked "Does who have a Facebook page?"

"You know damn good and well who I mean! Sam Ramsay!"

"Oh for God's sake, Liz! I have no idea!"

Liz shrugged her shoulders, and bent back over the basket she was working on. "I think you need to check it out."

"I have no idea why I would need to "check it out", and even if he did, what in the hell would I say? I'm also sure that he has a "person" who takes care of that stuff. He wouldn't personally post, or read his Facebook page. If he even has one." Sarah shrugged her shoulders right back at Liz, and gave her a glare.

Liz just looked at her and said "Okay. Whatever. But I still think you should. You have an itch that you need to scratch, Sarah. I can feel it rolling off of you in big itchy waves. I don't know what it means, but you need to pursue this. Something about this guy has gotten under your skin. You are one of the strongest, most sensible people I have ever met, and I have never seen you like this. I'm just saying. I love you, and I'll shut up now."

Sarah just shook her head and continued tying tiny bows.

~~~

Sarah got home later than she had planned, and she still had to unload the wood. She put on her gloves and got to work stacking it in the corral by the back door. After an hour of grunting, sweating, cursing and hurting, the task was done. Sarah was looking very forward to a long soak in a tub full of hot water and bubbles. She thought to herself that the next time she might take Mike up on his offer to deliver it and stack it for her, as she was getting to old for heavy, manual labor. She just didn't want to have to go out with him to get it done. She'd rather just pay him for services rendered with a check, and not boot bumping.

Sarah went in the house and washed up. She made a peanut butter and jelly sandwich and poured herself a glass of milk. She sat at the kitchen island and tiredly ate her sandwich, thinking about what Liz had said. Sarah still thought that Liz was crazy, and besides, she had a weekend in St. Louis to plan. Getting up, she made her way to the bathroom, where she ran a very hot bath with extra bubbles. She turned her Spotify on Billie Holiday and soaked for a good, long while.

After slipping on her underwear and one of David's old tee shirts, Sarah crawled under the covers with her laptop and a glass of whiskey. She did some price shopping, and made her reservations at the motel in St. Louis for Friday and Saturday night. With that completed, she logged onto her Facebook page. She spent a little time enjoying the pictures and cartoons, and responding to friends' posts.

Without even really thinking about what she was doing, she typed Sam Ramsay's name in the Facebook search engine. The first listing was "The Official Sam Ramsay." "Well," thought Sarah, "that's a little intimidating. He has an *official* Facebook page. La-ti-dah." She clicked on it and was staring at the face of Mr. Perfect. Sarah spent some time scrolling through all of his pictures, his posts, and a few videos. He was a busy, busy boy. He had been in Italy the week before, and was now in France, He would be in Canada next week, and the States the week after that. "Good Lord," thought Sarah. "I'd have sad eyes, too. I'd be worn out."

He was everywhere. Orphanages, benefits, cancer research fundraisers. Red carpet galas and premieres. He was pictured with celebrities and movie stars. Lots of women. Vacations on the Riviera, Thailand, and Italy. There were even pictures with him and his dog. Sarah had not seen any pictures with him and his damn ponies, but she was sure that they were somewhere. This man was living the Hollywood - or in his case- the London lifestyle. This man lived on a different planet than she lived. He lived in a different universe. It was like seeing someone from a book or a movie.

The one thing missing was Mr. Perfect and a steady relationship. She had only seen pictures of him and the same woman a few times. He was either gay, a man-whore or very, very private. Sarah had seen an interview on YouTube where he stated that he was straight, and he would have no reason to lie, so she figured he was just a horn dog. She couldn't find any scandal, or unkind words from anyone. You'd think one of the millions of women he had slept with would complain about *something*.

21

She scrolled back up to the comments section and stared at the screen. She started to type, but then stopped. "What the hell am I doing? No one will even see my comment, much less respond. And what in the hell could I write that wouldn't get the men with straight jackets after me ?"

Sarah froze with her fingers on the keyboard. The more she thought about it, the more she thought that she just might. Yes. She would write something. Because, as she had thought earlier, who the hell would even see it, except the hordes of girls who had posted about wanting to have his baby, or how beautiful he was. Or did he wake up looking like that. Or that they were available anytime he wanted. "Fuck! Have a little self- respect!" She could give a shit what they thought. They were just little girls. But Sarah was a grown ass woman, and she was going to write a fan letter. Kind of. Sarah took a deep breath and typed:

Mr. Ramsay: You do not know me, nor do I know you, except what I know of you in your pictures. And the you that is presented on your Facebook page, The OFFICIAL Sam Ramsay, and your Instagram account, that would be me, and 500,000 other people on this earth. I'm a photography nut from the middle of the United States, and the first thing I would like to say, is that you have a perfect face for the camera, and I would love to photograph you. But, I won't say that. I would like to say that you are one of the most beautifully symmetrical people I have ever seen, but I won't. I would like to say that you harken back to the era of Steve McQueen and Paul Newman. A man's man. But I won't. I won't say those things, because I am absolutely certain that you hear that all day, every day. Does that ever get

tiresome? For people to only see you for your face, your blue eyes and your body? (Which are all works of art by the way) Does anyone ever talk to you about sports? Or what you might think of politics? Or how you might feel about something other than your looks, fashion, or your workout routine? Do you even remember how to go about your day without posing? Have you lost yourself? Have you forgotten who you are? Are you lonely for just good conversation that doesn't revolve around your looks? Before I comment further, let me state that I am not intending this to be mean or angry. It is not a proposition and I am not a crazy fan. Though, I will admit that I am a fan of the way the camera loves you. Do you ever crave quiet? Solace? I might have it totally wrong, as you might REALLY love yourself and all of the hoopla and jet setting. You might be a complete narcissistic ass, but I don't think so. I look at you and see sadness in your eyes. A wanting. A needing. I know what it feels like to want something so bad it physically hurts. A need for something you can never have. My heart hurts for you and I don't know why. I have never written a fan letter in my life, and I feel totally stupid for writing these comments, but I have become obsessed with my heartache for you. I thought that writing these thoughts down, might get it out of my system and put my mind at ease. See what I just did? I've made this post all about me! What a weasel I am! Anyway, forget all the above words, as I'm sure you think I'm just a crazy cat lady who wants your body. By the way, I don't have a cat.

Before Sarah could change her mind, she hit enter and slammed the computer shut. "There! Are you happy now, Liz?" For some reason, writing the words did not help the obsession, as she tossed and turned all night thinking about sad, blue eyes.

February

Chapter 3:

The next two weeks thankfully flew by for Sarah. She was looking forward to her road trip to St. Louis. She always enjoyed the drive through the brown fields that had been wheat and maize and corn. Even the Interstate in Missouri was scenic. A good mixture of farms, small towns and big cities. The truck was loaded with her camera equipment and a change of clothes. Friday morning. 8:00 AM and she was ready to go. It would only take her a couple of hours to get to the city, and she couldn't check in to the motel before 3:00. But you never knew what or where pictures could be waiting. She also wanted to get down to the riverfront today for some quiet shots before the carnival tomorrow. She plugged her phone into the truck stereo, found Stevie Ray Vaughan on her playlist and turned it up loud. As she looked into her rearview she saw: a girl in a truck leaving dust on the gravel road. Sarah laughed out loud and sang "if the house Is a rockin', don't bother knockin......"

Three hours later, Sarah had parked the truck in the garage across from Busch Stadium. She unloaded her cameras and lenses and walked across the street to take pictures of the St. Louis Cardinals ball field. It always looked so different in the off season. It was strangely quiet, with no sea of red shirted fans enjoying a game. The quiet stadium in February had its own strange beauty. After snapping pictures around the stadium for an hour, she made her way to the Old Courthouse, and snapped some more of the beautiful old building. After one trip up and down Market Street snapping pictures of the store fronts and facades, Sarah made her way to the St. Louis Arch and the riverfront. It was quiet there, too. Most of the locals were still at work, and the February chill had kept visitors inside. The Gateway to the West Arch stood proudly erect overlooking the Mighty Mississippi. Friday afternoon had turned into a perfect opportunity to be left alone with just herself, her thoughts and her lens.

She took shots of the Arch, the river, and some great shots of a family who had ventured out with their children. The children were so bundled up they looked like snowmen. After asking permission, Sarah proceeded to catch some great moments. The big brother with his arm around his sister. The mom kissing the little one on her nose. Sarah hated posed pictures. Well, most of them. Mr. Perfect posed very well. Very well indeed. After getting the parents address, Sarah promised to mail them copies of the pictures. Digging a bottle of water and an orange out of her backpack, she found a bench to sit on and enjoy. She had noticed a lot of people and equipment earlier. They were set up between the Arch and river and were scurrying around like squirrels after nuts. Sarah just grinned and continued sitting. She figured that someone was taking photos for the *City of St. Louis Magazine.* A Blue Heron caught her eye. He was flying over the river looking for supper. Back and forth. Back and forth. Sarah stood and started trying to digitally catch his action. Across the dried, brown grass she stalked the bird like a lion in the jungle. Sarah backed up to catch him as he was flying away. Bam! Sarah had backed into a large solid wall of concrete. Twisting her ankle, she fell to the ground with a loud "Hmmppff!"

A menacing voice from somewhere above her growled "What the hell are you doing with that camera?"

Twisting her head, and trying to ignore the pain in her ankle, Sarah realized that the "wall" she had backed into was a very large man with a very large scowl on his face. He was mad. He was mad at her.

"What the hell??" snapped Sarah. "I'm just taking pictures. Did you not *see* me? I sure as hell didn't see you, as my *back* was to you, you ignorant oaf! Do you think you could help me up?"

The man hesitated for a minute, like he really didn't want to help her, which pissed Sarah off even more. "Hey! A little help here!" she shouted.

Finally! He held out his arm and helped her up. That arm was as big as a tree trunk. Sarah proceeded to limp her way to the bench that she had been sitting on earlier. "Good. I don't think it's broken, but it's sure gonna put a crimp in my day tomorrow. Thanks! Thanks a lot!" she said sarcastically.

"I need your camera," was all the man said, as he held out his hand and towered above her.

Sarah looked up at him as if he'd lost his mind. "What did you just say? It sure as hell wasn't 'I'm sorry' or, 'Are you okay'!"

The mountain man finally looked a little embarrassed, and said "I'm sorry. Are you okay? I need your camera."

"I am *not* giving you my camera, and why do you want it anyway?" Sarah was truly mystified.

"We can't have any unauthorized photos taken," was all the man said.

Sarah shook her head slowly and muttered "Unauthorized

photos? What does that even mean?"

"I saw you taking pictures. You can't keep those pictures," the mountain man repeated.

"I most certainly can! They are *my* pictures! Why would you expect, or even want, my pictures?"

Mountain man just growled "Because they're not authorized."

Sarah had never heard of having to get authorization to take pictures of landmarks and nature. Was it some kind of new city code? She was also having a hard time concentrating or even giving a shit what the mountain man said or wanted, as her ankle was throbbing and already swelling. She needed ice and aspirin. Like yesterday.

"I'm sorry, I don't understand. What authorization? Do I need authorization to take pictures of the arch and a bird?"

The mountain man finally realized that she didn't know what he was talking about and asked her "So you weren't taking pictures of the Oak Wood shoot?"

"No!" snapped Sarah. She hated to be so bitchy, but she was really in pain, and was trying to figure out how she was going to drive to her motel. "I don't even know what that is!"

Sarah noticed someone walking toward them out of the corner of her eye, but was so intent on trying to figure out how to get rid of mountain man, keep her camera, and make it to her motel, that she really didn't pay attention or care. "Just another person to growl at me."

"Are you okay? That was a nasty fall."

Sarah's heart stopped. It actually stopped, and she died for just a minute. She slowly turned her head toward that voice. Toward the voice that had just asked his question in a perfect English accent.

And looked right into the sad, blue eyes of Sam Ramsay.

"Oh my God! I *know* you." Sarah had to have hit her head when she fell. She felt a little dizzy. She was having an out of body experience that she'd always read about, but never believed.

Now she realized why "Oak Wood" sounded familiar, and why mountain man wanted her camera.

"I'm sorry. Have we met?" Sam Ramsay was kneeling in front of her and reaching for her leg. Sam Ramsay was going to touch her fucking leg.

"Uh, no, I mean yes, uh, no." Sarah could not think a coherent thought, and it was getting embarrassing. But it was Sam Ramsay! Sam fucking Ramsay! Sam Ramsay was in St. Louis! And Sarah had seen him naked. Arghh! All she could see in her mind was his dangling participle.

By this time Mr. Perfect had removed her boot and sock very gently. Sarah winced and looked at her ankle. It was already swollen and had started to turn an ugly shade of purple. Sarah felt it throb with every heartbeat, and as her heart beat quite rapidly, her damn ankle hurt. Badly.

"You said you knew me," Mr. Perfect gently felt her foot. "I'm sorry I don't remember your name."

"Oh! Sorry! No. You don't remember my name, as we've never met." Sarah starting to scare herself. All of her brains had just up and disappeared. She muttered, "Get a fucking grip, Sarah!"

Sam Ramsay knelt on the grass in front of her with her ankle on his nicely developed thigh. Sarah remembered vividly what that thigh looked like without the benefit of clothes. He was a large man, with large hands and long fingers that were surprisingly gentle on her foot. His shoulders looked like goal posts. His back had to be massive. Sarah wanted him to turn around so she could see that back; and that ass.

Sam cocked his head and looked at her. Confused, he asked "You know me, but we've never met?" He definitely thought she had a mental problem, but he had noticed that she had great legs. They were really long. She also had great cheekbones and purple hair for fucks sake!

She exhaled a loud breath, and tried to erase the picture that she had burned into her brain of a naked Sam Ramsay, Sarah tried to sound like a human. "Again. I am so sorry. No. We've never met. But I know who you are. I've studied your photographs Mr. Ramsay. I'm a picture geek. I'm sure the last thing you wanted to deal with today was another photographer." Okay, she thought, that sounded almost normal.

Sam smiled and looked at her. God! Those eyes! That mouth! Those hands! Those hands that were on her skin! Sarah started to lose it again, so she took a deep breath and stared at those beautiful blue eyes. He would think that she had a mental problem. An even bigger smile appeared on Mr. Perfects face. "I'm flattered that you know my work. Not a lot of people on this side of the ocean recognize me outside of New York City or LA. I'm working today. But I guess you figured that out, didn't you? And, please, my name is Sam. Mr. Ramsay is my father."

The mountain man cleared his throat and pointed back to the riverfront. Sarah had completely forgotten about him. She had pretty much forgotten her own damn name and her panties had turned to ash after her ovaries exploded.

"Just a minute, Rick. I'm done for the day, and we need to see about getting…? What's your name, darling?"

Oh my God! Sam Ramsay just called her darling! In a perfect English accent. "Sarah. Sarah Reid." She sounded like a ten- year-old. Shit! Shit! Shit!

"It is very nice to meet you Sarah Reid, but at this moment in time we need to get you where you need to be. You need ice and aspirin. And you need to elevate that ankle. I don't think it's broken, but you most definitely have a nasty sprain. Are you close by?"

That was the problem that had started to worry Sarah. "Uh, unfortunately, no. My motel is not close by, and my truck is parked in the garage a couple of blocks away. On the top level."

Sam stood thinking "Hmmm, that *is* a problem. Even if we could get you to your truck, there's no way that you could drive."

Sarah grasped at straws as her ankle continued to throb. "I can call Uber to take me, and I'll figure the rest of it out tomorrow." She leaned back against the bench and sighed.

Sam looked up suddenly and asked "You mentioned a motel? You don't live in St. Louis?"

Sarah felt a little sad that tomorrows plans were over. "No. I live a couple of hours away. I came down for the carnival tomorrow. I was planning on taking pictures. I guess I won't be doing that now. "

"Have you checked in yet?" asked Sam.

"No. I was getting ready to leave to do that when I backed into the mountain that you just called Rick."

Sam laughed. Sarah immediately noticed the laugh lines around his eyes. They actually crinkled. That made her smile like an idiot.

Sam smirked and said "Uh, yeah. Okay. I have this figured out. Where's your reservation at? Rick, type this in, and cancel that reservation, then call our motel and get Sarah a room there. Do whatever you need to do. Also ask them to have lots of ice, aspirin and a wheelchair."

Sarah protested "Oh, please! You don't need to go to all of that trouble! I'm already embarrassed enough."

Sam gently placed her foot on the ground, and stood up. He was really tall. He smiled again. "Well, I guess we could just leave you sitting here on the bench tonight. I'm sure you'd be in the same place when we came to check on you in the morning. We're going to the motel, anyway, so we're not going out of our way. And you're just going to have to put up with Rick and me helping you to the car. Sorry for any groping that may occur."

Sarah thought that groping would be very nice. "Groping will be fine. No offense taken, but, I must warn you. We can do nothing beyond that, as I can't wrap my leg around your waist at this point in time. Tonight you'll get no further than first base."

Rick snorted and tried hard not to grin. He failed. He started to laugh, then Sam joined in. Sarah looked at both of them and said "Wow! I didn't know that big ass mountains and trees could laugh!" Then she started to laugh.

Sam and Rick basically fireman carried her to the car they had parked at the photo shoot. No groping. All the nut carrying squirrels that she had noticed earlier were busy wrapping up cords, and tearing down lights. Their work was done for the day. The two men got her settled length wise into the backseat of the car, and Sam handed her the backpack. Rick drove, and Sam shared the front seat.

Sarah was impressed with the service she received at the hotel. When the car pulled under the portico, the staff waited with a wheelchair. Again, Rick and Sam helped her out of the back seat and gently placed her in the wheelchair. Sarah's ankle was elevated, and someone whisked her to the elevators to take her to her room. She turned to look for Sam and Rick to thank them for their help, but she didn't see them anywhere. "Well," Sarah thought, "that was surreal. I guess that was my once in a lifetime chance to see Sam Ramsay and I acted like a star struck teenaged fangirl." It made her a little sad and a lot angry with herself. Damn that man had been perfection.

A bucket of ice, a bottle of aspirin, and a well stocked mini bar waited in the room. There was also a fluffy, white robe laid across the bed. Sarah looked at it longingly. The sweet boy who had wheeled her up asked if she needed anything else. Sarah thanked him profusely and shook her head no. The first thing she planned to do was take three aspirin, hobble to the shower and then elevate her ice wrapped ankle. When the boy had closed the door, Sarah clumsily made her way to the table. She swallowed three aspirin with a whole bottle of water and slowly made her way to the bathroom. After she shed her clothes, she gingerly stepped into the shower. She turned the water on as hot as she could stand it then just leaned against the shower stall and let the hot water relax her. She could not wait to group text the girls. They would never believe her when she told them that she had met Mr. Perfect, and that she had stayed in the same hotel. She would text them first, and then try to figure out what she would do tomorrow.

Sarah had enveloped herself in the soft warmth of the fuzzy robe and wrapped her ankle in ice before she elevated it on the side of the bed. It already felt better. The throbbing had stopped, and the swelling had gotten no worse. Between the three aspirin and the numbing of the ice, she didn't feel half bad. She would have to figure out something regarding shoes, as she knew she would never get her foot back in her boot in the morning. A knock sounded at the door. She wondered who it was, as she expected no one. She knew it would take her a minute to get to the door to unlock it, so she yelled "Just a minute!"

She slowly made her way to the door, and opened it, only to see Mr. Perfect standing outside her door. He held the handle of a stainless- steel cart. "I'm *so* sorry I made you get up. Can I come in? I come bearing gifts." He gave her a crotch- tingling grin that made her heart stop for just a moment. The Pentagon could use that grin for a ballistic missile. It was definitely a weapon.

"Uh, of course," stammered Sarah. There she went again. She had completely lost her ability to speak to go along with her inability to walk. *Fuck! Fuck! Fuck!* Sam Ramsay knew how dangerous his smile was. She was a big, fat fucking mess.

Sam wheeled the cart in and then turned to help Sarah back to her chair. He put her leg back on the bed.

"I figured that you hadn't eaten anything this evening. With the aspirin, eating would probably be a good idea. You *have* taken the aspirin haven't you?" The whole time he was talking, Sam was taking lids off plates. The smell was heavenly, and Sarah realized that she was starving. All she had eaten that day was an orange.

"I didn't know what you liked, so I just got a little bit of everything. Do you mind if I join you? I'm famished!" Sam sat down in the matching chair.

Sarah stared at him. That seemed to be her modus operandi that day. Every hair of Sam Ramsay was in place. Even his stubble looked as if it had been drawn on one stroke at a time. He looked as if he had just stepped off the front page of GQ Magazine. Oh, wait. He had.

"What? Aren't you hungry? Am I keeping you from napping?" Sam asked with concern.

Before Sarah could answer, her stomach growled loudly.

They both stared at each other for a minute, before they both started laughing.

Sarah started to eye the dishes with a smile on her face. "It's pretty obvious I am. But you didn't need to go to all this trouble. I could have called room service. Though I'm glad to see you again. I thought that you and Charlie had ridden off into the sunset before I could thank you for your assistance this afternoon. You both went above and beyond."

Sam placed bits of this and bits of that on plates. He grinned again and handed her one. "Well, we both felt a little guilty. After all, it was Charlie that caused you to fall."He sank back in the chair next to Sarah and propped his legs on the bed next to hers.

She grinned back, "Oh, I see! You're just here out of guilt! Not for my incredible beauty or pleasing personality. That's okay. I don't care. I'm too damn hungry to care!"

They sat in comfortable silence as they ate hungrily. Sarah noticed his clothing. He wore a very nice pair of navy trousers with a grey sweater. The sweater had a zip up neck that wasn't zipped. You could see the bronzed skin of his chest peeking out. He had very nice brown leather shoes that now laying on the floor. His stocking feet were once again on the bed next to hers. He had nice socks. He had great teeth. Weren't the Brits known for their bad teeth? For some reason Austin Powers popped into her head. Really, Sam should smile more in his pictures. He had a great smile. He also had that hot, hot, hot thing where it looked like he clenched his jaws. It took Sarah a moment to realize that Sam had stopped eating and stared back at her with a raised eyebrow.

Sarah did something that she *never* did. She blushed. She could feel the heat start at her chest and slowly work its way up her neck, her ears and her face.

Exasperated, Sam asked "What?"

"You are just unbelievably pretty!" blurted Sarah. She wanted to crawl under a rock. She had actually said pretty. *Fuck!*

"Pretty?" he asked.

Oh, for God's sake, Sam Ramsay!" Sarah snorted. "Let's just get this over with. You know that you're unbelievably gorgeous. Don't pretend that you don't. If you are blind enough to not see that, then your line of work would dictate otherwise. And, yes, damn it! You are pretty. I don't care that I'm fifty five years old. I'm not fucking dead! Looking at you is like looking at someone with a huge hairy mole on their cheek. You just can't look away! Now that we've gotten *that* out of the way, can we please change the fucking subject? You're making me feel really defensive."

Sam grinned at Sarah with his fucking weapon of a grin. "Yes. I realize that I have that effect on people sometimes, and it gets a little embarrassing. None of us perceive ourselves the way other people perceive us. And I don't have any moles."

"Does *everyone* stare at you? That's got to be a little disconcerting, and probably weird." Sarah continued to stare at him, but also thought that he wasn't just a pretty face. He actually seemed like a nice guy.

Sam looked over at her and said "To tell you the truth, I try not to pay any attention. My job is my face and my body. That's all it is; my job. It's not like I save starving children or anything. But my job has provided me with more than I could have ever expected. I'm lucky, but I've also worked really hard to get where I am."

Sarah slowly nodded and murmured, "I get that. When you look the way you do, you have to compartmentalize. But I remember my trip to China, and being stared at everywhere I went; by everyone. I get stared at a lot for my height, too. Having your kind of beauty for a lifetime would drive me crazy."

Sam took their plates and put them on the cart. He poured each of them a cup of decaf, and went to the mini bar for two small bottles of Baileys. He poured a tiny bottle in each cup and handed a cup to Sarah, before he settled back down in his chair. "You are a beautiful woman Sarah. You, too, should be used to being stared at. You told me why you were here, and you told me you didn't live in the city. Where *do* you live, if you don't mind me asking."

That was slick, thought Sarah. He complimented her and changed the subject about his appearance. He looked a little uncomfortable. Sarah thought that Mr. Perfect might actually be a shy guy. Who would've thought?

"I have an eighty five acre farm in the country about two hours from here. So, no, I don't live in St. Louis, but I do live in Missouri. I love Missouri and the people here, but, I'm starting to think I could like a British guy, too." Sarah gave Sam a grin.

"Do you live alone? With a husband? Have a boyfriend? A Girlfriend? Children? Do you have livestock?" asked Sam excitedly.

Sam noticed the quick spark of pain in Sarah's eyes, before she laughed out loud and shook her head. "I'm sure you have better things to do with that body than sit here with an invalid and pretend to be interested in my 'livestock.' There's no beautiful woman waiting for you downstairs? No gala? You know the motel staff women, and probably half of the men, are waiting outside my door right now, just to get a glimpse of your delicious ass. Maybe you should just step outside and strut down the hallway to satisfy them. You would be the first man I've known that could actually sexually satisfy hundreds of women and men at the same time."

Sam sputtered and put his coffee cup down as he looked at Sarah in shock. He was quiet for a moment. Then he laughed. And laughed some more. He caught his breath and grinned a goofy grin "Tonight, Sarah Reid, I would rather be nowhere else."

Sarah could have sworn that he muttered the word "bawdy."

~~~

38

It was late when Sam left. He and Sarah had stayed up until the wee hours of the morning talking about everything. The weather, traveling, sights to see in the States, sights to see in England. Yes, they still had the red telephone booths. Sarah couldn't forget to tell Liz. Idle chit chat made the hours fly by. Sarah enjoyed Sam but she still didn't really know him. They had

discussed all kinds of topics, except anything of a personal nature. Nothing about family, or homes, friends or the state of the world. They skirted around things that led Sarah to believe that they were both feeling each other out. She thought they both knew this was a day- in- the- life scenario. They wouldn't run into each other again. Why get personal, and start something that they would never finish? That made for a morose Sarah. Sarah wanted to know Sam better, and to have more conversations with him. He had spoken on a variety of issues, and definitely had an opinion. She would make sure and tell Julie that Sam's brain was not a bowl of soup. Neither had made any other comments about Sam's looks.

Sarah studied him as he talked animatedly. The way he moved his mouth and hands. The way his laughter made his eyes crinkle. He was a quiet man who seemed to think about how he answered questions and was genuinely interested in what she had to say. She committed as much to memory as she could: sight, sound, smell. One evening was not long enough for her to solve the mystery of Sam Ramsay and his beautiful but sad eyes.

It was too late to text the girls, so Sarah took three more aspirin and limped to the bed. She would wait and talk to them in person once she got home. Her ankle felt considerably better, but not good enough to venture out on her own tomorrow. And she certainly couldn't go barefoot. After all, it was February in Missouri. She needed to be able to get her boots on. She had brought no other shoes. Under any other circumstance she would just have driven home, but that wasn't going to happen until at least Sunday. Thank God, she had an automatic. There was no way she could maneuver a clutch. So, she was stuck in a hotel with no familiar faces, except for Sam and Charlie who she would never see again. She was stuck in a hotel with no means of leaving. Sarah hated not being in control of her life. It was going to be a long, boring day, and she just wanted to feel sorry for herself.

The hotel room sheets were soft, and it was quiet in the hallway. Sarah opened her Kindle and went to Sam's Facebook page. It was a weird feeling looking at his posts and pictures when he had just spent several hours in her room. Really, really weird. What she now saw on the page was not what she had seen tonight. The pictures that stared back at her from the page captured images of stranger. They were not the Sam that she had eaten with, laughed with and talked with. The only thing that the two Sam's had in common were their eyes. Perhaps Sam was right. It was just his job. But, job or not, he couldn't put a mask on those eyes. Sarah felt a sudden surge of familial protection. That was just asinine, as Sam had mentioned in an online interview that he had a family. It would be silly if that was true. Who really knew if Sam had a family, or if his name was really Sam Ramsay? As much as Sarah knew the public Sam, she knew very little about the private Sam. No one did, and if they did, they didn't talk. His private life was just that, private. How someone who had lived his life in the spotlight could keep anything personal and private was beyond her. In this day and age of technology, you could find out anything on anyone. Sam did not need Sarah's protection. His eyes told the story.

He had done an extremely good job of protecting himself but at what cost? Who was Sam Ramsay? Was it the dapper playboy who posed at all the red -carpet events? Was it the face that stared back at you from magazine covers? Was it the laughing man that had spent the evening with her? It may have been all of them, but Sarah thought that it might not be any of them. She knew no more about Sam Ramsey than she did when she got to St. Louis. And that was before she had even met him. She just wished she'd had a little more time with him, as she knew she would be going home, and that she would continue to obsess over the mystery that was Sam Ramsay.

Sarah rolled over and turned off the light.

~~~

Sam walked into his room with a grin on his face. He loved bawdy broads. They were his favorite kind of women, and the rarest. You could have the blondes, redheads, and brunettes. You could have the models, actresses, and designers. Give him a bawdy broad anytime. It didn't matter what color their hair was, how old or young they were, rich or poor, large or small. He loved a woman who laughed loudly at him and themselves. He loved women who didn't take themselves too seriously. The women who cursed like sailors and told filthy jokes, but were also interested in real conversations and would tell you where to stick it if you got too full of yourself. He had just spent the evening with a bawdy broad in St. Louis, Missouri, and he was a happy man.

It was late and he was tired. His day had started at five thirty that morning. The photographer had wanted the early light. This was after he had been on a six- hour redeye from Ontario. Sam needed a shower and bed. He also needed home. Badly. What had it been? Two months? Two months since he had been in his own bed, walked in his own yard, or eaten his own cooking. He wasn't complaining, or maybe he was. He was tired in body and spirit. He worked hard at being a consummate professional. His hard work had provided the life that he had, a life that he had never even imagined. But right now, he just wanted to go home.

He had a shoot in Chicago on Monday, then on to Arizona and California. Five more days in the States, then finally two weeks at home, before the Oak Wood campaign started in earnest. Sam just looked forward to tomorrow. No work, no flight, and no craziness. Being in a city where no one knew him was complete awesomeness. Well, almost no one. Sarah had known him, and it had gob smacked him. Her being a photographer had given him pause until he realized that she took pictures for her own enjoyment, not to sell to the rags that were out there.

He made his way to the shower and relaxed under the spray of hot water. Thinking back over his day, he went over the photo shoot in his head. He always did that. He should have done this. He should have done that. He always picked apart all of the ways he could have been better. He could always do better. As he continued to unwind under the hot water, his mind wandered to the bawdy broad that had put him in such a good mood. Sarah Reid. Her name even made him smile. He had seen her taking pictures earlier in the day. He had noticed the tall, boot wearing woman with purple hair. Purple hair for God's sake! He liked her style. Sam knew style, and Sarah had it. She had stuck to the area on the other side of their shoot for several hours and he had realized that she was paying no attention to him or the crew that

42

were on the riverbank.

When the photographer had wrapped for the day and had been checking the digitals, Sam had watched the purple- haired woman. He noticed as Rick had walked toward her, and knew why. What Rick didn't know was that the purple- haired woman had paid no attention to them. Sam started to walk over to let Rick know it was okay. He watched as Rick got closer to her. The woman started to walk backwards with her camera pointed to the sky. Sam knew immediately what would happen. He started to laugh until he saw her ankle twist and saw her hit the ground. Charlie was a freight train. There was no give to the big guy. He walked a little faster. Rick was like a dog with a bone and would not give up until he had the pictures. Sam just wanted to make sure that the woman was okay.

As he got closer, he watched Rick help her up. He could hear the woman get loud. She limped pretty badly as she sat down on a bench. Sam hoped she hadn't broken anything.

When he reached her, he knelt and removed her boot and sock. They were nice boots. Well- worn leather. He noticed things like that. Her ankle had already started to swell and turn purple. The entire time he tried to talk to her, but she didn't make a lot of sense. He had wondered if she had mental health issues. She finally started speaking English and told him she knew his work. And that she was a photographer. Great. Just another someone who wanted to take his picture. But, he was kind of flattered that here in the middle of the United States, someone knew who he was.

When he really looked at her instead of her foot, his first thought was that she was stunning. She had beautiful eyes. They were blue, but aqua like the water of the Mediterranean and not blue like the sky. He smiled to himself, as her eyes were one of the first things he noticed. It was always the first thing everyone noticed about him.

Her ankle was already purple and swollen. He couldn't just leave her there, so they just changed her motel. Sarah had protested, but it really wasn't that big of a deal. She had slowly started speaking in complete sentences, and had seemed like a nice woman. Sam had exhaled a silent thank you for not having to deal with a crazy person. And when Sarah told him that groping her would be okay, but no leg wrapping, that's when he *knew*. Sarah was a bawdy broad.

Sam had planned to just take Sarah some supper. He was dead tired and just wanted a shower and bed, but he knew that she would have to depend on room service. The staff had delivered his meal, so why not just share? He hadn't expected to stay so long, but she was funny and the banter was great, and time just seemed to disappear. Sam had caught the quick spark of pain in her eyes when he asked about who she lived with. He also noticed that she quickly changed the subject. There was more to this woman, than the quick glimpse he had seen tonight.

 "Oh, well," Sam thought, as he crawled into bed. "I'll tell her goodbye tomorrow and make sure someone gets her home." He reached for his lap top. He needed to check in on his Facebook page. He had sadly neglected it for a few days.

"Sandalwood. That's what it is. She smells like sandalwood."

Chapter 4:

Sarah had slept like a rock. Between the pain, aspirin, and a late night, she had been exhausted. She stretched and thought of last night. It was a little bittersweet. She had enjoyed it so much, but it was over. Well, it would make a good story to tell the girls. She was in no hurry to get out of bed. She had no agenda for today. She stretched her ankle a little bit, and was surprised to find that it felt much better. She threw the covers back to take a look.

"Holy shit!" It looked awful. It was varying shades of purple, green and yellow. Thank God it looked worse than it felt. She might actually be able to hobble around her room. She might be able to make it down for breakfast. But, wait. She couldn't possibly get a boot on that ankle. "Shit!"

Someone quietly knocked at the door and Sarah slowly went to open it. A very tall man stood outside the door in nice trousers and expensive leather shoes. He held up a cardboard tray with coffee and a paper bag in front of his face.

"Could I help you?" asked Sarah with a grin.

Sam lowered his arms and grinned right back. "I brought you breakfast." Then he grinned even bigger as his eyes traveled from her face, lingered on her boobs, then down the rest of her body.

Sarah realized that she was wearing nothing but her standard sleepwear of panties and one of David's old tee shirts.

"Nope. I am *not* going to do it again," she said. She never took her eyes off Sam.

Sam took his time, and grinned like the Cheshire Cat as he continued to read her body like a book. Slowly. A page at a time. "You're not going to do what?" He finally reached her face and looked her in the eye with a smile that scorched.

Fuck! The man was capable of melting the panties off a nun. Sarah held her ground. "I am *not* going to blush."

Sam smirked, "That could be very attractive." He tried not to stare at her tits but he couldn't help it. From what he could see, they were perfect. They were large.

"Sam! Up here, Sam!" Sarah pointed to her eyes. "Do you like what you see?" She put her hand on her hip.

An embarrassed Sam growled. "Yes. Very much."

Sarah grinned and said "I'm kind of attached to them, too. I used to have good legs, too."

"You still have good legs. They're really... long. By the way, I could have been anyone standing out here. Do you always answer your door wearing nothing?" Sam grinned and made his way into the room.

"I didn't even think about it, and I *am* wearing something." Sarah limped to the chair and started to pull her leggings on. "I'm so happy you came by, because I didn't think I would see you again. I like you and think that in another time and place we could be great friends, and if I lived in a different universe. And that makes me sad." She stood up gingerly and zipped her jeans.

"How's the ankle feeling? It looks like hell." Sam was a little sad that she had covered up her legs. But the tits in the t-shirt were still staring him in the face. He liked that. A lot.

Sarah sat back down and looked at her ankle. "It actually looks worse than it feels. I still don't think I'm able to get around much, though." She sighed and then stuck her bottom lip out a little.

Sam handed her a pastry and a lidded cup of coffee. "Before the uh, accident, what were you planning on doing today?" He sat in the chair next to her.

"I wanted to find a place to snap some pictures of the carnival. The colors and characters would be fun to capture. You, know. Take pictures, breath the air. Just *be*." Sarah took a big bite of the pastry. "Holy shit! What is this?" She looked at the pastry and made very sensual noises as she chewed. She actually closed her eyes and moaned.

Sam chuckled. "Chocolate croissants. They're from a pastry shop down the street. It sounds like you're really enjoying them."

"I am," groaned Sarah. "Mine don't taste like this. These are heaven on parchment." She stuck her tongue out and licked a bit of chocolate from the corner of her mouth.

Sam coughed and asked "Oh, are you a baker?"

Sarah popped the last bite of croissant in her mouth and started to talk with her mouth full. "I am at home. I love to bake, cook, boil, steam. I love food. It's my second favorite thing, after my camera."

My God! She actually licked her fingers. And her tits still bounced pleasantly with each bite. Sam actually groaned inside. "I'm leaving. But I *will* be back, so don't try to do anything by yourself, okay? Give me an hour." Sam felt really hot and needed to leave quickly. Maybe he could find a closet and jerk off like a teenager.

This broad was killing him. How old did she say she was?

~~~

As promised, Sam was back in an hour with a wheelchair. He helped Sarah into it. "What are you doing? Where are we going? I have no shoes!"

He pulled a pair of blue plastic clogs out of the kangaroo pocket of the jacket he had put on. "These are the ugliest things I've ever seen. They cause me physical pain just looking at them. The Swedes have no sense of style. But they will do."

Sarah laughed and said, "I hope I don't cause you physical pain, as they will be on my feet."

"I just won't look at your feet." Sam pushed her out the door and onto the elevator.

As Sam pushed her out the front doors of the motel, Sarah was curious what this crazy man had up his sleeve. Sam chattered. He talked nonstop about nothing. Sarah realized that he was a little nervous. And that made her nervous.

"Sam? Didn't you have to leave today? I don't want to be any trouble, or get you into any."

"I have the day off. I don't fly out until the morning. I can't think of anything I'd rather do than get to know you Sarah Reid. Otherwise, I would be in my room, answering email, authorizing photos, and being interrupted by the staff all day. I want to, as you said earlier, just be."

He had pushed Sarah down the sidewalk for a while. Now he pushed her gently onto the grass. Sarah hadn't paid any attention.

She looked at the bench she had sat on yesterday. On the grass in front of it was a blanket, an ice chest and a basket. Sam had prepared a picnic with a perfect line of sight to the carnival that was just getting ready to start.

"Oh!" Sarah whispered. "Look what you did. Look what you did!" She looked up at Sam with wonder in her eyes and took his hand. "This is incredible. You are a nice man Sam Ramsay. How did you pull this off?"

He shrugged, smiled, and said "I know people. I figured you could use the ice chest to elevate your ankle. If you have a long-range lens, you should be able to get some shots. At least this would be better than being in the room all day."

He helped her sit on the bench. He opened the ice chest, removed a bottle of water and propped Sarah's leg on the top. He sat down next to her and sighed. "Can we just sit here for a little while? No talking, just being?"

"Absolutely."

~~~

They sat together in comfortable silence for an hour. They both watched the carnival. There were children in tutu's, and clowns on stilts. There were grown men on little motorcycles. Vintage cars and horses. They kept finding things to point out to each other. Sarah saw Sam relax as more time went by.

"Where are you off to next? I forgot," asked Sarah.

"I'm off to Chicago for one day, then Sonoma for two days. I finish up in Malibu before I get to go home."

Sarah leaned closer to Sam and asked quietly "How long has it been since you were home Sam? And where is home?"

He turned and looked at her for a minute. It was like he was trying to decide whether to really talk to her or not. Sarah waited.

"Two months. It's been a little more than two months since I've been home. And I live in London proper." Sam sounded wistful.

"I love to travel", Sarah said, "but I don't know if I could leave my home for that long."

Sam shrugged. "I'm used to it. I've been doing it a long time, and I'd never complain, but the older I get, the more I need a touchstone, someplace to land if only for a little while." He stared off into the crowd in front of them.

"My home, my daughters, and my friends are *my* touchstones. I don't know what I would do without them. As you get older, you realize what's important," Sarah replied. She kept looking at him. *Come back to me, Sam*, she thought.

Sam turned and asked softly "Your home, your daughters, and your friends? No husband?"

Sarah bit her lip, and suddenly got very quiet. Did she really want to go there? Would they be friends after today? She decided to take the leap. They would either be friends or never see each other again. Either way, it worked.

"I had a husband. David." A look of love so blinding that Sam could barely stand it shone from Sarah's eyes. He grabbed her hand and held it tight.

She smiled at him and said, "High school sweethearts. Thirty-five years of marriage. Three daughters. We built our dream home."

"What happened?" Sam held her hand more tightly.

Sarah whispered "An aneurysm. One day he was here, and the next day he wasn't. It's been almost five years."

Sam reached out and grabbed her, literally grabbed her. He wrapped her in those long arms and squeezed like he would never let go. Sarah squeezed right back. She was okay. She really was. It had felt good to talk about David to someone other than the girls. Sam didn't let go, and Sarah thought that maybe he needed the touch more than she did.

"I'm so sorry, Sarah," he mumbled into her coat. "I am just so fucking sorry."

After a little while, after they had both sat back on the bench and collected their thoughts, Sarah turned to Sam and asked, "Are we going to be friends Sam Ramsay?"

Sam looked at her, smiled and said, "Absolutely, Sarah Reid. Absolutely."

~~~

They continued to talk about everything. Sam had a mother, a father, and a sister. He had gotten into modeling on a bet. He had never aspired to be a model but had spent his entire life up until this point, in the industry. He knew nothing else. He had two good friends from childhood, and a best friend that worked with him in the fashion world. He loved to cook, and to make furniture. He liked a cigarette occasionally, and Irish whiskey. He did **not** have any ponies, but promised that he would look into it for her.

Sarah told him about her daughters and how they were the most hilarious people she knew. How they were her best friends. She told him that she liked a cigarette and a whiskey as well. She told him about her house, and her girlfriends. She also told him that they had all seen him naked.

Sam pointed out, that *everyone* had seen him naked.

Sarah laughed. "That doesn't bother you? Posing completely naked? That puts you in a pretty vulnerable place."

He shrugged. "I think we're all kind of hung up on body image. Americans, especially. It's just skin. And those photos were for a charity, so it was a good cause."

"Well, nobody would have a problem with their nudity if they looked like you. So that's easy for you to say." Sarah grinned at him.

"So, you have a problem with nudity, Sarah?" Sam asked very seriously.

Sarah thought about it for a minute, before she answered slowly. "No. I really don't. I'm an old woman. I have no unreachable expectations for what I should look like. I have earned this body. I bore three children and buried a husband. So, when I see my stretch marks, I think of the babies that I birthed. I have good boobs, but I see them in the mirror and remember feeding my children. When I see the scar on my stomach, I see the time my appendix burst, and I almost died. The lines by my eyes are from the laughter I've experienced, and the lines around my mouth are from the pain I've endured. My body is a scrapbook of my life. No one else's. I love my body and the story that it tells." She shrugged and looked at him.

Sam was quiet before he reached for Sarah's hand again. He expelled a breath and said "You just got me in the feels, Sarah Reid. That should be written in a book of poetry somewhere." He squeezed her hand. "What do you see when you look at my face? Please be honest. I don't want to hear about how pretty I am. Spin me a beautiful tale of truth amazing Sarah."

Sarah's heart did a slow, skidding stop. She looked at Sam. She stared deep in his eyes and memorized the pain that she saw there. She reached for his face, and asked "Do you mind?"

He shook his head no and held his breath as she took his face in her hands and caressed his cheeks.

"We really don't know each other, but, when I look in your eyes, I see sadness. I see pain. Only someone who has experienced it themselves would notice. You will tell me about that pain someday, Sam Ramsay, when you're ready, because we're going to be friends."

Sarah stroked the hard angles of his jaws. "When I look at this face I see a glimpse of the young, beautiful, fresh-faced boy that took the modeling world by storm. That boy is still there, under the surface." Sarah stroked the bridge of Sam's nose with her finger. "I see before me now, a man. I see a man who is not perfect. There is no such thing. I look at you with a photographer's eye and see that the man's face is so much more. The angles of your cheeks are like slashes made by a knife. They hold the light and shadow like a painting. I see the nose that didn't quite fit the boy's face, but is perfect for the man's." Sam was still quiet and watched Sarah with something like wonder.

Sarah continued. "As a woman, I see strength in this face, I see joy and pain. I love the face of the man, Sam. Age brings character and wisdom. I see that in your face today. I also see that some things are left unfinished, and it makes me almost want to cry in anticipation for this face to be complete." Sarah removed her hands and leaned back on the bench. She turned and looked at Sam.

Sam just sat there. He didn't say a word. He just looked off into the distance and wondered where this woman had come from. Did her friends know how lucky they were to share the same universe as her? Did her children know how incredibly lucky they were? Had David realized? He thought that David had probably known as a teenager that Sarah was a witch that needed to be held onto. Sam couldn't figure out how the two Sarah's coexisted. The bawdy broad that made him laugh, and the gift of the accessible woman that sat here with him.

He shook himself and looked at Sarah. "That was one of the sexiest things I've ever experienced. Thank you."

~~~

Sarah kept noticing people as they stopped, stared, and walked slowly past them. She started to giggle.

"What?' Sam asked.

"Does this always happen?"

"Does what always happen?"

"Every child, woman, and man has stopped and stared at you. Is this a normal occurrence?" Sarah shook her head.

Sam slouched down on the bench and scowled. "I try not to pay any attention, but, yeah, this is pretty much my life."

Sarah sat for a minute then slowly turned to Sam. She reached out and took his face in her hands again and considered the eyes that had been her obsession for two months. "Sam Ramsay. You are the most incredibly beautiful man I have ever seen. You should never make light of that. But your looks alone did not get you where you are. You've worked hard and given up much to get much. It's always a tradeoff. It's up to you to figure out when the tradeoff is dangerous. But, as beautiful as your face is, as beautiful as your body is, I find your heart to be even more beautiful. It's sad that most people don't see that beauty instead." She leaned in and gave him a soft, tender kiss on that cheek with the perfect stubble.

Sam quietly stared at Sarah for a long while. She waited.

Finally, Sam said very softly, "Sarah Reid, we are going to be the best of friends."

Sarah smiled and leaned back.

They ate their sandwiches and fruit from the cooler and watched the carnival for a little longer. Sam wheeled Sarah back to the motel with the cooler and blanket on her lap. He got her to her room and made her walk around until he was satisfied that she would be able to drive her truck home. Arrangements had been made for the motel shuttle to drive her to the parking garage. They exchanged phone numbers and promised each other they would talk the next day. They gave each other hugs and Sam said goodbye. He had an early flight.

~~~

Sarah just sat on the edge of the bed in a stupor after Sam left. Sam fucking Ramsay. Who would have ever thought that she would be friends with Sam Ramsay? Sarah knew that his looks were just icing on the fuck me cupcake that was Sam. It didn't matter to her. She truly liked the guy. He was funny, and thoughtful. He also was quite intelligent and had made wise decisions with his money and career. He had plans for his future after modeling. Sarah would have liked him no matter whom or what he was. Why he had spent time with her is what she couldn't understand. Why had he been drawn to her? It didn't matter, she was just glad that he did. It would be so nice to have a male friend in her life that didn't try to get in her pants. Sarah shook her head and headed to the shower. It was only then that she realized that she hadn't even taken her camera.

~~~

Sam let himself into his room and sat down. What the hell had just happened? What kind of witch was Sarah Reid? What spell had she put on him? If he was honest, when she opened the door this morning, in nothing but her panties and a T-shirt, Sam had been surprised. Surprised, and aroused. She had great tits. He had trouble keeping the tent that was in his pants from being noticeable. Sarah was fifteen years older than he was. He was forty, and could have any woman he wanted, whenever he wanted. He could have a young one, a middle aged one, or an old one. He could have five at a time if he wanted. In his younger days, he had used his looks and fame to take advantage of those women. He had mowed through women like a tractor.

But, he had gotten very selective. He had even gone through celibacy. He was very aware that loose lips sink ships, and he wasn't going to put his future in jeopardy for someone that was only in it for the spotlight and notoriety, or what kind of fame he could give them. If he was being honest, he was a hard guy to have a relationship with. He tended to be a perfectionist, and he wasn't in one place for very long. Long distance relationships were impossible. He shook his head. He didn't know what magic Sarah Reid had wielded, but he was glad that she had. She was all heart with a filthy mouth. But she listened. And she was sincere. And she *got* him. Somehow, she knew him. He didn't think she gave two figs for whom or what he was, and that she would have liked him no matter what. Sarah was comfortable in her own skin, and carried a confidence that was very attractive. David had been a lucky man. Sarah was the friend he had been searching for, and he hadn't even known it.

~~~

Sarah had just turned off the light when her phone buzzed. She rolled over and opened it. It was Sam. She grinned.

Sam: Are you asleep?

Sarah: No. Are you?

Sam: I'm texting you aren't I?

Sarah: Smartass.

Sam: I had a great time today.

Sarah: So did I. Thank you.

Sam: Can I text you every hour on the hour? Even in the middle of the night?

Sarah: If you need me, text me anytime.

Sam: I have a feeling that I already need you.

Sarah: You've already texted me, so we're good.

Sam: Smartass.

Sarah: Safe travels Sam Ramsay.

Sam: Sweet dreams Sarah Reid. Oh....... are you the same Sarah Reid that commented on my FB page a couple of weeks ago?

Sarah: Shit!

Sam: So it's NOT the same Sarah Reid? (sigh)

Sarah: You mean you actually maintain your page?

Sam: Why wouldn't I? It's my page.

Sarah: I just assumed that staff would be the ones monitoring it.

Sam: Nope. I do my own FB page and my own Instagram . So.... was that you?

Sarah: Yes. It was me. Shit!

Sam: Why shit?

Sarah: I'm kind of embarrassed. I don't do stuff like that.

Sam: What do you mean "stuff?"

Sarah: Write on strangers Facebook pages.

Sam: Well we're not strangers anymore.

Sarah: I hope not. We're mutual friendship virgins.

Sam: Do you believe in destiny?

Sarah: Hmmmm........Yes. I think I do. Why?

Sam: I think that we were meant to meet.

Sarah: Then I like destiny.

Sam: Me, too. I want to talk more about your comment, but I have to get up early.

Sarah: Are we good Sam?

Sam: We are SO good Sarah. Goodnight.

Sarah: Goodnight Sam.

Chapter 5:

Sarah was very happy to see her driveway. Home was always good. Her own bed, and her own pillows. That made her think of Sam, and how long it had been since he'd had his own bed and pillows. Sarah shook her head. That was his choice, but she couldn't help but think that he might be regretting some choices. She wondered where he was, and what he was doing. She remembered that he was in Chicago today then Sedona after that. She hoped he enjoyed the vibe of that calming area. She unloaded the truck, and made two trips into the house. Her ankle was still sore and swollen, and she didn't want to try to carry too much and fall.

After everything was put away and a load of laundry started, Sarah made herself a cup of coffee, and sat down in the kitchen. She wanted to text the girls, but didn't really know how to even start. It would be so much easier in person. She picked up her phone and group texted.

Sarah: Hey all! I'm home!

It was just a few seconds for them all to start responding.

Liz: Hey girl! Welcome home!

Julie: It's about damn time! Did you get good pictures? Did you get laid?

Karen: Glad you're home.

Bev: Tell us all about it. Lots of pictures?

Sarah: I don't even know where to start. I know it's Sunday, but I need to talk to you all . You will NEVER

believe what kind of a weekend I've had.

Julie: Sarah got laid!!!!

Sarah: LOL! No, I didn't get laid. It's better than that. Could you guys come see me this afternoon? I've got an

ankle I need to stay off of. I'll fix a late lunch?

Julie: I'm on my way. All I had planned was a date with my vibrator. I can do that later.

Liz: I'll pick up Bev.

Karen: My kids are little assholes right now. I am MORE than happy to leave for a bit.

The girls arrived en masse. As Sarah stood in the door and watched them all as they laughed and hugged, she thought for the millionth time how very lucky she was. They all walked in and headed straight for the kitchen.

Liz sat and looked at Sarah. "What did you need to see us for? And why did it need to be this afternoon, and what the hell did you do to your ankle?"

"Sarah said it was better than getting laid. I want to know what's better than getting laid." Julie lifted the lid on the pot of soup and stirred.

Sarah sighed and sat down. "I guess the easiest way to start is to just start at the beginning." Sarah began with the cold day, and the pictures she had taken. How quiet it was, and how much she had been enjoying her day. She stopped, and gathered her thoughts.

"Honey, just tell us. Now you have me worried." Bev looked at Sarah with concern.

Sarah continued with her backing up into Charlie and twisting her ankle. She then had to stop again. How the hell did she tell them that Sam fucking Ramsay had come to her rescue? "I had a knight in shining armor come to my rescue." Sarah just sat and looked at all of them.

Julie just stared at Sarah. "I hate armor. It's a pain in the ass to remove when you want to fuck the knight."

Sarah stared at Julie for a moment before she just said it. "It was Sam Ramsay."

You could hear a pin drop. Every single one of them just sat with their mouths open. Karen squeaked. "Sarah, if it wasn't you, I would tell you that you're full of shit."

"Well, if you think that's a load of shit, it gets better. We spent the weekend together." Sarah stared at them all and dared any of them to call her a liar.

For the first time since Sarah had known her, Julie was quiet. Then Julie whispered "You fucked Sam Ramsay? Sam fucking Ramsay? Good for you Sarah."

Sarah blew Julie a raspberry and said. "No! We didn't sleep with each other. It wasn't like that. I am an old woman for God's sake. Sam doesn't think of me that way. And I don't think of him like that. Well, sometimes I do..." She told them about the evening in her room. The conversation the next morning when she was just in her panties and T-shirt and the playful banter. They all laughed about that exchange. She told them about the picnic and carnival.

She did not tell them what she and Sam had talked about. That was Sam's story to tell. Not hers.

Bev had sat quietly listening, and then said, "Prove it. Where are the pictures? You don't go anywhere without your camera."

Sarah just stopped, before she shook her head slowly, "I didn't remember to take my camera."

"You didn't remember to take your camera?" Bev looked at her with a funny expression on her face.

Sarah slowly shook her head again. "No. I didn't take it." She looked at Bev, who sat and looked at Sarah with a funny little smile. Bev did not say a word, and Sarah knew why.

Karen made Sarah stay in her seat while she ladled the soup and put the sandwiches on a tray. "Is he gorgeous?"

Sarah looked up at her and sighed, "Yes. He is stunning. Even better in person, if that's possible."

"Did you get him naked to see if the rest of him was as pretty as his pictures?" Julie asked with a mouth full of soup.

Sarah shook her head again. Shit! All she could do was shake her head! "I know you think it's crazy, but it isn't like that. I feel like he's objectified by everyone. That is the world he lives in. Every single person who saw him stared at him. He actually had everyone do double takes. Oh, I see his beauty. You would have to be blind not to. But I see more than that. He's a really nice guy. He's more than nice. He's thoughtful and kind. He's really funny. He's also really smart, Julie. He is definitely not a 'bowl of soup.' I guess at the end of the day I'm wondering why? He spent an entire weekend with *me*! He didn't have to do that. Why did he do that? He had to have been really bored." Sarah had run out of steam and sat there looking at all of them.

Bev looked knowingly at Liz. They both looked at Sarah. Liz said, "You really don't see it, do you? You really, honestly, don't." It was Liz's turn to shake her head. "You are a good-looking woman, Sarah Reid. You've got legs that are longer than my car. You've got a certain style that no one else has. You don't take yourself too seriously, but you can be serious when you need to. You are a classy broad. Until you open your mouth. You are freakin' funny, but also the best listener I've ever known." Bev shook her head in agreement.

 Bev continued the comments that Liz had started." You can talk about anything, and you don't know a stranger. Anyone that has met you, immediately knows you have the biggest heart to go along with the biggest tits. Or at least the biggest *real* tits. After the pain that you've endured, I don't know how you have continued to keep that heart that is so good and pure. Most women would have gotten bitter and ugly. Sam Ramsay is the lucky one. *He* met *you*. And if he doesn't see that, and *you* don't see that, then fuck both of you! This could be whatever you both want it to be. It can stay a wonderful friendship, if that's what *you* choose it to be. It can be a short-lived inferno, or a long term , long distance something. It's nobody's business. But, you, Sarah, deserve to live your life. The entire, beautiful, painful thing. The sooner you realize that, the better." Bev had finally run out of breath, but quickly added, "*And,* you forgot your camera." She lifted her eyebrow and looked at Sarah.

Sarah sat in stunned silence as she looked at her friends. A tear slowly made its way down her cheek. She thought her heart would literally burst. It was almost painful. She couldn't catch her breath. The mother of the group had just been taken to school, and it was almost more than she could stand. "I love you all so much…" That's all she could get out, before being surrounded, in the arms of the people she loved.

After the soup and sandwiches had been eaten, the girls continued peppering Sarah with questions. Were his eyes really as blue as they were in his pictures? How tall was he? Did she make him read the room service menu to her with his English accent? She told them that they had exchanged numbers, and that they had texted, but she didn't share what they had talked about. It was still too new, and too private. She didn't want to share anything of Sam, unless he okayed it. Too much of him was already public, and Sarah was a little protective of his privacy. The girls understood that, and they thought it was the coolest thing ever. After talking about their class on Tuesday, they all hugged goodbye. Sarah knew that seeing them had been the best thing she could have done. They always put things in perspective. Plus, they had given her a huge ego boost. Sarah wasn't a person who needed her ego to be stroked, but it was nice to be petted once in a while. She smiled to herself as she loaded the dishwasher. And meowed.

~~~

Sarah had run a hot bubble bath. It was nice to be able to get in a tub without fear of falling. Her ankle still looked ugly, but it almost felt normal. She had washed her hair and was stretched out and lazy in the hot water. Ed Sheeran sang softly in the background. She still thought about what Bev had said, but quickly discounted it. It's not as if she would ever see am again. The texts would slowly stop and she would wonder about him for the rest of her life. That was the reality, but Sarah knew that the connection wasn't one sided. Sam had felt it, too. Her phone buzzed. Sarah thought about not answering, as she was so comfortable, but it might be one of her children. She looked at the screen and grinned.

Sam: What are you doing?

Sarah: You really don't want to know.

Sam: Are you flossing? Or is your face all covered with goo?

Sarah: LOL. No!

Sam: Then...what are you doing?

Sarah: I am bathing.

Sam: As in taking a bath?

Sarah: Yes.

Sam: (gulp)

Sarah: I said you wouldn't want to know! (smile)

Sam: I am picturing you being very... buoyant...

Sarah: Stop picturing it!

Sam: That's easier said than done.

Sarah: Then I will very skillfully change the subject. Are you in Chicago?

Sam: Yeah. Finished up the shoot just a little while ago.

Sarah: Early flight? Again?

Sam: 6:30. Arizona.

Sarah: I had the girls over this afternoon. I told them about meeting you. Was that okay?

Sam: You love them lots, don't you?

Sarah: Yes. Lots.

Sam: Then I love them, too. Share whatever you want. Except your body. Don't share that with them. Though, if

you decide to, can I watch?

Sarah: LOL! I'll try to get all of our schedules synced. (you are a funny man)

Sam: Did you ever wish you were somebody else? Or something else?

Sarah: Of course. Hasn't everybody? Why?

Sam: Right now, I wish I was something else.

Sarah: What do you wish you were?

Sam: Your bar of soap.

Sarah: Say goodnight Sam!

Sam: Goodnight Sam.

Sarah grinned as she hung up. Sam was a funny, funny man. She knew that what he had said was all in jest. She enjoyed the hell out of it. Hey, if the modeling didn't work out for him, he could always do standup. She added more hot water, and leaned back again. She thought of Sam and that beautiful face. She remembered the way that he always touched his face, or rubbed his hands together, or the way he leaned his head back when he laughed really hard and the laugh lines around his eyes. She started to think of his mouth, and the way he ran his tongue over his lips. She knew without a doubt, that he knew exactly what he was doing. He knew that he was a hunka hunka burnin' love. He was a bad man. He was a *very* bad man… Sarah pictured what his mouth would look like as he leaned in to kiss her. What that tongue would feel like in her mouth instead of his own. Her hands reached into the water and she gently touched herself. As she pleasured herself, she could only see Sam and those blue eyes. For the first time since David's death, there was no crying with coming.

~~~

Sam leaned back and yelled at the walls "Bloody hell!" He loved Sarah's honesty. But tonight, her honesty killed him. Why did she have to tell him that she was bathing? She could have lied. She *should* have lied. He stared at his dick staring straight up at him. He could go to the hotel bar and pick up a girl to take care of his soldier. But Sam continued thinking of Sarah in the hot, silky water, and he put the soldier at ease himself. Then he called his sister.

Chapter 6:

Sarah hummed as she did chores the next day. She'd dusted, and swept and mopped. Aretha Franklin blared on the stereo, and she danced with the mop. She couldn't remember the last time she had hummed. She caught a glimpse of herself in the mirror, and stopped as she stared at the reflection that stared back. She had a tie-dyed bandana on her head, a paint spattered T-shirt, and yoga pants. As usual, she was barefoot. Sarah stared and laughed. She looked like a homeless person. Well! She would just have to do something about that!

Sarah changed clothes, put on some mascara and lip gloss, and grabbed her keys and purse. First, she would visit Liz at the shop. She needed to know if Liz thought she was crazy. Sarah had begun to think that she had actually lost her mind.

The shop was busy, and Liz was with a customer. Sarah wandered the aisles and waited for her to finish. When Liz had taken care of the customer, she walked over to Sarah and hugged her before she asked, "Are you okay, chickie?"

"I think that I am more than okay. I think that I am great. But I think I've lost my mind, and I just need you tell me that's okay. To lose my mind, that is." Sarah was a little manic and chattered a mile a minute.

Liz took her hand and led her back to her office. She sat her down in the chair across from her desk, leaned over and asked. "What's going on, Sarah?"

"I am going to buy lingerie! I am going to buy new panties, maybe edible, and push up bras, and new shoes, and maybe a fancy dress. But mainly under things. I am going to buy new makeup, and then I am going to get waxed, buffed, and sanded." Sarah wrung her hands in her lap.

Liz put her fingers together, and leaned back in her chair. "Alright Sarah. Good for you. What's wrong with wanting sexy things? What's really the issue?"

Sarah took a deep breath, "No one will see them except me. But that's okay. I'm a woman who has had nothing sexy in my life for five years. I want my sexy back."

Liz smiled. "Did Sam text last night?"

"Yes. He texted while I was soaking in the tub. He's a funny man..." Sarah's voice trailed off.

"And?" Liz asked, with a questioning look on her face. "What did he say?"

"That he could picture me being buoyant, and that he wanted to be my bar of soap!" Sarah wailed.

Liz couldn't help it. She tried. She really did, but she couldn't stop the laughter that exploded from her lungs. "Well! That's quite the picture!"

Sarah sniffled, and said. "That's not funny!"

Liz got herself under control and asked Sarah. "How did the rest of the conversation go?"

"I told him goodnight."

"Okay, and the problem is...?"

" I masturbated in the tub. I had a spine-tingling orgasm. And I didn't think of David one time," Sarah confessed.

Liz expelled a loud breath and said, "Well. You had a better evening than I did, then!"

Sarah looked up, and laughed a little.

Liz lowered her voice and stared hard at Sarah, "I want you to listen to me. I want you to listen hard. You know I love you, so you know that what I'm going to say comes from that love. I don't think Sam thinks of you as a 'friend'. I don't think he knows what you are to him." Sarah jerked her head up and grimly looked at Liz. "I think that you have something that he needs. And I don't mean just your body. Your spirit. Your heart. Whatever. What I want you to do is to go for it. Go for it hard, Sarah! A month? Six months? A year? Two Years? Who the hell cares? You, better than most, knows that life is too damn short. Buy your panties, and eat the damn things yourself if you want! Buy those shoes, and wax yourself bald. It will make you feel like a woman, again. Just because David up and died on you, doesn't mean that your womanhood died with him."

Sarah jerked as if Liz had slapped her. "But..."

"No buts, Sarah!" Liz snapped. "Even if you fall hard, and it ends badly, wouldn't you enjoy the ride? Because if it does, nothing has changed. You have your home, and children that you love. You have all of us. And you will have opportunities. And through it all you will be wearing sexy underwear."

Sarah slowly nodded. "I feel like a woman again. I had lost her somewhere along the way. Maybe I buried her with David. But that's not fair. It's not fair to me, and it's not fair to David, who taught me how to be a woman. I like Sam so much. And if we do crash and burn, I can't imagine not being friends with him. He's the one who has created the wretched creature in front of you, and as crazy as it sounds, I'm thankful that he has. Plus, I don't know if I'll ever see him again." Sarah leaned back and sighed.

Liz got up and walked around to hug her hard. "Oh! Sarah? Do *not* buy a pushup bra. If you *do* see him again, and you wear a pushup bra, you might give him a heart attack!"

~~~

Sarah left the store with her head held high and drove into the nearest big town thirty minutes away. It was a college town, so she knew she could find what she was looking for. She hit pay dirt at the first store she found. She got panties. Lots of panties. Some were string bikinis. Some were boy shorts. Some didn't even have a crotch. And, yes, she bought several pairs of edible ones, too. She could always snack on them when she was watching a movie. She bought bras. Lots and lots of bras. Pink ones. Black ones. Polka dotted ones. Strapless, demi, cupped and some that had interchangeable straps. She bought camisoles and bustiers. She bought see-through gowns, and gowns with straps that tied at the shoulders. She bought 'love lotion'. She didn't know what it was, but she thought it sounded like it had possibilities.

She took her bags to the truck with a grin on her face and headed to the shoe store. Oh, baby! Sarah did love shoes! She got leopard print and zebra print. She got black satin and deep red velvet. She even bought the little clutch bags that matched them. All of the shoes had six-inch heels. She was gonna be a fierce, sexy, panty-wearing Amazon! And she loved it!

She drove across town, grabbed a bagel, and then hit the formal shop. The very first dress she saw was in the window. It made her gasp out loud. It was deep red that would match the shoes that she had just purchased. It had long sleeves, and a very high neck. Like turtle neck high. It was fitted through the waist and hips, flaring out at the thighs. But the dress had *no* back. Absolutely none. The dress fastened around the neck like a halter top, and then sloped down like the back of a one-piece bathing suit. As she entered she found the sales girl to ask if she could try it on. The young girl looked at Sarah, then at the dress. Sarah thought to herself, "If she says one disparaging remark, I will bitch slap her *so* hard. She will *not* ruin my day."

The sales girl sighed, looked at Sarah and said, "You don't know how happy it makes me that you love this dress. It's my favorite in the store. We've had a lot of interest, but you have to be tall to carry it off. No offense, but with your bust line and height....oh! This is going to be stunning!" Sarah felt a little guilty about wanting to slap her.

She took the dress down gently, like it was a sacred thing, and led Sarah back to the dressing room. She hung it on the hook, and stepped out. Sarah shed her clothes. She had to see the full effect. That meant no bra straps and no panty line. She slowly stepped into the crush of deep red velvet, snapped the strap around her neck and stood back to look in the mirror. Sarah saw the most beautiful thing on the planet. It was someone else, because it certainly wasn't her. The dress fit her like a glove. The color was perfect for her skin. She slowly turned to the side and almost cried. Her entire back was open. The back seam hit her right above her ass crack. Both of the dimples over her cheeks were bare for the world to see. It was if it had been made just for her.

She heard the sales girl ask if she wanted to see it in the three-way mirror. Sarah just nodded at the air, and stepped out. The sales girl gasped, and put her hands to her mouth. "Oh my God! You look like a movie star! Or someone out of a Disney movie!"

Sarah walked - no, she glided - to the three-way, and just stood there in a daze. It was even better. She turned to the side, and stared at her back. She had the appropriate amount of side cleavage. Just a hint of boob to tease the eye. Sarah immediately thought that if she ever got depressed, she would just put this dress on. It was an ego booster. She didn't care how much it cost. This was her dress.

She purchased the red dress, as well as a couple of others. Sarah had no idea where she would ever wear them. Maybe she could wear them to Tuesday night photography classes.

~~~

Sam was in a foul mood. He had done nothing but complain. It was too hot. It was too dry. The shots were shit. There was nothing to do in this god-forsaken city. He was also ashamed of himself. It was not like him to complain. Sam took pride in his professionalism. The crew had gone out for beers, but Sam wasn't interested in going. Charlie had walked up to him at the end of the shoot and grabbed his arm. "Take it easy, Sam. This leg is almost done. You're tired. We're all tired and just want to go home." Charlie looked him in the eyes and said, "You need to get home, but right now you need to go to your room and talk to Sarah."

Sam sighed, "Sorry, Charlie. You know this isn't like me. You're right. I need home. I miss my family, and I miss my own bed. "

Charlie continued to look at Sam before he clapped him on the shoulder. "Call Sarah, please. She will ground you." Then he went to join the others.

Sam walked up to his room as he shook his head. "What the hell is wrong with me?" He took a shower, climbed in bed and started to read his emails. He answered the ones that needed to be answered. He checked into Facebook to see if there was anything he needed to comment on. As he scrolled through, he came upon Sarah's comment from a few weeks ago. He read it again:

Mr. Ramsay: You do not know me, nor do I know you, except what I know of you in your pictures. And according to your Facebook page, The OFFICIAL Sam Ramsay, and your Instagram account, that would be me, and 500,000 other people on this earth. I'm a photography nut from the middle of the United States, and the first thing I would like to say, is that you have a perfect face for the camera, and I would love to photograph you. But, I won't say that. I would like to say that you are one of the most beautifully symmetrical people I have ever seen, but I won't. I would like to say that you harken back to the era of Steve McQueen and Paul Newman. A man's man. But I won't. I won't say those things, because I am absolutely certain that you hear that all day, every day. Does that ever get tiresome? For people to only see you for your face, your blue eyes and your body? (which are all works of art by the way) Does anyone ever talk to you about sports? Or what you might think of politics? Or how you might feel about something other than your looks, or your workout routine? Do you even remember how to go about your day without posing? Have you lost yourself? Have you forgotten who you are? Are you lonely for just good conversation that doesn't revolve around your looks?

Before I comment further, let me state that I am not intending this to be mean or angry. It is not a proposition and I am not a crazy fan. Though, I will admit that I am a fan of the way the camera loves you. Do you ever crave quiet? Solace? I might have it totally wrong, as you might REALLY love yourself and all of the hoopla and jet setting. You might be a complete narcissistic ass, but I don't think so. I look at you and see sadness in your eyes. A wanting. A needing. I know what it feels like to want something so bad it physically hurts. A need for something you can never have. My heart hurts for you and I don't know why. I have never written a fan letter in my life, and I feel totally stupid for writing these comments, but I have become obsessed with my heartache for you. I thought that writing these thoughts down, might get it out of my system and put my mind at ease. See what I just did? I've made this post all about me! What a weasel I am! Anyway, forget all the above words, as I'm sure you think I'm just a crazy cat lady who wants your body. By the way, I don't have a cat.

The last two lines always made him laugh. It had made him laugh before he even knew who Sarah was. She was good at that. Making him laugh. Sam lay back and seriously thought about what this relationship was, and where it could or would go. Was it a relationship? Did he want it to be? If it turned into something more, could they make it work? People would definitely talk. Everyone had tried to marry him off to every ingénue and starlet that had been popular. But, Sam didn't care. They had no gossip to talk about when it came to him. He had made sure of that. But, could Sarah handle it? Sam thought that Sarah could handle most anything. She already had.

Would Sarah want to pursue something more with him? She had made a good life for herself, and she knew what was important. It was one of the many things he respected her for. This want and need for Sarah had come out of the blue, and Sam was at a loss. He didn't understand his own feelings, so how was he expected to know what Sarah's were. One thing he was sure of, Sarah was in his life to stay, whatever kind of relationship it ended up being. He wanted to meet her children, and her girlfriends He wanted to observe her living her life. He needed to get home and talk to his sister about it. She could help with his confusion. In the meantime, he just needed to talk to Sarah. Nothing more. Nothing less.

Sam: Are you there?

Sarah: Of course. I told you any time you needed me.

Sam: I've been an ass today. What did you do?

Sarah: Why were you an ass? I went shopping!

Sam: I don't know why. I just need to get home. I'm beat. What did you buy?

Sarah: I bought panties!

Sam: PANTIES?

Sarah: Yes! Panties and bras, and lingerie. And shoes and dresses. Retail therapy.

Sam: Do you do that often?

Sarah: Actually, no. I don't remember the last time I shopped. I'm going to go get groomed tomorrow before class.

Sam: Groomed? Are you getting a flea bath ?

Sarah: LOL! No. I'm going to go get waxed, sanded, and buffed.

Sam: Oh. NOW I know what you mean. Where?

Sarah: I don't remember the name of the place. It's here in town.

Sam: No, I mean...WHERE?

Sarah: Everywhere. Does that make you hot, Sam?

Sam: Yes. Yes, it does. Do you always do this?

Sarah: What? Waxed?

Sam: No. You've left me with blue balls the last three nights. You are killing me.

Sarah: Hmmmm...I didn't know I had such power! I like it!

Sam: I would like it, too, if it didn't leave me with throbbing balls.

Sarah: I'm sorry Sam. We will have to discuss "your problem" in person. Maybe I can help?

Sam: I don't have "a problem". In person would be beyond great. I miss your filthy mouth.

Sarah: My "filthy mouth" misses you, too.

Sam: Oh, Sarah. You make me groan.

Sarah: I have you to thank for my sudden panty fetish.

Sam: Me?

Sarah: The innocent remark, or maybe it wasn't so innocent, about being my bar of soap?

Sam: Yeah. I meant that.

Sarah: You reminded me that I was a woman. I had lost that part of me somewhere in the last 5 years.

I had become so used to just being "the widow", that I forgot who I was.

Sam: Sarah, you are nothing, if not *ALL* woman.

Sarah: Thank you. My heart just did a little flip flop.

Sam: What are we doing?

Sarah: Shamelessly flirting.

Sam: No. I mean, yes. Yes, we are. But what are we DOING?

Sarah: I don't know, Sam. I'm just going to ride the wave and see where it takes us. The ball (not blue) is

in your court. I am open to suggestions.

Sam: This conversation does not need to be done via text. We need to talk. In person.

Sarah: I agree. How are we going to arrange that?

Sam: I am thinking. Will you be available tomorrow?

Sarah: Anytime, Sam Ramsay. I've been telling you that.

Sam: Say goodnight Sarah.

Sarah: Goodnight Sarah.

Sarah had rehashed the conversation with Sam last night over and over in her head. No. She didn't regret anything she'd said. And she couldn't read anything negative in Sam's remarks. It was flattering to think that she made him hot. And if he hadn't gone and picked up a girl in the bar to help him with his problem, well, then, that was flattering, too. Maybe he had, but, Sarah didn't think so. Sam sounded as confused as she was about their status. And that was somehow validating. It meant that Sam had thought about it, too. Sam Ramsay had been thinking about her.

Sarah was waxed, sanded, and buffed within an inch of her life. She wasn't completely bald, but she liked the look. Waxing was not enjoyable, but the results were worth it. She had forgotten how uncomfortable it was, and had let the mouth filth fly, but she was going to keep a standing appointment. It beat the hell out of having to shave every other day. She also thought that waxing people would be a horrible job. How many coochies could one woman look at in a day, before getting sick of them?

The girls waited for Sarah outside the classroom. They were all excited to see if Sam had continued to text her. Sarah showed them last night's conversation. They were all quiet for a moment, before Bev looked at her and said, "He's got it bad. Fucking Sam Ramsay has fallen for our Sarah."

"I don't think that either one of us knows what we're doing. But, I think it's going to be fun trying to figure it out." Sarah said with a big grin on her face. She turned and gave Liz a big hug, and whispered in her ear, "Thank you!"

Sarah looked at all of them, and shouted, "Guess what I did? I bought panties!" She filled them in on her shopping spree, and they all giggled as they walked into class.

Thirty minutes later, Sarah's phone buzzed. She usually turned it off in class, but she still hadn't heard from Sam, so she had left it on. She caught Liz' eye before she stepped outside to talk to Sam.

Sam: Sarah?

Sarah: I'm here Sam.

Sam: Sorry. I know you're in class.

Sarah: Not a problem. I've stepped outside.

Sam: Did you get waxed, sanded, and buffed?

Sarah: Yes, I did! I am quite...slick!

Sam: Bloody hell! You are KILLING me! Stop! Just stop! (smile)

Sarah: Sorry. But I really am. I made a standing appointment to stay...slick...

Sam: I am starting to picture you in all your glorious...slickness, but, we have more important

things to discuss..

Sarah: I'm all ears.

Sam: I finish the shoot in Malibu on Thursday. I am flying to London Friday morning. I have 2 weeks

before the grind of the Oak Wood campaign starts. I plan on sleeping in my own bed, living in

my own house and visiting with my family the first week. I would like you to come the second week.

Is that doable? Or, do you even want to? (please say yes)

Sarah: It's doable. Are you sure?

Sam: I have never been more sure in my life. I want to have you in my home, with me, just being.

Sarah: That sounds...really nice, Sam. (sigh) But no expectations, alright? No pressure on either one of us. I'm still not sure what "us" is anyway.

Sam: No expectations. I'm not sure either, but I'd like to work on finding out. I booked your flight out of St. Louis next Thursday at 2:15 PM. You will land in Heathrow at 8:30 PM. I will be waiting. I will be the tall chap holding flowers.

Sarah: Sam, I can buy my own ticket!

Sam: No! I want you to come to ME, so please let me do this. Besides, I already booked it.

Sarah: You're awfully sure of yourself, aren't you?

Sam: No. Just hopeful.

Sarah: Anything else I need to know?

Sam: No. Maybe... Shit! I have a charity benefit to attend. You can go with me, or not. It will

be formal. Big donors. Very boring.

Sarah: Not a problem. I've got just the dress.

Sam: I've never seen you in a dress.

Sarah: You've really never seen me in anything but a T- shirt and panties. We only saw each for two and a half days.

Sam: I loved that T- shirt...

Sarah: I'll be sure and bring it.

Sam: Will you call me later? When you get home?

Sarah: Should I be in the tub when I do?

Sam: Sarah! You really are killing me.

Sarah had just hung up when class let out. The girls filtered out and walked over.

"What's up?" Julie asked.

Sarah looked up in a happy daze. "I'm going to London next week!"

They met at Julie's where Ashley immediately went to mix up her mystery drink of the evening. They were all excited to hear about Sarah's trip, and wanted to know all the details. Ashley yelled from the kitchen, "Don't start without me!"

A few minutes later, Ashley came bearing a glass laden tray. Julie passed them out, raised her glass, and toasted "To Sarah! May she be screwed many, many times by a tall British model!" They all toasted. Karen asked. "What is this yumminess, Ashley?"

Sarah grinned, and looked at Ashley, "I know! It's a Sidecar. It's a British drink. You, Ashley, are awesome!"

They all started to talk at once. When was she leaving? Did she need a ride so she wouldn't have to leave her truck? Was she staying at Sam's? Would they be sharing a room? Was she taking her camera? Would they take in the sights? Would she meet any of his family?

"Hold on guys! Hold on!" Sarah exclaimed. "I have no idea! I will figure that out when I get there."

Liz piped up, "Well, you'll have plenty of panties to take! And I expect you to come home with less than half of them! I will be doing a panty count before departure and upon your return."

Sarah looked at her quizzically. "What on earth for?"

"Because I expect at least half of them to be ripped off!"

They all laughed and got comfortable. Sarah had suddenly gotten quiet.

Bev looked over at Sarah, and asked, "What's wrong sugar?"

Sarah looked up at all of them. "I'm a little nervous."

"Well, of course you are! You're flying off to a place to see a person that you really don't know. Look at it as a big adventure. Like Pee Wee Herman!" teased Julie.

"No, it's not that," sighed Sarah. "First, I don't even know what we'll be doing. I don't even plan on us sleeping together. I still don't know if Sam even sees me like that."

"Oh, honey! It's like riding a bicycle. It will all come back to you," Karen said sweetly.

Sarah shrugged her shoulders, and continued. "Second, I was with David for 35 years. He's been gone for five years. That's 40 years. And... I've never been with anyone else. We were both virgins when we made love for the first time when we were both 16." Sarah sighed. "David was my first, last and only."

"Darling girl!" said Liz. "That's about the most romantic thing I've ever heard. That's just so sweet! But, all you need to do is talk to Sam. If he's as thoughtful and kind as you say he is, he will make it a wonderful experience. There is nothing to be ashamed of. I can guarantee you that he won't think so either. He should feel honored."

Sarah whispered, "I just don't want to embarrass myself. I have no... experience, while Sam has 'experienced' hundreds I'm sure. I just don't want to be a lousy lover and disappoint him."

"If Sam cares for you, and evidently he does, because he's flying you to fucking London. He will care even more for you knowing that you are honest with him. And it will turn him on even more to realize that he has such a willing student!" Julie told her.

Sarah left for home feeling much better. She and Sam had been nothing, if not honest with each other. She would rather he know, so he would understand why she sucked at physical intimacy. If she didn't tell him, he would just think she was a lousy lay. Considering that she had nothing to compare it to, who knew? She might be a tiger in the bedroom. And who knew if sex would even be part of their activities. She told herself to stop over thinking it. She would go to London with no expectations and just have a good time.

When she got home, she laughed to herself wickedly. She went and ran a tub full of hot bubbles. She stepped out of her clothes, and slid into the silky water. A few minutes later she texted Sam.

Sarah: Sam? I'm home.

Sam: How were the girls?

Sara: Excited for me. And you.

Sam: I'm excited for you to come, too.

Sarah: Well... give me a minute... I am getting excited, too. And I may come...

Sam: You are in the fucking tub, aren't you???

Sarah: The water feels so good on all my...slickness.

Sam: I am groaning, Sarah. You are wicked.

Sarah: I am trying. But I've never done this sexting stuff and I don't even know if you're interested. How am I

doing? Should I stop? Am I grossing you out?

Sam: You are doing just fine. And you could never gross me out. But don't start something that you can't finish. I refuse to have throbbing balls tonight.

Sarah: I wish those throbbing balls and dick was here in the tub with me. Where are you? What are you doing?

Sam: I am laying in bed listening to you get your rocks off. And getting really excited.

Sarah: No rock offing, yet. I'm waiting for you to come rock climbing with me.

Sam: I can do that...

Sarah: Sam?

Sam: Sarah?

Sarah: I have become very... buoyant...

Sam: (groan)

Sarah: Can you see... my buoys?

Sam: Yes. I see your buoys surrounding my dick... Your skin is like silk and my dick is like steel. Softness against hardness.

Sarah: That's a very nice picture... I'm picturing my lips on your shoulder. You taste so good. I want to taste more of you. I want to feel all of you. Can you see how my hand movement makes the water move?

Sam: Yes.

Sarah: Can you see how that movement makes my buoys ... bob?

Sam: Can you see what my hand is doing? All I can picture is my mouth on you and wondering how long I can hold my breath. I know that you'll taste as good as I've been imagining.

Sarah: (moan) You've been imagining me?

Sam: (groan) Fuck yes. Every night. I've been imagining your taste, your noises and your feel and smell. I've been imagining all the things I could do to you and for you. Have you been imagining me?

Sarah: Constantly. I've turned into a cougar.....

Sam: I love soft, purring... pussies.

Sarah: I guess this means I can count on some orgasms when I come to London?

Sam: I hope so! If not, I haven't done my job. So much for expectations, huh?

Sarah: Talk to me some more Sam. Tell me all the dirty things you want to do to me, and I'll tell you all the dirty things I'm going to do to you.

So, they did.

~~~

Holy fucking shit! Sarah was going to kill him!. Sam still panted as he lay spread eagled on the bed. Like Sarah, he had never done the sexting stuff either. Oh, plenty of idiots had tried, but Sam wasn't interested in them enough to even participate. He would just hang up. He didn't think that anyone out there could have done it any better than Sarah just had. She *was* wicked. And he loved it. He laughed softly and wondered what the British press would say if they knew Sam Ramsay had just jerked off to phone sex with a fifty-five year old woman? He wondered what the press *was* going to say when Sarah started to appear on his arm in London and the States? Every woman in London would have jumped at the chance to share his bed. He wasn't being cocky. That was a fact. It had been that way for as long as he could remember. What no one knew is that Sam had never had a woman share his bed. Other beds, yes. But not **his** bed. They had never been to his home. and he never let them spend the night. He realized that he was thinking about his future with Sarah. What the hell? He wondered if she saw him in her future.

He was counting down the days until he was home. Three days. Three long days. He couldn't wait to see his sister and his niece and nephew. And of course, his mum and dad. But, his mind had already skipped ahead to the following week when Sarah would be there. He didn't expect anything from her. He wanted her to be comfortable and at ease. They didn't have to sleep together. Sam realized that she had been married to the love of her life for thirty-five years, and she had to be a little nervous. Sam was sure that Sarah had been faithfully in love with her husband. That's who Sarah was. He didn't want her nervous. He just wanted them to get to know each other. This whole thing had started so fast. It would be good to slow it down. But, fuck! If she was really like what she wrote, he didn't think he'd be able to keep it at a slow pace. No. He didn't want her nervous, because he was nervous enough for both of them. It would be the first time that a woman was in his thoughts for his future and it scared the shit out of him.

Chapter 7:

The week crawled by. Sarah had trouble concentrating. All she could think about was London and seeing Sam. They had only spent two days together. Two days. But they had experienced mind blowing sex more than once. On the phone. Sarah had enjoyed sex via text. It had been fun, and had given her a weird sense of control over the situation. Sam had certainly been open to the experience. They had learned quickly, but had kept it to sexting only. Sarah had told him that she didn't want to experience all of his naked beauty via SKYPE. She wanted to wait for the real thing. He had agreed.

Sarah shook her head, and wondered how this had happened so fast. On the one hand she wanted to scream that it needed to slow down. But on the other she wanted a fiery inferno. Her emotions were a never-ending roller coaster. She just needed one evening with Sam. An evening of just talking. She had a million questions, and she would not let this - whatever it was - to progress, until she had answers. Sam was a forty-year old stud, with more money than the Queen. He could have anyone. Why, at this moment in time, did he seem to want her? She suffered no insecurities, but he was Sam fucking Ramsay, the international jet setter and male super model who looked like a work of art. She was just Sarah Reid from Missouri.

Sarah had made her peace with David. David knew that she had a huge capacity for love. Sarah loved hard. Sarah loved forever. She also had a sexual appetite that had been stifled since his death. Sarah would want it for David. He would want the same for her. There would be no ghosts in Sarah's future. Sarah had prepared herself for heartache, but she hoped for happiness. She knew that what she had with Sam would not be sustainable. He was dedicated to London and his career. Sarah needed to know if she could go into this knowing it would end. His answers to her questions would tip the scales one way or the other. But, in the next moment, all she could think about was wrapping her legs around Sam's back and getting the high hard one. Regardless of the cost. Gaaah! He had her tied in knots.

The girls met at Liz's house after class. Sarah would miss next week's get together, so she needed a fix before she left for London.

"Are you all ready to go, Sarah?" Karen asked as she sat on the couch.

"I'll bet you've had your fucking bags packed since last week, haven't you? All you have to take is a carryon full of panties." Julie raised her eyebrows.

Sarah sank back into the leather chair. "I am *so* ready."

"Has Sam given you any idea what you two might be doing in London for the week? Besides screwing?" Bev asked.

Sarah thought before answering. "The only thing I know for sure is that we have a charity benefit to attend on Saturday evening. It's a formal gala. That should be fun, but I think Sam just wants to hang out. We really need to get to know each other. This has been a really fast ride, and we both feel like we need to slow down. I also feel like this is a "Sarah Test". I don't know what the questions are on this test, but I hope I pass."

"You shouldn't have to pass a test, Sarah! " Liz exclaimed.

"No, I understand the questions. I have some of my own. There are lots of basic logistical problems, schedules, and living in two different universes. Sam works more in the UK and Europe than he does in the States. I'm willing to meet him wherever, but I could never leave my home to live somewhere else. It's not likely I would be asked to do that anyway. But, I've made a life that I love. And I'm committed to that. He has different commitments. Work and family and a home of his own." Sarah sighed. "It will either work or it won't, and I have come to terms with it. I am just going to go with the flow and see where it leads me."

"Good for you Sarah. I am so proud of you." Bev got up to give Sarah a big hug.

Julie just couldn't resist. "You have balls Sarah Reid. Huge balls. "

"Oh! I have to do this before I forget!" Sarah muttered and pulled out her phone.

Sarah: Sam

Sarah: You are probably busy, but I needed to ask. Do you mind if I bring my camera?

Sarah: I would like to take pictures while I'm there. But, I will understand if that makes you uncomfortable. But you also know I do it for my own enjoyment. No one else.

Sarah: Call me later? The girls say hi.

Sarah looked up at the girls. "My camera. I wanted to make sure that it was okay with him if I brought it."

"Why on earth would he care if you brought your camera?" asked Ashley.

"Believe me. I understand why he would have an aversion to it."

Liz said. "The press in the UK is much worse than here in the States. They will say anything and sell anything about anyone. Headline: The Queen Mother pregnant with Prince Harry's son. They are vile. "

Plus, he's in front of cameras every day. Every stinkin' day. Sometimes for twelve to fourteen hours. Cameras are Sam's livelihood, but not his life."

~~~

Sam: Sarah?

Sarah: Sam?

Sam: Sorry. I was putting my niece and nephew to bed.

Sarah: That makes my heart happy. Are you at your sister's?

Sam: Yeah. I'm staying the night. Recharging. It's good.

Sarah: Recharging IS good.

Sam: I told my sister about you...

Sarah: Hmmm... how'd that go? Should I be worried?

Sam: LOL! No! My sister is the best. But you need to know that she is evil. She always gives me good advice. But, only when I ask for it.

Sarah: Did you ask for it?

Sam: No. I don't need her advice at this time, thank you very much. But, she wants to meet you.

Sarah: Whatever and whomever, Sam I am all yours for a week. For whatever *you choose to do.*

Sam: That sounds very enticing.

Sarah: In 2 nights. At this very time. I will be looking for a very tall chap holding flowers.

Sam: Counting down the hours until then. Good night Sarah Reid.

Sarah: Goodnight Sam Ramsay.

Sam hung up and looked up at the ceiling with a sigh. He took a drink of his scotch and played with his glass.

"You've got it bad, Sam. I've never seen you like this." Sam's sister sat down on the sofa beside him.

Sam turned and looked at Danni. He sighed again. "Yeah, I do. Did I tell you that she's 55?"

Danni patted Sam's arm. "Yes. Several times. And my question to you is, so?"

Sam raised an eyebrow. Danni continued. "Does she make you happy, Sam? Is she the first thing you think of when you get up in the morning? Is she the last thing you think of at night? Do you see things and think 'Sarah would love that'? "

Sam gave her a crooked little grin. "Honestly? All the time. But I don't really know her."

"Sam, you've already made your life choices. As has Sarah. She doesn't sound like some young, brainless thing that you have on your arm every night. She's a grown-ass woman." Danni held up

94

her hand when Sam started to interrupt. "I know! I know that most of those bimbos are sent by the agency for PR reasons. But, you've bedded half of them. What do you talk about when you get done screwing them? Hmm?"

"I haven't done that for a long time." Sam muttered. "You know that. And, there was nothing to talk about after screwing them. That's why they were never in my bed or my home, or why they never spent the night. And why I don't do that anymore."

Danni squeezed his arm harder. "But Sarah is coming for the week." She raised her eyebrow again. "Are you putting her up in a hotel?"

"Of course not! I would never do that to Sarah!"

"So... she's staying at the house?" Danni asked smugly.

"Well, yeah....Of course!" Sam said. Then he grew quiet and looked at his sister.

Danni leaned back against the sofa. "Well, that's a first." She looked at Sam from the corner of her eye. "I hope you know how to deal with a woman, Sam. Because Sarah is a woman. She doesn't sound like a hot to trot middle-aged gal who is just hoping to get laid by a sexy younger male model. She has a life. She has decided to let you into that life. This is a big deal. A very big deal. And I know that you've thought about the UK press. I don't think you need to worry about Sarah. It sounds like she has already experienced pain of the worst kind. She is a strong woman. It's up to you to decide what you're willing to put up with regarding your career. I see prioritizing in your future, Sam. It's time. You've made your millions. You have fame and fortune. You are a very smart man who has made smart decisions regarding your future, your money, your family and your charities.. What else is it that you're trying to prove? Are you as narcissistic as some of the press thinks you are? If Sarah can make you see the light, as to what's important in this world, then I want to fuck her to thank her. And don't deny it. You want to fuck her, too. You deserve happiness Sam. You've earned it."

Sam shook his head slowly. "Believe me, I know. We only spent two-and-a half days together, but we've talked every day since then. About everything. She makes me laugh, and she makes me think. I want to meet her friends, and her family. I want to see her in the house that she loves so much. I also admire the fact that she can talk openly about the husband that she lost. How she can still love him but live her life. Sarah has no ghosts going forward. She listens and she's very perceptive. She has the biggest heart. I want to use this week to slow down, and really get to know each other. I'm sure she has as many questions as I do. We need to figure out if this thing is possible."

"Sounds like you have it all figured out. I hate to tell you, but we never have it figured out. It's a process. Sometimes it's easy. Sometimes it's difficult. But, if there is 'meat on the bone' so to speak, it's so worth the work". Danni spoke softly.

Sam looked at Danni with a grin. "You know what's the best thing about Sarah? The absolute best thing?"

"What?"

Sam yelled. "She's a bawdy broad! And, did I tell you she has huge tits?""

Danni laughed along with him. "You are doomed big brother."

March

Chapter 8:

The six-and-a half-hour flight to London felt like twenty-four. Sarah was restless, and excited. She kept tapping her heel on the plane floor. She looked down and patted her knee to stop her foot. And then she grinned. She loved her boots. She had dressed for Sam. Sarah had always dressed for herself, but tonight was different. She wanted to make an entrance. She was wearing her standard black leggings with a long-sleeve, high-neck deep wine-colored tunic with a keyhole front. It showed just enough cleavage. Hey! If you got 'em, flaunt 'em! But the pièce de résistance was the boots. They were six-inch black suede leather stilettos. They went to the middle of her thighs and laced up the back. They were sex on heels. Sarah felt very sexy in them, and she had gotten more than a glance or two at the airport. Yep. They would do the trick.

After an uneventful landing, Sarah slowly made her way through customs. As she entered the last gate, the hairs on the back of neck stood up. She felt Sam, and as she looked up she saw a very tall chap holding at least two dozen stargazer lilies. There stood Sam In all of his six-foot-four-inch glory. He wore a fucking suit! A suit! He looked like James Bond waiting for one of the Bond girls. His blue eyes were almost black as they burned holes through hers. Those eyes traveled slowly over her body. He devoured her with those eyes. Sarah stopped breathing. She couldn't help it. Sam Ramsay was delicious. She couldn't wait to eat him up. She almost came as she stood right there in the airport. Especially when he slowly grinned that sexy, slow grin that turned her panties to ash. He knew exactly what he was doing. Sam was - what the books would call - smoldering. Yes. He smoldered, and he was making her body burn up. She did not even notice the cameras that were flashing at him. She wanted to kick the airport security and the custom agents. She panted and whispered to herself, "Hurry up! Hurry up! I want to fondle that gorgeous man standing over there. Slow down my ass!"

Sam saw her as soon as she turned the corner into customs. She was hard to miss. Sarah was a tall woman, but tonight she towered over everyone. Holy fuck! Sam had to swallow. Those boots! He couldn't wait to see Sarah in those boots again. Just the boots. He knew that he was watching her intensely. He couldn't help it. This woman exuded sultriness and sexiness. He knew that he had been in denial. He growled to himself, "So much for slowing down." He wanted to fuck her right there on the terminal floor. The paparazzi would love that! It was easy to ignore them, because all he saw was her. Sam had never seen an entrance like Sarah had just made. Sarah looked up and saw him immediately. A smile spread across her face as she watched him slowly fuck her with his eyes. He saw her shiver a little as if she knew exactly what he thought.

Finally! Sarah made it through the gate and Sam walked up to meet her. He leaned forward as he put his arm with the flowers around her back, and put his hand on the top of her ass. As she leaned into him, Sam enjoyed the tease of a breast that was now pushed against his chest. He looked in her eyes and kissed her with a slow, hot sweep of his mouth. God! She tasted and felt as sweet as he had imagined. He stood back and looked at her again with a question in his eyes. She nodded slightly. Sam kissed her again. This time more slowly and more deeply. His tongue met hers for the briefest of moments, and then he growled into her ear. "That was quite the entrance, madam. I would give you your flowers, but they're hiding the hard on that's in my pants right now. Let's get your luggage and get out of here."

Sarah giggled a little as the cameras followed them to the baggage carousel, where they waited for her luggage. Sam had not yet removed his arm from Sarah's waist. For this week, she was all his. He also noticed that the paparazzi took just as many pictures of Sarah as they took of him. And why wouldn't they? Sarah was stunning. Sarah was sexy. Sarah was unknown. She was oblivious to the fact that flashbulbs were everywhere. Her smiles were for him only, and he could not get out of the airport quick enough.

The luggage finally rolled through the chute. Sam put her bags on a cart and they finally left the terminal. Sam had parked close, and Sarah was thankful. Her legs wobbled, and she needed to sit. Sam's kiss had just about made her immobile. Sam had smelled of oak leaves, whiskey and sin. He tasted like heaven. She could still feel the scratchy tingle of his stubble on her cheek. She was a goner.

Sam had walked her to a blue Mercedes sedan and placed the luggage in the trunk. Flashbulbs still went off as Sam opened the door for her, but first, Sarah stopped and slowly turned toward the cameras. Sam saw her cock her hip and place one of those long legs out in all it's booted glory. She straightened her posture which pushed her magnificent tits even higher, and slowly smiled. The smile grew wider and wider. "Thank you all! It's my first time visiting London, and you've made me feel very welcome! Goodnight!" The flashes went crazy, and the reporters yelled questions at her. She never broke character. She slowly folded all six feet and four inches into the front seat as Sam shut the door.

He turned to face the cameras. "She's stunning, isn't she? You can quote me on that. And before you plaster 'unknown older woman" across the rags in the morning, her name is Sarah."

Sam was laughing when he got in the car. "You were amazing!"

Sarah looked at him and shrugged. "I figured that you came to pick me up at Heathrow yourself. You knew that they would be here. I guessed that you'd made a decision regarding how public we were going to be, so I just went with it. I hope that's okay."

"Okay? Okay? You're kidding, right? You were magnificent!" Sam couldn't stop his laughter.

Sarah leaned toward him and whispered. "It is so good to see you, Sam Ramsay."

Sam whispered back. "It is so good to see you, too, Sarah Reid."

They drove in comfortable silence for a few minutes as they collected their thoughts.

"Your hair is red." observed Sam.

Sarah laughed as she brushed her fingers through it. "Yes. I had it done when I got waxed, sanded, and buffed. Do you like it?"

"Yes. I do. But, I have to say, that I love those boots even more. Especially on those legs," growled Sam.

"I looooove these boots," Sarah sighed as she ran her hand up and down her leg.

Sam groaned a little as he watched her hand on that long leg. "I can't wait to see those boots on those legs... and nothing else." His heart pounded and he felt sweat on his back. "It's about a thirty minute drive to my house. I have food in the AGA. We'll eat, have a drink, and talk. No other expectations. Okay?" He glanced at Sarah to judge her reaction.

"That sounds wonderful," murmured Sarah. Her heart galloped like a race horse.

~~~

When Sarah saw the lights of London, she squealed like a tourist. Sam asked, "Would you like to see the sights tomorrow Sarah? You could get loads of pictures."

"I was under the impression that we would be staying in. You know, just being. Hopefully, I can catch the sights when I come back for the next visit. Plus, getting good shots would involve trying to outrun all the cameras, wouldn't it?" Sarah asked.

They had pulled up to an iron gate surrounded by a large red brick wall. Sam punched a button on the dash board and the gates swung open. Before he pulled the car forward, he turned in his seat and took Sarah's arm. "Are you coming for another visit, Sarah?"

Sarah brushed Sam's cheek with her fingers and whispered, "Oh, I hope so, Sam. I hope so."

Sam informed Sarah that the trunk of a car was called a boot in the UK. They removed her luggage, and Sam unlocked the front door. As they entered, the first thing Sarah noticed was the smell. Whatever Sam had put in the oven filled the house with the most delicious aroma. The second thing she noticed was that it was an absolutely stunning small home. Sarah sat her bag down and slowly turned in a circle, before she slowly started wandering her way through the house. Her eyes moved across old walnut wood wainscoting and leaded glass windows. She noticed the marble around the fireplace that blazed with flames. Lamps had been strategically placed by the chairs. There were soft pillows and comfortable leather furniture. Nothing heavy or too masculine like Sarah had pictured in her head. It was not a typical bachelor pad. It was beautiful. She noticed a beautiful old secretary that she guessed held the television. She went to rub her hands down the tiger maple wood. "That is a stunning piece!"

Sam looked pleased. "Thanks. I made that."

Sarah turned and looked at him with her mouth agape. "You made that? Where did you learn to do that?"

He shrugged his shoulders. "My dad. He can take anything and make it into something else. I like to do that with things that most people throw away. If it's good wood, it actually hurts me to see it junked. There's lots of that kind of stuff throughout the house." Sam was silently ecstatic that Sarah had noticed his work. "We'll take the bags up later. Let's eat!"

Sarah followed Sam to the back of the house. When she entered the kitchen, all she say was, "Wow."

It was a chef's kitchen, without being overwhelmingly full of stainless steel. Sam had kept the character of the age of the house, with a lot of white cabinetry, antique hardware, and old brick flooring. There were pot racks, white subway tile, and a farmhouse sink. The crowning glory was the massive AGA range in cobalt blue sitting in the middle of the cabinetry.

Sarah jumped a little and grinned. "I have an AGA, too! Of course, mine isn't as large, and it's red. They are wonderful in the winter. Mine keeps the whole kitchen heated."

Sam took pride in his home and Sarah's appreciation for it filled him with happiness. And, they both had an AGA. Go figure. They were pretty common over here, but not so much in the States. "Sit. I will pour us drinks, and get our plates."

Sarah sat at a beautiful farmhouse table and watched Sam work. He had taken his suit jacket off, and he had removed his tie. The top three buttons had been unbuttoned and his sleeves were rolled up. She could see the muscles of his back through his shirt. They rolled with his movements. Sam had a beautiful back, and it made her swallow. Her mouth had suddenly gotten dry. She also noticed the muscles in his forearms as he poured them each a glass of Jameson and sat her glass in front of her. When Sam bent over to take the food out of the oven, all Sarah could think was, "I would love to take a big bite of that ass!" It was such a nice ass.

Sam turned around, and caught her stare. He looked at her with a big grin. "I hope you like Beef Wellington as much as you apparently like my ass. They're both my specialty."

Sarah's heart flip flopped crazily. There he stood in an impeccable suit, with oven mitts on both hands, holding a casserole dish. He had done this for her, and she thought she would just melt.

"What?" asked Sam.

Sarah blurted, "This. This right here." She couldn't get any more words out, and she weirdly felt like crying. Sam was the most beautiful man she had ever seen.

Sam sat the dish down, and quickly crossed to Sarah. As he knelt in front of her he took her in his arms and rocked her gently. "Sweet Sarah. What did I do?" Sam's stomach was tightening, and he felt a little nervous. Really, he felt a lot nervous. He didn't know what he had done to upset Sarah.

"Oh, Sam!" wailed Sarah. "Just look at you! You in your oven-mitted, casserole-carrying, James Bond suit."

Sam shook his head. "Uh...what?"

"You did this for *me*. You dressed for me. You cooked for me. You even brought me flowers!" Sarah had gotten louder. Sarah was mortified, but couldn't quit babbling.

Sam continued to rock her, but couldn't help but laugh. Sarah felt his shoulders jerking, and accused him. "You're laughing at me!"

Sam sat back on his heels. "Yes, Sarah, I am laughing at you. You nutter. I wanted you here. I wanted to cook for you. I got the flowers so you would know who I was."

"Oh, Sam, Believe me. You didn't need to bring the flowers. I would notice you anywhere. You were the tallest man in the terminal who was fucking me with his eyes. I think every woman there wished she was me."

"And that's why I'm glad I brought the flowers. They were the only thing saving my bulging genitalia from being spread across the rags in the morning!"

"Sam?" Sarah sounded like an eight-year-old girl, and it kind of broke Sam's heart. It kind of pissed Sarah off, but she couldn't help it. "Can we eat your wonderful Beef Wellington, and drink our whiskey? And when we're done with that, could we have another glass of whiskey and make out for a while? We do need to talk, but the elephant in the room, is the sexual tension. Let's just make out. Then we'll talk. If you're lucky you might get to first base. You never even got up to bat when you carried me to the car In St. Louis."

Sam stood as he tilted his head back and laughed loudly. He caught his breath, and assured Sarah. "I would love to make out with you."

They couldn't eat in silence, so they peppered each other with questions.

Sarah wanted to know what else Sam cooked, because his Beef Wellington was to die for. He told her just about anything. Cooking was his second favorite thing to do.

Sarah asked what was his favorite. He wiggled his eyebrows, grinned and just looked at her.

"Oh," was all she said.

He wanted to know how often she saw her children. Sarah told him that they were always together for the holidays, and that they tried several times throughout the year to see each other. She told him about the long phone calls on the weekends. Sam asked if she had told them about him. She had. She was going to be away for a week. They would have noticed. They wanted their mom to do whatever made her happy. They were good like that.

Sarah asked about his sister and her kids. Sam told her that she was his favorite person, and that they had always been close. He was three years older, but Danni had always mothered him. Thomas was his six-year-old nephew, and Violet was his four-year old niece. He tried to see them as often as possible.

Sam asked about Sarah's house. She talked about building it with David with no regret in her voice, and without any awkwardness for him. She made Sam laugh about the big fight they had over the finish of the hardware. Sam asked who had won that battle. Sarah just grinned and said she did of course. She told him about the girls' slumber parties when it was her turn to host them. She told him that they always drank too much, and talked very dirty. Sam thought that could be great fun, and could they all talk dirty to him?

Sarah was curious about Sam's house. He told her it was built in 1802, and had been a mess when he bought it in an estate sale. He and his dad had done all of the interior work themselves. He told her that she was the only person, besides Thomas and Violet, to stay there. Sarah gulped, assuming that meant that he had finished the house in the last year, but Sam told her he had moved in seven years ago. Sarah gulped again.

Sam asked Sarah if she would tell him about David, but only if she wanted. Sarah just smiled at Sam, and told him about them being high school sweethearts. How funny he was and about his terrible jokes. And what a great father he had been and how much he loved her. She told him about the dancing and eating in bed. Sarah told Sam that she had no regrets. Thirty-five years was a lot more than a lot of people got.

Sarah wanted to know what a typical day in the life of Sam Ramsay was. He told her about having to be at a shoot early, just to do a lot of waiting around. He said some shoots were great, and some were awful. He loved the television commercials he did for Oak Wood. Marta, the female model that was in them with him, was a good friend. Sarah asked him about kissing all the women. Sam told her that he liked kissing, but that Marta's husband didn't. He also shared that it was always awkward, because of the number of people that surrounded them.

They finished eating. They both cleaned up and loaded the dishwasher. Sam poured them another glass of whiskey, and they went and sat in front of the fireplace. They sat in silence for a few minutes, as they nursed their whiskey.

Sam turned to Sarah. "I want you to know that I'm ready to make out now. We can make out as long, or as quickly as you want. I want you to know, that I will get to first base. That's to make up for St. Louis. I'll stop if you ask me to. And I won't stop if you say nothing."

Sarah just looked at Sam, and snuggled up by his side. "Let's just see how it goes."

Sam continued to look into Sarah's eyes as he leaned in and claimed her mouth. She was smooth, and hot, and moist, and tasted of whiskey. He dove deeper, and claimed those lips, and that mouth as his. She opened for him and he bit her bottom lip and moaned. His tongue swept hers and pulsated with the beat of his heart. Fuck! It was everything he thought it would be. Sarah enveloped him in sandalwood and heat.

Sarah groaned and moved closer to Sam. Her heart pounded. She just wanted to taste him, and lick him, and make love to his mouth and tongue. She nipped his bottom lip and raised her head to look at him.

Both sets of eyes were hooded, and Sam's blue eyes had gotten dark with desire. Their lips were swollen from the mutual ravishment that had occurred. They both panted. "That was so much better than I imagined," moaned Sarah. She placed Sam's hand on her breast, and said. "Your reward for fucking my mouth with your tongue. First base."

Sam moaned and slowly caressed her over her shirt. He felt her nipple harden immediately. It was Sarah's turn to moan. She moved and straddled him on the couch. Sam moaned again as he placed his other hand on her other breast and felt that one come to attention also. Her tits were so fucking responsive, and Sarah was making it extremely difficult to not grind into her.

Sarah thought of nothing except the exquisite pain in her groin. They both panted and moaned softly. Sarah suddenly pulled back and got quiet before she opened her eyes and looked at Sam. "We need to stop. Hopefully we can take this back up in a little while, but we need to talk."

Sam just coughed, adjusted his erection, gave Sarah a quick kiss, and said, "You start. Ask me anything." Bloody hell! His balls throbbed with his want, but he wouldn't push her.

Sarah leaned back against the couch. She still tried to catch her breath. Good Lord! The man had almost made her come with just his mouth. It had been a five-year drought for her, but she knew it was her reaction to Sam and not just lust. She cleared her throat and looked at Sam.

Sam reached for Sarah's hand. "Anything, Sarah. Ask anything."

Sarah started. "The first thing isn't so much a question. I just need to tell you something. Something about me." Sarah felt really nervous.

"David and I were high school sweethearts. We were both virgins when we made love at sixteen. David was my first, last, and only lover. I may talk a big game, but I am so scared. Not scared of the act itself. And I'm certainly not scared of you. You do nothing but make me feel desirable, and sexy, and pretty. You make me feel like a woman."

Sam sat and quietly looked at her with a soft smile. He squeezed her hand in encouragement as his heart skipped a couple beats.

"I'm scared that I won't know how to actually do it well. I am scared that I will be a lousy lover and disappoint you. I could never complain about my sex life with David. All we knew was each other. We had nothing to compare to. He always satisfied me. After so many years of marriage, we knew exactly what the other one liked. We never let our sex life get dull, and we experimented. But again, we had nothing to compare it to."

Sarah lowered her head and continued. "You've had a lot of sex. You're experienced, and you know what you expect from a woman. I don't know if I can meet those expectations. I want you to enjoy the sex, Sam. I am a quick learner and a willing student if you will have faith in me."

Sam just squeezed her hand a little harder, and took his time before he responded. Sam felt as if his chest was going to explode. How could Sarah ever disappoint him? How could she even think those things? He would be only the second man to have Sarah. He was honored but he was new to the emotions he felt, and he knew that both of them would go into this naked and vulnerable. It made him feel things for Sarah that confused him. He knew that she had been faithful in her love, and that turned him the fuck on. He looked onto Sarah's eyes. "You, Sarah, could never disappoint me. I'm also humbled with the trust you have in me. I will never crush that trust."

Sarah tried to look away, but Sam grabbed her chin and turned her head to meet his eyes. "This makes my heart clench, Sarah. You are such a special woman, and I am envious of David. He was a very lucky man. I think he knew that. I find before me, a creature of beauty, sexiness, faithfulness, and loyalty. That is very sexy. You have feelings for me. I have feelings for you. We are trying to figure out what that means. We are both going into this with emotions that neither of us has experienced. I'm nervous also. But I look at you and think I can't be nervous. It's just Sarah, and we will learn together. Okay?" Sam leaned and kissed her tenderly. Sam was surprisingly emotional.

"Yes. I have fucked a lot of … not women! Girls! Just little girls. I started off in my career screwing all of them. I was a boy whore. And I'm not proud of it. But the longer I stayed in the industry, and the better I became, the more selective I needed to be. I take my career very seriously, because I've worked too hard to get where I am. I've only had two serious relationships in my life. One in my twenties that was really just puppy love, and the other in my thirties. Some of the pain that you were referring to in your comment on my Facebook page has to do with my last relationship. We can talk about that later. I have even been celibate for a time. So, yes, I am experienced, but, not with you, Sarah. Not with you. I have never made love to a real woman. Please have faith in me." Sam's heart broke a little.

Sarah shuddered. Her heart was full. So full. How could someone say every single word so perfectly? She leaned over, with her heart in her eyes, and kissed Sam slowly and softly.

Thank God that was out of the way! Sarah straightened her shoulders and said, "Your turn. Ask me anything."

Sam set his shoulders and very seriously asked, "Are you the jealous type?"

Sarah laughed, "Are you kidding?"

Sam shook his head, and said, "No. I'm dead serious. I have to show up at functions and premieres sometimes with my female counterparts. The press always has an agenda, and will say all kinds of things for a headline. I also kiss and touch a lot of women in my photo shoots, and television commercials. You've seen what the girls say on Facebook and Instagram, and how they stare and pass phone numbers. Every billboard in London has me splashed across them. I am naked in calendars. I need to know if you're secure enough to put up with it."

Sarah chewed on her lip, and thought long and hard. Sam began to panic. Sarah finally said, "It's been so long since I would even have a reason to be jealous, but I am not that kind of person, Sam. It's your job, and I have faith in you. As you said, you are careful with your reputation, and I believe that you will be careful with mine. You've been doing this a long time. Long before you knew me. I'm too old to worry about stupidity. *But*, if we pursue whatever this is - *and*, if we go upstairs and do what I hope we're going to do, I cannot, and I will not, allow you to step out on me, Sam Ramsay. I have taken a bigger risk than you, so it has to be worth it." She smiled at him.

Sam did not even realize that he had been holding his breath. He let it out long and slow. "Okay, another question?"

"Do you not want a family, Sam?" asked Sarah softly. For a brief moment she saw that old familiar pain in his eyes.

Sam looked at the floor, and put his hands together. When he looked up at Sarah, the pain was back. This time he didn't try to hide it. "I thought we would talk about this later. I guess this is later. I have always taken my mum and dad's example seriously. They've been married for almost fifty years. That's what I always wanted. I thought I had that with Vanessa."

Sam continued, "I was in my thirties. We were pretty serious. I would have married her and started a family. She wanted kids, and so did I. I loved her. I still do. But, she couldn't handle the women, or the travel, or the work. She couldn't handle anything in my life. She tried. She really did, but she was jealous of everything and everyone. We called it quits after three years. I'm sure you've seen my interview in GQ?" He looked at Sarah. She shook her head no.

"I was a dick. I said horrible things about her, and made myself look like a narcissist. I didn't mean any of it. None of it was true. But I thought it might make her hate me enough to make it easier for her to let me go. It worked. The last I heard she was married with one son, and another on the way. I'm happy for her. Truly. Anyway, the last few years I've just been really lonely. The older I've gotten, the lonelier I've become. My career always came first, and I've almost waited too long to live my life. I've talked to my sister about it. I am forty years old. I don't want to be almost sixty when my child graduates secondary school. I would never have the opportunity to enjoy grandchildren. I don't want to start a family in my forties. I had hoped that you and David would share yours with me."

Sarah's heart melted, along with her panties. She looked at Sam in wonder. "You cannot be real. You should be an asshole. You should act like a king. You should be bangin' babes, and living the high life. But you are real, and you're not an asshole, and don't let me scare you, but I love you just a little bit, right now. I would be proud to share my children with you. But, let me warn you, they have filthier mouths than I do!"

Sam grinned. " I was going to talk about logistics: travel, work, vacations, scheduling... you know, all that mundane stuff, but I think that can wait until later." He stood and grabbed Sarah's glass. "This calls for more whiskey."

They had turned off the lights and watched the fire for hours, murmuring softly in between kisses. Sam stood up and reached for Sarah's hand. "Let's get your bags upstairs."

Chapter 9:

Sam and Sarah carried the bags upstairs. There was a large landing at the top with three bedrooms. A bathroom stood at the end. Sam looked at her and nodded to the room at the right of the landing. "That's the master bedroom. It has its own bath. The other two share the one at the end of the hall. Where would you like me to put your bags?"

Sarah stared at Sam. "Wherever you would like to put them."

Sam looked at her briefly, then nodded to himself. "In here." He walked into the master bedroom with her bags.

It was a large bedroom, with plush carpeting, large windows with room-darkening drapes, and lots of closets. The bed was the highlight of the room. A huge, walnut four-poster with a headboard that almost reached the ceiling. Intricate, carved details adorned the four posts, and a canopy of gossamer fabric fell to the floor. Two wing chairs sat in front of the bay window, with a book laying in one of them. A loveseat sat in front of the fireplace. One wall was floor to ceiling bookcases that were filled with all manner of literature and family photos. Everything was done in pale shades of cream and blue.

"Oh, Sam, this is beautiful…." Sarah sighed.

"We'll hang your things in that closet, and you can put your toiletries in the bathroom." Sam pointed to the doorway in the corner.

Sarah took the small bag, and walked into the bathroom. She stopped and just stared. The entire back wall was a glass enclosed shower. The entire shower was marble. It had a bench that spanned the entire length with multiple shower heads. Along another bay window sat a claw foot tub. But it wasn't any claw foot tub. This one was big enough for four people and it had jets. Sarah was getting moist just looking at that tub, and imagining her and Sam in it together. She swallowed. Across from the tub were two separate vanities with their own sinks and chairs. A chandelier hung over the tub. This bathroom was a marble masterpiece. She placed her makeup and hair products in the vanity drawer that was empty, then turned and walked back into the bedroom. Sam was standing looking at her.

"This is one of the most beautiful rooms I've ever seen Sam…" Sarah's voice trailed off as she looked around.

Sam had closed the drapes and started a fire. It was the only light. The light and shadow played off both of their faces. Tony Bennett softly sang "Fly Me to the Moon" in the background. Sam's eyes smoldered. Sarah's started to burn in response.

Sam slowly walked to her. "May I have this dance?"

Sarah slowly lifted her arms around his neck as Sam wrapped one arm around her waist and enveloped her hand with his. She laid her head against the softness of his shirt that smelled like oak leaves and whiskey. As he danced her slowly around the room, he sang along softly in her ear. Sarah felt so hot she thought she would melt. Sam's heart pounded as he slowly walked her to the bed. He sat her on the edge of the bed before he knelt, and proceeded to unlace the first boot. He slowly removed it, before he unlaced the other one. His hands were soft against her calves. "These are staying right here. For future use," he growled. He then slid her leggings down and laid them across the bed.

As Sam laid soft, hot kisses up her legs, Sarah became a quivering mess. It had been so long since she had felt a man's lips anywhere. She knew the knot of want that she felt in her lady bits was all Sam. She knew that no other man would turn her into the molten threads of need that ran through her veins. All she felt was want as she reached for his shirt to unbutton it. Sam stopped her with his hands. "No. Tonight is all about you, Sarah. Trust me."

"I trust you," Sarah whispered.

Sam stood her up, and put her arms up as he slowly pulled the shirt up over her head. Sarah heard him hiss. "What?"she whispered.

"I want this to be slow. I want this to be about you, but damn, Sarah. You're so beautiful I don't know if I can do slow. I want you more than anything I've ever wanted in my life."

Sam looked at Sarah as she stood in front of him; she was wearing nothing but her panties and bra. If you could call it a bra. It was a... half bra. It was now his favorite article of clothing, but it would have to go. But first, the panties. He took the top of her silken panties and slowly pulled them down. She never took her eyes from his as she stepped out of them. Fuck! Sam's first thought was to grab her and bang her against the wall, but Sarah deserved to be slowly savored. His heart pounded as he slowly reached for the clasp on the front of the bra. He slowly unhooked it and removed the lacy bit of material. Sam hissed again, and then moaned. Sarah was glorious. Sarah was an Amazonian goddess. He saw her shiver.

Are you cold?"

"No," whispered Sarah. "I'm burning. I'm on fire."

He bent down and kissed her softly. He heard her groan as he brushed her lips with his tongue. He kissed her neck and her collar bone. Sarah smelled of something earthy and deep. He realized again that Sarah smelled like sandalwood. Her skin felt like silk, and she tasted like heaven. Her legs quivered, and Sam thought he might come right then. He took a deep breath before he slowly took one nipple in his mouth and sucked. Her breasts were soft, but firm. He lightly bit her nipple that was a hard, pink pearl. Sarah gasped and arched her back. He lifted his head and looked at her. "This is for David." He softly licked the other nipple. Sarah gasped again, and Sam said, "This is for David." He sucked the hard, pink pearl into his mouth as he softly caressed the other with his fingers. She rocked into Sam's hardness before he quieted her with his large hands. He never lifted his greedy mouth from the nipples he licked. Sam licked then blew against them lightly. Sarah made little mewing noises that made Sam smile even as he grew harder.

He trailed kisses down her torso until he reached her abdomen. He gently kissed her stomach. Once, twice, three times as he whispered, "These are for your babies." He moved his head lower before he blew gently on her slickness. He still softly brushed his fingers across her breasts. Sarah cried out. He slowly and softly licked up and then down. Then again and again. He looked up at Sarah. "This is for me." Sam was ready to explode but he never took his eyes from Sarah's. She stood still as a stone, but never flinched or looked away. Tears ran like rivulets of rain down her cheeks.

"Sarah! I'm sorry! I'll stop!" Sam was horrified that he had made her cry.

"No, Sam. I'm not sad. You are trying to make me fall in love with you, aren't you?" Sarah whispered.

Sam stood to remove his socks. As he unbuttoned his shirt and removed it he never took his eyes from Sarah. He unzipped his trousers and pulled them down and stepped out of them. Sam stood in front of Sarah in all of his own vulnerable beauty. She looked at Sam, licked her bottom lip, and groaned. She decided that she would no longer be insecure about her own body around Sam. No one on earth could be as beautiful as him, so there was no comparison. He looked like a marble statue, but he felt hot, not cold.

"You are the most beautiful man I have ever seen Sam Ramsay."

"You're the most stunning woman I've ever seen, or tasted, or felt, Sarah Reid."

Sam slowly backed Sarah to the bed, where he finally broke and crushed her mouth with his. He bit, and sucked, and probed. Sarah opened to him, and matched him stroke for hard stroke. They made their way to the middle of the bed, where Sam laid Sarah on her back. The sheets were soft against her skin as he put her arms above her head, and assaulted the tits that he had been dreaming about. They were perfection. They were exactly what he had dreamed about. And tonight they were his. He bit, and sucked and kneaded. Sarah bucked against him, so Sam pulled back and looked at her. "Shhhh. We have all week." It occurred to Sam that he was only the second man to possess Sarah, and it made him pause. Sarah might have had her own nerves, but he had plenty of his own.

"Sam Ramsay, it's been five fucking years," muttered Sarah. "If you don't fuck me right now, I will literally explode."

Sam was more than happy to oblige. He lifted those legs that were six feet long. He spread them wide and looked at Sarah in all of her vulnerability. She was long and soft, and pink. He balanced himself above her, and entered her so very slowly. He whispered, "This is for you. Let me savor you, treasure you, make love to you." Sarah gasped and rocked against him. Sarah was hot, moist, smooth, slick and languid. He continued the long, slow thrusts, and when the time came, Sarah didn't need to be taught. She wrapped her legs around his waist and lifted her hips. Slow rocks, in and out, as they both panted. Their lips locked, and they groaned into each other's mouths as they exploded.

They lay tangled in the sheets and in each other. Sarah cried gently as she caressed Sam's chest and arms. Sam was hardness. All muscle, bone, and angularity. There was nothing soft about him, except his heart. Sarah cried a little harder.

"Sarah, please stop crying and talk to me." Sam murmured and held her tight.

Sarah looked into his eyes, and spoke softly, "That was amazing. It was more than amazing. That was the single most romantic, sweetest thing I've ever experienced. You, Sam Ramsay, are a heartbreaker."

Sam moved back. "I never want to break your heart."

"You just made my heart break in the most amazing way..." Sarah sighed. "David, and my children. And you. And me... I don't have the words." Sarah gulped and kissed his cheek softly.

"I want to be a page, Sarah." Sam whispered into her neck.

Sarah had stopped crying, and looked at Sam with a questioning look on her face. "A page?"

Sam whispered before he kissed her again. "I want to be a page in the scrapbook of your life."

Sarah lay on her side with Sam's arms holding her tight against his chest. His even breathing told Sarah that he was asleep. Sarah was... satiated. In mind, body, and spirit. She had just experienced something that was indescribable. Yes. Sam had fucked her. Sam had fucked her good. But he had done so much more. He had been romantic. And sweet. And aware of the past that Sarah proudly wore. Sarah knew that she had already fallen hard. That's what she did. But it changed nothing. She had made her decision to come to London, knowing what the likely outcome would be. No regrets. She was going to sop up as much of Sam's life as she could. She needed to fill her heart with as many memories as she could. Enough to last her lifetime.

Sam lay holding Sarah tight against his chest. He didn't want to let her go. His amazing, beautiful Sarah. Sarah, with legs as long as his. Sarah, with her big heart. He knew it had been difficult for her to tell him about her inexperience, but Sarah had not disappointed. She had been enthusiastic and passionate and giving. Sam somehow needed to make Sarah believe that what they were doing was not just about sex. Sam wanted more. He wanted to be part of her life, as he wanted her to be part of his. He would try to prove that to her the rest of the week.

~~~

Sarah roused slowly and remembered the night before. She

smiled with the memory and stretched out, raising her arms above her head. As she opened her eyes, she saw Sam on his side. He had his head propped on a hand and watched her. Those blue eyes blazed at her, and he grinned that slow, sexy grin. Sarah groaned. He was so hot! Sarah watched his eyes as they move lowered, and then his grin grew bigger. She realized that the sheet was around her waist, leaving the rest of her exposed. Her nipples immediately responded to his gaze.

"Damn! That's a great way to start the morning," Sam growled.

Sarah grinned back at him and stretched a little more.

Before she could unclasp her hands, Sam had them both in his and held them above her head as he straddled her. He was very happy to see her. "Oh! I had forgotten about morning wood," Sarah murmured.

Sam kissed her. Boy, did Sam kiss her. She had to come up for air, as he had made her breathless. She hoped she didn't have morning breath. Sarah moved and rolled over onto Sam's chest. She looked deeply into his eyes. "You did for me last night," she said. "Now it's my turn to do for you."

Sam looked up at Sarah in a haze of anticipation. Her hair stuck up in a really cute way, and she had a smudge of makeup on her cheek. She was beautiful. She straddled him proudly with those tits just staring him in the face.

She leaned down and licked his lips gently. She leaned further in and kissed his bottom lip. Sam groaned, as Sarah's nipples barely touched his chest. She saw his reaction and started brushing her breasts back and forth. She felt his hardness pulse against her inner thigh.

Sam reached for both breasts. One hand pinched her nipple and his other hand kneaded her as his mouth bit lightly. Now she was the one who pulsated.

Sarah reached for him, and Sam groaned. She lifted her hips, and without any hesitation, lowered herself rapidly onto him. Sam grunted. He actually grunted. He might have even yelled. He couldn't remember, it had been so fast and so incredibly sexy that he saw nothing. He felt only the sensations.

Sarah needed no instructions in the sex department. Sam opened his eyes to see Sarah as she laid on his chest. She sighed and smiled a little, before she muttered, "I love chopping wood."

Chapter 10:

They showered and went downstairs to fix breakfast. They both laughed and talked as they removed plates, bowls, and pots and pans. Sam fixed the eggs, and sausages, as Sarah toasted the bagels and brewed coffee.

They moved the meal to the table where they sat next to each other. Sarah picked up her fork and sighed as she looked at Sam with a grin.

Sam raised an eyebrow and asked, "What's the sigh for?"

Sarah put a fork full of eggs in her mouth and answered. "I think this is what's called the 'after glow'."

Sam bit a sausage and commented, "It's a good look."

"Thank you, Sam." Sarah spoke softly.

"If you're talking about last night, I think we both need to thank God, because that was heavenly," Sam continued to chew with a grin on his face. "You have nothing to be worried about, Sarah Reid. You know, in the sex department."

"Can we just stay in today? I don't know what you had planned, but I figured with the benefit tomorrow evening, that maybe we could just 'be' today. I want to explore your house, and find embarrassing pictures of you when you were a kid." Sarah stopped with her fork halfway to her mouth. "Though I doubt that you've ever taken a bad picture."

Sam laughed. "Explore to your heart's content. No secrets here. And you might very well find embarrassing pictures."

"I'd like to take pictures of you while I'm here, Sam." Sam looked up at her with a scowl. "No posing!" Sarah quickly reassured him. "I hate those. You'll never know when I snap them. I would love to have pictures to take back with me. I would love to snap photos of you in the home you love. Plus, they'll give me something to rub on my naughty bits when I get home. The other picture is worn out."

Sam choked on his coffee, laughed, and said, "I love your filthy mouth."

"I hope I can show you just how filthy my mouth *is*, before the weeks out."

Sam just shook his head and laughed. "That sounds very promising… Oh! Danni is coming for a late breakfast on Sunday. I hope that's okay."

Sarah was pleased that Sam wanted her to meet his sister. "Just her? She's not bringing the family? I really wanted to meet Thomas and Violet. And her husband. What was his name again?"

"Alex. His name is Alex, and no, just Danni on Sunday. I think she wants us to come out to their place later in the week. She thought that your first meeting without the chaos that is their children would be best." Sam finished his coffee and stood.

Sarah stood to help him. "You forget that I had chaos in my own home for a long while. I can handle it."

Sam walked over and wrapped her in his arms. "Sarah, I think that you can handle anything the world might throw at you."

Sarah had gone upstairs to retrieve her camera, while Sam went out for the mail. She heard him when he came in. "Fucking hacks!

God Damn penny dreadfuls!"

Sarah found him as he stood in the middle of the living room. He looked at a newspaper with a scowl on his face. She looked at him with a question in her eyes.

"You do not want to see this shit! I knew it would happen. I even knew what the headline would be, but it still pisses me off!" Sam was angry.

Sarah took the paper from his hands and looked at it. The entire front page was her. Her in her boots waving at the press at the airport last night. "Who is Sam Ramsay's Unknown Amazon Lover and How Old is She?" Sarah continued to read the article, and then threw the paper on the side table. She looked at Sam and asked, "Want to go outside with me? I wanted to check out your yard." She started to walk to the backdoor.

Sam looked at her in exasperation before he yelled, "That's all you have to say?"

Sarah glanced at the paper that still lay on the table before she looked up at Sam. "I look damn good?"

Sam stared at her and shook his head. "You are amazing. I'm used to this shit, but you shouldn't have to put up with it."

Sarah walked back to Sam and put her hand on his arm. "We discussed this. We both knew it would happen. It's happened. So what? Has anything changed since I got here last night? No. Are we looking forward to spending the week together? Yes. I don't care what anyone has to say. I'm here because I want to be. I also know who I am and what I am. I am not a love-starved 'older woman' who just wants to bang a younger man. I know I'm more than that. What the papers write is not who I am, or who you are. So. It doesn't matter. Okay? You have to make choices Sam. You're the one with the career. You need to make the wisest choices for you. Not me."

He stared at her and slowly shook his head. "You're trying to make it extremely difficult to say goodbye, aren't you?"

"I sure hope so, Sam."

~~~

They spent the day talking about the landscaping that Sam's mum had overseen. He was quite impressed with Sarah's knowledge about the different plants and shrubs. Sarah and his mum would get along swimmingly. Sarah told him about her gardening skills at home. Pulling weeds was her therapy.

She told Sam about all the girls. Bev who was the hugger, and Ashley with the profane mouth and magic hands for cocktails. She warned him about Julie, and to not be surprised by anything that came out of her mouth. How much she loved Karen's husband and kids, and Liz, the steady one, who always gave good advice. She told him that Liz was the one who encouraged the panty purchases.

Sam grinned and said, "Remind me to give her a big hug and thank her when I meet her."

"Be prepared to have your ass squeezed when that happens." Sarah grinned back.

They talked about travel, and were surprised when they realized that they had been to a lot of the same places. Sam, of course, had traveled much more than Sarah. Sarah was a little sad that most of his location shoots had been just work. No exploration of the local scenery. Sarah told him that he needed to branch out and absorb the local flavor and people. Sam had not been to Australia or Hawaii but he looked forward to going to both. Sarah told him that Italy and Venice were next on her travel "bucket list." She and David had planned for that trip when it was sadly interrupted. She still planned on going next year. Sam assured her that Italy and Venice would not disappoint. He had been there many times for the Oak Wood campaigns.

Sam told her about skiing. It was one of his favorite things to do and his favorite kind of holiday. Even though he didn't take holiday often, when he did, it was usually where there was snow. He also loved zoos. Sarah told him that St. Louis had a wonderful zoo that he would love. He loved hanging out with his sister's kids. Sarah looked forward to grandkids one day.

They both agreed that fall was their favorite season. Sarah told Sam about apple season on the farm and how delicious the house smelled when she made cider and canned apple butter. She told him about persimmons. He had never heard of them, so she had to tell him that they made delicious jelly.

"Did you know that persimmons can predict the winter?" asked Sarah.

Sam raised his eyebrows. "Now you're just pulling my leg."

"No really! They can!" Sarah said excitedly. "If you cut the seed in half, you can see one of four things. You will find a perfect fork, or knife or shovel. Sometimes, but not often, you'll get all three perfect images in the seed. If you find a lot of shovels, it means you'll get a lot of snow."

"What do the other ones mean?" Sam asked, suddenly serious.

Sarah just laughed and said, "I don't remember! I'm just always excited about the shovels."

"So I take it you like snow? Do you ski?" Sam asked.

"No. I've never skied. I've always meant to try it, though. I love snow if I don't have to clean off the truck." Sarah looked off into the distance, and mused. "I love being snow-bound. It brings out the nesting instinct in me. I bake and cook and read. It's so quiet. I've always felt that winter was when nature slept, but when it snows you can hear nature whisper."

Sam looked a little wistful. "That sounds like heaven. We don't get that kind of snow in London. Winter here just looks dirty. I would love to be snowbound with you, Sarah Reid."

"Well, we shall just have to make that happen, won't we?"

"Did you realize that our initials are the same? SAR?" Sam asked out of the blue. "Sam Aaron Ramsay and Sarah Anne Reid. I wonder what that means?"

Sarah looked at Sam and just shrugged her shoulders. "We wouldn't have to change the monograms?"

They both had similar tastes in music. Sam liked new music, too, but his favorites were standards. Tony Bennett, Frank Sinatra, Nat King Cole. He loved Billie Holliday. Sarah loved all of them, too, but leaned toward the blues.

Sarah asked Sam about the notoriety. Was he able to have a normal life, or did he just hole up with women and family? Sam told her he still went to the market, and his family visited all the time. No, he had never 'holed up'. And he didn't have women in his home. He was used to being followed by cameras, but he tried to keep his family and friends out of situations that could make them uncomfortable. His home was gated and set back from the road. He tended to stay out of the front yard. The backyard had his outdoor kitchen, lap pool, and garden. It, too, was surrounded by a wall and trees. No telephoto lens ability. The paparazzi never followed him when he went to his sister's. Danni lived in the country, and the reporters tended to lose interest after fifteen minutes on winding country roads. Plus, his car could go faster.

"I liked the fame in the beginning of my career. It was flattering. You know, ego boosting. I was such a young asshat. I loved the attention. But, it got old real quick. I've always tried to be professional and a gentleman. Especially to all the people who work behind the scenes. You know, the lighting guys, and makeup girls. They're just trying to make a living, too. My dad worked hard all his life. I respect hard work. If a child, or a girl, or a mum, or a guy stops me and wants a selfie, I try to oblige. At this point in my life, it is what it is. But if I could find a hiding spot to go to when I needed it, I would go in a minute." Sam sighed.

Sarah rubbed his nose with hers. "My place would be perfect. It is off the beaten path and I don't even think it's on GPS. I really live in the boonies."

Sam looked confused. "What is a boonie?"

"A boonie is where I live." Sarah laughed.

They had talked all day and into the evening, when Sam stood and reached for Sarah. "Upstairs. Go upstairs and run a bath. I've seen you ogling that tub. Fill it up and put whatever smelly things women put in bubble baths. I am going to start our dinner."

Sarah was disappointed. She was hoping to share that tub with Sam. Sam saw the look on her face. "If you think that I can stay downstairs in the kitchen, knowing you are being... buoyant upstairs in my tub, you have lost your mind." He reached for her mouth with his and burned her with a kiss. He pinched her ample bottom. "Go!"

Sarah squealed and ran up the stairs. She heard Sam laughing as he made his way into the kitchen. Sarah had started undressing before she was even off the stairs. She left a trail ofclothes. Her shirt draped on the steps. Her leggings landed in the middle of the bedroom floor. Her panties were left in front of the bathroom door, and finally her bra hung on the door knob. Sarah had lit candles that were scattered throughout the bathroom. The chandelier was gorgeous, but maybe for another time. Tonight, it was candles. She filled the tub and poured something that smelled good in the water. She stepped into the hot water, sighed and waited for Sam.

Sam had plated their dinner, and put it in the AGA to stay warm. He heard Sarah turn on the water and heard her singing and splashing. He could not get out of the kitchen fast enough.

Sarah heard Sam on the stairs, then she heard Ed Sheeran on the stereo. She caught her breath and waited.

Sam walked through the bathroom door and saw a vision. He caught his breath. No lights except for candles. Sarah in all of her glory surrounded by strategically-placed bubbles. It was a picture that he would never forget. It burned into his brain. His pulse quickened when he saw the way she was looking at him. She was molten lava that threatened to burn him alive.

Sarah was on fire. The anticipation made breathing difficult. It was one of the singular, most intense experiences of her life. Sam looked at her as if he would crush her with his eyes as he unbuttoned his shirt. He was a work of art in his naked glory. She watched his biceps as he removed his shirt. Sarah hissed out loud as she saw those obliques. She wanted to eat a meal out of those troughs of muscle. He stepped out of his pants, and she watched his thighs as he walked toward her and slid into the water.

It was nothing but sensation. Heat and silk created by their bodies and the water. They explored the curves and dips of each other with their hands, then followed with their mouths. Their mouths were hot as they both panted and moaned as the water made love to them both. Candle light flickered over Sarah's skin as she arched her back over Sam. Her head was thrown back as she moaned and moved. Sam was lost in the heat, in the fire, in the look of Sarah as she came. He muted her screams with his mouth, as he screamed into hers.

Chapter 11:

Sarah and Sam slept in the next morning. They ate brunch and went over the plans for the gala that evening.

Sam had to be there several hours before the festivities actually started. He and Marta had to be there for photos and meet and greets with the hosts of the event, which meant that he would be leaving shortly.

"You're more than welcome to go with me, but you would just be sitting somewhere for hours. Not knowing anyone would make for a long afternoon. Formal attire is not necessarily the best for a six-hour event. Marta's husband is coming later, too." Sam explained. "I've arranged for a driver. He will be here to pick you up at six o'clock. I've shown you how to buzz him through the gate. I'll be waiting for you when you arrive. You'll be able to see Big Ben at night. Make sure and bring your phone, so you can at least take a picture of that for your friends." He grinned at her.

Sarah replied, "Ooh! A driver! Lat-ti-dah! It will give me plenty of time to get glamorous. You know. All the girly things. Hair, makeup, jewelry. Do you want rock 'n roll, or classy?"

"Huh?" asked Sam looking at her.

"Rock 'n roll Sarah? Or classy Sarah?" she smirked.

"Sarah, you could arrive in your panties and T-shirt and be stunning. Dress for you tonight." Sam said seriously.

"Thank you, Sam, but tonight I'm dressing for you. I'll be all over the papers again tomorrow, so I want to make sure you're proud. This is, after all, your reputation." Sarah was serious.

Sam kissed her. "I could never not be proud to be seen with you Sarah. And you know I don't give a fuck about my reputation. Finally. Do I get a peek?"

"If you mean a peek at my dress, absolutely not. If you mean a peek of me, absolutely." Sarah opened her robe to reveal her naked body. She closed it again quickly and giggled.

"You are killing me!" Sam groaned. "You know I have to leave."

"Aren't you going to put your fancy duds on?" asked Sarah.

"No. I sent them over before you got here." Sam explained.

"Well, then I guess we'll both be a surprise." Sarah kissed him slowly, and deeply, with a little tongue thrown in.

Sam was a little exasperated and a lot horny. "You are killing me, woman! I will see you in a few hours. Remember, I'll be waiting on the steps. I won't have flowers this time, so please don't wear the boots. It might get embarrassing." He gave her a peck and got ready to leave.

After making out at the door for a little bit longer, Sam was finally able to get away. There was nothing he would like better than to stay in bed all day with Sarah, but this was a commitment he couldn't get out of. He hoped that Sarah wouldn't be too bored. He personally hated these things, but it was for one of his favorite charities, and he couldn't say no. He looked at his watch and started counting down the hours until he saw Sarah again. "Yep. I've got it bad," he said to himself.

Sarah showered and put on face moisturizer. She found some photo albums in the bookcases in Sam's bedroom. She sat and thumbed through them. They were of Sam, and a girl that Sarah guessed was Danni. Childhood photos in both albums. If Sarah had to guess, she would say that Danni was beautiful. She had the same coloring as Sam. Black hair and those same blue eyes. A beautiful complexion. Sarah was nervous, but excited to meet her tomorrow. She hoped she passed the Danni test as she knew how close she and Sam were.

Sarah got up to start the preparations for the night. She went to the closet and removed the tissue paper-wrapped confection. Sarah loved this dress. She had looked at it every day since she bought it. She never thought that she would have an opportunity to wear it. Life was funny like that. She had already realized that she could not wear a bra. Even the convertible strap that she had purchased clasped around the waist. This dress ended right above her ass. The sales girl at the shop had said that 'side cleavage' was a good thing. Sarah had plenty of that. Sarah unwrapped the dress and poured it over her head. She looked in the mirror and grinned.

~~~

Sam waited impatiently as he looked at his watch. It was six twenty. Where the hell was Sarah? "Sam, get a grip. She'll be here any minute," he muttered to himself.

The cameras had not stopped since he had walked out onto the steps. He was oblivious. He just wanted Sarah to get there. He finally saw the car turn the corner, and expelled a big breath. Why in the hell was he so nervous? He watched as the driver pulled up and got out to open the back door. All the cameras turned toward the car, hoping to get some pictures of the latest celebrity. The driver had gotten the door open, and he reached an arm inside to assist Sarah as she exited the car.

A very long, red-clad leg slowly showed itself, followed by another equally long leg. A pair of red suede stilettos punctuated the bottom of her legs like giant exclamation marks. Even the cameras had stopped flashing. It was as if everyone had been holding their breath. Sam knew he was. As only Sarah could do, she unfolded all six-feet- four inches of herself. As she stood up, the cameras started up again. Sarah was a vision of red from the soles of her feet to the high neck of her dress. The dress showed nothing but Sarah. Her hair was parted on the side and slicked down on her head. It reminded Sam of something from the 1920's. Diamonds sparkled in her ears.

Fuck! Sam thought he had probably said that out loud.

Sarah turned to the driver and gave him a kiss on the cheek.

"Fuck!" Sam did say that out loud, and he was sure that he heard other people say it. Sarah was bare from her neck to just above her ass. You could see her dimples. A long silver chain with a diamond on the end of it stopped right in between those dimples. Sam saw the profile of one of her breasts from the side of her dress. He swallowed. He had done hundreds - no thousands - of shoots with some of the world's most beautiful women. He had *never* seen anything like what had just gotten out of that car.

"Mine." Sam growled. It was if Sarah had heard him, because she turned and looked right at him.

When Sarah saw Sam, her eyes widened. He was standing on the top of the steps in a navy-blue velvet tuxedo that matched his eyes. He looked like fucking James Bond. She was going to start calling him James. His eyes were what drew Sarah in. When she looked into them, her eyes widened even more. He stalked her, yes, stalked her. It was as if he was a lion in the jungle creeping up on a gazelle. His eyes blazed and she could see his jaw as it clenched and unclenched. Sarah was immediately moist. He was a caveman coming to claim his woman.

Sarah thought that she might have swooned. As Sam walked down the steps toward her, she walked up toward him. They met in the middle. They heard nothing. Not the reporters hurling questions, nor the other people murmuring. They saw nothing. No other people, and no flashbulbs. They saw only each other. Sam grabbed her roughly and bent her over his arm. Her bare back was against his forearm and she could feel the soft hairs of his wrists against her skin and the soft cuff of velvet. Sam crashed into her mouth. There was nothing soft about the kiss. He plundered her mouth with his tongue and rubbed her skin where it ended at the edge of the dress. If they both hadn't needed air, Sarah believed they would've fucked in front of everyone. And not cared.

"You are killing me, Sarah," Sam said hoarsely. His body shook.

Sarah just smiled a dazzling smile as they walked up the steps.

They found their assigned seats. There were the name cards: Sam Ramsay and Sarah Reid. Nope. No "guest" for Sarah. Her name was right on the name card, and it made her look at Sam with a wide smile.

Sam was still trying to get it together, but he noticed Sarah's smile and just kissed her hand. Everyone stared at them, but Sam could see only Sarah. He loved her hair, and her dramatic makeup, but her in that dress was making Sam think he needed to find a hidden corner and bang her against the wall. Every time she moved, he could see the sides of her tits. Now that he knew what they looked like, and what they felt like, and what they tasted like, it made his cock stand up and say hi.

"Get a grip!" he whispered to himself.

Sarah could not take her eyes off Sam. The navy tuxedo made his eyes even bluer, and his hair was slicked back like a figure from Old Hollywood. No man on earth should ever wear a tuxedo again. Only Sam was made to wear them. Everyone else paled in comparison. He wouldn't let go of her hand, and Sarah felt the pulse in his wrist as it beat rapidly. He still had difficulty breathing, and Sarah still felt the moistness between her legs.

Sam leaned over and whispered hoarsely and masterfully, as he traced a finger down her bare spine. "I want to fuck you right here. In front of everyone. I want them to know that you're mine. Only mine. Do you have any idea how fucking hot you're making me?"

Sarah's skin shivered as Sam's fingers traced her spine. "I would sit on this table right now, Sam Ramsay, and place your head between my thighs if that's what you asked me to do. I would come in front of everyone and be proud and loud." Sarah placed her free hand under the table on Sam's upper thigh, and she felt his muscle tighten.

"You are a vixen, and I am tempted to do just that." Sam still spoke hoarsely.

They were thankfully interrupted by the staff as they brought their plates. The benefit had begun. They ate their meal in silence. They both stabbed their food and stared at each other. They had begun to draw a lot of stares, and their table mates had not said a word to them. Sam and Sarah were on fire for each other, but had started a slow burn in the rest of the event goers. Everyone felt it and was mesmerized by the sexual tension between the two of them. They were probably going to be responsible for a lot of lovemaking in London that night.

After the meal was finished, the silent auction was opened for an hour. An hour. Sam didn't think he could last for an hour, but he had to try. All he wanted to do was rip Sarah's dress off. As he thought those things, Sarah leaned into him and asked, "Don't you think we need to mingle? Who do you know? Care to introduce me?"

Sam shook himself. "It would probably be wise. Marta would kill me if I didn't introduce you. And I need to introduce you to Keith, my publicist. But. I'd rather leave."

"Me, too," Sarah whispered. "But I love this dress, so I want to show it off." Sarah wanted to get her emotions under control. She was a grown ass woman, not some love struck twenty-year old Sam Ramsay groupie.

He introduced her to their tablemates, and she conversed easily. Sarah asked as many questions as they asked, and she seemed genuinely interested in what they had to say. Sam just watched Sarah be Sarah.

They worked their way around the room, and Sam introduced her to Luca Moretti, the photographer and friend whom he had worked with numerous times. It surprised Sam when Sarah was familiar with his work, and she complimented Luca on some of his work she had seen at an art exhibit in Washington D.C. They discussed lighting and filters and argued lightly over digital or hard film. They exchanged numbers and promised to be in touch. Sam had never realized how knowledgeable Sarah was about her photography. Not only did she look stunning tonight, but she also charmed everyone he introduced her to. Sam wanted to shout to the crowd, "Yes! She is mine!"

They finally found a bored Marta and her husband as they stood in a corner. They looked up as Sam and Sarah walked toward them. Marta stared at Sarah, then she stared at Sam, and started to laugh.

She looked back at Sarah and said, "It's you! I saw you earlier, but didn't realize that you were the one who was here with Sam. Honey, I heard you made quite the entrance. Everyone is talking about you. I'm so sorry I missed it. Sorry, I'm Marta, and I'm so happy to meet the woman that Sam's been chattering about for the last month. You are stunning, and your dress is to die for."

Sarah thanked her and complimented Marta. She was introduced to Mark, Marta's husband, and then she started to chat with Marta about shoes and panties. Sam just looked at Mark, and shrugged his shoulders. Mark shook his head and sipped his drink.

After the two women started to talk about waxing, Sam leaned over and asked Sarah if she would like to grab some fresh air before they closed the auction. Marta just lifted an eyebrow at Sam, and said, "Fresh air, my ass! You just want to find a private spot and bang her! It's all over your face."

Marta turned to Sarah. "Let me give you my number. We have to get together when I'm in the States later this year, and if you can tear yourself away from the bedroom before you leave, we should do lunch." Marta was digging around in her purse for paper and pen. After scrawling her number down, she handed it to Sarah and then gave her a big hug. She whispered in Sarah's ear. "He's got it bad, Sarah. I have never heard him talk about a woman the way he talks about you. Please be kind, as he's a really great guy. And a great kisser, you lucky dog!"

Sarah said her pleasantries to Mark, as Marta hugged Sam. Marta whispered to Sam. "You grab that woman, Sam! Right now, you're just a giant walking hard on, but Sarah is wonderful. She could ground you."

Sam grabbed Sarah's hand and rushed her out the set of French doors, walking rapidly around the corner into the dark. He grabbed her roughly and pushed her up against the wall. She could feel the rough stone on her bare back but she didn't care. All she felt was the desire that passed like electricity between the two of them. He kissed her mouth roughly, and she moaned. Their heartbeats rapidly escalated as Sam groped for the hem of her floor length dress. He bunched it in his hand and pulled it up to her waist. He reached for her panties and realized she had none on. He growled as he bit her bottom lip, and ground against her. Sarah reciprocated. With no warning, he inserted a finger in Sarah's hot moistness. She groaned and bucked against his hand and finger.

"You are so fucking hot. You are so fucking mine. I want you to come right now. I want you to come loudly, so everyone hears, and then we are going to walk back in there and finish this damn benefit."

Sarah obliged.

~~~

They said their goodbyes, and tried to make their way outside. Everyone wanted to meet Sarah, and Sam had gotten very impatient. Finally! They ran down the steps toward his car that waited in front of the building. He got Sarah in and closed the door, and then got in behind the wheel. Before he started the car, he grabbed Sarah's head and plundered her mouth with another searing kiss. The hard angles of his cheekbones moved with the clenching of his jaws.

Sarah panted and was ready to straddle Sam right there in front of the building for everyone to see. She hadn't screwed in a car since she and David were in high school, but she was prepared to do it right then.

Sam finally started the car, and squealed his tires as they left. He cursed the entire way home, and continued to curse as he pushed the button to open his gate. He barely got the car parked, before he tore open his door. He ran and opened Sarah's door and drug her out. He fumbled with his keys, and continued to curse. Neither was coherent enough for speech. All Sam could do was curse.

He finally found the keys and got the front door opened. He dragged Sarah through and kicked the door closed. Their lovemaking up to this point had been slow and soft. This was not lovemaking. This was lust. This was pure sex. They both nipped each other's lips, and Sam kneaded Sarah's ass through her dress. She rubbed Sam through his pants, and he ground into her hand like a teenage boy.

They moved through the house as they pawed at each other. Sam stopped to rip off his jacket and tie. He ripped his shirt open and popped the buttons off. Sarah heard them all hit the floor and roll into corners. She threw her shoes off. Sam got his pants off and punished Sarah's mouth again. Sarah heard strange noises and then realized it was her. Sam did nothing but grunt as he grabbed and pawed her ass.

They continued to move until Sam stopped. He stepped back and glared at Sarah. " I'm going to fuck you. I am not taking it slow. I am not going to be gentle. I am going to fuck you hard, and I am going to fuck you good. I am going to ruin you, Sarah."

He reached for the snap behind her neck. The dress fell to the floor. Sam grabbed Sarah and pushed her roughly onto the kitchen table. He lifted her legs onto his shoulders and dipped his head to Sarah's hot wetness.

"This is what I wanted to do on that table at the gala."

He stabbed her core with a hard, wet tongue. He sucked and licked. Sarah thrust into his face. She could feel his stubble on her thighs but nothing else except pleasure and want and need.

Sarah was keening as she quickly spiraled out of control. It had been a five-hour session of foreplay, and she was beyond feeling anything except release.

Before she could slip over the edge, Sam abruptly stopped. "No! I want to see your face when I fuck you. I want to see you come."

There was no gentleness. There was no waiting. Sam thrust deep. Sam thrust hard. The table scooted a little on the floor. He punished her as he rammed into her over and over.

Sarah's eyes were open, but glazed over. She screamed his name as she exploded around his punishing hardness. Sam bellowed her name as he unleashed an entire night's worth of frustration into her body.

Chapter 12:

Sarah and Sam sat at the kitchen table as they drank their coffee and read the morning papers. Sarah had laughed so hard that she had to wipe the tears away. She even got Sam to laugh. They were everywhere. Every front page. Every second page. Every middle page featured pictures of them from last night's benefit. The Times of London had a picture of Sam bending Sarah over his arm with the headline "Sex on the Steps." The Daily Mail had them stalking toward each other on the steps with the headline "A Gala Global Warming." The Sun had somehow gotten a picture of them at their table. They were looking at each other intensely as Sam kissed Sarah's hand. The headline read "Sam Ramsay's Amazonian Vision in Red?" The looks on the faces of the people surrounding them brought peals of laughter out of Sarah.

They had not talked about last night. They were both strangely quiet other than their shared laugher about the headlines.

Sarah sat her cup down and looked at Sam. "You know we totally deserve this." She gestured toward the papers. "I was out of my mind with lust, Sam. I didn't see anyone but you on those steps, and my heart forgot to beat for a while. It was one of the most surreal moments of my life. Thinking back over it, it was like something out of a movie. But I keep telling myself, that it's my life. I wouldn't change any of it. I don't think I could. And look at those pictures! We are hot! I'll bet babies were conceived last night by people just watching us."

"I have never lost control like that Sarah. That's what you do to me. Do you understand what all of us saw last night? It was something that they will probably never witness again. I get to sit here and see it again." Sam was hoarse as he kissed Sarah's wrist on her pulse point.

"I wanted to make an entrance for you, Sam. I dressed for you last night."

"And then I *undressed* you for me." He winked wickedly.

Sarah's pulse quickened as she thought back to last night. She had never experienced anything as sexually intense. She could feel sore muscles on her back and hips from the unyielding table. Or it might have been from the bricks. She could feel her ears get warm as she thought about the table they sat at as it scooted across the floor. "Uh... did you wipe the table down?"

Sam needed the laugh, as he getting hot just thinking about last night. He had never done that to a woman. Never. But a woman had never done that to him, either. "Yes, dear. I wiped it down. Why? Were you wanting to use it again?" Sam stuck his tongue out at her.

"Perhaps I do!" Sarah said tartly. "But I need a couple of days for my back and ass to recuperate."

Sarah had prepared quiche and got the ingredients out for biscuits and gravy. Sam and Danni had never had it, and she didn't want to go home without feeding Sam some Missouri comfort food. Sam had fried the sausages and washed the fruit. They worked well in the kitchen together. They chattered away, oblivious to the world around them The doorbell rang, and Sarah looked at Sam expectantly. "Should I be worried?"

"Are you the worrying kind?" he asked.

Sarah just grinned and shook her head no. Sam muttered. "I

wonder why she just didn't come in? You women and your damn entrances!" He went to get the door.

Sarah heard them laugh as they walked to the kitchen. She turned to the archway. Sam and Danni walked in, and Sarah froze. It was like looking at a female version of Sam. Danni was beautiful. She had the black hair and the same striking blue eyes. A softer face than Sam. Without any of Sam's angles. She was tall, though not as tall as Sarah, and lanky. She was built like her brother. Sarah couldn't wait to meet Sam's parents. They had beautiful offspring.

She wiped her hands on a towel and walked forward to greet her. "Hi! I'm Sarah. You must be Danni. It's so good to meet you and put a face with the name. Sam talks of you constantly."

She couldn't stop staring. It was uncanny how similar they were.

Danni laughed. "I know it's disconcerting. We kind of look alike, uh? When we were children, everyone thought we were twins. I always tell people that I went into the wrong line of work. I should have been a model. I'd be making a hell of a lot more money than Sam, because I'm so much younger and prettier."

Sam laughed. "That is true. You are younger."

Sarah and Danni looked at each other before they looked at Sam and started to laugh. The ice had been broken. Danni followed Sarah back to the counter to see how Sarah made the biscuits and gravy. Danni asked about Sarah's home, and her children. Sam had evidently filled Danni in, which made Sarah feel a little weird, but in a good kind of way.

Sarah showed Danni how to make the biscuit dough; then she rolled the dough out on a floured board and cut the biscuits out with a metal glass she had found in Sam's cabinet. Sarah asked about Thomas and Violet, and Danni told her a story about their latest escapades. Sarah laid her head back and laughed. She told a similar story about her own children. They had discussed the difference between puff pastry and phyllo dough, and which one they preferred. They continued to talk and laugh as they both got the brunch together.

Sam had poured another cup of coffee and now leaned against the counter watching Sarah and his sister. He realized that Sarah could talk to anyone and make them feel at ease, but Danni was not an easy person to fool, and she was very protective of Sam. He couldn't help but think that Danni would have a lot to say. Sarah noticed Sam watching them and gave him a dazzling smile. It made his heart skip a beat. Danni noticed it, too, and smiled a bit to herself.

"The gravy is done and the biscuits will be ready in a few. You want to get the plates Danni, and I'll get the silverware and napkins? You just going to stand there looking pretty Sam, or are you going to plate up that sausage?" Sarah asked.

There was dead silence. Danni looked at Sam. They both shook their heads and began to shake with laughter.

"What?" Sarah asked as she looked quizzically at both of them. They just got louder. She finally realized what she had said, and just shook her head at them. "Oh, great! Another Ramsay who keeps their mind in the gutter. I should have said 'meat'." Peals of laughter greeted Sarah's remark. She looked at them both, smiled broadly, and sang – in the sweetest voice she could muster -, "Fuck you both."

After Danni and Sam finished off the biscuits and gravy, they leaned back to have a final cup of coffee. They discussed fast food restaurants and how they would destroy the world.

Danni looked at Sarah and asked, "Did you know my brother has never had anyone stay in this house except Thomas and Violet? And now you."

Sam started to say, "Danni, please no." Danni looked at him and said, "No! I'm going to say my piece. I think Sarah would like to know what I think. You, probably not so much."

Sarah saw Sam as he clinched his jaw. He looked like he would try to stop Danni, but instead he just sighed and shook his head. He knew it was useless to try to stop her. He propped his chin in his hand and prepared himself to be humiliated. She had been doing that to him her entire life.

"I've never even spent the night." Danni looked accusingly at her brother.

Sarah was serious when she told Danni, "Then I'm honored."

Danni slowly turned her head toward Sarah. "And you should be. Did you know that he's never even brought a woman here? They think he lives in the Oak Wood house in town. And I don't think he's even had anyone there in forever."

Sarah looked at Sam wide eyed. He looked at the floor so he wouldn't have to look at Sarah.

"Listen, you guys. I know it's none of my business, but that's never stopped me before. I might be assuming things that aren't even things yet. Sam and I are pretty close, Sarah. We always have been. We've always talked about everything. I think I'm the *only* person Sam talks to." Danni looked at Sam questioningly. He just shook his head yes. "Sam has done nothing but talk about you since you met in St. Louis. What's that been? A little more than a month? I have *never* heard Sam talk about a woman, much less every day. You've made quite the impression on my big brother."

Sarah started to reply, but Danni, again, held her hand up and said, "Let me finish." She took a deep breath and looked at Sam. "I like her, Sam. She's a woman. Not a little girl who doesn't know what she wants. Sarah has lived a life, and has endured things that I don't even want to imagine. And look at her. She knows who she is, and she knows what she wants. If she wants you - and I think she does - then you have to know that there is no way that she has not already thought about everything. The shitty aspects of your career, like the constant travel, and the women who never leave you alone, and living in London, and the press and your lack of privacy, and the age difference. I'm also sure that she has worried the most over what damage she could do to your career. *That* she cares about, the rest she doesn't. Sarah has a life that she loves, so she doesn't have to have yours for her happiness. I don't believe that Sarah would have boarded the plane if she hadn't already made up her mind. Damn the outcome. Sarah doesn't need you, Sam. She wants you. You need to realize the difference. She has much more to lose than you." Danni turned and looked at Sarah, who just looked a little shell shocked.

Danni continued to look at Sarah, and then she reached out and took Sarah's hands. "I love my brother, warts and all. He sowed his wild oats. But he stopped sowing a long time ago. He has been searching for something, and I don't even think he realizes what it is. Sam leads a life that is difficult for me to watch sometimes." Danni squeezed Sarah's hands a little.

"He lives in luxury, but he works too hard. He can't say no and people take advantage of him. He's also a little narcissistic and spoiled. And he's lonely. He needs to stop worrying about what the public will say about his life. Sam has achieved what he set out to do as a young man. This wasn't the career he wanted, but it's the only one he's ever had. It's all he knows. It's like a professional athlete who is washed up at thirty-years-old. What's he supposed to do with the rest of his life? Sam is forty-years-old and is still the number one male model in the world. He has lasted much longer than anyone would ever have guessed. I think he could do it for as long as he wanted. But at what cost? Sam has great ideas, he just needs someone to help him. I am so proud of him, and I love him so much. But a sister's love is not enough. He sees something in you, Sarah, that he needs. The age thing confused him at first, until I assured him it was because you were a woman. Sam is not used to having to deal with a woman, other than me."

Danni turned and looked at Sam. He still just looked at the floor. Danni turned back to Sarah, and didn't let go of her hands. "I think you could help him become a man. Because he isn't one yet. His work has kept him in the pretty boy bubble. The flashbulbs have fed into his narcissism. I want Sam to experience real life. With all of its bumps and bruises, and joy and pain. That's what makes us savor the pleasures." Danni squeezed Sarah's hands again. "You could be his home." Finished, Danni sat back in and released Sarah's hands, and looked at both of them.

It was uncomfortably quiet. It stayed that way for a while. Sarah finally looked at Sam. One single tear ran down her face. He finally looked up. He looked like a whipped puppy. Sarah got up and went to him. She stood behind him and wrapped her arms around him. She kissed him on the top of his head. She looked at Danni and said softly, "We are trying to figure it out. That's why I came. Sam and I are a work in progress. But you were wrong about one thing. I think I do need him."

She then walked over to Danni who had stood up and wrapped her in a tight hug. "Thank you," whispered Sarah in her ear. Danni hugged her back. Hard. Sam had walked over and was surrounded by the two women who cared for him the most.

Danni took a deep breath and yelled. "Have you two *seen* the papers this morning? Holy shit you guys! That's some sexy shit right there! You guys might just screw yourselves to death before you figure the rest of it out. You guys were so hot. Just looking at you two made me so horny. And that's a little weird, considering he's my brother, but I still went and climbed Alex' pole this morning. Oh! And Sarah? Has Sam talked to you about his obsession with bawdy women yet?" Danni laced her arm with Sarah's to go find the papers.

Sam just shook his head and groaned.

After they looked at the papers again with Danni, and laughed at the stories that she made up about the people around them in the pictures, she said goodbye. "You can both go upstairs now and fuck like rabbits, because I'm leaving!" She hugged them both hard and they finalized plans to be there for an early dinner on Wednesday.

Sarah turned and looked at Sam. "She is a force to be reckoned with."

Sam sank back onto the couch and ran his hand through his hair. "She wears me out."

Sarah grinned. "I like her. A lot."

Sam looked at her nervously, and asked "She didn't offend you, or hurt your feelings, did she? Danni has no filter."

Sarah sat down by him and thought for a minute before answering. "I don't know how you felt about what she said, but, I make no excuses. Everything she said about me was absolutely right on the money. I want you to know what I'm feeling, and I want to talk about where we go from here. But only if you see that happening. I came with no expectations Sam. I thought it was worth the risk. Because life is short, and I may not get a chance like this again."

Sam reached for her and moved her into his side. He breathed into her ear. "Ditto."

They talked for hours. Sam told her how he wanted to meet her friends, and her children. How eagerly he wanted to see her home and just spend time there. He wouldn't ask her to fly all over the world to meet him. That would not be fair, and would certainly be one sided. His schedule was fixed for almost the entire year. If he would ever have guessed that he would meet Sarah, he would have done things differently. But contracts were signed.

When they noticed that it was dark, Sam ordered pizza, and they ate it in the tub. They made love and they made plans.

Chapter 13:

Time went by much too quickly, and Sam had a difficult time imagining his home without Sarah in it. They didn't know when they would see each other again, and that made it much more difficult. Sam was smitten. Sarah had grabbed his heart. Everything that Danni had said was so true. He had been in denial. It had been easy for him because he just worked. When you're tired, it doesn't give you time to think. But, now, he realized how much more important life was. Next year was going to be different. He grinned to himself and thought, "Listen to me! Making plans for next year! I'm such an adult!"

The Oak Wood campaign was a month-long, non-stop promotion. Filled with nothing but television, magazine shoots, interviews, runways, and premieres; early mornings and late nights. Sam wouldn't give up the Oak Wood brand. They had picked him against type to model for their new Scotch. He was a beefy boy and they were a new distillery. They took a chance on him, and he never looked back. He had been eighteen-years-old for that first campaign. He was now forty. Twenty-two years with one brand just didn't happen. Like the excellent scotch that Oak Wood made, Sam was aging also. He had done their campaign every year, and he would continue until they didn't want him anymore.

He continued to think of ways to see Sarah. He didn't think it would be easy for him to fly to see her for one or two nights. She lived in a place that wasn't easy, or quick to get to. Sarah would have to be a destination, not just a flyover. He couldn't fly Sarah to a location for just one night. It wouldn't be fair to either one of them. He had gone crazy. He already missed her, and she wasn't even gone.

Sarah wanted to stop the clock. The hour hands went by much too quickly. She seemed to have a permanent lump in her throat. She knew it would be difficult to leave London before she came, but she didn't realize how emotional it would be for Sam. It was bittersweet. For him to be so upset was sweet, but leaving him upset was almost more than she could bear. Sarah had seen the pain reappear in his eyes, and she hated it.

One month. One month on the Oak Wood campaign. Sam was very loyal to the company, and she understood why. Loyalty was a very sexy trait. One month of only texts or phone calls. Not able to listen to him sing in the kitchen. One month of no Sam made her want to cry. There was no end in sight, and she couldn't figure out a solution. On the one hand, if she hadn't come to London, she wouldn't be feeling so shitty. You can't miss something you haven't ever had. But she had Sam, and she couldn't imagine not having him for months on end. Sarah shook herself and made two promises. First, she was going to enjoy these last few days. She didn't want to make it any worse for Sam. And secondly, she was going to figure out a way to see him after the Oak Wood campaign. She could last a month, but she couldn't last two.

~~~

On Monday they had stayed in bed all day. They only got up to raid the refrigerator. Then they ate in bed. They had showered together and then gone back to bed. They had talked. They had made love with desperation. They had laughed, and they had danced. They hadn't wanted to sleep and waste those hours.

On Tuesday, they went for a drive in the country. Sarah was almost giddy with the stone walls and thatched roofs. They had to stop to let cows cross the road. They stopped in a shady spot off the road, and made out in the car until a sheepdog startled them when it barked in their window. It was so wonderfully cliché. They had stopped to eat in a small pub in a little village. Some of the patrons had recognized Sam, but they just wanted to buy him pints of Guinness. Sarah never let go of her camera. She continued to add pages to her scrapbook.

~~~

Wednesday. Two more nights. Sarah sighed and Sam glanced at her as she sat in the passenger seat. They were on their way to Danni's for dinner. All they had wanted to do was stay home and be with each other, but they had promised. Sarah wanted to meet Thomas, Violet, and Alex.

"Sarah, I don't think I'm even capable of talking about it. My chest is so tight I can't breathe. I thought I was having a heart attack last night, but I realized it was heart-ache." Sam expelled a long, slow breath. Sam missed Sarah's quips, and her laughter. There hadn't been too many things to laugh about the last few days.

"I know Sam. Sorry. I want to be able to enjoy this visit. I really like your sister, so I know I'll like the rest of them. I really am looking forward to it." Sarah was quiet.

They drove the rest of the way in silence.

~~~

Danni's home was in the country about thirty minutes outside London. It was a beautiful drive, but neither Sam nor Sarah saw it. They made a left through an open gate with a cattle guard. They made their way up a long drive. Reaching the top, Danni's home was

spread out below
them. Sarah's eyes got wide. There were trees and a lake, and a
sprawling farmhouse with a wraparound porch. Sheep were
scattered around.

"This is so weird," Sarah said quietly.

"What's weird?" asked Sam.

"This reminds me so much of home. The long drive, the trees, the
water, and the house itself is very much like mine."

Sam just looked at her with a blank stare on his face. He finally
asked. "Really? This is what your home looks like?"

She just shook her head yes.

He stopped the car and turned toward her. "I can't wait to see
your home, Sarah. I would love it because it's yours. But if it looks
like this, then I really do believe in destiny, because this is my
favorite place."

He continued driving. As they got nearer, he slowed. "Shit! That's
just like Danni! Damn it!"

Sarah looked at him with concern, and asked "What? What's 'just
like Danni'?"

"Mum and dad are here." Sam muttered. "No pressure, Danni. No
pressure at all."

Sarah grinned and asked, "Pressure on who? You or your parents?
There's certainly none on me. I can't wait to meet the people who
made such gorgeous children."

Sam sighed and then grinned back. "Well, as long as you tell them that, everything should be fine."

As Sam was parking, two children came running outside, yelling "Uncle Sam! Uncle Sam!" He reached down and swung the littlest one in the air. The older one was grabbing his legs and yelling.

Sarah walked up to them, and Sam said very formally, "Sarah, the monkey on my leg is my nephew, Thomas, and the littlest monkey is Violet. Kids, this is Sarah." Both children got quiet, and turned shy quickly.

Sarah looked at them both and said, "It is very nice to meet you, Thomas, and it is very nice to meet you, too, Violet. Did you know that your Uncle Sam talks about you all the time?"

Thomas just looked at her very seriously. "You're really high."

She laughed and knelt down to his height. "I am high. But, look, I can get small just like you."

Thomas stuck his chest out and said, "I'm not small. Vi is small 'cause she's the baby."

"Don't tell her, but you'll always be bigger than her. But that's our secret, okay?"

As they continued their walk to the door Sarah looked at two miniature Sam and Danni's. The two children had the same raven hair and striking blue eyes. They were beautiful. Sarah looked at Sam. "If your parents have black hair and blue eyes, I'm going to start thinking that I've stumbled into the Stepford Family."

Sam leaned his head back and just laughed. "Oh, you just wait!"

Danni met them at the door. "Hey guys!"

"Hey guys, my ass." Sam snapped at her. "This was a dirty trick, Danni."

Sarah just laughed and gave Danni a big hug. "It's wonderful to see you again. I love your home. It reminds me of my own."

Danni lifted an eyebrow, cocked her head and looked at Sam. "Did you hear that, Sam? It reminds her of home?"

Danni and Sarah just stood there and stared at Sam. "Okay, okay! I know when I'm being ganged up on!"

The kids screamed and ran in circles around the house, the dogs barked, the sheep bleated, and Sarah loved it. Danni grinned at Sarah. "Welcome to my life!"

They followed Danni through the house. It was full of comfortable furniture and vintage finds. There were quilts on the couches, and big, soft cushions. Thomas and Violet's faces dotted the walls. It was a home that was lived in and loved. Sarah could spend time here.

They entered the kitchen that was bigger than Sarah's, but more modern. More stainless and a modern aesthetic, but with the same vintage finds scattered throughout. It was a great mix of new and old. A man stood at the sink with his back to them, and a woman sat at the enormous island with Violet in her lap.

"Hey, mum" Sam said as he went to hug her. "Dad, this is Sarah. Sarah, this is my mum and dad, but you can call them Ollie and Beth. Unless..." He looked sternly at his mother. "Unless they prefer Mr. & Mrs. Ramsay."

The man at the sink had turned around upon hearing Sam. He looked at Sarah as he was wiping his hands on a towel. "Hello,

Sarah. It's nice to meet you. Danni has been telling us all about you."

"Oh, I hope not!" Sarah chirped.

Ollie Ramsay stopped for a moment and looked at Danni. Then he grinned a Sam grin, and said, "I never believe half of what she tells us, anyway."

Sarah looked at Sam at the age of seventy-two. Sam's dad was tall, but not as tall as Sam. And his hair was salt and pepper with bold streaks of black still in it. Sam's same blue eyes crinkled with Ollie's grin. Sarah fell in love immediately. They all laughed, and Ollie clasped her hand with his. His hands were big and callused and strong.

Sam's mom put Violet on the floor and walked around. "I only make Sam call me Mrs. Ramsay. You can call me Beth, and it is wonderful to finally meet you. Danni's not the only one who's been talking about you." She gave Sam a smirk. Sam looked like he wanted to find a hole to climb into. Sarah snorted, and Sam glared at her.

"You don't know how happy it makes me to see you make your son so uncomfortable. Thank you for that." Sarah glared back at Sam. She looked back at Beth Ramsay to see her smiling at Sarah. She was an average height, with gray hair and hazel eyes. Thank God! But Sam got the shape of his eyes from her. The beautiful symmetry and his luscious mouth. These people could never have conceived average children.

"Are they here yet? I wanna meet this mystery woman ..." Alex's voice trailed off as he entered the kitchen and saw them all. He, too, was tall. About Ollie Ramsay's height. Brown hair and the most beautiful green eyes. He was big. A solid man. A large muscular back and neck. And arms. Alex was a muscular bear. But not hairy. Yep. Danni could've climbed his pole. Not a problem. There wasn't an average looking person in this family.

"Well, I guess that would be me, considering that the rest of you know each other." Sarah went to shake his hand, but Alex was having none of that. He grabbed her in a tight hug and swung her around.

"The woman who is responsible for my great breakfast, Sunday morning, deserves more than a handshake!" Sarah laughed breathlessly as Danni shook her head. Sam still scowled and Sam's mom and dad giggled.

Thomas stood by his grandfather and pulled on his pants leg. "Grandad. Sarah's high." Everyone stopped and looked at the little boy. "But she can make herself like me. But don't tell anybody." Ollie Ramsay shook his head and looked at Sarah with a question on his face.

Sarah saw them stare at her as Alex put her back on the floor. She had heard Thomas and immediately went to him before everyone thought she was a transgender on drugs. She knelt down next to the little boy. "See, I'm not high anymore, I'm just like you. But remember. Don't tell anybody."

Everyone relaxed, and Ollie Ramsay got tickled. He had to turn around so Thomas wouldn't think he was laughing at him. Sarah went and stood by him. "I love the repurposed furniture that Sam has in his house. They're beautiful pieces. He told me that you taught him. The interior finishes are wonderful, too."

Ollie looked at her for a little longer than was comfortable, but finally smiled and said, "There's quite a few pieces here, too. Would you like to explore?"

"I would love to, but only if Thomas can go with us. I'm sure that he would be a big help explaining things to me." She looked down at the little boy. Thomas took her hand, and yelled at everyone. "I'm gonna help Sarah and granddad. See ya later."

The rest of the family watched Ollie, Sarah, and Thomas. They were in animated conversation as they disappeared around the corner.

"Well. That's Sarah. She's already charmed her way into dad's heart because of her love of furniture." Danni went to pour a glass of water.

Sam's mother patted the bar stool next to her. He sat and looked at his mom. "So, son, how's it going so far?"

He just looked at her and said, "So far, so good."

"Sam Aaron Ramsay. Don't give me that bunk! No one told me or your dad, not even Danni, but she knows about your furniture, so she's been to the house. Is she staying there?"

"Mum!" I don't want to talk about this with you!" Sam wasn't really shocked. Danni had inherited her non-filter from their mother. But, still. It was his mother for God's sake!

"Sam!" His mother spoke sharply. Then she took his hand. "This family talks about everything. I'm not going to start beating around the bush now. Besides I'm too old for bullshit. You have never brought a girl to meet us or Danni. Never. And you have certainly never had one in your home. Sarah would be the first and only. Is she worth it?"

Sam looked at his mother with pain in his eyes. "So totally worth it, mum. I don't know if I will be able to stand the quiet when she's gone. It's always just been my house, but with Sarah there, it feels like home."

Beth Ramsay looked at Sam for at least a minute. Then she patted his hand and said, "Alright then."

The afternoon went by quickly. The dishes had been loaded in the dishwasher. Cocktails had been poured, and everyone lounged in the living room. Sam looked over at Sarah. She and his mother were sitting on one of the sofas and were discussing the finer points of shrubbery and plants. "I especially loved where you placed the hydrangeas in Sam's backyard. "

"I just love them! They're my favorite!"

"Me, too! I love that they're one of the few plants that give you such gorgeous color in shade. I love messing with the alkaline in the soil to see if I get white, blue, or pink blooms. They're like little surprises, because you just never know what you may get." Sarah was so excited.

Sam's mother was excited also. "Have you tried egg shells? I used them on my oak leaf hydrangeas and got the prettiest pale blush of pink. Just beautiful!"

Sam stared at the two of them. Why, oh, why, was he ever nervous? Sarah could take any situation and make it enjoyable. She remembered everything, and she was really interested in what everyone had to say. While he stared, little Violet had timidly walked over to her and slowly climbed up in her lap. Sarah never stopped the talk with his mother. She just snuggled little Violet in her arms and softly brushed her hair with her fingers as she continued to talk with his mum. God, Sam thought. She had to be a great mother. She would be an awesome grandmother. He continued to stare and watched as Sarah whispered something in Violet's ear. Violet lifted her little hand and brushed Sarah's cheek over and over again. Sam was surprised at the emotion he experienced as he watched Sarah and his niece, and was astounded to feel like he could cry.

Danni came and sat down by Sam. She scooted next to him and put her head on his shoulder. "I love her, Sam. Can I keep her?"

Sam just scooted her closer and responded. "No. I think I'm going to."

Sarah had convinced Violet that she really wanted to see the baby lambs, but that she was a little afraid of them. She would love to see them, but only if Violet and Thomas would go with her. Each child had one of her hands when they got their jackets and walked outside to see the babies that were on the hillside outside of the side door. The rest of the family walked outside to the porch. The men had cigarettes and a final scotch. Danni and her mom were having a cup of spiked coffee.

Sarah, Thomas, and Violet walked up the hill to see the lambs. Sam could see them as they sat in the grass and petted and rubbed the babies. All three of them animatedly discussed something of grave importance. The sun had begun to set. The sky was full of purples and pinks and reds. Sarah and the children had gotten up and had begun to run and laugh and chase each other among the sheep. Sam again felt like he could cry. His mother looked over at him and patted her heart with a big smile on her face.

"That is one helluva woman you got there, Sam." His dad sounded a little hoarse.

"Yes. Yes, she is," Sam agreed. He wished that he could capture this moment in time in a photograph like Sarah did. But he had captured it in his mind and in his heart. Sam was adding pages to his scrapbook.

Chapter 14:

Sarah and Sam said their goodbyes, with hugs for everyone. Sarah promised Thomas and Violet that she would be back to play. Danni looked at her and said gruffly in her ear, "You'd better!" She hugged Sarah hard.

As they headed for the car, Beth called them back to the porch. "Sarah, you don't need to bring Sam when you visit again. You are always welcome. With or without him." She gave Sarah another quick hug.

Sam and Sarah were quiet for the first few minutes of their drive home then they both started to talk at the same time. Sam pointed at Sarah. "Go ahead. You go first."

Sarah hugged herself, and turned to look at him. "Those children are yummy."

Sam grinned. "Yummy? Yes, I suppose they are. I kind of like them, too." He looked reflectively at Sarah. "You were really good with them. Violet takes a while to warm up to strangers. I'll bet you were great with your own children."

Sarah smiled. "I like to think that my children are the best things I had a part in. I like young people. Adults should be required to spend time with a child at least once a week. At least until they turn into beasts at puberty."

Sam laughed and shook his head. "Oh, God, I can only imagine."

They both laughed quietly before Sam got serious. "I'm sorry about Danni ambushing us. Sometimes I think her social skills never developed past the age of twelve."

Sarah shook her head. "It was fine. Not knowing that your parents were going to be there saved us both a lot of nervousness. They were wonderful, Sam. I enjoyed all of them so much. I understand why you're all so close. "Boisterous" is the word that comes to mind. "

"A pain in the ass is what I call them sometimes, but, yeah, we're close. I have never even asked about your parents. Or siblings." Sam looked at her inquiringly.

"I have my children, of course, and the girls that have become my family. That's about it. I was an only child whose parents had me late in life. They were wonderful. I have no sad childhood memories. My dad died of a massive heart attack when I was thirty. My mom passed the year before David. Cancer."

"Oh, man, Sarah. I'm sorry!" Sam was amazed by the strength Sarah possessed.

"No regrets, Sam. As I said, they were great. I think my mom gave me my strength. She handled my dad's death with such grace and dignity. Sadly, it took me about a year to even achieve half of that grace. I think losing both her and David so close together was a double whammy. I wallowed in self-pity for way to long. But thinking of her in her grief, gave me the incentive to pick up the pieces. I miss her." Sara smiled a soft smile.

Sam looked at her with the same soft smile. "I can't wait to meet all of your family."

Sarah smiled and laid her head against the seat rest.

~~~

They had eaten a late lunch, early dinner at Danni's, so they just plated up some fruit and cheese, grabbed the Jameson, and went back to the sofa. Sam lit a fire and they both cuddled. Sam had decided that Sarah had to see London proper. "Tomorrow, we will be tourists. You can't be in London a week and not see Buckingham Palace, Big Ben, or The Tower of London. Plus, the girls won't believe that you were really here, if you don't have some pictures."

"We don't have to do that, Sam, though pictures would be nice. But, I can only imagine the ruckus that your beautiful ass would create on the streets of London!" She laughed and nudged him in the ribs.

"I don't know what you think I do when I'm here at home, but I *do* go out. I'll put on a baseball cap and my sunglasses. It will be fine. But, I can't promise you that some people won't bother us. I'm used to it, and there *will* be selfies, but I don't want it to put a damper on your enjoyment." Sam looked hopeful.

"I'm game if you are! After all, there are no pictures or headlines that could beat Sunday's anyway!"Sarah laughed.

Sam winked at her. "That is so true!"

Sarah went upstairs, and Sam continued to think about the day as he went through the pictures in his head. Sarah with Thomas, Sarah with Violet. Sarah with his dad and mum. Alex swinging Sarah around as she laughed helplessly. And Sarah with Danni. He sighed. Those two were a lot alike, except Sarah's heart was more pure. Danni was just an evil wench. Everything that he had watched, listened to, and enjoyed had Sarah in it. He liked how comfortable and at ease she was in any situation. Sarah truly enjoyed her life. Sam wanted to fully enjoy his life. But Sam felt that to truly have that joy, he needed someone who was joyous to be with. Sam needed Sarah. Sam wanted to ask her to stay longer, to go with him on the Oak Wood campaign, but it would be thirty days of him going back to his hotel room dead of exhaustion. He couldn't ask her to do that.

"Hey, Sam?" Sarah called from upstairs. "Can you come here for a minute? I need some help."

Sam wondered what had happened, and took the stairs two at a time. He walked through the bedroom and saw Sarah as she stood by the bathroom door. Her hip was cocked and her chest stuck out. Every light blazed. She wore a pair of panties, a T-shirt, and those damn boots. It took Sam right back to the day that Sarah opened that motel room door with a swollen, purple ankle. That made him grin.

Sarah proceeded to *strut*. "Is this the way you do it? " She lifted her legs high, and wiggled her hips across the bedroom floor. "I figured you strutted in your underwear for the world to see, so I would strut in mine for you. I told you that the T- shirt would show up again."

She had continued to walk the entire time she talked. By this time Sam laughed so hard he had a hard time catching his breath, but he found it strangely arousing. Sarah looked damn fine in a tee shirt. She jiggled in all the right places. She walked up to him and started pushing him backwards toward the bed. Sam reached for her, but Sarah pushed him one last time. His legs hit the side of the bed, and down he sat. Sarah turned and strutted back the way she had come.

Sam very much enjoyed those boots on those legs. She bent really low to turn on the stereo. She gave her butt a little wiggle. Sam laughed and groaned at the same time. He loved Sarah's ass. Tom Jones started to sing "You Can Leave Your Hat On." Sarah whirled around and started to dance toward him. She danced her way out of her panties. Then she danced her way out of her T-shirt. She was a really good dancer, or in this case, a stripper. There stood Sarah in nothing but those fucking boots.

Sam stood up to rip his clothes off, but Sarah pushed him back onto the bed. She stood over him and slowly gyrated to the music as she peeled his T-shirt off over his head. Her tits were enticingly close to his face. Sam was a happy man. She took his shirt and rubbed it back and forth between her thighs and then threw it across the room. Sam bit his lip. How something so funny could be so hot was amazing, but that was Sarah. Sarah knelt on the floor in front of him, and slowly unbuttoned each of the five buttons on his fly. She peeled his jeans off over his bare feet, turned her ass to him and humped his pants. Then she threw them across the bedroom with his T-shirt. As was his standard operating procedure, he wore no underwear. Again, Sam reached for her. She backed up and danced her way to the sofa in front of the fireplace. Sarah proceeded to lay down on the sofa backwards and put her legs with those fucking boots over the back of the sofa. Sarah was a tall woman, so her head was hanging off the front. Sam started to laugh again.

"Hey Sam? Can you come and unlace my boots?"Sarah sounded a little out of breath. It must have been all the dancing. Or possibly all the blood that had rushed to her head.

Sam still laughed as he walked to the sofa. Sarah had one booted leg on the back by the right sofa arm. She had the other leg on the back of the sofa by the left arm. "Holy shit!" thought Sam. "She's doing the splits!" And then he remembered that she was naked except for those boots, and his laughing immediately turned into something else.

He walked to her and looked over the sofa back. Sarah was spread-eagled for Sam to feast his eyes on. And feast he did. Sarah was beautiful. Sarah was... slick. He slowly unlaced the first boot, removed it and threw it across the room. Something shattered, but Sam didn't care. He unlaced the second one a little quicker and threw it. He stood there and looked at Sarah in all of her nakedness. He slowly pulled her up the sofa, until she sat on the back. Sam looked at Sarah. She was a little flushed.

Sarah could feel the rough texture of the sofa as it rubbed against the back of her thighs. Sam never took his eyes from her as he knelt in front of her. She felt the pleasurable stick of his whiskers as Sam lapped her slickness with his beautiful mouth. Sarah groaned and jerked against his face. Sam's tongue continued to probe her softness before he hummed into her wetness. He fucking hummed! Sarah shrieked with the amazing sensation. She couldn't believe she was going to come in less than a minute. Sam had a magic tongue and his humming wasn't bad, either. Sarah jerked into Sam's face again and as she did she could feel her legs start to slide. Slowly at first, then she rapidly slid harder against Sam's face as the sofa started to tip, and Sarah started to fall off the couch. "Aaaaahhh!" she screamed . Sam licked and sucked harder. Then the sofa, which had been tipped to its limit, and Sarah who had slid as far as she could, ended up on the floor on top of Sam with the sofa on top of them both.

They were exhausted. They weren't able to stop laughing. They tried, but then they would start to howl again. They had turned the sofa right side up. Sam lit a fire and turned off the lights. He and Sarah curled up together in the beautiful four-poster bed that Sarah loved. She loved the softness of the sheets against her skin. They smelled of whiskey and oak leaves. They smelled like Sam. Sarah loved everything in Sam's house.

"For someone who models a lot of underwear, why do you never wear any?" asked Sarah.

Sam shrugged and held her tighter. "Don't know. It just feels better to free ball."

"I would think it would chafe." said Sarah.

Sam just laughed and kissed her behind her ear.

Sarah kissed Sam's shoulder. "Could I leave half of my panties here?"

"No, Sarah. I am *not* going to start wearing your panties. I do own underwear. I just choose not to wear them." Sam kissed her collarbone. Sarah shivered a little.

"You don't have to wear them!" Sarah nudged him and laughed. " It's just that Liz did a panty count before I left." Sarah licked Sam's neck. It was Sam's turn to shiver a little.

"Uh?" grunted Sam. "She actually counted your panties? Why?" He gently bit Sarah's shoulder.

"She told me that she expected half of my panties to be ripped off, and she counted them before I left. Of course, it was brought up that if we didn't hit it off, I could go to Scotland and bang a Scotsman. They informed me that the Highlander's don't wear any underwear under their kilts. So, I guess Liz figured if you didn't rip them off, a Scotsman surely would, as evidently, they don't like underwear." Sarah moved a little and nibbled on Sam's torso.

"It's true. You never wear underwear with a kilt. I never do." Sam licked the side of Sarah's breast.

Sarah looked up. "You have a kilt?"

"Any proper British bloke that has Scottish blood in their veins has a kilt." Sam ran a finger down Sarah's ribs.

Sarah sucked on Sam's ear. "Ooooh! That would be something to see."

"I would be honored to have your panties left right there in your cabinet. I might have to use them to satisfy myself." Sam brushed his fingers across Sarah's belly. She sighed.

Sarah ran her fingers up and down Sam's amazing obliques. "That's not fair."

"Why is it not fair? You leave 'em, they're mine to do with as I please." Sam brushed his fingers across Sarah's breast. Sarah moaned softly.

But then Sarah whined pitifully. "I won't be able to take any home and do the same, because you don't wear any." Sarah bent her head and licked both sides of those fabulous obliques.

Sarah had turned all the way around in the bed. Sam started to laugh. "Please don't do any more splits. I don't think I could take another fall."

"Sam, the only thing I'm falling for is you." Sarah rubbed Sam's calf. Then she kissed it, before working her way to the back of his knee, where she nipped and licked. Sam had gotten quiet, and waited. Sarah bit the side of his tight, round ass. Then she licked his ribs, and bit his nipple. As she looked at Sam, he stared at her.

"Are you really?" Sam asked very quietly.

Sarah stopped her ministrations, and asked, "Really what?"

"Falling for me?" Sam was still very quiet.

Sarah sighed and moved back under Sam's arm. "Yes. It's too late. You saw it. I have literally fallen for you."

"I'm serious, Sarah. We have tonight and tomorrow night. And then we have to work hard to figure out what we're going to do, and how we're going to do it. I need to know if you're in this." Sam was very serious.

She sat up and leaned back against the headboard. "I came here to London with no expectations. I really wasn't even expecting to sleep with you. And that would have been fine, too. Not great, but fine, because I had already decided that even if we didn't have … chemistry, I always wanted you as a friend. I didn't know if the age difference would get in our way, because I definitely thought about it."

"I like you so much, Sam. You make me laugh. You make me feel sexy. You listen to me. You like my family, and you don't even know them. You respect me, and you *really* liked me in my red dress." Sam growled and kissed the side of Sarah's ample ass. "You're kind, and respectful. You're polite to a fault, and you make a mean Beef Wellington." Sarah looked at Sam with a soft smile on her face. "I'm in this, Sam. I am *so* in this. I want to explore this further. You haven't been to me and mine yet. That has to happen. I haven't seen you work. Oh, sure, I see the finished product, but I would love to go to a shoot and watch you in action. I look around and I know I want to be able to come back here. I want to see your family again, those yummy little kids. And I'm sorry, but I love your sister. We could get into some righteous trouble together. "

"Oh, God. That's a scary thought."Sam had moved up to sit next to her.

"But, you need to see me in my comfort zone. I live in a totally opposite world than you, Sam. And you like the attention. The parties and premieres. My life is quiet. I like quiet. Sure, I love a good benefit, or a party. I love traveling, but then I get to go home to quiet. Could you do that? How have you done this last week with me, just being quiet?" Sarah leaned into him.

Sam leaned over. He kissed her softly. He stopped and leaned his forehead against hers and closed his eyes. "I have loved you here, Sarah. This is the first time that my house has felt like a home. I can hardly talk about what it will be like without you here. I am looking at my grueling schedule as a good thing, because I won't be here for a while to notice that it's just a house again."

Sarah sighed. "So, no expectations, Sam. But, do you want to pursue whatever this is?"

"I can't imagine how painful it would be if I didn't, and knowing that I would regret it the rest of my life. I hate 'what ifs'. I've already worked out some things for the future. Next year's contracts will be entirely different, and fewer. I can afford to be choosy. How much money do I need? You'll need to kick me in the ass, and make sure I don't cave. I am horrible at saying no. I've talked to Danni about financial things. She's better with my money than I am. There is a foundation that I've just started that I'm dedicated to, and I love England. I'm proud of my country. I can't ever see myself not living here. At least some of the time. You love your home. We've made our lives, Sarah. But I would love to see what we could maybe do together." Sam looked at her a little nervously.

Sarah's face shone. It actually filled with light, and Sam gasped. It gave him goose bumps. "If we can get through the rest of this year, we can actually make a plan of some kind. But, oh! This is only March. I can stand a month Sam, but what are we going to do after that? Sexting was fun, but in person is so much better."

Sam just groaned, and shook his head. "I'm working on it, Sarah. But, there are things I just can't get out of. We'll figure out something."

"Thank you, Sam Ramsay." Sarah whispered.

Sam stared at her. "For what?"

"For wanting me. "

"Thank you, Sarah Reid, for making me realize what I was missing." Sam had rolled her over on to his chest.

They made love slowly, and gently, with a little desperation, and a lot of hope.

Chapter 15:

made for a great way to start their day. They ate oranges and bagels and drank their coffee. They dressed in jeans, T-shirts, baseball caps, and sneakers. Sarah loaded up her bag with her cameras and lenses. She was surprisingly excited about sightseeing. Plus, it meant that she and Sam wouldn't sit around and dread tomorrow. It was a mild day for March in London. They had bundled up for the drive in, because Sarah wanted the top down on Sam's Candy Apple Red vintage Boxster convertible. It made Sarah feel so British.

They planned on Buckingham Palace, Constitution Hall, Royal Albert Hall, and Kensington Gardens. Then they planned to get to Big Ben and The Tower of London. It would be a full day of walking. Sam and Sarah held hands and Sam pointed out bits of history here and there. Sarah could feel the pride Sam had for his city. It was beautiful. Buckingham Palace was larger than Sarah thought it would be. It also had more tourists than she thought it would. They didn't stay long. Sarah excitedly snapped pictures of everything, but Sam noticed that she really enjoyed getting spontaneous shots of people. There was an old man feeding pigeons in Kensington Gardens, and Sarah snapped picture after picture. The man never noticed. Children seemed to be her favorite, and Sam could have watched her all day. She truly had a gift. They had been out for almost two hours when the first group of girls approached him for pictures. Sarah just grinned at him and offered to take the pictures for the girls. She took all their phones and snapped a group photo for all of them, and then one with each girl. Sam kissed every one of them on the cheek. Sarah then asked one of the girls if she would take one of them. Sarah showed her how to use the camera and asked her to just keep clicking until Sarah told her to stop. The giggly girl was happy to oblige. They moved on. They were on their way to the car to drive a little closer to Big Ben, when it happened again. And again, Sarah was happy to take the pictures for them. They were a little older than the secondary students. These were University age. They were a little provocative, and a lot suggestive, and a couple passed their phone numbers to Sam on folded pieces of paper. Sam was a gentleman, and treated them no different than the youngsters, but Sarah could see his jaws as they clenched. When the girls had left and they had reached the car, Sam threw the scraps of paper away and cursed. "Holy fuck! Have they no self-respect? They don't even know me!"

Sarah patted his arm, and gave him a kiss. "I was quite impressed with your self-control and your manners. Your mum would be proud."

"Well, I don't want to be rude, but it gets really tiresome being pawed." Sam huffed.

Sarah buckled up and said sarcastically, "I can only imagine."

Big Ben had wonderful opportunities for some great shots, and Sarah snapped in peace for almost forty-five minutes before the next group of horny girls accosted Sam. He looked to her as if he wanted her help, but she just looked at him and laughed. "You are on your own this time, buddy. I have places to go and people to meet." Sarah had spotted a pub across the street. It was so very British. It would make for good pictures. Sarah looked back at Sam. He glared at her. She just laughed and waved, as she left him surrounded by girls. Sarah climbed benches, and laid on the sidewalk and grass. She got some good shots of patrons as they emerged from the pub. She was changing lenses when Sam finally made his way to her.

"Bloody hell! Do you feel like getting a pint?" He nodded his head at the pub.

"A pint? In a pub? Are you freakin' kidding me? Of course I would!" Sarah grabbed his hand as she dragged him across the street. Sam grinned at her excitement.

It was dark and quiet inside. It was just like Sarah had pictured in her head, of what a typical British pub would look like. Dark walnut wood and hunter green vinyl. It smelled of malt and sausages. It was heavenly. Sam got their pints at the bar, and they went and sat in a booth. They clinked their glasses, said cheers, and sipped. Sarah noticed Sam's shoulders relaxing.

He looked at her and asked, "That didn't bother you? Seriously? The one girl actually tried to grab my balls!"

"I'm so sorry Sam. It must be so difficult to be so beautiful. Life would be so much easier if you were a hunch back with scales on your face, wouldn't it?" Sarah teased.

Sam just stared at her, and took another drink.

Sarah leaned over and took his hand. "I am teasing, but, before I knew you, when I had just seen the picture, I had thought that your beauty would be a sad cross to bear."

"Really?" Sam arched an eyebrow.

"Yes, I did. The idiots that do that shit are just girls, Sam. Everyone just sees the beauty that is your face and your body. I see it, and it sometimes takes my breath away. But then, I know something that they don't."

"What's that?" Sam asked. He was truly curious.

"I know your heart, and I know your humor, and the love for your family. I know *you*. And I also know that I'm the one that gets to go home and hump that gorgeous body. Me. Not them."

Sam touched her cheek, and said with wonder in his voice, "Where did you come from, Sarah Reid?"

Sam watched it happen. He knew it would. Sarah went up to get their second pint. Before the pub owner even had their glasses filled, he and Sarah were in animated conversation. "There she goes." Sam thought, full of pride. "Sarah being Sarah." Sam sat and watched as she got a tour of the entire pub. Upstairs, the kitchen, the basement. Then she got pictures of all of the staff, and even got one of the owner and his wife without their knowledge. She had a gift. After she got their address, so she could send them copies, she was bear-hugged by the man. Sarah didn't know a stranger.

As they walked back to the car, Sarah saw it. She squealed so loudly that she scared the pigeons. A red telephone booth. She made Sam take pictures of her in it. She took pictures of him in it. Then she grabbed a pedestrian and had him take pictures of both of them in it. There were many of Sarah's hands on Sam's ass, and Sam's hands on her chest. The gentleman taking the pictures just chuckled. Sarah planned on framing the most suggestive one for Julie.

They stopped at the market on their way home to get dinner makings. Sarah looked at the lemons. Sam was fondling the melons. He picked up two of them and turned to Sarah holding them on his chest. He grinned a stupid little grin and jiggled them up and down. "Look familiar?"

Sarah crossed her arms in front of her chest and looked at him sternly. "Really, Sam? Melons? How old are you? I don't need to look at your melons. I have my own." She reached for a banana and slowly unpeeled it, never taking her eyes off of him. She slowly slid the banana in her mouth. The entire banana. Sam gulped and dropped the melons. Sarah slowly slid the banana halfway out of her mouth. Then she bit it in two and grinned.

They both heard a snort from beside them. They had an audience. Several older women with baskets on their arms stood and watched them. The one who had presumably snorted was enjoying the show. "You better watch your P's and Q's with that one, Sam Ramsay. I don't think she's messing around."

Sam smiled that slow, sexy smile at the woman, and said, "Oh, I hope she'll mess around. Especially after that trick."

"I see what you're doing. You could melt the panties off a nun, couldn't you?" The woman continued. "I know who you are. I've seen that smile of yours on a million pages. But, this one," the woman nodded her head at Sarah, "She sees through that. You two are having fun. Life's too short to not enjoy it. Now take your woman home, and let her unpeel your banana." The woman laughed and laughed at her own joke. So did Sarah and Sam.

Sarah and Sam chattered as they worked on dinner side by side. Sam was in charge of the steaks and shrimp. Sarah would do something with asparagus and potatoes.

"Thanks for playing tourist today, Sam. I enjoyed it immensely." Sarah drizzled olive oil over the asparagus before she started to wrap the green stalks with bacon.

Sam put the water on to boil for the shrimp before he turned to her and grinned. "I enjoyed it, too. You tend to forget about the beauty that's in your own backyard."

"Tell me about Marta. How long have you known her?" Sarah sliced potatoes.

Sam poured them each a whiskey, and sat down at the table. Sarah finished putting the melted butter and cheese on the potatoes, and put them and the asparagus in the oven. She sat down with Sam, and put her bare feet in his lap. She took a sip of whiskey and leaned back.

Sam started to rub Sarah's feet absent-mindedly as he thought. "I didn't know her at all before Oak Wood. I worked with Therese' on the campaign for at least eight years. When she retired to start a family, they hired Marta. That's was almost four years ago. We hit it off immediately." Sam continued to rub Sarah's arches and in-between her toes. "I really detest most of the female models I've worked with. They're spoiled divas. They always make it about them, and what they need in order to do the work. They forget that it's about the product, and the owners of that product. Marta isn't like that. She's thankful for the work and is always professional. She will miss Mark like crazy on the campaign, though he usually manages to see hera couple of times. I like him, too. Yeah, if I have to keep the schedule that Oak Wood entails, I'm glad it's with her. She's a hoot. She's kind of like a little sister." Sam got up to wash his hands and put the steaks in the broiler.

Sarah took another sip of whiskey. "Well, it's got to be weird kissing your sister."

Sam laughed. "Yeah, sometimes it is. It's even weirder seeing each other naked, but we're usually laughing so hard by that time that it's certainly not romantic. It just looks that way on the page. It's just our job. I'm glad that it's Marta, and not one of the others. That would make for a miserable thirty days."

"I like her. She's going to call me when she's in the States, and I think I'm going to go see her and Mark. That doesn't bother you, does it?" Sarah got up to check on the food.

"Absolutely not! You two will enjoy each other. You both have filthy mouths. Plus you don't have to get my okay on anything, Sarah." Sam lifted an eyebrow at her.

They sat next to each other as they ate their dinner. They played footsie under the table, and continually touched an arm, or a leg, or a face as they talked. Sarah tried to get as much of Sam as she could. It was going to be a long time before she got anymore. Sam did the same thing. They each got quiet with their own thoughts as they cleaned up the kitchen and started the dishwasher. When they were done, Sam just reached for Sarah's hand and they went upstairs.

Sam reached for Sarah as they entered the bedroom. He just needed to feel her, as she did him. They stood that way for a while. They both were absorbed in the scents and the feel of each other. They needed enough to last until the next time. Sam took Sarah's face in his hands. "What do you want amazing Sarah?"

Sarah just lay her head on his shoulder and whispered, "You. All I want is you."

Sam led her to the bathroom. He turned on the taps in the tub that Sarah loved so much. He lit the candles, and turned on quiet, sensual, hypnotic guitar. Sam and Sarah stood face to face. Sam put Sarah's arms up, and pulled her T-shirt off. He unzipped her jeans, and she stepped out of them, along with her panties. He unclasped her bra and removed it. Sarah, in turn did the same for him. First the T-shirt, then the jeans. Sam and Sarah said nothing. They were utterly silent. The only sound in the room was the water running in the tub and the chords of the guitar. Sam turned off the water. Sam moved forward and touched Sarah's cheeks before he kissed both of them. He took her right arm and rubbed from the shoulder to her fingers. He could feel her pulse race, but she didn't move nor did she say a word. He took her left arm and did the same. He caressed her shoulders and down her silky, soft torso. Sarah did the same to Sam. She savored every hard muscle and crevice and all of his hard angles and soft skin. They stood and looked at everything the other had to give and it was good. Sam walked Sarah to the tub. They sat face to face and looked at each other. The flickering candlelight cast shadows on their faces and bodies as their mouths met. They kissed each other softly, until Sam turned Sarah around. Her soft back leaned against his hard chest. Sam poured water down Sarah's hair and body. He gently worked shampoo into her hair and massaged her temples before he rinsed her gently. He soaped her shoulders and her back and breasts, before again, rinsing her gently. Sarah trembled as she turned around and straddled him. The warm water and their breath had steamed over the mirrors and windows. It was hot, humid and sultry. They smelled of shampoo and soap. Sam reached for Sarah's face and greedily took her lips with his. His tongue swept hers with the beat of their hearts. He punished her mouth, and bit her bottom lip as he grabbed her ass with both hands and lifted her up and on him. Sarah cried out and arched her back. The only sensations they felt were wet, heat, muscle, and softness. Sarah was impaled and was helpless to stop. Sam lifted her up and down as the water splashed over the tub. As Sarah reached her tipping point, Sam left her mouth to move to her breasts. The crescendo of the guitar muffled their cries.

They added hot water as Sarah laid her head on Sam's shoulder. Sam rubbed her back, and wondered if a person could really die from a broken heart. Sarah was quiet as Sam continued to rub, lost in his own thoughts. He felt her shaking and turned her to see her face. Strong Sarah who could handle anything was quietly crying. "Oh, darling, please don't cry!" Sam was shaken. He kissed her tears.

"I'm okay. Really." Sarah wiped at her eyes with a closed fist. "I promised myself I wouldn't do this! It's just that this is so bittersweet. I am so incredibly sad that I will be leaving tomorrow. I can't seem to get the lump to leave my throat." She started to cry again. "But, the sweet is that I have had some of the best moments of my life this week. Without the bitter, I would have no sweet. Thank you, Sam Ramsay. You are officially my favorite guy." Sarah was inconsolable and couldn't stop.

Sam's heart was so tight in his chest that he couldn't seem to catch his breath. He lifted Sarah out of the tub. He grabbed a towel and strode into the bedroom with her in his arms. Sam dried Sarah and put her in the bed. He held her and rocked her as she slowly stopped crying. Sam was emotionally spent, as well.

Sam's voice was hoarse and shaky. "I don't know what to say to you, Sarah. I have no answers, and it's killing me! My life has forever been changed because of you, sweet girl. You have stripped the blinders from my eyes, and for the first time in my life, I know what's important, and I know what I'm going to do. And I want to do it with you." Sam put his head in Sarah's neck and breathed out heavily. "Do you have any fucking idea how hard it's going to be to see you get on that plane tomorrow and not know when I will get to see you again?" Sam wadded the sheets in his hands.

Sarah stroked his face, and just said, "Yes, I do."

Sam held her tightly. "Danni and I were talking about you the week before you came. She told me that if there's meat on the bone it's worth going for. And what she said on Sunday? About wanting me to experience the bumps and bruises of life? Oh, Sarah, I am *so* bumped and bruised right now."

Sarah gave Sam a scorching kiss, and then pulled back and looked deep into his eyes. "No expectations, Sam. Remember? I don't expect you to say it just because I do. I love you Sam Ramsay, I always will."

"Oh magnificent Sarah, I love you, too. I think I started loving you when you answered the door in your T-shirt and panties."

The morning came too soon, and they desperately made love before they showered. Sarah spent the morning packing, while Sam just sat and watched. His heart crushed when she took the red dress out of the closet and covered it with tissue paper before she put it in the garment bag. Sarah saw the look on his face. He was stricken. She rushed to his side and sat on the floor in front of the chair he sat in. "Sam? I don't know when and I don't know where, but I promise you, I *will* make another entrance for you. I will have a little time to think about it, and plan it, and I will knock

184

your socks off!"

Sam smiled a sad smile. "I am counting on it."

Sam took Sarah's bags to the car. He waited for her at the bottom of the stairs when she emerged from the bedroom. It broke Sam's heart but it made him grin. Sarah saw that slow, sexy grin, and thought to herself, "Yes! It worked!" She slowly made her way down the stairs. Sarah wore her standard black leggings. Her shirt was a deep fuchsia with lace inserts. The lace was a tease, as it showed the entire top of Sarah's ample bosom. It looked like her breasts were going to spill out. You couldn't see the strapless bra, only her deep cleavage. And the black suede, thigh-high, lace-up boots.

"Holy shit, Sarah! Put a jacket on! Or a bra! But wait just a minute before you do that." Sam met her at the bottom of the stairs and grabbed her. He wrapped one hand around her waist, and the other one he firmly planted on her left breast. He tried to get a peek of what was trying to spill out. "And the fucking boots! You are killing me, woman!" Sam groaned.

Sarah giggled. "I know that I'm now known in London as the woman in red who made an entrance. Well, I wanted to make an exit, too!"

Sam growled as he continued to clutch her breast. "I think we need to exit to the sofa over there and unbutton that shirt."

"Alas! We have no time," Sarah said, "though that does sound appealing."

~~~

They stood at the last gate as Sam could go no further. They had kissed continually since they arrived. Sarah put her head on Sam's shoulder and promised herself that she wasn't going to cry. Sam held Sarah and promised himself that he wasn't going to make it difficult for her to leave. The flashbulbs had found them, and they were surrounded by cameras. Neither of them had eyes or ears for anyone other than each other. Sarah kissed Sam's neck before she kissed his mouth. Deeply. Sam reciprocated.

"Text me as soon as you land."

It will be the middle of the night here Sam. I wouldn't want to wake you." Sarah murmured as she continued to nibble his lips.

Sam had a hard time getting his lip out of her mouth. "Like I'm going to be sleeping? I won't sleep until I know you're on terra firma." He went back in for more lip wrestling.

"Okay. It should be eight o'clock my time, so it'll be around two o'clock in the morning here."

Sam had to have one last kiss. "I will be waiting. I love you Sarah Reid."

"I love you, too, Sam Ramsay."

They could put it off no longer. Sarah had to go. As she walked through the final gate, she turned around and dropped the wrap from around her shoulders and gave Sam a shimmy of her shoulders and a beaming grin.

"God!" groaned Sam. "That bawdy woman is going to kill me!"

Sam watched Sarah until she disappeared from sight, then he turned and slowly made his way to the car.

Sarah had her ear buds in as she listened to Nina Simone sing softly. She would be home soon. But how would home feel to her now? Things had changed. Her life and her world had changed, and she already missed Sam. Everything had happened so fast. How could you love someone in three months? "Hah!" Sarah thought to herself. "I knew I loved David at fifteen. People thought that was crazy." She didn't care what people thought. She never had. Sam would have a harder time learning to let it go. His life had revolved around what other people thought for twenty two years. She sighed and closed her eyes, and watched the film reel play in her mind. She pictured Sam standing barefoot and shirtless in the kitchen. She remembered him as he played with Thomas and Violet, and how he looked at Danni. How cute he looked in jeans and a ball cap. She remembered the look on Sam's face when he saw her get out of the car wearing the red dress. It made her smile to remember the look of possession on his face. She could see the way his face and body looked over hers as they made love. Sarah had experienced wants, and needs and feelings that she had never experienced before. She wanted more.

Sam had poured himself two fingers of scotch and sat on the sofa. He had continually paced since he had gotten home. He told himself to get a grip. Perhaps the scotch would help. He sipped and relived some of the moments from the last week. He and Sarah had crammed a lot into that week. On one hand, it went by much too quickly, and on the other it seemed as if time had stood still. Sam leaned his head back on the sofa and remembered Sarah at the airport when she arrived. Those damn boots! He pictured her in his kitchen and how comfortable she was. He saw Sarah as she stood at the counter barefoot and showed Danni how to make biscuits and gravy. He loved how much she loved his house. It would be impossible to ever forget her on the steps at the benefit and how that night had ended. He had never felt, or acted upon feelings like that in his life. He didn't regret it. He pictured her and the kids in that field at sunset, and how it had made him feel. He had started to love her before that, but that night had pushed him over the edge. He pictured Sarah in the candlelight as she hovered over him in the bathtub. He saw the way the shadows highlighted and hid her secret places. He would never get in that tub again until Sarah was back to share it. Sam knew that the unknown was all on him. The reason for their separation was his career. Sam took a sip of scotch with a hand that trembled. He sat his glass down, leaned over and ran both hands through his hair and sighed. Then he put his face in his hands and he cried.

Chapter 16:

Sarah: I made it. Uneventful flight.

Sam: Thank God!

Sarah: I thought about getting a room, before heading for home in the morning, but I can be home around

ten, and I'd rather sleep in my own bed. So I'm going to head on down the road.

Sam: I'll bet it feels good to be back in Missouri.

Sarah: No. It doesn't. Things have changed. I left half of myself in a home in London.

Sam: The house is quiet. I hate it.

Sarah: Sam?

Sam: Sarah?

Sarah: I don't want to .....I CAN'T talk to you tomorrow, okay?

Sam: Uh...okay. Whatever you want?

Sarah: I am going to go home and I am just going to throw myself into a loud, horrific, snotty melt down.

I am going to do that tomorrow, because I'm too tired to do it tonight. But I need to do it Sam. I

have wants and needs now Sam, that I didn't have a week ago. And I'm soooo happy about that, but

I need to feel sorry for myself, if only for a day. Because now that you've made me have those wants

and needs, I know that they're not going to be easily gotten again. I need to get it out of my system.

Sam: I get that, Sarah. I have already started my, what did you call it? A pity party? (sigh)

Sarah: You've already started. I will have mine tomorrow.

Sam: I love you, Sarah Reid. You have no idea how much.

Sarah: I love you, too, Sam Ramsay, and if you love me half as much as I love you, we are fucked.

Sam: Goodnight amazing Sarah.

Sarah: Goodnight beautiful Sam.

Sarah slept like the dead. She had been physically and emotionally exhausted. When she slowly opened her eyes the next morning, she had to look around to remember that she was home. Home. With no Sam and no idea of when she would see him again. She could feel the ache start deep in her gut. She mentally slapped herself. She needed to text the girls to let them know she was home. They would start to worry if she didn't. But, she didn't want, or need, to talk to them. Not yet. She couldn't. Every nerve ending was raw. She felt like a burn victim, but no debridement would remove the pain.

Sarah: Hi all. I'm home. Made it in at about 10:30 last night. No offense, but I don't want to talk just yet. I can't respond to any texts yet, either. I'm a mess. And before you start thinking that the trip was

a bust. It wasn't. And that's why I'm not up to talking about it just yet. I'm raw. I am taking this

week to baby myself, and have my meltdown. I won't be at class this week. Can you all plan on coming to

my house next week? I know it's not my turn, but I can only tell you about my "adventure" once. Let's

do it Friday night, okay? Slumber party? I will need to get shitfaced. I love you all SO much.

Liz: (hearts)

Bev: hugs

Julie: ☹

Karen: ☹

Ashley: I'll bring the liquor. (hugs)

Sarah made her way slowly to the kitchen to make coffee. She sat at the island and waited. She had a feeling that was what she was going to being doing a lot of. That sounded like she blamed Sam, and she didn't. She knew going into this what Sam's schedule had to be and what his career entailed. She was just bitchy and pissed off. "Yep." She thought. "There's the first stage. "Anger. I should be doing real well by tonight." Sarah poured herself a cup of coffee. She could unpack. She could take a shower. She could dust. She needed to. She could unload the dishwasher. But all she really wanted to do was catch the next plane back to London.

~~~

Sam had drunk himself into oblivion and had finally passed out. It was after two o'clock in the afternoon and he felt like hell. "You deserve the pain," growled Sam aloud. "You're the one who let her go. You could've stopped her." He knew that he was being unrealistic. No matter how much he wanted her here, it didn't change the fact that he would leave tomorrow for the Oak Wood campaign. He had to pack, and he needed to eat something, but all he wanted to do was text Sarah. But, he had promised her he wouldn't. He wondered how she was doing. And then he didn't want to think about it. He hated to think about her in pain. She had experienced too much of it in her life, and he hated that he had caused her more. She deserved better. He went to the refrigerator to find something to eat before he swallowed three aspirin and some coffee. Sam opened the door and was greeted by a big stainless steel bowl of something. He remembered Sarah had put it in there with a funny look on her face. He took it out and removed the foil that was over it. It was full of whipped cream. Sam swallowed. Sarah had said something about a 'special desert'. As he continued to look at it, he realized that Sarah had probably been the 'desert" with the whipped cream on top. "Fuck!" shouted Sam as he threw the bowl in the sink.

Sam: Sarah? Can we talk now? Are you okay?

Sarah: No, I'm not okay, but I will be, and yes, we can talk. (sigh)

Sam: I'll be leaving in a few hours.

Sarah: I know. I've set one of my clocks to London time.

Sam: As soon as I get our itinerary, I will send it on to you.

Sarah: Okay.

Sam: What will you do today?

Sarah: I plan on staying in bed.

Sam: Please don't add worry to my heartache, Sarah.

Sarah: I'll be okay. But, I miss you. When I woke up yesterday, I thought I was still in London.

Sam: When I woke up, I had a raging hangover. I miss you, too.

Sarah: When I talk to you tomorrow, I promise I'll be in a better frame of mind.

Sam: I'll take you however I can get you.

Sarah: I hate me being this way. I haven't even bathed or combed my hair. If you saw me I would

scare you away.

Sam: You could never scare me away. Never.

Sarah: Bye, Sam. I love you.

Sam: I love you more.

~~~

As the week progressed, Sarah *had* gone through the motions. She had showered and washed her hair. She had unpacked. As she hung the red dress in her closet it had done her in. She went to bed for the rest of the day. Slowly, she was able to function. The texts from Sam were all that kept her from going insane. She missed her mom. She would know what to do. She had called the kids, but all she did was worry them. She still hadn't talked to the girls and had no plans to until Friday. She wasn't going to class again this week, either. She was too tired to even make the effort. She realized that she was depressed and that she needed to buck up, and realizing it was a good first step. She would get through this, but right now she just wanted to sleep all of the time. When she slept, she dreamed of Sam.

~~~

Sam was short and temperamental with everyone around him. He had even snapped at Marta. He couldn't concentrate. He didn't want to concentrate. He just wanted Sarah. She had him worried. She was too quiet, and she slept too much. And there wasn't a damn thing he could do about it. When he had snapped at Marta again she grabbed him and snapped back. "Come on! We are going to talk this out, whether you want to or not!" Sam followed her and pouted. "What the hell is wrong with you, Sam? As long as I have known you, you have never been rude. To anyone. You have everyone walking around on eggshells Spit it out, asshole!" Marta was furious.

Sam just shook his head and put his face in his hands. He was mortified to feel like he was going to cry. "Aaahh, Marta... I'm so sorry. It's Sarah. I'm worried about her. I can't seem to think about anything else, and I'm not sleeping." He proceeded to tell her about the last couple of days in London, and her behavior since she had gone home.

Marta leaned back in her chair. "She's depressed. That doesn't sound like the Sarah I met."

"She told me that she was going to get it all out of her system in a day or two, but it's been almost two weeks. She won't even talk to her friends or go to class. I don't know what to do. If I had time, I would fly over to check on her." Sam ran his fingers through his hair.

"You love her, don't you?" asked Marta.

"More than anything, Marta. She's a witch that's put a spell on me."

Marta whispered, "I love that you love her, Sam. It's about damn time! You deserve love in your life from someone other than me and Mark and your family. And I like her so much."

"It's killing me!" Sam paced back and forth.

"Would it help if I called her? Do you mind?" asked Marta.

"Would you? That would be great. She might be more honest with you, and I have no one else to ask." Sam had stopped pacing and looked at Marta with a hopeful expression.

"I'll call her when this press conference is done. Now get your ass in there and be nice!"

Marta: Hey chickie!

Sarah: Hey Marta.

Marta: Whatcha doing?

Sarah: Just hanging out in bed.

Marta: You been hanging out in bed a lot, Sarah?

Sarah: No. I'm just tired.

Marta: Sam is worried sick about you.

Sarah: There's nothing to be worried about. I'm fine.

Marta: You know I like you, and I feel like we could be good friends, Sarah. So, if we're going to be

friends, I'm going to be brutally honest, okay?

Sarah: Okay...

Marta: You are not the only one who is in pain Sarah! Sam's work is suffering. He looks like hell,

and he's not sleeping. Not only is he heartsick like you, he's now got the added pain of

worrying about your well being! That's not fair! You are being selfish, Sarah.

Sarah: I don't want him to worry about me. I'll be fine.

Marta: Too late. He's already worried. Do you know how much he loves you? I don't think you do,

 or you wouldn't be doing this to him!

Sarah: Now I feel even worse....

Marta: Stop it! If you love him, you are going to make this work! Do you hear me? Make him think

 of you at home being his beautiful Sarah, not the dirty, pitiful slug that stays in bed all day.

Sarah: Well, that's an ugly picture.

Marta: Sorry, but that's how he's picturing you right now.

Sarah: Oh, God! Marta, I feel so bad! I mean, I feel bad, But now I REALLY feel bad. I wasn't thinking

about Sam's pain. Only my own. What a selfish bitch I am!

Marta: LOL! Now that sounds more like the Sarah I met and liked. You two will get through this. Mark

and I make it work. But it's hard. But you don't strike me as someone who is afraid of hard.

Sarah: I am so glad you called me Marta. Thank you so much!

Marta: So does that mean we can still see each other when I'm in the states?

Sarah: Absolutely!

Marta: I'll talk to you later.

Sarah: See you!

Sarah got up and looked around her bedroom. She felt like she had finally woken up after two weeks of being in a nightmare. She straightened her shoulders and said to herself, "Okay, Sarah Anne. Time to plan the rest of your life!"

She made lots of coffee. She dusted, and finished unpacking. It had snowed a few inches overnight, and she went out and shoveled the walk. It felt good to move the muscles that had grown lax in bed. She unloaded the dishwasher and made a grocery list. She tried to keep her mind off Sam. She opened a can of soup and sat to eat it. She knew what she had to do. The girls would be here Friday, so first she would go to the store, and then come back to start on her photos. She needed to rip the bandage off.

The morning went by quickly with shopping and errands. Sarah put the groceries away, and went upstairs to her photo room. She sat down at the computer and plugged her first camera in. She took a deep breath and clicked "upload". Picture after picture of Sam, and his family, and the pub, and Big Ben. Sarah felt her breath hitch, and she started to cry. But it was good. This was her life she was looking at, and it was good.

Sam: Sarah?

Sarah: I'm here Sam.

Sam: What are you doing?

Sarah: I'm upstairs in my room looking at my life.

Sam: I'm sorry?

Sarah: I've uploaded all of my photos, and now I'm crying.

Sam: Please don't cry Sarah It breaks my heart.

Sarah: Oh, Sam It's good. It is so good.

Sam: I was so worried about you, Sarah.

Sarah: I'm so sorry, Sam, I was being very selfish. I don't want you to worry. I am finally okay.

Sam: Did Marta call you?

Sarah: Yes, She was wonderful. Thanks for that. I know you asked her to.

Sam: I didn't ask. She offered. Did she kick your ass, too?

Sarah: LOL. Yes, but I needed it.

Sam: Me, too. I was being a prick. Even to her.

Sarah: You better now?

Sam: So much better.

Sarah: Me, too. The girls are coming Friday for a sleepover. I'm ready. I went to the store and dusted the

house. Sam: This makes me so happy, Sarah. Can we SKYPE?

Sarah: That would be so cool! (I just yelled that out loud) It would probably also be safer. ☺

Sam: I'll try to oblige. Oh, Sarah, you've had made my life a lot better tonight.

Sarah: Ditto.

Sam: I love you, Sarah Reid.

Sarah: I love you more, Sam Ramsay.

~~~

Sarah stayed up late as she went through the photos. She laughed, and she cried, and sometimes she was just silent. She savored every sensation and emotion. She sucked it in like oxygen, because Sam *was* her oxygen. He had given her life. She looked at her London clock, and got up to call Danni and Marta.

Sam woke up after a good night's sleep for the first time in two weeks. His heart felt lighter after talking to Sarah. It was so good to get her back from whatever dark place she had been. He had been truly worried and thought that he would have to leave the campaign to go get her.

He would have to give Marta a hug and a big thank you. He didn't know what she had said to her, and he didn't care. If he knew Marta, it was the brutal truth. It had worked. Sam started to count down the days until this ordeal was over. For the first time in twenty two years he was tired of Oak Wood. He would do it next year, if asked, but it was going to be on his terms. No more thirty days away from everything and everyone he loved. They could afford to give everyone a week off after two weeks. Yes. Things were going to be different, and he felt incredibly lighter.

Sarah slept in after staying up so late. She had the day planned, and it started after a cup of coffee. She rummaged around upstairs and found what she needed. She found the rest of her supplies in the laundry room. She finished her project late in the day, and stood back and looked. She wandered from room to room. Again, she cried happy tears. She finished her plans for the day by prepping everything for tomorrow night. She put her laptop on the kitchen cabinet and called it a night.

Sam: Sarah?

Sarah: I'm here, beautiful Sam.

Sam: How was your day?

Sarah: It has been glorious. (sigh) How about yours?

Sam: Well, mine wasn't glorious, but people were much happier to be around me today. ☺

Sarah: I would be happy to be around you. Can you feel me hugging you?

Sam: Yeah, I can. Can you feel me hugging right back?

Sarah: Oh yes. (sigh)I have everything set up for tomorrow night. Text me when you're ready and I'll turn on

the laptop. And remember, I warned you!

Sam: I consider myself warned. I love you amazing Sarah. Welcome back.

Sarah: It feels good to be back. Love you more Sam Ramsay.

April

Chapter 17:

Sarah had sent a group text that instructed the girls to wait for each other before they came in. She would wait inside. Sarah was a little emotional as she sat in the kitchen. She was anxious to see the girls. She heard them as they came up the walk way, and it got quiet. She knew that they were reading the chalkboard by the front door. She had written, "The door is open! Come on in! Please move to your right and follow the Yellow Brick Road." Sarah heard the door open and waited.

Ashley, Julie, Bev, Karen and Liz opened the door to be greeted by hundreds of pictures. A line of jute was strung from the right of the door, and stretched around the room, over the fireplace mantle, and into the next room, as far as the eye could see. Clothespins held picture after picture. The girls couldn't move. Karen immediately started to sob. The others were silent, even Julie. They slowly started to walk. The first picture was a selfie that Sarah had taken at the airport in St. Louis. The next one was the lights of London from the airplane window.

"It's her life in London." Bev murmured.

There were pictures of Sam's backyard and his cars. There was a picture of Sam with his back to Sarah as he stood at the kitchen sink stark-ass naked.

"Jesus H. Christ." Julie hissed.

They felt like they were in church. There was picture after picture of Sam. Him in profile as he looked out his window and another as he stared through the lens at Sarah with his tongue stuck out. He lounged on the couch with a glass of whiskey and his bare feet on the coffee table. There was picture after picture of Sam's home. Then picture after picture of the Sunday papers with Sam in his blue velvet tuxedo and her in her red dress. It showed Sam as he stalked her down the steps, and then Sarah draped across Sam's arm in a smoldering kiss.

"Holy shit," breathed Liz. "Look at that. That's our Sarah."

They had made their way through the next maze of pictures. These were Sam's mom and dad, and Danni and Alex and Thomas and Violet and the farm. There were baby lambs with their mamas and dogs and a beautiful sunset.

There was Sarah and Sam as they groped each other and made faces in front of Prince Albert Hall. The next ones were in the same locale, but showed Sarah and Sam with their foreheads touching and their hands on each other's shoulders. They just looked at each other.

"I think I'm going to cry." Liz whispered.

Next came the outside shots of the pub. Then Winston and Miriam, the owners of the pub. The couple stood and held hands as they looked somewhere past Sarah's lens. There were children, and a man feeding pigeons. And amongst all of them were spontaneous pictures of Sam.

Bev started to sob and pointed at one of Sam looking at Sarah through her lens. "That man has nothing but love for our girl. That man has never taken a bad picture but that one is his best." She continued to sob, and went to Karen, who had never stopped.

Next were the ones in the telephone booth.

"Oh!" Julie whispered. "She found one!"

There were plenty of Sarah and Sam as they had put their hands down each other's pants, and ones of Sam as he grabbed Sarah's breasts and Sarah as she grabbed Sam's ass. But then they turned into Sam as he held Sarah's face and looked into her eyes. The next ones were of him as he kissed her hard.

As the girls got closer to the kitchen the pictures turned into selfies. Sam and Sarah lay in a bed on their backs with their heads together. Sam was shirtless and Sarah had a sheet that barely covered her. Another was of her as she sat on Sam's lap with her head on his shoulder.

The last two were of Sam sitting at a kitchen table as he looked out into space with tears in his eyes. It was almost a visceral reaction for all the girls. They felt the pain as it oozed out of the picture. They had all started to sob by this time.

The last one was of Sarah laying in twisted sheets with her hand over her heart as she cried. The other hand gripped the sheets so hard her knuckles were white. The heartache was palpable.

The girls couldn't move for a minute. They were all emotionally drained, but their girl needed them. They turned the corner to see Sarah sitting on a bar stool. She looked at all of them and just shrugged her shoulders and held her hands out as if in supplication. Then she started to cry.

No words were spoken for the longest time. There were just tears and lots of hugs. Sarah absorbed the pain and the love from her friends. She had wept so hard that she had the hiccups.

Liz was the one who spoke first. "I have no words, Sarah". Her voice broke. "You take beautiful pictures, but your life is more beautiful."

"Do you feel like telling us about any of it?" Karen asked softly.

Sarah was only able to whisper. "I just did."

Ashley went back to the front of the house to get her bag. She came back in and said, "I was going to do Margaritas, but tonight its gonna be tequila shots with salt and limes. We all need to get drunk."

Liz went and stood by Sarah. She rubbed the tops of her shoulders and asked, "Was it everything you hoped it would be, Sarah? "

Sarah just looked up at her with a sad smile and said, "It was more. So much more."

Karen very quietly asked the question that they were all wondering. "Is it over? And if it is, was it worth it?"

Sarah jumped up and grabbed the tequila bottle out of Ashley's hands. She grabbed a slice of lime. She smeared the lime over the back of her hand and doused it with salt. She licked the salt, took a big swig of tequila and squeezed the lime in her mouth. The tequila burned, and it brought tears to her eyes, but then that nice warmth started to spread in her chest and belly. Everyone stared at her like she'd lost her mind, but also because they were afraid of what she might say.

"It's worse, Karen. He loves me. And I love him. Now what the fuck do I do?" Sarah just looked at all of them.

"Pass that fucking bottle around, Sarah!" yelled Julie.

Everyone talked at once as Sarah sat there. They finally noticed that she had zoned out.

Bev put her finger to her lips. "Sssshhhhh!"

Bev looked at Sarah as she sat there quietly and asked, "Well of course he does, honey, but the more important question is, do you really love him? Or is it the sex? Or the comfort of a man's touch and companionship?"

Sarah hunched her shoulders, and smiled a quiet little smile. "I love him more than I ever imagined a person could love. He's funny and kind and respectful and sweet. He is the most well-mannered man I've ever met. He's an amazing cook and he has the best ass in the world. He loves his family. His kisses take my breath away, and the sex ain't bad, either."

"Oh, God, I'm a little bitter right now, Sarah. And jealous." Julie smiled at Sarah, before she asked, "Is he as beautiful in person as he is in his pictures?"

Sarah looked off into space with a sweet smile. " He's more beautiful than any picture. His face is perfect. His body is a work of art. But even better, is his heart. That's what I love the most about him. There is more to Sam Aaron Ramsay than a pretty face." She sighed and refocused.

"Tell us what you feel like telling us, Sarah. I would really like to know about the night you made those headlines! That is H.O.T.!" Liz fanned herself.

"All I feel comfortable sharing with you guys, about that night, is that I have **never** experienced anything like that in my life. And it ended fiercely..." Sarah grinned an evil grin.

"You're making me want to jump your bones just thinking about it." Julie said.

"Well before you do that, we have to let Sam know. He would want to watch." Sarah started to laugh. "Hey! Do you guys want to see that dress?"

They all continued to chatter as they made their way into the bedroom. Sarah told them what Sam had said about watching them. Sarah removed the dress from the tissue paper and held it up for all to see.

"Shit, Sarah! That's sex on a hanger!" Bev exclaimed.

"Pretty much, yeah. I wanted to make an entrance." Sarah sighed and rubbed the dress. "Okay! I am so glad you guys are here. Let's go eat!"

Sarah had made canapés and finger foods. After the tequila they were prepared to drink, it was probably a good idea. They all stood in the kitchen. They ate, did more shots, and listened to Sarah tell them about Buckingham Palace, the pub, and Sam's family.

"This Danni sounds like my kinda girl!" Liz said with a mouthful of pear and cardamom. "I love the fact that she ambushed you two."

Sarah's phone buzzed, and she left the girls as she picked it up and walked into the other room,

Sam: Sarah?

Sarah: I'm here Sam. Always.

Sam: I'm ready if you are. And can I ask a favor please?

Sarah: Absolutely. Ask away.

Sam: Can I just talk to you first? I just want to see your face and hear your voice for a few minutes, before

being bombarded.

Sarah: That would be lovely. The laptop is on. Fire away! See you in a minute!

Sam: Calling now.

Sarah walked back into the kitchen and heard the familiar pings of Skype. She walked over and turned to the girls. "Could you guys give me a minute with Sam? Then I will be more than happy to introduce you all. It will be the first time I've seen his face in two weeks. "

"What? We get to **meet** him?" Karen squeaked.

"Let's give them a moment, okay?" Liz herded them to the other side of the kitchen. They could still hear and see Sarah and Sam, but they tried to tune the couple out for their privacy.

Within just a minute or two Sam's face magically appeared on the screen. "Oh." Sarah just whispered. "Hi, Sam."

Sam grinned that slow sexy grin, and then touched the screen like he was touching her face. "Hi amazing Sarah. I've missed you."

"I've missed you, too." Then Sarah smiled that bright Sarah smile. She beamed.

Oh, darling, it's so good to see you. You look great. I was worried, you know." Sam frowned.

"Don't worry. I'm good. You look tired. Are you sleeping?" asked

Sarah.

"Yeah. I'd sleep better if you were with me, but I've slept good the last two nights. I am tired. I am counting down the days until this is over." Sam leaned back in his chair and ran his hands through his hair.

Sarah leaned forward and asked, "Where are you off to next? I forgot the schedule."

"Sarah? Could you move back a little? All I'm seeing is a screen full of tits. And while I love that, I am here by myself, you know." Sam was grinning from ear to ear.

"Hey, Sam? You know the girls are here, but maybe instead of 'texting', we could SKYPE - if you get my drift?" Sarah did a little shimmy.

Sam continued to grin and said, "I think we need to practice that. You know, to get it right?"

"I'm going to bring the girls over. Are you ready? Remember what I said?" Sarah raised her eyebrow.

Sam laughed. " I can't wait to meet them. It's great that they're with you tonight. Bring 'em on!"

Sarah waved the girls over. "Let me introduce you one at a time, then you can gang up on him. Sam, this is Karen. She's the sweetheart with the great kids."

Karen waved at Sam. "It is so nice to meet you, Sam! Sarah has been filling us in on the week in London."

Sam grinned. "I hope she hasn't filled you in on *everything*. And it's great to see a face with the name. I feel like I know you. Sarah talks about you all the time."

Bev and Ashley were next, and in pure, and perfect Sam fashion, he charmed their socks off. Then it was Liz' turn. Before she could say anything, Sam asked her. "Did you already count the panties, Liz?"

Liz started to laugh. "Not yet, But I will before I leave tomorrow morning!"

"Well," Sam purred. "I know you'll come up short with at least two pairs." And he held up a pair of Sarah's panties in each hand.

Liz gasped. So did Sarah. "Sam! Have you been carrying those around with you?"

Sam continued to purr. "They go everywhere I go. Whatcha gonna do about it?"

Sarah and Liz looked at each other and laughed loudly.

Julie walked up to the screen, and stopped. She studied Sam's face, and cocked her hip. "So, how does it feel to know that we've all seen you naked?"

Sam laughed. "Nice to meet you, Julie. Sorry, but as I told Sarah, you're not special. Half of the people in the world have seen me naked. But, Sarah has seen and felt the real thing. Not a photo. Ask her which one she prefers!" And then he grinned.

Sarah shook her head and cracked up. All of the girls huddled around the computer and peppered him with questions. "Is modeling difficult?" "Does it ever get tiresome having women throw themselves at you?" "Do people just see you as a face and body?" "Do you look like that when you wake up?" "What do you do in your down time?" "Do you have any down time?" "Do you like whiskey?" Sam tried his best to keep up, but finally he put his hands up in defeat.

"Ladies! Please! I don't mean to be rude, but write down anything you would like to know, and we'll go over each and every question when I see you in person, okay?"

"Will we see you in person, Sam?" Bev asked.

Sam smiled. "You can bet on it. I want to join your sleep over."

"That might get really interesting... will you model underwear for us, Sam?" Julie asked.

Sam leaned close to the screen and gave Julie a smoldering stare. Julie moaned a little. "I plan on it. I will even model Sarah's underwear."

"Holy shit, Sam! I just pictured you in Sarah's panties, and got moist." Julie sighed.

Liz pushed her way to the screen, and asked, "So, I take it you saw Sarah's story before we did. What did you think?"

Sam shook his head. "Sarah's story? What story?"

Liz looked at Sarah, who said "No! He doesn't want to see them."

Liz glanced back at Sam, who looked confused. "I think you need to see it. I think it's important. We all know how talented Sarah is, but this is...is...." Liz just looked at Sam with her hands out, and started to cry. "Painfully beautiful."

"Anything Sarah does is beautiful. Sarah? Whatever it is, will you share it with me?" Sam asked quietly. He touched the screen again, as if it was her skin.

Liz turned to the girls. "Okay everybody, let's do another shot and get some food. We need to let these lovebirds have the same experience we did. Let's leave them alone for a while. Sarah? Take Sam and that laptop down the yellow brick road."

Sarah looked at Sam for a long time. Again, she reached out to touch the screen. She could almost feel his face and his breath. Sam looked attentive. "Sarah?"

"Okay, Sam." She picked up the laptop, and turned it away. "We have to start at the beginning, so give me a second."

Sarah walked slowly into the front of the house before she turned to the beginning of the clothesline. "Sam?" Sarah sounded very vulnerable. "This is more than what you're going to see and experience. It's also what I do. It's an expression from my soul. That's what I do with my lens. I'm feeling a little nervous, sensitive and defensive. Please be kind."

"I would never be unkind to you, Sarah. Do you trust me?" asked Sam.

"Absolutely," Sarah answered.

She slowly turned the computer around and angled it, so Sam could see the first picture of her at the airport, then the lights of London, and on and on. Sam said nothing, and neither did Sarah, but she started to cry. She was proud of her work, but she was also still overwhelmed with the emotions that the images evoked. When she got to the pictures of Sam's family, Sarah heard him hiss. But she didn't stop or say anything. Sarah got to the last two pictures, and just waited. She hadn't looked at Sam or varied the angle of the laptop. She was frightened to look at him. Had she overstepped his right to privacy? Would he not like them? She kept going over question after question in her head. The silence had stretched too long. Sarah still wept.

"Sarah?" whispered Sam.

"I'm here, Sam. Always," Sarah whispered back.

Sam whispered back. "I need to see you, Sarah. Please let me see you."

Sarah slowly turned the laptop around. Sam's face was in his hands that still clutched her panties. In a muffled voice and without lifting his head, he said. "Do you know that these still smell of your soap? That's why I brought them. If I keep my eyes closed after I've gone to bed, I can still smell you here with me. "

Sarah couldn't catch her breath. She was unable to respond.

Sam finally looked up at her. Tears rolled down those chiseled cheeks. He wasn't able to speak in more than a whisper because he knew his voice would crack. He felt things that he didn't know existed. He had worked with hundreds of different photographers whose work spoke for themselves. He had never released a photo that he wasn't proud of. He had seen hundreds of other people's pictures. But none had ever elicited the emotion that Sam was feeling at this moment. These pictures would punch anyone in the gut, you didn't need to know their story to feel the love, the talent, and the care that went into the work, but, because this wasn't just Sarah's story, it was his also, it was almost more feeling than his body could hold. Sam couldn't begin to explain what he felt to Sarah. There were no words. It was just wave after wave of emotion as he continued cry. He could only touch the screen and say, "I love you so much."

Sarah broke. She sat down in the floor with Sam on her lap, and they both just felt together. Finally, Sarah was able to say, "I love you, and I love that I touched your heart. I love that you felt what I was trying to portray. I loved this week of our life, Sam Ramsay."

"Soon we will have more than just a week, Sarah Reid."

They whispered sweet nothings for a few more minutes, until Sam told her to get back to the girls, and enjoy the tequila. She had earned it. They promised to talk the next evening.

Sarah sat for a few more minutes, then smiled and turned the laptop off. It was time to start living again, and the girls waited.

~~~

Sam sat in his chair for a long time. It took him that long to get his emotions under control. He was impressed with Sarah's work. He knew she was talented, but he had no idea that she was that good. Of course, he was emotionally attached to the pictures, but if he looked at them objectively, they were really good. Sarah was gifted. He would love to have her do one of his shoots. Hmmm... Sam took out his cell and punched in a number.

Chapter 18:

Sarah had been busy. The last week had been full of phone calls back and forth to Danni and Marta. She had worked up a picture package for Danni and Sam, and had plans to go back to the dress shop where she had purchased her red dress. She had her standing appointment to get sanded, buffed and waxed. She had finished a grocery list, folded and put away her laundry and stacked some wood by the fireplace. April was around the corner. Sarah had been counting down the days until March was over. Sam had a birthday coming up. Sarah had big plans.

~~~

Sarah entered the dress shop and immediately saw the same girl who had helped her with the red dress. The girl remembered her and smiled before she walked over. "Hello again! Are you back for something else? Did you have a chance to wear the red one yet?"

Sarah grinned at her. "Hi! Yes, I might be interested in something else, but I'd really like to talk with the owner first. Would they happen to be here?"

The girl, whose name tag said "Lindsay", lost her smile. She looked a little nervous. "Yes, Lisa's here today, but she's across the street getting coffee. She should be right back."

Sarah reached out for Lindsay's arm. "I have no complaints, Lindsay! Please! I just have something I would like her, and you, to see. Maybe you can show me some things while we wait for her, okay?"

"Oh! Okay!"Lindsay's face brightened immediately. "Were you

looking for a specific color?"

"Not really, but something for spring, maybe? And sexy?" Sarah replied.

The bell rang over the door when Lisa came in bearing two cups of coffee. She smiled at Sarah as she sat the cups on the counter. "I see that Lindsay's assisting you. If you have any questions, please don't hesitate to ask."

"I have complete faith in Lindsay. She changed my life. I wanted to let her, and you, know that. I also wanted her to pick out another one for me." Sarah started to dig in her purse.

Lisa and Lindsay looked at each other, not really understanding what Sarah had meant.

"There they are!" Sarah huffed. She brought out copies of all the London papers that had come out the morning after the benefit. The papers with the pictures of her in her red dress and Sam looking like James Bond. She lay them on the counter and spread them out. Lisa and Lindsay walked over to see what the crazy lady was doing. When they saw the papers, Lindsay looked up sharply with a big grin on her face. "That's you! I knew you could pull it off! Please don't take this the wrong way, but, that is one of the sexiest things I've ever seen! Evidently, he thought so too!"

"Oh, he definitely did!" laughed Sarah. "And so did every newspaper in London!"

Lisa was impressed with the pictures but still confused about what exactly it was that Sarah wanted. "I'm so glad you're pleased."

Sarah turned to Lisa. "This young lady helped me when I needed it most. I saw the dress as soon as I walked in the store, but she's the one who insisted I try it on. She also said some other incredibly nice things to me. When I tried that dress on, I felt like a princess, but Lindsay, convinced me I was one. I purchased three other dresses besides the red one, because of her. The man you see in the pictures is Sam. He was already in 'like' with me, but that dress made him fall in love with me. He has changed my life, as I have changed his."

Lindsay's grin got bigger and bigger. Sarah continued. "I wanted to come back today to purchase more dresses from Lindsay, as she has impeccable taste, and is an honest salesperson. I plan on needing many more formal dresses over the next few years. I could purchase them in New York, but I won't, because I like to buy locally and I trust Lindsay's eye. But, if she is on commission, I will steal her from you, and get her a job wherever she chooses. I know people, now, in fashion."

Lisa and Lindsay's eyes had gotten very large. "Sam, the lustful fellow kissing me in that picture is the Oak Wood model, so please believe what I am telling you. If Lindsay's life dictates that she stays here, then I expect her to have a salary and benefits. She is much too important to your livelihood to lose. So! Lindsay? Let's shop!"

Lindsay grabbed Sarah's arm and dragged her to a rack. Lisa just stood there and stared. Sarah called over her shoulder. "I will check back with her next week, to see how things are going!"

~~~

Sam, as usual, had found a corner while he waited for someone to set something up. That was the story of his life. Hurry up and wait. He scrolled through his messages and emails, and thought of Sarah. He always thought of Sarah. Seeing her face via SKYPE had calmed him. He had been so worried about her. Seeing her had set his mind at ease. Now if he could just find a way to get a small break between the completion of the Oak Wood campaign and Prague. Or Prague and Paris. But three days just wasn't enough with the flying involved. He had three days after Paris, but would probably celebrate his birthday with twenty four hours of sleep. It wasn't even enough time to get to London. The time had started to crawl by, and Sam had become impatient. He wanted some sleep and some Sarah. He had never suffered through these press junkets before. He had always worked non-stop. It's why he had become successful. He didn't believe in luck, and he didn't believe in beauty. There were millions of good looking people out there. Hard work had given him his life. Sam had all the money he needed. He didn't have to work. He was tired of people telling him what to wear, how to act, how to pose, and where to be. He was tired of waxing and having his body oiled by someone else's hands. His fame was a tool to use for his charities. Oh, sure, it was an ego stroker. Sam wouldn't lie to himself. He could be a little cocky sometimes, but mostly he was just uncomfortable with it. He had earned the right to feel that way. But, by God, he had earned the right to say no, also. And he was going to do that. He was going to start saying no. He had more important things to do. He would be forty-one years old in a few days, and he was going to start living his life the way he wanted to - and with whom he wanted to.

Sam: Sarah?

Sarah: I'm here. Always.

Sam: What did you do today?

Sarah: This and that. I've been busy. I went back to the dress store last week.

Sam: Did you get anything?

Sarah: I really went to let the owner know how great her salesperson was. I also got sanded, buffed, and waxed.

Sam: Oh...,slick?

Sarah: LOL! Yes! I plan on staying that way. You never know when you might want to go pantiless!

Sam: The only person you'll be pantiless with is me, woman!!

Sarah: I hope that happens soon. I'm a little....frustrated.

Sam: We could always sext?

Sarah: Nope. Now that I've had the real Sam, it will continue to be the real Sam. I will wait. Can you?

Sam: I have been. (sigh)

Sarah: You have a birthday coming up. What? Three days, Paris time?

Sam: I'm so tired, I had honestly forgotten.

Sarah: Got any plans to celebrate?

Sam: I've got three days off after the premiere in Paris. I plan on sleeping through my birthday. I'll wake up in

time to fly to Milan. Yeah. I'm a party animal. Marta will probably try to surprise me with

something.

Sarah: Poor baby.

Sam: Say goodnight, Sarah.

Sarah: Goodnight Sarah. (kisses) Get some sleep, Sam.

Chapter 19:

Danni had gone into town to pick up some groceries and her mail. She was surprised to see a package from Sarah. She smiled as she thought about her. She was a devious little devil. Kind of like her. She couldn't wait to get home to open it and see what it was.

Danni put the groceries away, and went to feed the sheep. She enjoyed the quiet without kids. Thomas was still at school, and Alex had taken Violet to a play date by his office. They would all get home about the same time. She poured herself a glass of Jameson and water and went to open her package. After she settled down with her glass and a pair of scissors, Danni carefully cut open the box. It had FRAGILE stamped all over it. She hoped that nothing had been broken. The box opened, she looked inside to see lots of bubble wrap with an envelope taped to the top. She opened it.

Dearest Danni:

I miss all of you already! After having my little "breakdown", my first order of business was to upload my pictures. It was painful, but so fulfilling. I noticed the art you chose for your home, so I hope these little snippets of memories can find a place with the others. I love them. I hope you do, too.

Give those yummy kids kisses from me. And that hunk of a husband. And you.

I am feverishly waiting to see you all soon!

Lots of love. Your sister in bawdiness,

Sarah

Danni carefully unwrapped the plastic to find a framed picture of her and Sam. They were sitting on the couch with her head on her brother's shoulder, totally unaware of Sarah's camera. The lighting, the angle, and the quietness of the picture itself made Danni's throat constrict. Good Lord! Sarah was good! Danni loved this picture. She could feel the emotion in it. She laid it aside and opened the next one. It was she and her family on the side porch. Her mum and dad, Sam, Alex, and Thomas and Violet. They were all sitting quietly looking out at the field with the sheep and that beautiful sunset in front of them. Danni started to cry. It was an unbelievably beautiful photo. Sarah had a gift of picking the perfect shot. Danni wished that she was there with her. She would have hugged her hard. There was more, and Danni was almost afraid to unwrap them. She knew that they would be of her children. She was right. The first one was of Thomas on the swing. He was flying high and laughing. The pure joy on his face was breathtaking. The pure innocence of childhood encapsulated in a perfect moment. Fuck! Danni grabbed a napkin to blow her nose. The next one was of Violet curled up in her mum's lap. Again, neither one had been aware of Sarah's camera. It was another quiet moment that portrayed the love between the child and the grandmother. This would hang on Violet's wall someday. Danni was a mess by this time. There was one final picture. She took a deep breath before she unwrapped it. It was the largest print. Sarah had taken the shot from behind Thomas and Violet. They were sitting together on the top step of the side porch, framed again with that beautiful sunset. Danni remembered that Sarah and the children had just come back from playing in the field. Thomas had his arm around his little sisters back, and their heads were together. It gave a whisper of their little noses, and the curve of their mouths. It was almost in silhouette. It was the most beautiful thing Danni had ever seen. The love that Sarah felt for the subjects would be felt by anyone that saw them. Sarah had shared her heart.

When Alex returned home with the children, he found Danni at the kitchen island surrounded by the beauty that Sarah had shared. She still wept and continued to blow her nose. She picked up her phone and stabbed Sam's number in.

Sam answered on the third ring. "What's wrong?"

Danni stopped crying, and her ability to speak had returned. "Nothing's wrong. I've been sitting in the kitchen for the last hour weeping."

"Weeping? *You* were weeping? What the hell is wrong, Danni?" Sam was definitely worried. Danni did not cry.

"I received a package from Sarah today. Have I told you that I love her? Have I told you how incredible she is? Have I told you about her heart? Because she's got one. She's got a big fucking heart!" Danni was a little hysterical and had started to cry again.

"Danni! Stop crying! I know all of those things about Sarah. It's why I love her. Plus, she's got really big tits." Sam tried humor.

Danni laughed a little and sniffled. "She sent us a box of framed pictures, Sam! Sarah is fucking amazing! No! Not amazing. She has a gift. I mean a real gift. It's art, Sam! These pictures move me. And you know that's hard to do."

Sam was quiet for a minute. "If they're anything like what she showed me last week, I know. I've never seen photos like hers. And you know I've seen a lot of them. Her pictures are evocative. That's the only word I can think of. What did she send?"

"One of me and you that is wonderful. One of the entire family, and then the kids..." She cried harder. "Sam! Listen to me! She has got to shoot you. I don't mean 'shoot you', oh, shit! You know what I mean! You can slow down, not sign some contracts for next year. Have Sarah do a spread. It would sell immediately. You're already in the stratosphere, but for Sarah... she could write her own ticket. Her work needs to be seen. No! It needs to be *felt* by the world!"

"I've already made some calls, Danni. I agree with everything you just said. On the one hand, I would love to share her gift with the world. But on the other, if it takes her away from me, I would hate it. But I think Sarah would pick and choose wisely. She has to have an emotional connection with the subjects. She couldn't do it if she didn't. She's fucking amazing, and it makes me proud that someone that talented would choose to be with me." Sam sighed.

Danni blew her nose. "Well, you don't deserve her. You need to follow up on those calls. You do that, and I'll figure out the rest of it. But let's not tell her, okay?"

"I'll see what I can do and get back with you. I miss you guys." Sam said.

"We miss you, too, Sam. I need to call Sarah now. 'Thank you' seems to be so inadequate. I just wish she were here so I could maul her. Oh! We're all going to a drag show when we're all together again." Danni said seriously.

"Who is 'all'?" Sam asked.

"Me, Alex, you, and Sarah. It was her request. She wants to see the reaction of the queens when they catch a glimpse of your ass. She'll probably take pictures!" Danni snorted.

"Oh, God, Danni. Goodbye."

Marta: Sarah? Are you all set?

Sarah: I am SO ready!! He doesn't know, does he?

Marta: He hasn't a clue! He thinks I'm planning something for his birthday, but he has no idea it's you!

Sarah: Horning in on the premiere isn't going to screw you up, is it?

Marta: Oh no! Mark is coming, too! That's what I wanted to tell you. He's going to meet up with you at JFK.

You'll both fly out together! He'll enjoy the company.

Sarah: That's great! It will be nice to get to know him a little better.

Marta: A driver will be waiting for you at Charles DeGaulle. Mark has all the details. I cannot wait to

see Sam's face!!! I think I'm as excited as you!

Sarah: Marta, you are amazing! See you in Paris the day after tomorrow!

Marta: See you then!

Sarah had let the girls know what was going on. She would be missing class again. Sarah had a feeling she would be missing a lot of them. She had made up her mind that if she could fly to Sam when it worked for them both, she was going to do it. She was not going to miss being with Sam on his birthday. It would be his first birthday that they could spend together. He had three days off after the premier, and Sarah planned on keeping him occupied after he had his sleep.

Sarah was packed and ready to go. She could hardly contain her excitement, and kept looking at the clock wishing the time would go faster. Then she wished that it would stop when she got to Paris.

Sarah's phone buzzed. She smiled as she saw Danni's name pop up on her screen. She hoped it was about the pictures that she had sent. "Hey Danni! How the hell are you?"

"Sarah Reid! Have I ever told you that you are fucking amazing?" yelled Danni.

Sarah laughed. "I take it you got the photos?"

"My God, Sarah! You talk about them like they're my fucking snapshots from one of the kids' play dates! They are way beyond that. Your work needs to be in a gallery somewhere. You made me weep, and I'm a little bitter about that. Nobody makes me cry." Danni still yelled.

"Good! I'm glad you liked them. Please feel free to make copies for Ollie and Beth if you want, but I've been putting a box together for them also." Sarah smiled.

"I'm not saying a word to them. They need to experience their own emotions when they open their own box of love. Because

226

that's what it is Sarah. Love. I felt your heart in these photos. Thank you."

"I can't wait to take more. Thomas and Violet have stolen my heart." Sarah said.

"They haven't stopped talking about you. You need to call them in the next few days. Speaking of the next few days. Are you all ready? Are you about to piss your pants, because I am. I could piss my pants for you. Do you know what Sam is gonna do? Be prepared to have hot sex on the red carpet." Danni laughed.

Sarah laughed with her. "Well, it will be difficult to top the benefit in London, but I'm positive I'll surprise him more this time. He was expecting me in London, but Marta assured me that he has no idea I'm coming to Paris. The clock can't move quick enough!"

"Girl! You have set the bar for 'entrances'! I can't wait to see what the papers will have to say Saturday morning." Danni smacked air kisses at her and said goodbye.

Sarah chuckled to herself.

May

Chapter 20:

Mark was waiting for Sarah when she landed at JFK. He gave her a big hug and told her he was happy to have someone to talk to on the flight. They found their connecting flight, boarded and settled down in their seats. Eight hours would give them plenty of time to visit and nap. Sarah needed it. She had left home at three in the morning to catch her six a.m. flight to JFK. She had too much nervous energy to have slept well. She and Mark would land at Charles DeGaulle around four in the evening. It would give her four hours to make herself beautiful.

Mark filled her in on the details. He seemed sincerely excited. Marta didn't want to take the chance of putting Sarah in Sam's room. He might be staying in until having to leave for the premiere. She had planned to put her in with the makeup artists. Their room was next to Marta's, so it would be easy for Marta to keep Sarah up to date with any changes that may occur. After Sam, Marta and Mark left for photos, a hotel staffer would escort her down into the crowd of reporters and photographers lining the red carpet. Then Sarah was free to make any kind of entrance she chose. The staff would move her luggage to Sam's room after she had left.

"You have no idea how much I appreciate your wife. I couldn't have pulled this off without her," Sarah told Mark.

Mark laughed. "She loves this kind of stuff. And she loves Sam, so this was a no brainer."

"I know how much she means to Sam, too. It's great that they get along so well. That could make for a miserable job, if they hated each other." Sarah leaned her head back.

Mark got comfortable, too. "It used to bother me. You know, her and Sam. He sees my wife naked more often than I do."

"That doesn't bother you?"

"Not anymore. I know how much she detests most of the other models she works with. She always looks forward to the Oak Wood campaign. It's long, and it's grueling, and she wouldn't do it if Sam wasn't doing it with her. I know he takes care of her, and that makes me feel better. Plus, he's a great guy. You do realize that he's *never* taken a date to a premiere? You're the first."

"Well, he's not actually taking me to this one. I'm kind of crashing it. I don't know, Mark. I think Sam is basically a shy guy, and even after all these years, a little uncomfortable in the limelight. If he's comfortable with me around, and it makes his job easier, then that makes my heart happy." Sarah smiled and closed her eyes.

Mark patted her hand before he closed his own eyes. "I think you make his heart happy, too, Sarah."

They slept the rest of the flight, and were woken by the attendants announcing their descent. The lights of Paris below were beautiful, and Sarah's heart started to beat faster. It was going to be almost unbearable to be just down the hallway from Sam, and not be able to see him. "It will all be worth it, Sarah! Don't screw it up!" she whispered to herself.

After they deplaned, Mark and Sarah made their way to the baggage carousel. The driver was there with a cart for their luggage. He loaded up, and they followed him to the waiting limo.

As the driver had received his instructions from Marta, Mark and Sarah were able to enjoy the cushy interior of the vehicle. Soft as butter leather seats. A refrigerator and a good stereo system. There was a bottle of champagne in an ice bucket. Two glasses waited to be filled. "Shall we?" asked Mark.

"Absolutely!" Sarah smiled.

Sarah got the glasses while Mark uncorked the champagne. After filling their glasses, Mark raised his glass and toasted. "To true love and all that entails!"

They clinked their glasses and drank. Sarah loved the first bite of champagne. She always breathed the first bubbles up her nose. It was like inhaling little bubbles of sweetness.

Mark looked at her, and asked, "So, have you decided upon your entrance, yet?"

Sarah shook her head no, and answered. "I'm still thinking about it. The moment itself may dictate what I'm going to do."

They stopped at two glasses. Sarah had a lot of preparation ahead, and Mark wanted to screw his wife sober.

The ride to the hotel was fairly quick, and the traffic wasn't too bad. Paris traffic was loud, but Sarah craned her neck to see everything she could, and didn't hear anything.

Mark asked, "Is this your first time in The City of Lights?"

"I was here with my husband a long time ago. We were young and only here two days. This feels like my first time in so many ways. But to tell you the truth, I don't care if I never leave the room!"

Sarah laughed. "I can see the sights anytime. They'll still be here when I come back."

"You are a woman after my own heart, Sarah! We'll plan on seeing each other for breakfast. That will be the only time we venture out. You know, we have to eat to keep our strength!"

Sarah was still laughing when the limo pulled up to the hotel entrance. The bell hops were there to take their luggage. They were aware of where Sarah needed to go. A pretty French girl named "Catherine" approached her. She was a little agitated as she asked in a cute French accent. "Ms. Reid? I'm afraid that Mr. Ramsay is sitting in the lobby reading the papers. I'm so embarrassed, but do you mind if we sneak you through the kitchen? You are still wanting to be secret?

Sarah became paralyzed. Sam was no more than a few feet away from her. She wanted to run as fast as she could into that lobby and wrap her legs around him. She could almost smell the scent of whiskey and oak leaves that she loved. She could almost feel his stubble against her cheek. Sarah wanted to scream his name as loud as she could.

"Ms. Reid? A secret?" Catherine brought her back to earth.

"Oh, of course. Don't be embarrassed. The kitchen is fine." Sarah picked up her camera bag and purse that she had dropped as she followed Catherine to a side door.

"Is the entire hotel staff in on this?" Sarah asked.

"Oui! It is… " Catherine tried to think of the right word. "Romantic?"

Sarah smiled back at her. "Thank you all so much. Please be sure to tell everyone that."

"Of course, Ms. Reid." Catherine had entered the elevator that was marked "Staff Only".

They rode up in silence. The elevator stopped on the twelfth floor. Catherine turned left, and Sarah followed her down the hall. The hotel was luxurious. The carpeting was plush, as were the light fixtures and accessories. There were touches of gold everywhere but not overdone. It was quite nice and smelled heavenly.

"Here we go, Ms. Reid. One of our staff will be back to get you before Mr. Ramsay makes his entrance. And may I say that he is a very nice man. Not all the celebrities are so nice. He is very polite." Catherine smiled.

"Yes, he is. Thank you for saying so." Sarah opened the door to start her preparations.

The entire room was full of equipment and makeup tables. Two women sat in front of the mirrors. The first one got up and walked to Sarah. She had wild curly black hair that stuck up everywhere. She was as wide as she was short. "You must be Sarah?" She put her hand out and Sarah shook it.

" I'm Barb. I've been doing Sam's makeup for almost ten years, even though Sam doesn't really use any. It gives us a chance to sit and visit." She laughed loudly. "That's Sharon. She's my assistant."

"Hi Sharon." Sarah gave her a little wave.

Sarah saw her luggage by the side of the door. As she walked over to her bags, Barb walked with her. "We're here to help with whatever you need."

"I've never had my makeup done before." Sarah said.

Barb and Sharon grinned at each other as Barb said, "Let's see your dress."

Sarah walked to the largest bag, opened it and brought out a tissue-wrapped hanger. As she unwrapped the dress, Barb and Sharon's eyes got big, and they exhaled in unison. "Wow!"

"That explains the hair!" laughed Barb.

Sharon giggled and said, "This is gonna be fun!"

~~~

Sam threw the papers on the hotel lobby table. He was already dressed in his tuxedo. It was classic black with silk lapels, shiny black shoes, and socks. Sam had picked a white waistcoat instead of a cummerbund. He hated cummerbund's. He always felt like he was wearing a rubber band that would snap at any moment. He had paired a beautiful aquamarine silk shirt under the waistcoat with a black silk tie. Sam was pleased with his choices. He loved the unexpected pop of color.

People had started to arrive for the premier and the flashbulbs had started to explode. "Bloody hell!" growled Sam. He would go back to his room until the cluster-fuck was over. He was done.

He walked to the registration desk and made arrangements for staff to come for him when it was time for him to be the dancing monkey. He took the lift to the twelfth floor and turned left out of the elevator to go to his room. As he passed the makeup room he heard Barb and Sharon giggle. What were they doing up here? He knocked at the door as he passed. "Hey! You guys are having too much fun in there!" As he continued on to his room he could have sworn he heard Sarah. He turned around to go back, and then thought, "You have lost your fucking mind Sam Ramsay! Sarah isn't here. It's just your wishful thinking. " He just shook his head, and continued to his room to wait.

The girls got quiet when Sam knocked. Sarah became paralyzed when Sam knocked. She wanted to throw the door open and jump in his arms, but she had been here too long to blow it now. Thank God he had walked on by. She looked at Barb and Sharon, and they all exhaled together. Sarah looked in the makeup mirror. It didn't even look like her! The silk caressed her skin like a mother's touch, and of course she loved the shoes. But the makeup was magic. It didn't look like she was wearing anything other than a smoky eye. Her jewelry was the star of this ensemble. She laughed and turned to Barb and Sharon. "You guys are miracle workers!"

"Everything works together perfectly!" said Sharon. "I can't wait to see the papers in the morning!"

They heard a knock at the door. Sharon opened it and was met by a very pretty young man who was there to escort Sarah to her destination. The girls hugged one another, and Sarah took a deep breath. It was time. Sarah started having doubts about over-stepping boundaries, but then just said out loud. "Screw it!" She linked her arm with the young man's.

Pierre and Sarah took the lift down to the ground floor, and he led her down a hallway to a side door. He pushed his way through the throng of reporters and photographers, telling them that a hotel VIP was coming through. Sarah got quite a few looks, and she swore there were a couple of people who recognized her. She just grinned and put her fingers to her lips. "Ssssshh!" She found her spot. Then she waited.

Hotel staff retrieved Sam and walked him to a side door. Reporters were waiting to ask a few questions. Sam politely answered, stood still for the cameras, and then waited for Marta and Mark to catch up. When Marta answered the reporter's questions, she and Mark walked out with Sam. The screaming started immediately. Hundreds of men and women were behind the ropes as they lined both sides of the red carpet. Sam did what was expected of him. He posed for photos, and had selfies taken. He kissed cheeks. He smiled. All while he slowly walked the gauntlet of people.

Sarah, who still stood in her designated spot, heard the screams start. Then she heard someone yell out, "I want to have your baby!" She shook her head, and grinned to herself. Yep. Sam was on his way.

When Sarah finally saw Sam she gasped, "Fuck!" He was beautiful in his tuxedo, but the shirt made her giddy and suddenly moist. She continued to watch him make his way closer and closer to where she was stood. Pierre still guarded her from being pushed and shoved. He was see her amongst the reporters, but Sarah could smell the oak leaves and whiskey.

"Now", she said to Pierre. Pierre opened the gold cord, and Sarah, in all of her six-feet-four-inch glory, walked up behind Sam before she quietly made her way to his side. He hadn't seen her as she had said nothing, but the crowd had gotten quiet. It was as if they had inhaled collectively. The flashbulbs still exploded, but they were aimed at her, not Sam. She softly put her arm around his waist and waited. Sam automatically put his arm around Sarah's waist, thinking it was Marta, as he continued to pose for pictures.

It took him a second to realize just whose waist he was holding. Sarah felt him stop breathing. He stopped posing. He grasped

her a little tighter. Sarah felt the tension in the arm around her waist but he didn't turn. It was if he was afraid that she would be an illusion. He continued to stare at the crowd as he whispered, "Sarah?"

Sarah whispered back, "It's me. Sam. Always."

Sarah saw him swallow, and then he slowly turned his head.

Sam saw a goddess. "Fuuuuck, Sarah!" She was dressed in an aquamarine silk dress. It matched his shirt perfectly. There is no way she could have known, because Sam dressed himself. No one knew what he was going to wear. Sam stood and undressed her with his eyes. Her ample cleavage was barely contained by her strapless gown. A large aquamarine stone lay between her beautiful tits. Sam looked at it hungrily. Matching chandelier earrings dangled from her ears. Sam wanted to lick those ears. Her hair was swept back from her forehead. It was now a deep brunette with a chunk of teal on the side. Sam wanted to mess up that hair. Her eyes were rimmed with smoky black kohl, with a hint of the same teal color in the corners of her eyes. Sam wanted to see those eyes glaze over with pleasure when he made her come.

He looked back down her body slowly. Sam wanted to knead her ass. There was a slit from the hem of the dress cut all the way to her waist. It made her long legs look even longer. Sam growled. And Sarah, who loved her shoes, had six inch opalescent stilettos. They reflected silver and aquamarine.

As Sam smoldered, so did Sarah. She looked blatantly at his ass in the perfectly tailored trousers. She leaned forward and rubbed her hand down his waistcoat to the top of his pants. She rested her hand on that hard abdomen, and growled at Sam. "Mine!" She felt like a she wolf in heat. The shirt made his amazing blue eyes contrast even more with his black hair. Sarah wanted to tug on that hair as it lay between her thighs. She had turned into a wanton hussy.

They both panted as the crowd grew even quieter. It was like they were waiting to see what was going to happen next. Sarah and Sam did not disappoint. Sam moved his arm from Sarah's waist, and placed his hand on the top of her ass. He grabbed her chin with his other hand and crushed her mouth with his. This was not just a kiss, this was possession. His heart pounded, as he ground Sarah's body into his. Sam did not come up for air. He continued to plunder her mouth with his tongue, and to inhale the earthy scent of sandalwood that was Sarah.

Sarah's heart beat just as hard and in sync, with Sam's. She opened her mouth to accept the punishing kiss, and met his probing tongue with her own. She tugged on his hair and whimpered. Sarah felt Sam's hardness when he ground her into his body.

They both finally stopped to breathe. Sam took a breath before he kissed her again. Small, sweet, nips. "I love you so much amazing Sarah."

"I love you, sweet Sam."

"Let's get this shit over with. Two hours Sarah, and I am going to fuck your brains out." Sam took her hand as they rushed inside.

Mark and Marta had watched and waited. They both wore huge

grins. Mark leaned into Marta and asked. "Did that make you as hot as me? Can we go back to our room and do what they just did in public?"

Chapter 21:

Sam shoved Sarah up against the elevator wall as he kneaded the ass that he'd been staring at for the last two hours. He couldn't even remember what had transpired between the time he saw Sarah on the red carpet and now. He had stayed in a constant haze of lust the entire evening. He saw nothing but her. Sarah had worked her hand down the front of Sam's pants and was palming him. As was usual, no underwear. Sam groaned against her mouth. "Sarah, we'll talk. Later." Sarah just moaned and ground her pelvis into Sam's groin.

The elevator dinged and the doors opened. Then they shut. The elevator started moving down. Sarah pulled her mouth away from Sam's. "Oh, fuck! It's going down!"

"It's going down right here, right now." Sam ran his hand up the slit in Sarah's dress.

"No, Sam! The elevator! It's going down! I can't wait much longer," panted Sarah.

The elevator slowed at the fourth floor. Sam quickly punched twelve again before the doors opened to let a group of people in. He and Sarah moved to the back of the car. He made sure to stand behind Sarah to hide the bulge in his pants. He never stopped kneading her ass. The man at the front of the car punched in ten and eleven. Sarah turned and looked at Sam with panic and mouthed "Fuck!"

They both still panted as Sam reached around and grabbed Sarah's hand and looked at her. Her lips were bruised and swollen from his punishing kisses, and her eyes had glazed over. She was so damn sexy. He growled under his breath. The woman in front of him turned and looked at Sam. Then she looked at Sarah and slowly smiled. She turned back around when they slowed down at the tenth floor. As she walked out, she turned and whispered to them. "Have fun!" Then she winked.

Half of the group got off on ten. Sam nervously tapped his foot on the floor and chewed on his bottom lip. Finally the car emptied on eleven. Sam moved to Sarah again.

"No!" she laughed as she pushed him back. "Let's make sure we exit this time. I don't want to do it in the elevator."

When the door opened, Sam ran, dragging Sarah with him. He fumbled in his pocket for the key card. "Fuck! Fuck! Fuck!" He finally got the door opened, and drug Sarah in after him. He turned and kicked the door shut.

Sam continued to drag Sarah. He stopped at the table in the corner of the room, and turned on the lamp that was sitting on it. He shoved it to the back. He smothered her panting mouth with wet, hot lips that tasted of whiskey.

Sarah was lost in the smell of Sam, in the feel of his mouth, and the scorching heat of his skin. She had missed him so much that she couldn't stop touching him. She whispered into his mouth. "I love you, Sam. I missed you so much."

Sam couldn't get enough of Sarah. He lingered on her lips, and breathed in the earthy smell of her skin. She felt like heaven to him. "Oh, God, Sarah, I can't be away from you this long. This has been the longest month of my life."

Sam rubbed Sarah's thigh that was exposed by the split in her dress. He gathered the dress in his hands and pulled it up to Sarah's waist. Sarah was bare beneath the dress. "Oh, God, Sarah!" moaned Sam. "I 'm sorry, but I need you so much."

Sam lifted Sarah and positioned her on top of the table. He pulled the top of her dress down, exposing the beautiful cleavage that had been on display all evening. He moaned and bent to taste the sweetness.

Sarah hissed and arched her back. All she could feel was Sam's heat, and the coolness of the wood under her. She reached for the front of Sam's waistcoat and feverously unbuttoned it. "I need to feel your skin against me. Please!" Sarah lamented. She grabbed the shirt and ripped it open, exposing Sam's beautiful torso. She caressed his musculature with her hands while she kissed his neck.

Sam continued the onslaught of Sarah's nipples as he pulled her forward on the table. He unbuttoned his pants and pulled them down before he raised his head to look into her eyes. Sarah looked into the indigo of Sam's eyes as he buried himself within her in one deep thrust. Sarah's eyes widened and she cried out before she wrapped her long legs around Sam's waist. The intensity of Sam's gaze and three deep thrusts brought Sarah to a throbbing, clenching orgasm. She sustained the gaze and watched Sam as his thrusts became faster. With each thrust he grunted, until she felt the tortuously all consuming fire build up again deep in her core. As Sarah came again, Sam roared and exploded inward.

They stayed wrapped in each other until their panting subsided. Sam caressed Sarah's breasts and shoulders. Sarah rubbed Sam's abdomen and back. They couldn't touch each other enough. Sam stepped back and looked down. "Sorry about that Sarah, I didn't mean to drag you in here and bang you on the table." He ran his hands through his hair and looked at his pants puddled around his ankles. He hadn't even gotten his shoes off. "I wanted it to be better than that, but you just drive me crazy with wanting you."

Sarah looked at Sam's pants, then she looked at herself and chuckled softly. She looked like she had a giant donut wrapped around her waist. All of the beautiful aquamarine dress was bunched around her middle. Her shoes were still on, too. "Sam Ramsay, do not *ever* apologize for giving me a double whammy."

Sam duck walked to the bed where he sat and removed his shoes and socks, before removing his pants. Sarah had laid the dress on the table and walked her way to Sam. He looked up at her in all her bare beauty. He took her hand before pulling her into the bed with him.

Sam cupped Sarah's faced and kissed her. A sweet, delicious kiss. "How did you do this? I mean, you totally blindsided me. Feel free to blindside me anytime."

Sarah shrugged. "I couldn't have done it without Marta and Danni. Especially Marta. She's amazing, and I think she was as excited as me."

Sam pulled Sarah onto his chest and stroked her back. "Then I love her even more, but, I feel a bit guilty."

"Guilty? Why?" Sarah pulled back and looked at Sam.

Sam pulled her to him again. He couldn't get an acceptable amount of her smell or skin. "This is twice that you've come to me. You can't spend your life following me. I have to be a participant in this relationship, too."

Sarah nestled into Sam's neck. "I know that. I expect you to come to Missouri as soon as your schedule will allow it. You *need* to come to me, but until then, I'm able to do this. Please let me do this. "

"Oh, Sarah, I love it. I love that you're here. For the first time in more than twenty years, I have hated the grind of this campaign. I tried to tell myself that's it's because I'm getting older, and that's part of it. I found you, and I realize that because I'm getting older, my chance with you may never come again. I want different things now. Things that are more important than my career. I have started to prioritize." Sam's fingers whispered against Sarah's cheek. "That should make Danni happy. She's been bitching at me for years to slow down."

Sarah caressed Sam's arm. "I have always grabbed the brass ring. It's just who I am, but after David died, and after I had a clear mind again, I made a conscience decision to only do the things that I wanted to do, to surround myself with people who fed my spirit, and to stay away from negative things and people. I have been content." Sarah looked up at Sam and smiled. "But you've made me realize that content is not necessarily happy. I had forgotten that I was a woman, with wants and needs, and passion. A part of me had disappeared. I can't ever go back to content. I deserve more than that. I *need* more than that. And I have you to thank." Sarah cupped Sam's face. "It's more than the mind blowing sex, Sam. Though I'm not complaining. I love talking to you. I love your stories, and your passion for your charities, and your humor. I truly like you. I can't imagine going through the rest of my life without you banging me on a table. But if you disappeared tomorrow, I now know what I need." Sarah smiled that Sarah smile that was like sunshine.

Sam hugged Sarah and whispered, "I will never disappear."

After cuddles and more kisses, Sam asked, "When do you have to leave?"

"I purchased a one way ticket, Sam." Sarah smiled. "I am open to whatever you need or want. "

Sam grinned and sat up. "You can go to Italy?" Sarah shook her head yes. "This is great! I'll have more down time the rest of the campaign. Oh, Sarah this is great! I'll be able to show you Milan, and Rome and Venice! I'll be able to help you check off one more item on your bucket list!" He was so excited that he bounced like a toddler.

They talked long into the night and made plans for tomorrow and the next week. They discussed plans for next month and the next year. They both knew that Sarah couldn't stay for the duration, and that they would be apart for long stretches. That fact had not changed. But they would figure it out.

They had curled up together, face to face, and had started to drift off to sleep when Sarah whispered, "Happy Birthday, Sam Ramsay. Happy Birthday to you."

Sam grasped her firmly, and whispered back, "I don't ever want another birthday without you. I love you, Sarah Reid."

~~~

Sarah woke up before Sam. She let him sleep. She knew he was dead tired and hadn't gotten much rest. She didn't even shower. She threw on some clothes, brushed her teeth, and ran a comb through her hair, before she went downstairs to get some coffee and pastries from the motel café. Sarah felt lighter. It was as if she had been waiting for something the last month and she had finally found it. Coffees in hand and pastries in a bag, she headed back upstairs.

Sam and Sarah drank their coffee and ate their pastries, while they went over the plan for the day. They planned to see the Arc de Triomphe, Notre Dame Cathedral, Montmartre and Moulin Rouge, and they would finish up at the Eiffel Tower. They both wanted to see it at night. They wanted to find a neighborhood café for dinner, so they could sample authentic French food. They wanted meat, potatoes, and heavy cream sauces. The Europeans had a different outlook on celebrity, so playing tourist wouldn't be as full of interruptions as it had been in London. Sarah and Sam showered and headed out for a day of adventure.

Their first stop was the bank that the hotel staff had recommended. Sam had argued with Sarah that she didn't need Euros, as he had money. Sarah insisted. "I might want to buy things for my friends and kids. I don't want you to have to purchase those for me. Besides, I'll need Euros in Italy, as I'm sure I'll be on my own sometimes."

Sam grinned. "Italy! You're going to Italy! With me."

Sarah and Sam walked to the bank. They both had seen the Eiffel Tower in the distance. There was hardly anywhere in Paris that you couldn't see it rising above the city. Sarah stopped several times to take pictures. After she exchanged money, they found the Metro that the bank teller had pointed out. Yes, it was as dirty and stinky as the New York City subway system, but everything that Sarah had read, said it was the quickest way to get around. They purchased tickets each from the machine in the station, and started looking for their color of their Metro line. Just like in the States, they had many different-colored lines to choose from.

Sam was no help, as he had never ridden the subway in Paris. He had never even taken in the sights, except from a car window as he was being driven from one function, or job site, to another. Sam grinned at Sarah. "It's like I'm seeing Paris for the first time. And I kind of am. I'm just chuffed to bits."

Sarah raised her eyebrow, and looked at Sam questionably. "Chuffed to bits?"

"Sorry." Sam's grin grew bigger. "Excited. I'm excited to see it with you."

"Oh, okay then. Ditto." Sarah laughed, and pulled his hand toward the subway that had just pulled up. "That's us."

Sam and Sarah had to shade their eyes as they exited the dark subway station. They walked a little, and Sam told Sarah about British slang. She was only interested in the naughty ones, and the cursing. As they rounded the corner, the Arc de Triomphe rose up from the Champs Elysee. Sarah had her camera in hand quickly. It was surprisingly not crowded. The tourist season hadn't started yet, so she was able to move about freely.

"Did you know that the Arc de Triomphe is the biggest arch in the world?" Sarah asked Sam.

"Are you going to be a walking, talking tour guide, Sarah?" Sam asked with a grin. "How did you know about the Metro and this?" He pointed to the Arc.

She smiled and shrugged. "After I knew I was coming to see you, time seemed to stop. I had my bags packed a week before I left. Nervous energy. So, I read up on Paris. It helped me pass the time. Now, you're stuck with me."

Sam grabbed Sarah around the waist and kissed her. "There's no one I'd rather be stuck with."

Next was the Notre Dame Cathedral. Sarah was mesmerized by the French Gothic architecture, and she rushed to get shots of the famous Rose window. She informed Sam that it was built from 1163 to 1345. He just laughed and found a bench to sit on. He could have sat and watched Sarah all day. He loved her excitement, and her joy. She had found a group of children taking a field trip. Sam leaned back and just delighted in Sarah's ability to talk to anyone. Language barrier be damned. The children were enthralled with her, as were the teachers.

Sarah wandered her way back to him. She sat down by him on the bench and leaned her head on his shoulder. "I'm sorry. Are you bored? We can move on if you like. I don't want to be the only one doing what I want."

"I could never be bored around you, Sarah. I love watching you with your camera. We can stay as long as you'd like." Sam rubbed the top of Sarah's thigh. She shivered a little. God! She loved it when he touched her.

"Just a little longer, then?" She saw an older couple walking toward the church. She rushed off to charm them, Sam was sure.

Pictured out, Sam and Sarah decided to get some fruit and cheese and wine, and go eat in the park under the Eiffel Tower. They would work their way to Montmartre and the Moulin Rouge after eating, and then back to the Eiffel by dark.

They found their food and drink and used Uber to get to the Parc du Champ de Mars, the beautiful park under the Eiffel Tower. The River Seine flowed quietly by, and the park stretched as far as they could see. They found a spot under a beautiful oak tree and unpacked their lunch.

"I'm starving!" Sarah said as she grabbed a handful of grapes.

"It's all the chin-wagging you've done." Sam grinned. "Do you want to fill me in on this place? I didn't even know it was here."

"I just knew there was a park. I don't have any details for you! Chin-wagging? I think I know what that means." She stuck her tongue out at Sam.

"You are a cheeky little devil, aren't you?" Sam leaned back against the tree and pulled Sarah to him. He kissed her sweet and long. "I love this. I love being here with you. I could just watch you, being you, forever."

She sighed. "It's all I know how to be. Just me."

"Just you is perfect." He kissed her again.

They stayed in the park for a while. Sam knew how important quiet was to Sarah. He was thrilled to share her quiet.

They walked to the nearest Metro and headed toward Montmartre. As they walked toward their destination, Sam turned and told Sarah very seriously, "I know about Montmartre. You don't need to tell me, unless you feel the *need* to do so. It was an artist colony for lots of famous artists."

"Okay, smart ass," said Sarah as she hugged herself. "Like who?"

Sam grabbed Sarah by the waist and whispered in her ear, "Renoir, Modigliani, and even Picasso. Paris has designated this entire area as a Historic District. What you see is what it looked like a hundred years ago." He kissed her neck. "Did you find that information sexy?"

"I actually am a little aroused right now, Sam." Sarah kissed Sam and laughed. "But you can't get us distracted. I want to see the Eiffel at night."

~~~

Sarah took picture after picture. She had she and Sam's caricature drawn. She bought a few small original paintings from a very pretty young man with a beard, who kissed her on both cheeks. So French! She bought bracelets from a woman who used fresh lavender flowers to make the beads. Sarah bought one for all the girls, and she talked with the woman for a long time about the process. Enough broken English was used that Sarah could follow along. She was intrigued by the woman's work. Sam stood off to the side and watched her with a smile on his face.

Sam was getting some attention from locals who recognized him. He couldn't complain. He hadn't been interrupted all day. They were very polite, and they didn't want a picture. They were interested in his work. He explained the long lulls in between the actual photography. They asked him about makeup and Photoshop. He told them that he didn't use makeup and that he didn't allow Photoshop to be used for his pictures. He was charming. Sarah stood and watched him. He was completely at ease talking about his work instead of about his beauty. Sarah was determined to join him for a day of work. She wanted to see him in his "office".

They wandered off the main street, and down a side street. Sarah was entranced by the colorful doors. Deep azure, yellow, green, and purple. They were beautiful. Sarah couldn't take enough pictures. They continued walking and found an amazing courtyard. Old brick with a bubbling fountain in the center. The boxwoods were perfectly manicured, and Sarah could only imagine what it would look like in the summer, with all the window boxes lush with trailing vines and blooming flowers. She and Sam decided that they would return in the summer. If not this year, next.

After turning around to go back, they realized that they were hopelessly lost. Sarah laughed. "I can't imagine a better place to get lost."

Sam saw a group of people ahead of them and walked faster to catch up. Sarah watched him shake hands with a gentleman, and cheek-kissed his companion. Sam made a lot of hand gestures, and then he laughed loudly. Sarah loved the way he laid his head back when he did that. She wasn't close enough to actually see it, but she knew what the laugh lines around his eyes looked like when he did that. Sam didn't laugh enough. Sarah was going to remedy that.

Sam walked back. "I asked for their recommendation on a café. They're on their way to eat, so they asked that we join them. I've always found that if you eat where the locals eat, you'll probably have good, authentic food."

Sarah just leaned into Sam and brushed his cheek with her hand. "I love you Sam Ramsay."

They joined the Parisians at a corner café called The Canard Sauvage. They all sat a large wooden table with bottles of house wine already there. They poured the wine, and one of the English-speaking men toasted, "A toast to new friends and new adventures!"

Sarah, as usual, had already taken her camera out, and she wandered around the café with her glass of wine, talking to everyone and laughing. Sam, as always, watched her. She was like a magnet, drawing everyone to her.

The locals ordered for them, and they started with soup of some kind. It was delicious. The wine flowed freely, and so did the conversation. Sarah finally sat next to him when the main course was served. Parsnips and carrots with rosemary, and, as the name of the café implied, duck. After taking her first bite, Sarah turned to Sam. "Well, it's not in a heavy cream sauce, but it's divine!"

Sam laughed, and said, "France is like Italy in that different regions have different foods. You'll find the heavy sauces here in Paris, but I would venture to say that the owners are not originally from here. They probably cook the way they were raised."

"Of course! I should have realized that. Italians have the seafood in the south, with the heavier sauces the further north you go. It's all about what's grown, or caught in the area. I'm going to ask about it when I'm done eating." Sarah stated.

"Of course you will," smiled Sam. "And you will truly be interested. You are a charming woman, Sarah Reid."

Sarah smiled that sunbeam smile. She leaned over and kissed Sam gently on his nose, then his bottom lip. The women at their table sighed and then tittered amongst themselves. Sam and Sarah heard "amour". They knew what that meant, and they smiled at each other.

Sarah and Sam waited outside the café for their taxi. Sarah had gathered everyone's names and addresses to send pictures. She had just finished hugging and kissing everyone goodbye, again,

when their ride appeared. Sam opened the door for her and climbed in after. As they settled into the back seat, Sam took Sarah in his arms and kissed her a long, lingering kiss. Sarah's heart sped up, and Sam felt it.

He smiled and said, "How do you do it?"

"Do what?"

"Make everyone you meet love you."

Sarah's eyes widened, and she sucked in her breath. "Do I?"

"Yes. Especially me." Sam kissed her again.

The taxi had them back at the Eiffel quickly. Sarah and Sam walked around the base for a while looking at the beautiful iron lattice work. Sarah busily snapped pictures of the tower and the people. She took several of Sam and he took several of her. They had a local take a few of them together. Sam again found a bench, and watched Sarah. It was one of his favorite things to do. Just watch Sarah. People would start showing up to see the Eiffel lights come on, so she was taking this opportunity to shoot as many shots as she could without having to deal with the crowd. Sarah came and sat down beside him, and leaned her head onto his shoulder. "Thank you for today, Sam. It has been spectacularly lovely." Sam kissed the top of her head, and they waited.

Every night, every hour on the hour, the Eiffel Tower was covered in golden lights and sparkled for five minutes. Like a lighthouse, the Eiffel had a beacon on the top that pointed two light beams in opposite directions. Sarah kept her seat by Sam, and took pictures, changing the lens occasionally. Sam took her hand and kissed it. Sarah leaned in, and they kissed each other. Then they just sat and watched.

They sat long enough to see the lights come back on the following hour. Sarah whispered in Sam's ear. "Please take me back to the hotel. I keep thinking about what you said in Montmartre. About the artists? I am still strangely aroused. "

Sam opened the door to their room, and waved Sarah in first. They had been strangely quiet on the ride back. Sam grabbed Sarah's hand and asked, "Is everything all right? "

Sarah smiled and kissed Sam. "Everything is wonderful. I am still just absorbing all of the sights, sounds, and smells of Paris. It's a little overwhelming, to have had one of the best days of your life. You know?"

"Every day since I met you, Sarah, has been one of my best. I love watching you. I love the way you are with people, and how you see things differently than anyone I've ever known. And I'm humbled," Sam patted his heart. "Humbled Sarah, that you see something in me that is worth flying half way across the world to spend time with."

Sarah wrapped her arms around Sam's hard waist. "Don't you know? I would fly around the whole world for you Sam." She kissed his ear and whispered, "Now take me to that bed and let's end this perfect day in Paris."

Chapter 22:

Sam and Sarah ate breakfast in the hotel café, and decided on their itinerary for the coming week. They had wanted to drive from Paris to Milan, but it was an eight-hour drive, and Sam's schedule started early on Tuesday, so that plan had been nixed. Sam had planned on flying before Sarah had gotten to Paris, so she would fly out with him. Sam had phone calls to make. Some work stuff, and he planned on checking in with Danni. Sarah needed to call her children and the girls to let them know what she had decided, and to arrange for someone to water her plants and get her mail.

The morning had gone quickly. Sarah's children were so excited, and all three had talked to Sam on the phone. He had assured them that he would try to keep her out of trouble, but had told all of them that he was very concerned about her running off with an Italian lover, and leaving him heartbroken. The girls were good, though Karen had been nursing a sick kid, and was tired. Liz would take care of things at the farm. After Sam had checked in with Danni, Sarah took the phone and proceeded to "chin-wag" with her for another thirty minutes. When she hung up she turned to see Sam sitting at the table with his chin in his hand grinning a goofy grin.

"What's all that about?" Sarah pointed to his face.

Sam just kept grinning. "All what?"

"That shit-eating grin," Sarah raised her eyebrows.

"I love that you and my sister can talk like two old women for thirty minutes. I've never heard Danni talk to anyone that long, unless she's lecturing someone." Sam just kept smiling.

Sarah laughed. "Oh, I remember sitting in your kitchen listening to one of her lectures. I like her a lot. I can't wait to get to know her even better."

Sam shook his head. "So what's on the agenda for today? The flight doesn't leave until three. It's only an hour and a half trip, so we could make plans for today, or tonight, or whatever you want to do."

"What would you be doing if I wasn't here?" Sarah asked.

Sam leaned back. "I would have made the same calls I just made, and probably just hole up here in the room. I'm a party animal, you know."

"I don't know about the party, but I do know you're an animal." Sarah laughed. "Why don't we find a café and get some lunch, and just walk for a while around here. Then we could just come back to the room, watch French television and order room service. I want you to relax and rest before the next leg of the campaign."

Sam laughed, "Sounds good to me, but I can't make any promises about resting."

Sarah and Sam window shopped as they walked hand in hand. They passed many clothing stores, and a store dedicated to just vintage hats. Sarah stopped and looked in and then turned to Sam and said, "Only in Paris would a store solely dedicated to antique hats be able to stay in business. It's a shame, because they're beautiful." She shook her head as they continued to walk. Sam took her hand and kissed it, but he didn't let go.

They went into several antiques shops. Sarah fell in love with some bistro chairs. They were weathered and so French. Sam tried to talk her into getting them. "You can always have them shipped to the States. The cost would be minimal, as they don't weigh much." Sarah just said that she didn't need them. The next store was Sarah heaven. Sam watched her as she found a huge ornate mirror in the back corner. It was leaning against the wall and was taller than her. It had once been painted with gold leaf, as some was still clinging on precariously. There was generation after generation of paint. Some white, some yellow, some green. The original mirror was still in it, and the silvering had come off in places. Sarah just stood and rubbed the wood. She turned to Sam. "This would be so awesome over my fireplace." She turned and looked at it again. "It would also look awesome in your entryway."

"Sarah, I can tell by the way you're rubbing it, that it excites you. Let me get it for you." Sam walked to her side and looked at her.

Sarah just continued to stare at it. "It's not because I don't want you to buy it for me Sam. You can buy me things. That doesn't bother me. But, I *want* it, I don't *need* it. So, thanks, but no thanks." She squeezed his arm and continued to browse.

As they walked to the front door, Sarah squealed. She actually squealed and ran toward the vintage camera that was on a shelf by the front door. She lovingly picked it up and studied it. She was so excited that she trembled. Sam stood with his arms crossed and just grinned. Nothing made him happier than seeing Sarah excited.

"What is it? I mean, I know it's a camera, but is it special?" Sam asked.

Sarah was almost reverential. "It's a nineteen forty Graflex Crown Graphic. It was made in New York, so it's funny that it's here in Paris. I haven't ever looked for one, because they would be nonexistent in my neck of the woods. But I understand why they're so collectible. This is amazing. It even has the accessories and the bag. Oh, my..." Her voice trailed off.

Sam grinned at her. "I'm not going to tell you to buy anything else. You either will, or you won't. You're kind of acting like I do when I spot a piece of old barn wood, or walnut. You could probably get a deal, as it looks like it's been here a while."

Sarah slowly put it back on the shelf and sighed. "I'll bet someone used it in the war. What stories it could probably tell."

"That makes sense to me. Right time frame. Why are you putting it back Sarah? It obviously gives you joy."

"It does." Sarah sighed. "And I want it. I can afford it, but, again, I don't need it. But it was great just seeing one, and touching it." She grabbed Sam's arm and kissed him quickly. "Let's grab some lunch. I'm starved."

"You're always hungry woman!" Sam laughed. "I noticed a creperie across the street. We could do savory and sweet?"

"Crepes in Paris? Hell yeah!" Sarah drug Sam out the front door.

Sam and Sarah walked hand and hand back to the hotel after having eaten a spinach and cheese crepe, and a salted caramel crepe. They were both pleasantly full and in no hurry. They strolled slowly, talking about some of their favorite things about Paris. Sam remarked, "I am going to take your advice and start absorbing some of the locales, Sarah. Hopefully you'll be sharing most of those experiences with me. I've enjoyed these last three days so much. I feel rejuvenated and ready to finish the last leg of the campaign."

Sarah leaned her head into Sam. "If you are rested and relaxed, and have had a good time, then I'll let Danni know that I've done my job. She worries about you, Sam."

"I know she does, but, in the coming year, things are going to be different. More time off. See, I've got this big-hearted, big-chested woman that lives in the States. In the *middle* of the States. I'm kind of arse over tits about her, so I plan on spending a lot of time with her."

Sarah grinned. "I'm going to hold you to that Sam Ramsay."

As they entered the lobby, Sam turned to Sarah. "Do you mind going ahead and getting the lift? I'm going to check with the desk about any mail I might have. I'll be right there."

Sarah was still waiting for the elevator when Sam walked up. They rode up together and continued to chatter. As they entered their room they both kicked off their shoes. Sarah had noticed the first night that she met Sam that he was a barefoot kind of guy. As much as Sarah loved her stilettos, she loved taking them off. She, too, loved going barefoot. Sarah pulled her pants off, and crawled up in the bed. She squished the pillows up behind her back and waited for Sam. He had taken his jacket off, and untucked his shirt, before crawling up beside her. He got settled next to Sarah.

"Milan is going to be the most chaotic part of this trip. It's Fashion Week, so it will be nuts. Lots of meet and greets, a photo shoot and a runway show. That will run Tuesday, Wednesday and

Thursday, with another premiere Friday evening. Are you ready to make another entrance?'

Sarah grinned and said, "I have just the dress. It will be nice to have all the lust taken care of *before* the red carpet this time!"

"Yeah, I don't know if my heart, or my dick, can take another one of those surprise entrances, Sarah. Red and aquamarine will forever be my favorite colors." Sam leaned over and kissed her gently. "You had asked about seeing me work. Are you sure you want to spend that much time being bored out of your mind?"

Sarah shook her head vehemently. "Absolutely! You wouldn't get in trouble for taking me would you?"

"I'm a grown-ass man, Sarah! I can take anyone I want to. It's not like they could fire me!" Sam scowled. "Anyway, I only have the one shoot in Milan, so it might be the best time for you to go with me. Plus, Luca Moretti will be the photographer."

Sarah smiled. She had been introduced to Luca at the benefit in London. Sarah knew Luca Moretti's work, and was excited to see him again. "That would be wonderful! I enjoyed meeting him, and it will be exciting to see him work. I think he takes my favorite photos of you."

"I'm reminding you again of how boring it will be. You can bring your camera, if you want. Luca seemed to be interested in what you used when you two talked." Sam said.

Sam got up to get them some bottled water. As he walked back to the bed, a knock sounded at the door. Sarah gave Sam a questioning look. Sam just grinned that slow, sexy grin that melted Sarah's panties off. Sarah heard Sam open the door and murmur, and then close the door. Sam   walked back with a beautifully wrapped box. He sat it on the table, and poured two glasses of Jameson.

As he brought the water and whiskey to Sarah, she raised her eyebrows. Sam grinned bigger and crawled back into bed and toasted, "Here's to Milan. May it go quickly." Sarah looked at Sam over the rim of her glass as she took a sip. She didn't say anything. Sam continued to chatter away about Milan, and Italy, and crepes, and all manner of bullshit.

"Enough! I can't stand it anymore! What is that?" Sarah yelled.

Sam laughed and got up. "You just couldn't take it anymore, could you?" Sam handed the box to Sarah and sat on the edge of the bed. He had a silly grin on his face as he watched Sarah unwrap the box. He was excited to have gotten her something. This was his first gift for Sarah. He planned on many more.

Sarah slowly untied the yellow bow, and laid it on the bed. Then she proceeded to pull the tape that was holding the beautiful yellow, purple, and aqua paisley paper that wrapped the box. She slowly opened the lid to be met with tissue paper. She looked at Sam with wide eyes, before she ripped the tissue out. She looked down and stared into the box. She lifted her head. "Oh!" That's all she was capable of saying. "Oh."

She lifted the Graflex camera out of the box and continued to stare at it. All of the accessories and the bag were in the box with the camera. She lifted her head with tears rolling down her cheeks. "Why Sam?"

Sam leaned over and caressed her cheek, before he kissed her softly. "Because you wanted it. You didn't need it. Well, I wanted to get it for you. It gives you joy, Sarah. I wanted to be part of that joy. I plan on many, many gifts, so get used to it."

"Oh, Sam… I don't know what to say." Sarah whispered. "I love it so much. But I love you more. How did you get this without me knowing? I've been with you all day."

Sam was as excited as a teenage boy getting to cop a feel from his girlfriend. "I suggested the creperie across the street from the shop, so I could see the name and address. When I checked my mail, I had the desk staff call the shop with my credit card information. One of the staff walked over and got it and brought it up."

"You are a sneaky little devil, aren't you Sam Ramsay? I'm going to have to remember that." Sarah laid the camera back in the box and put the box on the bedside table. She crawled over to Sam and laid her head on his hard chest. "Thank you. You continue to surprise me every day. In so many ways."

"Many ways, uh?" Sam asked teasingly. He started to caress Sarah's back. "I hope my sexual proclivities are the main surprise. They're a lot better than you thought they'd be, aren't they?"

Sarah laughed before she got serious. "It surprises me every day that you want to be with me. It's obvious that there's an attraction, but it surprises me that *any* forty-year old would give a fifty-five year old widow a second look, much less *the* Sam Ramsay who could have any female, and probably male, that he wanted. I still don't understand, but I love that you surprise me every day by loving me."

"No! We are not having this conversation again, Sarah! Give yourself a little credit, for fuck's sake!" Sam was exasperated and a little sharp. "Have you ever looked at yourself in the mirror? *Any* man would give you a second look. You are stunning. That's the first thing I noticed. Your beauty. The second thing I noticed was that you might have had some mental health issues, but you dispelled that pretty quickly. Then, oh God! That mouth of yours!"

Sarah laughed a little. Sam continued. "I love your heart. I love your tits. I love your spirit. I love your ability to talk to anyone. I love the relationship you have with my sister. I love that you love my family. And I especially love that you love me. A man would be crazy not to give you a second look." Sam cupped Sarah's cheeks. "I never want to have this conversation again."

Sam leaned back against the pillows and crossed his arms and glared at Sarah. She knew that he wasn't really mad, but he was serious. He wasn't done. "I've been on billboards in Times Square, and I've made more magazine covers than I can count. I've been with Oak Wood my entire modeling life. That just doesn't happen. I've gone viral more times than I care to remember. I have had more women than I care to mention. I can be a narcissist and cocky sometimes. I'm a clothes junkie. I like to look good when I go out. I know I look good in a suit, and I work hard to make my body look good. But..." He still glared at Sarah.

"As I told you before. I don't believe in luck. But I did get lucky with my genes. My black hair and my blue eyes catch people's attention. That's the luck I got from my mum and my dad. But I look in the mirror and I see a man with big ears, wonky hair, and a huge nose. I have scars on my face, and large pores. I fucking moisturize! But the camera loves my face. So, I got lucky with that, too. I ended a relationship with someone I cared about deeply, because of that fucking camera. I've restored a house that I rarely stay in because it's not a home. I'll not have children because of that fucking camera. I can be a big fucking prick, Sarah! But the biggest thing that I lucked out with is you. You saw past the superficial and saw me. Warts and all. That afternoon at the carnival in St. Louis?" Sam looked at Sarah with anguish in his eyes. She shook her head yes.

"You told me what you saw. The boy I had been, the man I was now, and the man you were excited to see completed. I want to be complete with you, Sarah Reid, because you saw my possibilities. I treasure you Sarah. So, no! Don't ever talk to me again about me wanting you. I think you've saved my life by wanting me. I want the rest of your scrapbook to be filled with page after page of us." Sam put his head in his hands.

It was Sarah's turn to rock Sam. She had always been a good rocker. She had practiced plenty on her children. She rocked Sam in her arms and gently combed his hair with her fingers and murmured soft things in his ears. Her heart was broken for him, but oddly moved, too. She knew how difficult it had been for him to say the things he'd said, and she was touched that he loved her enough to say them. She loved him so hard that it was a physical pain. How the hell would she ever be able to go home? Their relationship had progressed further than it had after London. Sarah couldn't fall into a bed of misery again. She continued to rock him until his breathing evened out.

Sarah leaned back and took Sam's hand. She turned and smiled that blinding, beaming smile. It took Sam's breath away. The only time he had seen that smile that blinding was when Sarah talked about David.

"Oh, fuck Sarah!" He grabbed her face and kissed her with scorching lips. Sarah gasped and drew back and looked at him.

Sam looked at her in wonder. He knew she loved him, but in this moment he knew that she loved him hard and deep and forever. "I have never said those things out loud before. Not even to Danni." He kissed her again. "Sorry about that. I'm really not a puss. But I love you so much it hurts."

"How the hell can I go home? How the hell can I leave you? On the one hand, I tell myself that this isn't reality. But on the other hand, I don't give a flying fuck. But, I do have to go home sometime. Maybe we can go back and forth?" Sarah had begun to get a little hysterical.

Sam kissed her again. "We have been given this wonderful thing called us. We will figure it out Sarah. We will."

Sarah leaned over Sam and unbuttoned his shirt. She leaned him forward and took it off. God! She loved the massiveness that was his back. She slowly licked him from his collarbone to the waistband of his pants. Sam's skin shivered. She looked up at him and removed her own shirt. Sam started to breath heavier as his eyes darkened. She rolled over on her back and removed her jeans and panties. Sam rolled over toward her but she pushed him back before she peeled his jeans down, and then off. Sarah straddled Sam's gorgeous torso, as she unclasped her bra. Sam reached for her breasts and moaned. Sarah arched her back and sighed. She loved his fingers. They were long and slim and soft as a baby's butt.

Sarah lowered her head and kissed Sam a soft, sweet kiss. Sam responded by nibbling her bottom lip and tweaking her nipples. Sarah trailed kisses down Sam's sharp cheek bones, and his chin before she worked her way down his neck and chest. She reached for her glass of Jameson and slowly poured some in Sam's belly button. Then she filled each of those obliques with the rest of the whiskey. She looked at Sam with a wicked smile. He grinned back. "I've been wanting to do this since I saw that first picture."

Sarah lapped the whiskey out of his belly button. She could see the goose bumps appear on his skin. She chuckled as she trailed her tongue to his right oblique and swept her tongue up and down. The whiskey burned so good, but Sarah burned hotter. She trailed her tongue to the left oblique, and sucked the amber liquid. She then lowered her head and took Sam's hardness in her mouth. Sam bucked once and groaned. All he felt was Sarah's wet heat. He grabbed her head. Sarah felt hot. She felt powerful. It was so fucking good.

Sam looked down to see Sarah's head moving up and down between his legs. Her hands caressed his hips and the obliques that she had just used as her shot glass. She made little panting noises and had started to writhe her pelvis on the bed. Fuck! It was so sexy, and it felt so good. As Sam neared his apex, he reached for Sarah and rolled her over onto her back.

"I want to be inside you." He kissed her hair, her eyes, her cheeks. With every kiss, he told her he loved her. Her skin felt like hot velvet. He tongued her nipples until she cried out and arched her back. Sam caressed her arms and her belly, before he spread her legs and kissed her thighs. They both panted and cursed. As Sam balanced over Sarah, she smiled. "I love you Sam Ramsay."

As Sam plunged into Sarah's hot wetness, he whispered hoarsely, "I worship you Sarah Reid."

~~~

Sam and Sarah could not stop touching each other. They stood in the shower and soaped each other. They washed each other's hair, and they stood and held each other as the shower jets rained hot water down on their bodies.

They ate room service in bed. They talked and fed each other sausages and cheese. They had another whiskey and passed grapes and cherries from each other's mouths. They were inebriated with lust and intoxicated with each other.

Chapter 23:

Sarah left Sam still asleep as she went to shower. She was happy for a few minutes of just Sarah time. She needed to try to absorb the emotional coupling of last night. Something had changed in their relationship, and Sarah was petrified by the depth of Sam's emotions. She was even more petrified by hers.

Sarah had never dreamed that she and Sam would be permanent. She knew that they had chemistry. She knew that they had experienced amazing sex, and great conversation. They had similar tastes in music, food, and travel. Sarah knew that Sam loved her. He told her all the time, and he showed her all the time. She had fallen into this madness before she even knew they loved each other and had prepared herself for a good heartbreak. She felt as if she had experienced whiplash. She would now be able to look further into the future than just the coming year. She and Sam had a visceral reaction to each other. Sarah had never even experienced that with David. She couldn't believe that at this stage in her life she had been given another great love. Because that's what it was. She had found it in Sam. He was her heart.

She had become addicted to an enticingly hot man who was also, kind, funny, and smart. And he loved her as much as she loved him. She didn't know what she had done to deserve her life. She'd had the good, the bad, and the ugly. But losing David had made her appreciate and treasure what she had with Sam. She squared her shoulders, and said out loud, "I love Sam Ramsay. He is mine!" Sarah resolved to do whatever it took to keep them both happy.

Sam heard Sarah go to the shower and turn on the water. He realized that he and Sarah had stepped over an unseen line last night. Things had shifted. He remembered Sarah's clothesline of pictures after her London visit. They had made him weep with the emotional gift she had given him. Then he had wept last night. Sarah would think she was banging a sissy boy but Sam didn't care. Sarah was part of him, and they had melded into one entity last night.

He thought of her beauty, her heart, and her generosity, and it made him strangely emotional. He was now forty-one-years-old and had resigned himself to the fact that the baggage he carried around would ultimately leave him with a lonely life. Fame and looks were fleeting. It's what came after that was important. Love, family and friends were ultimately all that mattered.

Sarah had changed his life. He felt that their life together was destined a long time ago. He felt as if he had been waiting for her forever.

~~~

Sam and Sarah walked down to the creperie they had eaten at the day before for an early lunch. They planned on dinner after they got checked into their Milan hotel. By the time they got back and packed, it was time to go. Sam gave Sarah a look as she came out of the bathroom. He then gave her a wolf whistle. She wore black leggings with an orange empire waist blouse. It had a low neckline that showed off her beautiful cleavage that Sam had enjoyed just a short time ago. He grinned his slow, sexy grin.

"What's that grin about Sam? I know it's either something dirty, or something ornery!"

Sam kept looking at her as she sat and put her feet in orange and white polka dotted patent leather heels. Only four inches this time. Sam shook his head and said, "I love your unique style Sarah."

Sarah stopped buckling the strap on her heel and looked up at him. "Too much? "

"Never! Unique is good. You're comfortable in your skin, and I'm quite comfortable with your skin, too. I think confidence is one of the sexiest things ever. Plus, you always look damn good."

Sarah laughed and then grinned. "Thanks! Seriously. The dapper gentleman that's known the world over for his design style, telling me that he likes mine, is truly a great compliment."

"Just telling you the truth, darling. I, if nothing else, tend to be an honest man." Sam zipped up his suitcase, and looked around for anything they might have missed. "Well, it's time to go join the chaos that's Milan during Fashion Week."

~~~

After an uneventful ninety-minute flight, Sam and Sarah took a taxi to the hotel. The driver commented that he thought the traffic might make their ride to the hotel longer than their flight. Sam had explained to Sarah how many people would be milling about at all hours of the day and night. There would be a million cameras and reporters. Finding a place to eat would be difficult, and there would be no sightseeing this time. Fashion Week in Milan was a global affair. There would be no let up for the four days they were there. The only break Sam would get would be at the photo shoot.

Sam had already made arrangements for Sarah to have a front row seat at the runway show. He didn't do runway anymore, except for Oak Wood. He wanted Sarah to see what he had made his living doing for so many years. Runway modeling had given him his life. He had also talked to Luca about Sarah coming to the photo shoot. Luca had been beyond gracious. Sam was excited for him to see Sarah in action with her camera and her charm. Sarah would be by his side for the meet and greets. He didn't want her stuck in the room for four days, and he couldn't bear knowing she was in Milan and not have her with him.

The hotel lobby wasn't too crazy yet. Most people would start showing up later in the evening. Sam and Sarah checked in and went to their room to unpack and steam and hang up their formal clothes. Sam suggested a drink in the bar downstairs before it got nuts. They could tell the crowd had picked up when they stepped out of the elevator. Flashbulbs already flashed, and reporters were everywhere. Sam was stopped several times by people he knew. He introduced Sarah to all of them. She was positive that she wouldn't remember any of them. He didn't stop for any of the reporters. He was very nice, but just told them it was his day off, and that he would answer questions at the press conferences tomorrow. He never let go of Sarah's hand. They finally found an empty table in a corner of the bar. They each ordered two fingers of Jameson neat. Sarah also asked for a glass of ice. After receiving their drinks they leaned back and exhaled.

"Wow!" Sarah laughed. "If that is just the beginning, I can't wait until tomorrow!"

"Are you serious? That didn't bother you?" Sam asked incredulously.

Sarah continued to chuckle. "Not at all. No matter how nuts it gets, it will be over in four days. It took me four days to have my first child, so anything else is easy."

Sam grinned and took Sarah's hand. He turned it over and kissed the pulse point on her wrist. Sarah shivered a little. "You are an amazing woman Sarah Reid."

"Yeah, I'm pretty amazing, aren't I?" Sarah cocked an eyebrow. Sam laughed loudly. "I guess we're what the press would call *official,* aren't we?"

"Oh yeah. We are definitely official. I think that was pretty apparent in London. But you've been with me in Paris, now in Milan. There will be a feeding frenzy." Sam sipped his whiskey.

"Are you okay with that? It's your career, after all."

Sam sighed and leaned back in his chair. "I've had my career for too long, to have it disappear overnight. It's mine to worry about, not yours. But, no, I'm proud to show you off, and I'm ecstatic that you're here with me. It will be nice to have an ally."

"Always, Sam. Always." Sarah sighed and leaned back, too. She sipped her whiskey and looked at Sam through the glass.

Sam hesitated, then squared his beautiful shoulders and looked at Sarah. "Please don't take this the wrong way. I'd never dream of trying to tell you what to do, but... I've always kept my private life private. It's all I have that's not out there for everyone to see. It's also been my way of protecting Danni and her family and my mum and dad. I will introduce you to anyone you want to meet. You are Sarah Reid from the States. The woman I love. They don't need to know where you live, because I don't care if you live in the boonies, they would track you down. It could drive you crazy. My suggestion is to leave it at that. *not* because I don't want people to know who you are, but just to keep the privacy that I need." Sam looked at her expectantly and a little nervously.

It was Sarah's turn to reach for Sam's hand. "I agree one hundred percent." She caressed his forearm. She felt the muscles, and the soft skin and whisper of the fine black hairs. She loved his arms. "Before I met you, when all I had was an eight-by-ten glossy nude of you, I was trying to find out who you were. When I did, I researched you, and the first thing that jumped out at me, was that you've never had a hint of a scandal. How can that be? After all the women you've bedded, and even in business deals, there's been nothing. How do you do that?"

Sam just shrugged. "I've always tried to be a gentleman, and I've always been honest about my career coming first. It's the way I was raised. My mum and dad instilled honesty, hard work and professionalism. And when all else failed, I paid them off."

"Really?" Sarah was surprised.

Sam snorted. "Sarah! Of course I didn't pay them off. Ultimately, it's just because I'm a really, really nice guy. And humble."

"Oh! So humble!" Sarah cracked up."But seriously, you are a gentleman who's a really nice guy."

They sat and nursed their drinks for a little longer and decided to call it a night. They would just order salads at the front desk, and eat in the room. First presser started at nine in the morning, and it would be non-stop the rest of the day.

~~~

The next morning Sam and Sarah watched each other dress. No one wore a suit like Sam Ramsay, and unlike any man that Sarah had ever known, Sam loved them. She had stopped counting at ninety when she had been in London. Sam had at least ninety suits.

Today, Sam had chosen a brown plaid pattern with a very subtle baby blue stripe. He had paired a baby blue shirt, a dark brown tie, and a waist coat in the same plaid. Sarah sighed as she watched him as he put beautiful gold cuff links in the French cuffs. Sarah had chosen her ensemble before she saw what Sam would be wearing.

Sam watched Sarah walk out of the bathroom. He had to swallow. He had seen her as the most beautiful woman in formal attire. She was also the most beautiful woman he had ever seen in a T-shirt and panties. And no one rocked leggings like Sarah Reid. As he watched her walk to the dresser he finally realized that Sarah looked beautiful in anything. She wore a pair of wide-legged, high-waist sailor pants. They had two rows of gold buttons on each side of her belly. The trousers were the exact color of brown as Sam's suit. She paired the pants with a completely sheer long-sleeved, baby blue blouse that matched Sam's shirt. It had a slit from the neckline to the high waist band of the pants. She was wearing a darker blue spaghetti strap, lacy something underneath it. It was subtly sexy. And Sam was sure she didn't even realize it. She wore plain gold hoop earrings, and -Sarah being Sarah-, she wore brown plaid heels with a subtle baby blue stripe. She had spiked her hair up into a faux hawk. Sam loved the classic outfit with the little bit of rock and roll. Sarah lifted her head to ask if Sam would button up all the tiny gold buttons that ran down the back of her blouse. Sam was speechless as he continued to stare.

"What?" asked an exasperated Sarah.

"It's beginning to freak me out a little. I know that you saw what I was wearing last night, but what are the odds that you would have packed an outfit that coordinated exactly? How would you have known?" Sam was wide-eyed.

Sarah shrugged. "I know, right? Remember you asking me about believing in destiny?"

"That seems so long ago, but yeah, I do."

Sarah walked over to Sam and kissed him softly. "I remember what you said. You told me that you thought that we were destined to meet. I am convinced that there are forces at work Sam. Like all the planets have aligned and that the Gods want us together. It's a little frightening, isn't it?"

Sam whispered as he put his arms around Sarah. "It could never be frightening, but it is definitely very exciting. You look amazing. How can you be so classy, but so bawdy? I want to spend the rest of my life trying to figure that out."

As they walked off the elevator they were surrounded by a throng of reporters, cameras, models, and staff. Sam squeezed Sarah's hand. He leaned over and whispered in her ear, "Are you ready?" He kissed her cheek, and the cameras went crazy.

They made their way to the hotel conference room where they were peppered with questions from the reporters.

"Who's your friend, Sam?"

"Care to introduce your lady?"

"Are you quitting the business?"

"Hey! Are you going to be joining Sam for the rest of the campaign?"

"Are you a lover or a friend?"

"Does the age difference bother either of you?"

"Do you wake up looking this good?"

"How do your families feel about your relationship?"

"Where did you guys meet?"

It was a cacophony of noise. Sarah observed several women pass Sam pieces of paper. Sam just slipped them in his pocket and never skipped a beat. Sarah and Sam kept smiling as they made their way to the conference room. Sam had never let go of her hand.

The press that had followed them from the elevator stopped at the doorway to the conference room. There would be no entry for them. The room was already full of chairs with the press that had been given access. The staff shut the doors on the noise outside, and the cameras busily followed Sam as he walked Sarah to a chair at the end of the front table. Sarah sat and crossed her long legs. She never stopped smiling as Sam kissed her cheek and made his way to the middle with all of the microphones. He sat and smiled at the crowd.

Sarah leaned back and prepared to watch Sam do what Sam did. She loved how self-deprecating he was. He continually rubbed his hands together, or rubbed an eye, or the stubble on his chin. She knew that he hated the hoops that he had to jump through, or as he called it, "being the dancing monkey". He would look at her every few minutes and smile.

When Sam looked at Sarah, she smiled back at him. She was cool as a cucumber! Sam loved that Sarah didn't need this. She wasn't with him for the notoriety, or the headlines, or what she could gain from a relationship with him. She was there for him. She was his ally, and Sam knew without a doubt, that she would become a bear if someone tried to do or say something that was an attack on him. He smiled at Sarah again and leaned back in his chair and waited for Luca and the Oak Wood reps to get seated.

The room quieted, and one of the Oak Wood reps started the conference by talking about the Oak Wood brand, their long relationship with Sam Ramsay, and the spring lines of spirits and fashion. They then opened the conference for questions.

A reporter from a local Milanese paper asked, "Sam, this isn't the first time we've seen you with the beautiful woman that's sitting to the side. Both of you burned up the papers in London." There were chuckles from the press. "Care to give us an introduction?"

Sam smiled, and Sarah saw the crinkles at the corner of his eyes. She sighed. She loved his laugh lines. Sam looked over at Sarah. "She's stunning, isn't she?" The gallery of reporters murmured amongst themselves. You could feel the curiosity ripple through the horde like a stone being skipped on a river. "Ladies and gentlemen, allow me to introduce Ms. Sarah Reid."

The murmurs grew louder. "Where did you meet?" asked another local reporter.

"We met at a shoot in the states. Let's just say that she fell for me." Sam looked at her with a smile on his face. Sarah laughed out loud. All the cameras pointed at her.

"So you're an American?" someone asked. Sarah just shook her head yes.

Another asked if they had coordinated their clothing, which made both of them laugh.

A journalist from *The Stag* stood up, "Sam, you have a global image as a quintessential British gentleman. You have been called the world's sexiest man, the world's most beautiful man, and the number one male model for decades now. Are you concerned that Ms. Reid will dampen the allure or appeal that your fans have for you?"

Sam sighed and leaned back in his chair. He rubbed his hands together and played with his lapel before answering. "No. I'm not concerned, nor do I care. My fans will either find me appealing or not. I would be more concerned if Oak Wood found me unappealing. I'm forty-one-years old. I've never been married. I've had no children. I've worked my ass off. I deserve happiness as much as the next guy. Sarah makes me deliriously happy." He looked at Sarah in all her relaxation. She raised her eyebrows as if asking a question. Sam just smiled at her and said. "I think Ms. Reid would like to say something."

All the cameras again were pointed at Sarah. She continued to sit with those long legs crossed. She took a deep breath. "I might not be an ingénue, but I am a woman. I know what sexy looks like. I actually like sexy. Sam Ramsay was sexy as hell twenty years ago. Sam Ramsay was sexy as hell yesterday, last night, and today. I dare say that he will still be sexy tomorrow." The press again chuckled.

"Our relationship will not change the fact that he's a panty-melter. " The room burst out in laughter. "But, what all of you, and his adoring fans," Sarah swept her arm out at the reporters, "fail to see, is that there's more to Sam Ramsay than sex appeal. There's more to Sam Ramsay than that perfect face, or exquisite body, or the blue eyes and black hair. He has a brain, and a wicked sense of humor. He likes his whiskey. He has a heart and an old fashioned sense of honor. He is loyal and mannerly to the extreme. I feel so lucky to know all of that, and to experience Sam for who he truly is. I feel sorry for all of you that will never see that. He's worked hard for his career, and sacrificed a lot to be where he is today. He deserves to grab his brass ring. No matter who or what that might be. Hell, guys! Give him a break!"

She looked at Sam as he sat at the table with his chin in his hand wearing a huge grin. Sarah gasped a little at the look in his eyes. The rest of the front table had grins on their faces, too.

Sarah wasn't done. "In conclusion, let me just say, that we are all here today to talk about Sam and the wonderful people at Oak Wood. Could we perhaps address that? I'm just a middle-aged widow from the States. I'm not nearly as exciting as the people sitting in front of you."

Sam watched the Press Corps chuckle, and turned back to the front table. He shook his head and grinned. Sarah had done it again. As impossible as it sounded, she had charmed the shirts off the press. Luca, who was sitting to Sam's left, leaned over and asked, "Can I have one of those, too?"

Sam laughed as he continued to look at Sarah. "Sorry, Luca, there's only one Sarah. They broke the mold with her."

The presser had concluded. Sarah had been hugged by everyone employed by Oak Wood, and she had been mauled by Luca, who had fallen in love with her a little. Sam watched him and Sarah as they talked animatedly. He walked up to them and wrapped his arm around Sarah's waist. They were talking about tomorrows photo shoot. Sarah beamed as she looked at Sam. "Luca has given me permission to snap pictures tomorrow Sam! I'm so excited! Of course, I'll have to sign a nondisclosure about selling them. Can you please assure him that I don't sell my photos?"

Luca took her hand and kissed it. "Tesoro, I believe anything you tell me. But the attorneys would have a sequestro. A seizure, you know? I remember talking about lenses and angles at the London benefit. I'm so sorry that I don't recall much of that conversation, as everyone there was busy, how you say it? Sbavando. Drooling. Over the red dress. I wished that I had my camera, as you, carissimo, were a vision." Luca looked at Sam and laughed. "For the first time in years, someone was prettier than you Sam!"

Sam squeezed Sarah's waist. "The vision that was Sarah that night will stay with me forever. Especially the way it ended." Sam growled, and kissed Sarah's neck that had suddenly grown very warm.

Luca put up his hands and laughed. "I can only imagine, damn it! I know what would've happened at my house, if that dress would've gone home with me! But, seriously, Sarah, when you come tomorrow, can you bring some of your work? Did you bring any? I've heard from several people about your talent. I would love to see it. Especially any you might have of my adopted son, Sam."

Sarah looked at Sam with her eyebrows raised. "I have them on my laptop. I would love for you to critique my work."

Sam looked at Luca. "Sarah doesn't work like any photographer I've ever been around. You forget that she has a camera in her hands. You'll be surprised at what, or who, she decides to shoot. She has many special gifts, but her emotional attachment to her subjects is very special."

Luca bear hugged Sam and kissed Sarah on both cheeks, and they all said their goodbyes until tomorrow.

Sam and Sarah had to maneuver another change of clothes for the next luncheon and a press conference for the print campaign. It would be held in the same location as the first one. As they hung up the clothes that they had just removed, Sam stopped and looked at Sarah. He walked to her and bent her over his arm for a deep, scorching kiss. Sarah could smell the oak leaves and whiskey that was pure Sam. The cashmere of the suit felt like the worlds softest blanket against her neck, and Sam's tongue made Sarah forget where or who she was. The sensations overwhelmed her. She murmured something and Sam lifted his head to look at her glazed eyes and swollen lips. He wanted to ravish her on the carpeted floor. But, they didn't have time.

"Do you have any idea how proud you make me? How fucking amazing you are? That stuff you said at the presser, were some of the nicest things anyone has ever said about me. And because it came from your mouth makes me want to show you how grateful I am. I want to show you how grateful I am in that bed over there."

Sam could have shown her his thankfulness in the hallway if he wanted. She was lost in a vortex of Sam. She shook her head to get her bearings, and then chuckled. "I can't wait to see what we wear." Sam laughed, too, and patted her ass.

Sam changed into a classic black Italian wool suit with silk lapels and a white shirt with a blood red tie. He placed the same red pocket square in his breast pocket. He had finished putting in sterling silver cuff links, when Sarah walked out of the bathroom. They both stood in silence for a moment before they started to laugh. Sarah just shrugged and said, "Well, it is what it is."

Sarah wore a black column dress that ended just below her knees. It was long sleeved with a rounded neckline. A simple, classic dress that made her impossibly long legs look even longer. She had added a blood red scarf of a lacy material, dangling ruby earrings, and blood red stilettos. Sam stared at Sarah's legs as he imagined them wrapped around his neck. "You peeked, didn't you?"

Sarah laughed. "No! I swear I didn't, but I thought that black would go with whatever you were wearing. I could match a scarf and shoes if I needed to. I'm just not going to question it anymore. We just both have exquisite taste."

It was the same scenario as before. They were peppered with questions on their way to the luncheon. Sam, ever the gentleman, had been polite as he propelled Sarah through the crowd with his hand on the small of her back.

They entered the conference room and were met with a long table of delicious-looking food and coffee. Sarah looked at Sam, but before she could say anything, Sam said, "I know! You're starving!"

As they filled their plates, Sarah murmured, "I'll be fine. If there are people you need to talk to or meet, please do so. I can always find someone to talk to. You don't need to protect me from the reporters."

"I have no doubt that you could talk to most anyone, and you are perfectly capable of protecting yourself, but, I want you with me." Sam was determined to not let her out of his sight.

They found some seats and proceeded to enjoy their breakfast when Walter Lemons, an older gentleman in his seventies and the owner of Oak Wood, approached them with his wife. "Do you mind?"

"Of course not, Mr. Lemons! Please!" Sarah indicated the empty chairs. She was impressed with herself that she had remembered his name. "I don't think we've been introduced yet. I'm Sarah." She held her hand out to Mrs. Lemons.

"It's so nice to meet you, Sarah. Please call me Sally, and that old man talking to your Sam, is just Walter." She smiled broadly at Sarah. "I've been dying to talk to you since London. We didn't get a chance at the benefit." She raised her eyebrows at Sarah. "It looked as if you were preoccupied with... other things."

"Oh, God!" Sarah laughed. "I think that red dress will be my legacy!"

Sally patted Sarah's hand. "Honey, the dress was absolutely divine, but the legacy is the way Sam was taking it off of you with his eyes. People are still talking about it."

Sarah put her face in her hands and shook her head. "I refuse to be embarrassed about it, but everyone I've met has mentioned it."

"Don't ever be embarrassed! It was H.O.T.!" Sally roared with laughter. "But after this morning's press conference, I told Walter that we were going to track you down. I *had* to meet you. You were fabulous!"

"Thank you so much! I hope I didn't overstep my bounds, but Sam and I knew what the press would be most interested in. I wanted to address that, but I also felt that a little, uh, redirecting, was in order. It is the Oak Wood campaign after all."

"All of the Oak Wood people are still talking about you. I have to say, you're charming. You charmed the press, which is impossible, and you charmed everyone at Oak Wood, and Luca won't stop talking about you. If you weren't with Sam, I think he'd convince you to run away with him."

"If I didn't have Sam, I don't think it would take much convincing to run away with him. I have a bit of a crush on him, and I know how much he means to Sam." Sarah finished up the last of her breakfast.

"I don't want to butt in, but I'm going to anyway." Sally said, and they both laughed. "I've known Sam since he was an eighteen-year-old pretty boy. I watched him as he was thrust into something he had never even thought about doing, much less having as a lifelong career. He has done it with grace, humility, and hard work. We love him like a son. We are so proud of what he's accomplished and what he wants to continue to do. He is loyal to us to a fault. He considers himself lucky to have us, but we are just as lucky to have him. None of us would be here without the other. It is a symbiotic relationship."

"He is extremely loyal to Oak Wood. He feels like you're family." Sarah responded.

"We are. We love Sam. Especially the Sam that no one else sees. But you've seen it. We are the family that Sam has never brought a woman home to meet." Sally raised her eyebrow. Sarah waited. "You are the one and only. He has never even talked about a woman, much less present her to the world. He never uttered a word about his previous relationship, and they were together for several years. All we knew is what we read in the papers. You're not what we, or the world, expected. Walter and I thought that you had to be pretty special, and now that I've talked to you, I know why he loves you so much. Because he does. I can see it in his eyes and in his body. He's more relaxed and grounded. You have given that to him Sarah, and we are so happy for you both. Sam is such a lovable man, and I am thankful that you see that. He deserves happiness, as do you."

Sarah's eyes filled with unshed tears. These people loved Sam so much. For Sam, not what he gave them. She leaned over and hugged Sally hard. "Thank you for sharing him. I love him so much, because of *what* he is, not *who* he is."

Sam and Walter watched their women as they talked and laughed. Sam could not get rid of the shit-eating grin that had taken up permanent residency on his face. Walter looked from Sarah to Sam. "She's a charmer, Sam. But more than that, she's honest. And she honestly loves you. And I think that you honestly love her. I can see it in both of you. You've changed, and I like it."

"Oh, Walter, I don't think I could ever go back to what I was before I met her. She's the most incredible woman I've ever met."

Sam continued to stare at Sarah. She felt him, and turned to look at him with that beaming smile. It made him swallow. "The age thing doesn't bother the Oak Wood investor's? Because if it does, I'm afraid my relationship with them might change."

"I was going to ask you if she made you happy, but after that eye exchange, I don't need to. You deserve your happiness, dear boy, and age is just a number." Walter enveloped Sam in a big hug.

~~~

Sarah was in the same chair. Sam had taken his place in the middle. Again the Oak Wood rep talked about Sam, Oak Wood and the spring lines, before opening the conference up for questions.

A reporter from *Human Magazine* asked Sam if he would continue his relationship with Oak Wood.

Sam smiled and answered. "I started with Oak Wood as an eighteen-year-old boy. I am now a forty-one-year old man. I think we have the record for the longest-running collaboration. I would be honored to stay with them as long as they want me." As the press started getting loud, Sam held up his hand. "But I do plan on making huge changes in the coming year. My scheduling will be considerably slower, and I plan on being very selective on the contracts I sign. I will continue to promote my charities and British menswear. Let's face it guy's, you see this face on something every day. You see interviews in print weekly. You have got to be fucking sick of me! I know I am!"

A local reporter asked, "Would that have anything to do with Ms. Reid?"

He turned and looked at Sarah with a blinding smile before he turned back to the crowd. "Absolutely."

Europe Magazine asked, "So you're going to slow down because of Ms. Reid?"

Sam took his time before he answered. He rubbed his hands together and brushed the stubble on his chin. "Let's just say that my family and I have been discussing it for a while. I'm not twenty, or even thirty anymore. I have been blessed with a good income, so I don't have to work. I set out to make changes in the male modeling arena, and I've done that. I have nothing left to prove. Sarah just helped me see that anything was possible. I'm ready for those possibilities."

"Would Ms. Reid like to comment?" asked a reporter from a Milan paper.

Sarah looked at Sam. She hadn't planned on commenting at all. She had said her piece earlier in the day. Sam looked at the reporter. "Ask her yourself."

The reporter looked at Sarah. She took her time before answering, and when she did, it was said softly. "I learned almost five years ago that life is fleeting, and can be gone in the blink of an eye. My experience has taught me to treasure anything that makes me happy, and that feeds my spirit. I have *chosen* that. I refuse to surround myself with negativity. I have wonderful children, and great friends that I thought kept my soul full. I didn't realize until recently, that I wasn't full. Sam is helping me with that." Sarah smiled that blinding smile at Sam. "Sam deserves to have whatever and whomever he treasures. But much more than that, he needs to be full. You all do. Sam is working on that. I recommend that you all do the same."

It was quiet for a long time. Sarah had caused everyone to pause. Sam finally stood up and said, "You all are very familiar with the Oak Wood campaign as I see you every year. You know how I feel about the company. With that said, we are done. I have to go kiss my woman." Sam strode to Sarah, who had stood up when he did. He wrapped her in his arms, crushed her to his hard chest and kissed her a long, slow kiss. He leaned his forehead against hers. "*You* are my treasure, Sarah. You feed my spirit every day, and I love you. That's all I need."

Sam and Sarah did not stick around to chat with anyone. They went straight back to their room and whispered sweet nothings to each other as they made love. They absorbed each other's touch and smell and caress. They just needed to be.

Chapter 24:

The meet and greet that was scheduled for Tuesday evening was just for the staff, runway models and their agencies, and the Oak Wood people. It would be low-key, with good food, music, and dancing. Sam and Sarah looked forward to it, as the city was too busy to do anything outside of the hotel.

This time, they didn't match. Thank God. Sam rocked a pair of jeans and black v-neck T-shirt. Sam being Sam, he donned a black jacket and black Cuban heels. All of the black with his blue eyes made Sarah want to lick him. She wore skinny jeans with a tight-fitting turquoise T-shirt and those damn black boots. Her hair looked like they had just finished making out. Sam didn't know what to look at first. Those boots or Sarah's tits. He grabbed her and growled. "Let's just stay in, so I can take that shirt off."

Sarah laughed and backed up. "No way! I'm ready to let my hair down, drink some tequila, and dance!" She stopped and looked at him. "That's okay, isn't it?"

"Tequila! I can't wait! Come on amazing Sarah! Let's get drunk and hump each other on the dance floor."

Reporters still milled about in the lobby. Sam and Sarah were more than happy to stop for some pictures. They could hear the music thumping already, and the sound of lots of voices. They opened the doors and were met with all manner of dress and age. Sarah had never seen so many half-naked women. She looked at Sam and commented, "I've never seen so many boobs and legs in one place in my life."

"Ah, but the best legs and boobs in the room are yours. Hopefully, later, the legs will be wrapped around my waist, and the boobs will be in my mouth." Sam laughed at the look on her face as he dragged her into the room.

They found a table before Sam asked what Sarah wanted. She grinned wickedly. "I was serious, Sam. Bring a bottle of Patron, shot glasses, some sliced limes and a bowl of salt. We are going toe to toe buddy!" Sam laughed all the way to the bar.

"Hi Sarah! Can we party with you guys?" Sarah turned to see Walter and Sally Lemons headed her way. Sarah couldn't help it. She tried. She honestly did, but she started to giggle as she got up to hug Sally.

"If you want to party with Sam and me, you better be prepared to drink some tequila. I'm trying to get Sam drunk tonight, so I can take advantage of him."

Walter and Sally howled with laughter, and they were still howling when Sam got back with the tray full of Sarah's requested items. "What's so funny?" Sam quizzically asked. That just set them all off again. Sarah jumped up and said over her shoulder as she walked away. "I'll get two more glasses for the party animals."

Several people who Sarah recognized but whose names she didn't remember, said hello as she walked through the crowd. She smiled at everyone and waved. She had a lot of eyes on her as she stood at the bar and waited for the shot glasses. Sarah felt someone come up behind her as they whispered in her ear. "Hello beautiful." As it had been whispered in a lyrical Italian accent, Sarah didn't turn around. She waited for her glasses and said, "Hello Luca! You better save some dances for me. And when we're done doing that, will you run off to South America with me?" Sarah got her glasses and turned around.

Luca laughed as he kissed her cheeks. "I will run off to anywhere you wish, Tesoro. Your wish is my command."

Sarah raised her eyebrows at him. "You could be a dangerous man, Luca. I'll keep that in mind. Should I get another glass?" She indicated the shot glasses.

Luca looked and grinned. "I don't know what we'll be partaking in tonight, but it could get interesting. Sign me up!"

Sarah got another shot glass and Luca followed her back to the table. As she approached their table, Sarah chirped at Sam and the Lemons'. "Look who I found trying to pick up the ladies."

Sam growled. "I'm sure the only lady he was trying to pick up was you."

Luca looked at Sarah, Sam, Sally, and Walter. He grinned broadly. "This is going to be fun!"

Sally watched Sarah set up the bar. "I love margaritas, but I don't really know what you're doing with the salt and limes." Everyone howled with laughter.

"Sally, I love you, but I don't see you staying long tonight. And I want you to know that it's okay. I just wanted to tell you that before we start. Alright?" Sarah filled up the shot glasses. Sam snorted, as did Luca and Walter. "Sam, I think we're going to need another bottle and more provisions, because something tells me that Luca will keep up with us for a while."

Sam stared at Luca and then at Sarah. He turned his gaze back to Luca. "You're trying to get me drunk to get in my pants. Or you're trying to steal my woman. Either way, it could get dangerous!" Sam left everyone laughing as he went for more tequila, limes, and salt.

When Sam returned, Sarah explained to Sally how to do a shot of tequila. "First, lick the top of your hand. Like this." Sarah licked, and Sam and Luca stared at her tongue. Walter noticed both of them, and started to snort. He looked forward to watching his wife do her first shot of tequila at the age of seventy-three, and he was definitely going to enjoy watching the testosterone fly between Luca and Sam. Walter didn't have the heart to tell Luca that it was a losing battle.

"After you put the salt on your hand you lick it, then you shoot the tequila." Sarah tipped her head back and downed the shot. "Then you suck the lime. Like this." Both Luca and Sam swallowed. "It's kind of like mixing a margarita in your mouth. You just don't need a blender."

Sarah turned and looked at the men. "That one will put me ahead of you gentlemen all night. And could you both put your dicks away? I can feel you two marking your territory under the table!" Walter choked, and Sally squeaked. The men stood there with their mouths agape.

Sally was able to partake of two shots. Sarah hugged her and told her how proud she was of her and promised to find her at the runway show. Walter gave Sarah a kiss on the cheek, and told her how much fun he'd had, and how great it was that she had given Sally a first. He assured her that they would see her Thursday. They said their goodnights. Sarah smiled as she watched them slowly walk out of the venue.

Sarah turned to Sam and Luca. "I just love them! I want to be just like them when I grow up."

"You do realize that they're my bosses, don't you? And they're elderly? You just made one of my elderly bosses do two shots of tequila. What do you have to say for yourself?" Sam stood with his arms crossed and frowned at her.

"I would say that she's fucking awesome. I would say that her husband adores her. And I would say that they both adore you. You are their surrogate son, because Sally told me so. So, I did with them what I do with my children. We drink, we eat, and we curse! Drink up bitches!"

Luca and Sam silently stared at her, then each other, before they burst out laughing. After doing two more shots of tequila, Sarah stood. "I love this song! Let's dance!"

"Sarah, I don't know how to dance. Only slow dancing." Sam wished that being tipsy would help with the dancing, but he knew it wouldn't.

"Okay! I'll grab you for the next slow one. Come on Luca, you're gonna shake your money maker!" Sarah grabbed Luca and dragged him away. Luca looked helplessly back at Sam as he was swallowed by the crowd.

Sam sat grinning at nothing. How he loved that woman! When was the last time he'd let his hair down? He couldn't remember. He liked his alcohol. He was British, for God's sake. And he had gotten drunk many times. But he couldn't remember the last time, except for the night that Sarah had left London. He was tipsy, and relaxed, and having fun. Because of her. It's like she knew exactly what he needed. He noticed that the crowd had stopped around the dance floor. He wondered what was going on, so he walked over to see.

There was Sarah and Luca in the middle of the dance floor, dancing to One Republic's "When Love Runs Out." Or rather, Sarah danced while Luca tried to keep up. Sarah gyrated and stomped and moved her head and body in ways that Sam had never seen. Bloody hell! Sarah was an amazing dancer. Sam realized that Sarah did everything well. She certainly danced well. No, not well, not good. She was fucking great! Evidently everyone else at the party thought so, too, as they had moved off of the floor to watch her. The song over, Sarah grabbed Luca's hand with a smile on her face. She hadn't even noticed that they were the only ones left on the dance floor until everyone started to clapped. She looked around and grinned. Instead of being embarrassed, she took a big bow and blew kisses to everyone. She walked up to Sam, wrapped her arms around his neck and kissed him. He grinned against her mouth.

Sarah had a different dance partner for the next four songs, as all the young men wanted to dance with her. There had been no slow songs yet. Sarah was able to lick her salt, and down her tequila and lime juice in between songs. She was still one up on Sam and Luca. Sam enjoyed watching her, and Sarah knew he watched. She was so happy that he was relaxed and having a good time. She was having a blast. She was in her element with all of the young people. She fed off their energy, and it made her miss her kids.

Sarah made her way to the table when the last song ended. She needed a breather. A pretty young man walked up to ask for the next dance. Sarah laughed. "I'm an old woman! I need a break! But come get me in a little while, okay?" The young man smiled and assured her he would. Sarah asked Sam, "Do you know him?"

Sam smiled and said, "I know most of them. They'll be on the runway Thursday night."

"It'll be nice to recognize faces then. They're all great. Ready for another shot, gentlemen?"

Luca groaned, and shook his head. "I am done, Tesoro. I am not embarrassed to be outdone by your drinking prowess. I am not embarrassed to be outdone by you, beautiful woman. I am an old man, and I am drunk, but if it doesn't work out with Sam, you know we'll be in South America in a heartbeat."

Sarah wrapped her arms around Luca, and kissed him gently on the mouth. Luca sighed and looked to the heavens. Sam just grinned stupidly. "Yep," he thought, "we're shit-faced."

After telling them that he could only imagine the headache he would have in the morning, he moved the photo shoot to the afternoon. After hugs all around, Luca said goodnight.

Sarah sat back down next to Sam. She put her chin in her hand and looked at him. She grinned a goofy grin and said. "I love you, Sam Ramsay."

Sam grinned back. "I love you more, Sarah Reid. And I'm drunk."

"Ready for another?" Sarah asked as she was filling up the shot glasses.

"God, woman! You're trying to kill me. But, unlike Luca, I'm not quitting. Hit me!" Sam did his shot while he watched Sarah do hers. They both grinned at each other with the limes in their mouths like teeth. They giggled. The music turned into a slow song, and Sarah's eyes lit up. "Come on! It's a slow one!" She grabbed Sam's hand and took him to the dance floor.

As Sam wrapped his arms around Sarah, he heard her whisper, "Oh! "Funny Valentine" is a tossup for my favorite song ever."

"Me, too," said Sam. He started singing in her ear as he danced her around the floor.

"Sam, you have a beautiful singing voice! I'm serious." Sarah leaned back at looked at him. "You need to sing to me often. Okay?" Sarah was also impressed with his dancing skills. He had marvelous rhythm. She grinned to herself, and thought, "I *know* he has rhythm."

"Every day, amazing Sarah. If that's what you want." Sam kissed her neck. They slowly worked their way across the floor. Sam was very drunk, but he felt Sarah's heart beat next to his. Her skin was soft, and her breasts pushed against his chest. It was like dancing and feeling sensations in syrup. Thick, warm, and smooth. Sam reached for her lips, and assaulted her mouth with his tongue. She tasted of tequila and salt. Sarah moaned a little.

Sarah felt Sam's hard chest against hers. Her hands were clasped around the tight muscles of his back. She was drunk, but aware enough to feel the sensations that Sam created in her gut. When Sam kissed her, she opened freely and participated willingly. It was like everything was in slow motion, and she never wanted it to end.

The song ended, but Sam and Sarah stayed on the dance floor rocking each other.

Sarah was feeling ornery, and she knew it, but she insisted on one more shot. She knew Sam wouldn't say no, if she was doing one, so she filled the glasses. They did their shots and slammed the glasses on the table.

Sarah cocked her head and asked, "Sam, I'm going to ask you to do something. Please just go with it, okay? Trust me?"

Sam was curious, but he trusted Sarah more than anyone. "Okay. Whatever you want Sarah."

"Whatever?" she teased.

"Outside of murder, pretty much anything. I can't say no to you."

"Come with me. Don't ask questions. Consider this therapy." Sarah got up and took Sam's hand. They walked up to the DJ at the sound system. She released Sam's hand and walked up the steps to his sound board. She talked with him briefly. They both smiled at each other and Sarah came back to Sam. "Sam, remember, you said you trusted me. Please just go with it."

Sam was very drunk. Drunk and confused. What was Sarah up to? When the song ended, the DJ picked up a microphone. "Ladies and gentlemen. We have a treat for you tonight. I believe you all know Sam Ramsay. Most of you have probably worked with him. He's here with Sarah, who I believe you are all getting to know. They are going to entertain us with a couple of songs. Sam? Sarah? Are you ready?"

Sam just stared at Sarah with his mouth open. "There is no fucking way I'm going to sing! I'm not that drunk!"

Sarah pouted prettily and said, "You're going to make me do it all by myself? That seems so mean."

The people had started to clap and chant, "Sam! Sam! Sam!"

"Bloody hell!" Sam thought he was going to puke. But he walked up the steps to take a microphone. He couldn't say no to her.

Sarah had the other microphone. She smiled at him. "I will help you start, but then you're on your own. Please sing it for me, Sam. It reminds me of our first night together."

The music started and Sarah started singing "Fly Me to the Moon."

Sam just stared at her, but finally joined her.

Sarah slowly walked off to the side and watched Sam with her heart on her sleeve as the man she adored sang one of their favorite songs to her. He was wonderful. He had a beautiful singing voice. Sam had been born in the wrong generation. His suits, his style, and his choice of music harkened back to old Hollywood. He was simply a cool dude.

After Sam finished the song he walked over to Sarah and laid a scorching kiss on her. Sarah shivered, clapping and whistling with the rest of the people at the party. It had been that good. When it got quiet again, Sarah sat Sam in a chair in front of her. She took his microphone and gave it back to the DJ. She nodded her head to let him know that she was ready. She had done karaoke a thousand times. She wasn't nervous to sing, but she was nervous to see Sam's reaction. He just sat and watched her with his constant shit-eating grin.

The music started, and Sarah began to sing "You Make Me Feel Like a Natural Woman."

The room was absolutely silent as Sarah finished singing the Aretha Franklin song. Sam sat in stunned silence. Sarah handed the microphone back to a silent DJ. The room erupted, and Sam slowly stood up. As she walked to him, he grabbed her, and put his head in her neck. "Holy fuck, Sarah! You're incredible! You need to sing for a living. I'm so drunk. Is it time to go?"

They stumbled to their room. Sam fell onto the bed and moaned. Sarah got his shoes off, and his jacket. After fumbling with his buttons, she finally got his shirt off, and then his pants. He never moved. Sarah was very inebriated, but not so much that she couldn't admire Sam laying on the bed in all his naked glory. He was absolute perfection. His face was beautiful, and his body looked like a sculpture in marble. She could always appreciate a work of art. No matter how drunk she was. She stripped her own clothes off, and threw them with Sam's on the floor. She turned off the light and crawled in bed next to him.

Chapter 25:

Sarah sat at the table the next morning with a cup of hot coffee when Sam slowly moved and opened his eyes. He squinted as he noticed her. "What time is it?"

"It's ten-thirty. I have water, aspirin, and coffee for you. In that order." Sarah walked over and sat on the side of the bed.

"What time did you get up?" Sam hoarsely asked.

Sarah smiled and said, "Around eight. I showered and went to find food and coffee. How are you feeling?"

"Not as bad as I thought I would. How much tequila did we drink last night?" Sam slowly stretched.

Sarah grinned. "A lot. We went through one bottle of tequila between you, me, Luca, Walter, and Sally. You, me, and Luca went through another, and me and you might have finished one by ourselves. I can't remember."

Sam slowly stretched all of his muscles and then stopped. He opened his eyes and looked at Sarah with panic in his eyes. "Oh my God! Did I sing last night? Did I really sing to a room full of people that I work with?"

"Yes, you did, and quite beautifully. You have a wonderful voice, Sam." Sarah walked to the bed and started to massage Sam's temples.

Sam groaned and closed his eyes, "Just kill me now...fuck."

Sarah laughed quietly. "I'm serious. You were good. I would never let you embarrass yourself Sam, especially with co-workers. But, I was pretty inebriated, too. My judgment might have been askew."

Sam sat up before he winced. "Wait a minute! You were unbelievable. You were like a professional singer! How'd you learn to do that?"

Sarah chuckled. "Thanks. I've always sung. I grew up singing with my folks, and in church. Then David and I puttered around with a couple of bands. I've done a few local musicals. I've just always sung." She shrugged her shoulders like it was no big deal. "You took your first step last night, Sam."

"My first step?"

"Your first step in a new relationship with your co-workers, and part of a relationship you'll have with my kids. Karaoke is a family tradition. I have a karaoke machine at home. We eat good food, drink a lot of alcohol and sing karaoke." Sarah continued to massage his temples.

Sam asked, "Do they sing as well as you?"

"Oh, they're much better than I am, but when you're drunk, it really doesn't matter. It's about the fun and the bonding. Last night was the first of many, Sam. You and Gemma are going to love each other. She's the middle daughter. If you think I'm bawdy, just wait!" Sarah got up to get Sam's water and aspirin. He took them gratefully before he sipped his coffee with a sigh.

Sarah continued. "I'm going to get my hair done. The front desk made arrangements for me. My suggestion for you is, take a shower, then hit the gym downstairs. Sweat the toxins out. I know you're used to going to the gym, and I feel like I've disrupted your routine."

"It's been a beautiful disruption." Sam sipped his coffee and smiled at her. "That actually sounds like a great idea. You'll be okay?"

Sarah smiled. "The shop is just around the corner, so I can walk. I'm lucky the staff pulled it off. It's a little crazy in Milan right now!" She stopped and looked at him. "You're not mad at me are you?"

"Why would I be mad at you? Never mind the why. I could never be mad at you." Sam got out of bed slowly and stretched in all his naked glory. Sarah swallowed and licked her lips.

"I think there will be a different vibe around the others now, Sam. They all enjoyed you so much last night. It's good to let your hair down and just have fun. And to show everyone that you're human. A real person that can have fun. Not some insane image of perfection." Sarah kissed him gently.

Sam hugged her. "I can't even remember the last time I let my hair down. Last night was fun, but I'm going to have to talk to Luca about keeping his hands off my woman!"

Sarah laughed as she picked up her bag. "Ciao!"

Sam stood in the shower and let the hot spray wash some of the previous night off. He couldn't believe that he had actually sung in public. With a microphone, no less. And he had gotten drunk. With co-workers and his bosses. The longer the water ran, the more he realized that he didn't care. He'd had a great time, even though he was paying for it this morning. Danni would be proud of him. She would also understand exactly what Sarah had done for him. He shook his head as he washed his hair. He didn't know what he had done to deserve Sarah, but he was prepared to make big changes in his life. Sarah had been the first big change, last night had been another.

~~~

Sarah sat in the salon chair with foil in her hair. She thought about last night, and the importance of it in Sam's life. Everyone who encountered Sam commented on what a gentleman he was, and he truly was. But, he could seem a little aloof to the younger models and staff. He had set the bar so high that everyone was a little intimidated. She knew that he wanted to keep his public and personal life separate. But having fun, and letting your guard down, if just a little, made for a better working environment. Sarah was sure after last night, that the rest of his work year would be much more pleasant. Everyone had thoroughly loved and enjoyed Sam last night.

~~~

Sam worked out for about an hour, showered again, and felt almost human. He looked up as Sarah came in. He grinned when he saw her new hair color. "Do you like it?" Sarah puffed her hair up with her hand and cocked her hip at him.

"I always like your hair. It's like bedding a different woman every month." He grinned.

Her hair was a lighter brunette, with the tips being pink. It wasn't a loud pink or a fuchsia, just a subtle hint of pink. Sarah showed Sam her toes. "My toes match!"

Sam continued to grin. "I'm sure there's a reason for the pink. You never do anything without thinking it through, so I look forward to the surprise."

Sarah laughed, bent over and gave him a quick kiss. "Feeling better?"

"Feeling and smelling much better. Did you eat? I inhaled the fruit and cheese you left on the table."

"I had a cup of coffee and ate before you got up. Luca said there would be stuff to eat at the shoot, so I can wait for lunch. Are you ready?" Sarah was reaching for her camera and her laptop.

Sam took the laptop from her. "After you, madam."

~~~

It was organized chaos in the room where the photos would be shot. Women scurried around with lights and spray bottles. Men uncoiled electrical cords and put up screens. There were props of all kinds: chairs, couches, tables - even a bed. French doors opened out onto a balcony. Against the wall was a garment rack full of all manner of men's clothing. The other wall had a table set up covered with food. Sarah imagined that it was kind of like craft services on movie shoots.

Luca was in the corner at a table. He said something in Italian to the man who sat next to him. Sarah walked up behind him. She wrapped her arms around him, leaned in, and whispered in his ear. "You shouldn't drink so much the night before, if it's going to make you this grumpy."

Luca stood and turned with a smile on his face. "Tesoro! I see that you survived. I did not think I had when I woke this morning." He kissed her cheeks and walked to hug Sam. "I heard that I missed the best part of the party last night. Who knew that you could sing? And you?" He turned back and grinned at Sarah.

"Bloody hell!" Sam groaned. "I guess everyone's talking about it? I'm so happy to be the topic of conversation this afternoon."

In unison everyone in the room started to clap and laugh.

"You two were amazing!"

"We didn't know you had so many talents Sam!"

Sam looked over at Sarah, shrugged his shoulders, and grinned. Sarah grinned back. Sam turned to the crew and took a deep bow. "I am a man of *many* talents." He turned and smirked at Sarah. "Thank you. Thank you very much. Now! Can we get to work?" The ice broken, Sam walked crossed the room and started to thumb through the clothes rack.

Luca was still laughing when he noticed Sarah's laptop. "Oh, good! You didn't forget! I would really love to look at them now, but I would like to take my time. Can you stay when we're done? I don't know what Sam's schedule is today."

"I made sure that this was all he had scheduled for today. We are yours as long as you need us." Sarah put the laptop on the table.

Luca walked closer and grasped her shoulder. "Thank you, Tesoro."

Sarah was confused. "For what?"

"You have made my Sam... lighter. He is more relaxed and not quite as uncomfortable with his skin. You have eyes like me. You see more than just the beauty on the outside. You see Sam." He looked over at Sam before he turned back to Sarah. "Amore! I love that Sam love's you. And I love that you love our Sam."

Sarah hugged Luca. "Please don't let me interfere with your work.

I want to be an unseen stalker. So if I distract you, please let me know."

"Oh, Tesoro, you are always a distraction to me!" Luca laughed and went back to his work.

Sarah walked around quietly. She recognized most of the people from the night before. She had even danced with several of them. She stopped to chat, and sometimes she would snap a picture of something. Sam watched her as he sat in front of the stylist to have his hair done. She hugged a few of the people there. She was so incredibly comfortable that Sam felt like he had absorbed some of it from her. Like osmosis. This was the first time that he didn't have butterflies or that he wasn't tense for a shoot.

Sarah felt Sam's looks. It was like they had an unseen string stretched between them. They could feel where each of them were without even looking. Sarah turned to see Sam's eyes blazing into hers. She mouthed "I love you." Sam mouthed back. "I love you more."It did not go unnoticed by most of the people there. Sarah heard the women sigh.

Sarah conversed with a lighting tech about the angles, and wattage. She looked up to see Sam across the room naked. His back was to her as he stared through the French doors, deep in thought. A woman sprayed his back and arms with an oily substance before she rubbed it into his skin. The substance made the muscles in his back, neck and arms look more defined, as it redirected the light and shadow of the hard planes of his shoulders. Sarah gasped and her pelvis clenched. No matter how many times she saw Sam's body, it still took her breath away. The lighting tech squeezed Sarah's arm. "I've been working with Luca and Sam for fifteen years.

I can't count how many times I have seen him naked. Sam, not Luca! He was a pretty boy, but he's a gorgeous man. I've never seen anyone as perfect as Sam. He is a work of art."

"Yes. Yes, he is," Sarah whispered.

Sam had changed into a short-sleeved shirt and trousers. He lounged on the couch. Sarah watched him stroke his chin, rub his hands together, or play with the ring on his finger in between takes. When he stood, he always crossed his arms or put a hand in a pocket. He very rarely smiled. Sam was almost always intense. But it had worked for twenty-two years. Sarah continued to walk around quietly.

During a break, Sarah caught Sam leaned up against a ladder checking his phone. He was barefoot and completely oblivious that she was there. She set her camera up on a table across from him and set the timer. She had the remote in her hand when she walked to him. He heard her and looked up with a blinding smile. Sarah stopped and patted her heart as she continued to look at him. He cocked his head and curled his finger. She knew what he thought. "Come here, woman!" She walked slowly up to him and leaned her head into his neck.

"Are you bored yet?" he asked.

"I could never get bored with you in the room, Sam." Sarah sighed and caressed his cheek with her hand, before she kissed him softly. Sam didn't stay soft. He grabbed her waist and pulled her into his chest before he started an exploration of her mouth with his. He put his hands on both sides of her head and kissed her another long, slow kiss. "I love having you here."

"I hope that none of these people have cameras, because

someone could get rich selling the pictures." Sarah stood back to catch her breath.

"The only people in this room that have cameras are Luca and you. Cell phones aren't even allowed, except for Luca and me. Not for my privacy, but because this is Luca's shoot, and no one else's. I'm somewhat surprised that he's allowed you to take pictures." Sam leaned back against the ladder.

"That's because he wants to ravish me in South America. He's trying to butter me up."

The afternoon went by quickly. Sarah couldn't believe it when Luca shouted "That's a wrap! Thank you everyone!"

Sarah grabbed an orange from the food table, and watched Sam talk to one of the clothing assistants. Sam was naturally soft-spoken, but he loudly expressed an opinion to the poor man. Sam finally clapped him on the shoulder then shook his hand, before he walked to Sarah. "What was that all about?"

"It was about the same thing that I've talked to him about before. No polo shirts for this shoot. I have told him, and told him, that I will not wear them. Not only will I never wear them, Luca hates them. I think he got my point."

Sarah would remember that. "I get it. I will never buy you a polo shirt."

Sam took her arm with a grin, "Time to work with Luca. You can help choose the shots from today."

"Oh, I thought this was Luca's shoot."

"It is, but I have the final say. Luca and I are usually always in agreement." Sam walked her to the table that Luca sat at. Sarah just gaped at Sam. She thought to herself, "Smart man! Final say, uh? He's definitely not just a pretty face."

Sarah sat and watched Sam and Luca go through the first third of the photos. They immediately discarded the ones they didn't like. Then they did the same with the second third. As they went through the final third, Sam grabbed Luca's arm. Luca grinned and said. "Ah! I thought you would like these." Luca then looked at Sarah. Sarah saw the look on Sam's face. She got up and walked around to stand behind both of them.

The pictures were of her. There were pictures of her as she used her camera, and talked to the crew. There were close-ups of Sarah as she stared into space. Luca had snapped some of her and Sam. There was one of her as she sat in a chair with her arms thrown over the back and her legs stuck out. The pictures were amazing. Sam looked up at her. Sarah had started to sniffle. They didn't look like her. The pictures were of a beautiful woman who was in control of her world. They presented confidence, beauty, and grace. Sarah knelt by Luca and took his face in her hands. "Thank you, dear friend for making me look so beautiful. To have the great Luca Moretti have enough interest in me, to take my picture, is beyond humbling. Thank you dear, dear man."

Sam was speechless. Sarah looked like a goddess. She photographed beautifully. All of her outer and inner beauty shone like a light for everyone to see. "I have to have all of these." Sam said hoarsely.

"Of course, but, I would truly like to take more of your Sarah, and the two of you together. I see, perhaps, another avenue for Oak Wood." Luca stared at Sam, and Sam slowly shook his head as he continued to look at the photos.

Sarah stood by the French doors and drank a tepid cup of coffee. She waited for Sam and Luca to make their final selections. Sarah didn't need to watch. Sam didn't take a bad picture. She had known from that first glossy, that the camera made love to him. He made it look so easy, but Sarah had finally seen it. His hands as he rubbed them together. His fingers as they played with his ring. His hands as they rubbed his stubble or as he put them in his pockets. After twenty-two years of modeling, Sam was still not comfortable. The work itself made him feel vulnerable and uncomfortable. Sam had confidence in who he was, but not so much in what he was. His beauty made him uncomfortable.

"Sarah! Bring that beautiful body over here! I want to see your work." Luca called her over.

Sarah laughed and walked over. "Alright, you dirty old man!"

Luca and Sam sat on each side of Sarah. She pulled her laptop over and grabbed her camera. "I have a lot on the laptop, but my camera has what I took today."

"Are the London pictures on there?" Sam asked.

"Yes. Even the sad, ugly ones." Sarah said softly. She was very nervous. She felt like she was at a job interview. She knew that she wanted constructive criticism and that Luca would be honest. That's what scared her. It was kind of like wanting compliments for your ugly baby. You wanted the truth, but not really.

She powered up the laptop, and started the slideshow. She was silent as her pictures rolled across the screen. If Luca wanted her to stop, he would say so. They started with pictures of her children, and David. Sam grabbed her hand. He didn't let go. They continued with pictures of her life. There were sunrises, and sunsets. Sam squeezed a little harder. No one said a word. Luca had not asked her to stop on any of them. Sarah's heart broke a little.

There were lots of pictures of Liz, Bev, Julie, and Ashley. Close-ups and moments in mutual admiration. There were lots of children. Then the London pictures started. Sam squeezed so hard that he starting to hurt her hand, but Sarah didn't care. These still felt raw. Next were the pictures of Sam's family. There were a lot of Thomas and Violet and Sam. All of her clothesline pictures were in the same order on the screen, ending with the selfies of her and Sam, and then her in her bed of pain. Sarah heard Sam sniff. Then the Paris pictures. Sam had not seen them. They were fantastic, especially the ones at the café. There were a lot of him. He hadn't even realized that she took them. None of them were posed. They were open and happy and vulnerable. Sam laughed with one of the locals, and with one of an elderly local women who had patted his ass and laughed at him. The slideshow stopped. All Luca said was, "Camera please."

Sarah uploaded her pictures to her laptop and started a slideshow again. There were pictures of the crew with their heads together as they worked. There were pictures of the lighting techs, makeup artists, and assistants. There were pictures of the city off the balcony. Again, lots of Sam. She had taken close-ups of Sam when he was naked. It showed the profile that Sarah loved so much. Sam looked like he was a million miles away, and Sarah had wondered where he was, and what he was thinking. She had taken a long shot of his nakedness after the woman who had spritzed him left him alone to dry. Sam stood with his arms out, and his legs spread, in all of his naked beauty. He looked like DaVinci's Vitruvian Man. Sam's naked loneliness had touched something deep inside of Sarah. He was surrounded by people, but so alone. There were several of Luca. An extreme close-up showed him in profile. Every white hair of his beard looked like brush strokes, and his eye looked like a glacier.

The final ones were of Sam against the ladder as he looked at his phone, the barefoot Sam that she loved, and him as he looked at her and cocked his finger. The last photos showed the two of them as they kissed and held each other. The pictures were done and they all just sat there. Sam was silent but still squeezed Sarah's hand. Sarah felt as if she had died just a little. Luca hadn't said anything. He just sat there. The silence grew uncomfortable. Sarah finally said, "Thanks for looking at them, Luca. I appreciate you taking the time." Sarah started to unplug the camera cords.

Luca grabbed Sarah's hand and looked at her. "Tesoro... do you trust me enough to leave these with me? I'd like to take another look at them in the quiet of my room. I can get them back to you tomorrow." Luca was strangely distracted.

"Of course you can. Keep them as long as you want to. And again, I feel honored that you would take the time. I'm just a small-town girl from Missouri who just had her pictures looked at by the great Luca Moretti. Swoon!"

Luca smiled at her and squeezed her hand. "Sam, can I speak with you before you leave. I have a few questions about your pictures."

Sarah went to get her bag and grabbed a bottle of water. Her heart still ached a little, but she knew that she wouldn't stop taking pictures. Photography gave her joy, but she had been hoping that Luca would at least like some of them. He didn't have to love them. She stood and watched Sam and Luca in deep conversation. They still sat at the table and occasionally Sam would shake his head vehemently. Luca patted Sam on the back. He looked at Sarah and blew her a kiss. Sarah smiled a brittle smile back at him.

Sam and Sarah had been quiet on their way back to the hotel. When they got in the room, Sarah finally exploded. "He could at least have said *something*! That my pictures suck. They're okay. Something." She felt like she might cry. Her photos were like her children. And her children had just been ignored.

Sam wrapped Sarah in his arms. "I've never seen Luca do that. I don't know what it means, but let's just wait until we see him tomorrow. I know that it was hard sharing them with him. But let's just wait." He kissed her forehead.

Sam and Sarah called a taxi to head to the outskirts of Milan for a late dinner. They would be assured of a seat outside the city proper, and they needed to get out of the hotel for awhile. They hadn't eaten anything from the shoot, so they both felt famished. Their driver had recommended a neighborhood ristorante that had good house wine and Cotolettaalla Milanese. Sarah wanted to try the famous Milan veal, and the driver assured her that she wouldn't be disappointed.

They shared a booth and ordered their veal and a risotto dish. They poured their wine and leaned back together in the booth. Sarah sipped her wine and leaned into Sam's chest. They talked about the day as Sam caressed Sarah's neck. Sarah had enjoyed it very much, but she knew without a doubt that Sam did not. He was uncomfortable in his skin in front of the camera. He loved the finished product but not the actual modeling. The scowls and hand rubs were not part of his pose, it was because he didn't quite know what do with himself. He knew that it worked. But she would never let him know that she knew. They talked softly and kissed frequently as they waited for their food.

Sam knew that the dinner had been a good idea. It was quiet, and he knew that Sarah needed quiet. It had been the chaos of the Oak Wood campaign for three weeks, and he was tired. He knew that she had to be, too. She had been with him for almost all of it. As he necked with Sarah, he smelled the sandalwood and felt her soft skin. He had found that he liked the quiet very much, too. Recharging was a very good thing.

Chapter 26:

Sam and Sarah got up early. They showered and had already sat down in the hotel restaurant for breakfast. There were only a few people there so it was quiet.

"What's on your agenda today? I know the runway show starts at four. How early do you have to be there?"

Sam leaned back in his chair, and held his coffee cup in his hands. "I was thinking about hitting the gym again this morning. As far as the show, I have to be there a couple of hours before. Do you mind going that early? I can always have a car bring you later."

"I'd like to go with you. I want to absorb the flavor of a runway show in Milan during Fashion Week. I'm sure I'll find someone to talk with. Walter and Sally will be there won't they?"

"Yeah, they'll be there, but probably not that early. I'll make sure you sit with them in the front row." Sam sipped and continued. "If you don't mind seeing a lot of naked men, you can wander around in the back if you want." He raised his eyebrows and wiggled them at Sarah.

She wiggled her eyebrows right back. "Naked men? Yes please! But the only *man* that will be back there will be you. The rest are just boys."

Sam laughed. "Why, thank you, madam. It's sad, but true. The rest will be eighteen to twenty-year-olds that don't look old enough to shave."

"I would love to see the chaos that goes on back there. I figure everyone already thinks I'm a cougar, so what's it going to hurt?"

Sarah grinned.

"I think cougars are beautiful animals." Sam snorted. "I love petting them, and stroking them, and making them purr." He looked at Sarah over the top of his coffee cup.

Sarah laughed loudly as his phone rang. He looked at the number and then at Sarah. "I think our morning plans might have changed. It's Luca." Sarah's heart sank when she thought about her photos and Luca's silence.

Sam and Sarah held hands in the elevator. They were on their way to Luca's room for coffee and to get Sarah's laptop. Sam gave Sarah's hand a little squeeze. He could feel her tension. Sarah looked up at him. He stood and stared off into space with a funny look in his eyes. "Sam, are you okay?" Sarah whispered.

Sam shook himself a little bit. "Sorry! I zoned out for a minute. More importantly, are you okay?"

"I'll be much better after I get my laptop back." She grimaced. "I just want to get this over with. I would hate for this to change mine and Luca's relationship."

Luca opened the door wearing boxer shorts and a bathrobe. Sarah tried to hide her grin but didn't succeed. Luca looked down and smiled. "I've been busy making lots of phone calls. Give an old man a break!" He hugged Sam and kissed Sarah on the cheek. "Come in! Come in!"

Luca poured them coffee and they sat down at the table. Sarah's laptop was open and the slideshow of her photos was on. "So?" Luca asked as he looked at Sam.

Sam shook his head no. "No. I didn't say anything. And I hate myself for that. But I want Sarah to discuss it with you, and make her own decisions, with no bias from me. These are her pictures, and her life. Not mine."

Sarah looked back and forth at the two men. "What the hell is going on?"

"Tesoro, please." Luca swept his hand at the laptop. "I can only imagine what you thought of me yesterday. I didn't say a word to you, and that hurts my heart, because I know it hurt you. I didn't even think of that until this morning. I wanted a chance to look at all of your photos here in the privacy of my room. I've been looking at them all night."

"All night?" Sarah whispered. "Why?"

"I want to look at them again, with you, Sarah. Not all of them, because I don't need to. I don't want to talk about lenses or angles, or light and shadow. I want you tell me what you were thinking when you took them. Can you do that for me?" Luca asked earnestly.

"Of course."

They went through Sarah's pictures on her laptop. Some they scrolled through, others would grab Luca's attention, and he would ask Sarah, "What were you feeling?" She would answer, and Luca would continue scrolling. When they got to the London pictures, Luca slowed the speed down, and asked even more questions. Then the Paris pictures. Luca had more questions. Then the pictures that she had taken the day before. Luca stopped on all of Sam's pictures and the pictures of her and Sam, just as he had with the London and Paris pictures. Finally, they were done.

Luca had offered no opinions, only questions.

Luca leaned back and looked at Sarah. "All of your pictures are good. They got better over the years, as you gained confidence. You have a very good eye, and you choose your subject matter carefully. But, more importantly, you have emotion attached to your photos. You don't take a picture unless you feel something. That translates to the people looking at your finished photograph."

Sarah looked at Sam with a huge grin, then back at Luca. "Thank you so much! The great Luca Moretti just told me that my pictures are good. I can die happy right now!"

"I'm not done, Sarah." Luca scrolled to the London pictures. "Your life changed in London."

Sarah turned and looked at Sam. "Yes, it did," she whispered.

"As did yours, Sam." It wasn't a question.

"Yes," whispered Sam.

Luca looked at Sarah intently and leaned forward. He took her hands in his. "So did your pictures. I do not want to belittle your life, and your family, as I can see in your pictures how much it all means to you. But something was missing, Sarah. Please do not take offense."

She stared at Luca as a tear rolled down her cheek. Sam saw it, and went to her. He glared at Luca. "Enough!"

"I am not trying to hurt her, Sam. I think Sarah knows that. She knows exactly what I am saying. And she knows that it is true, don't you, Sarah?" Luca looked back at her.

She shook her head, as the tears made rivulets of pain down her face. She had known in her heart, but now her secret was out there for the world to see.

Luca squeezed Sarah's hands. "Please tell Sam why your pictures changed. He needs to know, and you need to tell him."

Sarah had started to panic. Her heart beat erratically and she had a cold sweat on her forehead. She knew what Luca had asked her to do, but she didn't know if she could. She was so afraid. Afraid of what Sam's reaction might be. She couldn't even form the words in her own mind much less say them to Sam. What would she tell her children? She had been trying to come to terms with it in her own brain for several weeks, but hadn't been able to form the complete sentences. It was if the alphabet was missing half the letters. Now the Italian in front of her had seen it in her pictures, and it suddenly made all of the letters reappear. She gasped, removed her hands from Luca's grip and hugged herself as she sobbed.

Sam could feel his anger grow. He wanted to punch Luca in the face. A man that he loved had hurt Sarah, and that just wasn't acceptable. He wanted to sweep her up and take her back to their room and just cradle her in his arms. But, under the anger, was confusion, as he didn't understand what Luca had asked of Sarah.

"Sarah?" whispered Sam. "What is it? It doesn't matter. Whatever it is we'll figure it out, but you have to stop crying. It breaks my heart. Please, Sarah!"

Sarah finally looked up at Luca and stared at him for a long moment.

Luca said again, "You need to tell him, Tesoro. Tell him now, then we will talk some more." He got up and closed the door as he went into the bedroom.

Sarah loved Luca, but right now she hated him just a little, but he was right. He must be a fucking psychic, as he had figured it out by looking at her pictures. No, it was because he saw things as she did. Now that she comprehended what her brain and her heart had been trying to tell her, she needed to tell Sam. Her alphabet was back and she had to start making sentences. They had always been honest with one another, and Sarah wasn't going to start lying by omission.

Sarah slowly turned toward Sam and looked up at him. Sam leaned over and placed her in his lap. "Please Sarah, tell me," he whispered.

She took a deep breath and started. "I adored my husband, Sam. You know that. Our life together was everything that we wanted it to be. It wasn't perfect, because nothing is, but it was more than good. He gave me my three daughters, which is the best thing that ever happened to me. We loved each other deeply, and forever. And I miss him every day."

"I love your capacity for love, amazing Sarah, you know that." Sam continued to cradle her as he rubbed her back..

Sarah exhaled loudly. Her breath hitched a little. She just said it. "I love you differently than David." Sam suddenly got very quiet. "I never had the gut reaction to David that I have with you. I can physically feel your pain, your frustration, your insecurities, your love. It's like I have a magnet in my body that is always trying to connect with you. Wherever you are, I know where, because I *feel* you. It's more than physical, it's as if the other half of my soul is yours. I've been waiting for you for a long time." She swallowed.

"I never felt that with David. Never. But with you, it's as if I've found my last jigsaw puzzle piece. You are me, and I am you. Two halves that make a whole." Sarah whispered, "Please don't be scared Sam, as I honestly think I might die, but I love you more than I've ever loved anything or anyone. It's so big it hurts."

Sam finally lifted her off of his lap and placed her in the chair in front of him. He hadn't said a word, which made her start crying again. Sam knelt on the floor in front of her. He took Sarah's hands. "Please look at me, Amazing Sarah." She did.

Sam whispered, "I told you I believed in destiny, and that I thought we were destined to meet. I knew that the moment you opened that hotel room door in St. Louis. I *knew* it. I told you that I thought that you were saving my life, Sarah, and you have. You just said exactly what I've known, but couldn't find the words. I'm a different person when you're not with me. It's as if I'm sleepwalking, or I'm missing a battery, not fully charged. I'm not Sam without Sarah."

Sarah whispered hoarsely, "It's as if we've always known each other. I feel as if we've kept missing each other over lifetimes. It scares the hell out of me."

~~~

Luca had been in the bathroom a long time. He cleared his throat as he came out. He found Sam and Sarah wrapped up in each other as they laid side by side on the bed. He sighed and smiled.

"Sarah, I want to hire you to work with me, and I want to do a layout with you and Sam as the models. I also want to talk to you about doing Sam's next shoot on your own, wherever you would like to do it." Sarah slowly turned to Luca. Her eyes were swollen.

"Now go to your room and fuck like rabbits, because Sam has a runway show to do, and you don't have a lot of time. Sam can fill you in on some of my ideas. Think about it, and we'll talk tomorrow. Now get out!"

They held hands in the elevator and stared at each other. They were silent until they entered their suite. Sam turned quickly and wrapped Sarah in his arms. "Damn it! I'm so sorry I didn't say anything, Sarah! I know how upset you were. I thought this was between you and Luca. I'm gutted. Was I wrong?"

She nestled closer into his chest. "Oh, Sam, I understand. I think I'm still in shock. My only complaint is that you said this was my life and my decision." She looked up at Sam's face and caressed the sharp plane of his jaw. "You're wrong. This *is* my life, but it's also yours, and my children's. We need to make decisions together, as a family. This is *our* journey."

Sam's eyes widened. "As a family?"

"Like it or not, you've acquired three daughters and a son-in-law. Along with a woman who is a little shell-shocked right now. I don't even want to start the conversation, because we don't have time. Luca might want to talk tomorrow, but he's going to have to wait. There are people we need to talk to, and I need to ice my eyes before I get ready."

Before she could extricate herself from Sam's arms, he grabbed her again. "You are amazing, Sarah. Forget what Luca said. I never want to fuck like rabbits. They do it very rapidly. Five seconds and they're done. Granted, they do it many times a day, but I would rather do it slow once or twice." He kissed Sarah's cheeks, her nose and finally her mouth.

~~~

Sarah was the only one who needed to dress for the show. Sam's designer duds that he would be wearing on the runway were already at the venue. He had on trousers, a T-shirt, and flip flops. His clothes for the after-party were in a garment bag that he would take with him. They had decided to attend the party for a little while, but they were going to make it an night early. They had a lot to talk about. Sarah asked for one of Sam's dress shirts, and had gone into the bathroom to get ready.

Sarah emerged dressed in a black wool men's suit. Black trousers draped her legs and a black suit jacket with silk lapels cinched in at her waist looked as if it had been tailored just for her.. She wore Sam's white shirt. Boy did she wear it. Sam looked at her and gulped. He shouldn't have been surprised, as Sarah was a stylish woman. She wasn't wearing a tie. The shirt was unbuttoned half way down the placket. She was wearing a lacy black bra that revealed her cleavage. Sam growled. "Damn, Sarah! I just want to eat you up."

Sarah slipped her feet into red stilettos. "If you're a good boy on the runway, you can do that later." She slipped pearls in her ears and on her wrist, grabbed a red clutch bag, and out the door they went.

Sam and Sarah made their way to the backstage area. It was already a cacophony of sights, sounds, and smells. There were boys in all manner of dress and undress, hair product, deodorant, makeup, shoes, and rack after rack of designer clothes. All they heard was a continuous buzz of people talking over each other.

Sam looked at Sarah and said, "Welcome to the backstage of the runway show in Milan during Fashion Week."

Sarah grinned and looked around. "How on earth does anything get done?"

"Disorganized organization." Sam laughed. He took her hand and made his way to the back corner. Even the great Sam Ramsay didn't have a dressing room. His clothes were hung on racks just like everyone else. A makeup table with the lights ablaze waited.

"Will they oil you down and do your hair and makeup like they did at the shoot?" Sarah asked.

He shook his head. "No grease. It would get on the clothes. You know I don't use makeup. Though, if I get sweaty, they'll powder me. Stu will coif my mess of hair, and Paul will help with my changes. It's always really rushed. The women will go first, then the men."

Sarah shook her head and grinned broadly. "I would love to stay and watch all the goings on, but I'm more excited about you walking that catwalk. All the women -and most of the men - will be drooling over you, and they'll all want to scratch my eyes out. It'll be really hard to hear anything with all the ovaries that are going to be exploding."

"Why would they want to scratch your eyes out?" asked Sam uncertainly.

Sarah laughed a deliciously wicked laugh as she kissed him full on the mouth. "Because I'm the one going home with you. I'm the one that gets to see your beautiful naked body. The only ovaries in close proximity to the Sam Ramsay will be mine. Ciao!" Sarah waved a little wave, and walked off to explore.

As Sarah walked around and talked to a few of the people she knew, the flashbulbs went off in her face. All the reporters wanted to talk to her. She spoke to a few of them, and told them that it was her first time in Milan for Fashion Week and how excited she was. They asked about her designer, and she laughed and told them that the suit had been purchased a long time ago from Macy's and that the shirt was Sam's. And that, yes, she was more excited to see the men's fashion. That remark elicited a few chuckles from the press.

Sarah spotted Sally and Walter Lemons, and together they found their seats. They were at the very end of the catwalk in the front row. They would have an unobstructed view of Sam as he walked the length, stopped, posed, and walked back. She was strangely excited. Sarah knew that the runway had been Sam's bread and butter, and how he paid his bills all those years ago. Plus, there was *no one* who wore a suit like Sam. Sarah sighed, smiled a quiet smile and leaned back in her chair. Sally looked at Sarah and patted her hand.

The lights dimmed as the designer came out to introduce his fashion line and the sponsorship of Oak Wood. Techno music blared, and the women started their walks. First came swimwear, then loungewear, before it ended with formal wear. Sarah liked some of the dresses, but couldn't wrap her head around the fact that they were all so skinny. As the women's portion ended, and a buzz went through the room. It was the Sam Ramsay show. Everyone was more excited to see him then the actual fashion, as Sam did not do any other runway anymore. This was a yearly treat for all the fashionista's. Sarah felt a sense of pride in Sam's hard work. He had earned the accolades.

As before, the designer came out and introduced his spring collection, but also thanked Sam personally for participating. The crowd erupted with cat calls, wolf whistles, and applause. Sarah swallowed as she remembered that Sam was a big deal. The lights dimmed, and the first few bars of Stevie Ray Vaughan's Riviera Paradise started. The audience hushed, and Sarah's lungs stopped working. She loved Stevie Ray Vaughan. A little "Oh!" escaped Sarah's lips and her eyes got large. Sam came out from the side of the stage in nothing but tight boxer briefs. You could hear a collective gasp, as he walked languidly down the smooth white runway. That body. That face. Sarah had still not taken a breath. She was mesmerized by the pure sexuality that was Sam. He slowly walked toward Sarah. Their eyes met from the moment he had walked out. The closer Sam got, the darker his eyes became. He scorched her with his heat. He stopped at the end and stared at Sarah so intensely, that she felt the heat start at her pelvis and work its way up her torso, her breasts, and her face. Sarah heard Sally say, "Oh, my....." as if she was far away.

You could have heard a pin drop after the men had finished modeling the underwear. Sam had walked three times, and each time was as intense as the first. Everyone had begun to stare at Sarah, but she had tunnel vision. She noticed no one but Sam. She had not been this lustful since the Red Dress Benefit. That's what she and Sam had started calling it. In capital letters. She wanted to hunt him down, strip him naked, and fuck him on the runway for everyone to see.

Stevie Ray Vaughan continued to play over the speakers. "Little Sister" started the swimwear presentation. Sarah knew that Sam had to have pulled some strings for the music choices for the entire presentation. She knew that it was for her. Sam entered the runway in blue trunks and met her eyes again with that sexy as hell grin. It made Sarah flex her thighs together. She knew they were both going to hell for the lustful images that were playing like a porn movie in their heads. He reached the end of the runway and winked at her. She would have to kill him later for putting her in such a painfully, frustrated position. She would kill him after she rode him.

Sarah looked forward to the formalwear, and also for the music selection. Sam walked out before the music started. He stood there and stared down the runway at Sarah. The speakers pulsed out the first beautiful chords of "Lenny." Sam was dressed in a white wool jacket with black trousers and shoes, a white shirt, and black tie. He was classic, old Hollywood. He wore the famous intense Sam scowl. He stalked Sarah down the runway. The audience had gotten the idea that Sam was going to get to the end of the runway and devour her. Sarah felt it. He stopped and continued to stare intensely at her. She never stopped looking up at him. She couldn't. It was as if she had been hypnotized, and was not capable of breaking the spell that Sam had put her under.

The next ensemble was a dark gray tuxedo jacket and trousers, with lighter gray piping on the lapels. It was set off by a white shirt, and a gray and white waistcoat with a gray tie. There was a red pocket square in the breast pocket. Sarah wanted to lick Sam. Everywhere.

When Sam walked off to change into his last ensemble, Sarah finally exhaled and collected herself. She had the feeling she would need it.

Sam walked out in a classic black wool tuxedo, with a white shirt, black bow tie, and a white pocket square. He held a red rose in his hands. "Fly Me To the Moon" started to play over the speakers as he walked straight to Sarah. Sarah swallowed. Sam walked straight to the end of the runway and stopped. He crouched down on his heels and crooked his finger at her. Sarah slowly got up and walked the few steps to him. She was incapable of doing anything else. She looked up at him as he put his hand behind her neck, gave her a long, slow kiss, and handed her the rose.

Sarah was still in a lust-filled daze when the show ended. Everyone tried to get to her, and a million people asked her questions. As her legs were still jelly, she continued to sit in her seat. She heard everyone as if they were background noise. She didn't care what they said. She didn't care what they asked. She felt Sam before she saw him. She looked up and saw him as he made his way to her. Everyone parted as if he was Moses parting the Red Sea. He strode to her and roughly jerked her body to his roughly. She knew that she would have bruises on her arms the next day. She didn't care. All she felt was Sam's pounding heart and his hard arousal. He scorched her mouth and growled in her ear. "We're not going to that fucking party."

Chapter 27:

Sam had taken Sarah's hand and not let go. The elevator ride was silent. They stood with their fingers entwined and stared at each other. In silence. The sexual tension was so thick that you could cut it with a knife. When they entered the room Sam turned on the table lamp in the corner. He didn't want darkness. He wanted to see Sarah when he made her come. They stood as Sam pulled her jacket off and slowly unbuttoned the rest of Sarah's buttons. He pulled her shirt out of the waistband of her trousers and threw them on the chair. Sarah proceeded to pull Sam's T-shirt over his head and unzipped his trousers. He stepped out of them and pulled Sarah's panties down. He unclasped her bra to see that her nipples were already hard. Sam brushed his knuckles softly over them and heard Sarah moan.

She ran her hands down Sam's hard torso and sighed. She lightly used her fingertips to brush across the hard muscles of his abdomen. It was his turn to moan. They looked and touched and memorized every hard plane and angle; every soft and silky curve.

Sam was intoxicated by the woman in front of him. She was beautifully excited, and her eyes were glazed. She offered him everything. He treasured her body, her mind, and her heart. He inhaled the sandalwood and felt the silkiness of her collarbone before he leaned down and licked it.

Sarah looked at the man in front of her. He took her breath away, and the way he looked at her made her lose her mind. She thought about what she had just experienced on the runway. She lusted after Sam. He made her ache in ways that she had never ached before. Sarah loved the way that his blue eyes could change shades depending on either the light, or his mood. Right now, they were almost black with desire.

Sarah took Sam's hand and led him to the bed. As he lay down, Sarah straddled him and leaned over and kissed his bottom lip. Her breasts teased him, and Sam groaned. He reached for her, but Sarah said hoarsely, "No. Right now, you're mine." She kissed his ears and then his jaw line. She loved the way his stubble tickled her body. She ran her fingers through his black hair. She loved it in the mornings when it hung over his forehead in all of its wild abandon. She kissed and caressed his chest and stomach. She could die a happy woman if the last thing she saw was that torso. She licked the obliques that she lusted after. She kissed and licked her way from his collar bones to his wrists. She took his fingers one by one and sucked them into her mouth.

Sam groaned, "God, Sarah! I need to touch you." She shook her head and continued her travels down his body. She was ready to explode, but she wasn't done. She made her way down his thighs before she kissed then licked his erection. Sam bucked and groaned. She kissed him behind his knees, then his calves and feet. She worshipped his body as she kissed and licked her way back up to his face. She licked his mouth with her tongue before Sam caught her tongue with his own and took her breasts in his hands. He lowered his head and took one of her breasts in his mouth as he fluttered his fingers gently across the other one. Sarah moaned as he switched. She lifted her hips and slowly lowered herself, inch by slow inch. She felt Sam's thigh muscles tighten before he grabbed her ass with both hands and groaned. She moaned and rolled her hips for several beats before she rocked slowly then moved up and down. Again, she rocked and moved up and down.

She moaned against Sam's mouth, "So hot; so full; so good."

Sam gritted his teeth and watched her with his black eyes as he felt her grip and convulse around him. Sarah was spent, but Sam was not.

He looked into her eyes and growled, "Turn around. Get on your hands and knees."

Sarah's eyes grew large at his demanding tone, but she did as he asked. She turned with her head toward the foot of the bed and rested on her hands and knees. Sam loved that she trusted him. She asked no questions. She was only interested in pleasure. Sam stopped and looked at Sarah's ample ass. He kissed and fondled each cheek. As he hovered over her he whispered in her ear. "Look up, Amazing Sarah. I want to see our faces when we come together."

As she lifted her head she was met with the mirrored image of her and Sam. Her lips were swollen, and her eyes looked drugged. She was addicted. Sam hovered over her as he watched them both in the mirror. He had his hands on each side of her ass. He gave one hard thrust and they both lost their minds together. It was pure wanton sex. There was nothing but grunts, sweat, and the slap, slap, slap of skin on skin. Sarah watched as Sam's body met hers with each thrust. As Sarah spiraled over the edge, Sam gave a loud grunt and roared, "Mine!"

Sam lay on Sarah as they tried to catch their breath. They were tangled in the sheets and each other. Sam held on to Sarah's ass. Sarah hadn't unclenched the sheets from her fisted hands. She turned over and looked at the ceiling. A small drop of sweat rolled slowly between her breasts. As Sam rubbed it with a fingertip, he asked her quietly. "Are you okay, Sarah?"

"I feel like such a slut. But that was hot." Sarah grinned up at him. Sam snorted and held her closer. "When did you notice the mirror?"

Sam shrugged. "Tonight, when you were on top of me. I saw the reflection of your back. I've never done that before." Sarah looked at him incredulously. "No! I mean, I've done *that* before, but I've never used a 'prop' so to speak." Sam cupped Sarah's cheeks, and said hoarsely. "I don't ever want to not be able to see your eyes when I pleasure you Sarah, but I don't want you to ever feel uncomfortable. That would kill me."

"Sam," whispered Sarah. "That's the last thing you would ever do to me. You couldn't. You're too much of a gentleman. Well...outside of the bedroom, anyway."

Sam exhaled, chuckled softly, and asked, "I guess I just took for granted that it was a new experience for you, too. Was it?"

Sarah smiled. "I've experienced the "bow wow wow". I think most men like it. To be honest, I'm no novice to props. I was married a long time. David and I worked hard to keep the spark lit for both of us. But no mirrors. That was unbelievably sexy."

Sam wiggled his eyebrows. "Hmmm...props? That has piqued my interest. In the future, maybe you can show me some of these props?"

Sarah giggled. "Oh, you just wait! Come on! Let's shower. We need to talk before I call the kids tomorrow."

They showered and made their way back to bed. "Before we start talking about Luca and his ideas, I need to ask you something." Sarah leaned over on Sam's chest. "Did you pick out the music tonight Sam? Was the rose your idea?"

Sam rubbed his fingers up and down Sarah's arm. He couldn't stop. "Of course I did, and yes, it was. Tonight was all for you, Sarah. And a little bit for me. It was the last runway I'll do. What better way to end it than with you."

Sarah sat up and looked at Sam very seriously. "Tonight was bittersweet. It broke my heart in many good and different ways. You know how much I love Stevie Ray, and my two favorite songs of his are Riviera Paradise and Lenny. I can't believe you remembered me telling you that. And, are you serious? Your last runway? You owned that room. There were moments, Sam, when you could hear a pin drop. You are a big, fucking deal. I was so proud to experience it."

"Ah, Sarah, I remember everything you tell me. And, yes, that was my last runway. It's the only one I do anymore. I've been thinking about it for a couple of years, but meeting you has made me finally start making some decisions. I'll still do the campaign, but no more runways. I'm over them. Plus, everyone is going to be talking about this one for a long time. It was as much about you, as it was me." Sam leaned over and kissed her.

"Sam, do you realize that you haven't read a paper, or done any kind of interview, other than the press conferences, this entire campaign?"

Sam stared off somewhere over Sarah's shoulder. "Huh. I hadn't even thought about it. If you hadn't come, that's all I would have done. It always helped to pass the time." He refocused on Sarah. "See what you've done to me? You've helped me start living a life." Sam embraced her, and stroked her hair as he murmured over and over again how much he loved her.

They laid together for a long time, before Sarah brought the conversation back to Luca. "Was he serious, Sam?"

"He was. I've known Luca for a long time, and I've never seen him look at someone else's pictures. He's excited, Sarah. He's excited about you, and I don't know how I feel about that."

"To be honest, I'm not sure how I feel about it either."

"Sarah? If we're going to have a serious conversation, you're going to have to put some clothes on. I find you very distracting."

Sarah laughed and slid out of the bed. She walked slowly across the room and swayed her hips a little more than usual. Sam groaned. Sarah laughed again, and put on her T-shirt. She came back to the bed, and asked. "Better now, Sam?"

"Yes. Thank you very much." Sam grinned and got comfortable. "What do you not feel comfortable about?"

She thought before she answered. "We're in this together, right?"

"Always." He leaned over and kissed her softly.

"And you have to stop kissing me," Sarah sighed, "if we're going to have a serious conversation."

"I can't make any promises, amazing Sarah." Sam twined his fingers through hers and laid back on his pillow.

"Okay. My biggest concern is that while you're slowing down your schedule, I would be speeding up mine. We'd be right back to where we are now. Except that you'd be meeting me somewhere.

I love my home, and I've been away from it a lot lately. But being away because I love you, and I want to spend time with you, is different than being away because I'm working."

Sam played with her fingers that were clasped in his own. "Those were my thoughts exactly. But I'm being selfish. I want to spend as much time with you as possible."

"Was he serious about the layout, Sam? Why on earth would he want me in your pictures?"

"Did you not *see* them Sarah?" Sam was incredulous. "You honestly never even looked at yourself, did you?"

"I was taking the pictures of you, Sam, not me."

Sam shook his head, and reached for Sarah's face. "When I saw those pictures yesterday, all I could see, and I all I could feel, was the love that was on your face. And the love that was on mine. We were beautiful together."

"You're always beautiful, Sam. I've never seen a bad photo of you. Even the outtakes, and unpublished ones are amazing."

Sam shook his head. "I've never had a picture taken by anyone, including Luca, that captured my feelings like you did. Of course, I've never been in love before. But Luca took my pictures yesterday, too. He didn't capture what you captured. We need to do the spread. I want the world to see what we are together."

"Can I choose what, where, and when?" asked Sarah.

"I think you could ask Luca to shoot us in the loo, and he'd be thrilled," Sam laughed. "He wants you bad, Sarah. So, yes, I think he'll go for whatever you want."

"Okay. I'll let him know that the spread is a go, but I have to talk to my children and the girls about the scheduling. He'll just have to wait. This is a group decision that can't be rushed." Sarah was firm in her resolve.

"Any ideas yet?" Sam asked as he hugged her. " I know you, and I can see your wheels turning."

She pinched his arm. "Well, actually, yes." She raised her eyebrows. "Where will we be next week?"

"Venice?"

Sarah laughed and nodded yes. "It will be my first experience being a professional, in a place I've wanted to go to my entire life. And to be in love? Life is good."

~~~

Sarah had the laptop open on the table the next morning. She group texted her children the night before, and now waited for the familiar ping of SKYPE. She, Sam, Charlie and her husband Trace, Gemma and Harper would discuss her options. She wanted input from everyone. But she was a little nervous. Sam had talked, via text and phone calls, to all three of her daughters. The girls had all done their research, so they knew who Sam was, and what he looked like, but this would be the first in-person conversation. Sam had been warned.

Sam and Sarah heard the ping, and connected with Harper. Then Charlie and Trace and Gemma were connected. All three of the girls started to scream at the same time, as they tried to say hello to their mother.

Charlie and Trace were first. "Mom! How the hell are you? We miss your face!"

"What's up, bitch?" Gemma asked, grinning.

Harper waited for them to get that out of the way as she studied her mother's face. When it got quiet, she looked at Sarah, and leaned close to the screen. "Yep. You've been getting laid. You've been getting laid a lot." She looked at Sam as he sat next to her mother. "Are you the Sam that's been giving her the high, hard one? Or would that be another Sam?" Harper lifted her eyebrows as her sisters cackled in the background.

Sam looked at Sarah, who by this time had her face in her hands. Her shoulders shook with laughter. "I hope I'm the only Sam who's giving her the high, hard one!"

It was quiet for a moment, then everyone started laughing. Sarah grinned at Sam. "I told you."

Sam stared at the screen in wonder. He had seen lots of pictures of Sarah's family, but it hadn't prepared him for the real thing. Charlie, Gemma, and Harper were beautiful women. They were beyond beautiful, they were stunning. They all had hair as dark as him, and all three of them had eyes that were sapphire blue. They could grace the covers of magazines. But Sam's next thought came straight from his brain and out his mouth. "Oh fuck!!! I've died and gone to heaven! I'm surrounded by a bunch of bawdy women!"

After everyone caught their breath, Sarah reported what Luca had in mind. All three of the girls, and Trace, agreed with Sam immediately.

"Mom! Do the photo spread!" Trace exclaimed.

Charlie grabbed Trace's arm and leaned forward. "Now the whole world can see what we've always seen. How absolutely stunning our mother is. I'm getting a little weepy just thinking about it."

"I've been trying to get her to see in herself what I saw immediately, but she needed to hear it from you guys." Sam lightly kissed Sarah's neck as she caressed his cheek.

After the girls finished cooing over the display of love between the two of them, Gemma looked at Sam and asked, "Hey, Sam? Could you get the room service menu?"

Sam looked quizzically at Sarah. She just shrugged her shoulders. She had no idea what Gemma was up to. Sam stood up and leaned over the computer to get the menu. As he did, all three girls started to wolf whistle and moan suggestively. Trace just grinned and looked down at his feet. Sam sat back down with the menu and cocked an eyebrow at Gemma.

"Good Lord, man! Just read the fucking menu out loud with that Colin Firth, Hugh Grant, Michael Caine British accent. I haven't had a man in a couple of months, and your voice makes me want a vibrator and a cigarette."

Sam looked at Gemma with his mouth open. Then he shut it. "That's a first. I've had a million women want my body or my face, but I have never had anyone want to pleasure themselves with my voice. Thanks for that, Gemma. Perhaps I will hire a voice coach to fine tune what you obviously think is a gift."

They all laughed and then got serious and went through everything item by item. When they were done with that, Sarah had a pretty good idea of what her demands would be. The girls basically just wanted her to do what made her happy, but had brought up a few things that Sarah hadn't thought of. They made plans for the next visit and started their goodbyes, when Sam asked, "Trace? "

"Yeah, man?" Trace responded with a grin on his face.

Sam grinned back. "Considering you're the lone man in this bevy of intelligent, independent women, I would normally tell you to hang in there. But to be honest, I'm a little jealous."

"Oh, you don't know how happy I am, to have some more testosterone in the mix. I'm exhausted." Trace sighed.

Sam and Sarah shut the computer down, and sat in silence with their own thoughts. Sam looked at Sarah. "I love your family. It's like being surrounded by three more Sarah's. I predict wicked shenanigans in the future."

Sarah called Luca to give him her ideas for the photo shoot, and to let him know she had talked to her family and would work out the rest of the details later. Luca was open to Sarah's ideas, and was more than happy to wait. They could discuss it in further detail at tonight's premier.

~~~

Sarah had asked for another white shirt from Sam. He had just finished putting silver cuff links in when Sarah emerged from the bathroom. It didn't even surprise them anymore. Sam was wearing a classic tuxedo. Black wool with silk lapels, white shirt and black bow tie and shoes. Sarah was again wearing Sam's white dress shirt. It was tucked into a classic, full, floor-length black skirt. She had rolled up the sleeves to her forearms, and left the top three buttons undone with the collar up. She donned a pair of black, patent-leather stilettos and complemented the outfit with hammered silver and turquoise jewelry. Sarah stopped to stare at Sam in a tux. His narrow hips, broad shoulders, and tight ass always made her heart skip a beat. She couldn't help herself. She ran to Sam, and scorched his lips with a hot, wet kiss.

Sam kissed her soft lips right back. He stepped back and whistled. He believed Sarah could wear a burlap sack and somehow make it look elegant. Her hair was classic Sarah. It kind of stuck up a little everywhere. It looked like she had just gotten fucked. Oh, wait. She had. "Understated elegance. Very nice, Ms. Reid. Very nice indeed."

It was the first time that Sarah had actually walked the red carpet with Sam. No surprises, no grand entrance, just Sam and Sarah holding hands. Sam kept his other in the small of her back as she smiled and posed like a pro. Sarah laughed out loud when she heard a couple of women offer to have Sam's babies. Once inside, names and numbers folded on slips of paper became plentiful. Sam handed the folded pieces of paper to Sarah who just grinned at the girls as she placed them in her clutch. It was all quite entertaining. Sam thought it was sexy how Sarah handled the aggravation with grace and humor. He turned and squeezed her hand. He raised an eyebrow as he reached over and whispered in her ear. "I think it's time to give the paps a picture worth taking, don't you?"

Sarah purred. "Absolutely."

Sam gathered her in his arms and leaned her back against his shoulder. Sarah opened her mouth enticingly for Sam to explore. He did not disappoint. He leisurely enjoyed Sarah's mouth, with a few gentle nips of her bottom lip. Sam was not usually one for public displays, but Sarah and her red dress changed that a long time ago. He couldn't get enough of her smell and her skin. The flashbulbs went crazy, Sarah panted and he had sweaty balls. Sam was a happy man.

~~~

At the after party, Sam and Sarah sat with Luca and a couple of younger male models. Sam was happy that the models had approached them and asked to sit together. Sarah, as usual, had been right. The vibe had changed, but Sam had no plans to sing again. Sarah was happy to be in a Sam and Luca sandwich, but at the moment she was on the dance floor using her voodoo. They had done shots of tequila, but they had no plans to drink as much as last time. As she once again left for the dance floor, Sarah laughed over her shoulder and said, "You know I could drink you both under the table!"

Sam grinned and sighed. Luca turned to Sam, and said, "If I was a few years younger, I would challenge you to a duel for that one, Sam."

"And I would accept. I would be sorry to kill you, Luca. As much as I love you, I have never loved anyone the way I love that woman. How did I get so lucky?"

Luca clasped Sam's neck and brought him close. "Because Sarah sees more than your pretty face, Sam. She sees the most important thing about you. Your soul. Don't fuck this up. If you do, I really will take her to South America."

"In your dreams, Luca. I'm in this for the long haul." Sam's face lit up when he saw Sarah return to the table.

As Sarah sat to catch her breath, Luca asked her, "So, have you made a decision on what we talked about?"

Sarah grinned as she poured a shot for herself, Sam, and Luca. Their table mates had left to dance. "I have, as well as my children and Sam, but, before we get into that, I just wanted to let you know something." She licked her salt, drank her shot, and sucked her lime. She smiled sinfully at Luca. "We did fuck after leaving your room. But it wasn't like rabbits. It was much nicer, and lasted a lot longer, but thanks for the suggestion."

Sam looked at Sarah. Then he looked at Luca. Luca looked at Sarah, swallowed and then looked at Sam They both burst out laughing as they did their shots. Luca looked a little sweaty.

"Okay." Sarah set her shot glass down, took Sam's hand, and turned to Luca. "First, I am honored and humbled that you even looked at my pictures. I'm shocked that you want me to take pictures with you, and I'm in denial that you want to take *my* picture. I think Venice will be a good place for the spread shots. We'll all be there, so it will be convenient. It's Venice, for God's sake! What better place than one of the most romantic places on earth? Plus, I will be going home after Venice. I've been gone long enough."

"I agree, Sarah. Not a problem." Luca responded wistfully. "I will miss you, Tesoro."

Sarah squared her shoulders. "Second, I don't want to work all of the time. Photography is my joy. I don't want it to become my burden. I also don't want to work all of the time, while Sam is trying to slow down. I would like to do a shoot with you every three months. And I would like this year to just be pictures of Sam, until I don't feel so intimidated being with you and your camera."

Luca grinned. "I think that's doable."

And not to sound demanding, but I'd like to have some input in the locations, if I could. I have some great ideas for Sam. Something that he would find comfortable."

"Tesoro, none of what you just said is demanding. Are you interested in doing something in Venice other than your photo spread? I would like you to take your camera when it's just you and Sam being tourists. I would love to see what catches your eye."

"I take my camera almost everywhere, so of course I'll take pictures." Sarah's shoulders slumped and she sighed. She leaned over and kissed Luca on the cheek. "That was easier than I thought it was going to be. Thank you Luca, I truly am honored."

Their tablemates returned and shots were poured for all. Sarah kicked off her shoes, and tucked her leg under her in her chair. They raised toasts and paid no attention to the crowd around them until the chanting started. "Sarah! Sarah! Sarah!"

Sarah wondered what was going on, until someone walked up and gave her a microphone. "Sing us a song, Sarah!"

Sarah looked at Sam and grinned. Sam held up his hands and shook his head emphatically. "You promised! No way am I singing. They want you, not me."

"Okay then!" Sarah slid off her chair and took the microphone. She addressed the crowd. "I'll be more than happy to sing a song, but first, I think we should all sing one together." The crowd cheered, as Sarah made her way to the DJ booth. Sam lost sight of her in the crowd. He leaned back and waited. The first chords of "Bohemian Rhapsody" stated, and the crowd erupted. By the second verse, everyone was singing along, including Sam and Luca.

The cheers died down, and the crowd got quiet. Sam still could not see Sarah, but it didn't matter. He just needed to hear that voice. Then Sarah started to sing "Fever." Her voice was low, and sultry. Sam felt electricity course through his veins. His skin broke out in goose bumps.

Sam stood up. He could hear Sarah as she got closer. She continued to sing about fever, and love. Sam was dealing with his own kind of fever as Sarah appeared before him. She swayed and did a hip grind that immediately made his dick stand at attention as she continued to taunt him with the lyrics. Sam sat back down immediately.

Sarah leaned over Sam and straddled his thigh. He felt her breath on his face as she continued to sing the last verse. Fuck! He hungered for this woman. As she finished the last line of the song, she dropped onto his thigh and kissed him deeply. "Take me back to the room Sam Ramsay, so you can eat your desert," she whispered in his ear.

Sam growled loud enough for the people around them to hear. He picked Sarah up and strode out of the ballroom to a roar of applause, whistles, and cheers.

Sam had gone into the bathroom to hang up his tuxedo. Upon his return to the bedroom, he found Sarah laying in bed in all her naked glory. He had his desert first, and then they both had the main course.

June

Chapter 28:

It was an uneventful flight into Marco Polo Airport, but Sarah was almost giddy. She looked intently out the airplane window at the canals and the dome of St. Mark's Basilica. She could even see the white vaporettos and black gondolas. And people. Thousands of people. "Holy shit!" Sarah looked at Sam.

Sam smiled. "Yeah. The tourists are crazy. The best time to experience Venice is early in the morning, or at night, unless you get lost. That's the best. The dead ends, the small chapels, the colorful homes."

Sarah poked him in the ribs with her elbow. "I thought you didn't soak up the local culture in your travels, Sam."

"I don't, and I haven't, but I've been doing some research. I want to make this place extra special, Sarah. For you, and for David."

"And that right there." Sarah sighed and leaned her head on Sam's shoulder.

Sam raised an eyebrow. "What?"

"What you just said. That's why I love you. You have the best heart."

Sam and Sarah's luggage was picked up and taken to the hotel. Their driver drove a quick trip for them to catch their vaporetto. Vaporetto's were water taxis. They and the gondolas were the only means of travel in Venice, unless you walked.

Sarah grinned at Sam. "I've already turned into what I hate. And I don't care."

"What have you turned into?" asked Sam, with his own big grin.

"A fucking tourist."

The vaporetto pulled up to their hotel. The Gritti Palace was a fifteenth century palazzo. Sarah stood and stared with her mouth open. It was just so Venetian. There were red geraniums in boxes that lined the railings that ran along the Grand Canal. It was directly across from St. Mark's Basilica on The Grand Canal. Staff was waiting to assist with their arrival and check-in. A young man offered his arm to Sarah to help her up and continued to help her up the stairs. She and Sam entered the palazzo lobby as the doors were opened by staff. Sarah gasped. Terazzo tiles lined the floors, and huge marble pillars surrounded the doors. Everywhere that Sarah looked, she saw luxury. Deep, dark woods, and red velvet; gold braiding and opulent mirrors. Even the ceiling was incredibly beautiful.

The concierge waited for them and escorted them to the private elevator that whisked them directly into their attic apartment. "Buon giorno, Mr. Ramsay and Ms. Reid. You will be in The Redentore Terrazza Suite. Please do not hesitate to let us know if you need anything." He unlocked and opened their door. S he handed the key cards to Sam, he quietly stated, "Please enjoy your stay at the Gritti Palace."

Sam and Sarah walked in and stood still before they slowly looked around their home for the next week. A living room opulently decorated with dark woods and red velvet. A large Murano glass chandelier hung from the ceiling. Sparkling prisms of light reflected off of the dark wood on the walls. They walked slowly into the bedroom where red floral fabric and velvet surrounded them in tasteful luxury. Their luggage had already been unpacked and hung in the closets and placed in the drawers. Even their toiletries had been arranged in the bathroom that was completely ensconced in green marble. As they walked their way back into the living room they noticed the black iron spiral staircase in the corner. They held hands and slowly made their way to the top. A door opened up to their own private rooftop terrace. It looked out over the Grand Canal.

Sam's eyes lit up as he and Sarah stared at the bottle of Prosecco nestled in an ice bucket. There was a basket of chocolates, towels, and two white fluffy robes strategically placed on the end. "Sarah! Look! It's a giant bathtub!" Sam's eyes twinkled.

Sarah's eyes gleamed as she clapped her hands together. "Oh my God! It's a two person swimming pool! We will definitely be using that."

Sam laughed as he grabbed the Prosecco and chocolates as they made their way back down the stairs.

"Holy hell, Sam!" Sarah fell back on the brocade sofa in the living room. "I've never seen, much less stayed, anywhere this fancy!"

Sam opened the bottle of Prosecco and poured them both a glass. He handed Sarah hers, as he sat down beside her. He raised his glass and toasted. "To Sarah, and to me, and to big bathtubs on roofs!"

They sipped as Sam looked around. "I've stayed in some pretty swanky places, but, like you, I think this one takes the cake. I'm a little gobsmacked."

"I can't imagine that the whole crew is staying here, are they? Somehow I can't imagine the lighting techs, or makeup gals being allowed to set their stuff up in a place like this."

"No. It's just us, though I would imagine that Luca is here somewhere." Sam grinned.

Sarah sat her glass on the coffee table before asking, "Why are we the only ones?"

Sam shrugged. "I told you I wanted to make this extra special Sarah. I think we're off to a great start."

"You are a dear, dear man, Sam Ramsay." Sarah looked at Sam with her heart on her sleeve. "You do know that I want to do it everywhere in this apartment, don't you?"

Sam smirked. "By *it* and *everywhere*, what do you mean?"

Sarah giggled. "Fucking, screwing, making love. Mad monkey sex. In that bed, that spiral staircase, the floor, this sofa and especially that pool."

"Well, Ms. Reid, I will do my best." Sam removed his shoes and leaned back on the sofa. "What do you *need* to do in Venice, and what do you just *want* to do?"

They talked about St. Mark's Basilica, the Bridge of Sighs, the Doges Palace, Murano, Burano, and of course the Rialto. Sarah couldn't leave Venice without some tall Italian leather shoes. Sarah wanted to hire a private guide to get her to some of the smaller neighborhood chapels. She hadn't planned to attend all of Sam's press conferences, so she had a couple of mornings free to explore to her heart's content. Sam didn't have any early morning, or late night junkets, except for the premier, so that left

348

him with time to explore with Sarah. It also meant that they could see Venice late at night, without having to get up early. They made their plans for the week, and made no mention of the fact that Sarah would be flying home on Monday while Sam flew to Prague.

After eating a delicious meal in the hotel restaurant and then braved the crowd and walked to St. Mark's. Sarah and her camera were in a Venetian frenzy. St. Mark's onion domes stood in all their Byzantine glory as they reflected the warm Venetian sun. The smell of unclean water did nothing to dispel Sarah's happiness. She had found children so she was in her element. Sam stood and watched her. He decided that watching Sarah was another one of his favorite things. He watched as she spotted a scene that was so perfectly cliché. Sam watched as she approached an old man feeding pigeons. Sarah hadn't had time to learn more than a few words in Italian, but Sam had no doubt that she would charm the man in a matter of minutes. He grinned as he watched her. A common language was not necessary for Sarah. When Sarah finished taking the shots she wanted, she turned to Sam and gave him the smile that made his heart stop. He walked to her and kissed her gently as they made their way into St. Mark's. Sarah wanted to see the mosaic tiles in the interior. Sam would never deny her anything. They spent the rest of the afternoon at the Doges Palace and the Bridge of Sighs.

As Sarah snapped pictures she turned to Sam and said, "I know that it got its name from the prisoners walking over it into their prison cells, but all I ever think of is Robin Trower."

Sam squinted. "What is Robin Trower?"

Sarah was shocked. She squeaked a little. "Oh, Sam! We will

definitely be listening to Robin Trower when we're trying out that pool tonight. This old lady is going to expose the young pup to good music. And Robin Trower is a Brit."

They stood together with their hands entwined and watched the sunset. As they made their way back to the hotel, they noticed that the crowds had dispersed, and all that was left were lovers holding hands, and locals who were returning home after work. They heard the lapping of the water against the wooden piers of the canals, and the last of the gondolas as they made their way home. Venice had become magical in its quiet. Sam stopped Sarah and wrapped his arms around her before resting his chin on her shoulder. "You have bewitched me, Sarah Reid. I am completely under your spell."

Sam retrieved the robes from the rooftop so they could don the soft white fluffiness after shedding their clothes. After climbing the spiral stairs they were met with the Venetian stars twinkling over the inkiness of the Grand Canal. They disrobed and sunk into the warm water of the pool. Sarah reached over and hit play on her phone.

"Robin Trower?" Sam asked with a smile on his face.

"This song is called 'Bridge of Sighs'." She moved close to Sam and tangled her legs with his. "You were checking out my ass going up the stairs, weren't you?"

"Sarah, I always check out your ass. It's one of my favorite things." Sam reached for her and pulled her over to straddle him. He gripped the ass that was the topic of conversation. "I love checking out your ass, but I love touching it even more."

Sam continued to caress Sarah's ass and back and shoulders as he listened to the song. It was a sexy, melancholy, moody tune that encapsulated everything he was feeling, knowing that Sarah would be leaving. They were both in a completely different emotional place this time but it didn't make it easier.

Sarah laid her head on Sam's shoulder. She stared out at The Grand Canal and looked at all the lights from the stucco facades of the buildings sparkle on the water. She felt as if she was in a bubble of quiet where all she felt was Sam and the dampness of the saltwater in the air. She sighed. "I'm so glad we're here together."

"Me, too, Sarah."

"I'm glad my first visit to Venice has been with you. I'm glad that it was with you, and that it didn't happen years ago." Sarah wrapped her arms around Sam's neck.

Sam grasped her tight. "I know you wanted to experience this with David, but I'm so happy you're experiencing it with me."

"I think I needed the years to pass in order for me to appreciate the experience, and especially to appreciate it with you, Sam." She continued to keep her arms around his neck.

Sam felt Sarah's hands tighten around him and then felt her tears. "Please, Sarah, don't cry. You know it breaks my heart."

Sarah whispered. "Do you know how I hunger for you? I have this need that's raw and wild. It's as if I've been empty my whole life until I met you. You are my sustenance."

Sam gripped her hard, almost painfully as he pulled her face to his. He captured her mouth with his and plundered her heat. He

351

felt the silkiness of her wet skin and smelled the sandalwood that was uniquely Sarah. He gripped her hair and pulled her head back to lay scorching kisses on her neck. He whispered hoarsely, "Loving you scares me, Sarah. It scares me that I feel so much. It scares me that you feel so much for me. I have become lost in the madness that is us."

Sarah could feel Sam's hard length against her stomach. She was almost dizzy with her want and her need for him. She pressed herself onto Sam's hardness. Sam gently stopped her and looked into her eyes. "I want to savor you slowly tonight." He turned her around on his lap, so that her back was against his chest. "Let me love you."

He stroked her arms gently under the warm water, and then her stomach. Sarah laid her head back and Sam felt her shudder. As he cupped her breasts and circled her nipples, she arched her back and moaned. Sam was dizzy with his own desire but he wanted to draw out as much pleasure for Sarah as he could. "Beautiful", growled Sam as he gently stroked the inside of both of her thighs. The water made his strokes liquid and smooth.

Sarah arched again, as Sam lightly teased her center with a feathery stroke. "I need..."

"What do you need, Sarah?" Sam continued to stroke Sarah with soft, light fingers.

"You. I need you." Sarah lost her mind with the sensations of the water and Sam's fingers.

Sam slowly increased the pressure and the rhythm of his fingers as he kissed Sarah's back and neck. Sam felt her tighten and then felt the tremors that were like waves on the ocean. They started small, but grew bigger before they crashed. Sarah cursed quietly and panted as she lay back against him.

He let her catch her breath before he turned her around again to face him. He held her and continued stroking her everywhere. He needed to touch her. He needed to taste her. He picked her up and carried her across the pool where he set her down on the edge of the pool deck. He stayed in the water. Sam looked up at Sarah with a devilish grin. "I want desert again, before the main course."

"Oh, God, Sam!" Sarah looked at him with a grin as Sam lifted her legs over his shoulders. He kissed her thighs as his fingers joined his mouth and tongue. Sarah moaned as she braced herself with her arms on the pool deck. This man drove her into a state of oblivion. She wanted to move to that state and take up permanent residency.

Sam looked at Sarah as he ministered to her wants and needs. She looked down at him. He knew immediately when he had driven her to the edge. Her eyes got glassy and she squeezed the sides of his head with her legs as she started to moan loudly. He could watch her come forever. Fuck the way she dressed. Fuck the color of her hair. His favorite Sarah look was her naked with her legs wrapped around his head as she came.

Sam didn't give her time to catch her breath before he was moving them back across the pool. Sarah was limp as a rag when he had her straddle him. He slowed everything down to let her come back to earth, but he was as hard as a steel beam. He rubbed her back and kissed her neck, and gave her the time that she needed.

"Do you think people can overdose on orgasms?" Sarah

murmured.

Sam chuckled softly. "What a way to go." He kissed her mouth softly, and brushed his knuckles gently across her breasts. She was pliant and soft and returned his kisses.

"It's time for the main course, Sam. Let me serve you." Sarah's kisses got deeper, and hotter as she felt Sam's hardness with her hand.

He moaned, "Fuck....."

Sarah lifted up and slowly lowered herself onto the hardness that she needed. As she filled herself with Sam she realized that he filled her in every way. She sat up straighter and looked at Sam as she slowly rocked. "Tell me what you feel."

"Hot." Sam was hoarse. "Fluidity." He reached for her breast and suckled the tip. Sarah hissed and increased the rhythm. Sam looked at Sarah as he grabbed her hips. "Tight."

They both looked down to watch their bodies as they joined in the age old dance. Sam looked up at Sarah in the Venetian moonlight and suddenly wanted to cry with the emotion that the image evoked. "Love."

Again, they both looked down at their bodies, as Sam's hold on Sarah's hips tightened. With each thrust, Sam grunted. "Mine."

~~~

They slept in the next morning, showered and walked to a pasticceria in St. Mark's Square for an espresso and a bigne al cioccolato. Sam always enjoyed Sarah's moans, but her moans of enjoyment as she ate the pastry filled with chocolate cream made him grin. Sarah made eating a sensual experience.

They returned to their apartment to dress for the press junket. Sam and Sarah looked at each other in anticipation as they took their clothes out of the garment bags. Sam held a baby blue suit with navy trim. Sarah held a baby blue dress with navy trim at the bottom. They both laughed and shook their heads. Sam's cufflinks were silver, as well as Sarah's jewelry. A private vaporetto waited to take them on a short ride to the venue.

Again, they were met with the cameras and reporters. Sarah recognized one of the men from Milan and Paris, and stopped to chat with him for a moment. Sam stood and watched her talk easily with the gentleman. He would ask a question, Sarah would answer, and the reporter would chuckle. Sam should have been used to the fact that Sarah didn't know a stranger, but it still made him shake his head in wonder. He continued to watch as Sarah and the reporter engaged in a long conversation. The reporter did not take notes, or turn on a recorder. He animatedly described something to Sarah. She touched the reporters arm with a smile on her face, as the reporter leaned and kissed her on both cheeks. Sarah returned to Sam with the reporter on her arm.

"Do you remember Jean Luc? From Paris?"

"I'm sorry, but after so many flashbulbs, and so many questions being yelled, and so many years, I do not. It's nice to meet you." Sam raised his eyebrows at her as if to ask why she had brought him over.

Jean Luc laughed. "I understand. Sarah and I were discussing a bed wetting problem my three year old was experiencing."

"Excuse me?" Sam asked quizzically.

Jean Luc chuckled and said, "You can discuss it with her later, but I wanted you to know how lucky I think you are. Sarah is not only a vision to look at she is one of the most incredibly real people I've ever met. Yes, you are a very lucky man."

"Jean Luc, I consider myself the luckiest man I know. Thank you." Sam shook his hand, and then placed his other on Sarah's back to guide her into the venue. It was basically a rehash of the previous pressers. Sarah sat at the side up front, as Sam was, as usual, in the middle. It was the same questions, the same reporters, and the same tedium. Sarah zoned out until she heard her name mentioned. Someone had asked about her singing. She just grinned and looked over at Sam.

Sam grinned and addressed the questioner. "Sarah has many talents. And she's good at all of them. That includes, but is not limited to, her singing. And, no, she won't be singing for you today."

The reporters still chuckled when the presser concluded.

~~~

They changed into casual clothes and comfortable shoes and headed out for the Number One vaporetto. It would take them on a slow, leisurely tour of the entire length of The Grand Canal. They planned to take another to Murano. They both leaned back and relaxed as they took in the sights, and smells of the main street in Venice. Sarah's camera was her constant companion. She had moved to the back of the water taxi for some different shots. Sam stayed in his seat as he enjoyed the wind in his hair, the colors of the water and facades of the buildings, and total relaxation. Sarah returned to her seat and leaned into Sam. She gave him her brilliant smile and squeezed his arm. Sam wrapped his arm around her and continued to stare at her. She was more beautiful than anything he could see outside the boat.

The tour seemed to end much too quickly, but they were eager to continue their adventures. They grabbed gelatos at a kiosk and walked the neighborhood. As in Paris, they were hopelessly lost within ten minutes. They weren't worried, as at the end of every block there were signs with arrows pointing out the vaporetto stands and gondola piers. They turned a corner, and entered a large square with a well in the middle. There were window boxes of flowers everywhere and three boys played soccer in a corner. Sarah turned to look at Sam. He just laughed and waved her on. Within five minutes Sarah kicked the ball with the boys. He joined the three boys to gang up on her.

After they dribbled and kicked for thirty minutes, they shook the boy's hands and continued on their way. They took the first vaporetto they saw and made their way to Murano. As the water taxi slowed to dock, Sam and Sarah stared at their destination. The facades were bright red, and azure, and yellow. There was pink and purple and green. It was one of the happiest looking neighborhoods they had ever seen. As they walked up the steps, Sarah asked, "Can we sit for a moment and get something to drink? That kicking made me parched."

There was a cafe within twenty feet of the vaporetto stand. Sarah sat at one of the outdoor tables as Sam went in to get their drinks. As they sipped, they people watched. Sarah would snap a shot occasionally. Sam could never tell exactly what it was that caught her eye. He would have to wait to see the finished product.

Their drinks finished, they continued their walk. It was quieter on Murano. Sam and Sarah quickly bypassed the glass shops that had hordes of people and continued to look for a demonstration of glass blowing that didn't have so many tourists. Sarah knew what to look for, and told Sam to be on the lookout for a decal in the window with "Vetro Murano Artistico" on it. This assured her that it would be authentic Murano glass, and not a knockoff. Sam found a decal, and they entered just in time to see a demonstration. He thought it strangely hypnotic, and would have stayed for another, if Sarah hadn't tugged on his hand. "Come on! We're going shopping for the girls!"

Shopping occurred in the shop next to the demonstration. Murano glass was everywhere. They took in vases, miniature animals, jewelry, glasses, bowls, pitchers, sconces, and of course the chandeliers. Sam was struck silent by the beauty of the ceiling covered with hanging chandeliers. Prisms of reflective sunlight bounced off all the glass and cast sparkles over the entire shop. It was like being surrounded by fireflies in a fairyland. Sarah immediately spotted an aquamarine chandelier and grabbed Sam's arm. "Oh! That would look stunning in your entryway at home."

The first thought that went through Sam's head was that Sarah had called his house 'home'. The second thought was that she was absolutely correct. It was graceful, with no ostentation, and the color reminded him of the necklace that Sarah had worn to the premier in Paris. He had to have it. He looked at Sarah and said, "I have to have it. Every time I look at it will remind me of you in Paris."

Sarah beamed, "I can't believe you remember my necklace, but it is the perfect aquamarine to go with all of the gray and white in your home." She continued to shop. She purchased earrings and necklaces for her daughters and the girls. She also purchased four sconces to be mailed home. She would put two of them up on either side of her fireplace. She would give Liz the other two for her shop. The owner spoke enough English for Sarah to converse with him regarding small supplies to the States. Sarah thought that there would be a market for the beautiful pieces in Liz's shop. She left her information with the owner, and he gave his to her. Sarah had charmed him, as he kissed both of her cheeks.

After Sam purchased the chandelier and made the arrangements to have it shipped to London, they continued their walk back to the café they had stopped at earlier. After they ate a late lunch, they headed back to The Gritti on the vaporetto.

They ordered a bottle of Jameson from room service and savored the warm, smoky whiskey as they sat on the sofa in the living room. Sarah sighed and laid her head back on the sofa. "What a wonderful day. Beautiful weather, no flashbulbs, and you."

After Sam poured doubles, he kissed Sarah gently and then again, followed Sarah up the stairs to the pool. They stayed in the pool, until the bottle was almost empty, and then finished it, and each other, in the bedroom.

Chapter 29:

Sam and Sarah ordered breakfast. They sat and drank espresso outside on the terrace of The Gritti. Sam had another presser, and Sarah planned to explore the churches with the guide that the hotel staff had arranged.

"Your press conference will only last a couple of hours, so what else is on your agenda?" Sarah asked as she sipped her coffee.

"I thought I'd hit the gym, and catch up on social media and emails. Marta will be getting in shortly, so I'll probably have lunch with her."

Sarah frowned. "I didn't know she'd be here today. I hate that I'll miss her. Maybe I should reschedule."

Sam laughed. "She'll be here for the rest of the week. She mentioned something about going shoe shopping with you on Thursday. You've been waiting a long time to see your chapels, and Marta will be here until we fly out on Monday. Go have fun, and enjoy your quiet pursuit of all things church-related."

The waiter brought their plates, and Sam watched Sarah pick at her food. She still had a frown on her face. "What's going on, Sarah?"

"I'm just keep thinking that we only have six more days together, and I'm going to be leaving you alone. I hate to squander the time."

Sam reached over and stroked her cheek. "Do you want me to go with you? I really have no agenda today after the presser."

"No." Sarah sighed and smiled. "You need to catch up, and quiet will do you good. I'll be back sometime this afternoon."

Sarah's guide showed up as they were finishing breakfast. Sam clasped Sarah to his chest and kissed her temple. "Enjoy yourself, Sarah. I will be here waiting." He smiled and suddenly, Sarah just wanted to stay in their apartment and make Sam pay up on the promises he made with his smile. He just laughed at her and swatted her ample ass.

Trista was the guide, a true Venetian. She had been born - and spent her life - in Venice. She watched Sam kiss Sarah. She grinned as she looked at Sarah. "Ah! Amore! Bellissimo!"

They chatted as Trista led the way to their first church. After she asked Sarah exactly what she was searching for, Trista had suggestions on some small neighborhood chapels she thought Sarah would like. "The mosaic work in some of the smaller chapels is exquisite, but most tourists aren't aware of it. I'm glad you asked. I will enjoy seeing it again with you."

San Giovanni Bragora, with the Baptism of Christ, was beautiful, as was Titian's Annunciation in San Salvador. Sant' Apollonia followed, with lunch in San Marco Piazza.

As they ate, Sarah asked Trista a hundred questions about Venice and what it was like growing up there, versus the difficulty of living there now. Trista was patient, and enjoyed answering all of Sarah's questions. Sarah admitted that she had fallen in love with the "Serenissima", and was thinking of coming back for an extended stay. Trista suggested that if she was going to stay for longer than a week, she should consider renting an apartment in one of the palaces. It was more affordable, and would give her the true Venice experience. She offered to assist Sarah with the planning and the paperwork. They exchanged numbers and then continued on to the smaller chapels.

~~~

When Sam heard Sarah open the door, he laid his laptop on the coffee table and met her with a kiss. He stood back and looked at her nose that was rosy with a slight sunburn; her eyes shone and she smiled. "It looks like you had a good day."

"Oh, I did! Trista was so patient with me, and took me to some fabulous places!" Sarah set her camera and bag down so she could hug Sam hard. "I need water and the sofa. My feet are tired!"

Sam got her a bottle of water and joined her on the sofa. "Did you get done what you wanted to get done today?" Sarah asked as she drank half of her water in one gulp.

"I did. I got an hour in the gym. Marta says hi and is looking forward to Thursday. I caught up on my Facebook page, and I posted a few pictures on my Instagram account." Sam lightly rubbed circles on Sarah's wrist.

"Anything interesting?" Sarah leaned her head back and took off her shoes before putting her feet on the coffee table.

Sam lifted an eyebrow. "Just the same old same old. But I feel obligated to my fans. Speaking of my fans, I noticed that you don't follow me on either page."

"Why follow you?" Sarah laughed. I've got the real thing. But I am a fan of Sam Ramsay. I guess I need to change my status and start following you, just to make sure you don't post any naked pictures of me."

"Why post naked pictures of you when I can see you naked right now?" Sam said devilishly.

"Down, boy!" Sarah laughed. "I need a shower and a nap. Care to nap with me?"

"Whatever you wish, amazing Sarah."

Sam spooned Sarah in the exquisitely appointed bed. She had just showered and Sam basked in the earthy smell that clung to her. He threw his arm over her and tugged her tight against his chest. He wanted to absorb as much ofSarah's skin as possible, as often as possible. Sarah sighed and said, "I'm ready to go home."

Sam stopped and held his breath.

"If I could pack you in my suitcase, and take you home with me, I would in a heartbeat, Sam Ramsay." Sarah caressed Sam's forearm and snuggled deeper into his body.

Sam clasped her tighter before he asked, "Are you tired of this, Sarah? Have you had enough of me and my life?"

Sarah flipped around quickly. She looked deep into Sam's eyes before cupping his cheeks. "I could never have enough of you. Are you crazy? I've loved being with you as you've done your job. But I feel as if we've been in a bubble. Does that make sense to you?"

"I understand what you're saying." Sam maintained eye contact. "That's kind of my life. I live long stretches in an alternate reality, and small stretches in the real world. It's all I know."

"Sam, you get waxed and oiled, told what to wear, where to be, and who to see. You get your teeth whitened and have your picture taken wherever you go. You are surrounded by people who never tell you no. I'm not belittling that. But that is *your* reality, not mine." Sarah continued to speak softly as she looked at Sam.

"I know, Sarah. It's all true, but I'm getting more impatient by the day to experience your reality, and hoping that we can find a happy medium." Sam kissed her softly on the cheek.

"We'll make it work, Sam." Sarah smiled a soft smile. "That's why this time I don't think going home will be as devastating to me. I know what we have, and I know what we want. I hate the thought of leaving and not knowing when we'll see each other again. But this time I know we *will*."

"I will come to you next time." Sam sighed and closed his eyes. "It's my turn, and I can't wait."

Sarah leaned back and continued to lightly rub Sam's forearm. "I love it here. I love the idea of the pictures that will be in my scrapbook. I cherish this entire trip and I have no regrets whatsoever, but, I miss my home, the girls, and my life. It's time."

"Let's make the most of these last few days, and then I will do the planning for the next act." Sam closed his eyes.

They napped.

Sarah was awakened by Sam as he softly kissed her neck. "Wake up, sleepy head. We have dinner plans."

"Where are we going? Do I need to change?" Sarah asked sleepily.

Sam looked at Sarah in her leggings and T-shirt. "You're perfect.

Throw on a jacket and your boots, and we're good. But, come on! Time's a wasting! Oh! And you'll probably want your camera. As if I have to tell you that."

Sam led her to the elevator and out the front door. They walked to the vaporetto stand in front of The Gritti Palace, where a gondola waited. But it wasn't any gondola. It wasn't the typical black gondola that Sarah and Sam had seen everywhere in Venice. This gondola was a work of art. It was painted royal blue with gold accents.

Sam pointed out the gondolier who stood at the back. He was such a cliché and such a treat. He wore short black trousers, a red and white striped shirt, and a straw hat with a red ribbon. He was everything one expected of a gondolier. Sarah was giddy.

Sam explained that the gondolier's oar rested in an elaborately carved wooden rest called a forcola. The counterweight at the front of the gondola was beautifully carved brass called a ferro. It was carved in an "S" shape, representing the shape of The Grand Canal. Sarah stared at him as he continued his history lesson. "All gondolas were ordered to be black centuries ago. If you see a gondola any other color it means that it has been in the same family for centuries. These different-colored gondolas were 'grandfathered' in, so to speak. You could say we are taking a sunset ride in a piece of Venetian history."

"Wow, Sam! You really did your homework! That is amazingly awesome." Sarah's eyes shimmered as Sam and the gondolier assisted her into the gondola and onto her seat. Sam sat by her and pointed out the basket in front of them. The hotel staff had prepared them dinner, and the gondolier and his water craft were theirs for three hours. Enough time to enjoy the sunset and

Venice from the water at night. All she was capable of saying was "Oh." She kissed Sam softly and laid her head on his shoulder as the gondolier rowed away from the stand.

Sarah took picture after picture. *Everything* in Venice was a postcard. Sam could not stop grinning at how excited Sarah was. The gondolier had gone the opposite way from St. Mark's, so they experienced a different part of the city. Sarah had been in some of the Venice neighborhoods earlier in the day, so she hadn't seen any of this part of The Grand Canal. Every time they passed under one of the hundreds of bridges, Sarah kissed Sam. She explained to him that it was good luck. He doubted that, but didn't care, until he looked at the gondolier who assured him she was correct. They relaxed and looked at everything. They never stopped holding hands.

The gondolier stopped the gondola so they could watch the sunset on the horizon. As they watched brilliant yellows and oranges turn into purples, pinks, and blues, the gondolier picked up a twelve-string guitar and started to play and sing "Santa Lucia" softly. Sarah looked at Sam with tracks of tears on her cheeks. Her heart was in her eyes. "This is so perfectly perfect. Thank you, Sam Ramsay, for giving me this perfection. I'm going to have to start another scrapbook."

Sam groaned softly as he took her in his arms. "I love the fact that we've filled the pages of your first one, and have to start another."

They unpacked their basket and enjoyed fruits and cheeses, and a bottle of Prosecco that hotel staff had prepared for them. They had even included some of the chocolate pastries that Sarah loved so much. As Sarah put a different lens on her camera, the gondolier started singing "O Solo Mio." Sarah snapped picture after picture. He was more than happy to oblige and continued to sing all the way back to The Gritti.

They walked slowly back to the private elevator with their arms around each other's waists. After the elevator left them in their apartment they slowly walked to the bedroom where they stood face-to-face as they slowly removed each other's clothes. They moved to the bed where they held each other, kissed each other, and touched each other. They loved each other.

~~~

The next morning, Sam and Sarah made their way to the old theatre that Luca had picked for the photo shoot. Sarah stopped as they entered. It was all tarnished gilt, worn velvet, and rough plaster. The theatre was a dowager that was in beautiful decay. It featured muted, worn colors, and frayed edges, smoky mirrors and flaking gold leaf. It was a dark and moody place with an old, slightly musty smell. Sarah fell in love immediately.

After the pleasantries with Luca were over, an assistant led Sam and Sarah to the back of the stage, where several clothes racks displayed items they would wear for the day. Sarah was stunned. There was an aqua chiffon ball gown; yellow, pink, and lavender spring dresses; and lingerie. So much lingerie. Sarah swallowed, suddenly nervous. Sam was used to being naked and vulnerable. She was not. Sam sensed her unease, and walked over to her, putting his arm reassuringly around her waist. "Do what you are comfortable with, Sarah. There is nothing to be nervous about. But, you do realize that only me, you, Luca and two other people are here, don't you?"

Sarah looked around and realized Sam was right. This was beyond a skeleton crew. She saw Sharon standing by the makeup station with a grin on her face. Sarah smiled back and waved. Sharon had been instrumental in the makeup that matched the aquamarine dress in Paris. It was good to see a familiar face. Sarah turned and smiled at Sam. "This will be fun. What do we do first?"

Luca walked over to the two of them with a smile. Before he could say anything, Sam scowled and rumbled, "I see what you're doing here, Luca! Lingerie? You think you're getting a peek at my woman in all her naked glory?" Sarah giggled.

Luca roared with laughter and then pointed out the screens that were set up for their privacy. "Damn! What was I thinking? I shouldn't have thought about those! Seeing Sarah in, as you said, -all her glory- could have sent me to heaven a happy man!"

He explained that he wanted Sam and Sarah to do what they felt. There was no schedule or program. He just wanted them to have fun. He also made it clear that he wanted Sarah to share any ideas she might have for lighting, angles, and locations. Luca wanted a total collaboration. Sam stood with his arms crossed as he listened to Luca and Sarah talk. He interrupted. "So, as usual, I'm just the pretty face, with no say?"

Sarah winced and rushed to him. She hated that he had thought that. "Sam! I'm sorry! Of course I want your input!"

Luca smirked. "Oh, Sarah! Don't believe a word he says. Sam *always* has a say. And he always says it!"

Sarah told Luca that she wouldn't wear bows or girlie things because she was a woman. He responded by saying, "Oh, tesoro, you are definitely all woman!"

She also decided to not be shy about the lingerie. She knew she would never look like this again, so why not go for it? She knew that she didn't look twenty, or thirty anymore, but she looked damn good for fifty-five. She was not ashamed of her body, and Sam seemed to like it just fine.

The first scene involved Sam and Sarah as they danced under a two-hundred-year-old Murano glass chandelier. The candlelight was the only light used in the shot. Sam wore a white robe and black boxer shorts. Sarah wore a long, white peignoir set. A sheer dressing gown over a sheer, spaghetti-strapped gown flowed down her body, ending in a puddle at the bottom. A lacy, white thong, and black-and-white zebra-patterned stilettos completed the ensemble. Sam visibly swallowed when he saw that she wasn't wearing a bra. He crushed her to his chest and hoarsely whispered, "Jesus H. Christ Sarah!"

They next shots were on a settee covered with faded red velvet. It was edged in peeling gold leaf. Sam lounged on it wearing nothing but a pair of unbuttoned jeans. Sarah wore her black leggings and a sheer blue tunic. Sharon had smudged a little makeup under Sarah's eyes. They were both barefoot and had bed head. It had been Sarah's suggestion for Sam to mess his hair up. He was always well-coiffed in his photos and in public. She wanted to show the world what he looked like when he woke up. Sometimes she thought his hair had a life of its own. She loved seeing it in the mornings, the way it stuck up everywhere after she had been tugging on it all night.

They changed into spring dresses, trousers, and button-up shirts. Suits and waltz=length party dresses. Luca photographed them on the floor, the balcony, a chair, and on some scaffolding. Luca shot for hours, but Sarah wanted three more scenes.

Sam wore a white tuxedo, with a white bow tie and white shirt. The only color was an aqua pocket square. Sarah was a vision in the aqua chiffon ball gown. They stayed on the empty stage as Sarah sang so that only Sam could hear. Sam spun and dipped her and held her close. They lost themselves in each other. When she finished singing they stood and held each other for a few minutes.

For the penultimate scene, Sarah instructed Sam to wear only black tuxedo pants. No shirt, no jacket, no shoes or socks. She asked him to take a seat in the front row and wait for her. As he sat and waited, Luca waited on the stage. Neither had any idea what she had up her sleeve, but both were excited. As Sarah finally came out from behind the screen, Sam and Luca let out audible groans upon seeing her, and said in unison, "Fuck!"

Sarah wore a black lace demi-bra with a matching black lace thong. A black lace garter belt held up thigh high sheer, black stockings with seams up the back. She wore a pair of six-inch red patent leather stilettos.

Sam watched Sarah strut across the stage. He noted that Luca gasped and tried to take pictures at the same time. Sam's entire blood supply went straight to his dick. It stood at attention and was hard as steel. He couldn't take his eyes off every man's fantasy that walked across the stage. Sarah evoked pure, wanton lust.

As she reached Sam she bent over and kissed him before biting his bottom lip. His eyes went straight to her tits, as they almost tumbled out onto his face. He didn't let her get away with a soft kiss. She could *not* look like that and expect him to be a gentleman. He growled, grabbed the back of her head, and twisted her hair in his hand as he kissed her mouth. By the time they both came up for air, she was splayed across his lap with her legs laid out in the empty seat next to them. Luca got himself under control, and went crazy with his camera. At least he had a brain that worked, as no one else in the theatre could speak. It took them a while to regain their senses. Sam lifted Sarah and said, "I have no idea what you have in mind for the final shot, but I can't wait!"

Sarah laughed. "What do you want to do right at this moment, Sam?"

Sam was only able to growl. "I want to fuck your brains out!" As he looked at her face he raised his eyebrows. "Oh, hell no! We are *not* screwing in front of Luca. He'd have a heart attack!"

"We're just going to pretend, Sam." Sarah got up, and strutted back behind her screen.

Sam watched her ass wiggle across the stage. He ran his hands through his hair and said, "Bloody hell! This woman is killing me!"

Sarah had noticed a beautiful old wool rug that was rolled up, propped up in a corner. Sam and Luca rolled it out in a corner of the stage where some of it was in shadow. Sam and Sarah stripped down to nothing, and came out with just sheets wrapped around them. They lay down on the rug and let Luca do his magic. She laid her head on Sam's chest and looked into his eyes. She whispered. "Do you know how I ache for you?"

"It can't be any greater than what I feel, or what you've given me, amazing Sarah. You are my reason, my insanity, my craving and my pain."

Sam, Sarah and Luca decided to grab a late lunch and finish the shoot outside. Sam and Sarah changed back into their jeans and T-shirts. Sarah grabbed her camera as they headed out.

After food and several cups of espresso, the three of them started a leisurely walk. Sarah took pictures of whatever captured her eye, as did Luca. It was an easy afternoon of absorbing Venice, with all of her sights, sounds, and smells. After plans were made to go through the photos the next morning, they said their goodbyes. Luca went his way, and Sam and Sarah headed for Harry's Bar. They wanted a bellini before heading back to The Gritti.

~~~

Sam was stretched out on the sofa with his legs on the coffee table. He had his laptop out and scrolled through the headlines of the day. Sarah sat at the table looking at the pictures she had taken that day. Sam got up to join her. "So, how do you feel about the shoot, Sarah?"

"It was more fun than I thought it was going to be! But, I think it was fun because I did it with you and Luca." Sarah whispered caresses on Sam's cheek as she smiled at him.

Sam rubbed his face into her hand. "You were wonderful. I've never had a photo shoot quite like the one we had today."

Really?" Sarah asked.

"I've never wanted to fuck the ladies I've done shoots with, and I've never had a steel beam for a dick on set before." Sam laughed.

Sarah looked at Sam with her mouth agape. "All the beautiful women you've had your hands and mouth on, and you've never wanted to bang them? I find that hard to believe, and also kind of humbling."

Sam shook his head. "Nope, I've told you, it's just my job. Being with you is not a job. Remember? I know how you taste, how you feel, and how you sound when I'm inside you. That's all I could think about."

They both turned to the computer screen as Sarah scrolled through her days pictures. Sam was astounded by the shots she had taken of him in the theatre. He hadn't even realized she had taken them. He saw no scowls, or hands that didn't know what to do with themselves. No hands in pockets, no hands rubbing his stubble. They were just him. Being. As they went through the pictures she had taken outside, one caught his eye. She had taken a picture of him leaning on the railing overlooking The Grand Canal. His hands were clasped in front of him, and his hair was blowing in the salty breeze. He was in profile and was staring at something on the horizon. He was naked in his vulnerability and his eyes were far away.

Sarah looked at him and asked, "What were you thinking about Sam?"

Sam shrugged. "You."

After she caught her breath she turned back to the screen. "I think this one needs to be in black and white." Sarah continued to study the photo.

He shook his head. "I don't know how you do it."

"Do what?" she asked.

"Get the shots that you get. I didn't see you take any of these. Are you some kind of ninja?"

"Ha! Funny, Sam. I just try to be inconspicuous and not get in anyone's way. Plus, you're my favorite subject." She kissed him softly and then sighed.

Sam cupped her cheeks and deepened the kiss. "I love that sigh."

Sarah touched her forehead to Sam's and whispered, "I have forgotten all of the other mouths I've touched. Yours is all that I remember. I kiss you short and sweet, and I kiss you long and intense. I kiss you because it's love in its purest form. Kissing you has changed my world. My mouth dances and sings when I kiss you. I want to kiss you silent, and I want to kiss you loudly. I want to kiss you until you moan and you're lost in me, and the only map you have is me. Kissing you is saying everything that my heart feels, but that my voice can't say."

Sam swallowed hard as he took Sarah's hand and led her into the bedroom. They kissed each other into oblivion.

~~~

Luca looked at Sarah at breakfast the next morning, and asked, "So, how do you feel about your first photo shoot?"

"Well, I don't know Luca. How do *you* feel about it?" Sarah arched her eyebrows.

"Well, tesoro, all I can say is that I don't think I've ever been quite that...excited at a photo shoot."

"Hey! That's my woman you're talking about!" Sam grimaced.

Sarah patted them both on their arms. "Seriously, I guess the proof is in the pudding. The pictures are either good, or they're not. I'm not expecting much, but it was fun."

"Oh, they're good, tesoro, they're good. Did you bring yours? Let's look at those first." Luca made room for them to huddle at the table. Sarah opened up her laptop and started the slideshow. Just as he had the first time, Luca was silent as he watched them. He would stop occasionally, and then continue on. Sarah was just as nervous as before.

When Luca had seen enough, he went back to the one of Sam at the railing. He looked at Sarah. "What's your thought on this one?"

"Definitely black and white. Other than that, nothing. No editing. I love it just the way it is." Sarah was firm in her answer.

All Luca said was "Hmmm", as he asked her about some others. He then looked at Sam and her, and asked them if they were ready.

Sam laughed. "I think this is the most nervous I've ever been about a shoot. Maybe I'm nervous because it's so personal for us." He inhaled deeply. "Let's rock and roll, Luca."

Luca turned on the computer and sat back to watch their faces. He didn't need to look at the screen. He had already looked at the images a hundred times.

Sam and Sarah grabbed each other's hands and hunched over the computer as image after image floated by. They were silent for the first few minutes, until Sarah couldn't stand it anymore. She hit the pause button, looked at Sam and then Luca and then yelled. "Holy Mother of God! We fucking rock!"

There was not a bad picture. Sarah was stunning, and Sam had never looked as good as he did when he gazed at Sarah in them. He had never been as relaxed, or oblivious to the camera. They were perfection. Sarah felt as if she was looking at someone else. All that looked familiar was the way she looked at Sam in the photos.

Sam continued to hold Sarah's hand as they finished looking at the rest of them. All he could say was, "All of these are because of you. You are fucking amazing, Sarah Reid. I want these on billboards everywhere. I want the world to see what you are to me. I can't wait for the girls to see them, and my mum and dad, and Danni and Alex, and your kids, oh my God, your kids are going to be so fucking excited." He babbled, but he couldn't help himself. He was so proud and excited that the woman that sat by him had loved him enough to do the shoot. As he looked at them, he was in awe that the goddess in the pictures, was his.

After they finished looking at the rest of the photos, they all leaned back and exhaled loudly. Sam looked at Luca and asked, "Now what? What do you suggest we do? These need to be out there. These are some of the best pictures I've ever taken, but Sarah is... Sarah is, just... unbelievable."

Luca rubbed his beard with a finger and thought for a moment before speaking. "I agree. I've been thinking about it all night, and trying to decide what would be the best option. If I'm being truly honest, I don't think that you, Sam, have ever taken pictures like these. Not to toot my own horn, but I've always felt that my relationship with you has made my pictures with you better than anyone else you've worked with, But, I can't compete with the pictures that Sarah takes." He pointed at Sarah's laptop. "But, it's apples and oranges. We have two different things going on. So, are you guys ready for my thoughts?" He raised his eyebrows as he looked at them.

"Luca, you know if I didn't have Sam, I would run off to South America with you in a heartbeat. Because you know I love you, you have to know I trust you. So, as Sam said earlier, let's rock and roll."

"Tesoro, you know if I were younger, I might have to fight Sam for you." The burly Italian grinned and leaned over and kissed her on the cheek. "Remember what I told you about your photos capturing Sam's heart? I have captured yours in these photos. Not because of how great a photographer I am, even though I am." They all laughed, and Luca continued. "It's because of who you are. Of what you are. Your heart and your spirit are bigger than anyone I've known. I don't think anyone would take a bad picture of you, because you're bigger than what any picture can capture. It's why your pictures of Sam are the best I've ever seen."

Sarah's mouth dropped open as she stared at Luca. Sam sat with a grin on his face and shook his head in agreement. "I love him, and I know his heart. It's why my pictures of him have always been very good. But you, Sarah, have Sam's love. I think that Sam is in love for the first time?" He looked at Sam questioningly. Sam lowered his head and nodded. Sarah's heart stopped as she saw the beautiful boy that was just under Sam's skin. She got off her chair and kneeled between his legs. She took his head in her hands and held him as she whispered sweet things to him. Silence settled over the room for a few minutes, as everyone tried to regain their composure.

377

Luca wiped his eyes, and looked at Sam. "Boy, you know how much I love you. I am so fucking happy for you, but I'm happier that it's Sarah that you love." He took a handkerchief out of his pocket and blew his nose. He clapped his hands. "Okay, here's my ideas. First, the photos that were taken yesterday at the theatre will be in GQ Great Britain and America. But only if you guys are willing to do the interview that will go with them. We're talking about ten pages in the middle of the magazine."

Sarah looked at Sam with enormous eyes. Sam had been quiet, with only a grin on his face.

"Second, I have been on the phone all night and early this morning with some friends in New York. Sarah, it's time. It's *your* time. I think you must do a gallery show. I want to send the curator all of them."

Sarah was dumbstruck. She looked from Luca to Sam. Sam saw that she had tears in her eyes. She finally swallowed and looked back at Sam. "I don't know what to say. Absolutely yes to the gallery showing. But the interview and pictures are Sam's decision. They are just as much his as they are mine."

Amazing Sarah, I hate sharing you with the world. I hate sharing you with anyone, but I vote a huge yes." He stood and pulled her into his arms.

She leaned into his hard chest, and quickly soaked it wet with her tears. She hoarsely whispered. "Look how you've changed my life, Sam Ramsay! My photographs are a part of my heart, but you are all of it."

Sam whispered back, "Look how you've changed my life! Look at how you've changed me."

Sarah turned and walked slowly to Luca. She sat down in his lap, and turned her head into his broad chest. She wrapped her arms around his neck and whispered in his ear, "Thank you, Luca. Thank you for believing in me, but more importantly, thank you for believing in Sam. He has so much more to offer. I love you, Luca, you're now my family."

"Ah, tesoro, you make me weep with joy." Luca wept and embraced her hard.

~~~

Sam couldn't stop smiling, but Sarah was still quiet. He asked, "Can I call Danni? She will shriek, then she'll dance, and there will probably be a lot of happy cursing. Or do you want to call your kids first?"

Sarah laughed as she hugged him. "I would love to hear some happy cursing!"

Sam called Danni. Sarah heard him tell her about all of the pictures Sarah had taken, and what Luca wanted to do with them. And then he told her about the photo shoot at the theatre. "Make sure you buy every fucking copy of GQ , because there will be ten glorious pages of yours truly and the next top model. *And*, it'll be the middle spread."

Sarah could hear Danni all the way across the room. She shrieked. Loudly. Then she loudly proclaimed that she was doing a happy dance. Then the cursing started. "Holy fuck! That's fucking awesome! Are you fucking kidding me? Cocks and ballss, Sam! Fucking cocks and balls! Fuck me runnin'!"

Sam laughed at Sarah, who had laughed so hard she cried. Sam held the phone out to her, because he couldn't speak, but Sarah couldn't either and kept shaking her head no.

Danni got quiet on the other end of the phone, because she heard their hysterics. "Are you guys fucking laughing at me? You are, aren't you? What did you tell her Sam? You ass wipe!"

This made them laugh even louder. They couldn't catch their breath. Sarah sat on the bed with her head between her knees, and Sam was on the floor holding his stomach. Danni got quiet again, and then they heard her laughing. It took all three of them a few minutes to regain a little control. Sarah got the hiccups, and that made all three of them laugh again.

Sarah was finally able to take the phone from Sam. "Oh, shit, Danni! I can't wait for you to meet my girls. Sam will think he's died and gone to heaven. Surrounded by bawdy women will either give him a heart attack, or a permanent boner! You're the only other person I know besides my girls that says 'fuck me runnin'!"

Danni wanted to know what her girls thought, but Sarah told her that she was the first person they had called. Danni got quiet, and then said, "I love you, you Amazonian Goddess. I see many adventures in our future. And, hey, Sam! Can you still fucking hear me? Don't forget about the drag show! Pin Sarah down for her next London visit, because it is on, you ass wipe!"

They chatted a few more minutes before they hung up. Sarah sent a group text to the girls, and waited for them to respond. "I love your relationship with your sister, Sam. You ass wipe." She got tickled again, and her giggles made him laugh some more. Sarah heard the ping notification and opened her phone.

Gemma: Hey, old woman! What's up?

Charlie: Hey mama!

Harper: Sup old woman?

Sarah: Hey girls! How is everyone?

Charlie: Well, we're not in Venice. We're all fine, but we would be even finer if we were in Venice.

Gemma: Especially if we were getting the high hard one every night from that yummy Sam!

Harper: All is well, mom. Is Venice everything you thought it would be?

Sarah: It's even more than I've imagined all these years. It's been an incredible trip. I'll tell you all about it

later, okay?

Charlie: Is everything okay, mom? Are you leaving Sam to run off with Luca?

Sarah: LOL! Not yet! Nothing is wrong. Actually, everything is beyond great.

Gemma: Did you and Sam get married???

Sarah: Ha! No! Remember I told you about Luca looking at my pictures? Well, I took some

more. Of everything, but a lot of Sam. Anyway...it looks like I'll be having a gallery showing in New

 York. I am beyond excited, and it will be a great way to see all of you. You will come, won't you?

Gemma: Holy shit, woman! Of course we'll come!

Harper: Holy shit is right! That is beyond awesome!

Charlie: Oh, mom! I ALWAYS knew how talented you are, it's so great that someone else saw it, too.

Sarah: There's more.

Gemma: You're pregnant???

Sarah: Gemma, you are a funny, funny girl! Please say hello to the next female super model, and her dashing,

younger male super model.

Harper: What???? What does this mean???

Sarah: Luca asked Sam and I to do a photo spread in an old Venetian theatre yesterday, It was fun. It was exciting. It was sexy. We had beautiful clothes. And a LOT of very skimpy lingerie.

Charlie: I can't wait to see the picture, mom. I'm sure they're gorgeous, because you are.

Sarah: Thank you Charlie. But the whole world will be seeing the pictures.They're going to be the middle

pictures in GQ . Ten pages, along with an interview with me and Sam.

Harper: Is Sam there with you? That was a stupid question. I know he's with you. What do you think of my

beautiful mama? She's not going to be embarrassed is she? I'm a little protective.

Sarah: Harper, it's Sam. The pictures are stunning, just like your mum. I would never let anyone

embarrass her. You will be very proud of her.

Gemma: I want to say something dirty, Sam. But, you just called her 'mum' in that fucking British

accent. Then you called my mother 'stunning'. I think I love you.

Charlie: I love you, too, Sam. You 'get' her. She's pretty damn special. But you knowing that, makes you

special, too. I am just so excited for you guys! Not just for the pictures, but for the adventures you

two are going to have. And the love. My mom has earned that. And, I think that maybe you have, too.

Sarah: It's still Sam, and you, Charlie just made me want to hug you. Tight. I can't wait to get to know all

of you.

Sarah: Okay. Back to Sarah. My heart is joyful. So joyful. I love you all. I will be flying home Monday. I will

check in with you when I get home okay?

Harper: Safe travels, mom. You, too, Sam. Hope to see you soon.

Gemma: Safe travels you two love birds. See you soon Sam!

Charlie: Love you, mom. Safe flight, and watch for deer on the drive home. Sam, safe flight. Get your ass to the

farm. You need to see my mom in her element. And YOU need to start practicing your karaoke!

Sam and Sarah sat back in their chairs. Sarah was elated, and Sam was thoughtful. "I love your daughters, and I don't even know them. They love you so much, and they have so much fun with you." He looked up at Sarah. "That's a testament to good parenting skills. You and your family are so similar to mine. I think that's pretty cool."

"It is, isn't it?" Sarah grinned. "I think that's why I loved your family immediately."

They sat and smiled at each other for a while.

Chapter 30:

They decided that you couldn't go shopping in The Rialto without dressing up a bit, so they did. They were supposed to meet Marta at St. Mark's, and then walk over the Rialto Bridge to hit the designer boutiques. Sarah was determined to take home a pair of Italian leather shoes. They went to the restaurant downstairs in The Gritti, and grabbed a quick bite to eat. Sarah was surprised that Sam wanted to go shopping with her and Marta, but then again she wasn't. He was a clothes horse. He loved fashion, and why wouldn't he? He and Marta would be able to give her great advice. She mentioned this to him as they ate breakfast.

"I don't need to advise you on anything, Sarah. I love your style. Don't change anything!"

They finished their lunch, and spotted Marta immediately in St. Marks square. Sarah and Marta hugged and laughed. As they walked, Sam and Sarah filled her in on all that had transpired over the last few days. Marta squealed, "Luca! Luca loves your pictures *and* you! That is phenomenal! I can't wait to see them. I'm thinking that your showings in New York will coincide with my trip to the States. Can I come? Please!"

Sarah hugged Marta again. "That would be wonderful! Then I can be sure that at least five people will be there."

Sam looked at Sarah funny. "Five?"

"Yeah. Five." Sarah stopped and thought. "Charlie and Trace. That's two. Gemma. That's three. Harper. That's four. And Marta. That's five."

"Sarah! I'll be there! Why would you think that I wouldn't be there?" Sam was a little annoyed.

Sarah grabbed his arm. "I didn't think your schedule would allow it. Are you serious? Oh my God! That would be wonderful!"

"So that's six!" Sam grinned.

"No! Seven. Mark will be there, too!" Marta informed them.

Sarah grinned, and looked both of them. "Look how lucky my life has become." Marta and Sam shook their heads at her, and the three continued to walk.

They walked over the Rialto Bridge and headed to the Armani store first. They had fun looking at everything, but Sarah knew the price tags were a stop sign for her. Marta and Sam weren't interested in anything, either. They went into the Prada store next. All three of them decided before they went in that they were going to have fun, and try everything on. So they did.

Sam tried on a charcoal-colored velvet tuxedo that made Sarah's heart stop. He was truly one of the world's most beautiful men. It's not that she forgot how gorgeous he was, because she was with him every day, but sometimes his beauty was blinding. Sam looked good in anything, but suits and tuxedos always made him look like a work of art. on his body. Sam stood and posed in goofy positions. But Sarah couldn't laugh. All she wanted to do was climb him like a tree. Damn! What this man did to her! Evidently he did it to all the sales girl's, too, as they all giggled like school girls the moment they walked in the store.

Sarah swallowed. "You need to get that tuxedo, Sam. it's just so... sexy."

"You know I need another suit like I need a hole in my head! And you also know that I try to purchase British fashion." Sam watched her as he fingered the lapels. "Though, I'm sure I could find a use for it eventually..."

Sarah walked up to him and rubbed her hands up and down the front of the jacket's beautifully soft velvet.

He bent over and whispered in her ear. "You really need to stop doing that, or I'm going to have to find a chair and a newspaper."

Sarah whispered back, "I want you to wear this to the premiere tomorrow night. And all night I want you to think about the fun we could have with this luscious material back in our apartment."

"I'll take this one!" Sam yelled at the giggling sales girls.

Sam quickly had the suit fitted with alterations and arranged for delivery to the Gritti.

The Gucci store was Sarah's heaven. She found a pair of deep wine stilettos that had gold heels and trim. They were so sexy, and she knew they would look great with almost any color. They also looked good on her. She saw Sam swallow hard when she put them on. But, she would never pay a thousand dollars for a pair of shoes. Sarah stood and petted them for a while, before she sadly had the sales girl put them back. Sam didn't try to talk her into buying them, as he knew once she made up her mind, it was made up.

Sarah and Marta found the sale items, and became children in a toy store. They both found purses, and Sarah found a belt. Sarah figured that if she didnt go home with Italian leather shoes, she would go home with Italian leather accessories. Sam stood by the door and patiently waited for Marta and Sarah to pay for their treasures. He watched them with a grin on his face. As they all walked out, Sarah noticed the bag that Sam carried. "What did you get, Sam? I didn't even notice you looking at anything."

"Oh, it's a pair of shoes that Alex asked me to pick up for him. He had ordered them and they were holding them in the back. It kind of surprised me, as I never knew that Alex was into Italian shoes. Go figure." He shrugged his shoulders as they continued on to their next destination.

Sarah was so excited to be able to enter Dittura. She had been ordering Sells furlane for years on line, but she thought being able to see them made and bought in the same store was the coolest thing ever. She explained to Sam and Marta that Sells furlane were the traditional gondolier velvet shoes. They were soft and supple, and if you weren't a gondolier, you would wear them as house slippers. As Sarah was a barefoot girl, and didn't wear house slippers, she had always worn them as shoes. She bought a pair of dark green with gold sequins, and a pair of deep eggplant with red sequins and roping. Marta loved them so much that she bought a pair for her and Mark. Sarah wanted to buy a pair for Sam, but he was a barefooter, too.

Next was Mondo Nova, the Carnival mask store. Marta made it out with four masks, and Sarah purchased ten. Sam raised his eyebrows when she bought that many. She laughingly explained that three would be for her daughters for Christmas, and the other seven would be used as décor in her house. Sam grinned. "I can't wait to see your house. You decorating skills are probably as unique as everything else about you."

The last stop was Ruga dei Speziali. The aromas hit their noses as soon as they opened the door. It was a sensory overload of coffee, cardamom, cinnamon, and nutmeg, and all manner of spices. Sam and Sarah were in spice heaven, and proceeded to fill their baskets. Sam hadn't known about the shop, and he was excited to take all the wonderful smells home to his London kitchen. Marta laughed as she watched them. She didn't cook, but she enjoyed the sights, sounds, and smells.

Sam was accosted by shrieking girls on their way to find pizza. They all wanted their picture taken with him. Marta laughed and pointed to a pizzeria up the street. "I'll order for you." Sarah took each girl's phone and took everyone's picture. She then asked one of them to take her camera and take her and Sam's pictures. Finally able to break free, they made their way to Marta and inhaled their pizza before heading back to The Gritti. Marta had booked a room at the motel next door so they parted ways with hugs and promises to eat together after the junket that evening.

~~~

Sam and Sarah had kicked off their shoes when they got back to the apartment. They curled up together, face to face on the couch. Their legs were entwined, and Sam brushed his fingers through Sarah's short hair.

"Your hair is so soft. I love feeling it in my fingers."

"Hmmm. Feels good," Sarah murmured. She was ran her hand softly up and down his chest.

They continued to talk softly and touch each other. It was if they wanted to store up as much touch, scent, and sight as they could. Sarah slowly unbuttoned Sam's shirt and opened it so she could feel his skin against her hand. She caressed the hard planes of his stomach and chest. Sam unbuttoned Sarah's blouse, so he could kiss the soft skin of her collar bone. They softly discussed the changes that had occurred in their lives in just the last few days. They talked about the future, schedules, and food they liked or hated. They talked politics and religion. They talked music and sports. Sarah told him how painful it was to get sanded, buffed, and waxed. He knew how it felt, as he had his chest or legs waxed often for pictures, and he couldn't imagine how it felt for her lady bits. He wondered why she continued to do it, if it was painful.

"You don't have to trim the lawn for me Sarah. I don't have a preference." Then Sam stopped and thought for a minute. "Well, maybe I do. I've never seen you with anything other than a landing strip, and I know I like what you feel like." He gave her a wicked little grin. "I also fucking love the way you look when you are all sanded, buffed, and waxed. You're beautiful in all your slickness, and I love looking at it."

Sarah smiled as she unbuttoned and unzipped Sam's jeans. "I started doing it again before I went to London to see you. So, yeah, I did it for you. But I love the way it makes me feel. I love the way a thong, and a landing strip makes me feel when I'm walking down the street. It makes me feel sexy. And when I don't wear anything... I love the way your eyes get almost black when I see you picturing me in all my slickness. So, it's a win-win."

Sam had pushed her skirt up around her waist, and lightly rubbed her stomach. The next sound was Sarah's lacy panties being ripped down the front. "Let's head into the bedroom, and you can show me all that slickness." He grinned as he stood up and took her hand.

~~~

Sam and Sarah changed for the press junket. Sam wore a camel-colored wool suit jacket and trousers. He paired the suit with a black shirt and a black-and-camel-colored striped tie. He wore two-toned brown and black oxford shoes and gold cufflinks. Sarah wore a black pencil skirt that ended below her knees and a pair of camel-colored heels. She paired a three-quarter sleeve, camel-colored, high-neck silk blouse. The only jewelry she wore was gold earrings. Sam looked up at her and whistled. "Very elegant, Ms. Reid."

She laughed and said, "Thank you, Mr. Ramsay." She did a slow turn to reveal the cowl in the back. It opened all the way to the waistband of her skirt.

Sam strode to her and caressed the exposed back. He watched as goose bumps appeared on Sarah's skin as he caressed her. It made him feel proud that he could elicit that kind of response from her. But, he was having a response to her, too. He always had a response. He stayed in a constant state of arousal when he was around her. Sarah turned, and Sam slowly grinned. Then his mouth dropped opened as he stared at her magnificent tits. The silk of her blouse could not conceal the obvious proof of her arousal. Her nipples stared straight at him.

Sam reached out a finger and rubbed it across one of the peaks.

She laughed as she picked up her clutch. She grabbed Sam's hand. As they walked out the door, she leaned into Sam's ear and whispered, "I'm not wearing any panties, either."

Sam looked up at the ceiling and growled, "Bloody hell, woman! You are killing me!"

When they stepped out of their private elevator, they saw the regular paparazzi horde. The press didn't notice Sam and Sarah until they started to make their way through the decadent lobby. Then the flashbulbs and questions started. They didn't stop for pictures this time. They made their way through the gauntlet of people, and the maze of hallways in The Gritti. After they entered the conference room and the doors shut, the sounds were immediately muted.

Sam held Sarah's hand to lead her to her designated spot at the front, and he grinned as he overheard remarks about Sarah's ensemble. She looked like an elegant lady when she walked toward you, but when she walked by you, she looked like an elegant sex kitten. She was a total juxtaposition.

Sam took his place in the front and leaned back to wait for everyone to arrive and get seated. He looked over at Sarah who sat with a smile on her face and her long legs crossed at the ankles. Her eyes had never left him. Sam felt a sudden burst of sublime joy. It was almost painful how much emotion he had for her. As he watched her watch him, it nearly made him want to weep with pure happiness. He knew in that moment that he would move from London to be with her wherever she was. He would retire to be with her. If she wanted him to grow a beard to his knees, he would do it. He was hers completely. It was terrifyingly wonderful to be so in love.

Sarah watched Sam's face, and wondered what he had just thought. She saw his eyes grow wide. It looked as if he had experienced an epiphany. When he refocused on her again, the look that he gave her was raw, honest, and breathtaking. She knew in that moment that she would move to London to be with him. If he wanted her to become a hermit in his home and wear nothing but an apron, she would do it. If he wanted her to give up the plans with Luca, she would do it. If it meant seeing her children only once a year, God help her, she would do it. She knew in that moment that she wasn't whole without him, and it scared the hell out of her. Everything that she had attained, everything she had worked for, meant nothing to her, if she wasn't with Sam. Her eyes widened and her mouth opened as she continued to look at the beautiful man in front of her.

As they stared at each other, they both saw at the same time, the utter, and complete submission into each other. Sarah gave a quiet little "Oh!" Sam stood up and quickly walked over to her. He knelt down in front of her.

"I love you amazing Sarah. I will go wherever, and do whatever you want. I am yours to do with as you wish." Sam picked up her hand and kissed the knuckles of each finger. As he looked up into her eyes, he choked out, "Do you know how lost I would be without you?"

Sarah leaned her head into his neck and whispered tearfully, "Ditto, Sam Ramsay. Ditto."

They just absorbed each other for a few minutes, until they both realized that it had gotten quiet. As they looked around, they saw that everyone had stopped their activities to look at them. Flashbulbs flashed bright strobes of light, but no one said a word. Sam stood up. He looked at Sarah and kissed her softly on her cheek before he made his way back to his chair.

"I'm sorry, everyone. I just had a life-changing experience. I never thought that would happen in a room full of reporters." Sam grinned as he looked at Sarah again. She was still teary-eyed, but smiled back.

"That was pretty intense, Sam. Did you pop the question?" a reporter in the back asked.

Sam chuckled as he looked at Sarah. "No. I did not "pop the question", but I will right now if that's what Sarah wants. I just realized that I would do whatever she asked of me."

Sarah laughed and shook her head. "Sorry. Sam and I just experienced a very private moment that wasn't private."

The reporters laughed. A reporter that was familiar to Sarah stood and asked. "Sarah, I know what you're going to say before I even ask it. I realize that this is about Oakwood and Sam. I promise we will get to that, but first, could you tell us a little bit about yourself? It might help with the dodgy headlines. As you and Sam are not shy about your relationship, it would be nice to know you a little better."

Sarah looked at Sam as he smiled. She looked back at the reporter. "Okay, I will answer your *one* question, but then it's back to the Oakwood Campaign, okay?" She watched everyone turn on their recorders, and the few old schoolers who had paper and pencil.

"I was an only child of wonderful parents. I married my high school sweetheart. David and I went to college, and traveled a bit. We had a wonderful marriage that lasted almost thirty-five years. I have three beautiful, professional daughters and a son-in-law that are my best friends. None of them live in Missouri, but I enjoy my road trips to see them. No grandchildren."

The reporters murmured amongst themselves. "My husband and I had just finished building our farmhouse on land that has been in my family for generations when David passed away from an aneurysm. I was an adoption liaison for twenty-five years, but retired when my husband died. I'm five-foot-ten, but I do love heels, so I'm usually taller. I tend to have a different color of hair every month. I dabble in photography, and I cook really well. I love to travel, as you all have probably noticed." The reporters laughed.

" I have a small circle of great girlfriends that I'm missing very much. I have had a good life that I was content with, until I met Sam by bumping into him in St. Louis. Literally. We liked each other immediately, I think." She looked at Sam, who nodded his head yes. "He's funny and kind, and a true gentleman, and he was so incredibly nice to me when I was an invalid. Yes. I am a cougar." The room erupted in laughter.

Before the reporters could ask more questions, Sam reminded them again of why they were there. They proceeded with the standard questions that he had answered a million times. But, ever the gentleman, he patiently answered and joked and passed a lot of it off to Marta and the Oakwood people. He was able to stare at Sarah when someone else answered a question. He had decided that looking at Sarah was one of his favorite things.

Sam and Marta saw a reporter walk up to Sarah when the presser was over. They could hear her chatting with him. "Watch her. She'll have him eating out of her hand in a matter of minutes."

Marta clasped Sam's forearm and stared at him before she looked back at Sarah. "If you would have told me six months ago, that you would be with an older widow, I would have thought you'd lost your mind. But Sarah is one of the most genuine people I think I've ever known. Did you notice that I didn't say anything about her being gorgeous? Or that I didn't say anything bitter about her legs? If you screw this up, I want her, okay? I'm sure that Mark wouldn't complain at all to be sandwiched between me and her."

They heard the reporter try to find out the name of the town Sarah lived in. Sarah just laughed and told him, "You don't need to know that, as I'm sure you'll find out on your own. I don't live in a town. I live in the boonies, but the small town that is closest to me, doesn't even have a motel. It has two stop lights, and a great coffee shop. But if you were thinking of coming, I thought you'd like to know that you wouldn't have a place to sleep."

The reporter laughed, and said, "That sounds as charming as you Sarah."

"Why, thank you sir!" Sarah turned to Sam and Marta.

Sam looked at Marta. "See! I told you so!"

~~~

They were so tangled in each other that you couldn't tell where one began and the other ended. They had left a trail of clothes across the floor of their apartment that led to the bedroom. Sarah wore only her silk blouse. Sam had made her keep it on, and she was happy he had. The silk against her bare skin elicited fabulous sensations.

They had revealed their private public moments in the press junket. They stared at each other when they both realized that they had come to the same conclusions.

You would truly leave your children for me, Sarah?" Sam asked hoarsely as he nestled his chin into her neck.

"I wouldn't be leaving them, Sam. It would just be more difficult. I wouldn't see them as often. They're grown women with their own lives. I've done my job as a mother. Now it's my time. I'm not being selfish, it's just that I don't think I could live without you." Sarah whispered against his hair as tears ran down her cheeks. She felt totally vulnerable with the feelings that had been swirling around in her head for the last few hours.

Sam had to catch his breath before he spoke. "You have so much more to leave than I do. Mine is mostly just work, but yours is flesh and blood of your body. The love you have for your daughters has to be a visceral, physical thing, and that brings me to my knees. That you would do that for me...."

"It's not for you, Sam. It's for us. This -thing - between us is something bigger than physical attraction, or our enjoyment of each other. It's as if we've found pieces of our soul that we didn't even know were missing. I feel as if I've finally found my way home."

"La mia casa e' dove sei." Sam whispered in Italian. "My home is where you are."

Chapter 31:

They sat at the table and ate eggs benedict and drank their espresso.

"Do you have anything on your agenda today?"

Sam shrugged his shoulders. "I thought you could just tell me what you wanted to do. I'm game for anything."

Sarah wiggled her eyebrows. "Anything, Sam?"

"Well, almost anything. You wore my ass out last night."

Sarah put her hand on top of his that was sitting on the table. "I'd like to stay in today. We'll have a late night tonight. I'd like to shoot some pictures here in the apartment. Just you and me. The only pictures we have together are the ones I've had other people take."

"Just us?" Sam was confused.

"Uh, we would be in a state of undress. I want to shoot us in all the places we've made love. Lets see... that would be on the staircase, in the pool, in the bed, and on the couch." Sarah's eyes twinkled.

Sam grinned. "Don't forget the table and the floor."

"Oh, the table!" She sighed deeply. "These would be just for our enjoyment. I thought they may be nice when we're texting each other, if you know what I mean. But nothing pornographic. Nothing I'd be embarrassed to show people."

"You know I can't say no to you." Sam looked at her over the rim of his coffee cup.

Sarah smiled a little sadly. "I don't want to share you with anyone else today. Not even Venice. Just you and me."

"We're my favorite duo." Sam grabbed her hand across the table and softly rubbed the top of it.

They spent the next hour checking their social media and texting friends and family. They worked in silent companionship until Sam started to laugh. Sarah looked over at him with a grin on her face. She knew he had found the surprise she had left him on his Facebook page.

"I see you started following me, Sarah! Boy, did you start following me!" Sam kept looking at the computer screen. A picture had been posted on his page. It was black and white, and it was beautiful. It was an extreme close up of Sarah's bosom. There were no nipples, and it wasn't pornographic, it was just Sarah's amazing cleavage. She had angled the camera where you saw no face.

"This is beautiful. You should definitely shoot nudes, Sarah. You continue to surprise me with your artistry." He clicked on the picture as Sarah watched, and saw him change his home page picture to her breasts. "The fans are *not* going to like seeing tits on my page, but I don't care. This is art."

Sarah looked at him quizzically and asked, "How did you know it was me?"

"Hell, Sarah! I know every inch of your body. Especially those creamy orbs of goodness!" Sam kept his eyes on the screen.

Sarah burst out laughing so hard that she snorted. Sam looked at her like she'd lost her mind. "What's so damn funny?"

She continued to laugh and snort. "Creamy orbs of goodness? Holy shit, Sam! You need to write bodice rippers. Are you going to start calling your dick the 'love rod'? Or will you start calling yourself my 'sex stallion'?" She clutched her stomach and tried to catch her breath to no avail. She couldn't gather her composure.

He started to laugh. "No, from this moment I shall start calling my dick "the battering ram."

Sarah laughed even harder. "Then you shall start calling my lady bits the "pink pearl."

"Will your bosom heave with want for me?" Sam had slid to the floor with his hands across his stomach.

"Oh! My melons will tremble with the wanting of your manhood. My 'pink pearl' will clench in silent spasmodic wonder as it sees your heaving, pulsating man steel!"

"We have got to fucking stop! I'm dying! I seriously can't breathe!" Sam was in pain from the laughter.

They lay on the floor as they clutched their stomachs and tried to catch their breath. Sarah looked over at Sam. "I think we might have to start new careers. We need to write erotica!"

Sarah left the room to track down her camera, tripod, filters, and remote. After Sarah had everything set up, she knelt on the floor by Sam and started to remove his clothes. He lay there quietly and watched her pull down his lounge pants. He didn't have a shirt on, so she made quick work of him. She then stripped off her tee shirt and panties. As she lay down next to him, he reached for her with his beautiful ice blue eyes, now a steely gray. "Huh uh, buddy! I have plans for tonight, but pictures to take right now!"

Sam grinned and Sarah almost caved. But she didn't. She lay down by him and wrapped an arm around his waist and put her head on his chest. "Is your pink pearl wanting my battering ram?" Sam playfully asked.

"My pinkness is always in want of your ram, but right now we're just going to talk." Sarah pinched his skin over his rib.

"Ouch! I thought you wanted to take pictures. What's up with the talking?"

Sarah looked up at him seriously. "Because I don't want you to go into your pose mode. I don't want your hands placed perfectly on my body or the scowl that you're so famous for. And I better not see your hands anywhere on your face! You'll never know when I take the pictures, so let's just lay here and 'be'."

They stayed on the floor and continued to talk quietly. Sarah moved occasionally, which made Sam do likewise. They then moved onto the table in front of the window. Their backdrop was The Grand Canal, with St. Mark's and Venice herself. Sarah led Sam to the couch and cuddled with him. The entire time she kept him busy with conversation, and occasionally kisses and caresses. They went into the bedroom, then onto the spiral staircase, before going onto their rooftop terrace, and into the pool. Sam was relaxed, and happy, in awe of Sarah's gift of taking his mind off of the camera. Three hours of holding, kissing, and touching Sarah was the best way to spend his time. He couldn't wait to see the images she captured.

~~~

Sam went to the gym for a quick workout, so Sarah showered before she started to transfer pictures to her laptop. While the images transferred, she steamed her dress. She stood in the bedroom with the steamer in her hand when Sam returned. He was sweaty and sexy and held a garment bag and two brown paper sacks. He stopped as he saw the dress that she was steaming. He slowly grinned and opened the garment to reveal the charcoal velvet Prada tuxedo that had been delivered to The Gritti after altering. It was the tuxedo that Sarah had insisted he buy.

"Now I know why you insisted on this tux!" He smiled at Sarah as he walked over to her. He held the velvet softness next to her gown. Sarah's dress was a floral confection of wispy layers of chiffon. Layer after layer of pastel blues, yellows, pinks, greens, and lilacs. In the center of each sheer flower was a dot of the same charcoal color of Sam's tuxedo.

Sarah stood with her mouth open as she looked between the gown and tuxedo. "I had no idea! I swear! I meant what I said about having fun with that jacket. I'd never noticed that this gown had any charcoal in it."

Sam shook his head as he looked at her. "I'm not going to question it anymore, either. It's just what we do. I had a surprise for you, but I don't think they'll work with this dress."

"Oh goody! Goody! I love surprises!" Sarah turned off the steamer and waited as Sam walked to the closet and removed the bag he had left the store with yesterday. "I thought that was for Mark?" Sarah looked up at Sam.

"I have learned not to try to talk you into something after you have made up your mind. But I knew you had to have them." He opened the shoebox to reveal the heels Sarah had loved at the Prada store.

Sarah grabbed them out of his hands and quickly set down on the bed to put them on. They were a work of art, and Sam knew they would never look as good on anyone else as they did on Sarah. Wrapped up in the fluffy white robe, the shoes made her long legs look like they went on forever. The black boots had just got moved into second place, because these shoes were meant to be wrapped around his waist.

"Oh, Sam. I love them so much. And you're right, I did pet them. A lot. I'm not going to complain about the money that you spent on them, because I love them, and you, so much. And I know that it gives you pleasure to give me pleasure. Thank you, Sam. You sure know how to treat a girl."

"I love to give you pleasure in everything, Sarah. Thank you for not complaining. I have plans for those shoes." Sam looked at her lustfully.

"Hmmm. They would look great with your tuxedo."

"Sarah, as much as I love those shoes, and you, I am *not* going to wear them tonight. I'm not ever going to wear them, no matter how much you might beg."

She grinned broadly. "I won't ask you to, but I definitely have plans for tonight. Just keep thinking about that." She looked over. "What's in the sacks?"

Sam's had completely forgotten about the sandwiches. "They're sandwiches and a bottle of Jameson. We haven't eaten since late morning, and our dinner will be late. It's probably a good idea to eat a little something. Do you want a drink?"

They nursed their drinks as they looked at the images on the laptop. Sam should have been used to seeing the beauty that Sarah drew from her subjects, but he was again struck by how the images were sexy yet emotional at the same time. They looked at all of the images before Sarah went back and selected her favorites. She had caught Sam as he lay on the floor, holding his stomach as he laughed. His head was back and his mouth was open. You could see the crinkles around his eyes that only came from laughter. In another, Sam kissed Sarah's hair. Her head was on his chest as they lay with their legs entwined on the couch. The curve of Sarah's ass and the softness of her breast against his chest was in soft focus.

The bedroom evoked a different kind of response from them both. They were sexy, but not graphic. Sarah's favorite was her on the bed with one arm over her head and the other around Sam's neck. She had her eyes closed and had thrown one leg around his waist with the other leg spread out. Sam laid over her with his hand on one of Sarah's breasts, the other covered by his body. His head was turned in profile. He, too, had his eyes closed. The muscles of his back were flexed, as well as the gluteal muscles in his ass. The smoothness of Sarah's stomach and the back of Sam's neck made them both look as if they were composed of silk. They both sat and stared at the image.

"It reminds me of the mirror in Milan. It's so sexy."

Sam nodded. "I thought the same thing. It's definitely got a rise out of me." He looked down at his trousers, where they could both see the extent of his arousal. "We're fucking beautiful together, Sarah."

"We are better together than we are apart." Sarah sighed and took his hand. "This is one of my favorites. I'll go through my final few picks." She clicked on the arrow and opened up the photo on the table in front of the windows. She and Sam were in shadow. He had laid on his back on top of the table. His long legs were stretched out, showcasing his fabulous thigh muscles. His eyes were glued to Sarah. She straddled him on her knees, with her back to the camera. He had his hands around her waist and her head was in profile. It showed Sarah's beautiful back and ass, as well as a significant amount of a breast, with a hint of a nipple. But the star of this photo was the backdrop of Venice with The Grand Canal, St. Mark's, and the piazza. The sunlight reflecting of the dome of St. Mark's gave a golden glow to everything outside the windows.

"I love this one, because we're almost in black and white, but everything else is in that golden Venetian glow. I don't need to do anything to this photo. This one is going on the wall at home." Sarah squeezed his hand.

"Me, too. This will sit on my bedside table." He kissed her cheek and turned quickly back to the screen.

The next image was of them in the pool. Sarah was straddling Sam with her hands clasped around his neck and her head on his chest. Her breasts were pushed against his chest, and her eyes were focused on something in the distance. She looked far away. Sam's arms were around Sarah and, he, too looked at something in the distance. Sam's shoulders, and again the backdrop of Venice, were partners in the picture.

The last one that they looked at was of them on the staircase. Sam gasped when Sarah brought it up on the screen. "Damn!"

was all he could say. He suddenly understood why Sarah had made them get in the shower before they had made their way to the stairs. Their hair was wet and wild, and their bodies glistened. Sarah leaned back over the railing. One hand clutched at the iron as she stared intensely at Sam, while her other hand grabbed his hair. One of her long legs was bent on a step, and the other was extended out onto the next step down. Sam loomed over her like an animal, intent on devouring her. One hand clutched her breast, and the other arm encircled her waist. One long leg was placed in between Sarah's and the other was stretched onto the step below. The light and shadow played off his magnificent physique. His deep obliques and his jaw looked as if they had been etched with a knife. The bunched muscles of his back and shoulder, and the tight roundness of his ass communicated his intent.

"I see ravishment. I see lust. I see intent. I see sex. I *feel* fire." Sarah whispered as she looked at Sam.

 "I look at this and all I want to do is finish fucking you, because this picture is the preamble. This picture is fucking foreplay. I'm proud of these pictures Sarah! They need to go in the showing." He looked at her intently.

She slowly shook her head. "I think so, too. They're perfection, and they're us. Do you know how long I've wanted to take pictures like this? A lifetime. But they were so worth the wait. And so were you."

~~~

Sam paired his new charcoal tuxedo with a pale lilac shirt, a gray bow tie, and black shoes. He had just finished putting in silver cufflinks when Sarah walked out of the bathroom. "Sam? Can you lace me?" She had her arms wrapped around her chest to keep her gown from falling off. Even though not completely dressed, she was a vision. She turned around, and Sam saw that the top of the gown was a bustier that laced down the back. The laces were charcoal ribbon. Sam laced the bustier tight and finished it off with a bow that stopped at Sarah's tail bone.

Sarah bent over and shook her tits to get them where they needed to be. She stood up and looked at Sam. The entire gown was the sheer floral fabric, including the form-fitting bustier. The full, multi-layered chiffon fell from the bottom of the bustier and gathered to make a small train. She paired the outfit with pale lilac heels and a large amethyst pendant and matching earrings. Sarah had let her hair air dry, and it was soft, wavy, and unkempt. She was a spring vision.

"You never screw up, do you?"

"Never screw up?" Sarah asked quizzically.

"You never make a false step. Not in your fashion sense, in your friends, in your photographs, in anything."

"Oh, Sam, I am *not* perfect! Believe me. You just haven't seen me in the real world yet. But thank you for that." She reached up and kissed him softly. "I can be a bitch sometimes. Just like any woman."

"Oh, God, I hope so. It's impossible to live up to you. I'm looking forward to a little bitchiness."

As they made their way down the elevator, he couldn't take his eyes off her. Sam shook his head. "I don't understand how you can look like a spring princess with your tits hanging out. But somehow you do." Sam felt different about this Sarah. Her other gowns had been pure wanton sexiness, but this one made him want to cherish, treasure, and love her. Slowly. And preferably all night.

"It's a little girlier than I normally go for. But I thought it a perfect gown for Venice. I feel pretty in it." Sarah smiled.

As the elevator door opened, she continued to look at Sam with a grin on her face, and added, "By the way, I'm still not wearing panties."

Chapter 32:

Sam and Sarah made their way to the red carpet. They heard the familiar noise and bustle of reporters and crowd outside. They waited for their cue before starting the routine Sarah had become familiar with. Sam never took his arm from around her waist. He smiled when he noticed the cameras wanted as many pictures of her as they did of him. As they slowly made the walk, he heard a voice yell something about potty training. He looked at Sarah with a raised eyebrow. She broadly smiled at a man in the crowd before she walked to him and kissed him on both cheeks. After a brief conversation, she again kissed his cheeks before she returned to Sam's side.

"What was that all about?" Sam was curious.

"That's Jean, the reporter I met in Paris. Remember? He was having a potty training issue with his three-year-old. He wanted to let me know that my suggestion had worked." Sarah continued to slowly walk and smile for the cameras.

Sam shook his head and squeezed her a little tighter.

They found a table with Luca at the after party. The music already blared, and they felt the beat of the bass at their table. Sam went to the bar to get a bottle of Jameson, some glasses, and Sarah's camera that the staff had left with the bartender. She was anxious to show Luca the pictures she had taken. It was a funny feeling to not be nervous. He had validated her talent and had given her a huge burst of confidence. She knew the pictures were good.

Sarah watched Sam as he made his way through the crowd. He stopped and talked several times to the people that approached him. She saw him laugh before he saw her. She watched his jaw clench. He held the bottle under his arm while his hands held the glasses. Her camera was hung by the strap around his neck. "Yep," Sarah remarked to Luca as she grinned and put her chin in her hand. "I am fucking smitten. I'm a smitten kitten."

Luca looked at Sarah and laughed loudly. "Have you noticed how much more relaxed Sam is around everyone? Getting drunk and singing in front of your coworkers works every time. If I didn't know better, I'd say you did that on purpose." Luca's eyes twinkled devilishly.

Sarah looked innocently at Luca. "Who? Me?" She turned back to Sam to watch him walk the last few steps to their table. Her head stayed in her hand and she continued to grin at Sam stupidly. He smiled that slow, sexy smile that made Sarah's knees go weak.

"What's up?" He set down the bottle and the glasses, and unwrapped the camera strap from around his neck.

Luca snorted. "She's a smitten kitten."

"I thought you were a cougar. You need to make up your mind which feline you want to be. I don't have a preference, as both of them purr." Sam leaned his forehead against Sarah's and kissed her on the tip of her nose. Sarah purred.

As Sam poured the whiskey, Sarah brought up the pictures on her camera. Sarah toasted. "Here's to love. The love of new friends, new adventures, and the love of a good man. May everyone be as blessed as me."

"Hear! Hear!" the men exclaimed.

Luca scrolled through the pictures as Sam and Sarah sipped their whiskey and talked quietly. "These are phenomenal, Sarah! But you know that, don't you?" He looked at Sarah, who nodded her head yes. "You don't need to have me critique your work, sweet girl. Anything that you think is good is going to be good. These need to be seen. Are you two okay with that? Are these too personal?"

"They are personal, but we love them." Sam looked to Sarah for confirmation. "We think they're beautiful. For the first time in my entire career I haven't been concerned about what I do with my body. With Sarah, I'm focused on her, or on something else entirely, other than me."

Luca looked at the two of them. "Sarah, you are incredibly beautiful in your photographs. You are a beautiful woman, but lots of beautiful women don't photograph well. You are taking the pictures, and I have no idea how you pull that off. As a man who has made a very good living with his camera, I am humbled by your talent."

With tears in her eyes Sarah whispered. "Tiamo, Luca. Tesoro mio."

"Well, in order to start crying in our whiskey, we need to have some of it in our glasses." Sam refilled their glasses. Before Sarah could take a sip, a young man walked up to their table and asked Sarah if she was going to sing again.

Sarah laughed. "Maybe. But I don't want to be a spotlight whore!"

The man told her that some of them brought guitars and were hoping for a little jam session. "That sounds like fun! I'll sing, but only if Sam sings with us."

"As long as it's not a solo, I'll do it. But let's wait a little while, okay?" Sam looked at the young man.

"Of course!" The man obliged. "I actually came to see if Sarah would dance with me."

"Let's go, handsome! Prepare to get your groove on!" Sarah looked over her shoulder at Sam, as she to the dance floor. "The next slow one, sexy, and you're all mine!"

Sam grinned, and whispered, "I'm already all yours."

Sam talked Luca into staying so he could hear Sarah sing. They walked to the edge of the dance floor to watch her become art in motion. Luca was mesmerized, but Sarah always mesmerized him. "Does she do anything badly?" He never took his eyes off of Sarah.

"She's told me that she can be a bitch sometimes, but I've yet to see it. She's set the bar very high, Luca." Sam feasted his eyes upon the banquet in floral chiffon.

Luca grabbed his arm. "Stop it! Just stop it!"

Sam looked at Luca with surprise on his face. "What the hell are you talking about?"

"Sarah is unique. Everyone who meets her knows that. But, boy, you are selling yourself short. You're the nicest, kindest, most genuinely humble and well mannered fellow I've ever met. The fact that you've been able to retain those qualities with your beauty and fame amazes me. Everything that you've attained is because of the way you look. Oh, you've worked hard, but I wouldn't want to be you, as weird as that sounds. Anybody else would be the cockiest jackass on earth. But not you, Sam. I think it would be hard being you. That's why I love you. As beautiful as you are, you've never been quite comfortable in your own skin."

Sam was quiet as he looked at Luca. "A very smart and beautiful woman once told me that the way I look would be a hard cross to bear. It is sometimes. There is more to me than this face. Plus, my parents would be so disappointed if I was a rude bloke, Luca."

"You and Sarah are good together. She grounds you. She adores you. And you adore her. But you also give her joy. In two or three years, you two are going to be so syrupy that it's going to be sickening." Luca laughed and wrapped Sam in a big bear hug.

The music slowed to a slow instrumental. Sarah was by Sam's side in an instant. "Come on, sexy man!"

They wrapped their arms around each other and glided across the floor. With each dip and twirl, Sarah's dress floated as if stirred by an unseen breeze. This was another of Sarah's favorite things. Dancing with Sam was heavenly. She loved the way he smelled, the way his back felt under her hands, and the way his chest felt against hers. He had removed his bow tie and unbuttoned the top three buttons of his shirt. She leaned in and kissed him in the hollow of his throat before he twirled her again. Luca cut in, and danced her the last few times around the floor. She lay her head on his broad chest and patted his heart with her hand. As the music ended, they walked off the floor together and made their way to Sam.

The three of them had just caught their breath and had taken a sip of whiskey when the young man from earlier brought Sarah a guitar. "A song, Sarah?"

Sarah laughed. "Alright, but just one, then it's every man for themselves." Someone else brought her a microphone that she proceeded to stick in her cleavage to leave her hands free for the guitar. She moved her chair out so she was facing Sam. "Well, everyone, it has been great fun! I'm flying home on Monday morning." The room erupted in groans and someone shouted, "You're not coming to Prague?"

"Not this time. I have a home to get back to. But I promise I'll see most of you again!" The crowd clapped and whistled. Sam, in that moment, felt a pain in his heart at the thought of her leaving. He had tried not to think about it, but Sarah's departure was eminent.

Sarah continued. "I've had the experience of a lifetime. It's been so much fun and I thank you for that. I'm going to sing a Garth Brooks song that a lot of you probably won't know, but I think it very appropriate in this place and time. Please listen to the words, and forgive me for changing some of the lyrics, but know that a little of it is for you guys, a little for Luca, and a lot for Sam Ramsay."

Sarah started strumming the strings, and then began "The Dance." As she sang about the memories made and having to say goodbye, the room was in utter silence as Sarah's clear voice soared over them. Sam sat stiffly, staring intently at her with his hands clasped tightly in his lap. His heart was in his eyes that had started to tear up. Luca, too, was emotional, and Sarah, didn't know if she would be able to finish the song, but she tried. As she finished the next verse, she took a deep breath, and her voice cracked a little as she finished singing about chances.

Sarah handed the guitar to someone in the crowd. She knelt in front of Sam and they bowed their heads together. The room was silent except for a few sniffles from around the room. As the two gathered their composure, the room was errupted in a roar, as everyone clapped and stomped.

The applause continued as Sam stood up with Sarah wrapped in his arms. "I love you amazing Sarah."

"Ditto, Sam Ramsay. Ditto." Sarah whispered.

Sarah was enveloped in a sea of people who wanted to say goodbye. Sam stood wrapped in Sarah's spirit. She was someone who was simply loved by all. Sam wondered what his life would look like if he'd never met her, or if he'd never gone to her motel room that morning with breakfast. That simple act of kindness had changed his life. It had changed his world, and he was suddenly so thankful for his parents who had taught him to be a gentleman. Because his life would have continued to be empty and he would never have been given the gift that was Sarah.

Sam and Sarah were quiet on the elevator. They held hands as they leaned against the cool stainless and gazed at each other. When the doors opened, they both kicked their shoes off and headed for the bedroom. Sam took his jacket off and lay it on the bed, then went to Sarah to untie her laces. As he picked up the velvet jacket, Sarah asked, "Could you get some water Sam, while I hang my dress. I'll get your jacket, too."

Sam went to get the water. He turned off the lights, and picked up their shoes before he headed back into the bedroom. Sarah had turned off the lights before going into the bathroom. Sam sat her water on her bedside table, removed his pants and laid back on the luxuriously soft sheets. He waited for Sarah. He could see the light under the door, and he heard her hum something softly. God, he was going to miss her. She had slid into the routine of the

415

Oakwood Campaign like a seasoned warrior. She had come, she had seen, and she had conquered. It was if she had been doing it all her life, and to have done it with as much grace left Sam missing her before she had even left.

He saw the light go off, leaving the apartment in darkness except for the table lamp on the credenza outside the bedroom door. It cast a golden glow across the bedroom floor. The door opened and Sarah walked out slowly. Sam sat up quickly. "Holy shit!" His heart rate sped up, and he immediately became hard as steel.

Sarah walked to his side of the bed and stared down at him. She was wearing nothing but Sam's velvet tuxedo jacket. The jacket did not close across her abundant cleavage. Sam stared at her hands as she caressed the velvet lapels over her breasts. He could see a hint of her nipples and realized that she was as aroused as him. His eyes traveled slowly down her smooth stomach to the juncture of her thighs. He swallowed and continued to look at her calves and ankles, to stop on the gold trimmed heels. "I told you I had a date with a velvet tuxedo jacket. It feels so soft and sexy against my skin. Would you like to feel it, Sam?"

He moved to the side of the bed. "Yes, please." He brushed his knuckles across one of the velvet lapels over Sarah's breast. He could feel her nipple through the fabric.

Sarah took her phone out of the pocket and started her playlist. "Dance with me?" She reached out her arms, and Sam was more than happy to reach back.

They slowly moved in time with the music. Sarah gently brushed Sam's cheek, before caressing his shoulders and back. She gripped his ass as Sam did his own exploring, his hands staking their own claim on Sarah's breasts. He popped open the only button keeping the jacket closed. He caressed her stomach and the top of her thighs, before grabbing Sarah's ass.

He leaned his head on Sarah's collar bone. "I have never been with a woman that is as much fun as you, Sarah. You're always a surprise. Whether it's your clothes, your hair, your body, or your words, you always keep me guessing, and I love it."

Sarah breathed fast as she replied. "I want you to enjoy me. I want you to always be surprised. I want you to always want me, as I want you. You take my breath away, Sam."

Sam kissed her. He kissed her hard. He bit her bottom lip, and licked from her ear to her collarbone. "Every time I look at you, my heart stops. All I want to do for the rest of my life is to make you smile. To make you sigh. To make you moan. To make you scream. I just want to spend the rest of my life loving you."

Sarah hooked her leg around Sam's waist. "Love me now, Sam."

Chapter 33:

Sam felt the length of Sarah's warm body pressed against his as he slowly woke up. His arm draped across her ribcage and he could feel her deep breaths. He enjoyed the quiet moment. As he watched her sleep, he noticed a wad of gray under her head and started to laugh under his breath. Sarah's breath hitched and she slowly stretched and opened her eyes, before turning to Sam. "Was I snoring?"

Sam grinned at her. "No, I just noticed your pillow cover."

Sarah rubbed the side of her face back and forth across the velvet tuxedo jacket. "Hmmm. It feels so good." She stretched like a cat. Sam expected her to purr. She had purred plenty last night. As he thought about it, so had he. That velvet had been over them, and under them and between them. He would never look at velvet the same way. Who knew it could be an aphrodisiac? Velvet and Sarah's stretched out length against him were a perfect combination.

"Feel like chopping wood?"

They went up to the roof top with their coffee and breakfast. It was early, and the beautiful city of Venice was still quiet. The sun was reflecting off the dome of St. Mark's, and only a few gondolas had started to make their daily rounds. They sat in comfortable silence, knowing that there were no more obligations for them until they flew out on Monday morning. The weekend was theirs to do with as they wanted. Sarah's Oak Wood campaign was over.

Sam leaned back in his lounge chair and turned to Sarah as he took a sip of coffee. "You need to pack an overnight bag and your camera. Our train leaves at ten."

"Our train?"

"I thought we'd spend some time tonight in Verona. I booked a room in a bed and breakfast for the night. It's only an hour and a half by train. I thought it would be nice to see a little more of Italy, and to have a little bit of quiet and just be." Sam said. "I thought we could find a table outside, order some local wine, people watch and just enjoy each other. And maybe make some plans."

Sam? You are a hopeless romantic. The city of Romeo and Juliet? With you?" Sarah beamed. "Making plans with you sounds like a plan." She sighed happily.

~~~

The train ride took them through beautiful countryside. Sarah busied herself taking pictures out of windows and researching Verona on her phone. They checked in to the Hotel Gabbia D' Oro. It was next to the Piazza delle Erbe, so they wouldn't even have to walk far. It was a charmingly elegant, ivy-walled jewel. The rooms were not large, but the owner's special touches were perfection. Antique laces, and faded glory. It was the perfect room for Verona.

After they purchased some apricots and berries, they found a table outside of Caffe Tubino. Gourmet coffee in Italy was bliss. Sam could drink his weight in coffee in a day, and Sarah was almost as bad. They shared their love of coffee and Jameson. Both were manna from heaven.

Sam opened up his calendar on his phone. "I'm anxious to start planning, Sarah. I have to have a goal before we leave on Monday.

I can't see you get on that plane again, not knowing when I'll see you again. It's too gut-wrenching."

"I agree. Let's start with the easiest and work our way backward." Sarah opened her calendar. "I have nothing that can't be rescheduled, except for my showings. I guess we'll have to figure that out when it comes. I was thinking Thanksgiving and Christmas, even though I know you Brits don't really celebrate Thanksgiving."

"I had planned time off from the middle of November until the New Year. What do you think about coming to London for Thanksgiving? I had hoped to spend Christmas with you at the farm." Sam looked hopefully at Sarah.

Sarah grinned and put her chin in her hand. "A perfect birthday, and a perfect Christmas."

"I know!" Sam said excitedly. "Your family needs to come to London for Thanksgiving! All of them! Charlie and Trace, and Gemma and Harper! They can stay at Danni's. She would love it! Bloody hell! My mum and dad would love it!"

"Sam! Calm down! I need to check with them, and you need to check with Danni, but I think it would be amazing." Sarah grabbed Sam's hand. "The thought of a house full of family makes my heart joyful. You are fucking brilliant Sam Ramsay."

They continued to drink their coffee, make plans, and watch the people go about their day. They walked and talked as they made their way back to the piazza and La Fontanina for lunch. They had their choice of carpaccio, venison, Foie gras, calamari, and sea urchin. They couldn't make up their minds, so they ordered the tasting menu and a bottle of delicious local wine. They took their dessert of berries in a paper sack with them, and with sun kissed skin and full bellies, they made their way back to their room for a nap.

Rested, they freshened up and changed for dinner. They had not done any fine dining together, so after some research online, they picked a restaurant right around the corner from their room. As they waited outside for their table, they enjoyed some more of the locally-produced wine with the evening breeze and quiet murmurs of the other patrons around them. Sarah sat with her head on Sam's shoulder. He had placed his arm along the back of Sarah's chair and absently rubbed the back of her neck. "Thank you for this, Sam." Sarah said quietly. "It's been lovely not having to be anywhere, a schedule to keep, or people to see."

"I'm in denial about your departure. But we have tonight and tomorrow night. I just want you all to myself." Sam continued to rub her neck and inhaled the earthy sandalwood of her.

Sarah smiled against his shoulder. "I've tried not to think about it, too, and I hate that I'm going to be missing Prague. It's another city on my bucket list, but maybe we can come next spring or fall?"

"Most definitely! I actually have a shoot with Luca there in June. You'll probably be working with him by then, so we can just extend our stay. Prague is a city you don't want to miss. I actually have soaked up the culture in that city and taken a lot of my own pictures. You would adore the photo opportunities and the food." Sam stood up and took Sarah's hand as the hostess came to seat them at their table.

Everything on the menu sounded delicious, and after they had eyed some of the plates on other people's tables, they decided that they probably couldn't go wrong with whatever they ordered. Sam ordered chestnut ravioli with shrimp, and Sarah ordered pork belly with white truffles. They both ordered fried artichokes and risotto.

"I can't wait to cook risotto for you, Sam. I make a really mean parmesan spinach risotto, and usually pair it with bacon wrapped asparagus and country cured pork belly. Do you like asparagus?"

Sam grinned at her, and kissed her on the cheek before answering. "I like most everything, except squid ink pasta. Nope. Don't like that. But I'll try anything once. Food should be fun and enjoyable, don't you think?"

"Absolutely I think that cooking food, eating food, reading about food, and talking about food are some of life's greatest pleasures. Food is sexy. Charlie, Gemma, Harper, and I have always said that our plan was to eat and drink our way around the world." Sarah sipped her wine. "I'm about two-thirds of the way there."

"I never thought of eating food as sensual, but after watching you with those chocolate croissants in St. Louis, I changed my mind. Do you know how much that turned me on? You actually moaned with pleasure, and all I wanted to do was rub the chocolate all over your body and lick it off. And I didn't even know you." Sam turned serious as he looked at Sarah. "Where would we be right now, Sarah, if you hadn't gone to St. Louis? What if you hadn't hurt your ankle? What if you hadn't been so fucking funny?"

Sarah put her hand on his cheek. "You would be spending a lot of time alone in your room, and I would be content. Only content, not happy. It's a sad thought, isn't it? When I think about it, and I think about it a lot, I think how much I love your parents."

Sam looked confused. "My parents?"

"Yes, because they worked hard to provide for you and Danni, and you haven't forgotten that. You have their work ethic. Your parents raised an amazing son, who is a gentleman with manners, and principles. And because, after all of the fame you've achieved, you remain nice and kind and humble. And *that's* why I love your parents. If you weren't such an incredibly nice man, you would never have come back to my room to check on me. This relationship has happened because of you, Sam, and your parents for instilling that goodness in you."

Sam stared at her for a long minute. "I had this same conversation with myself last night as I watched you on the dance floor. I hope I don't sound cocky, but I pride myself on good manners. Yes. I went to your room the first time to check on you, because I'm a nice guy. But it was all you that made me go back the second time."

As the waiter sat their plates on the table, Sarah whispered in Sam's ear. "Cocky is the last thing you could be, but you implied that you came back because I was funny. And, all this time I thought it was my tits!"

"Well. That's a given." Sam grinned and sipped his wine.

The food was exquisite and they left not a hint of food on their plates. When the waiter came to ask them if they wanted dessert, Sarah groaned. Sam asked for the check and they walked slowly back to their room.

They kicked off their shoes, as Sarah looked at Sam and asked,

"Can we undress each other and eat our berries in the middle of the bed and then make love?"

"How fast do you want me to undress you?"

"Very slowly, Sam. Let's make it last long enough to sustain us until we see each other again." She had started to pull his T-shirt over his head.

"I'd much rather forget the berries, undress each other quickly, and make love slowly." Sam rumbled.

Sarah stopped and thought about it for a minute. "I guess I can live with that!"

~~~

Sam joined Sarah in the shower the following morning. They tended to shower together more often than not. Today, Sam couldn't take his eyes off Sarah as the water ran down her body in glistening rivulets. He would miss this. Sarah and water were his favorite combination. He reached for her and caught the water that was between her glorious tits with his tongue. He looked at her with no makeup, her hair wet and slicked back on her head. It was a vision that would haunt his dreams after she had gone. He continued to lick the water from her stomach and belly button. He saw her skin break out in goose bumps, and it made him moan. He lapped the water from her ear lobes, her neck, and shoulders before standing back to look at her under the jets of water. He would never tire of her and the stories that her body told.

Sarah watched Sam as he watched her. He was her private masterpiece. She reached out and ran her finger down the center of his abdominal muscles, before she dipped into the oblique muscles that looked like they had been scooped out of his body with a spoon. His eyes were so dark they were almost black, and Sarah knew he wanted her. The flat muscles at the sides of his ass clenched as she stroked him and heard him hiss.

They crushed into each other and felt nothing but sensations. Wet lips, tongues, and wet, slick skin lent their own kind of heat and fire. As Sam turned Sarah to face the shower wall, he cushioned one of her breasts with his hand, before he grabbed the side of her ass with the other. He sent a silent thank you to the gods for giving Sarah her height, as it was just so damn easy to go to the place that would quench the fire that consumed them.

~~~

They couldn't keep their hands off each other as they packed. They would stop to kiss or to caress a breast or squeeze a butt. They finally left for the train station. For the hour and a half ride back to Venice, they touched, kissed, and laughed quietly. The fellow passengers were their audience and Sarah caught an occasional glimpse of a smile or a sigh. Italians adored their lovers, and Sam and Sarah did not disappoint.

They rode the elevator up to their apartment, where they threw off their shoes and sank onto the couch. "Fuck! I feel like a randy teenager again Sarah! Look at me!" Sam looked down at the tent that his pants had made.

Sarah leaned her head back against the back of the couch and laughed deep and long."I remember being a teenager. I'm not *that* old." She turned and scowled at him, then grinned. "David and I couldn't keep our hands off each other."

"Do you ever regret it? Being so young, and only being with

David?" Sam asked softly. "Did you ever wish you'd been more experienced?"

"Never." said Sarah softly. "We didn't know if we were good at making love or not. We knew we liked it, and we knew we gave each other pleasure, but we had no one else to compare it to. How can you miss something that you never had? We loved each other. That's all we needed."

Sam reached for her and pulled her into his shoulder. He stroked her hair softly. "You taught each other well. Making love to you, and with you, is the most pleasurable and satisfying sexual experience I've ever had. You're the first woman I've been with that I have such an emotional response to. It makes me feel so proud to be the only lover you've had besides David. That you picked me." He turned her face to look at him. "But this life right now isn't all about sex with you, Sarah. You know that, don't you? You are so much more to me than just someone to fuck. I love fucking you, but I love your heart, your laugh, and your humor. I love your body. I love talking with you and hearing your opinion on things. I love your artistry, and the way you love your family. I love the way you love my family. I love all of you, Amazing Sarah."

Sarah sniffed. "If it was just sex, I wouldn't be here right now. London would have been the end of us. That's why I think I fell apart after that trip. The sex was more than I imagined, but *you* were more than I imagined. I got a taste of you in London, and I realized that I wanted the whole meal. I wasn't sure if you wanted to be my dinner partner, or not. You were wonderful to me, and I knew that you liked me, and wanted to see me again, but liking me wasn't going to be enough for me. You gave me something that I'd never had, and after I got home I knew that I couldn't live without that something. You had started a fire that I wouldn't be able to put out, and it burned me up. I knew that you lusted after me, but do you know when I knew you loved me?"

Sam whispered. "When Sarah?"

"I knew you loved me when you had Marta call me. And you reinforced it for me when I showed you my clothesline of photos. The images of our life in London that week caused a visceral reaction in you just like me."

Sam leaned his forehead against Sarah's. "Sweet Sarah, it was so much earlier than that for me. And it was so many more things than that. You answered the door in your T-shirt and panties. Damn! That image still makes me hard. You actually came to London. The way you were with my family. When you left London, my house was just a house again, not a home. You brought life to it. I drank myself into oblivion, because I knew I had found what I'd been looking for, and it had left with you on that plane. But, fuck, those pictures -"

"If I didn't know better, I'd say it was love at first sight, except my first sight of you was all your naughty bits in an eight by ten glossy."

"I think you would've intrigued me with just your Facebook post. I would have tried to find out who you were." Sam smiled. "Face it, Sarah, serendipity, karma, destiny... Whatever it is, we were meant to be, and as with most things, the longer you have to wait for something, the sweeter it is."

She kissed the chiseled jaw of Sam's hard cheek. There was nothing soft about his face or body. But Sarah knew how soft his heart was. "The leaving is bittersweet this time, somehow easier and more difficult. Easier, because I know you love me, and I know we're going to make this work. So I can go home without that uncertainty. But leaving you will never be easy for me, Sam. I could become suffocating."

Sam kissed the tip of her nose. "Too late. You have already taken my breath away."

~~~

Sam and Sarah stood in line at Cocaeta. It was a small unimposing hole in the wall that all the travel sites recommended. A trio of young girls with violins were performing an impromptu concert for the patrons. While Sam waited, Sarah left the line to take pictures of the crepe maker. Each crepe was made to order, which was why there was always a line. The gentleman noticed her as she took pictures of his hands on the skillet. He laughed and then offered her a beer. She grinned, took the beer, but didn't engage in conversation. She didn't want people to get aggravated with her monopolizing his time. She continued to take pictures until Sam made it to the register to order. Sarah ordered a white chocolate, hazelnut, and strawberry, and a potato gnocchi, spinach, cream, and ham for her and Sam to share. As the crepe-making king prepared their order, Sarah peppered him with questions. Sam stood and watched and listened.

They took their crepes and beer to a table. They unwrapped the crepes and tasted. Sam waited for it. "Oh my God!" Sarah moaned, as she closed her eyes and tipped her head back. He chuckled. Yep. Food porn. The savory crepe was a nugget of gastronomical perfection. He finished his half first and took a bite of the white chocolate. He almost groaned with the sheer goodness on his tongue. He leaned back with his arms crossed and waited for it.

"What?" she asked.

"Please try to remember that we are out in the open, surrounded by people with children. I adore your orgasmic affair with food, but if you can't be quiet with your food orgasm, please wait to eat yours back in our room."

"It's that good?" Sarah whispered with her eyes wide.

"It's that good," laughed Sam.

"I'll try, Sam." She took a bite of the delectable white chocolate and hazelnut-filled pancake. She froze. "Fuck!" whispered Sarah as she looked over at Sam.

There it was. Sam slapped his thighs and threw his head back.

"Sam! People are staring!" Sarah said with her mouth full of crepe.

"It's better for them to stare at a man laughing than at a woman with a mouthful of cream having an orgasm!" Sam continued to convulse with laughter.

Sarah stared at him for several seconds. She was stunned. "I can't believe you just said that. You are a nasty, nasty man, Sam Ramsay."

This set Sam off again. He clutched his sides and gasped for air. He had begun to draw a crowd. Sarah finished the last bite of her crepe and stood up. She loomed over him. "Come on! Let's get you back to your room. I can't take you anywhere!"

Her remarks didn't help matters. Sam honestly thought he would die from laughter or the lack of oxygen to his brain. He grabbed Sarah's hand and let her lead him back to The Gritti. As they entered the elevator, he finally got his laughter under control. As he turned to Sarah he saw the tears as they streamed down her face. Her shoulders shook. When she noticed that he had caught her in her fake indignation, it was her turn to shriek with laughter.

They were still laughing when they entered the apartment. They kicked off their shoes and fell onto the sofa. They grabbed each other's hands. "I love you Amazing Sarah." Sam kissed her knuckles. "And I am a nasty man."

"The nights not even over, and it's already been an amazing day. I love laughing with you. Actually, if I think about it, I love doing everything with you." Sarah sighed and smiled.

Sam continued to hold her hand, and looked off into the distance. "Let's order room service and stay in the pool until we look like raisins. I don't want to share you tonight. All I want is to see you in the water in the moonlight. The morning will be here too soon."

"I love that pool," Sarah groaned as she stretched out her long legs. "I especially love that pool with you in it. I have a soaking tub in my master bath, but I'm thinking of getting a heated four-season pool put in. What do you think?"

Sam grabbed her and brought her to his chest. "I'm thinking that there can't be enough places on this earth for you to be in water. It's your best look. All that glistening, wet slickness. Yes! You definitely need a pool."

They weren't interested in their food. They were only interested in each other. They touched an arm, or a back. A shoulder, or a lean into a neck. The soft brush of lips across a cheek, or mouth.

The soft, quiet murmurs of sweet nothings. The thick air of resignation almost choked them. The whiskey was poured, and the siren song of the beautiful iron spiral staircase called their names.

As Sam and Sarah slid into the smooth, glassy water, they had no eyes for the beauty that was Venice. They only had eyes for each other. Sam placed Sarah on his lap and wrapped his arms around her. "This delicious madness that is you, is the sanest thing I've done in my life. I am mad for you, Sarah."

"As the morning gets closer, I find myself wanting to change my mind - to stay with you and go on to Prague." Sarah closed her eyes and inhaled the oak leaves and whiskey that was Sam.

He massaged her arms and kissed her neck. He closed his eyes and exhaled before he whispered in her ear. "Love me Amazing Sarah, and let me love you. Let me see you over me in the moonlight."

Sarah turned to Sam and gave him a long, soft kiss as she rested her hands on the hard planes of the chest she loved so much. She cried quietly as she lifted up. She kissed his mouth and slowly lowered herself. Sam looked up at the vision over him. Sarah moved slowly and fluidly over him. He felt pain and pleasure in the act they performed and it was heartbreakingly beautiful.

Sarah loved Sam softly. Sam loved Sarah with hardness and desperation. Climax and tears were achieved, but satisfaction wasn't.

~~~

They had a difficult time dragging themselves out of bed the next morning. They couldn't quench the need to touch each other. They reluctantly started the process of packing. Sarah would box up a pair of shoes and say, "I love you, Sam!"

Sam would put a suit in a garment bag and say, "I love you more."

As Sarah was folding up leggings, and panties and T-shirts, she would smile that beaming smile. "I love you so much, Sam Ramsay."

That smile broke Sam's heart. "Ditto, Amazing Sarah. Ditto."

They finally completed the process of leaving the beautiful apartment that had been their oasis for the last ten days. They stood together and looked at all of the memories they would leave with and slowly made their way one last time to the roof top. As they stared out over the Grand Canal, Sam wrapped his arm around Sarah's waist. "I'm going to make sure that we aren't apart any more than thirty days. I don't care if it's only one night, thirty days is the most I can survive. I never want to see you cry because of goodbyes again. "

 "I'm going to start counting down the days until Thanksgiving. I know I'll see you before then, but extended time with you is something I'm looking forward to." Sarah squeezed his arm. They turned and made their way down the staircase, and out of the beautiful golden city of Venice.

Chapter 34:

Sarah woke and slowly stretched. She reached for Sam before she realized she was home in her own bed. Her heart seized for a minute, but then she smiled and thought, "No way, Sarah Reid! The only thing to be sad about is that Sam isn't in bed with you!" She headed to the shower to get the cobwebs out of her head and to loosen up her tight muscles from the long flight and drive home last night. She had to get her inner clock back to Missouri time, but she had a ton of stuff to do, and it couldn't all get done today. But she needed to start.

After she had showered and poured her first cup of coffee. She wandered out to the glass porch off the kitchen. She curled up in a wicker chair and texted the girls.

Sarah: Hey all! The globetrotter is home safe and sound! And I am bearing gifts!

Liz: Welcome home, chickie! I've missed your face!

Julie: Welcome home, you hussy! When do we get to see you and what did you bring me?

Ashley: It's about damn time! Are you able to walk, or has so much sex made you an invalid?

Bev: Yeah!!! I've missed you and your hugs! What Julie said, when do we get to see you?

Sarah: I've missed all of you so much! Sleepover Friday night? Also, the jetlag won't let me be atclass tonight. I actually don't know if I'll be going back to class, but that's a story for Friday night.

Karen: Sorry, guys, sick kids are going to be the death of me. I'm exhausted. I'm glad you're home, Sarah. If the kids are feeling better, I'd love an evening away from them. I hope you took lots of pictures!

Liz: It's Sarah! Of course she took lots of pictures! Yeah for sleepovers! I'm there!

Ashley: Hell yeah! I'll think of cocktails and try to come up with something.

Julie: Wouldn't miss it!

Bev: Of course I'll be there!

Sarah: Hey Ashley! Don't worry about the cocktails, as I feel that Jameson will be the drink of the evening. I have plenty. I can't wait to see all of you!!! Friday evening anytime after six!

Sarah smiled as she sipped her coffee and looked out over the creek in the backyard. She heard the buzzing of the bees and the cardinals' sweet song as they rustled in the lilac bush by the corner of the house. David had given her the lilac for Mother's Day the last year he was still alive. She smiled as she remembered. David would be so happy for her. All he had lived for was her and their children's happiness. She had always been a content optimist. But Sam had made her truly happy and joyful. David would be joyful for her. As she finished her coffee, she went through her list of things to do and stood to start her day.

She started with dusting. Almost a month of being away had left a layer on everything. The girls had taken care of her plants, but now that it was spring in Missouri, she spent the next few hours carrying them outside and repotting the ones that were root bound. She hummed as she worked and smiled to herself often.

She took a break to open a can of soup she found in the pantry. She turned on some music as she sat at the island spooning her chicken noodle. She would have to go to the store today if she wanted to eat anything else. The larder was bare. She raised her head and smiled. Then she laughed. One Republic's "When Love Runs Out" played. She got up and danced her way across the floor. She spun. She gyrated. As she continued to move her feet and smile, she said out loud, "Thank you Sam Ramsay."

Sam: Hey, Amazing Sarah.

Sarah: Hey yourself.

Sam: Is it good to be home?

Sarah: It is wonderful! All I did today was work myself to death. But it was lovely work.

Sam: What did you do?

Sarah: Just the usual stuff for this time of year. I dusted, and moved and repotted plants. I went to the grocery store. Hey, do you have to do that when you're away from home for so long? Or does Danni do your dusting for you?

Sam: That's funny! Do you honestly think Danni would do my dusting? I have someone come in once a week to dust and take care of the plants. What are you doing right now? Please don't tell me you're in the tub!

Sarah: Not yet! I'm sitting on the back porch with a glass of iced tea listening to the peep frogs and watching the lightning bugs.

Sam: I know what peep frogs are, but what are lightning bugs?

Sarah: Fireflies, Sam. They've just started coming out tonight. I've heard a whippoorwill and the barn owls are out hunting tonight. It's very peaceful. What are you doing?

Sam: You know. Laying in bed in my room. One of the things I do very well.

Sarah: I wish you were here with me. Just being.

Sam: Me, too, Sarah. I can't wait. Now that I've had a glimpse of what I want, I can hardly stand being away from you. But, it's better this time, isn't it?

Sarah: Oh, so much better! Do you know what else I did today?

Sam: Texted the girls?

Sarah: Of course I texted the girls. Sleepover Friday night! Wanna Skype?

Sam: A Friday night sleepover Skype? Can you all wear sexy lingerie? If the answers yes, I'm all in!What else did you do today?

Sarah: I danced! One of my favorites came up on my playlist, I stopped eating my soup, and danced my way around the house. I haven't done that since David died. Thank you, Sam Ramsay.

Sam: I love watching you dance. Why are you thanking me?

Sarah: For giving me joy! For giving me love! For giving me you!

Sam: Ditto, Amazing Sarah.

Sarah: Say goodnight Sam. I love you more than you'll ever know.

Sam: Goodnight, Sam. I love you more.

The week went by quickly. Sarah did yard work and grocery shopping. She walked the fence lines to make sure that trees didn't need to be cut out. She painted the wicker furniture and the shutters. She went to her favorite clothing store in the city to say hi to Lindsay and get some more dresses. She also let Lisa the owner know that she had dropped the stores name all over Europe. She didn't want them to be surprised if they started getting phone calls from across the ocean.

She got sanded, buffed, and waxed, and her hair was now navy blue with a patch of blonde. She popped in to give Liz a quick hug. But Liz wasn't having any quickness.

Liz hugged her hard when she saw her. "You look stunning! Love is a good look for you, Sarah."

Sarah chuckled and hugged her back. "I missed you so much! And, yes, love is better than any anti-aging cream."

"So, you can get into the details when we're all together Friday, but is this thing with you and Sam going to work?" Liz stared at her earnestly.

"It looks like we're stuck with each other. We've both decided that we're forever kind of people." Sarah smiled.

"Oh my God, Sarah! I am so stinkin' happy for both of you! You are a total inspiration for the rest of us broads over thirty-five! Maybe I need to expand my horizons and start taking up some young men's offers!" Liz laughed. "Not that I want marriage or anything, but I'm going to stop putting limitations on myself. Fuck it! And maybe I'll fuck them!"

Sarah howled with laughter. She hugged Liz again and told her she would see her Friday. "Oh! I almost forgot! Make sure and bring lingerie."

"Lingerie?" Liz asked curiously.

Sarah laughed. "Yep. And because Sam's going to be the brunt of my joke, please keep in mind that he will be seeing you in your lingerie. He doesn't know it yet. So, nothing with cut out boob holes, or crotchless panties. Not that any of that would bother him, but I don't want to see your boobs or you in crotchless panties, okay?"

"I like the way your mind works, Sarah. Under that stunningly elegant and beautiful exterior, lies the heart of a real slut! I love it! See you Friday." Liz hugged Sarah again.

Sam was busy doing the regular pressers, interviews and a few television interviews. He went out and wandered around the city. He ate and drank the local offerings. But something was lacking. Without Sarah he found no joy in wandering around alone in Prague. Still she would be proud of him for making the effort. Stick a fork in him, he was done. He was done living in hotel rooms. He was done sitting alone at after parties and watching everyone else. He was done hearing himself talk about himself. He was done with the life that had made him famous and rich. He just wanted to live a life with Sarah. And he missed his family. Sam was not twenty-eight, hell, he wasn't even thirty-eight, and he was tired. He just needed some time to 'be', before he picked and chose what *he* wanted. He was looking forward to Saturday morning. It would be great to see Sarah's face and hear the girls. Maybe they would bring him out of his funk. He and Marta would attend the premiere together, and that helped a little. But he needed the next few months to go by quickly. When the middle of November came, then time could slow down.

~~~

Sarah spent Thursday cooking and stripping the beds. She had plugged her camera into the computer upstairs to upload her photos. In between beds she made crème' brulee. She shredded pork and made cole slaw. Finally, as the last of the pictures uploaded, she fixed herself a sandwich and a glass of Jameson and sat down in front of the computer screen. She was prepared this time. No tears. She would only allow herself laughter. As the images moved across the screen, Sarah stopped at the ones that caught her eye and moved them into a separate folder. She didn't want to subject the girls to hours of boredom looking at all of her photos. But they would want to see some, and Sarah knew as she looked at them, that they, too, would be seen by other people besides her friends and family. Sarah was confident in her ability to capture the images that spoke to her. Luca had instilled that confidence.

Sam: Hey woman!

Sarah: Hey man! ☺

Sam: What are you doing?

Sarah: I just poured myself my second glass of Jameson and I'm looking at my pictures on the computer. What are you doing?

Sam: Getting ready for the after party. I don't want to go.

Sarah: You need to go, Sam. Those young boys worship you. Just put in an appearance, and then leave.

Sam: I guess I could do that. How are the photos? Any that catch that wonderful eye of yours?

Sarah: I think I'm going to have to have another showing... You are a revelation in these.

Sam: That good, uh?

Sarah: Yes. They're that good. Are you okay, Sam?

Sam: No, I'm not. I'm tired. I'm tired of long hours. I'm tired of after parties. I'm tired of being dressed. I'm tired of being oiled and waxed. I'm tired of missing my home and my family.And I'm tired of missing you.

Sarah: Oh, Sam! I'm GLAD you're tired of it all!

Sam: What?

Sarah: Danni told me that you wouldn't prioritize until you got sick of it. I'm glad you're sick of it.But I'm sorry that I'm not there to rub your head and kiss your neck.

Sam: That would be lovely. I'd prefer you here to kiss things other than my neck.

Sarah: Hmmmm. Yes. That would be wonderful. Soon, Sam, soon. Take it in small increments. You know the saying: one day at a time. That's the only way I'm not going to lose my mind.

Sam: I can do that. I'm looking forward to starting my morning with you and the girls Saturday. I guess it will be your Friday night. Anyway, maybe that will help with my funk.

Sarah: I love you, Sam. We went more than a month before, we can do this.

Sam: I love you, too, sweet Sarah. I know we can do it, I just don't want to. I don't WANT to wait a month. The pictures of you in my head are all that's keeping me sane. But at least I get to see Marta at the premiere.

Sarah: Oh, good! Give her a hug for me.

Sam: I will, but I'd rather give you a hug.

Sarah: I'm hugging you right now. Can you feel me hugging you tight, Sam?

Sam: I can. I went out and walked the city today.

Sarah: Yeah! Did you soak up the local flavor?

Sam: I tried, but it's not the same without you.

Sarah: Next year. Next year we shall globetrot together.

Sam: Now that's a plan. I love you, Amazing Sarah. I miss you.

Sarah: I love you, Sam Ramsay

Sarah didn't like the way Sam sounded. She couldn't hop on a plane every week just because one or the other of them was heart sick. They had to deal with Sam's schedule. But Sam wasn't a morose man, and tonight he was morose. Hopefully seeing each other's faces tomorrow night would help, but she would call in reinforcements. She called Marta and then Danni.

Danni called her back a little later. "You were right, Sarah. He's depressed. I chewed his ass, but I don't know if I need to hop a plane or not. What do you think?"

"I can empathize with him, Danni. I was a mess when I came back from London. I was a mess for two weeks. I was in a very bad place, but Sam talked to Marta about it, and she offered to call me. Boy! Did she call me! I remember her calling me a slug." Sarah laughed as she remembered their conversation. "I think I'll wait to hear from her. She's going to the premiere with him tonight, so she's already in Prague. She promised that she would call me. I don't expect either of them to go to the after party. If I have to hop a flight tomorrow, I will."

"I understand you guys missing each other, but this isn't like Sam. I've only seen him like this one other time, and that was a long time ago." Danni exhaled loudly.

"I know what you're talking about. He told me that was a bad time for him, but he was just a boy. He told me he was done last night." Sarah continued. "He said he was done with hotel rooms, and long hours, and talking about himself. I think that now that he's realized that he wants something more, he wants to be done like yesterday. But, he won't break his contracts, so he's stuck. He just needs to understand that this too shall pass."

"He told you he was done? Really?" Danni asked excitedly.

"Yes. He's tired, and he just wants a life." Sarah sadly said.

"Is it weird that I'm happy, but worried, too?" Danni asked.

"No. That's exactly how I feel. I'll let you know after I've talked to Marta. Thanks so much Danni. I wouldn't have called if I wasn't worried. We're also supposed to Skype tomorrow night, so we'll see how that goes." Sarah sighed.

"Family sticks together, Sarah. You're family. And may I say that I'm so fucking proud of you! It took loving you for Sam to grow up. He may be having growing pains. Let's hope so. Love ya, chickie!"

"Love you, too, Danni. I'll talk to you later." Sarah hung up and waited for Marta's call.

Marta knew immediately that something was wrong with Sam. He was quiet and lethargic, and a little unkempt, which was totally unlike him. Marta would have thought him ill if Sarah hadn't called her. "What's wrong with you, Sam?" she asked him as she went and sat down by him. "Are you not feeling well?'

"I'm fine. I just want to get this over with." Sam said sullenly.

"You are *not* fine, and I would have known even if Sarah hadn't called me." Marta glared at him.

Sam looked up at her. "Sarah called you?"

"Yes, she did. She's worried about you. Does this conversation sound familiar? She's ready to hop a flight she's so worried, and she's only been home three days. You've done this to her, Sam. What is it with you two?" Marta sighed. "I'm going to tell you what I told her. You know I love you, but you also know I'm honest. Grow the fuck up, Sam!" Marta said loudly.

"What the hell are you talking about, Marta?" Sam asked with a scowl.

"That right there. You never scowl at people, Sam! You're being selfish. You are causing the woman that you adore to be worried sick. Do you not think that she misses you as much as you miss her? Do you not remember how you felt when she was in her bad place after London?"

"I was worried sick about her. She had me scared." Sam hoarsely whispered.

"Well, that's what you're doing to her. I told her she was being selfish thinking she was the only one in pain. Well, guess what? You're the one being selfish now, and belittling the pain that she feels. You guys love each other. You'll figure it out. This is just a bump in the road that you'll get through." Marta grabbed his hands and looked at him gently.

"Bloody hell! I would never intentionally cause Sarah pain! I remember how helpless I felt when she was depressed, and it kills me that I've done the same thing to her. I am such an ass!" Sam rubbed his hands through his hair, messing it up even more.

Marta grabbed a comb off the table by Sam's chair. "I'm going to comb your hair into some semblance of order, and you're going to call your woman. Then we're going to walk our asses up that red carpet. Then we're going to make a brief appearance at the after party. Then my ass is going home to my wonderful." She started combing Sam's hair. "Call her now!"

~~~

Sarah's phone buzzed, and she answered quickly, without even looking to see who it was. "Marta? How is he? Do I need to come?"

"I love you, Sarah. I'm so sorry I've worried you. Can you forgive me?" Sam asked softly.

Sarah started to cry. "Sam! You had me so worried! I remembered the bad place I was in, and to think that you were living in that same pain was killing me. Don't do that again! And, yes, I forgive you. And I love you, too."

"Please don't cry, Sarah. You know how that hurts me."

"I can't help it! I love you so much. Your pain is my pain." Sarah's sobs slowly stopped.

Sam swallowed, and spoke a little stronger. "I think I'm at an intersection. I've come to so many realizations that I think I became overwhelmed. I won't do that to you again. Did you know Marta is a magician?"

Sarah laughed shakily. "Yes, I know. Why do you think I called her and Danni? I figured if Danni couldn't yell some sense into you, Marta could wield her power."

"We just got our cue. It's time for the dancing monkey routine. I wish you were here, but Marta will do in a pinch. I'm glad she's here tonight. I love you, and I'll talk to you tomorrow night. Your time. Thank you, Amazing Sarah, for loving me." Sam whispered.

"Ditto, Sam Ramsay."

Sam: Sarah, are you up?

Sarah: I'm up. I went to bed fairly early last night, so I was up with the roosters this morning.

Sam: You didn't tell me you had roosters! That's so cool!

Sarah: No! I don't have roosters! But I'll get some if you want them, you silly man. You get really excited about livestock and poultry. Should that worry me?

Sam: LOL! I guess I'm just imagining the entire farm experience. Have you ever had livestock or poultry?

Sarah: I briefly had chickens, but having them is a hassle when you travel. It's easy to get someone to water your plants and get your mail, not so much

445

to gather eggs.

Sam: I would like a dog someday. I like dogs.

Sarah: It's good to have you back, Sam.

Sam: It's good to be back. I'll talk to you tonight.

Sarah: Until tonight. ☺

Chapter 35:

Sarah wore a T-shirt and panties. She was a vision in boobs and legs, and she knew it was Sam's second favorite look. "Oh, my God! You're stunning!" Karen exclaimed when she walked in the kitchen. Sarah turned to see Karen wearing lacy blue boxer shorts and a tiny yellow tank top.

"And you are too cute for words!" They hugged each other and giggled. "I've missed you Karen! How's the family?" Sarah sat her down on a bar stool and waited.

Karen shook her head, and sighed. "We've been fighting flu bugs for a month. First me, then the hubby, and now the kids. I'm so ready to kick back tonight. This was such a great idea. I'm so glad you're home. This place always recharges me."

"Yeah. It recharges me, too. I sat out on the back porch last night and listened to the owls and whippoorwills. It was lovely. And the lightning bugs were fabulous!" Sarah smiled as she got Karen a glass. "Do you want whiskey yet? Our lingerie party for Sam won't be until midnight, so you might want to pace yourself."

"I think I'll start with some of your apple cider, Sarah. If I start drinking now, I'll be asleep in an hour."

"Yo, Bitch! Get your ass up and give me hugs! I've missed your face!" Julie strode through the kitchen and enveloped Sarah in a tight hug. Sarah laughed as she stepped back, then she grew silent, and her mouth dropped open. Julie stood tall in a black bustier with chains, black fishnet stocking, matching stilettos, and a riding crop. She wore dramatic makeup and donned a black bobbed wig.

Sarah swallowed and grinned. "You look sexy and scary all at the same time. I'm thinking I probably need to hide that crop somewhere before the night's over. The lingerie party starts at midnight. Whiskey or something else?"

Ashley was next, then Bev. As they walked into the kitchen together, they both saw Julie. They stopped and stared and then started to laugh. Their reaction made Sarah laugh again. She figured that laughter was a better option than running.

Ashley was a raven-haired angel. She had left her black hair down and wore a white silk gown that ended above her knees. The straps were tied in bows on each shoulder. She was elegantly beautiful.

Bev was dressed as everyone expected her to be. Big hair and a complete floor-length black peignoir set. She completed the look with black mules. The shoes even had the feathers on the toes. She was a gorgeous cliché.

They talked and laughed until Liz finally arrived. She stood and watched all the women who were so dear to her and it made her smile. Sarah finally noticed her. "Wow! Just wow!" Sarah walked to Liz for a hug and then stood back holding her arms. "You look like you just stepped out of a 1940's move. "

Liz wore pale pink silk pajamas with black trim on the lapels. She had worn black smoking slippers, and held a long slim cigarette holder and a champagne glass. "I got pulled over."

"What?" All of the girls asked as they rushed to her.

"Yeah, Bob pulled me over to let me know I had a tail light out. When he walked up to my window, he did a double take."

"Oh my God, Liz! That's awesome! Did he ask why you were in your pajamas?" Sarah chuckled.

"No, he didn't. But he did a slow look down my chest." The girls broke out in wolf whistles and cat calls. "I told him about our lingerie sleepover here. I think he'll have very pleasant dreams picturing us in all our pajamaness."

"He'll be fantasizing about you for a while. I'm sure he already has. He's got the hots for you, Liz. Don't pretend you haven't noticed, because everyone else has. You need to tap that ass!" Ashley poured herself some whiskey and raised her glass in a toast. "Here's to tapping asses! Wherever they may be!"

"I'll drink to that!" Julie shouted.

"Well, I always thought I was too old for him, but Sarah has made me see the light. The next time he asks me out, I'm going to say yes. And, I just might… tap that ass!" Liz howled.

Sarah looked at her. "Don't wait for him to ask. Go get it yourself!" All of them agreed with Sarah.

As Liz walked by Sarah, she leaned close and whispered in her ear, "I went and got sanded, buffed and waxed today. You want to go panty shopping with me Monday?"

"Good for you!" whispered Sarah. "And, yes, I'll go panty shopping. I need to get new ones."

Liz cocked an eyebrow at her. "I thought you bought plenty?"

"I did, but Sam either rips them off or keeps them. I think he hates underwear. He doesn't wear any, and he doesn't like me to either." Sarah groaned. "I love pretty panties, but I can't keep them in one piece around him. "

All of the girls heard Sarah's last remark, and gathered around the island to hear all about Sam's aversion to panties, and the sordid, sexy details of Sarah's time with Sam.

Sarah clapped her hands and said loudly, "Okay! Before you all start peppering me with questions, eat!" She pointed to all of the food she had prepared. "The lingerie party starts at midnight, and Sam has no idea. I just want you all to know that he will find us all strangely arousing. Especially you, Julie. I think a dominatrix outfit will be on his Christmas list. God help me!" Everyone laughed and talked as they filled plates. Sarah stood against the counter and watched them all. She had missed them.

After everyone had their plates in hand, Sarah fixed her own. She turned to see them all looking at her. She took a big bite, and then looked back at all of them. "What?"

Liz blew a raspberry at her. "For fuck's sake, Sarah! You've been gone for almost a month. We want to hear all about it! Every intimate detail. Start talking!"

Sarah took her time. "I can either take your questions one at a time, or I can go through the timeline and tell you the highlights. Then you can ask questions. Which do you want?"

In unison they yelled "Timeline!"

Bev interrupted. "Start with your surprise for Sam on the Red Carpet in Paris! Did you knock his socks off?"

Sarah lost her focus for a minute as she remembered the look in Sam's eyes when she saw her. She smiled quietly before she reached for a manila folder on the kitchen counter. She had printed off a few pictures, as she knew the girls would want instant gratification.

"Paris was amazing, romantic. and…. intense." Sarah spoke quietly as she started to remember. The girls were quiet as well. "The hotel staff was great, as well as the Oak Wood makeup girls. The hotel was elegant and very rich-looking. I definitely surprised Sam. He didn't even know it was me behind him on the Red Carpet. He thought it was Marta until he wrapped his arm around my waist. The look on his face was priceless. He whispered my name before he turned to make sure it was me, and not just his imagination."

"Oh, my God, that is so sweet," sighed Karen.

Sarah pulled out a Parisian newspaper and put it on the island. It was the two of them in their matching aquamarine clothes as they kissed. The girls oohed and aahed when Sarah threw a glossy of her and Sam in the same clothes. It showed Sarah's amazing cleavage with the aquamarine stone between them. You could see the same color of Sam's shirt and pocket square. You could also not take your eyes off Sam. His eyes were on Sarah and they were filled with pure hunger.

Liz picked up the picture. "Holy fucking shit, Sarah!" she whispered. "That man looks as if he wanted to eat you up! Please tell me the night ended with you being ravished. You both look like a romance book cover."

"I *was* ravished." Sarah smiled. "Let's just say that I was very happy to have people on the elevator with us and that tables can come in very handy." She sighed and shook herself a little. She told them about exploring the city, getting lost, and the local eateries. She gave them the picture of the Eiffel Tower at night, and told them that Sam had bought her an antique camera. She told them about her remarks at the press conference and about the after party.

"I'm so happy you sang for them, Sarah! Everyone should get an opportunity to hear your voice!" Bev declared.

"That was a very good party. And it was an even better night after." Sarah remembered the mirror. "I think everyone should try a mirrored bed from the seventies. Very hot."

"This elegant hotel had beds from the seventies?" Ashley was confused.

"No. It *was* elegant. But they had some beautiful ornate antique mirrors in the rooms. They were hung at a perfect height." Sarah clenched her thighs together as she remembered the images.

She continued to tell them about Milan, and showed them a photo of Sam in his black and white tuxedo, and her in her black skirt and Sam's white dress shirt.

"You could wear a fucking trash bag and look elegant." Julie whined a little. "It's just not fair."

Sarah got even quieter. "The last ten days we were in Venice, Sam rented an apartment at The Gritti Palace. It had a private rooftop terrace and pool." She looked around at her friends as they sat with their mouths agape. She showed them the photos of their room and some shots of Sam she had taken throughout their stay. "I've already called a company about installing a heated pool here at the farm. Sam and I wouldn't feel comfortable anywhere without a huge tub and a pool. We love the water. Well, Sam loves *me* in the water."

"Fuck me!" Julie hissed out. "That is so hot."

Sarah talked about walking around the city, the shopping, the press conferences and the premiere. She told them about Murano and their overnight stay in Verona. She gave them photos to look at. She then told them about taking pictures at Sam's photo shoot with Luca.

"I can't put into words the way I feel about Luca. He's the best in the world at what he does, and Sam loves him like a father. I respect him so much. But if Sam and I didn't work out, I would run away to South America with him." Sarah chuckled a little and wiped a tear from her eye.

"Is he a hot older man? Could you give him my number?" Liz teased.

Sarah laughed. "He reminds me of a burlier Ernest Hemingway. But he is all Italian. He's a big old flirt, and I love him so much. Anyway, he loved my photos from the shoot." She placed a few pictures of her and Sam down on the island.

The girls were silent as they passed the photos back and forth. Julie looked up at Sarah. "These are really, really good. They look like professional photos."

"Thank you, Julie. Luca liked them so much that he wanted to shoot me and Sam together. He rented an old Venetian theatre that was beautifully decaying. You guys would have loved it. Anyway, here's a few of Luca's from that day." She placed the photos of her and Sam in front of them, and leaned back against the counter. A tear slowly rolled down her cheek.

Karen was the first one to sob, then the rest of them followed suit. Liz got up to walk to Sarah. She enveloped her in her arms and rocked her back and forth. Liz stepped back but kept her hands on Sarah's arms. "You are a stunning woman, Sarah, but you're the one always taking the pictures. Who would've thought to put you in *front* of the camera? The world needs to see these." She kissed Sarah on the cheek and leaned back against the counter with her. Liz took Sarah's hand and didn't let go.

Ashley looked at Sarah seriously. "I agree with Liz. There's nothing in GQ or Harpers Bazaar that is as beautiful as these pictures are. I don't think I've ever seen Sam look so good. He never takes a bad picture, so that's saying something!"

"Thank you, guys. I mean it. It's funny that you would say that, because they *are* going to be seen." Sarah went on to tell them about the upcoming photo spread and her gallery showings.

The girls went crazy, and the bottle of Jameson was officially opened. Julie yelled over all the noise, "Don't forget about us little people when you're rich and famous!"

"Never, Julie. You guys are my family, my touchstones, so as much as my life is going to change, the more it will stay the same. I think Sam needs this. I'll show you a few more, then we can go upstairs and look at the rest of them. I thought you guys would like to see what the actual people and cities look like." Sarah put the nude photos she had taken of her and Sam in the apartment in front of them. Again, there was silence as the girls looked at the images.

Again, Julie spoke first. Her eyes were big as she asked quietly, "Please tell me that he's as good a lay as that body implies, because that would just be a damn shame to have something like that and not know what to do with it."

Sarah chuckled. "Oh, we definitely know what to do with it."

"And to think you were worried about your experience, Sarah!" Liz said. "These are *hot.*" She fanned herself with one of the pictures.

"We are pretty combustible when we're together, that is true. But as beautiful as that man is physically - and he is - he takes my breath away sometimes. His heart, though, is so much more beautiful than his face or body. He could have been an average Joe, but after our first night in London together, I would have been swept off my feet. It's private, but he was the kindest, sweetest man. He had my heart from that moment." Sarah sighed and smiled. "Okay! That's my last month in a nutshell. I'm pouring Jameson for all, and anyone who wants to go upstairs and look at a few more pictures is welcome to. They're already scrolling across the screen. Sorry, I didn't have time to print them off."

The girls grabbed their whiskey and headed upstairs to look at more photos. They were so excited to be getting a sneak peek at the next world-famous photographer's photos. Sarah stood behind and snapped pictures of all of them in their lace and silk. And one of them in her leather. Sarah shook her head and laughed.

Sarah had picked up the newspapers, pictures, and all of the plates before she got out the crème' brulee and the cheesecake with varying accompaniments. The girls came back downstairs and were met with the many gifts Sarah had bought for them.

"Hey, Sarah? Who were the people in the café?" Bev asked.

"Sam and I got lost in Paris. It was great. We wanted to find a local café, because you'll be guaranteed good food. Sam saw the six of them in front of us, and ran up to ask them where we should eat. They were locals from the neighborhood and they were on their way to eat, so they invited us along. That was before we finished the night at the lighting of the Eiffel. It was a wonderful night." Sarah started handing out sacks.

Bev smiled as she took a sack. "I'm sure you got everyone's names and addresses, and charmed the socks off of them, because that's what you do." Sarah chuckled and blew Bev a kiss.

The girls opened their Murano glass earrings and necklaces. Everyone loved them. Sarah reached for the box on the floor and handed it to Liz. "I have the owners contact information. He was excited about having the chance to work with you. I think these would do well in your shop. I only brought you one, the other two I'm putting up over my fireplace."

Liz unwrapped the tissue paper and reached in. She gingerly brought out the beautiful Murano glass sconce. The lights over the island reflected the myriad of colors off the ceiling. Liz looked at Sarah with tears in her eyes. "Oh, Sarah! It's beautiful! Look at the craftsmanship, and the colors! And it has the decal on it! You knew what you were looking for didn't you? And you thought of me? That is just so sweet! I love it." Liz stroked the beautiful glass before putting it carefully back in the box.

Sarah passed candy, chocolate, and trinkets and poured another glass of Jameson for all. Everyone got caught up on each other's lives.

Bev had gone out with an attorney from the neighboring college town. Yes, another attorney. She assured them it wasn't serious, just sex.

Julie told them she was giving serious thought about celibacy.

Karen was tired and just wanted her family to start feeling better.

Liz had convinced herself to ask the officer out, and Ashley was strangely quiet. They all thought that Sarah should guest teach one of their photography classes, which made her laugh. They made plans for a spa day and a trip into St. Louis for shopping, food, and music. Liz mentioned the county fair, and asked if Sarah was going to sing with the locals. She told them yes, if she was home. She still didn't know when the gallery event was going to be set up, so she would have to wait and see. The whiskey flowed, as did the conversation and affection. It was good to be home.

Sarah looked at the clock and clapped her hands. "It's time to get in position, girls! Remember, Sam will enjoy this, so let's try to make him a little uncomfortable, without getting raunchy. Okay Julie?"

Julie shrugged. "You're no fun. I wanted to slip you the tongue. I've always wanted to kiss you, you know." Everyone stared at her until she started to laugh.

Karen shook her head. "I never know if you're serious or not."

They were all a little inebriated and a lot excited to see Sam's face. How could they not be? The familiar ping of Skype rang out on the laptop. Everyone took their positions, and Liz brought up the screen.

The first thing Sam saw was a group of beautiful women as they stood in front of the computer with lingerie on. The second thing he noticed was that Sarah wasn't among them.

Sam looked at the girls. They were all incredibly beautiful women, and Sam enjoyed their lingerie very much. Liz started rubbing Karen's arm very suggestively and gyrating her hips. As he watched, all of the girls started touching each other, and kissing each other's cheeks. They were moaning and groaning, and Sam was confused and aroused. Where the hell was Sarah?

"Uh, Sarah?" Sam literally yelled. "Sarah?"

Sarah appeared from the corner of the screen. "It's so good to be home, Sam."

She groaned seductively as the rest of her body appeared. She was wearing a T-shirt and panties. Sam found her outfit the sexiest of them all.

"I missed my girls so much." Sarah started rubbing against Julie's leather.

"What the hell is going on, Sarah?" Sam asked loudly.

"Well we were going to have our lingerie sleepover tonight anyway, and you keep telling me how you'd like to watch, so we thought we'd oblige. Would you like us to continue or stop?" Sarah hadn't stopped rubbing against Julie. Neither had Liz.

Sam leaned back and squinted his eyes. He crossed his arms over his chest. "Yes, please."

Sarah leaned over into the screen. God, she was beautiful! "Yes, continue, or yes, stop."

"Please continue. You guys are getting me hot. I'd really like to see Julie ride one of you like a pony and spank you with that riding crop. I like whips, and I really like spankings." Sam raised his eyebrow.

All the girls froze and nervously looked at Sarah. Sarah continued to stare at Sam. She started to smile. The smile got bigger and bigger. "We had you going at first, didn't we?"

Everybody started to laugh, and then Sam asked for each one of them to model their lingerie for him. "I'm serious. I will critique, as you know I'm a professional."

It would be hard for any woman to say no to Sam Ramsay, so Karen started first. She shook her cute little butt in front of the screen. "Good job, Karen. Very cute. Cute is sexy. I've always been a sucker for boxers and a tank top. It reminds me of University. Thank you."

The next one up was Julie. She high strutted in front of the screen and then whirled and looked at Sam while she cracked her whip. Sam cleared his throat nervously. "You scare me a little Julie, but I find you weirdly sexy. You just need to find the right guy. Maybe you should start looking at rodeos. I think a cowboy might do well with you."

It was Bev's turn. She slowly waltzed her way across the screen. She stopped and cocked a hip, raised an eyebrow and stared at Sam. "Oh, Bev! I love the Old Hollywood glamour of your peignoir set. Classic is always good. I can't see, but I would bet money that you have feathered mules on, don't you? Yes, I know what mules are. I told you I was a professional." Bev reached down and showed Sam her shoes with a grin on her face. "Ah, very nice. Very nice, indeed."

Liz walked slowly across the screen with her cigarette holder and glass of Jameson. Sam sighed. "I love this, Liz. It evokes Doris Day and that era. You can *never* go wrong with classic silk. The only thing that would make it perfect are smoking shoes." Liz grinned a

459

wicked little grin as she held up her shoes. Sam sighed. "I think I love you Liz."

Ashley walked slowly to the front of the screen and then turned in a circle. Her hair floated in black waves down her back. When she stopped she pulled her hair to one side exposing the ties at the shoulder of her gown. Sam sighed and leaned forward. "This is beautiful, Ashley. Virgin and vixen all rolled into one." Ashley smiled and left the shot.

Sarah was next, and Sam swallowed hard. Sarah's long legs glided into view, and Sam could see the bounce of her magnificent tits. The T-shirt stopped high on her thighs, showing most was home. She still didn't know when the gallery event was going to be set up, so she would have to wait and see. The whiskey flowed, as did the conversation and affection. It was good to be home.

Sarah looked at the clock and clapped her hands. "It's time to get in position, girls! Remember, Sam will enjoy this, so let's try to make him a little uncomfortable, without getting raunchy. Okay Julie?"

Julie shrugged. "You're no fun. I wanted to slip you the tongue. I've always wanted to kiss you, you know." Everyone stared at her until she started to laugh.

Karen shook her head. "I never know if you're serious or not."

They were all a little inebriated and a lot excited to see Sam's face. How could they not be? The familiar ping of Skype rang out on the laptop. Everyone took their positions, and Liz brought up the screen.

The first thing Sam saw was a group of beautiful women as they stood in front of the computer with lingerie on. The second thing he noticed was that Sarah wasn't among them.

Sam looked at the girls. They were all incredibly beautiful women, and Sam enjoyed their lingerie very much. Liz started rubbing Karen's arm very suggestively and gyrating her hips. As he watched, all of the girls started touching each other, and kissing each other's cheeks. They were moaning and groaning, and Sam was confused and aroused. Where the hell was Sarah?

"Uh, Sarah?" Sam literally yelled. "Sarah?"

Sarah appeared from the corner of the screen. "It's so good to be home, Sam."

She groaned seductively as the rest of her body appeared. She was wearing a T-shirt and panties. Sam found her outfit the sexiest of them all.

"I missed my girls so much." Sarah started rubbing against Julie's leather.

"What the hell is going on, Sarah?" Sam asked loudly.

"Well we were going to have our lingerie sleepover tonight anyway, and you keep telling me how you'd like to watch, so we thought we'd oblige. Would you like us to continue or stop?" Sarah hadn't stopped rubbing against Julie. Neither had Liz.

Sam leaned back and squinted his eyes. He crossed his arms over his chest. "Yes, please."

Sarah leaned over into the screen. God, she was beautiful! "Yes, continue, or yes, stop."

"Please continue. You guys are getting me hot. I'd really like to see Julie ride one of you like a pony and spank you with that riding crop. I like whips, and I really like spankings." Sam raised his eyebrow.

All the girls froze and nervously looked at Sarah. Sarah continued to stare at Sam. She started to smile. The smile got bigger and bigger. "We had you going at first, didn't we?"

Everybody started to laugh, and then Sam asked for each one of them to model their lingerie for him. "I'm serious. I will critique, as you know I'm a professional."

It would be hard for any woman to say no to Sam Ramsay, so Karen started first. She shook her cute little butt in front of the screen. "Good job, Karen. Very cute. Cute is sexy. I've always been a sucker for boxers and a tank top. It reminds me of University. Thank you."

The next one up was Julie. She high strutted in front of the screen and then whirled and looked at Sam while she cracked her whip. Sam cleared his throat nervously. "You scare me a little Julie, but I find you weirdly sexy. You just need to find the right guy. Maybe you should start looking at rodeos. I think a cowboy might do well with you."

It was Bev's turn. She slowly waltzed her way across the screen. She stopped and cocked a hip, raised an eyebrow and stared at Sam. "Oh, Bev! I love the Old Hollywood glamour of your peignoir set. Classic is always good. I can't see, but I would bet money that you have feathered mules on, don't you? Yes, I know what mules are. I told you I was a professional." Bev reached down and showed Sam her shoes with a grin on her face. "Ah, very nice. Very nice, indeed."

Liz walked slowly across the screen with her cigarette holder and glass of Jameson. Sam sighed. "I love this, Liz. It evokes Doris Day and that era. You can *never* go wrong with classic silk. The only thing that would make it perfect are smoking shoes." Liz grinned a wicked little grin as she held up her shoes. Sam sighed. "I think I love you Liz."

Ashley walked slowly to the front of the screen and then turned in a circle. Her hair floated in black waves down her back. When she stopped she pulled her hair to one side exposing the ties at the shoulder of her gown. Sam sighed and leaned forward. "This is beautiful, Ashley. Virgin and vixen all rolled into one." Ashley smiled and left the shot.

Sarah was next, and Sam swallowed hard. Sarah's long legs glided into view, and Sam could see the bounce of her magnificent tits. The T-shirt stopped high on her thighs, showing most of her long legs. She was glorious. "I'm sorry, girls, but this is my favorite. This is a woman who looks good in anything, so why not wear what she wants. This woman doesn't need any added decoration, as she is all the decoration needed. I love it. Well done, Sarah, and thank you."

All the girls clapped and blew Sam kisses. He grinned that slow sexy grin, and Sarah felt her knees start to buckle. "That should be against the law Sam Ramsay!" Liz hissed him.

"What?" Sam asked, grinning slyly.

"That fucking sexy as sin, panty melting, make a nun a whore, moist crotch clenching, knee buckling, ovary punching, lose your morals and your mind, moan making grin! Just stop it!" Liz looked at Sarah who was bent over clutching her stomach in laughter.

Liz looked at Sam who was roaring with laughter. "Oh, Liz! I can't wait to meet you in person. You are going to be fun."

Sarah pointed at Sam. "He knows exactly what he's doing. I could be pissed as hell at him, and all he'd have to do would be grin that fucking grin, and I'd climb him like a lineman climbs a telephone pole. I think it's the reason he doesn't smile very much in his pictures."

Liz looked confused. "Why doesn't he smile in his pictures?"

"Because the world would have a panty shortage! With all the panty melting going on! And the church would be scandalized with all the bail money they'd have to put up for the nuns turning tricks! And the Emergency Rooms would be over filled with all the punched ovaries and buckled knees!" Sarah screamed with laughter, and the girls lost control.

"Oh! And the world would have a shortage of panty liners! Oh, my God! No panty liners because of all the moist crotches!"

Ashley gasped, "You could very well be the downfall of the world, Sam!"

It took them some time to calm down. Just when they thought they had it under control, someone started to giggle, and it set them all off again. Sam laid his head down on his arms to catch his breath. Every time he looked at all the beautiful, lingerie clad women in front of him, it just make it funnier. He saw Sarah with her camera out of the corner of his eye. How on earth she could take pictures with all the alcohol and laughter, he had no idea, but her camera was like an extension of her body, so she probably didn't even realize it.

Sarah left the girls gasping and pulled a bar stool up to the screen. She sat down and put her feet on the rungs of the stool as she looked at Sam with a drunken smile. She looked like she was sixteen. It made Sam's heart catch. She continued to smile and stare drunkenly.

"I love you, Amazing Sarah. I needed this, and I love the girls for doing this. I haven't laughed this hard since you toppled the couch over on us in London." Sam chuckled softly.

Sarah continued to smile. "That was pretty funny, but, damn! I tried, didn't I?"

"If I recall, that night ended quite well. I'm just glad there were no injuries. That would have been hard to explain to the doctors." Sam sighed and smiled back at Sarah.

"I have so much fun with you."

The girls had surrounded the computer, and they all had the dazed, confused faces of drunkenness.

"Thanks, ladies. It's been awesome! "

"We can't wait to meet you in person, Sam. You love our Sarah, so we love you. But be prepared. There *will* be ass grabbing." Liz blew him a kiss. Sam grinned. Liz started to mutter as she walked away.

"Are you good Sam?" Sarah looked at him with concern.

"I am so good, Sarah. I know you did this on purpose, so I thank you. But most importantly, I love you so much." He heard the girls sigh in the background, but he didn't care.

"I love you. Remember that. We have bumps in the road for just a little while, but those will even out. "

Sam leaned into the screen. "You are one in a million, and you're mine. I will remember that."

Sarah beamed. "I love you, Sam Ramsay."

Sam replied. "I love you, Sarah Reid."

Sarah had thought ahead. Thank God. She had prepared breakfast casseroles to pop in the oven Saturday morning. The house filled with the heavenly smell of bacon and sausage. She would usually would make eggs benedict or brioche French toast, but she had guessed they would all feel like ass, and they did. Sarah made a pitcher of mimosas and had the coffee hot, as one by one the girls slowly and painfully made their way to the kitchen. Most of them didn't talk, and a few just growled. No one spoke until the first mimosa and cup of coffee were drunk. As Sarah pulled the casseroles out of the oven, she sat the bottle of aspirin on the island.

Liz lifted her head out of her hands and looked slowly around at the girls. She winced, as she realized that even her eyelashes hurt. "I don't care how shitty I feel this morning, last night was totally worth it."

"I had so much fun. Sam is definitely a keeper, Sarah." Karen slowly sipped her second cup of coffee.

Sarah sipped and shook her head. "I plan on keeping him."

"He's a hoot, Sarah! I never thought I could get past his beauty, but he had me rolling last night! You two were meant for each other." Ashley gingerly walked out to the glassed-in porch. Her stomach felt like she'd done a million crunches.

Bev looked up at Sarah. "You two give me goose bumps. I've never seen two people look at each other the way you two do. It's like you're magnetized." Sarah gave a little snort. "Not to bring up anything uncomfortable, but we all knew David. I know how much you loved each other, and what a good marriage you had together. I don't want to take anything away from what you had, but I never saw that between the two of you. And before you say that it was because you'd been married for thirty-five years, don't. Because that's not why. You and Sam have something rare, and it's powerful to be around."

The girls all shook their heads as Sarah stared at Bev. "It's funny you should say that. I had a very painful epiphany in Paris. Luca saw it, and I guess I knew, too, but hadn't acknowledged it. Out of guilt perhaps, but I'm not guilty about it anymore. I never loved David the way that I love Sam. That's not taking anything away from David, but with Sam it's just *more*. It's a physical pull, a visceral reaction. I can only compare it to my feelings for my children, but it's different. We are two halves of a whole. I just don't know how I'm going to explain it to my children." Sarah sighed.

Liz said quietly, "You won't have to. They'll see it, and they'll feel it."

~~~

By the time Sarah got the house cleaned and the dishes done, it was mid afternoon. She took a shower and put on some leggings and a sweater. It was overcast and had gotten a little chilly. She fixed herself a cup of tea and took her e-reader and tea to the glassed porch. She started afire in the small fireplace and curled up in a chair and read for a couple of hours. It was quiet and had finally started to rain. Sarah loved rain. She loved the way it smelled, and how it washed the dust off of nature. She sat and watched the drops roll down the windows. She could see lightning in the distance. She watched the rain in silence, and was happy. Her joy would return with Sam, so for now, she was content with being happy.

Sam: Are you there?

Sarah: Always.

Sam: How are you feeling?

Sarah: I feel surprisingly good! How about you?

Sam: I'm good. I'm in my own bed, in my own house. Finally!

Sarah: You're in London?? ☺

Sam: Took the red eye. I have three days before I fly to South Africa.

Sarah: Going to Danni's?

Sam: I'm staying the night tomorrow night. You know. Recharging.

Sarah: Recharging is good. Please give Danni and Alex and those yummy children hugs from me. I'm sitting in my kitchen porch watching it rain. It's getting ready to storm. You can smell the ozone in the air. I love storms. They're exhilarating.

Sam: I feel the same way! I love storms. Thank you again for last night. It was unforgettable. What are your plans for the week?

Sarah: I'm going panty shopping with Liz tomorrow. I need to get the tires rotated on the truck. I plan on going to class Tuesday evening, and I'm going to organize my photos. That will take a few days. You know. Just life. Have you been to South Africa before?

Sam: I love it so much, I've taken holiday there several times, all over Africa, actually. The people are wonderful, and the vistas are breathtaking. It's one of my favorite places.

Sarah: Are you telling me that you've taken in the local flavor, Sam? ☺

Sam: Not while I'm working. But when I went the first time for work, it intrigued me, so I planned a holiday. I've been going ever since.

Sarah: I would love to stay in one of those glorified tents in the savannah. Boy! What a place for quiet and just being.

Sam: I have done that! We will definitely put that on our bucket list. I would love to experience that with you.

Sarah: Oh, Sam, "we" now have a bucket list, and it hurts so good. I love you, Sam Ramsay.

Sam: I love you, Sarah Reid.

July

Chapter 36:

Sarah was surprised that time had gone by so quickly. She had gone shopping with Liz, and against her better judgment, she had purchased more panties. Class was great. The truck had the tires rotated and the oil changed. Sarah felt as if she was rushing to wait. Waiting to start living her life. She wanted time to go quickly so she could begin.

She pulled the weeds out of the flower beds all afternoon. Dirt therapy was always fulfilling. She smiled as she dead headed the hydrangeas and thought about Beth Ramsay. She couldn't wait to see Sam's family again. She would have to find something special to take to Thomas and Violet.

Sarah had just finished a shower when her phone buzzed. She picked it up and saw Bev's number on the screen. "Hey Bev! What's up?"

"Sarah! We need to get to the hospital!" Bev's voice was strained.

Sarah sat down on her bed. "Slow down. Who's in the hospital?"

Bev started to cry, and that really alarmed Sarah. "It's Karen's daughter, Ava."

Sarah inhaled sharply. "What happened?" She started to throw on clothes and ran a comb through her hair.

"Well, you know how the whole family has been fighting that bug that was going around. I think it went through their family twice.

Somehow the virus settled in little Ava's heart and it's touch and go right now." Bev started to cry again.

"Listen to me! Buck up! Karen is going to need us. We don't need to be a wailing mess. You go ahead to the hospital. I can't fit you all in my truck. I'll meet you there. I'm out the door now!" Sarah grabbed her keys, locked the doors and headed for her truck.

When Sarah entered the PIC Unit waiting room, the only person there was some other child's family member. She had arrived first. She walked to the nurse's station and asked someone to please let Karen and Jack know that she was there if they needed anything. She went and sat down on an uncomfortable plastic couch and waited.

Jack came out about twenty minutes later. His normally happy-go-lucky personality looked as if it had been stomped on. His face was gaunt, and dark circles ringed his eyes. His clothes were rumpled and he needed a shave. Sarah stood up and wrapped him in her arms. She rocked him back and forth in silence. What could possibly be said? As a mother, she couldn't imagine the pain that they were both going through, especially when it was such a young child.

"Jack, please go down and get a cup of coffee, or take a quick walk outside, but do something for a few minutes to get out of here. I'll go sit with Karen. You don't need to be gone long, and I know you don't want to, but you need to." Sarah hugged him again and whispered, "Go!"

Sarah entered the darkened room quietly. All she heard was the beeping of the machines, the whooshing sound of oxygen and the soft crying of a mother in pain. Karen was huddled in a chair at the top of Ava's bed running her fingers through the beautiful red hair that was just like her own. Ava looked like a tiny little toy. She was dwarfed by the oxygen mask on her face and the blankets that were mounded over her. Sarah moved a chair next to Karen. She didn't say a word. She simply touched Karen's shoulder. Karen leaned back into her and continued to stroke her daughter's hair. Sarah sat and stroked the mothers.

~~~

Sam: Are you there?

Sarah: Oh, Sam, I wish you were here.

Sam: What's wrong?

Sarah: I've been at the hospital since yesterday afternoon. Karen's little girl Ava is very, very sick. It's heartbreaking. I have just come out to my truck to smoke a cigarette. I wish I had a glass of whiskey.

Sam: Is Ava going to be okay?

Sarah: There's been no change since I got here yesterday, and I've been here all night. The virus that she had has settled in her little heart causing a lot of damage. It doesn't look good. She's fucking 4 years old! The same age as Violet.

Sam: Sarah! I'm so sorry. Have you had a chance to shower, or eat?

Sarah: No. Karen seems to want me near, so Jack -that's her husband - and I, have been doing shifts in the room.

Sam: I'm going to let you go to her. I will keep texting, but respond only when you can, okay? I love you.

Sarah: I love you, too.

~~~

The next day was just like the previous one. Sarah sat and rubbed Karen's shoulders and combed her hair with her fingers. Jack kept trying to get Karen to go for a walk, or a drink, or to leave the room for a little while. Sarah finally told him that he needed to stop. Karen wasn't going anywhere. If it had been one of Sarah's children, she wouldn't have either. Liz, Bev, Julie, and Ashley had rotated in and out of the waiting room. They kept bottles of water and snacks supplied for everyone. Bev had rented a room at the motel across the street for showers and naps. Karen's mom and dad had come, as well as Jacks mom. They would go in for short visits, and then they sat with the rest of them.

Liz sat with Sarah in the waiting room on Saturday night. Sarah had her blankets and her pillow and had made her preparations to sleep where she'd been sleeping for the last three nights. The beeps, soft padded shoes, and quiet conversations of the nursing staff had become Sarah's background music. Liz and Sarah sat and talked quietly for a few minutes before Liz left. Everyone else had gone to their motel rooms or home, but Karen wanted Sarah there, so Sarah stayed. She had grabbed a quick shower yesterday morning, but hadn't had a meal or a full nights' sleep for the last three days. As Liz and Sarah continued to huddle together in quiet conversation, Sarah felt it. She gasped and sat up. Liz cried out. "No!"

"It's not Ava, Liz! It's Sam! He's here! I feel him!" Sarah finally, for the first time started to cry.

Liz looked at Sarah and thought she might have reached her breaking point. She made no sense, as Liz knew that Sam was in

473

Africa. Sarah continued to sit and wait, knowing that Liz thought she had lost her mind, but Sarah knew that her tired body and mind weren't playing tricks on her. She continued to cry with exhaustion, grief, and hope.

She saw him before she heard his steps. She smelled oak leaves and whiskey. Sam walked briskly down the hall straight for her. He reached down for her. He picked her up like she was a child and sat with her on his lap. He rocked her and whispered sweet things, and Sarah cried all of her pain out onto his shirt. When Sarah had finally stopped, Sam looked into her eyes and asked, "Are you okay, sweet girl?"

"No, I'm not. My body is tired, my heart is tired, and I stink."

Sam turned to Liz who had cried her own tears. "I'm glad I get to meet you first, Liz. Though I hate that's it's under these circumstances." He leaned over and gave her a gentle kiss on her cheek and squeezed her shoulder.

Liz sighed. "I'm glad you're here for our girl, Sam. She needs you. Karen won't let her go, and Sarah's dead on her feet. Maybe she'll get some sleep now that you're here."

"I'll make sure she does. I don't plan on leaving." He looked down at Sarah, who couldn't stop touching his cheek.

Liz stood and gathered a big bag and her purse. "I'll see you tomorrow, Sarah. Please let Sam sit watch while you sleep. Jack or the doctors will wake you if they need you. You won't be any good for Karen, if you make yourself sick. Sam, I'll see you tomorrow, too."

Sarah's eyes were still on him when Sam looked down at the sad woman on his lap. She was beautifully broken. "How did you get here?" she whispered.

Sam smiled gently and kissed her temple. "I flew. On a plane. Close your eyes, sweet Sarah. They will come and get you if they need you. We'll talk when you wake up."

Sam must have fallen asleep as he held Sarah, because he was woken by a soft squeeze on his shoulder. It was Ashley. "Sam? You need to wake Sarah up. Jack is asking for her."

Sam looked at his watch. It was six in the morning. "What time did you get here?" he whispered.

Ashley answered. "Just a few minutes ago. I came early, hoping to give Sarah time for a shower and some coffee, but the doctors went into Ava's room as I got here, and Jack just came out for her, but didn't want to wake her."

As Ashley finished talking, the doctors left the room, and she and Sam heard the guttural screams that came from the room.

"Oh, my god!" Ashley put her hand over her mouth. Her eyes filled with tears as she sank down on the couch next to Sam.

Sam leaned into Sarah's ear that was next to his heart. He whispered ever so softly, "Sarah? You need to wake up. Do you hear me? Karen needs you now, more than ever." He kissed her temple gently and saw Sarah's eyes slowly open. As she focused on him, she smiled the soft morning smile that Sam loved. But just as quickly, she heard Karen and her eyes immediately filled with pain and she gasped.

"Sweet Sarah, go give that heart of yours to your friend. She needs you fiercely right now. I'll be here waiting." Sam kissed her gently.

Sarah stood as Ashley stood by Sam with her head in her hands. Her shoulders shook. Sarah glanced at Sam. "Go to Karen. I'll be here with Ashley."

Sarah slowly walked to Ava's room. She was torn between the need to go in and the want to not intrude on Jack and Karen's horrendously painful private moment. As Sarah rounded the corner and entered the room, she saw Karen laying over little Ava. The room was quiet. No more beeps of the machines, and no more whoosh of oxygen. Just utter stillness except for Karen's guttural sobs. The pain that Sarah felt in the room was like a punch to her gut that made her knees buckle, and she had to grab the door frame to keep from falling. She took a deep breath and walked over to Jack, who was staring helplessly at his wife. Sarah touched his arm, and Jack turned to her. Sarah wrapped her arms around him, and without word gave him her heart and love. She stood and rocked him as he sobbed great heaving sobs.

"She's gone, Sarah! She's gone, and Karen..." His voice trailed off and he looked dazed. "I don't know what to do."

Sarah continued to hug and rock him as she whispered, "You just need to love her, Jack."

Sarah continued to hold Jack, until his shoulders stopped shaking. He stepped away from Sarah and looked down at his wife who keened over their daughters little body.

He put his hand on his wife's shoulder. "Sarah's here, Karen."

Jack looked up at Sarah, before he straightened and walked to her. "What do I do now? What's the procedure when one of your children die? Do they give you a handbook on the death of a child?" he asked crying.

Sarah took Jack's arm and led him to the door. "Sam and Ashley are in the waiting room. Have them call the other girls and anyone else that needs to be called. Give Sam or Ashley your phone, and tell them who to call for you. You need to call Karen's mom and dad, and your mom. I believe all of them are across the street in the motel. The hospital will be coming to talk with both of you. They are going to ask some tough questions that will need to be answered. Be prepared Jack. This day is going to get rougher. Go. Do what you need to. Give me and Karen a half hour before you come back in here, and ask Sam if you need anything. He flew a long way to be here. He'll want to help."

Jack gave Karen one long, last look before leaving the room. Sarah went and stood behind Karen. She bowed her head and touched Karen's back with both hands. Karen immediately sank back against Sarah. Karen's whole body trembled, and she couldn't, take her hands off of Ava, who looked as if she were asleep. Her beautiful red hair was spread out around her perfect little face. Sarah's heart clenched and she inhaled sharply. She had to keep it together for Karen's sake. She could fall apart later. Sarah sat and gently pulled Karen onto her lap, gently wrapping her arms around her slender shoulders.

"Oh, sweet girl, I'm so sorry. I'm not going to tell you that you'll get through this, because you will. You're a strong woman with two other children at home. I'm not going to tell you that you'll get over it. You won't. But, you will get *through* it. Your life from this day forward will forever be changed, but you will go on. It will just be different."

Karen wrapped her arms around Sarah's neck and continued to sob. "Keep talking Sarah. You're my magic, and you always make me feel better. I think it's because you've suffered so much pain, you know just what to say. So, just keep talking."

"I love you Karen, and you know that. You were there for me, I will be here for whatever you need me for. But right now, I'm going to tell you what's going to happen, and what you need to do. Can you just listen?"

Karen shook her head that she had rested in Sarah's neck. Sarah's shirt was wet with her tears. "Jack, and Ashley and Sam are out in the waiting room making phone calls. I told Jack to give us a half hour before he came back in. The hospital staff will give you all the time you need, but you need to do it quick. They will make all of the arrangements, but you have to give them direction. Can you do that? Please don't lay all of the decision making on Jack's shoulders. He's in pain, too."

Karen cried softly, but whispered, "Yes. I don't want him to do this by himself. I can give direction. I can help, Sarah."

"I won't be in here when you do this. This is something you and Jack need to do together. They will want to know what funeral home you want to use." Karen cried harder. Sarah gave her a minute, and continued to hug her. "They will also ask if you want to donate her organs." Karen stopped breathing for a moment. "I know that's not something you ever think of with a four year old, but you will need to give them an answer. You and Jack can talk about it."

Karen slowly lifted her swollen eyes to Sarah's and touched her cheek. "Thank you. I don't think I would want anyone else to tell me these things." Sarah smiled gently at her and reached for the box of tissues. "I'm sad to be doing it Karen, but so honored that you're letting me. These first few days will be a circus."

Sarah lifted Karen up and sat her in the chair. She got a cold washcloth and wiped Karen's face. "That feels good. Thank you." Karen's breath was still shaky, but it was stronger.

Sarah leaned over and looked in Karen's eyes. "Can I love Ava now, Karen?"

Karen smiled a sad, bright smile. "Please!"

Sarah walked around to the other side of the bed and looked down at little Ava's body. She was a miniature version of her mother. Sarah combed her fingers through the child's beautiful red hair and caressed her cheek. Sarah sat on the edge of the bed before she stretched out beside the little one in the big hospital bed. Sarah embraced Ava, rocked with her, and whispered sweet words that Karen couldn't hear but could feel. It was as if Sarah was enveloping the room in a blanket of love. Sarah smiled at Karen as she sang a lullaby that she used to sing to her own children and then placed Ava back down on the bed, tucking the blankets around her.

She walked back to Karen, who had started to weep again. She smiled at Sarah through her tears. "Go home tonight and fall apart with your husband Karen. We will take care of tomorrow, tomorrow. Do you understand?"

Karen smiled at Sarah. Then she stopped suddenly before she asked, "Wait! You said Sam was helping Jack? Your Sam?"

It was Sarah's turn to whisper, "Yes. My Sam. You can't ask me anything else, because I don't know. I fell asleep as soon as he got here last night."

"Oh, Sarah! That one's a keeper."

"Yes, he is. Should I send Jack in?" Sarah stood up.

Karen nodded sadly, and then squared her shoulders. "I know I'm going to need you, but I want you to go home tonight. I might ask you to go to the funeral home tomorrow. Would that be okay?"

"Whatever you need me for, sweet girl. I'm going to take your advice. I'm going home to shower and eat. Then I'm going to cry for you. And then you're going to take my advice and go home with your sweet husband, love on your kids, and grieve."

Sarah walked around the corner to the waiting room. Jack sat in a corner on his phone. Sam sat next to him clutching a piece of paper as he talked on his own phone. Ashley was on the couch where Sarah had left her, making her own phone calls. Bev, Liz, and Julie sat in quiet conversation. Karen's mom and dad sat with Jack's mom. They looked sad and lost. Sarah stood and looked at all the people that she loved so much, and her heart swelled with a multitude of emotions. Sarah gave everyone a tired little smile. Sarah approached Jack who had ended his call. He looked sad, but hopeful. Sarah sat down and took his hands in hers. "She's ready, Jack. Go be with your wife." Sarah hugged him hard, before Jack walked back into the sad room that held his wife and daughter.

Sarah stood and looked at everyone else. "Karen is doing better than you'd think. None of us will know anything until tomorrow afternoon. Everyone needs to go home, get some rest and be joyful in the knowledge that we all knew and loved Ava. I love you all, but I want to cry hard. I want to do that at my home."

Sarah turned to Sam and was smothered by his strong arms. Sarah inhaled the scent she loved so much. She closed her eyes, and whispered, "Take me home, please."

Chapter 37:

Sam picked up his suitcase and garment bag at the nurse's station on the way out. As he and Sarah exited the hospital, she had to stop and think for a minute. Sam looked at her as she stood there. She shrugged her shoulders. "I forgot where I left my truck." She hit the alarm on her key fob and saw her lights flash and the alarm sound.

As they walked to the truck, Sam asked, "Do you want me to drive?"

She smiled as she unlocked the doors. Sam put his suitcase and bag in the backseat. "I don't mind. It's not a long drive, but it's a pretty drive, and I want you to enjoy it." She walked around the truck to lean against Sam. "I can't believe you're here, but I'm so glad you are."

Sam held her for a moment. "Let's talk on the way home. We both need sleep."

Before Sarah started the truck she leaned over and kissed Sam on the lips she had missed so much. It was a sweet kiss with under currents of desperation. Sarah pulled out of the parking lot and headed home. "How long is the flight from Cape Town, Sam? Have you had any sleep at all? What about the campaign?"

Sam put his hand on her thigh. As he spoke he watched out the truck window as the city faded away to Interstate, and rolling hills. "It's almost twenty-four hours from Cape Town to St. Louis, and then a short flight from St. Louis to here. I slept a little on the plane, but I've been frantic to get to you. It made it hard to sleep." He squeezed her thigh and smiled.

Sarah whispered. "What about Oak Wood? It's your last campaign stop this year."

"Really, Sarah?" Sam cocked an eyebrow. "Do you remember who owns the company? Walter and Sally Lemons send their love, and they sent a huge donation to a children's hospital in Ava's name."

Sarah stared at the road. "Oh!" escaped her mouth and a tear rolled down her cheek.

"They love you Sarah, and they love me. They arranged for the flight and got me to the airport. They can finish the campaign without me."

"I love that you're here, but I'm sorry you're missing a place that you enjoy." Sarah was hoarse with emotion.

"Sweet Sarah, I never enjoy the locale when I'm working. Unless you're with me. I'm all yours for almost three weeks. If you'll have me." Sam, too, was hoarse.

Sarah slowed and pulled onto the shoulder of the highway, yanking the truck into park. Sam looked at her in confusion. She leaned across the seat and threw her arms around Sam's neck. "If I'll have you? If I'll have you?" Sarah shrieked. "I didn't know how badly I wanted you here until just now! I knew I wanted it, but, holy shit Sam!" She finally kissed him. A real, toe-curling kiss that left them both shaking.

Sam continued to hold her as the cars zoomed by on the highway. "I was afraid to kiss you the way I wanted, Sarah. I thought it inappropriate, under the circumstances, but, bloody hell! I'm glad you just did that."

Sarah leaned back in her seat and sighed. "I understand. I'm so tired that I might not make any sense, but a sweet little girl has died. I feel the pain of her mother and father. But as hard as it is for you to realize it when you're in the middle of it, the sun will come up tomorrow, and it will set. People will die, and babies will be born. Karen and Jack will get through this, and they will learn to live their lives differently. The man that I adore just flew twenty-four fucking hours to be with me in this pain. This man that I adore left a campaign that I'm sure he has never missed before, to be with me. This man that I adore is here because he loves me. So I plan on loving him. For many, many hours. *After* we've showered, eaten, and napped."

Sam grinned the grin that Liz hated. "Are you sure you want to do it in that order?"

"God, yes, Sam. I'm beat, and you have to be. Shower, food, sleep."

Sam just smirked and muttered, "We'll see."

The Interstate turned into county road. Sam was entranced with the hills and valleys of Missouri. The trees, blue sky, and wildflowers in the road ditches were beautiful. He kept asking Sarah what kind of flowers they were, or what kind of trees. Sarah was happy to answer his questions. She loved Missouri, it was a beautiful state. As they rounded a sharp curve on a hillside, Sam saw them. The whole hillside was full of black and white cows. He yelled so suddenly, and so loudly, that Sarah almost ran off the road. "Livestock! It's fucking livestock! What kind of cows are those? They're bloody beautiful! Our cows don't look like that back home." Sam bounced in his seat, and Sarah cracked up.

Sarah yelled back at Sam, "They're Holsteins, Sam! Holsteins! They're dairy cattle. I might as well warn you, so you don't pee your pants, that we will be seeing horses, sheep, and buffalo."

Sam turned to her with his eyes wide. "Buffalo? They have buffalo in Missouri? I've never seen a buffalo. Except in a zoo." He turned and looked backward out of the window and watched the cows disappear from view.

"They're raised for their meat, Sam. You're in farm country now. Everything you see is raised for it's meat, milk, or it's wool. Everything you see planted, like that alfalfa in that field, is used to feed that livestock, or sold in order to buy more livestock or feed. These are all generational family farms. They're all self-sustaining farms. We were green, before green was cool." Sarah smiled at Sam.

"I fucking love Missouri." Sam continued to stare at everything. Sarah found it hard to imagine that the man who sat next to her, the man who had been all over the world, was so excited about rural Missouri.

Sarah slowed as they entered her small town. She pointed out the post office, and the salon where she was sanded, buffed, and waxed, and had her hair done. She pointed out the coffee shop, and her mechanic, and then Liz' gift shop.

"This is quite charming." Sam said seriously.

They had just made it through town, when Sarah made a left onto gravel. Sam looked at her with his mouth open. "You live on gravel?"

Sarah laughed loudly. He was so stinking cute. "Well, I don't live *on* gravel. I live in a house, on grass. But you have to drive on gravel to get there."

"Smartass."

Sarah slowed as they neared the entrance to her drive. It was a long drive, and you couldn't see the house for a while. She was strangely nervous. "Were you nervous to show me your house Sam? Because right now, I'm nervous to show you mine. I want you to love it."

"You're asking me this? The man who had never had anyone *in* his house? Hell, yes, I was nervous. My house is a labor of love, just as yours is. You love your home, Sarah, and I love you. Therefore, I'll love your home. Now drive."

Sarah made a right turn onto her gravel drive. They drove under a massive arbor that spanned the drive. It was covered with a jungle monstrosity of wisteria in full bloom. The entire arbor looked as if it was covered in a million clusters of lilac grapes. On both sides of the drive were redbud trees with their gnarled trunks and branches. The drive went up hill before leveling off and making a sharp left turn. To Sam's right was a pond with a covered shelter on the bank. It was currently occupied by mallard ducks catching bugs that skated on the water. Below them lay the farm that Sarah called home. She stopped the truck and looked at Sam.

"Now you know why I love Danni's place so much. It looks familiar, doesn't it?"

Sam just stared and whispered, "I love it already."

The white two story farmhouse sat at the bottom of the hill. The red shuttered windows had flower boxes overflowing with all manner of color. The house had a wraparound porch with a swing at one end and lots of white wicker furniture. Boston ferns hung the entire length of the porch. The drive curved around to the side of the house. Planter beds of all kinds surrounded the drive and house. There were more redbud trees, and ginkgos. Maple trees and birches. A three-tiered fountain sat in the front yard surrounded by a plethora of hostas. Sam could hear the gurgle of the water and the splashing sound as it dripped from one tier to the next.

Sarah drove to the side of the house, where the porch continued. There was more wicker and some rocking chairs. To the left of the driveway, and down the hill, was a large lake. Sam could see a dock with a canoe tied to it. A creek meandered its way at the back of the house.

"I spend more time back here than I do in the front." Sarah said as she parked the truck in front of a two-car garage that looked like a red barn. Another small red out building was to the side of the garage. Stepping stones went from its door toward the back of the house. Sam guessed that it probably went to a kitchen door. Sam could see a chimney, and it, too, had flower boxes under the windows. "What's that?"

"That's the craft room that David insisted I have. I do my scrapbooking and gift-wrapping type stuff. Let's get your bag and luggage, and we'll walk around to the front and go in the front door." Sarah grabbed Sam's garment bag, and he followed her through the yard. Everywhere he looked, there were trees and plants and flowers surrounded by manicured lawn. As Sam and Sarah walked up the front steps Sam stopped her. He dropped his luggage and took his garment bag from Sarah's hand and laid it on a wicker chair. He took her in his arms and breathed in her earthy scent, then whispered in her ear. "I could get used to this. It feels like home."

Sarah's breath hitched as she smiled and unlocked the door. She kissed Sam, then took his hand and led him in. The foyer was fairly large with oak hardwoods that stretched into the house. The walls of the foyer were covered with rusty tin, and both side walls had shelves with baskets in them and shelves for display. There were photos, old tins, books, and rocks. There were grates in the floor under the shelving, and Sam noticed two pairs of boots sitting on the grates. Sarah kicked her shoes off. Sam did the same.

As Sam followed Sarah into the house proper, he noticed the open door to the left. He guessed that was the bedroom, as it was the only wall in the whole downstairs. The rest of the house was completely open with old oak ceiling beams and hardwood floors. Sarah stood to his right with her arms crossed. The front of the house was floor to ceiling windows, with stained glass at the top. He had noticed them when they arrived. A window seat was built in under the windows. Directly in front of him was a massive stone fireplace surrounded by built-in shelves. Sarah had hung her Murano glass sconces on either side of a mirror that hung centered over the fireplace. A comfortable looking, well-worn black leather sofa sat in front of the fireplace with an old oak chest as a coffee table. Two wing chairs in faded gray suit fabric sat on each side of the couch. Everywhere he looked, he saw different shades of gray, with pops of black and white and wood that grounded everything.

The wall in the back of the house held all manner of guitars and a wall of old clipboards hung on old doorknobs with sheet music, photos, and play bills. There was a pool table in the middle, and bar chairs lined the walls. There was an old upright grand piano in the corner, and a karaoke machine sat on an old Victrola. The room continued to the left into the kitchen. It was massive and white, with antique hardware, and old leaded glass upper cabinets. The stars of the kitchen were the red Aga range in the middle of the back wall and the massive island. It was an old store display case that was topped with a well-used butcher block. All of the countertops were black granite. The backsplash was classic subway tiles, but they had been turned vertical instead of horizontal. Rusty tin covered the wall behind the Aga.

The porch was actually an extension of the kitchen and had three walls of glass with a fireplace built into the corner. A television hung over the mantle. Sam could see Sarah's craft room and the creek which had a wooden bridge leading to a gazebo that was covered with wild honeysuckle. Sam could smell it, and it made him smile.

Sam walked to a loveseat on the porch and sat down. He looked up at Sarah and took her hands. "Can I live here? I'll move in right now." Sam loved Sarah's home. It wasn't too feminine or too masculine. It was homey and comfortable. You could walk in and immediately know that you could prop your feet up. "Your home is like you, Sarah. It's inviting, and full of heart. It's made to be enjoyed."

Sarah sat down by him and exhaled. She leaned her head against Sam's hard chest. "You just get me, Sam. You can move in right now."

There was a winding staircase between the kitchen wall and the wall Sam had seen when he came in. He followed Sarah up the stairs and looked at the craftsmanship. He wished he had done his staircase in London like Sarah's. The treads were reclaimed oak, and the banisters were painted white with black spindles. The stairs ended on a large landing with a door in front of them. Two bedrooms were on the right with their own baths, as well as two more bedrooms on the left with baths. Sarah called her room the "studio". She led Sam in, and Sam's knees buckled. He had to sit in an overstuffed chair to the right of the door. He was all over the walls. These were the pictures that Sarah had taken when they had walked Venice with Luca. There were also many of Sam and Sarah that Luca had taken of the two of them with Sarah's camera. The vintage camera that Sam had bought for her was displayed on a shelf with an old Brownie camera. Sarah had installed a spotlight over them.

"Sorry. I'm really not a stalker. I just hadn't finished before I left for the hospital." Sarah sat in Sam's lap and kissed the hollow of his neck.

"It'll take me many days to explore this house. There are treasures everywhere. This place is perfect." Sam kissed Sarah's collarbone.

Sarah was fading fast. She was bone tired. "Come on! Let's get your stuff off the front porch. Shower, food, and nap."

Sam laughed devilishly as he followed her down the stairs. He was worn out, but not that worn out.

Sam followed Sarah into the master bedroom. He stopped immediately. The whole house was Sarah, but this room was somehow more. She had continued the gray, white and black color scheme, but had added pale aqua and pale blush pink. Three of the walls were painted dark gray, and one wall was matte black. It was dark, masculine, and sexy. She had added just the right amount of aqua and blush, and accessories to add a touch of feminine. Sam knew fashion well enough to know that this room was stunning.

It was a large room that held a king-sized bed with a very tall, padded, charcoal gray suede headboard. It faced another fireplace that was clad in dark mica. Sam could see the glittering flecks in the stone, and he knew it would be beautiful at night with a fire. A large iron chandelier hung from the middle of the beamed ceiling. On the tall chimney were hung the six nude pictures that Sarah had taken of them in their apartment in The Gritti. White mats in eleven-by-fourteen black frames made them the centerpiece of the room. Sam stood and stared at the photos. They still made him catch his breath. Sarah took his hand and smiled softly and sweetly. "I got them hung on Monday. I love them."

Sam squeezed her hand and continued to look around the room. A chaise lounge covered with hounds tooth was another perfect touch in a room full of perfection. An eight-foot-tall silver antique mirror was propped up in the corner. Mirrored side tables flanked the bed with matching mercury glass lamps. Sam walked over to look at a piece of painted wood propped up against the base of one of the lamps. It said, "Hello there, handsome". Sam turned and grinned at Sarah. "I guess this is my side? Or were you expecting someone else?"

Sarah smiled. "You can have any part of the bed you want, because you're the only one I was expecting."

The reclaimed wooden floor was covered with a lush wool rug in faded colors of gray, aqua, and blush. It was heavenly under Sam's bare feet. Antique barrister cases held books and treasures with more signs propped among Sarah's photos. Sam noticed another painted piece of wood between a piece of petrified wood and books on Winston Churchill. It said, "I wish I was kissing you instead of missing you." Sam strode to Sarah and kissed her silly.

Sarah wilted under his ministrations, so he slowly undressed her and sat her on the chaise as he undressed himself. He helped her up and into the bathroom shower. Sam barely noticed the bathroom, but he knew it was big, and that Sarah's shower had more jets, sprays, and nozzles than he had ever seen. A built-in bench wrapped itself around three walls of the shower. He saw that the walls and floor were concrete. He sat Sarah on the bench and tried to figure out how to turn the damn thing on.

Sarah laughed quietly as she got up to turn on the water and the rain heads in the ceiling. Sam took a hand held sprayer from the wall and bathed Sarah. He gently and lovingly lathered and rinsed and kneaded her tired muscles. Sam couldn't resist the sight of Sarah's wet body. He always adored her, but he worshipped her wet. He sprayed and kissed her shoulder, then her neck, before he kissed her lips. Sarah quivered as she leaned back against the wall. She took his face in her hands. "I've missed you so much. Food and a nap can wait for just a little while."

As Sam leaned in, he saw a print encased in acrylic hanging on the wall of the shower over Sarah's shoulder. It said, "Push me against the wall and kiss the hell out of me." So he did.

Chapter 38:

Sam slowly woke up to the feel, the sound, and the scent of Sarah. His chest pushed against her softness and he felt her deep, even breathing. Sam loved the times when he woke before her. He could watch Sarah sleep for hours. Satisfied that she was still soundly asleep, Sam quietly got out of the bed and put his jeans on. He wandered into the kitchen to see what he could fix for them to eat.

Sam threw together a pot of soup and brewed coffee. He looked at his watch and saw that it was two in the afternoon. His internal clock was so screwed up after Venice, Prague, London, and Cape Town; he had no idea if it was morning or night. All that mattered was that he was with Sarah in a place that he could fall in love with. He poured himself a cup of coffee, and began to look around.

As he sipped his coffee and wandered through the house, he was not surprised that Sarah's taste was eclectic. It was as artful and unexpected as her. His father would love what Sarah had done. She had placed a feather by a crystal pendant. He found rocks displayed artfully by an antique hand-painted fan. Sarah had mixed old and new, ornate and country into something that worked. She had stacked suitcases on top of each other and attached them to the wall for display space. On the wall going upstairs she had attached at least thirty open books in a haphazard display. It looked as if they were flying off the wall. It was pure artistry. It was pure Sarah. Sam was sure that the books were sentimental to her.

As he made his way back through the front, he noticed the walls on each side of the windows. He stood and smiled. She had hung all of the Venetian masks with pictures of Venice interspersed among them. It was beautiful. Sam realized that what Sarah had done was to stage vignettes of her life, and he also realized that he was everywhere in the house. There was a small photo of him in profile on her bedside table. There were pictures of them in every bookcase and on every shelf in the house. He had been placed with pictures of her children, and pictures of the girls. Sam had only seen two pictures of David, but she had placed his picture beside one of David's in a middle shelf of the bookcase by the fireplace. On another shelf Sam found another piece of painted barn wood. Sam was sure that Sarah had painted all of the little sayings he had found throughout the house. The wood read, "I think I'd miss you even if we'd never met." It looked and felt as if he lived here, too. He sighed as he took a sip of coffee. He was home.

Sam sat at the island drinking a second cup of coffee when Sarah walked into the kitchen in a T-shirt and panties. Sarah in a T-shirt was an instant turn on for him, and when she stretched, a quiet groan escaped from his lungs. Sarah stopped mid stretch and looked at Sam intensely. The man sat on a bar stool in her kitchen in nothing but a pair of jeans that he hadn't bothered to button. There went her breath again. Sarah walked to him and kissed him gently on the corner of his mouth. He held her and rested his chin on her shoulder. "You have no idea how much I've missed you in your T-shirt and panties."

"Hmmmm," moaned Sarah, as she inhaled the oak leaves and whiskey that was all Sam. She raised her head. "Is that coffee? And what else do I smell? Is that soup?"

Sam got up and poured her a cup of coffee. "I made a pot of soup. It was the easiest thing I could think of. We had our shower and our nap, but not our food. I'm famished."

Sarah sighed as she inhaled the deep flavor of the coffee. "What time is it? I really need to call the children."

"I already called them from the hospital, Sarah. I don't know if all of them are coming, but I'm sure that one or two will be here." Sam sat down on the bar stool next to her.

Sarah looked at him in teary-eyed wonder. "You're just - just so - gah! How'd you get their numbers?"

"Liz gave them to me. That's who I was on the phone with when you came into the waiting room. I called them, and Danni, Walter and Sally, and a list that Jack had given me."

Sarah smiled softly. "I love that you're here. I didn't think it was possible to love you more than I do, but knowing how difficult it was to get here makes me love you even more." Sarah sipped her coffee while Sam filled their soup bowls. She noticed that the clock said four o'clock. "I would have expected Karen to have called by now. Maybe she and Jack were able to go it alone."

"Oh! I forgot to tell you, Jack called me. They're doing okay, but plans have changed. I told him that you would call Karen later this evening. You were still asleep, and thankfully, so was she. Neither of us wanted to wake you guys up. I wish I'd met him under different circumstances, because I really like that guy. He sure loves his wife." Sam picked up the empty soup bowls and took them to the sink. Sarah watched him rinse them out and put them in the dishwasher. When he turned, Sarah still watched him. "What? Do I have chicken in my teeth?"

Sarah smiled. "No. I love the fact that you called my kids. And that you have my friends' phone numbers, and that you like, Jack. I'm thinking that I really like you here." Sarah watched Sam in all of his barefoot, no shirt, unbuttoned jeans glory, as he leaned back against the counter.

Sam looked around the home that Sarah had made. "I'm thinking that I like being here. I like feeling that I'm part of your home. I see bits of me everywhere here. Do you know how that makes me feel? "

Sarah brushed away a tear and shook her head no.

"It makes me feel loved. It makes me feel like I'm home. I love that, Sarah Reid, and I love you for including me." He finally walked to her for the sweet kiss that her lips had been begging for.

When they came up for air, Sam continued to touch her. "Did you guys use a firm from the city for your house plans? It's an amazing floor plan."

Sarah shook her head. "No. David was an architect. I had twenty-five years to figure out what I wanted and needed. I told David, and he made it happen. This house sits where the old homestead sat, but that house was unsalvageable. Though it did provide our floors, some doors, and the stained-glass windows in the front room."

Sam nodded as he looked toward the front of the house. "I thought they looked original, but I knew this house was new, so that makes sense."

"I used what I could of the hardware for the drawers and cabinets, and the leaded glass in the upper cabinets. Some of the stone in the front fireplace is from the old one that collapsed. I have a lot of weird stuff in the craft room, but I love it." They wandered through the house, as Sam pointed things out and asked a million questions.

"Are you really curious, Sam, or are you just being nice?"

"I." He kissed her nose. "Really." He kissed her cheek. "Want." He kissed her shoulder. "To." He kissed her hair. "Know." He pulled her T-shirt down and kissed the swell of her breast.

Sarah cleared her throat as looked around at her home. "I can't tell you why I choose to do the things I do. I just do what speaks to me, and what makes me happy. It's that simple."

"Oh, Sarah, you do things from your heart, and I know that your heart is not a simple thing." Sam laid his hand against that heart and kissed her softly.

~~~

Sam grabbed the bottle of Jameson, and Sarah grabbed the glasses and a pack of cigarettes. They went and sat on the porch swing off the kitchen. They sat close and pushed the swing in a rhythmic arc. Sam smelled the water that enveloped the house. He smelled the newly mown grass and the whiskey in their glasses. They listened to the babbling of the creek and the peep frogs that were singing their night song. The sun had almost set, and it was as if the world had stopped in a kind of limbo. No longer day, and not quite night. They were quiet as they listened to the night things awaken.

The first flicker of light appeared in front of them, then was gone.

"What was that?"

Sarah laid her head on Sam's shoulder. "Just watch," she whispered.

The flickers of light started with a few here and there, but in a few short moments they were surrounded by hundreds and hundreds of lightning bugs. It was like being in the middle of fireworks that didn't burn. There was enough light coming from the kitchen window that Sarah could see Sam's eyes. They were wide open with wonder and a huge grin spread across his face. His face reflected an innocence that made Sarah want to cry.

"Lightning bugs, Sam. Welcome to Missouri."

They continued to rock while Sarah called Karen. Sam was entranced. Sarah leaned against him as she dialed. Sam put his arm around her shoulders. Jack answered the phone. "Hey, Sarah. Did you rest?"

"I did, Jack. I slept for several hours, thanks to you and Sam. Did Karen get any rest?" Sarah asked softly.

"She did. She actually got up just a little while ago. Let me get her, she's been waiting for you to call."

Sarah waited, as Sam kissed her temple. "Hey girl." Karen's voice was soft and raspy.

"Hey back atcha. How you doing, girlie?" Sarah's voice was soft, too.

"I'm doing better than yesterday." Karen said sadly.

Sarah sighed. "Oh, sweetie, I'm so honored that you wanted me there. It was one of the sweetest gifts I've ever been given. Thank you, dear girl." Sam squeezed her shoulder.

"Sarah, life is going to be chaotic over the next few days, so I want to tell you something while I can. Please don't interrupt me, okay, as I think I'll only be able to say it one time." Karen took a breath.

Sarah exhaled. "Whatever you need."

Karen was silent for a minute before she began. "I love you for staying with Jack and me. I know I expected a lot from you, but I really don't think Jack and I could have made it without you." Karen started to weep softly, which made Sarah cry.

"You loved our daughter." Karen cried harder. Sarah clutched Sam's thigh. He continued to squeeze her shoulder. "The moment you crawled into bed with Ava and sang to her, it was if a weight was taken from my shoulders. I felt peace and love. Yes, I've loved you for a long time, but after experiencing this with you, that love is deeper. You are my sister, and you are Jack's sister. You said that you were honored for the sweet gift of sharing this with us. You are a gift to us."

"I love you so much, and my heart is breaking for you guys. But I also feel peace knowing that you and Jack are going to get through this. I learned through David's death, and my parents, you never get over something like this, but you do get through it. Life just gets different. You and Jack lean on each other, and feed each other the strength you're going to need." Sarah was hoarse with unshed tears.

Karen sniffed and Sarah heard her blow her nose. "I need to ask you something. Please tell me hell no if you need to, and I will completely understand."

Sarah smiled. "Anything you need, Karen."

"We didn't go to the funeral home today, but I guess you figured that out as I didn't call you. We donated all of Ava's organs. Jack and I couldn't stand the thought of other parents having to go through what we did. She will be cremated tomorrow."

Sarah choked. "My God! You two are so strong, Karen!"

"We're trying to be. What I want to ask you, is, will you sing for us and Ava? And will you do it at the farm?" Karen got quiet.

"Of course, but I'm don't really know what you're asking, Karen." Sarah was completely confused.

"We just want a memorial service. A celebration of Ava's short life. We want music and food and just close friends and family. Then we want to scatter her ashes and release balloons. We'd like to do this at the farm." Karen's voice trailed off.

Sarah swallowed and looked over at Sam. "How many people are you talking about, and how soon? I'm honored that you've asked me, by the way."

"Because of the cremation, we can do it anytime. I'm guessing maybe around thirty people?"

Sarah thought over lists in her head, and made mental check marks. "Of course, Karen. You and Jack should be in a better place emotionally that you might enjoy it more. Also, it would be nice for people to not have to get up early the next morning. They could stay and enjoy the love and friendship."

"Oh, Sarah! That's why we asked you! You think of things that we wouldn't." Karen had stopped crying and sounded stronger.

"What time do you think, and let us know how much money you'll need for food and drink. Or do you want us to have it catered?" Karen asked.

"Sam and I will take care of everything. Let's choose to start at 4 pm. I don't want any money from you guys. Let me do this in memory of Ava. We don't need catering. You know I love cooking for people. With just me in the house, the only people I get to cook for anymore are you and the other girls. Oh! Can you email me pictures of Ava? I want to use them for centerpieces. Karen, I don't want this to sound like a party, but I'm so excited to be able to do this for you guys. You will be surrounded by friends and love. It will be a good thing." Sarah said this firmly.

"It's just what Jack and I want! A happy day! And, Sarah? I can't wait to hug Sam. Jack really likes him, and he told me what a huge help he was."

Sarah smiled at Sam. "I will tell him, Karen. He said the same thing about Jack. I'll be checking in with you, okay? Get some rest, and love those kids and your sweet hubby."

"Thank you so, so much Sarah. We love you so much. Goodnight."

Sarah sighed loudly and leaned back against Sam.

"This isn't going to be too much is it, Sarah? I will help with anything I can, but do you need to call in reinforcements?"

Sarah chuckled. "Oh, I'll definitely call in reinforcements, but if any of my kids are coming, I won't need to. Gemma and Harper are organizational wizards."

"Hmmm." Sam cocked an eyebrow at her. "I wonder where they get that from?"

Sam poured them another whiskey, and they smoked another cigarette and enjoyed the night sounds before heading in. Sam was still enthralled with the lightning bugs and an owl they heard as it hunted for its nightly mouse dinner. He was intrigued with how loud it was in the dark if you really listened. As Sarah and Sam cleaned up, she told him about the pool plans. Sam's eyes lit up, and that made Sarah laugh.

"I love you in the water, Sarah. " Sam said hoarsely

"If you play your cards right, we can enjoy the water together in a few minutes."

They made their way to the bedroom, stopping so Sam could ask questions about particular objects and decorations. He was correct in thinking that everything meant something to Sarah. The rocks that he had seen had all been brought to Sarah by her daughters when they were little. Some had been saved by her grandparents. Sarah turned on the bedside lamps and lit the pillar candles in the multiple mercury glass stands. She had even filled the fireplace with candles. Sam followed her into the bathroom so he could really look at it. He remembered that the shower was concrete. The only other thing he remembered about the shower was Sarah's wet body.

French doors had been used instead of shower doors. The shower itself had two huge rain heads, three jets that came out of the wall, and two hand held sprayers. Concrete shelves were built into the walls to hold soaps and shampoos. The bathroom was pale gray, with more tin as the backsplash behind the sinks. Two old water troughs functioned as sinks. They had been installed in two old dressers that had so much peeling paint, it was hard to tell what color they were. A ten-foot-tall old oak apothecary cabinet sat in between the sinks. An old ladder leaned against the wall with soft, fluffy white towels hanging from it. Beautiful gray veined tile covered the floor. He asked her if they were heated floors. She grinned and told him of course.

The masterpiece was the bathtub. It sat in a bay window of old leaded glass. An iron rod across the middle of the window held a curtain of black and silver damask pushed off to the side, leaving the view outside unimpeded. The walls that surrounded it were painted a dark matte charcoal. It was framed by an archway with antique corbels at the top. A small chandelier hung over the center of the tub, and a huge wicker cone full of ferns and trailing ivy hung from the wall at the end of the tub. It was big enough for four people, with jets and nickel hand sprays.

The tub itself looked as if someone had taken a huge iron claw foot tub and draped a sheet of white porcelain over it. The porcelain poured over the edges in pleats and folds. It was the most amazing thing Sam had ever seen. He stood and gazed at it with his mouth agape.

"That tub is a work of art." Sam gawked.

"It is pretty amazing." Sarah grinned as she lit the bathroom candles. Sam could smell the sandalwood from the bedroom and now the bathroom. As he watched Sarah, he noticed the antique wicker dress form that stood in the corner by the tub. It wore a sheer white lace bustier and matching thong with a garter belt. Sam swallowed hard.

Sarah walked into the bedroom and rolled open a set of barn doors to show Sam the walk-in closet. The only items on the right side were Sam's garment bag and his luggage. "This is your side of the closet. I bought you some jeans, T-shirts, and a couple of flannel shirts. I also got you a proper pair of muck boots. I hope you don't mind, but knowing you, I figured you would come with only trousers, designer T-shirts, and very expensive leather shoes."

Sam was gob smacked. "You bought me clothes? You bought me farm clothes. And you bought me the ugliest fucking pair of boots I've ever seen, and I love them! And for your information, I brought jeans and a pair of sneakers."

"Feel free to unpack. I'm going to run the bath. I'll be back in a few minutes."

Sam lounged in Sarah's bed and scanned the objects in her room. He noticed another painted sign on one of the barn doors. It read, "A kiss is a secret told to the mouth instead of the ear." Sam wanted to tell Sarah's mouth a lot of secrets.

Sam heard the water run, and Sarah hummed softly. The sandalwood was thick in the air, and it was quiet. There was no traffic, no neon, no muted conversations behind closed doors or in hallways. Sam had lived in hotel rooms for so long, and was home so rarely, he had forgotten what darkness and quiet was like. The room was dark except for the candlelight, and the mica in the fireplace glittered like diamonds. This room was meant for love making.

The bathroom door opened and candlelight was Sarah's backdrop. She wore the white lace-topped thigh high stockings and a sheer white lacy garter belt. The matching thong left little to the imagination, and the bustier was so sheer, that Sarah might as well have been naked. Sam groaned in anticipation.

As Sarah walked out of the bathroom she moaned a little and had to stop to catch her breath. Sam was naked in her bed. She swallowed before she walked to him. She slowly reached out her hand and ran it down his chest and abdomen. Sam's muscles quivered. Sarah bent over and ran her tongue over his obliques. Sam moaned as she stood and said, "You should never wear clothes. You should never be allowed to cover up the perfection that is your body. You make me lose my mind, Sam Ramsey."

"You make me lose my patience, Sarah Reid." Sam growled, as he sat up and pulled her toward him. His teeth took the bustier and his hands took the panties. Sarah heard and felt the rip of fabric.

The darkness, quiet, and the scent of sandalwood lent an air of languid sensuality. Slow caresses, and deep kisses. Tongues and fingers that were in no hurry. The only sound was the occasional spit of a candle, and Sam and Sarah's quiet moans. Time had stopped and had no meaning, as they were lost in each other. The flickering light of the candles highlighted all of Sam's hard planes and angles as he raised himself over Sarah. The sharp angles of his cheek bones left the hollow of his cheeks in blackness. Sarah's shoulders and the tops of her breasts gleamed with a golden glow as she lay softly under the hard man. As she slowly rolled over Sam, he caressed her hips and tugged her hair gently. They moved in the bed until they lay side by side.

Sarah looked into Sam's eyes that had darkened with lust. She touched his cheek and whispered, "Sharp."

Sam gently tugged on Sarah's breast with his mouth and whispered back, "Perfect."

"Crazy." Sarah moaned as she touched Sam's abdomen.

Sam gripped Sarah's ass. "Soft."

"Hard." Sarah hissed as she gripped Sam's length.

Sam groaned. "Good."

As he touched Sarah's wetness with a finger, she arched. "Pleasure."

Sarah wrapped her leg around Sam's waist as they continued to lie face to face. "Longing," moaned Sam.

Sarah moved her hips and Sam moved slowly into the heat of her. They both moaned and rocked gently back and forth as they continued to watch each other. His eyes were hooded and he bit his bottom lip. "Tight. Wet. Pleasure." Sam was slowly losing his mind.

Sarah's eyes grew wide as she looked into Sam's. "Hard. Hot. Mine." As Sarah slowly lost herself in Sam, he grabbed her face and whispered, "Love."

The candles burned low, and Sam and Sarah still talked softly with their legs wrapped in each other. "You're going to have to run more water. It'll be freezing."

Sarah grinned. "It's heated."

They went and immersed themselves in Sarah's tub. The water was hot and silky, and the jets were turned low. They both groaned as they slid down to their necks in the water.

"When did you buy me clothes?"

Sarah's eyes were closed as she luxuriated in the hot water. "I bought them after London. After my pathetic meltdown, I found it helpful for my emotional well-being to buy you clothes. It gave me hope that you would be here someday to wear them."

She straddled his lap. She kissed his shoulder and put her cheek against it. Sam reached for the soap and a washcloth. He started to lather her back and neck. "I've bought you things, too."

Sarah lifted her head and smiled. "Ooh! What did you get me? Tell me! Tell me! Pretty please?"

Sam laughed as he continued to lather her body. "You'll just have to wait to see when you come back to London." She pouted a little as she lathered his shoulders and arms.

He started to rinse the soap and continued to ask questions. "I want to live in your bedroom. It's more masculine than I thought it would be. I guess it shouldn't surprise me."

Sarah laughed loudly as she moved to lean back and look at Sam. "My bedroom has never been girly, but it looked totally different two weeks ago. I painted the walls, and got all new bedding and a new headboard. I painted all of the little signs. I wanted it to be your room, too, and I wanted it to be sexy for us. First it was for David and me, then it was mine, now it's ours. I'm glad you like it. I think there shall be some picture taking in that room."

"That room was made for sex. I plan on having a lot of sex. We'll see if we have time for pictures."

August

Chapter 39:

They were busy for the next few days. There were lists and phone calls and a trip into the city for various things. They dusted and stripped beds and cooked together. But as hectic as it had been, they both sat on the back porch every night. They sipped whiskey, smoked cigarettes and enjoyed the night sounds and each other.

On Friday Sam pulled round tables out of the garage. He washed and sat them up around the yard. Sarah went to the kitchen to check on Sam before she went upstairs to work on the pictures for the centerpieces. She stood and stared as he rolled the tables out of the barn. He was barefoot and shirtless. All he wore was a faded pair of jeans. Sarah watched the muscles in his back and forearms ripple, and she immediately wanted him.

She rushed down the back steps when Sam looked up and saw her. His heart stopped. She wore a pair of cut off jean shorts and a T-shirt, and all he wanted to do was strip her clothes off and screw her in the grass. She reached him, threw her arms around his waist, and kissed him. Her mouth was hot and wet. He reached to pull off her shirt, but Sarah just giggled and ran back in the house. Sam grinned and shook his head. He wiped the sweat of his forehead and continued to roll tables across the grass.

Sarah heard the car. It was still down the road a bit, but it would turn in the driveway soon. She smiled and got up. Sarah reached the front gate when Gemma put the car in park. She opened the

car door and stood up and looked at her mother. "'Sup woman?"
Then she smiled and rushed into Sarah's arms. Sarah rocked with
her for a few minutes before they walked onto the porch.

Sam had heard the car, too, and had come in the backdoor.
"Sarah? I think someone's here." As he rounded the corner from
the kitchen, Sarah and Gemma walked in the front door. Sarah
looked up at him and smiled happily. Gemma made it through the
front door before she saw him. She stopped. She stared. Her
mouth dropped open. She didn't say a word, but she whimpered a
little. She looked at Sarah with a guilty look. Sam grinned and
crossed his ankles before he crossed his arms across his chest as
he leaned up against the wall. He raised his eyebrows as he
looked at Sarah, who started to laugh uproariously. "I do believe
this is the first time that I have ever seen Gemma speechless!"

Sam chuckled as he walked to Gemma and gave her in a big hug.
He whispered in her ear, "Hey Gemma. It's so good to finally meet
you in person." He stepped back and told Sarah, "I'll go put on a
shirt."

Both women said in unison, "No!" They looked at each other and
started laughing.

After he put on a shirt, Sam took Gemma's luggage upstairs. The
women sat at the island when Sam came back in. He leaned over
Sarah with a hug and a kiss to her temple before he got icy beers
for all. He sat down next to Sarah and absentmindedly picked up
her hand and kissed her wrist.

"How long are you staying Gemma?" Sam asked before taking a
swallow of the cold beer.

Gemma shook her head and took a deep breath before she

squared her shoulders. "Okay! We're just going to have to get this shit out of the way. You, Sam Ramsay, are the most beautiful man I've ever seen. The British Parliament should make a law that you can never wear a shirt. I am having lustful thoughts about you, and I don't feel fucking guilty! A girl can dream, can't she? And I'm a little bitter, and a lot jealous that my *mother* is tapping that!"

They were still laughing when Charlie, Trace and Harper arrived. Charlie hugged her mother hard and then turned to Sam. She hugged Sam hard and said, "My mother has always been stunning and kind. But now she's joyful. Thank you for that, Sam." Charlie kissed his cheek gently.

Trace gave Sam a hug. "Thank God!" Sam said. "Some testosterone!"

Harper hugged her mom before she grabbed Sam, kissed him full on the mouth and grabbed his ass firmly. "Now we've got that out of the way!"

Sarah walked to Sam, who grinned, and reached around his waist as she laid her head on his shoulder. "I warned you."

~~~

The women started supper. Trace and Sam sat in the living room talking. They heard a lot of giggles, curses, and whispers. Sam raised an eyebrow at Trace. Trace grinned and said, "You know they're in their talking about us, don't you?

Sam chuckled and turned to look at Sarah. She stared at him and smiled. "God! I hope so!"

"I got lucky marrying into this family," Trace told Sam. "Those four women are one and the same, and they will someday kill me. But what a way to go!" Trace grinned and watched the women dance in the kitchen.

"I'm the luckiest bastard on the planet. I don't know what I did to deserve her, but I'm thankful."

"I'll give you that, but I think Sarah got lucky, too, Sam. She's happier than I've ever seen her. You got a once in a lifetime chance, and she got a second one."

After supper, they all sat at the big farmhouse table Sarah had made out of barn doors. She sat by Sam with her head on his shoulder and watched her children laugh with Sam. Sam gave as good as he got, and Sarah's soul was full.

The night ended with the karaoke machine being put to good use. Sam even sang "Fly Me to The Moon" with Sarah. Her daughters all had beautiful voices and sang lovely harmonies together. Sam and Trace leaned back against their chairs and watched the four women drunkenly sing their rendition of "Unchained Melody." Sam couldn't take his eyes off Sarah. She beamed as she made her way to him for a gentle kiss.

~~~

The next morning started the way the evening had ended. There were lots of laughs, songs, and dances in the kitchen as they all helped with breakfast. Sarah went over the list of things to do, and Charlie quickly went into overdrive as she assigned tasks and chores. Gemma and Harper offered their own ideas. Sarah leaned against the counter next to Sam. "The reinforcements have arrived."

The memorial service preparations had been completed, and

everyone went to their respective bedrooms to shower and change. Trace and Sam went outside to wait for the women. Soft background music played. The food and bar was set up in the garage, along with one long table covered with framed pictures of Ava. Interspersed with the photos were some of Ava's stuffed animals, toys, and books. Pink and white balloons hung from the rafters, and pink and white candles glowed everywhere. All of the tables were spread throughout the backyard. They were covered with pink and white gingham tablecloths. The centerpieces were fresh cut flowers from Sarah's garden that framed pictures of Ava. Sam and Trace had lined the path down to the dock with candles. Adirondack chairs sat around a low table with more balloons and candles. The men had also lined the foot bridge and path to the gazebo with candles and had tied up hundreds of balloons. The men had looked at each other and grinned. They were pleased with the results.

They heard the laughter of the women as they approached the back door. As the women emerged, both Sam and Trace in one voice, muttered, "Fuck!"

Sam had been to hundreds of parties, galas and fundraisers. He had been surrounded by the world's most beautiful women, but he had never seen anything like the four women who walked down the steps toward them. They all wore simple sundresses that bared their shoulders, but the beauty and style of the Reid women made *nothing* simple. For the first time in his life, Sam experienced what the world experienced when they looked at him, except four times greater. The four women had more beauty than he could fathom.

He looked at Trace, who grinned, and shrugged his shoulders. "Just wait until we all go out to eat sometime. It gets almost embarrassing. You're gonna make it even worse."

Sam looked at Sarah with his arms crossed and his heart in his eyes. Sarah did a slow, lustful look down his body. Sam saw her lick her lips, and it made him want to lick them. Sam wore khaki trousers with a basic white button-up shirt. The top three buttons were undone, and he had rolled the sleeves up on his forearms. Sarah gave Sam a kiss and said, "Thank you."

He wrapped his arms around her waist and kissed her bare shoulder. "For what?'

"For being here. For working so hard this week. For loving me."

"I'm afraid I'm fucked, Sarah Reid. I adore you, and I'm already in love with your daughters. Hell, I'd even, what does Gemma always say?" Sam's soft laughter against her shoulder made her skin break out in goose bumps."I'd tap Trace he's so great."

~~~

The service was beautiful. Everyone ate and cried, but there had been a lot of laughter, too. Jack and Karen were overcome with emotion when they saw that Charlie, Gemma, and Harper had come. The three of them and Sarah sang songs and lullabies until the sky was dark. Sam and Trace went around to light everyone's pink and white Chinese lanterns. Sam held Sarah as they watched them float off into the night sky. They reminded him of big lightning bugs. He had become very fond of those fiery little insects. He would miss them when he left.

Sam and Sarah walked Jack and Karen to their car to say goodnight. Sam held a sleeping Bryce, Karen and Jack's six-year-old son. Sarah talked softly with Karen as Jack buckled the kids into their car seats. Jack hugged Sam hard, and said gruffly, "Thank you, man. I don't know what we would have done without you and Sarah. Don't fly off without saying goodbye."

Sam hugged Jack back. "I might fly off, but I will always be back. You'll see me again, and I think Sarah wants to have you over for dinner before I leave. Tonight, you go home and love that sweet wife of yours. And after you do that, go watch your kids sleep."

Sam and Sarah stood and held each other as they watched the tail lights disappear up the driveway. They smiled at each other as they walked around to the back porch to join the others for a night cap.

Charlie and Trace were curled up on a wicker love seat. Liz talked softly with Gemma and Harper, and Bev, Julie, and Ashley murmured on the porch steps. Sarah and Sam made their way to the porch swing and gratefully took the glasses of whiskey Gemma handed them. Sarah lit a cigarette for Sam, and then herself. Gemma reached for it and smiled before Sarah lit another.

"It was beautiful, you guys, Perfect weather, delicious food, beautiful décor, and tears through laughter. The best kind of tears."

Bev looked at Sam and said, "You're a hell of a guy Sam. You flew half way around the world to be with this tribe. That takes balls."

Sam grinned slowly and said, "Thanks, Bev. I've always been strangely fond of my balls."

Liz pointed at Sam. "No! There you go! That "I know I'm fucking sexy, and you want me" grin. That's not allowed! It's so fucking unfair!"

Gemma laughed and pointed at Sam. "No grinning, Sam!"

Sam continued grinning at Liz as he pulled Sarah closer to him. "Tell him to stop that!" Liz muttered.

Sarah laughed as she stood up with Sam. "We're going where it's dark." As they walked down the steps, Sam turned and grinned at Liz again.

"Fuck you Sam Ramsay! I saw that!" Liz wailed. Sam and Sarah heard the laughter as they made their way down the candle lit path to the dock.

Liz sighed as she leaned back in her chair and looked at Gemma and Harper. They looked at Charlie with upraised eyebrows.

Charlie sighed and smiled. "I think I love him. My mom is joyful you guys!"

Gemma was strangely introspective before she responded. "Does anybody else *feel* it? It's like the air around them is magnetized. It's like they both know where the other one is. All the fucking time."

Ashley told them about Sarah's clothesline of pictures and the lingerie Skype party. "I don't know if you guys want to hear it or not, but I know with all of my heart, that Sam Ramsay adores your mother. And she adores him. I would never have believed that a forty-year-old supermodel would fall for a fifty-five-year-old widow, but who do you know that doesn't love your mom?"

Harper leaned forward and took her time. "I'm going to talk about my dad, so if you don't want to hear it, too bad. My dad was an amazing dad who adored my mom. It's the kind of love and marriage I want one day. They loved each other for a long time, and it always gave me hope that something like that was possible." Her voice cracked a little, as Gemma stroked her back. "I adored my dad, and I adore my mother, and I don't think I'm going to take anything away from what they had together. But I think what Sam and my mom have goes beyond that. I noticed it immediately."

Everyone quietly agreed and nodded their heads. She continued. "I think mom has found her destiny." Harper continued. "I know she loved my dad with all her heart. But I think her and Sam love each other with their souls."

Liz patted Harper's back. "Your mom and I discussed this. She finally realized it when she was in Venice, and as much as it fulfilled her, she also felt guilty. She loved your dad, but it's so different with Sam. She felt guilty, and she had no idea how to tell you guys that without it sounding like it lessened your father. I told her that she wouldn't need to. And she didn't. You can see it and feel it. And it's a little overwhelming, isn't it? Are you guys okay with all of this?"

Charlie kissed Trace softly on his cheek then smiled at all of them. "I'm more than okay with it. I would never get in the way of destiny. And, yes, their vibe is thick."

"Well, you women are getting too deep for me, but I know he adores Sarah. And, hell, I think I've fallen for the guy. I'd fuck him." Trace grinned.

"Does it not bother *any* of you that she's getting more than any of us?" Julie asked. "By a man who looks like that? I'm fucking bitter."

"Oh! Believe me! I'm bitter! You all know they're down there skinny dipping don't you? But, seriously, as bitter as I am, is it weird to be so fucking proud of my mom?" Gemma looked toward the dock that was now in darkness. She heard splashes in the water.

Bev smiled. "I've always been proud of your mom. Now I'm just so damn happy for her."

A trail of clothes was scattered across the dock. The candles were blown out. They both knew that the water would call them. Sarah's legs were wrapped around Sam's waist. His feet were on the bottom rung of the ladder. As he slowly thrust into Sarah he watched her eyes look back at his. Sam caught his breath as he looked around her. They were surrounded by hundreds of lightening bugs.

"What?" whispered Sarah.

Sam continued to slowly move in Sarah as he looked around them in wonder. "Pages, sweet Sarah. Pages for our scrapbook."

~~~

The next morning Trace and Sam sat in the kitchen with their coffee. Everyone had eaten earlier, and the four women went out to the gazebo with their coffee to say their goodbyes. Sam watched Sarah as she walked over the foot bridge with her arm wrapped around Charlie and the other two following. Trace watched him watching them. "We talked about you last night, you know."

"Oh, I'm sure. I hope I passed muster." He turned to watch Sarah as she sat in the gazebo with her daughters. "But, honestly? Even if they hated me, I couldn't leave her."

Trace took a sip of coffee, and looked at him over the rim. "Charlie, Gemma, and Harper would never put Sarah in a position of having to choose, Sam. They love her too much. It's so obvious to all of us how you two feel about each other. My God, man! You flew all the way around the world to be here! Welcome to the family, Sam. And you've got to stop grinning at me like that. I'm starting to have lustful thoughts about you, and that makes me really uncomfortable."

~~~

Sarah sat down and looked up at her daughters. She sighed as a tear rolled down her cheek. She hoarsely mumbled. "I'm not ashamed. I'm not ashamed that he shares my bed, and I'm not ashamed that I love him. I'm not ashamed that I'm a fucking cougar. And, God forgive me, I don't care what you guys think. At this point in my life, I only care what I think."

She looked up at her daughters who all openly cried. "We have always been open and honest with each other, and I'm not about to start lying to you guys, now. I would expect the same from you. But, please be gentle, as I'm feeling really, really vulnerable right now."

The girls surrounded her. Charlie put her arms around her mother and said, "We all feel that you deserve all the happiness that comes your way. Sam makes you happy. That's good enough for us." Sarah's breath hitched a little as she looked up at her oldest daughter.

Harper knelt in front of her mom and took her hands. "Dad would be ecstatic." Harper started to softly weep. "We talked last night about the thing that's going on between you and Sam. It's not the sex, though the sexual tension is thick. It's more than that. It's a physical pull that we can all feel. Even Trace. I don't think I've ever experienced anything like it. It's almost scary. You and Dad loved each other, but you and Sam need each other. You two are like puzzle pieces that fit together perfectly." Sarah rested her forehead against Gemma's.

Charlie smiled. "He loves you so much, Mom. There is so much more to Sam than the beauty everyone sees on the outside. He is even more beautiful on the inside. You see the inside of him, and I think he's been waiting for someone like you. He is so kind. We love him, Mom. And we're so proud of both of you. You each had hurdles to get over to even start this relationship, and that is inspiring to all of us."

They all hugged and made plans for the next visit. Sarah guessed it would be the first gallery opening. The girls hadn't seen those pictures yet, so they headed back to the house to look at them before their departure.

Sam could tell that they had all been crying. Sarah walked to him and laid her head on his shoulder. He exhaled quietly and kissed her forehead. She took his hand and pulled him. "We need to show the girls and Trace some photos before they leave. We've been so busy, I forgot about them."

They all went upstairs to Sarah's darkroom. "Looking at them on the computer will be easier than going through the hard copies. Pull up some chairs."

Sarah started with the clothesline pictures from London. The girls chattered and asked questions. The room got very quiet as they looked at the image's from Danni's. Sarah continued to scroll through the selfies ending with Sarah's tortured form in her bed sheets. Sam squeezed Sarah's shoulder. Charlie clasped Sam's other hand tightly. Harper and Gemma wept.

"That was my timeline of London. I can look at them now without pain."

She then scrolled through various photos of Paris, Milan, and Venice. "These are wonderful! I knew you were talented, but these are stunning!" Trace looked at her in awe.

Sarah reached for a large portfolio under her desk. She pulled out the hard photos of the shoot with Luca and spread them out on the large table in the middle of the room. "These are Luca's that will be in the magazine." She walked back to Sam and wrapped her arm around his waist.

"Wow!" Gemma hissed. "You two are sex personified! These pictures are perfect."

Harper turned and looked at them with wide eyes. "You guys are H.O.T."

"I can't wait to buy up all the magazines in my neighborhood." Charlie and Trace stared at the pictures.

Trace turned and looked at Sarah. "Okay. Now I'm officially uncomfortable. I had started having lustful thoughts about Sam because of that grinning thing he does. Now I'm having lustful thoughts about my mother-in-law. You two are turning me into a pervert. Damn!"

Sarah led them downstairs to show them the photos that she took in the Gritti Palace apartment. As the family walked in behind her, Harper stopped and looked around. "Wow! You've completely changed this room! It's amazing!"

Gemma hissed and glared at Sam. "This is a room made for sex! You're having sex in this room, aren't you?"

Sam grinned as he leaned up against the wall.

Gemma muttered, "Liz is right. That fucking grin needs to be outlawed."

Charlie and Trace made their way to the fireplace to look up at the photos. Charlie was silent as she turned to look at her mother. "Holy crap, Mom! How do you do that?" She pointed at the photos.

Sarah smiled as Sam put his arm over her shoulder. She looked at him and said, "It helps to love the subject you're taking pictures of."

Trace made his way out of the bedroom. He stopped and looked back at Sam and Sarah. "Okay. It's gone beyond uncomfortable. It's almost painful. I want to do you both at the same time. Was that the emotion you were going for Sarah?" He shook his head disgustedly as he walked out with the laughter following him.

They put the luggage in cars and started saying goodbyes. Sarah held Charlie and spoke softly in her ear as Sam and Trace hugged each other. "Thank you, guys, so much for coming." Sam said. "I know how much it meant to Sarah and Jack and Karen. It's been great meeting you. We'll let you know when the date for the gallery opening is set and plan on seeing you then." Sam shook

Trace's hand.

He hugged Charlie hard and whispered in her ear, "You are so much like your mother Charlie, that you have a special little place in my heart."

Charlie grinned as she kissed him on the cheek. "We'll see you soon at the opening. Thank you so much for calling us in the middle of all the sorrow. It meant the world to us."

Sam hugged Harper as Sarah held Gemma. Harper gripped Sam's ass and leaned into him. "Welcome to the family Sam Ramsay. Thanks for the joy you've given my mother. I know how much you love my mom, therefore I love you. I'll see you soon."

Gemma walked slowly to Sam and just looked at him. "I'm not going to say anything flippant or profane, Sam. And unlike my sister, I'm not going to grab your ass." She reached for Sam as she started to cry. Sam hugged her and rocked her a little. Gemma sniffed and quietly continued to hold him. "I love that you have changed my mom's life. We've always known how beautiful she is inside and out. We have always known how talented she is, but living here, she would have continued to be a hidden gem. Because of you, the world will get to experience Sarah Reid. But, more importantly, your love for her has given her confidence and joy and spontaneity. You are a special man, and I think you *both* got lucky."

Sam clasped the back of her head as he kissed her on her cheek. "I wish I could have met your dad, Gemma. The three of you are a product of both of your parents and what an incredible job they've done. I've loved getting to know you and watching you girls with your mom. You all have a very special relationship, and it reminds me so much of my own family. My heart is full."

Sam and Sarah stood and watched the cars as they disappeared up the driveway. He kissed the top of her head as they turned to go inside.

Chapter 40:

They immediately started to break down the tables. Everyone had pitched in last night to help with the cleanup, so they didn't have a lot to do. Sarah gathered up all of the tablecloths and held them clutched to her chest as she watched Sam roll the last table back inside the garage. He turned to see Sarah watching him.

He reached for the table cloths before kissing her gently. "We make a good team." Sam told her.

Sarah smiled with tear filled eyes. "Yes, we do."

Inside, Sam went to the laundry room and Sarah started a sink of soapy water. She was wiping off the kitchen table when Sam came out of the laundry room. He stopped and grinned at Sarah bent over the table. He walked up behind her and wrapped his arms around her and growled in her ear. "*Nobody* rocks a pair of Daisy Dukes quite like you."

Sarah giggled. "I wasn't aware that Brits were familiar with Daisy Dukes."

Sam was serious as he slowly pulled down her shorts and panties. "Every male in the world knows who Daisy Duke is. It wasn't all about the General Lee." As he held her hips and kissed the cheeks that were now bare to his eyes, he silently chuckled to himself as he said, "It's time we broke in *your* table."

So they did.

~~~

They stripped the beds and did the laundry. They loaded the

dishwasher and washed, dried, and put away the rest. They dusted, swept and mopped the floors. Sarah told Sam that it was like they were cleaning the pain away. She folded clean tablecloths and watched Sam as he watered the window boxes. He hadn't shaved, or styled his hair. He was handsomely messy and hairy and Sarah's heart did a little hitch as she watched him with the hose. He was comfortable with doing the little things that her life consisted of. He looked up and saw her through the window. He grinned that slow, sexy grin as he turned off the hose. Sarah's heart flip flopped as she watched him walk through the door.

"What are you looking at?" Sam grinned.

She sighed. "It's always you I look at, Sam. Don't you know that?"

"I do know that sweet Sarah. I, too, only have eyes for you."

"This first week has been chaotic. Definitely not a typical week in the life of Sarah. The next two weeks will be different, and I'm afraid you'll be bored. Sometimes I don't leave the farm for a week at a time. Can you do that?"

Sam took her shoulders in his hands. "Sarah, I could live in a mud hut on a deserted island and be perfectly content, as long as you were there with me." He grinned and kissed her. "I love it here. I thought it was quiet at first, but if you stop and listen you can hear everything. You can hear the buzzing of the bees and the melodies of the birds. I love the croaks of the bullfrogs and the quacks of the ducks on the pond. Hell, I even love the sound of the sprinklers on the grass. This place was just what I needed, and I didn't even know it."

Sarah caressed his cheek. "I love how your hair has a life of its own, and that you haven't shaved or worn shoes for three days. I'll only begin to worry if you start wearing overalls."

Sam laughed as he walked into the kitchen. "My goal is to wear nothing at all."

Sam and Sarah ate leftovers, cleaned the kitchen and made their way to the back porch for whiskey and cigarettes. They sat in the dark and quietly talked about their families and friends, their goals for the future, and Sarah's gallery showing. They went over Sam's schedule for the rest of the year. They were both excited that it would be possible to see each other every month for the next few months. They could work with that. Sam swallowed the last of his whiskey before he sighed and leaned his head back. He squeezed Sarah's shoulder. "Life is good."

~~~

The next morning as they drank their coffee, Sarah heard the noise of a vehicle as it came down the driveway. She raised her eyebrows as Sam looked at her questionably. "I have no idea who it is."

She opened the door and saw a large delivery truck. Two men carried a large paper-wrapped box up on the porch. After verifying that she was who she was, they returned to the truck to unload an even larger box. They went back one final time and came back with a box apiece. After signing, Sarah pulled a chair up to the first box. The first thing she noticed was the French postage. She looked up at Sam, who leaned against the door frame with his arms crossed. He lifted an eyebrow. All the boxes had French postage on them. She knew Sam had something to do with whatever was in the boxes, but she had no idea what they might be. Sam returned with a knife and proceeded to cut the tape from the largest box.

"What did you do, Sam?"

"Why would you think it was me?" Sam grinned down at her.

As she ripped the filler out of the box, she stopped with a gasp and looked at Sam with wide eyes. Sam helped her lift the antique French Bistro table out of the box. It was the one that she had looked at in the shop in Paris. Sarah gently touched the ornate iron work as she rubbed her eyes.

"I can't believe you did this!" Sam helped her open the chairs and placed them around the table. Sarah threw her arms around his neck and peppered his face with kisses. He just laughed and held on.

"Holy hell, Sam Ramsay! You are the most wonderful man. How did you do this? I was with you the entire time!"

Sam laughed. He enjoyed the feel of her breasts pushed tightly against his chest, and all of the little kisses she was placing on his face and neck. "I didn't go to the hair salon with you, now did I? Open the other one!"

Sarah beamed. "Cut it! Cut it open!"

"Yes, ma'am. Your wish is my command." He cut the packing tape. "Let's move this one inside. It's really heavy, and we'll probably have to lay it down."

They moved the box very carefully into the living room, and Sam slowly pulled out the very heavy, very old antique mirror. Sam sat beside Sarah down and said softly, "I want to buy you gifts, Sarah. It makes me happy."

Sarah climbed into his lap and leaned her head in his neck. She laughed quietly and whispered, "You have a package waiting for you in London, too. I can't wait for you to open it. I was so disappointed when I called about this mirror to be told that someone had bought it. I wanted this badly, but I knew it would look great in your foyer."

Sam smiled. "Great minds think alike."

Sarah continued to whisper. "Let's not hang it up today. Let's lean it up by the fireplace. I have *very* fond memories of a certain mirror in a certain motel room in Paris. I think a proper thank you is in order. "

Sam swallowed. "Yes ma'am. Your wish is my command."

~~~

They weeded the flowerbeds all day. Sarah told Sam she called it dirt therapy. They worked quietly for several hours, only breaking for lunch, and Sam thought that she was absolutely correct. It was hot, but he enjoyed the sweat. He enjoyed the heat of the soil on his hands and under his fingernails. He enjoyed the noises Sarah made as she stuck the spade in the ground. He also enjoyed her soft songs as she methodically moved from one bed to the other. He enjoyed the slow pace, the lack of any kind of schedule, and the absence of people.

Sarah loved the feel of the dirt on her hands and the sound of the bees buzzing in the honeysuckle. She loved that Sam knew the difference between weeds and plants. She loved that this quiet time on the farm had seemed to be good for him.

They completed their tasks and sat on the bottom step of the back porch. They were both happily tired and extremely dirty. Sam softly wiped a spot of dirt off Sarah's cheek, then placed his dirty mouth on the corner of her dirty mouth and kissed her gently. "Thank you."

Sarah smiled.

~~~

The sky filled with storm clouds, and the temperature dropped. Sam thought a fire would be nice, and Sarah had started a bath. A big crack of lightning knocked the power out, they both went through the house lighting candles. Sam and Sarah discarded their clothes in the bathroom floor before they slid into the hot water that Sarah had run before the power went out. Sarah leaned back against Sam's hard chest with a deep sigh. "I love you, Sam Ramsay."

Sam massaged her neck and shoulders, before he ran his hands down her ribcage and outer thighs. He felt the goose bumps as Sarah shuddered. He kissed her neck. "I love you, Amazing Sarah. Let me show you how much."

Sarah turned to straddle him, but Sam stopped her with a kiss. He reached for the shampoo and proceeded to wash and rinse her hair. He lathered her back, arms, and legs with a sandalwood-scented body wash, before gently rubbing her breasts. Sarah moaned and arched her back against his chest. She could feel Sam's desire against her hip. She reached for him, but he stopped her hands. "No. Let me love you."

He continued with soft brushes against the inside of her thighs. He felt her legs quiver. There was nothing on earth as sexy as

Sarah in the water. With his mouth on her neck and a hand on her breast, the other hand did what Sarah was begging for. Sam couldn't see her eyes, but he loved the sounds she made when he pushed her over the edge.

Sarah caught her breath, and used the same soap to wash Sam's dirt away. She gently washed his face before she pulled him forward to slip in behind him to wash his back and his hair. She stood up in all of her glistening wetness and looked down at him. Sam swallowed. "You are a vision, Sarah Reid. You should always be in water and candlelight." She reached for his hand as she stepped out of the tub.

Sam followed Sarah into the living room. He stood over her as she lay down on the rug in front of the fire. The shadow and the light of the fire reflected off of the water still on her body. Sarah was so beautiful that it was almost painful for Sam to look at her.

Sarah looked up at Sam as he stood looking down at her with so much desire that his blue eyes were almost black. He stood like a Greek God in all his naked, wet glory. The flames of the fire, the flashes of lightening, and rolling thunder had created a thick, charged and sensual atmosphere. "Just let me look at you, Sarah. Do you know how fucking beautiful you are? Do you know how much I love you?"

Sarah whispered feverishly, "I am full of fire and want Sam. I feel so much sometimes that it's like I'm burning up with my love for you." She had gotten up and knelt in front of him as he still stood looking down at her.

"I don't want gentle. I don't want nice." Sam growled at Sarah as he grabbed a handful of her hair and kneeled down with her. His eyes burned. "I want to fuck you, Sarah."

Sarah pointed to their reflection in the mirror, before she got on her hands and knees. She looked at Sam in the mirror. "Then fuck me hard, Sam."

The lightning flashed, and the thunder roared. The torrential rain drummed on the metal roof above them. It was primal, visceral and erotic, as Sam and Sarah created their own storm.

Chapter 41:

The storm had left branches and tree debris strewn about the yard. The air still smelled of rain, and the grass was wet under their feet. They started on the cleanup, and Sarah watched Sam as he stood at the back fence with an arm full of branches. He stared off into the distance lost in thought. Sarah had noticed him check out several times the last few days. "Where does he go when he does this?" Sarah wondered as she slowly walked up to him and wrapped her arm around his waist.

Sam looked down at her and smiled a sweet, quiet smile before he looked off into the distance again. "What's your favorite time of year, Sarah?"

She thought about Sam's question. "I always love it here, but if I had to choose, it would have to be fall or winter. As beautiful and vibrant as it is now, I love the colors, the smells, and the settling of fall. You smell like fall to me, Sam. I always smell whiskey and the earthiness of oak leaves on you. But I also love the snow, the beauty, and the quiet of winter. It's a difficult decision. Why?"

Sam continued to stare into the distance as he squeezed Sarah's waist, and softly said, "Just thinking about our future."

Sarah sighed and softly said, "I love that it's *our* future."

Sam showered while Sarah cut out biscuits for the gravy; the bacon was in the oven to keep warm. Sarah hummed as she worked before she lifted her head with a big grin. She looked up and whispered, "Thank you David!"

Sam walked out of the bedroom with a towel around his waist.

Sarah noticed that his hair had gotten quite long. He stopped in the doorway as he listened to Frank Sinatra crooning. Sarah walked out of the kitchen wearing only an apron. Sam's grin got bigger as Sarah approached him and asked, "Wanna dance?"

~~~

They lay in bed with their long legs wrapped up in each other. The towel and the apron had ended up on the floor somewhere in the living room. Sarah turned and laughed. "Damn! I'm proud of myself!"

Sam lifted an eyebrow and smirked. "And evidently humble."

"No, you goofy man! I'm amazed that I was able to get into some of those positions! My picture should be in the fucking Kama Sutra! Yep. I'm proud!"

Sam bent his head back and roared with laughter. "As am I, Sarah! As am I!"

Sarah's stomach growled loudly. "I forgot about breakfast. I'm starving."

Sam growled as he rolled her onto his chest. "I'm always starving. I'm starved for you."

Sarah giggled. "That's very sweet Sam, but right now, I'm starved for bacon!"

They continued to laugh as they made their way, naked, into the kitchen to finish breakfast.

They went into town to see Liz at her shop before they headed to Karen and Jack's for supper. Sarah had insisted that Sam pack an overnight bag as she had planned a surprise road trip. It was time to get him off the farm. Sam loved Liz's shop and had thoroughly enjoyed Karen, Jack, and the kids.

"I think that they're going to be good, don't you?" he asked as he watched the scenery fly by his truck window. He had begged Sarah to tell him where they were going, but she wouldn't give him a clue.

"Yeah, I do, too. I think it helps to have someone else at home who depends on you. Those kids will be their salvation. Gemma, Harper, and Charlie were all adults when David died, but it helped me knowing that I had to get my shit together for them."

"That makes sense. Speaking of the girls, let's call them and Danni."

They talked to each of the girls and then Danni. Thomas and Violet wanted to talk to "Aunt Sarah", so they monopolized the conversation with talk of a new swing and new lambs. Sarah promised them she would see them soon. The calls made the time go by quickly, and as they finished up the conversation with Danni, the St. Louis Arch appeared in front of the truck with the beautiful Mississippi river as its backdrop.

"I know what that is!" Sam grinned as he looked intently. "And I know where we are!"

"I thought we could come back to where we started." Sarah smiled. "Right smack dab in the middle of the chapter that has changed both of our lives."

"I love that," Sam said. "And what is "smack dab"?"

She laughed loudly. "It means right in or right on."

Sarah had booked the same room at the same hotel they had stayed at when they met in January. After they checked in, and made their way to the room, Sarah sat her bag down and plopped back down in the same chair she had sat in all those months before. She kicked off her shoes and put her feet up on the same bed.

Sam stood looking down at her with a funny little grin on his face. "I think I knew from the moment I walked into this room that I would love you forever. I had no idea what kind of love, but I knew that I had to have you in my life. Now…" He shook his head as he sat down in the chair next to her. "Now, you *are* my life."

Sarah reached for his forearm. "Did you never have qualms about our age difference? I never did, but half the world doesn't want to fuck me either."

Sam shook his head. "Of course I thought about it. But only to wonder what *you* would think. I haven't thought about it since. And, believe me, when that photo spread comes out, half of the world *will* want to fuck you. But the only person who gets to fuck you, is me."

So he did.

~~~

The sun had lowered in the sky as Sarah took Sam's hand and led him to the elevator and out the front door of the lobby.

"What do you have up your sleeve, Sarah?" Sam squeezed her hand lightly.

She laughed and stopped to kiss him softly. "I told you. We're going back to where we started."

As they continued to walk, Sam noticed the bench that they had sat on months before. As they got closer he saw a blanket, a cooler, and a basket. He turned with a grin. "How did you pull this off?"

Sarah smiled. "The staff remembered us when I called the hotel last week. They were thrilled to be able to help me pull this off."

They sat on the bench. Sarah laid her head on the shoulder she loved so much. They sat in comfortable silence as they both relived their own memories of the last time they shared the bench.

Sam rubbed small circles on Sarah's shoulder. "When did you fall in love with me, Sarah?"

She smiled. "Truth?"

"Always."

Sarah settled back against the bench. "I think I fell in love with your ass when I saw the glossy for the first time." Sam laughed softly. "I mean, really. You have a perfect ass. What's not to love? But, seriously, I loved you when you came to the room that night to check on me. You're such a nice person. And then the next day, when you brought me breakfast, and then brought me here. I guess I thought after that night we had on this bench, and with the age difference, we would just have a long-lasting friendship."

She sighed loudly. "The moment that I fell hard was the moment you saw me at Heathrow. I felt like your eyes were burning me up. My panties turned to ash and my legs turned into jelly. I knew that my life would never be the same."

"Damn, Sarah," Sam growled. "I remember those legs in those

fucking boots! I wanted to fuck you right there on the floor of the airport."

"How about you, Sam? When did you fall for me?"

He replied without any hesitation. "When you answered the door in that fucking t-shirt."

The sun had set as they had made their way back to their room. The staff had a bottle of Jameson and strawberries waiting for them. Sam removed his shirt, socks, and shoes, poured the whiskey and relaxed back in the chair with his legs stretched out on the bed. He wondered how his life had gotten to this point. He turned on Sarah's playlist. She had a much better selection than he did. He saw the light go out under the bathroom door and grinned as he wondered what surprise she had in store for him. The door opened, and out she stalked in nothing but a T-shirt and legs.

She stood in front of him and stared down as she threw back her whiskey in one swallow. Sam only grinned as his eyes slowly traveled from her eyes, to her tits, down her stomach and thighs. He was already hard. How could she make a forty-one-year-old feel like a horny teenager? No other woman had ever gotten him so excited so quickly.

Sarah turned toward the table and bent over to set her glass on it. Sam swallowed loudly. She smiled wickedly when she heard him notice she wasn't wearing anything under the T-shirt. She slowly bent all the way over to touch her feet with her hands.

Sam groaned. "Jesus H. Christ, Sarah! I'm going to explode! Do you have any idea what you do to me?" He reached for her ass with both hands before he laid his cheek against her cheeks.

Sarah slowly turned around and turned the music up and the lights low. She reached for the button on Sam's jeans and slowly unbuttoned it and pulled the zipper down. She knelt and pulled his jeans over his hips before pulling them off of his legs. She reached for his hand and led him to the bed. Sam's eyes were almost black as he scooted toward the headboard and watched her pull her T-shirt off over her head.

"Do you know how beautiful you are? Do you know what you do to me?" he whispered hoarsely.

Sarah straddled the hardness of his chest. She ran her fingers through the hair that had started to curl. "I love that your hair is crazy. I would love it short or long, or in between, or shaved bald." She kissed his head softly.

She continued to kiss the sharp angularity of his cheeks. As usual, they were covered with black stubble. "I love your stubble and I love you clean shaven. Though I do love the way your whiskers feel against my breasts and against my thighs when your head is between my legs." Sam continued to watch her with his black eyes.

She gently kissed his lips. "I love your lips whether they're smiling or scowling, because I know what they feel like on mine. I know what they feel like on my body, and I know the words that come out of them."

She kissed both eyes and sighed softly. "I love these eyes that look at me with desire. I love the way they turn dark when you want me. I love when they're light with laughter. Love is all I can see when I look into your eyes."

She slowly licked his sculpted chest that was no longer waxed. She felt the soft hair as she kissed him. She moved on to the obliques and kissed them gently. "I love your strong chest whether it's covered with hair, or waxed, because I love the heart that lies under it so much."

Sam stroked her cheek gently but was quiet. His heart was beating rapidly. He couldn't speak.

She continued to kiss both of his shoulders, arms and hands. "I love your arms and shoulders because of their strength. I love that they hold me in pain and in love. Their strength gives me strength. I love the hands that hold mine and that paints my body like an artist with a canvas. I love the pleasure that those hands and fingers give me."

Sarah turned him slightly and gave a gentle bite on his ass cheek. "I love your ass because it's perfect and a wonder to look at, whether it's clothed or not. I love wrapping my legs around it when you're making love to me. I love to watch you walking away from me, because I get to see the perfection of this ass."

"I love these legs and feet because they're your foundation. And they have given me a foundation for my future. I love that they walked you to me so many months ago and have continued to walk *with* me."

She slowly kissed her way up Sam's stomach, neck, and lips. She sat up and looked into the black depths of his eyes. "I love that you are a beautiful work of art, Sam, because you are. But I love you because you are more than your beauty. You are just you. You are my Sam."

Sam looked up at the vision that was Sarah. He couldn't speak. As a single tear rolled down his cheek all he could do was to show her how much he loved her with his mouth, hands, and fingers.

He did not leave a single inch of Sarah to go un-kissed or un-worshipped. He loved her slowly and he loved her deeply. He loved her in silence, as he didn't have the words.

Sarah felt the sun on her face as she slowly stretched the next morning. She opened her eyes to see Sam staring at her. "Good morning, handsome! How long have you been awake?"

"About an hour."

"Why didn't you wake me up?" Sarah softly touched his cheek.

"I love to watch you sleep, Sarah. The quiet moments are sometimes the memories that last the longest." He rubbed her forearm lightly and continued to look into her eyes. "Last night you were hellfire, Sarah. This morning you are my holy water."

Sarah was taken aback by the quiet desperation in Sam's voice. "Which one do you prefer?"

He reached for her and whispered into her ear. "I prefer both. I love the inferno that you burn me up with, then the coolness as you drown me."

~~~

They left the hotel in the early afternoon to be met with a sea of red. Sam and Sarah wore cargo shorts and red St. Louis Cardinals shirts and hats. Sam stood on the sidewalk and grinned. As far as he could see was Cardinal red. Young men, young women, families, and seniors all connected by their love of a game and a team.

"Who are the Cardinals?" he asked excitedly.

"You mean to tell me that after all your trips to the States you have never been to a baseball game?" Sarah asked incredulously. "Not even New York or L.A.?"

Sam almost jumped with excitement. "Never! I know nothing about the game, but I know that Americans are baseball crazy. Come on! Hurry up!" He grabbed her hand and pulled her into the crowd.

They settled into their seats behind first base. They both wore sunglasses, and Sarah had her scorecard and camera ready. She explained to Sam that the vendors would sell their wares, but that if he wanted a hot dog or nachos he would have to go get them. He looked at her with her scorecard. "You really take this game seriously, don't you?"

Sarah looked at him sternly. "Oh, hell no! It's all about the amount of fine, young man ass." She sighed loudly and looked out at the players doing their pre-game stretches. "I just love the tight pants with all the firm, young asses. It really does something to me. You know how I love ass. I could care less what they do in the game."

Sam stared at her with his mouth open, and a look of incredulity on his face. He was speechless.

Sarah roared with laughter. When she could compose herself, she gasped, "I'm only kidding Sam! I love the game. I love the smells and the sense of community among everyone here." She patted his arm as she continued to laugh. "You just provided me with another page in the scrapbook."

Sam smiled as he shook his head and murmured under his breath. "You are something, Sarah Reid."

Through the first four innings, Sarah explained the game, and the strategy for the offense and defense. She tried to explain the different pitches for different situations and batters. As the fifth inning started, Sam got up and told Sarah that he was going to find snacks and get another beer.

The sixth inning had started by the time Sam made his way back. "Holy shit, Sam! Did you buy out the stadium?"

He grinned as he stood above her with a box. "I heard someone say that beers needed to be bought before the seventh inning stretch."

He had hot dogs, nachos, baked potatoes and pizza. He sat down and chuckled. "I figured I could share." He gave her a hot dog and a beer before he took the same for himself. He passed the box to the guys in front of him and told them to share.

The rest of the afternoon passed quickly. Sam got to see the left fielder hit a three-run home run for a Cardinal win. He stood with the rest of Cardinal nation and cheered loudly. He looked at Sarah with a huge smile on his face. "Even I know what a home run is."

They ended their evening drinking with other fans at a bar across from the stadium. They closed the bar down and talked quietly as they walked back to the hotel.

~~~

As they finished their breakfast the next morning Sarah leaned back and thought out loud. "We could go to the zoo, or walk the riverfront."

Sam looked at her, before he reached over to touch her cheek. "Let's go home, Sarah."

Chapter 42:

They rowed out to the middle of the lake where they shed their clothes to swim in the cool water. Sam sat in the canoe with Sarah leaning back against him. The sun felt good on their skin as they sat in silence, naked in the boat. They watched the dragonflies skate across the water as Sam tattooed a soft touch with his lips across Sarah's shoulders.

"Two more days, Sam." Sarah had her eyes closed as she absorbed the warmth of the sun, the smell of the water and Sam's touch. "But I'm okay. How about you?"

He sighed. "I hate leaving, but, it's going to be really busy in three weeks. The magazine spread comes out next week, then the gallery opening..."

"Is it okay that I'm a little scared?" asked Sarah quietly.

He kissed her neck. "I think nervous would be a better word. The Sarah Reid I know is never scared of *anything*. The next three weeks will change both of our lives in a good way."

"I hate the thought of waking up without you for the next three weeks. I have also had little anxiety pangs over the perfection that we have turned into. I keep waiting for something to happen. I know that's silly, but we haven't even had a fight. *Nothing* can be this perfect." She nestled deeper into his chest.

He chuckled softly. She could feel his chest rumble against her back. "Well then, I will definitely have to think of something to piss you off later today. I've heard make up sex is the best."

Sarah just muttered, "I thought we'd been having the best."

"Sarah, Sarah, Sarah. It could be fun to find out." He shook his head and laughed at her. "We don't need to fight, or pick each other apart, or feel insecure in our relationship. With age comes wisdom." He looked down at her. "We both know what we want, and who we want it with. And that, right there, *is* perfection."

~~~

That evening Sam filled the tub with steamy water and sandalwood scented oil. He lit the candles and turned on Sarah's playlist. He walked back into the bedroom to see her as she stood in the doorway. He growled as he walked to her. "I will never get tired of looking at you Sarah Reid. I will never get tired of the scent of sandalwood, as it always reminds me of you. I will never tire of your laugh, and the way you moan underneath me."

He watched her as she moved above him in the water as the candlelight flickered over her face. He inhaled the scent of her as she softly laughed above him before moaning her pleasure along with his.

They ended the evening on the porch swing with whiskey, cigarettes, and lightening bugs.

Their last day was filled with touching, kissing, and talking. As they lounged on the couch they coordinated their schedules. Every few seconds they would stop to caress or gently kiss each other. There was a quiet desperation in their need for each other.

Sam led Sarah to the bedroom where he sat her on the edge of the bed. He slowly removed her clothes, then his own, before he kissed the mouth that he loved so much. He knelt on the floor in front of her and placed her long legs over his shoulders as he looked up at the woman that had become his life.

"I am going to worship at your altar, Sarah Ramsay. You are my church. You're my religion and communion. You're my salvation."

~~~

Sarah had gotten as far as she could go with Sam. His next stop was through security before heading to his departure gate. They stood and held each other as they murmured quietly amid the bustle and noise of the airport.

"The photo spread comes out tomorrow. Are you ready?" Sam asked.

Sarah sighed before she answered. "I guess I'm as ready as I'll ever be. It feels like it's happening to someone else. It's like I'm looking through a window into someone else's life. It's surreal. I'm not sorry about any of it, it's just a weird feeling."

Sam shook his head. "You kind of just explained my entire career. Twenty three surreal years."

373

Sarah felt a piece of her heart break. It was a physical reaction to the sadness that was in Sam's voice. "Oh, Sam!" she whispered. "I hope that you're beginning to see the possibilities of the wonderful man that you are."

Sam smiled a crooked smile. "You've made me see that life is an *endless* possibility, Sarah."

She hugged him tight. "Text me as soon as you're on terra firma. I will see you in three weeks."

Sam kissed her long. "Three weeks might as well be three years. It will be painful. But it will be doable."

Sam: Are you there?

Sarah: Always. Are you home?

Sam: I am standing in my foyer looking at a very beautiful mirror that has been hung over the entryway table.

Sarah: Oh, good! Danni told me she would get that taken care of. Does it work?

Sam: The reflection from the Murano chandelier is quite beautiful. I would never doubt your eye Sarah.

Sarah: You shouldn't. My eye caught you, didn't it?

Sam: Where are you? On the porch? Watching the lightening bugs?

Sarah: Yeah. I miss you already. Putting off going to bed by myself.

Sam: Oh, God... I can still taste you... I've stayed hard the entire flight.

Sarah: Three weeks, Sam. Three weeks. We can do this.

Sam: I know we can do it. I just don't WANT to.

Sarah: I love you, Sam. Say goodnight.

Sam: I love you more. Goodnight, Sarah Reid.

Sarah walked slowly through the house on her way to bed. Everywhere she looked, she saw pieces of Sam. His boots were sitting in the entryway, and a rock that he had found was sitting on a shelf. As she showered, she saw his shampoo and his razor. Every little thing that she noticed made her smile. It was more than her home now. She crawled into bed in one of Sam's shirts. It smelled of him and was another tangible bit of evidence that he had been there. As she settled onto her pillow she noticed the letter propped up against her bedside lamp. She grinned, because she would know that horrendous scrawl anywhere. She was such a mess when it came to Sam that she even thought about his tongue touching the flap as he had licked it to seal the envelope. She laughed out loud and opened the letter:

My magnificent Sarah Reid:

*I already miss laying there with you. I can see the way you mush up your pillows before laying your head on them. I know you're wearing a T-shirt and panties. You should **never** wear them to bed again. The only thing that should be touching those sheets is your magnificent naked body.*

I already miss the lightning bugs, and the noisy silence of the farm. I miss the smell of the fresh mowed hay and the sound of your laughter. I miss seeing your long tan legs in your cut-off jeans. I already miss the world that is just you and me, the scrapbook of our life. I already miss just being.

You took a chance on me, and I am so thankful. You saw something in me that I didn't see in myself. You gave me something that I didn't even know I needed. When I look forward in my life all I see is you. You have given me a life full of anticipation.

You have given me the most precious gift of all. Yourself.

548

Goodnight. I love you more than lightning bugs.

~~~

As Sam walked through his living room, he noticed a picture frame on the fireplace mantle. He reached for it and saw that it was a picture of thousands of lightning bugs in the dark sky of the farm. He could just see the outlines of the out buildings. There was a sliver of the arm of the porch swing and Sarah's long legs stretched out into the darkness. A glass of whiskey and a pack of cigarettes sat on the porch post. He smiled and sighed. He would have to call Danni. He knew that she had placed the picture. He needed to thank her for making coming home a little easier.

He poured a glass of whiskey, grabbed his bag, and went upstairs to shower off the airplane grime. As he set his bag on the bed, he noticed several frames on the bookcase shelves. The first picture was a close up from the rear, of he and Sarah with their foreheads touching. He knew that it was from Ava's celebration, because he recognized the dress that Sarah wore. He remembered taking it off her that night on the dock when they left their friends and family on the back porch to make love in the lake. Sam could still see her dress as it lay bunched up on the wooden slats. He smiled as he set the picture down before he moved on to the next.

The next one was another shot from the rear. It was him in just a pair of jeans. No shirt. No shoes. He was standing and holding onto the back fence of the farm looking off into the distance. His hair had gotten long and curly, and he noticed that his hands were dirty. He and Sarah had been cleaning up the storm debris. He continued to smile as he went to the last picture.

The last one made him walk to the bed and sit down. He clutched the picture in his hands and looked at the beauty that they were together. He remembered Sarah taking pictures that day but he hadn't seen any of them. She deleted so many that he hadn't thought anything of it. They had been in the canoe. Sarah had placed the camera at the front shooting back at them. Sam was in profile with his arm around Sarah. The right side of his chest and shoulder, and a hint of the oblique held Sarah between his legs. It was the *implication* of nudity that was so arresting. Sam's arm covered Sarah's breasts. Her knees were bent and her head lay against his chest. Sam's long legs were crossed under hers. The delicious hint of just the curve of her ass and waist and her long arms made his heart stop for a moment. She was so fucking talented. He sat and looked at the picture for a long time before he placed it back on the shelf.

He had gone to unpack his bag when he noticed the final picture on his bedside table. He smiled and ran his finger down the glass as he looked at Sarah's breast. No one else would know it was Sarah, as there was no face in the picture, but Sam knew. It was a black and white close up of the side of Sarah's left breast. It showed the bottom of her chin, her torso, and her right arm that lay across her breast. Only the nipple was covered, and it was so fucking sexy. Sam laughed softly.

He had gotten to the bottom of his bag when he felt the envelope. He grinned as he read it:

I love you more than lightning bugs.

Chapter 43:

Sarah got up early the next morning and drove into the city to go shopping. She bought one hundred and sixty two copies of GQ.

She stopped at Liz's to see if she wanted to grab a quick cup of coffee. Liz was with a customer, but told Sarah to go ahead and she would be over shortly. Sarah waited impatiently. She couldn't stop her knee from shaking. The girls knew there was going to be a photo spread this month, but they didn't know exactly when. She wanted to share her excitement, and the pictures, with Liz first. Sarah hadn't had the nerve to open the magazine yet. She wanted to share this moment with Sam, but considering he wasn't here, her next best choice was Liz.

Sarah looked up as the bell tinkled to see Liz walk in. Sarah stood up and gave Liz a long, hard hug. Liz grasped Sarah's shoulders and looked at her with a huge smile on her face. "You are glowing! I take it Sam's visit was a good one? Under the circumstances anyway."

"Oh, Liz! The death of that little girl was one of the worst experiences of my life, and one of the most precious ones. And, yes. Sam was exquisite. And yes. I am cuckoo for cocoa puffs in love with him." Sarah's phone buzzed with a text message from Charlie. Before she could answer it, she got a message from Gemma, then Harper. Her phone had turned into a notification tsunami. Liz looked at her with a raised eyebrow. "Am I missing something?"

Sarah pulled a copy of GQ out of her purse and slowly handed it to her. "Oh, my God! It came out today?" Liz grabbed it and squealed. "Do you love it? Is it great?"

Sarah looked down at her coffee nervously. "I haven't looked at it yet. I wanted you to see it first, to give me your opinion before I look at it."

"Oh, honey! There is no way that any picture of you or Sam will be bad. It gets me in the feels that you wanted me to see it first."

Sarah stared at Liz. "None of this would have happened without your encouragement. You listened to me. You gave me my confidence back. You insisted on the fucking panties! You insisted on going for it. Looking back, I now realize just how damn bossy you were!"

Liz looked down at the cover to see Sam and Sarah. It was the shot of them as they danced under the Murano chandelier. Sarah had on the aqua chiffon ball gown and Sam wore the white tuxedo. "This is beautiful." She slowly opened the magazine and thumbed through the pages to the middle.

Sarah had opened her phone and texted all three of the girls about the SKYPE call she would make when she got home. Before she could close her phone, a text appeared from Sam.

Sam: Are you there, Sarah?

Sarah: Yep. Sitting in the coffee shop with Liz. I have the truck filled with a hundred and sixty two issues of fucking GQ!

Sam: What do you think?

Sarah: I haven't looked yet. Just the cover.

Sam: Look at the fucking pictures, and read the article, then text me back. Do it now!

Sarah: Good Lord! Between you and Liz, I now realize I'm surrounded by such

bossy people!

Sam: Yes, you are. Look at the damn pictures and text me back. Actually, call me. I'm at Danni's.

Before she closed her phone, another text, this time from Danni popped up.

Danni: Open the FUCKING magazine!!! OMG Sarah!!!!

Sarah: Okay! Okay! Okay!

"Oh, my God! Are they that bad?" Sarah's heart beat very fast, and she felt like she could have a panic attack at the look on Liz's face.

 "Scoot over here by me! We'll look at the pictures and read the interview together."

"What do you think of the cover?" Liz asked Sarah before she opened the magazine to the middle.

Sarah sighed. "I love it. That dress was to die for. Sam in a tux is sex in Italian wool. I see us. Together. In love. It's going to be so hard to look at these objectively. I just don't want to be the reason that the pictures are mediocre. Sam has never taken a mediocre picture in his life."

Liz looked at her exasperated. "I am going to slap you! Not another word! Nothing. Zilch. Nada. Nil. Look and read and keep your mouth shut until you're done." Liz slowly opened the magazine.

Liz watched Sarah's face as she slowly thumbed the pages. Sarah chewed her bottom lip, and then smiled a little as she softly ran her finger over a picture. When she flipped to the last two pages, she gave a little gasp. One full page was the shot of Sam ravishing her mouth, as she lay across his lap in the bustier. Sam held her head with one hand, and grasped her ass with the other.

The other full page was Sam and Sarah wrapped up in the sheets on the floor. Luca had taken an extreme close up of their profiles and had it printed in black and white. Sam was over her with their foreheads touching. His lips barely touched hers as they stared into each other's eyes. His hair fell over his forehead, and her hair was messy. The light and shadow was exquisite. The angle was perfect, but Sam and Sarah were the stars of the photo.

Sarah looked at Liz before she flipped back to the beginning and slowly read the interview. When she finished, she shook her head at Liz and called Sam. He picked up on the first ring.

"Hey, babe! What do you think?"

"Oh, Sam!" Sarah's breath hitched before she started crying.

"I love them, Sarah." Sam whispered softly. "Luca might have taken the pictures, but they are all you. I'm so fucking proud of them."

"I love them, too. He made me look so beautiful, Sam. And you made me feel so beautiful."

"You are fucking gorgeous, Sarah! No one made you look that way. And the interview was great. I'm so damn proud!" Sam almost crowed.

"It's not fucking fair that you look the way you look." Sarah heard Danni shout in the background. "Then you add my ass wipe brother, and it's almost more than the world can stand! H.O.T.! I'm surprised that the damn magazines haven't spontaneously combusted!"

"So, are you happy with it, Sarah? " Sam softly asked.

Sarah quietly answered. "So, so happy. I just didn't want this to be your first taste of mediocrity, but Danni's right. They are H.O.T. I wish you were here right now, so we could be wrapped up in sheets."

Sam sighed. "Babe, look at that picture. I'm wanting you just as bad. I would suggest that we SKYPE tonight?"

Sarah laughed. "No way! I'm in love with the real Sam. No SKYPE. I'll wait for the real thing."

She heard Danni yell in the background again. "Get a room you guys! Oh, wait! You can't! Bloody hell!"

Sam chuckled. "I'll text you tonight. Or morning. Depending on what part of the world we're in. I love you, Sarah, and I'm in awe of your courage."

"Thanks, Sam. I love you more. I'll talk to you tonight. I'm going home and calling my daughters, and then I'm calling Luca." Sarah hung up and looked at Liz.

Liz sat with her chin in her hands. She wore a huge grin. "What?" asked Sarah.

"I'm just so fucking happy for you. You deserve this more than anyone I know. You know I love you, and I know you'll tell me it's none of my damn business if I ask you the question I'm getting ready to ask you."

"Ask away." Sarah laughed.

"Is he as perfect in bed as the rest of him? It would be a real shame for him to look the way he does, and be a lousy lay."

Sarah laughed loudly. "Well, considering that he's only the second man I've ever had sex with I really have nothing to compare to. But... hell yes! He's amazingly creative, and his number one goal is always my pleasure first. And second. And third." She sighed and closed her eyes. "But, Liz, it's almost spiritual. I can't really explain it. I just know I can't live without him." She shrugged her. "It's more than the sex."

"I gotta find me some of that," Liz muttered.

Sarah went home and talked to Gemma, Charlie and Trace, and Harper. They were all beyond excited. She texted replies to all of her messages. Marta had sent a picture of her holding open the middle pages of the magazine with her eyes crossed and a huge grin on her face.

Marta: These pictures are fan-fucking-tastic Sarah!! H.O.T.

Sarah: LOL! That makes me feel so special!

Sarah: OMG!! I miss you so much! How's Mark??

Marta: He is as usual, perfectly yummy. We are both so excited for the gallery opening!!! Mark's also ecstatic that there will be MEN around!!! Poor guy, when he married me, he had no idea he'd be marrying a lot of other women, too.

Sarah: LOL!! I'm sure he loves it!! I can't wait to see you! I can't wait for you to meet my family.

Marta: I can't wait to meet them, too!! If they're anything like you, I foresee a LOT of fun in NYC!!

Sarah: See you in a couple of weeks.

Marta: Ciao, bella!

Sarah made the hotel reservations in New York and had finalized the dates and times for the show with Debra Wagner at the gallery. She had texted all of that information to Sam. She needed to get the photos mailed and she needed to be there before the show to okay everything. She had learned from Sam, to be smart about her stuff. She had final say on which photos would be shown, and also how the groupings would be displayed. She had made it clear to Debra that *none* of the pictures of Sam or her children were for sale. Everything else was available to the highest bidder. Sarah would let Debra set the prices, because she didn't care. She just wanted to network a little to be able to get some more contacts for future endeavors. She was excited about the possibilities, and excited about the ability to say no.

September

Chapter 44:

The two-and-a-half hour flight to JFK was uneventful. Sarah was excited to see the gallery, but she was more excited to see Sam. "Three more days, Sarah. Three more days." She texted Sam to let him know she had landed.

Sarah kept craning her neck to stare out of her cab window. New York City was not going to disappoint. Her driver grinned at her in the rearview mirror. "First time in the Big Apple?"

Sarah grinned back. "Yep. It's weird, I just got back from Paris, Milan and Venice, but I've never been to New York City."

"Wow! You're a globetrotter. Why did you gallivant all over Europe? Vacation?"

Sarah's grin turned to a soft smile. "A man."

"Ah! Love! Husband?" he asked.

Sarah leaned forward and looked at him in the mirror with a serious look on her face. "No. A lover. A much *younger* lover. I'm a cougar."

The driver laughed. "Good for you! Love has no age!"

"Not unless they're under twenty-one. That would be illegal." Sarah sat back against the seat before she laughed at the look on his face. "He's forty-one for God's sake!"

The driver shook his head and grinned before he looked at her again. "If he's forty-one, you can't be that much older than him."

"Oh, I am, but you've made my day."

"He's a very lucky man."

"Sam will be here in three long days. I actually am here for business." Sarah still felt excited to say that. "I have a photography exhibit at a gallery down town in a few days. He'll be here for that. He's a Londoner."

The driver continued to grin. "Those Brits always get the babes. It must be the accent."

Sarah's driver had her luggage on the sidewalk before she was even out of the car. He rushed to open her door. As she thanked him, he looked over her shoulder and grinned. "I'm guessing he's with you."

Sarah turned to see Sam on the sidewalk in front of the hotel. He wore low-slung jeans that fit his slim hips so well. A T-shirt and well-worn leather jacket had never made casual look so damn sexy. She actually squealed as she ran toward him. Sam wrapped his big arms around her and squeezed her hard.

"What are you doing here? I didn't expect you for three more days. Oh! Who the hell cares? I'm so happy you are!" Sarah kissed him fiercely. Whiskey and oak leaves. Immediate sensory overload.

Sam kissed her back, and as he felt her skin and breath, he thought, "I'm home. Wherever Sarah is, that's my home."

They made their way to their room. Sam had also booked rooms for the family, but not on the same floor. He knew how he and

Sarah exited elevators, and he didn't want to take any chances on running into family. Trace and Charlie would arrive the next night in case Sarah needed anything. Sam had made reservations for the four of them for dinner tomorrow night. Everyone else would make their way in the next two days.

"I could get very spoiled, Sam." Sarah sighed as she laid her head against the hard chest of the man she adored.

"I don't want you to worry about anything. I want you to enjoy it and to soak it in. This is all about you, Sarah." Sam held her gently as he inhaled the underlying scent of sandalwood. Earthy and grounding. "I think I'm as excited as you are."

Sarah stepped back and looked at him. "How did you get out of three days of work?"

"It was with Luca. We just rescheduled. I think he wants to come to the farm sometime. I don't know if his intentions are honorable with you.... I'm going to have to watch him like a hawk." Sam tried to scowl but couldn't keep the grin off his face.

"You know I love him," Sarah laughed. "South America is always my Plan B, but in the interim, I'd love to introduce him to Liz. What do you think?"

Sam closed his eyes and threw his head back as he laughed loudly. "I think that Liz would be the closest thing to you that Luca could ever have. That could be *very* interesting!"

"Oh, no! She's much nicer than I am." Sarah said seriously.

Sam took her face in his hands as he looked into her eyes. "Sarah, *no one* is nicer than you. But Liz is right up there with your bawdiness! Luca would have his hands full! Come on! Let's go see your gallery."

When the cab pulled up to the front of their destination, Sam held the door open for Sarah. As she exited, she saw huge posters with her name and picture on them. Every window was covered with her. She stopped in her tracks and gaped.

Sam looked at her and then looked at the front of the gallery. He was so fucking proud of her. She was so cute with her mouth hanging open and her eyes as big as saucers. "Give me your camera. I want to take your picture with your picture." He grinned. Without a word she handed him the camera and slowly walked to the windows.

"How do you do it?" she whispered.

"Do what?"

"Go through life seeing yourself like this? It's surreal." Sarah continued to stare at herself plastered all over the front façade of the building.

He shrugged. "It was weird at first, but then I realized that it was always someone else in the pictures. It wasn't me. It was just someone doing a job." He snapped her picture. "Though I have the luxury of pretending to be something else. Until your pictures. Those are all me. This is all you, babe. You and your camera."

Sam stood and held Sarah when Debra Wagner stuck her head out of the door with a grin on her face. "Sarah?"

Sarah walked to the petite blonde and gave her a big hug. "It's so great to see a face with the voice. This is Sam. Sam, this is Debra."

Debra shook his hand and chuckled. "I know who you are. I've been looking at the two of you for the last two weeks. You're both as beautiful as your pictures. I'm so excited for your ideas, Sarah. Let's go in. I'm anxious to get your thoughts."

It was a larger space than Sam had imagined. It was also very white. The two women chattered excitedly as Debra took Sarah to a corner. Sam watched them as they pointed animatedly. Everywhere that he looked he saw Sarah's pictures propped against walls. Every corner, every space, occupied by Sarah's heart. It looked as if the furniture was still covered in sheets, just waiting to be placed for the best views. He looked up and caught Sarah smiling at him across the room. She looked at him questioningly. He slowly smiled and shook his head. He didn't need to help her with any decisions. This was all Sarah.

As Sarah looked at him her heart did a slow roll. He leaned up against a door frame with his legs crossed and his arms crossed on his chest. The worn leather jacket did something to her insides. He smiled his slow, sultry grin. She shivered a little and wondered if she would always come undone when he did that. She hugged herself with her arms and returned his grin before she turned back to Debra.

It only took Sarah an hour to go over all the final details. They had called and emailed so many times that all Sarah had left to do was to see the space herself to give Debra final instructions. After they said their goodbyes, Sam and Sarah walked out to catch a cab back to the hotel. As they stood with their arms around each other, a city bus stopped down the block. Sam chuckled into Sarah's hair as he saw her notice the bus.

"You need to close your mouth, sweet Sarah. You might swallow a fly."

She looked up at him in disbelief. "We are on the side of that damn bus!"

"That we are. I love that picture." Sam growled softly into her neck.

Sarah continued to look at the picture of her and Sam that Luca had taken in the theatre in Venice. It was the one of her in the bustier and garters as she lay across Sam in the seats. It still made her lady bits stir every time she saw it. Evidently it made Sam's bits stir, too. She felt it against her thigh.

"I don't know how you do it, Sam. I know what it does to me being on the side of a bus. I can only imagine what being on a billboard does to you."

As Sarah snapped a few pictures of the bus, Sam laughingly said, "Those billboards do nothing for me. I'm up their all by myself. That would be a little weird. But that damn bus makes me want to get back to the hotel as quickly as possible."

As the cab pulled up, Sarah leaned into Sam and whispered a little breathlessly. "Now that I'm a big star, will you take me back to our room and ravish me like one?"

He kissed her with heat. He kissed her with want and desire. He kissed her with love. Sarah's legs wobbled as they got in the cab. "You have always been my star, Sarah. I am more than happy to ravish you."

~~~

They sat in the middle of the bed eating their room service. Sam stared at Sarah's golden shoulders and cleavage that the sheet that was wrapped around her couldn't quite cover. He loved the times they were alone. He loved the easy conversations and the quietness of their voices. He also loved the loudness when they weren't conversing. He smirked a little as he thought about the decibel level that had been amped up less than an hour ago.

Sarah looked at him and stopped her forks forward progress. "What are you so cocky about Sam Ramsay?"

"I was just thinking how much I love our quiet conversations. But, I love your loudness." He grinned a cocky little grin.

She pouted her lips, before she grinned back. "You weren't so quiet either!"

"No. No I wasn't. I'm loud and proud!" Sam sighed as he leaned back in his chair. He smiled softly at her as he took her hand to spread soft kisses on it. "Do you know what my favorite Sarah sound is?"

"My singing?"

"No. It's those quiet little moans, then the soft intake of your breath as you whisper my name. That, quiet Sarah, is my undoing."

~~~

The next day gave them both a chance to see the sights of New York City. They made their way to Ellis Island and the Statue of Liberty. Then they went to Central Park and ate lunch they got from a street vendor. They went to Times Square and Fifth Avenue. They did all of the touristy things that they both wanted to do. Sam was stopped several times for pictures and autographs, and some people even asked for Sarah's. They remarked on the magazine layout and the picture on the busses.

It was Sarah's first request for an autograph. Sam told her to get used to it. They went back to the hotel for a nap, after Sam had informed Sarah that he had sent a car to pick up Trace and Charlie. They would meet them in the lobby to go to the restaurant.

Sam met Trace and Charlie in the bar while Sarah finished getting ready. They quietly talked until Sam saw Trace's eyes get big as he looked over Sam's shoulder. Sam smiled at Charlie and asked, "She's fantastic looking isn't she?"

"My mother always looks fantastic, but since she met you, she glows. It's like a light has been turned on in her soul." Charlie squeezed Sam's forearm. "Turn around and look what my mother can do with a little black dress. I don't think she'll come in, if you don't."

Sam noticed that every man in the bar had gone quiet and their eyes were fixated on the bar entrance. He slowly turned to see Sarah staring at him. Sam grinned as he looked at his woman. Her dress was a simple, black boat neck with three-quarter-length sleeves. That should not have put lustful thoughts in every man in the bar. The dress was very short, and she wore those fucking boots. She didn't wear any jewelry, except for small diamond studs in her ears, and a yellow clutch purse. She was nothing but long legs, boots, and hair that looked as if she had just been bedded. Sam slowly got up and walked to her.

"Hey, beautiful."

"Hey, handsome."

"I see that you've made another entrance." Sam growled as he bent her over his arm and kissed her mouth. He thought he heard sighs emanate from the bar. He laughed softly into her mouth.

The four of them enjoyed dinner. Trace and Charlie thanked Sam for the driver and their room, but protested that they could pick up the tab themselves.

"Sam! You don't need to do this!" Sarah kissed him on the cheek. "It's sweet, but unnecessary."

"Nope, I don't want to hear it. This is all about you, and I want to do this. You have been a very cheap date, Ms. Reid, and I'm a very cheap guy, so it's all good. If you don't stop your protestations, I will have to kiss you into silence." Sam cocked an eyebrow at her.

"Gah! You just sounded so British! Protestations? Really? But being kissed into silence doesn't sound too bad." She kissed his cheek again, and whispered, "Thank you. I feel very cherished."

"I'm going to have to remember that "kissing into silence" thing." Trace turned to look at Charlie with a smile.

As they waited for their cab Sam whispered in Sarah's ear. "I expect that dress and anything you have on underneath it to be off by the time I lock the door to our room. Except the boots. Leave those damn boots on."

Sarah looked up into Sam's eyes and sweetly whispered back. "I'm not wearing anything underneath the dress."

~~~

Sarah had to be at the gallery for most of the morning and afternoon and had made it clear that Sam wasn't allowed in the building until the opening. She wanted it to be a surprise for everyone. Sam would sight-see with Trace and Charlie before he made sure that Gemma, Harper, Marta, and Mark made it to the hotel with no issues. They planned to meet up later in the day and spend the evening with everyone for dinner and cocktails.

That evening Sam stood in the bathroom doorway and watched Sarah shower. He found it difficult not to join her, but people waited for them in the bar downstairs. As she stepped out of the shower and reached for a towel, he, as always, was stunned by her beauty. He would never tire of looking at her. He would go to his grave feeling the overwhelming, sublime suffocation that was Sarah.

She noticed Sam as he watched her. He had on faded slim cut jeans with a red T-shirt and black tweed jacket. Sarah swallowed and knew that no one wore a pair of jeans like he did. Hell, if she was being honest, she knew that no one wore clothes better than Sam. No one wore no clothes better than Sam. She had the sudden urge to unbutton those jeans and slide them down his muscular thighs. She wanted to kneel at the throne that was Sam Ramsay. She shook a little as she realized that she was staring at his crotch. As she raised her head her eyes met his. She knew that he realized exactly what she was thinking, as his eyes had gotten dark and a small smile played across his lips.

Sarah breathlessly chuckled. "I guess dessert will have to wait."

~~~

It took Sarah, Marta, and Mark a long while to say hello to one another. There were lots of kisses and hugs among the three of them. It took longer with Gemma and Harper, but they eventually made it to the restaurant. The alcohol flowed, as did the conversation. Marta and Sam kept them all entertained with tales from some of their photo shoots. Mark interjected with some salacious tidbits from the dressing rooms that had them roaring with laughter. Sarah leaned her head against Sam as she caught her breath. She wore a big grin the entire evening.

Harper smiled lovingly at her mother. "You look so happy, mom. Are you nervous?"

"Not really. More like excited. Now that I know that at least six people, or seven with Debra, will be there, I feel considerably better. Hey! Sam and I are on the sides of city buses! What more could I want?"

"Do you know how many pictures I took of those fucking buses? So cool, Sarah! So cool." Trace was loudly excited. "Now I think we need to find someplace with karaoke and dancing! I need to get my groove on." Trace looked slyly at Sam. "And then after I'm done with Sam, I'll get my groove on with you, Sarah."

~~~

Sam spent the day talking quietly and touching Sarah softly. He knew she was nervous. He could sympathize. There was no feeling like putting yourself out there for other people to judge. He had lived with that insecurity for a long time, and he knew that it never got easier. He calmed her fears with the quiet faith that she was talented and that her photography made her happy. It filled something in her, and replenished her, and that was all that mattered.

They stood and looked at each other as they prepared to leave. Sarah wore very tight black tweed cropped pencil trousers with one of Sam's white shirts. She thought the shirts brought her luck. She had rolled up the sleeves and paired red stilettos and chunky red beads around her neck. They were her only pop of color. Her legs looked even longer than usual.

Sam donned black trousers and shoes with a red shirt and black tweed jacket. Sarah had requested no tie. She wanted to be as casual as possible. She unbuttoned one more button as she looked at him, kissed him in the hollow of his throat and then made him turn around so she could get a long look at his perfect ass.

Sam kissed her gently. "How do you make classy look so damn sexy?"

"I could say the same to you, Sam Ramsay. You make me breathless."

Sam put her arm through his as he opened the door. "Are you ready for everything in your life to be different?"

"As long as I'm with you, my life will be perfect." Sarah took a deep breath as they left for the newest page, in the next chapter of their life.

Chapter 45:

Debra met Sam and Sarah at the side door in the alley. She escorted them into the elevator to take them up to the private room that had been prepared especially for them. As she unlocked and opened the door, she turned to them. "I can't begin to tell you how excited I am. I've been doing this for more than twenty years, and this is the most unique and beautiful project I've ever been involved with. You, Sarah, have an impeccable eye. Please enjoy the ambience, and come down whenever you're ready."

Soft candlelight bathed the small room in a golden glow. Champagne chilled in an ice bucket, with a plate of chocolate covered strawberries beside it. A small velvet love seat sat in the corner and Tony Bennett sang softly in the background. Sam turned to Sarah with a soft smile. "You're responsible for this, aren't you?"

As he continued to hold her hand, he walked to fill up the champagne flutes. A small silver framed picture sat off to the side. It was the picture of the two of them naked in the canoe. He turned to Sarah and held her face with his slender fingers. "Who are you?" he asked wonderingly. "And how did I get so lucky?"

"That picture is a reminder. It reminds me that no matter what happens after this night, no matter where life might take us, that we will still be those two people in that canoe. Just two people who adore each other." Sarah covered Sam's hands with her own. "That picture exemplifies what is the most important thing in my life. You." Sarah leaned into Sam, and gently kissed the lone tear that had traveled down his cheek.

Sam bowed his head and touched her forehead with his before he closed his eyes. "It's when you render me silent Sarah, that my heart is the fullest."

They snuggled on the love seat as they drank their champagne and ate their strawberries. Sarah stood as she took Sam's hand. "Come see what I've done for you, Sam. I wouldn't be here without you, so this night is as much about you, as it is me. Come see what I feel when I look at you."

They took the elevator down to the ground floor and walked to the door that stood in front of them. Sam saw Sarah take a deep breath as she opened the door. "Welcome home, Sam."

Black, white, and gray. That was the first thing that Sam noticed when he walked through the door into the gallery. Everywhere he looked, he saw fabric. Soft, sheer gray tulle with twinkle lights. Black and white tweed and herringbone. Black and white buffalo checks. And the photographs. The damn photographs. He came to a sudden stop before he clutched Sarah's hand. He turned and whispered, "You have fucking lightning bugs in the gallery, Sarah."

She smiled at him and brushed his cheek. "Let me take you on a tour, though I'm sure that everything will be familiar to you."

As she took his hand and led him slowly throughout, he realized that Sarah had created vignettes. Each grouping of photographs was in their own room. The photos she had taken of them in their apartment in Venice were surrounded by soft gray silk. A crystal chandelier hung from the ceiling bathing them in a soft glow. A black velvet settee sat in front of them with mercury glass tables on either side. Sam was silent, as he was transported back to the sights, sounds, and smells of Venice. A sudden vision of Sarah gliding over him in the rooftop pool made his heart pound.

The photographs from Paris were surrounded by black and white damask with antique sconces in between every photo. Two bistro tables and chairs were placed in front of them with vases of hydrangeas.

The Milan photographs were hung on walls of black silk. An ebony buffet sat underneath them with silver lamps. A low bowl of blood red roses sat in between them. A booth of red leather seats and a scarred wooden tabletop faced it all. Sam could remember the taste of the risotto and the tenderness of the veal that they had shared in their one quiet moment in that city.

There was London. Pictures of Danni, Alex, Violet, and Thomas; sheep, pubs and dogs. They were surrounded by tweed and herringbone suit fabric. A tuxedo jacket of Sam's was thrown over a leather love seat. A large table sat underneath the photographs with Sarah's red dress draped across the end of it. A bottle of Jameson and two glasses were sat near the dress. "Holy shit!" Sam stared in the corner. "How the hell did you get a red telephone booth?"

"Go look at it." Sarah giggled.

The glass door was covered with an enlarged photograph of them groping each other. Sarah was grabbing Sam's ass, and he had his hands up her shirt gripping her tits. It looked as if they were in the booth. Sam turned and grinned from ear to ear.

As they continued to the front door they were met with Sarah's clothesline of pictures. No fabric surrounded them, just the bareness of the white walls. It was stark and emotional, and painful. Sam squeezed Sarah's hand a little harder as he looked at the last picture of her selfie in her bed. Two rows of old wooden folding chairs sat in straight, hard lines. Sam was mesmerized.

Sarah's photos always evoked emotion, but her vignettes, instead of battling with the pictures, fed the emotion.

The next room was Sarah's kitchen. Black and white buffalo check fabric surrounded the pictures taken at the farm. A farmhouse table was covered with chaffing dishes of pulled pork, BBQ ribs, baked beans and cole slaw, fresh sliced tomatoes and fruit. And there were biscuits. Lots and lots of biscuits. The second table was covered with all manner of beverages. The glasses were mason jars of varying sizes.

The last vignette was charcoal, gauzy fabric imbedded with thousands of twinkle lights. A piece of porch railing held a pack of cigarettes and another bottle of whiskey and glasses. White wicker faced the rest of her pictures. They had traveled home.

"I know that we came in the back. But when people come in, they will be directed to travel to their right. It will all be in chronological order..." Sarah was stopped by Sam's lips. They were hot, and wet, and a little desperate. Sarah felt his heart pound and felt hers pound as well.

"Fuck!" Sam gasped as he looked around. "I've never experienced anything like this in my life. This shouldn't have worked. There's just so *much*. But, somehow it does. Of course, it does! It's your vision, and that *always* works. I am completely gob smacked. And I am completely in love with the artist who created all of this."

Sarah grabbed her camera off one of the tables and proceeded to snap away until Sam stopped her a little later. "We need to get upstairs, so you can make your entrance, darling. The doors will be opening in ten minutes."

As they made their way onto the elevator, Sarah muttered, "Fuck!

I hope somebody comes. Otherwise we have a lot of damn food to eat."

Sam just stood silently with a small smile on his lips.

As they enjoyed another glass of champagne, they heard a a soft knock before Debra popped her head in. "Can I come in for a moment?"

"Of course. I would pour you a glass of champagne, but we have no other glasses." Sam looked around for something to use.

Debra giggled. "It's quite alright. I don't need it. I Just wanted to let you know that it's time, and to give Sarah a hug." She reached for Sarah and squeezed tightly. As she stepped back, she continued to hold Sarah's forearms. "Thank you for this experience. I hope that you always use my gallery for your art. Your work is special, Sarah."

Sarah reached for another hug, as Sam said, "We appreciate all of your hard work. I can't imagine how difficult it was to put all of this together."

"Oh! Not difficult at all. Sarah had everything delivered, and an artist rendering of where it all went. I just followed directions!" Debra opened the door for them.

Sam shook his head as he took Sarah's arm. "Of course you did."

Sarah could hear the low murmur of voices as they waited at the door for Debra's introduction. She took Sam's hand and took a deep breath. He smiled and stood silently.

They heard Debra ring a bell, and the murmurs stopped. "Ladies and gentleman, before I bring the amazing artist and perhaps her favorite subject out..." Light laughter was heard. "I just wanted to express how much joy this project has brought to me. I am so grateful for Sarah's vision. Her photographs evoke a visceral reaction from everyone who sees them, but the place settings for her art actually put you in the picture itself. This has been a labor of love for Sarah and me. But a bigger love is between Sarah and Sam. You can see and feel that in her pictures. So, without further ado, ladies and gentlemen, the amazing artist, and her amazing subject, Ms. Sarah Reid and Mr. Sam Ramsay!"

Sarah's legs had gone numb, and she breathed rapidly. Sam placed his hand on the small of her back. "I'm right here. Let's go eat some fucking biscuits!"

Sarah looked up at Sam and laughed when they walked through the door to loud applause. She wondered how so few people could make such a loud noise. Sam's hand was still warm against her back as her eyes slowly focused on her surroundings. The first people she saw were her daughters and Trace, who rushed to her to hug her.

"Holy shit, mom! I am so proud of you!" Gemma was almost beside herself. She hopped up and down. Charlie softly cried, and Harper was stunned into silence.

Mark and Marta rushed up for their hugs and to give congratulations. As she and Sam thanked them for all their support, a pair of beefy arms encircled her waist from behind her and a soft, stubbly kiss was laid on the back of her neck. Sarah's eyes got big and her mouth opened as she looked at Sam. He just stood and smiled at her. "Luca?" She slowly turned around to find the burly Italian looking at her with a beaming smile. "Luca!" She threw her arms around his thick neck and peppered his beard with little kisses.

"Tesoro, tesoro." Luca murmured softly as he wrapped her tightly into his chest. "What you've done here is magical. But not surprising, as you are magical. I'm so proud of you." Sarah sniffed loudly, as Luca let her go to wrap his arms around Sam. As she stood and looked at the two men, she felt her legs get tugged. "Aunt Sarah!"

She looked down into the faces of Thomas and Violet, and immediately started to sob again. "Don't cry Aunt Sarah. Unless they're happy tears. Mum always says happy tears are the best." Thomas was very serious.

Sarah squatted down to pick Violet up in her arms and to give Thomas a kiss on the cheek. "They are very happy tears, Thomas. I'm just so happy to see you both again." Violet laid her head into the crook of Sarah's neck. The little girl continually caressed her cheek. As Sarah stood up, her eyes were met by the eyes of Sam's family. Danni and Alex stood and grinned, as did Beth and Ollie. She again, was surrounded by hugging family.

Sarah stood and chatted animatedly with Sam's family. Sam and Luca stood and watched with smiles and sighs. "Isn't she something Luca? Can you believe that she didn't think anyone would be here? She has no idea how loved she is by so many."

"Oh, my boy. I think that Sarah has so much love in her own heart that it's hard for her to see past that. You know I still want to whisk her off to South America, don't you?" Both men continued to watch the woman that they loved as she was hugged and kissed by everyone.

Sam saw the elderly couple enter the gallery first. He went to greet them when Sarah noticed him walk to the front door. She looked to the front and gasped, before she put her hand over her mouth. "Oh wow!" She ran to join them as tears ran down her face. She was immediately engulfed in Walter Lemons arms. "I can't believe that you guys came all this way! But I'm so glad you did!" She reached for Sally and kissed her cheek.

"Oh dear! We wouldn't have missed this for anything! You're now family, girlie. Congratulations on the magazine layout. It was spectacular!" Sally kept Sarah's hand clasped in her own.

Walter looked at Sam, who stood with his long arm wrapped around the older man's shoulder. "We'd like to talk to both of you about the Oak Wood campaign, but later. Right now, could we have a look around?"

"I would be honored. Let's start at the beginning of this journey." Sarah continued to hold onto Sally's hand as she led them on a private walk through. Sally couldn't believe all the attention to detail that she noticed everywhere, and the beauty of Sarah's photographs. She asked a million questions, and noticed even more. As they ended in the "kitchen", Sally looked around before she looked at her husband. "Looks like a trip to the states will be on the agenda for next year. I absolutely have to see this heaven that's Sarah's home."

Sam walked to Sarah and put his arm around her waist. Sarah smiled through her tears as she looked at the sweet couple in front of her. "You are welcome anytime. For as long as you want to stay."

She had just finished introducing the Lemons to her daughters when she heard the loud giggles enter the space. Several voices in unison said quite loudly, "The bitches are here!" Sarah looked up with a grin to see Liz striding toward her. She was clad in black leather and feathers. Feathers. But somehow it worked. She was one hot mama. Julie, Ashley, Bev, Karen and Jack followed her. "And one man!" Liz yelled as she wrapped Sarah up in her arms and planted a big, fat, wet kiss right on her lips. Julie grabbed Sarah's ass as she hugged her, and Ashley and Bev each pinched a boob. Jack and Karen stood quietly with her for a few minutes, before they all walked toward Sam. Luca stared at Liz, then turned to Sam and asked. "Who is that and can I have her?" Sam caught Sarah's eye as he shrugged his shoulders, and Sarah giggled.

Several hours later, Sarah stood next to Sam as she continued to be hugged and kissed. She had shaken so many hands that her fingers were numb. She couldn't believe how many people had come; family, friends, and so many of the models from Paris, London, and Milan. She had already promised to go dancing with them later in the week. Everyone loved her art and the venue. Sarah was a wet, emotional mess. She sighed and hiccupped as she laid her head on Sam's shoulder. She breathed in the familiar smell of oak leaves and whiskey. That always grounded her. "This is almost overwhelming."

Before Sam could respond, Debra skipped over with a grin on her face. "Every single photo that was for sale has sold Sarah! I can't wait to see the papers tomorrow! The press that was here are all in love with you, and everyone was blown away by the "rooms" you presented them in. Enjoy this. You have earned it!" She gave Sarah a hug before she went to mingle once again.

Sarah looked at the floor, then up at Sam. "Fuck...." Then she grinned.

Sam grinned from ear to ear, before he walked his way to pick up a mason jar and a knife. He bounced the knife off the side of the jar to get everyone's attention. He swallowed, looked at Sarah and said, "Sarah and I want to thank each and every one of you for coming tonight. Most of you have traveled long distances to share in our happiness, and that means more than you will ever know. The artist standing here with me tonight has stolen my heart. And I'm pretty damned sure, that she's stolen all of yours. That is her greatest artistry. Her heart that she gives to all of us, and the hearts that she collects from us. What a wonderful gift it is for all of us to be loved by Sarah Reid. "

Sarah smiled and cried as she watched the man that she adored profess his love and pride in her to all their friends, family and strangers. Sarah knew that this was one of those moments. The quiet words spoken from a quiet man who loved her.

Sam continued. "Sarah tells me she loves me every day. Yeah, I'm the lucky bloke who gets to love and be loved by her. And she shows it. She feels it. She says it. Every fucking day." Sam's voice broke, and he stopped to get control of his emotions. He looked over at Sarah. She continued to smile and cry. Sam could hear soft sniffles throughout the room.

"She brought me something that I didn't even know I wanted or needed. She has given me a life. An amazing life full of family and friends. A life full of quiet moments of perfection. A symphony written by the notes of her heart. I am humbled, Sarah Reid. Humbled by the miracle that is you. "

Sarah slowly walked to Sam. He took her face in his big hands and kissed her softly but thoroughly, as everyone catcalled, cried and cheered.

After Sam finished devouring her mouth, he took her hand and continued. "I'm just so fucking proud of her! Look around you! Is this just the most amazing thing you've ever seen?"

Everyone clapped and cheered. "I've reserved the two floors of the hotel for family and friends. My mum and dad are taking the children back with them for the night. Take advantage of that Danni and Alex." Everyone laughed. "I've rented the bar and ball room at the hotel for our enjoyment. Open bar and late-night food. A little bird also told me, that there may be karaoke and dancing. And, if we're lucky, we might get Sarah and her daughters to sing for us. All of you are invited! Let's kick off our shoes and get this party started!"

Sam kept kissing Sarah in the back of their cab. He couldn't get enough of her taste, her smell, or the feel of her skin against his hands. "I'm so proud of you, Sarah Reid."

"I'm proud of me, too! I know Debra thought I was nuts, but I could see the entire venue in my head. I'm happy you're proud of me, Sam. I wanted to do it for you."

Sam laughed as he kissed her gently on the mouth. It was a sweet kiss, which quickly turned into heat and desire. "How about we go up to our room and change clothes for the party?"

As Sarah rubbed her hands up and down Sam's chest, she whispered, "Yes please."

It was déjà vu all over again. Sam had Sarah pushed against the elevator wall with her shirt unbuttoned, and her bra bunched around her waist. She ground her pelvis into his thick thigh and groaned as his mouth performed CPR on her tits. They both panted in desperation. As the door dinged and opened, Sam stuck his head out to make sure that the hall was empty of people. He saw that the coast was clear, so he grabbed Sarah's hand and proceeded to drag her to their room. His shirt was completely unbuttoned and pulled from his pants. His fly was open and his eyes were glassy. Sarah held her shoes in her free hand, and her lips were swollen in a sexy pout. Sam couldn't help but think about those swollen, pouty lips being anywhere on him. He muttered as he inserted the key card. "This is why I got our room on a different floor. We definitely have an erotically dysfunctional problem with elevators."

~~~

The two of them had changed into jeans and T-shirts after an hour-long shower. The party was in full swing when they entered the bar downstairs. Mark, Marta, Danni, Alex, Karen, and Jack turned and looked at them as they walked in. All of them started to laugh.

Danni walked up slowly before she stopped between the two of them. She put her hands on her hips and looked at Sam, and then at Sarah. Then she sniffed loudly. "You two smell like sex."

"Impossible," Sarah said sweetly. "We fucked in the shower." Sam looked at Danni with a smirk on his face as they continued to hold hands as they walked by the group of laughing people. They leaned on the bar.

"And that is why I fucking love her!" yelled Danni. "She gives me a lady boner! Seriously, Sam. Can I have her?"

Sarah held the bottle of Jameson tight against her chest, and Sam held the glasses. They looked at the friends and family they loved so much. Sarah grinned an evil little grin, as she asked for another bottle and more glasses. They all laughed as they walked into the ballroom.

Sam had done nothing but watch Sarah for the last thirty minutes. He guessed that she had spoken personally to, and hugged or kissed, everyone who was there. Every few minutes, she would turn and find his eyes on her. She always accused him of using his smile as a weapon against her, and he did. But she had no idea what that beaming Sarah smile did to him. Sarah had her own weapons, and he loved being the target of them.

She was slowly swallowed up by the young men. A driving beat had started, and the men wanted to dance. They wanted to dance with her. Sam saw her shoes fly out of the middle of the huddle that was moving en masse to the dance floor. He threw his head back and laughed.

"She is a magnificent being." Luca walked up to stand by his side. "I hate you and I love you."

Sam continued to laugh as his eyes watched Sarah become art on the floor. He felt as if he watched an ethereal creature from another planet. He was physically unable to stop watching her.

"She is perfection, Luca. I feel like I am going to wake up, and this will all have been a dream."

Liz walked out of the crowd toward him, and he heard Luca hiss. He raised his eyebrow as he looked at him and laughed. As he turned back to Liz, he was met with leather clad arms that reached around his neck. "Are you as proud of our girl as I am?"

"I'm always proud of Sarah. Every day, every moment." He kissed her cheek and squeezed her waist. "You are a leather-clad vixen tonight!"

Liz giggled as she turned to Luca. "Come on you sexy Italian man! Come dance with me. I might even let you pinch my ass!"

"Cazzo! Let's hope so!" Luca looked back at Sam with a grin on his face.

Sarah returned to the tables that they had pushed together. Sam sat with Danni, Alex, Mark, Marta, Karen, and Jack. Charlie and Trace mingled. Harper and Gemma stayed on the dance floor with some of the models. Liz was still on the floor with Luca, Bev danced with some pretty boy, and Ashley and Julie danced with each other. Sarah thought that was probably safer for everyone. She poured shots of Jameson for all.

"Are you trying to get me drunk and take advantage of me, Sarah Reid?" Sam asked slowly.

Sarah grinned at him. "Too late. We're all a little drunk, and I've already taken advantage of you tonight."

Karen reached across the table to take Sam's hand. "Thank you sounds so inadequate Sam. But thank you. We can all get as wasted as we want, and all we have to do is get on the elevator. You are a very giving man, Sam Ramsay, and not with just the plane tickets and the hotel rooms. Jack and I don't know what we would've done without you, well... you know."

Sam stood and wrapped petite Karen in his arms. He rocked her and whispered in her ear. Jack joined in, and everyone else sat and experienced the remnants of sadness. Sarah watched her big man and wondered how on earth she could love him more than she did.

"Wait…what? Did you say plane tickets and hotel rooms? Sam?" She looked at Sam as he sat back down with a sheepish look on his face. "What am I missing?"

"Sam bought the plane tickets for me, Charlie, Gemma, Harper - all of us." Karen said. "I would bet that he got them for Danni, Alex, and his mom and dad, too." Danni looked at Sarah and nodded her head yes. Sarah's eyes had grown to twice their size.

Trace continued. "He also reserved the whole floor of rooms for all of us." Trace leaned close to Sarah's ear and whispered. "Don't be mad at him. He wanted to do this because he loves you that much. Let him have this, Sarah."

"He's a fucking millionaire who doesn't spend money on anything except fucking clothes Sarah! He can afford it! Now come on! I want you and me to dance with my husband!" Danni drug Sarah off Sam's lap and then grabbed Alex.

Alex looked back at everyone with a grin on his face. "This is gonna be fun! I'm gonna be the creamy center of a Danni and Sarah sandwich cookie!"

The whiskey flowed, and dancing continued. Sarah, Gemma, Harper, and Charlie made a quartet of beauty with their looks and their harmonies when they sang "Moondance". Sam and Sarah ended the night dancing to "Riviera Paradisio."

As they fell into bed, Sarah looked at the ceiling. "Wow. What a night. Most of our guests will pass out from alcohol, and a few will probably make babies."

Sam grinned before falling asleep. "I have definitely had too much alcohol, but I'd be glad to practice conception. Tomorrow."

~~~

After they ate brunch with everyone, they went back to the gallery with Luca. Sarah had discussed an idea that would take care of the rescheduling of Sam's shoot, and would be her first assignment with Luca. She had packed her cameras and a bag with a few different items of clothing and the clothes that they had worn the night before.

"So.... I was thinking that pictures with pictures would be kind of cool. But, if you think I'm full of shit, just tell me." Sarah looked nervously at Luca.

Luca laughed loudly before he hugged her in his thick arms. "I could never tell you that tesoro. I love you too much. I also trust you eyes. Let's do it."

Sarah immediately started to set stuff up and empty her bags. "You and Sam can occupy yourselves while I get everything ready."

Sam frowned at Luca. "See! She's already got an attitude. One little photo spread, and one gallery opening, and she thinks she's all that."

Sarah stuck her tongue out, and Sam laughed softly at her before he and Luca walked across the gallery in conversation.

~~~

Sarah sat with Violet in her lap as the rest of their families sat around the dinner table later that evening. Sam filled them in on their schedule for the rest of the year.

"I'm going back to the farm with Sarah for a week when we leave tomorrow. Mark and Marta will be joining us before we all head to the Oak Wood campaign in LA."

Danni grinned. "I can't wait to see what kind of entrance Sarah makes at that one!" Everyone chuckled as Sam continued.

"After LA, I have a charity function in London. Sarah will be coming with me for that. She'll stay until I finish up the few contractual obligations I have in the UK. Then, our life will turn into something almost normal. I have nothing until I renew contracts in January. Sarah and Danni will be helping me with those. A change is in the air, folks, and I can't wait." Danni and Sarah looked at each other with small smiles on their faces.

Sam continued. "I will be at the farm for October and some of November. I have been told that I am required to learn how to make apple butter and cider." As everyone grinned, Sam took Sarah's hand. "I can't think of anything else I'd rather do."

Sarah continued to stroke Violet's hair as she spoke. "We are planning on spending Thanksgiving in London. Danni has graciously offered up her home for the festivities. We know the Brits don't celebrate, but as it's all about being thankful, we thought it appropriate to spend it all together."

Ollie and Beth held hands as they looked around the table. Everyone had smiles on their faces. "We would like to celebrate Christmas at the farm." Sarah continued. "Sam is dead set on experiencing clean snow for Christmas. I'll try to see what I can do about that."

Harper raised an eyebrow as she said, "Knowing my mother, I'm sure she already has it all figured out. Right, mama?"

Sarah grinned. "Yeah, I do. We have four bedrooms at the farm, and my craft room will sleep two. We've also got the basement. If we get snowed in, we have plenty of floor and air mattresses."

Sam grinned. "It's going to be so much fun!"

"You're just so stinkin' cute, Sam!" Sarah giggled.

"I am *not cute.* I am devilishly handsome."

Chapter 46:

Sam, Sarah, Marta and Mark spent the morning and early afternoon walking Sarah's land. They waded in the creek and picked wild flowers. They saw a red fox and rabbits. The cows on the neighboring land softly lowed, and the scent of freshly mown grass filled their senses. The girls listened to the bees buzz as they lounged on a blanket on the creek bank. They watched Sam and Mark as they talked and walked on the other side.

"This is a little piece of heaven, Sarah. It's just what I needed." Marta sighed as she closed her eyes.

Sarah closed her eyes as well as she lay back. "I'm so glad you're here. I love to share my life."

Marta turned and looked at Sarah. "Are you guys going to get married?"

Sarah opened her eyes as she looked back at Marta. "Huh. I hadn't even thought of that. I'm sure Sam hasn't either." She lay back down and looked up at the soft clouds that dotted the blue sky. "I don't think it matters, does it?"

"No. I really don't think so, either. I was just curious if you guys had talked about it. I know he adores you. I'm pretty sure you like him a little bit, too." Marta grinned.

Sarah smiled back at her. "And in the end, that's all that matters, isn't it?"

Sarah smiled and hummed quietly as the others napped. She was in a place of peaceful happiness. Simple pleasures like good food and good friends. A beautiful whoshe loved, and a late summer afternoon. Life was so good.

"Hey beautiful. What are you doing?" Sam asked as he pulled her against his chest and wrapped his arms around her waist. "You smell like grass and sunshine."

Sarah closed her eyes and laid her head against his hard chest. "Hey handsome. I was just thinking how lucky I was. And the simple pleasures of life."

"I like simple *pleasures*, too." Sam growled softly as he nipped her ear lobe, and slowly ran his hand up her ribcage. He stopped at the side of her breast, before softly running his knuckles across her nipple.

Sarah softly gasped as goose bumps broke out on her forearms. She turned to look at him. He grinned, but his eyes were dark with desire. "You make me feel like a sixteen-year-old girl Sam Ramsay. I walk around with tingly naughty bits all the damn time! Maybe there's a pill for that."

Sam looked down at her sunburned nose and shoulders. "Let me see if I can help you out with your naughty bits." He slowly turned her to the kitchen island and placed a hand on her lower back. He gently pushed her down, as he nibbled the sun-kissed shoulders and the back of her neck. As he tasted and touched her silken, sun-warmed skin, he knew that he would never tire of her smell, her taste, and her little gasps and moans. He would forever love the hidden places that she shared with only him. When he was old and feeble, he would still want her and love her as desperately as he did right now.

"What if Mark and Marta come in?" Sarah whispered.

"I told Mark not to bother us for two hours." He continued to kiss her neck as he unbuttoned her jeans.

"Well! That was rude! And very confident. Two hours, huh?" She moaned softly as her jeans puddled around her ankles. Sam's fingers made it impossible for her to continue to speak. Sarah heard his zipper, and felt his lips on her lower back, before they moved further down. Her legs buckled a little, but he held her up with one arm, as his tongue began its onslaught.

Sarah exploded as Sam continued, but it wasn't enough.

"Please, Sam!"

"Please what, sweet Sarah?" Sam held her hip with one arm and kept the other one on her lower back.

"I want you. Not your fingers. Not your tongue. You."

"Your wish is my command." A hard, deep thrust without warning sent Sarah spinning. She couldn't tell if it was her grunting or Sam. Perhaps it was both of them. She wondered if it would always be like this for them. The need for the deepest connection. A connection on another plane of existence. She reached the point where no thought was attainable. It was only the emotion and the sensations of utter and complete pleasure.

The four of them went into the city. They walked around the historic district and then went to Sarah's dress shop. Then they went to Sarah's favorite brewery. They sat at a table on the patio and listened to Sam complain about watery American beers.

"There is no good beer in the States." Sam lifted his nose. "The UK is the only place that knows how to brew a proper beer."

"Well, Mr. Snobby, why don't you try the milk stout, then complain to me about American beer."

Sam was pleasantly surprised by the smooth, rich taste, and ordered another. Time passed quickly, so they ordered dinner before they headed back to the farm.

Their days were spent with relaxing and good conversation. They enjoyed the lull before the flight to LA, and the chaos that would be the final leg of the Oak Wood campaign. As they all lounged on the back porch, Marta looked at Sam. "A little birdy told me that Oak Wood might shake things up a little next year. Do you know anything about that, Sam?'

Sam looked concerned. "The Lemons approached Sarah and I about doing something together... that doesn't mean they're firing you, does it, Marta? We won't do it if that's the case. We would feel incredibly guilty!"

Marta looked at Mark before turning to look at Sam and Sarah. "Actually, it's perfect timing. I'm not renewing my contract, Sam."

"Oh, Marta! Sam can't do Oak Wood without you! You keep him sane." Sarah sat up straight on the porch swing.

"He'll be fine, because you're going to do it with him. Besides, I can't imagine how exhausting it would be for me and Mark to try that campaign with a five-month-old to deal with." Marta looked at the both of them with a smile on her face.

Sam and Sarah looked at each other. Then they looked at Mark and Marta, who had huge grins on their faces.

"Fuck! Congratulations!" Sarah wrapped Marta her in a hug. "I'm so happy for you both. You guys are going to be such good parents."

"You both realize that she's going to go crazy buying baby things, don't you?" Sam joked. "And she'll want to have all kinds of parties. She'll want a pregnancy party, a baby party, a one-month-old party..."

~~~

Sarah stood in the bathroom and smiled to herself. They had been gawked at everywhere on the trip to LA. People stared at them in the airport in Missouri, on the plane, and especially in LAX. She had expected Sam to be leered at in LA, as that city, as it was, like New York, more celebrity and fashion conscious. What she hadn't expected was for someone to ask for an autograph from *her*. She had been asked numerous times along with a dozen selfies. It was all a little surreal. Instead of freaking out she chose to laugh about it. Sam had grinned from ear to ear, as he reminded her of the magazine spread. She decided she would have to just enjoy the interplay between fantasy and reality.

~~~

Sam walked into the bathroom, and stopped suddenly. Sarah didn't have to do anything. She simply leaned against the vanity and held his world in her hands. She was a vision in rust-colored tulle and gold. Layer upon layer of autumn-colored tulle. It was strapless with a simple gold belt around her waist. Her sun kissed cleavage was its own accessory. He felt his hands clench as he tried to get his breath back.

"You intoxicate me, Sarah Reid."

Sarah sighed as she turned to look at Sam in his chocolate tuxedo. He wore a cream-colored shirt and a rust-colored vest. He had finished his look with a gold, cream, and a rust-colored bow tie. She held her breath as she looked at him. She found it hard to believe sometimes that she had somehow made him love her.

She brushed her lips softly against his and laid her hands on his chest, before she inhaled the scent of oak leaves and whiskey. "And you are my book of wonder, Sam Ramsay. I want to spend the rest of my life reading each word, each page, and each chapter. I want to dog ear the corners, and return to my favorite passages again and again, to relive each and every moment."

~~~

They shared a limo with Mark and Marta. As they waited in the traffic that had slowed to a crawl, Sarah realized that she had never attended a premiere in the States. She hadn't experienced nerves at any of the others, and she wasn't nervous now. But she was excited.

When the limo stopped, the driver got out and opened the door for Mark. He exited and held a hand for Marta. They heard the crowd and saw flashbulbs. Sam got out and held his hand for Sarah. As she stood and brushed her hands down her dress, the cacophony started. As usual, there were many women. They screamed loudly. As Sarah laughed, she heard another loud voice. "Marry me, Sarah!"

She stopped with her mouth open. Sam laughed before loudly replying to Sarah's suitor. "Sorry, mate. She's going to marry me!"

Sarah looked at him sharply as they made their way up the red carpet. As they entered the venue, Sarah continued to look at Sam. "Do you think that maybe we should talk about that?"

Sam chuckled and patted her arm that was still held by him. "Probably."

~~~

The after party was in full swing and Sarah was already on the dance floor. Sam had watched her all night. He nursed his whiskey and smirked to himself. He knew that she had thought about nothing other than the marriage remark. He wanted her to think of nothing else. He found a perverse satisfaction in knocking Sarah off kilter. She was always so sure of herself, and comfortable in her own skin. He loved that he had gotten her a little wobbly.

He needed her to say yes for a myriad of reasons. He adored her, and could never imagine his life without her, but marriage or no marriage wouldn't change that. He knew that Sarah had never even thought about it, and he hadn't either until the last few days. Mark had asked him if they had talked about it. Sam had been surprised when he realized that neither of them had ever brought it up. Their whole relationship had happened so fast, they were just now catching their breath. And other than the quiet moments at the farm, and the few days in London, they had been living in the fantasy that was his career and the beginning of hers.

But Mark, being the ever-practical man had brought up some very unromantic but important issues. The longer Mark talked to him, the more importance it had for Sam. He loved Sarah. He wanted to take care of her by loving her and pampering her. But, he had grown to love her family as well, and that was something he wanted to be a part of. He could do everything he wanted without marrying her, but he wanted what Danni and Alex had. And what his mum and dad had. He wanted what Sarah and David had experienced. He wanted a home. Sarah was that home.

Sam needed to know that he would wake every morning with her in his arms, and go to sleep every night with her in his bed. He wanted to make decisions with her and share her friends and family. He wanted someone to come home to, someone to celebrate with, and someone to cry with. He wanted the touch and smell of her skin to be his balm and her smile to light up his heart every day.

~~~

Sarah couldn't stop thinking about what Sam had said. Marriage. Did she want that? Did she need that? Yes or no wouldn't change the way she felt about him. It's not as if he had asked her. He had stated it, sure. But that wasn't a question. She didn't have anything against marriage. She had experienced a good one. Did she want to do it again? Sam had put her on edge, and she didn't like it. She really didn't know why. She was usually good at thinking things through and not getting hyped up, but, damn it! Sam had hyped her up!

She knew that the thought of not having him in her life made her sick to her stomach. She couldn't imagine her life without the ability to touch him or feel him in her body. The sensual experience of Sam Ramsay was a miraculous thing, but his kindness, his tenderness and his love for her were even more miraculous. She didn't know what she had done to deserve two great loves in her life, but her life was a walking, talking miracle.

She walked back towards Sam who sat at their table. He smirked at her behind the rim of his glass. She stopped and narrowed her eyes at him. She had a sudden epiphany. Had he done it on purpose to make her life tilt a little? He looked just a little too pleased with himself. Yep. They were most certainly going to talk about it. She continued her walk and arrived at the table at the same time that the Lemons walked up. She loved them, but she wished they would go away for a little while.

She looked at Sam and found him trying to cover his laughter with his hand. She hugged the Lemons and poured a double.

They were interrupted all night by the familiar faces who wanted to dance, drink, and to talk. The first moment that they had alone was in the elevator as they made their way to their room.

Sarah took a deep breath before she turned to Sam. Before she could say a word, he put his fingers to her lips and softly said, "I would prefer to talk about it when we're home in London. I just want you to think about it. Mull it about in your head. As soon as the presser is done tomorrow, we'll be on our way. "

But —" Sarah was stopped again by Sam's fingers.

He grinned. "Plus, I haven't asked you, have I?"

Sam felt her lips as she pursed them behind his fingers. She glared at him. That smile of his was a weapon that completely disarmed her. It stopped any questions she might have had, as well as any coherent thought except shedding him of his clothes.

"Fine!" Sarah hissed. "You got what you wanted. You are so unfair."

"How am I unfair?" Sam crossed his arms across his chest as he leaned back against the elevator wall. Then he grinned at her again.

"That right there, you ass! " Sarah tapped her foot impatiently.

Sam laughed quietly as he stared at her. "I don't think I've ever seen you like this. You're really cute when you get aggravated."

As the elevator door opened, Sarah stomped out before turning to look at him. "You better be naked and in the bed by the time I get my dress off."

"Aren't you a bossy little thing! Are you going to hurt me, Sarah?" Sam continued to laugh as he dug for the key card.

Sarah stopped suddenly. "I would never hurt you, Sam." But then she poked Sam's chest and glared at him. "But I am going to fuck your brains out."

"Oh, thank God."

So she did.

~~~

The press conference was scheduled for eleven o'clock. Sarah and Sam admired each other on the way down. Sam wore brown trousers with an unbuttoned cream shirt with a brown tweed jacket. He finished the look with brown Cuban boots.

Sarah wore a brown pencil pants with matching stilettos. She paired a cream-colored, skin-tight, short-sleeved turtleneck.

All of Sarah's questions swirled like a tornado in her brain. But Sam had asked her to just think about things until they could discuss it more in London. As much as she would never admit it to him, she thought he was probably right. She would have a ten-

and-a-half-hour flight to try to figure out why she was so anxious about the marriage word. The anxiety alone made her even more anxious. "Gah!" she thought. "Get a grip!" This was so unlike her, and she needed to figure out why.

Sam stood and smirked at her. As she caught his look, she snapped. "What? Do you find me funny?"

He shook his head with a grin on his face. "I know that brain of yours is going a mile a minute. I have gob smacked you. Thank God, I kept you busy last night. You probably would have stabbed me in my sleep if I hadn't worn you out."

Sarah snorted. "You're probably right, but don't be fearful of sleeping on the flight. My murderous tendencies have calmed down. For a while, at least."

As they stepped off the elevator they were met with the usual throng of flash bulbs and loud questions. They were both friendly as they answered a few questions and posed for a few pictures. Sam's hand never left Sarah's lower back.

They entered the room for the press conference. Sarah started to make her way to her usual spot at the side in the front. Sam stopped her and pulled her gently to follow him. She gulped as she saw her name card next to Sam's in the front. She slowly turned to look at him, but stayed quiet as he pulled her chair out.

As he sat he took her hand in his. He loved the feel of her skin under his fingertips and the look on her face. Of, course, he loved her face with whatever look was on it, but surprising Sarah twice in a twenty-four-hour period was very satisfying. He loved that he could knock her off kilter because it reminded him that she was human.

For the first time in a long time, he was excited to see what the Oak Wood campaign would bring in the new year. Doing it with Sarah would be fresh, exciting, and satisfying. He appreciated that Walter agreed to breaks in between cities. He and Sally loved Sarah, and were almost as excited as he was to have her join the team. Sam looked forward to the changes in the brand and his life.

There was no sense of déjà vu. Instead of a staffer introducing the panelists to the press corps, she introduced Walter Lemons, owner of Oak Wood. As Walter leaned into his microphone, he looked at Sam and Sarah and winked with a smile on his face. They both smiled back at him.

"I usually just let Sam handle the bulk of these things, so forgive me if I'm not as smooth." Walter waited for the chuckles to die down.

"Sally and I started our little company twenty-five years ago. Who knew, huh?" Walter turned and looked at Sam.

"When we developed our first ad campaign, we both wanted Sam. We wanted him because of his looks. I mean, who wouldn't? He not only looked good on paper, he looked good on film. He was different."

"We've done something that no one else has. We have continued to work with Sam for decades. Sam is more than just a pretty face. He was a boy with character who has turned into a man of character. He has a work ethic and is unfailingly polite. Sally and I love him like a son. We are so proud of him. Because of him, we have worked hand in hand with the best designers from all over the world. He has been good for our little company."

"Things are going to change in the coming year. Sam has worked endlessly for Sally and me. I feel as if we've taken advantage of him. He is going to have some time off in between cities. He has earned that." Walter continued.

"But that's not what we're discussing here." Walter grinned at the sea of faces in front of him. "Marta came on board six years ago, and she has been wonderful. She's a hard worker, Sam loves her, and they look great together. But I'm afraid that's about to change." Walter waited for the low murmurs to quiet.

"Marta is going to have the chance to enjoy more time with her husband, because they're going to have a baby and start a family. Congratulations, you guys! You will be wonderful parents."

The crowd applauded loudly, as Mark and Marta smiled back at them. Walter again, leaned forward. "Just as our scotch has matured, so has Sam. It is our greatest wish for him to be happy. Happy with his life and happy with Oak Wood." Walter stopped to take a drink of water.

"We will continue to work with Sam as long as he wants to work with us. In the coming year, Oak Wood will again feature Sam. The only change is that Ms. Sarah Reid will be the new female face of Oak Wood. Sally and I are overjoyed that she has accepted our offer. Please help Sally and I welcome Sarah."

The room was loud with conversation and questions. Walter raised his hands. "Please! You know how this works. One question at a time, when you're called. We can start with Phil who is right down front."

Phil clicked on his recorder as he stood up. "This is for Sam. I'm not trying to be rude, as I've met Sarah, and find her unfailingly nice, but, was she chosen because she's your girlfriend?"

Sam frowned at the reporter. He looked at Sarah, then back to Phil. "I'm sorry, but that *was* rude. First, I don't get the final say. That would be Mr. Lemon's call. Sure, I have input, but I'm not the deciding factor. Secondly, I would never jeopardize the relationship I have with Walter and Sally, or Oakwood, with an emotional objective. Sarah is not my girlfriend. You make it sound like she's my toy. She is so much more than that. Thirdly, have you seen her photos? And finally, have you seen the magazine spread?" Sam leaned back in his chair with his arms crossed over his chest and a smile on his face.

There were a lot of "Hell, yea's, cat calls and wolf whistles. Sam leaned forward again. "Okay, now that you've objectified us, can we talk about the campaign?"

The next question came from a female from *Ravaged*. She laughed. "I think that was all for Sarah, not you. That's got to feel a little different, huh?"

Sam reached for Sarah's hand and kissed her pulse point. His heart beat rapidly. "I love it. I want to whistle every time I see her." He smelled the sandalwood as his lips touched the soft skin on her wrist. He could feel her heart beat quickly. As he looked in her eyes, he saw nothing but desire, love and excitement in her eyes. He was so damn proud.

The reporter from *Ravage* finished her question. "Is Sam taking more time off because of your relationship, Sarah? Are wedding bells in the future?"

Sarah smiled, but took her time before she answered. "Sam is not taking *more* time off. He's taking time off. He's never done that before, and, yes, it's because of our relationship. It's our priority. As far as wedding bells, I will keep that private. Whether we do or don't doesn't pertain to anything regarding Oak Wood."

"Are you excited?" "Have you always wanted to model?" How does your family feel about all of this?" All the reporters talked over each other, before Sarah stopped Sam with a hand on his arm.

"Hey people! Let me try to answer all of your questions in one try, before moving on to someone else, okay?" Sarah waited for them to sit down.

Sarah sat forward in her chair, and took Sam's hand. "No. I have never wanted to model. I had never even thought about it, and had never been exposed to it, until I met Sam. My priorities had always been my family, especially my girls, after their father died, and my photography. Those are still my priorities. Insert Sam into family, as he has quickly catapulted into mine and my family's hearts."

She squeezed Sam's hand as she continued. "Because of Sam, I have experienced things, and met people that I would never have had the opportunity to meet. He has changed my life in many, many ways. Because of him, I have traveled more in the last few months than I have in my entire life. Those travels provided me with photographic paradise. Plus, just his face alone... I mean, hell! Look at that face."

The press corps erupted in laughter and flashbulbs exploded. "Because of him, I met Luca, who, along with Walter and Sally, have become my family. Though, I must admit, Luca is really cute." Laughter, again, ensued. Sarah looked down the table and blew Luca a kiss.

"I did the magazine shoot, because Sam and Luca asked me to. I trusted them to not make me look bad. I was surprised to find I enjoyed it. I won't be doing layouts like that with anyone other than Sam."

Sam growled into his microphone. "You better not!"

"So, to say that I'm excited would be a gross understatement. I have met people who I'm now in love with." She turned and looked at Mark and Marta. She held her heart, as Marta blew her a kiss.

"If Sam breaks my heart, I now have a man that I will run away with." She blew another kiss to Luca, who actually blushed.

"Because of Sam, I now have Walter and Sally Lemons in my life. My parents are both gone, and they have wiggled their way into my heart. I appreciate their confidence in me, and I want to make them proud."

Sarah paused, before continuing. "I now have extended family that I love so much. I'm excited for a new chapter in my life. My world is full of possibilities. And, I am having so much fun! Thank you Sam Ramsay."

Sam leaned over and kissed her softly before grinning at the crowd in front of them.

Chapter 47:

It was late when they landed at Heathrow. They had rushed after the presser and talked for most of the ten-and-a-half hour flight. They had both caught a nap, but they were dead on their feet when San unlocked his front door.

"Leave the bags. I'll get them in the morning." Sam locked the door behind him.

Sarah sighed. "Oh, thank God. All I want is a whiskey, a shower and bed."

"I'll pour the drinks, you can go on up. I'll meet you in the shower." Sam was already on his way to the kitchen.

Sarah slowly walked up the stairs and inhaled deeply. Sam's house smelled like him and was just as beautiful as she remembered. She walked into the master suite and slowly started to undress as Sam walked in with their glasses. He set them on the table and followed suit. Sam took her hand and led her into the shower.

"Oh, God. I love this bathroom," Sarah murmured.

They stood under the rain heads and washed the airplane grime off their bodies. They both wrapped up in soft, fluffy towels and walked back into the bedroom. Sam toasted. "Here's to London and good conversation. Tomorrow." They clinked their glasses, drank the whiskey, and dropped their towels where they were before they crawled into the sheets that smelled of Sam.

"Good night, Amazing Sarah."

"Good night, Sweet Sam."

The two of them slept late and basically did nothing all afternoon. They still had a bit of jet lag but had made it to the grocer. Sarah sat and watched Sam prepare supper. She loved his skill in the kitchen, but when he bent over to find a pot, Sarah sighed softly. A few seconds later he reached up to get a glass out of the cabinet. Sarah sighed again as she watched the muscles in his back ripple under the thin cotton of his shirt. He had a beautiful back, and even better shoulders. She sighed again. Sam set his glass down and started to flex his arms like a body builder.

"What are you doing?" Sarah asked, laughing.

Sam whirled around. "I can hear you, you know."

"Hear me?"

"Yes. You keep sighing. It's making me feel slightly sluttish. Is that all I am to you Sarah? Just a pretty face and body?" Sam pouted and stuck his lower lip out a little.

Sarah shrieked with laughter. "That's right! You're my boy toy. I like 'em slutty."

Sam put his finger to his bottom lip and stuck his hip out. "You make me feel so dirty."

"Oh, my God! You've got to stop! I can't breathe!" Sarah had collapsed with her head on the table.

After she had regained her breath, she looked up to see Sam staring at her with a serious expression. "What is it, Sam? What's wrong?"

"This." He waved his arm between the two of them. "This right here. This is perfection."

"Oh, Sam." Sarah walked to him and patted his chest. "It is."

He looked into her eyes and stated seriously, "We're going to eat an absolutely perfect meal, in an absolutely perfect kitchen. Then we're going to sit on an absolutely perfect couch, before an absolutely perfect fire, with an absolutely perfect glass of whiskey. Then I'm going to talk about our absolutely perfect life together, made even more perfect by an absolutely perfect marriage. It's time for that conversation."

Sarah swallowed and whispered, "Okay, Sam, whatever you want."

Sam didn't taste his food. He couldn't even remember what he had cooked. His stomach was in knots, and he didn't know why. He had trouble explaining the importance of marriage in his own mind, much less to Sarah. Maybe it was the tradition. He was a traditional man, after all. Maybe it's because he wanted to proclaim to the world that she was his. He had thought about it constantly since they left the farm, and he at one time, thought about a prepared speech. But he didn't want their conversation to sound like he had prepared it. He would just pour out his soul.

Sarah's food tasted like cardboard, even though she knew that Sam had prepared an absolutely delicious meal. It stuck in her throat, making it difficult to swallow. And breathe. She had thought of nothing else except marriage since Sam mentioned it. She respected Sam's admonishment to think about it, and to mull it over. That's all she had done. She realized that married or not, it wouldn't change her absolute adoration of him. But, this wasn't just about her, this was his life, too, and she needed to remember that.

Sarah was already comfortable on the couch with her long legs stretched out on the coffee table. She looked up to take her glass from Sam and smiled. His heart stopped for just a minute and suddenly he felt calmer.

He sat down next to her and poured their whiskey. He pulled Sarah close to him and kissed her on the head. "You ready? "

Sarah swallowed and nodded her head yes.

"I don't want you to feel as if I'm trying to pressure you into anything, Sarah. Though I'm still trying to understand why you're so against marrying me." Sam stared into the fire.

"Oh, my God, Sam! I feel awful that you feel that way! I love you so much, and I have no idea why I'm so anxious about this discussion. I'm not against it, I'm just fucking jittery, and it's driving me crazy." Sarah absently rubbed his forearm. His smell grounded her instantly, and she took a deep breath. "Let's toast to us and good conversation."

As they clinked their glasses, Sam turned to her and quietly began. "You've experienced a wonderful marriage. I haven't, and I want to. I want what you and David had, and what Danni and Alex have, and what my mum and dad have. I've waited so long, and I feel as if I deserve that. No matter what our decision is, it will never change the way I feel about you, or the need I have to be with you. Do you understand?"

"I do, Sam." Sarah took a sip of the smooth whiskey, and licked her bottom lip.

Sam groaned and closed his eyes. "But you can't do that. You will not distract me, you little minx."

Sarah just grinned as she turned to face him on the couch. She folded her long legs under her and waited for him to continue.

Sam turned to her and began. "I don't believe there are accidents in this life. I don't believe that we met each other accidentally, even though there was an accident involved." Sarah chuckled.

"Everything has led me to this moment. All my choices, joys, fears, and sorrows. All my loneliness." He never took his eyes off her as he sipped his whiskey.

"I feel as if our souls met a very long time ago, and our bodies have been trying to find each other again. You are my destiny, Sarah."

Sarah was still and quiet. She didn't blink, and Sam couldn't see her breathe, but she never stopped looking at him.

"I crave you, Sarah. It's like the dull ache of hunger that's never satisfied. I don't think it ever will be. You are my sustenance." Sam shuddered a little, and got even quieter. "I watched you sleep last night."

Sarah's eyes got large as a tear rolled down her cheek, but she didn't say a word.

"When I watched you sleep, I knew that I needed nothing else. You have stolen my heart, Amazing Sarah, along with my soul, my reason, and my shirts. I'm a pretty old-fashioned guy, so I want the tradition of marriage. It's important to me to be able to show the world that you're mine, and I am yours. I want to make you my everything, including my wife, and show everyone our commitment to each other." Sam stopped and took a breath before he reached into his pocket.

He got off the couch and turned Sarah to face him as he knelt in front of her. "Sarah Reid, will you marry me?" He looked up and saw her crying. He opened the small black ring box.

Sarah never looked down as Sam put the ring on her finger. She never stopped crying, and she never stopped staring into his beautiful blue eyes. She finally whispered, "Yes. It would me my honor to marry the man that I have been waiting lifetimes for. Yes, Sam Ramsay. I will marry you."

Sam kissed her lips gently. He whispered, "Thank you."

They held each other for a long while, lost in their own thoughts, before he asked her, "Aren't you even going to look at it?"

"I've already seen it countless times, Sam. I don't think it's grown since this morning." Sarah arched her eyebrow at him before he roared with laughter.

She looked at the ring that Sam had placed on her finger. He took her hand. "I know that topaz is your birthstone, but I wanted a blue one. It reminds me of the water you love so much, and the clear blue of the sky at the farm. Yellow citrine is also a November birthstone. I wanted them surrounding the blue, because they reminded me of the sunshine that always seems to be you. Then, of course, it's a damn engagement ring, so there had to be diamonds. I got a platinum setting, because I know you're not a fan of gold."

Sarah looked down at it, then back up to Sam. "I can't believe that you put that much thought into it. Wait. Yes, I can. You think everything through. I love that it's not traditional. I love the colors, I love the ring, and I love you."

They talked late into the night. They made their plans, and set their schedules, before Sam took Sarah's hand and led her upstairs. "I think it's time that I made love to my fiancè."

October

Chapter 48:

The first two days back at the farm had been filled with nothing but sleep, food, and love making. They had only left the big feather bed to fix food. Today would be spent with Jack and the girls. The plans were to pick apples and make cider and apple butter. A meal and cocktails would accompany kitchen duty. Sarah had put out a few fall decorations, but as they would be gone until after Thanksgiving, she hadn't gone crazy.

Sam and Sarah sat at the kitchen island as they drank coffee and smiled at each other. They were both rested and satisfied. The kitchen counters were covered with glass canning jars and half gallon jugs. The AGA had every burner covered with pressure cookers and ceramic pots. Sam had been amazed at the science involved in canning. He couldn't wait to see Sarah in her element.

He watched as she got up and refilled his coffee. As she turned to pour, Sam watched her ass in the jeans that she wore. It was such a fine ass. He noticed that it had gotten quiet, and he looked up to see Sarah staring at him with a smirk on her face. "Like what you see?"

Sam growled as he stood up and walked to her. He grabbed that ass with both hands. "I always like what I see. How soon until everyone gets here?"

Sarah laughed as she gave him a quick kiss. "I swear to God, Sam, if I didn't know better, I'd swear you were twenty. Have you not had enough of me? Are you not tired?"

"I feel twenty. Are you complaining?" Sam gave her a slow, wet kiss.

She pushed him away laughing. "No complaints. My man keeps me very satisfied, but the gang should be here anytime. It will just have to wait until later."

Before he could respond, they heard the first vehicle. "I am going to hold you to that, Sarah Reid, then I'm going to hold you to me." Sam wiggled his eyebrows, as Jack and Karen walked into the kitchen.

After another pot of coffee, and with everyone there, they all headed out with their own bushel baskets. The air was crisp enough for just a jacket, and the leaves had just started to turn. The maples were already on fire, and the birch trees were gold in their autumn foliage. The sumacs were so red they looked as if they were bleeding. Sam stopped to take a deep breath, and he realized that the farm looked different and smelled different. October in Missouri was a wonder to behold.

By early afternoon, everyone had filled their baskets and Sarah had filled another with bittersweet for the fireplace mantle. They headed back to the house for some lunch and an assembly line of peelers, dicers, and stirrers.

The sandwiches were eaten, and the Bloody Marys were poured. Sam watched in amazement as everyone automatically took up a task without having to be told. "It looks like you guys have done this before."

Karen giggled. "Every year, Sam. Once you get a taste of Sarah's cider and apple butter, you'll understand."

Jack grinned as he looked at his wife. "I think he's already tasted Sarah's cider and apple butter."

Liz groaned from her spot at the counter. "You can tell you have kids at home, if that's what you're calling it."

Sarah made Sam the official stirrer as she continued to sort the apples. The house slowly filled with the enticing bite of fresh apples and cinnamon. It suddenly felt like fall, and Sarah wondered where the time had gone. She and Sam had not even known each other for a year, and here he stood in her kitchen, with her friends, in her home. She sighed a happy sigh.

Of course, there was apple pie for dessert and baskets of apple butter and cider for everyone to take home. Everyone filled their whiskey glasses again and lounged around the pool table. Sarah sat next to Sam with the guitar on her lap. She softly strummed as she talked with Ashley. It had been strangely quiet without Julie. She had a continuing education class, and hadn't been able to make it.

"Hey, Sarah, we're heading home soon. How about a song before we go?" Jack asked quietly. His eyes were closed and his head lay on the back of the chair.

Sarah strummed and softly sang. Sam watched her become immersed in the song, as he became immersed in her. He loved this. He loved all of it. Because of his love for Sarah, he had the love of her friends and family.

He continued to smile as Sarah finished the song. He looked around at the group of people that he had grown so close to before turning back to her. "I love you, Sarah Reid."

She looked at him before leaning over to kiss him softly. "I love you, too, Sam Ramsay."

Jack and Karen said their goodbyes. Everyone else had consumed too much, so they all found their bedrooms for the night. Sarah took Sam to bed, before turning out the lights and locking up. When she returned to the bedroom, she found Sam still stretched out where she had left him.

She took off his shirt and his pants. He opened one eye. "Are you going to take advantage of me? You are a Mrs. Robinson, after all. I always thought Anne Bancroft was hot. Not as hot as you, but still..."

Sarah laughed before she undressed. As Sam crawled between the sheets, she crawled in next to him. She snuggled up next to him and laid her hand on the hard muscles of his stomach. She could feel his heart beat slowly under her head and felt his even breathing as she inhaled the smell of oak leaves and whiskey. Her soul was so full. She fell asleep to Sam's heartbeat.

~~~

The days were filled with more cider and apple butter making. They packed up boxes to mail to Danni, Alex, Beth, and Ollie. They walked the farm in the cool, crisp air. Sarah took pictures and made a lot of soup. They spent an afternoon at Liz' shop, and took her into the city for a late dinner. They spent an evening at Karen and Jacks where they enjoyed a good meal and played with the kids. They had had dinner with Bev, Ashley, and Julie. Everyone made their Thanksgiving plans and started their Christmas agendas.

They finalized their Thanksgiving plans with Trace and Charlie,

Gemma, and Harper. Sarah had been in constant contact with Danni and Beth. Sam always shook his head when she talked to his sister. It was like they had grown up together. She and Danni were so much alike.

~~~

The fireplace crackled with flames and the kitchen had been cleaned. Sam lay on one end of the couch with his laptop, and Sarah lay on the other end reading a book. Billie Holiday sang softly in the background. They would catch each other's eyes and smile. Sam brushed her feet with his own making Sarah sigh. He watched her intently as she laid her book aside.

"I agree." Sam shut the laptop.

Sarah raised her eyebrow and asked, "Agree? What do you agree with?"

"I haven't experienced winter at the farm yet, but so far fall is my favorite. It's crisp, and the colors are different. It even smells different. It smells sharper somehow." Sam moved his big body down the couch and crouched over her. As he brushed his fingers across her collar bone he saw the goose bumps appear.

"I love seeing you in your element. Here at your home, with your friends, doing the things that you love," Sam said softly as he started to slowly unbutton her shirt. When the last button was undone, he rained soft kisses over the swells of her breasts. He could feel her heart beat get faster as he slid a bra strap down her shoulder.

He stopped and crouched back on his knees as his eyes looked into hers. "I want you to stand up for me, sweet Sarah. Stand and please take your clothes off. Slowly."

Sarah stood as she continued to look at Sam. His eyes were almost black and filled with desire. The look that made her lose her mind. "Well, since you said please." She smiled as she stood and turned her back to him. Billie Holiday was replaced by Etta James. It was something slow and sultry. Sarah started slowly dancing. Sam leaned back against the couch with his arms behind his head. He stretched his long legs out and a small grin appeared on his face.

Sarah slowly pulled one arm out of the sleeve of the shirt, before she gave Sam a sexy look over her shoulder. He kept grinning calmly, but inside his pulse rate had skyrocketed and the crotch of his jeans had gotten quite snug. She slowly removed the other sleeve as she continued to dance toward him. She put the shirt on the arm of the couch, before she danced her way around the couch behind him.

Sam felt the heat from her body but she hadn't even touched him. She slowly dropped her leggings in his lap. Then her bra. Sam swallowed. "Holy fuck!" Next, she dangled her lacy little white panties off of her fingers in front of his face. Sam growled quietly as he grabbed them from her hand. She reached over him and slowly pulled his T-shirt over his head. His shirt joined hers on the couch.

The heat from her body was overwhelming and the touch of her breasts on the back of his shoulders was like a fiery brand. He groaned and leaned his head back to get a glimpse.

"Oh no! No peeking Sam Ramsay!" Sarah slowly danced her way around the side of the couch with her back to him. Her hips slowly gyrated as she lifted her arms over her head to the beat of the music.

"Fuck, Sarah! Do you know what that ass and those legs do to me? All I want right now is for those legs to be wrapped around my head." Sam rasped as he licked his lips. "Turn around and look at what you do to me." He had to get his fucking jeans off, before he busted the zipper. He was in pain, and all he wanted was to be inside of the vision that was still slowly dancing with her back to him.

Sarah slowly turned around with her hands clasped over her tits. Sam almost laughed, because there was no way in hell anyone's hands could cover them. As she slowly danced to him, she turned her back once again. Sam had no idea what she had in mind, but he knew it would be fucking brilliant.

"Unzip your jeans, Sam." Sarah's voice was husky and breathless, and he had no problem with obeying her command. She kept her back to him and continued to gyrate as he unzipped his fly. He gave a little exhale, as some of the pressure was off his cock. He swore there was a zipper imprint on it. He was hard as steel. He growled, "Enough of the teasing Sarah. I want to taste you."

Sarah continued to dance slowly with her back to him, before she backed up, straddled his legs and slowly bent over. All the way to the floor.

"Bloody fucking hell!" Sam's mouth dropped open at the sight that was in front of him. He and Sarah had been adventurous, but the sight of her long legs, her ass, and everything else in front of him for the taking was damn sexy. She reached for the legs of his jeans and began to pull them down his legs.

Sam reached for her ass as Sarah gave another jerk of his jeans. They came off his legs quicker than anticipated. Sam slid off the couch, and Sarah did a complete somersault before she stopped her forward momentum. She landed on her back, on the rug in front of the fireplace, with Sam's jeans wrapped around her head.

It was silent for a moment, before Sam exploded with laughter. "I knew you'd do something that would surprise me, but I didn't expect that."

Sarah's voice was muffled, as her mouth was covered with his denim jeans. "I did that on purpose. Stuck the landing."

Again, there was silence, and then they both laughed uncontrollably. Sam had tears and Sarah snorted as he crawled his way to her. He wrapped the denim around her eyes a little tighter. "Laughter with sex. That's the absolute best. And, yes, you're right where you need to be, but please don't get up. Just lay there, and let me take it from here."

November

Chapter 49:

Sam stood against his kitchen counter with a cup of coffee and smiled. He and Sarah had picked up her daughters and Trace at Heathrow a little earlier, and now he heard nothing but cursing, laughter, and footsteps. Sarah had gone up to assign bedrooms, while he got the whiskey and glasses out.

He felt Sarah's arms around his waist before she said, "What are you doing?"

"I loaded the dishwasher, made coffee, now I'm getting the glasses and bottle. I'm also grinning a lot."

"Why are you grinning, Sam?"

He kissed the corner of her mouth. "This house has never been loud. Well, except when we're alone."

Sarah laughed and smacked his arm. "You do plenty of moaning and groaning, too, Sam Ramsay. But, I'll admit it. You do delicious things to me. I can't help but scream. I'm loud and proud."

He kissed her again. "I love you loud, and I love the sound upstairs. It sounds like a home."

Sarah stepped back and took his hand. "Trace and the girls want you upstairs for a minute. They have something they want to give you."

As they started up the stairs, Sam stopped. "I love this, Sarah. Look at what you've given me." He shook his head and took her hand. She pulled him into the master suite where Trace and Charlie, Gemma, and Harper were sitting around the fireplace. Sarah had him sit on the couch. She couldn't help but chuckle, as she remembered that couch on top of them.

All of the girls and Trace grinned as they looked at Sam. "What are you guys up to?" Sam looked at each of them.

Trace reached over and picked up a wrapped box with a big multicolored bow. He handed it to Sam. "Open it."

"Okay! Okay!" He ripped the ribbon and the paper off and took the lid off the box. As he removed the tissue paper, he pulled out a folded green T-shirt. He looked up at all of them with an eyebrow raised.

"Oh, Sam. Unfold the damn thing." Sarah laughed at him.

He slowly unfolded the red shirt and held it up. In large, black, graphic letters it said: "World's Most Handsome Grandfather." He swallowed before looking at Sarah and Charlie. They both had begun to cry.

"Does this mean what I think it does?" he whispered.

Trace grinned from ear to ear. "Yep. There's another one in there."

The second T-shirt was yellow. It said: "Super Model Grandpa."

Sam laughed loudly before he rapidly walked to Sarah and Charlie. He kissed them both on the cheek before he whispered "Congratulations." He gave Trace a tight hug.

He whispered in Trace's ear. "Thank you for including me."

Trace stepped back and looked at him. "Fuck that shit, man. You're family."

"When's the due date? My schedule will be cleared for the month before and after." He felt like his chest was going to explode.

Charlie smiled and said, "May fifteenth. A spring baby. You do realize that you bypassed fatherhood and went straight to grandfather, don't you? Are you okay with that?"

"I love it." Sam stopped for a minute as he tried to get his emotions under control. "I don't ever want to presume anything, but I'm honored and humbled, and right at this moment, I'd really like to have known your dad."

Everyone was quiet as Sarah walked to him and kissed him gently. She hugged him tight."I love you so much."

~~~

It was a beautiful, surprisingly warm November day in the English countryside. The men obeyed Danni's orders and took their cocktails and cigars to the porch. Sam listened with one ear to his dad, Alex, and Trace as they talked football and politics. With the other ear he listened to the murmurs and laughter of the women in the kitchen. He could see Sarah through the window. She held Violet on one hip as she stirred something in a big bowl. She smiled as she talked with his mum. The smells of the season wafted out of the doorway, and Sam's stomach growled. He smiled to himself as he sipped his drink and watched his dad walk to him.

Ollie grabbed him in a tight hug and kissed his cheek. Sam

reciprocated with an even tighter hug.

Ollie whispered. "Thank you."

Sam stepped back as he looked at his dad with a questioning look.

Ollie looked through the kitchen window, before he turned and looked at Alex and Trace and Thomas. "For this. Your mom and I have wanted this for you for so long. You deserve your happiness son. We're so proud of you."

Sam swallowed. "I've always known that dad. Before Sarah, the one sure thing in my life was my knowing that you all loved me and were proud of me."

Ollie said gruffly. "But we've never been prouder of you than we are right now. You took a chance that a lot of people in your station wouldn't have. And look at what you've got. "

Sam looked through the window again. He grinned as he looked back at his dad. "She took a chance on me, too, dad. I got really, really lucky."

Ollie sipped his drink. "I don't believe in luck. I believe in hard work and destiny."

~~~

The children sat at the island with Beth and Ollie. The rest filled the seats around the farmhouse table. The home was filled with loud laughter, conversation, and the wonderful aromas of roasted turkey, apples and cinnamon. Beth got everyone's attention by tapping her knife against her glass.

"We don't celebrate Thanksgiving here, but I love the idea of taking one day out of the year to celebrate what we're thankful for. I think we need to do this every year. Occasionally, Yanks come up with a good idea."

Everyone laughed as she continued. "I'm going to start with what I'm thankful for, then Thomas and Violet want their turn." The two children wiggled on their seats with excitement.

Beth lifted her glass in a toast. Thomas and Violet lifted their cups of cider. "I am thankful for my family that has suddenly gotten significantly larger, because at the end of the day, that is the most important thing in life. Thank you all for making my life full."

Everyone toasted and waited for Violet.

The little girl was very serious. "I thank my mummy and my daddy. I thank my grandpop and nana and my Uncle Sam. And my Aunt Sarah." The little girl scooted off her bar stool before she ran to Sarah, climbed in her lap and hid her face in Sarah's neck. Sarah squeezed her tight before she looked up with tears in her eyes.

Ollie cleared his throat. "Your turn, Thomas."

Thomas was serious as well. "I like my mum and dad. I like my grandpop and nana, and Uncle Sam and Aunt Sarah. I like the lambs, and my tractors. I like that I tie my own shoes. Oh! And I like ice cream!"

"Me, too!" Violet yelled.

Ollie stood and took his time as he thought of his words. "I'm thankful for mornings. Every morning that I wake up is a day to be thankful for. It means I have another day to try to get it right. Another day to be a little kinder. Another day to be a little more helpful. Another day to love my wife. Another day to love Danni and Alex, Thomas and Violet. And now, another day to treasure Sam and Sarah and her amazing family. Another day to love my life."

"Oh, my." Sarah whispered.

Harper leaned back in her chair and patted her full stomach. She looked around at each person, before she stopped at Sam. "Thank you, Sam. I'm thankful for this right here."

Alex stood with his glass. "I am thankful for my hot, horny, foul mouthed wife. The mother of my children, the daughter of the best in-laws ever, and the sister to Sam. He's almost as good looking as I am." Everyone laughed before he continued. "I'm thankful for the addition of Sarah and her family. Especially Trace. We need all the testosterone we can get."

Trace laughed. "I am thankful to be among all of these fierce women. Especially my hot wife." He raised Charlie's hand and kissed her knuckles.

Charlie looked lovingly at her husband and then her mother. "I am thankful for life. Old and new."

Danni stood. "Now you all know that I'm not a sentimental... bitch - "

"Danni!" Beth looked at Thomas and Violet.

"Anyway. Of course, I'm thankful for my yummy husband, children, and mum and dad. But, today I'm thankful for my brother. He brought me the sister I always wanted, as well as her extended family. It's weird. It's like they've always been around, and they're so much like us, it's freaky. I love you, Sarah Reid!"

Sam smiled at Sarah. "I want to go last, so it's your turn."

Sarah looked down at Violet's small head that was still against her neck. The little girl's curls were soft against her skin, and the smell of sweaty little girl made her think of her own children when they were the same age. Time went by so fast, and sometimes she missed those times. She lightly brushed the little girl's dark hair.

"I have had a good life. A lot of the time, a great life. But there are times that I miss my mom and dad so much. Lately, I've been missing my husband for a plethora of reasons." Sarah felt Sam's hand squeeze the top of her knee. "I've been missing all three of them because I would like them to see what my life has become. Because of Sam, I have another family and a great sister."

Sam growled, "Danni is not great! She is evil."

Sarah arched an eyebrow at him. "That's one of the things I love about her. As I was saying, I have a wonderful son-in-law, and that bear of a man named Alex sitting over there just makes me a little breathless."

Alex puffed up his chest and slowly ran his hands down his hard, chiseled chest. Danni punched him and smirked at him.

"What am I? Chopped liver?" Ollie puffed out his chest and rubbed it. Beth snorted and Sarah laughed out loud. "I look at you and see Sam in twenty years, Ollie. You, sir, are filet mignon."

She continued. "I hope that David and my parents know what my life feels like now, because at this moment I have never been happier or more thankful. Thank you, Sam, for loving me."

Sam stood silent, much as his father had, as he tried to form the feelings in his heart into words. "I don't want to sound ungrateful, or to make light of my success. I've been lucky, but I've also worked hard. I have a wonderful family. But, there's been something missing from my life. That spark. That heart. Time had gotten away from me. I looked up and I was forty-years-old with nothing except a million pictures as my legacy."

Sarah looked up at the man she loved.

"I found my spark, my light, and my heart when this tall, leggy, beautiful woman opened her hotel room door for me wearing nothing but a T-shirt." He caught his breath.

Alex groaned, and muttered, "Shite! That must have been something!"

"Oh, my God, man! It was!" Sam groaned as he looked at Alex.

Harper raised an eyebrow at her mom. "You definitely have to tell us that story later."

"I asked her to marry me, and for some strange reason, she said yes. Sarah and I have been busy. Some time ago, with Danni's help, I set up trust funds for Thomas and Violet. My mum and dad, Danni and Alex allowed me to do a little something for them, too. Sarah and I have started on a gift for you, Gemma, and you, Harper. We've also done that for you and Trace, Charlie."

Sam stopped and looked at the floor for a minute. As he looked up, tears were in his eyes. He looked at Sarah. Her heart, as usual stopped for just a moment. "This has been the best year of my life. I am most thankful for Sarah Reid. For some reason, she loves me. We've started a scholarship fund in David Reid's name at the small school where Sarah lives."

Harper gasped, and he saw all three of Sarah's daughters with tears in their eyes. His family had nothing but big smiles. Danni looked strangely satisfied.

"We've also set up a trust fund for the peanut that will be arriving in May. Mum, dad. Danni and Alex? I'm going to be a grandpop!" Sam walked to Charlie and Trace and stood behind them with his arms across their shoulders.

As everyone congratulated the parents to be, Charlie stood to hug Sam hard. "I am so thankful that you and my mom took a chance on each other. Honestly though, we expected nothing from you, Sam. Loving our mother is more than enough."

Sam kissed her cheek. "I never do anything that I don't want to, sweet Charlie."

"Presents! Presents!" Thomas and Violet shouted as they carried wrapped gifts to Sarah.

"Why am I getting presents?"

Violet cocked her little hand on her hip. "Because it's your birthday, silly!"

"Open mine first!" Thomas clapped his hands.

Danni laughed as she continued to place wrapped packages in front of Sarah.

"How did you know it was my birthday?" Sarah asked, embarrassed, before she started ripping into the packages. Beth placed a tiara on her head that spelled out 'Birthday Girl', before she brought out a cake and cups of spiked coffee.

Sam stood and watched her laugh and make jokes with his family. He loved them so much for making this so special for her, and he loved her so much for accepting their love with grace and happiness.

Thomas and Violet had given her funny socks and leggings.

Gemma had filled a bag with all things sandalwood. Candles, bath salts, and essential oils.

Harper gifted her with a beautiful aqua sweater and matching leggings.

Trace and Charlie had filled a box with silver frames for future baby pictures.

She received a beautiful white cashmere sweater from Danni and Alex. Danni set another small bag in front of her, before she said slyly, "Open this after you get home. It's as much for Sam as it is for you."

Sarah's eyes got large as she glanced at Sam.

Beth placed a small package in front of her. As she ripped the paper, she saw an old, worn blue velvet box. She lifted it carefully out of the paper and opened it. Inside was a very old, very beautiful silver necklace. A large Lapis lazuli was surrounded by small blue diamonds. Sarah could tell that it was very old, very beautiful and much too generous. She looked at Beth. "I can't accept this. It's too much, Beth."

Beth patted her hand and smiled. "It was my grandmothers. I had two necklaces. I gave the rubies to Danni. I thought they would look nice with her dark hair. The blues will look beautiful with your eyes."

Sarah swallowed and looked at Sam. He smiled softly at her and shook his head yes. "Oh, Beth! I don't know what to say. Thank you seems so small."

Sarah stood and hugged the woman that had started to fill the hole in her heart where her mother had once been. She kissed her cheek and softly said in her ear. "Thank you for this day. Thank you for your gift, and thank you for your son."

Beth patted Sarah's cheek. "Oh, sweet girl, I thank you for making him so happy. Happy birthday."

"Hey Sam. Where's your gift?" Alex teased.

Sam grinned. "Her birthday's tomorrow. She'll get it then."

Sam, Sarah, Trace, and the girls all lounged in front of the fireplace back in London. They nursed their whiskey as Charlie had hot cider and talked about what a great day it had been. They decided they would go sightseeing without Sam or Sarah. Londoner's loved Sam, and Sarah wanted them to have the opportunity to have all day to enjoy London without the interruptions of autographs and pictures.

Sam and Sarah looked forward to cooking for everyone. She couldn't think of a better birthday gift than to cook for her family. They would eat then head out to a pub with karaoke. The families' flights left the next afternoon, so they could play a little.

~~~

Nat King Cole crooned softly in the background as Sam and Sarah danced around the kitchen. The aroma of Beef Wellington swirled around them, and Sarah laughed at Sam and tried to catch her breath. Sam looked at the smiling beauty of Sarah, and he stopped and grasped her tightly against his chest. He kissed her temple.

"You make me drunk, Sarah. You make my knees shake. When I look at you, I see the rest of my life," he whispered against her hair.

She felt his heart beat as she laid her palm against it. "Where would I be, if I hadn't met you? My life would be content, but my soul would still be searching for you Sam."

They slowly rocked in each other's arms as they continued their quiet murmurs and kisses, before they were interrupted by laughter as the front door opened.

The laughter continued as the enjoyment of communion over food and drink was had by their family. Sarah leaned against Sam as her daughters and Trace told them the details of their day, and the sights they had seen. They had seen Sam and Sarah's picture on the side of several busses, and had seen a cardboard Sam in a window of a suit shop. They had also found the pub with karaoke that they could walk to. No sober chauffer or taxi would be needed.

Sam and Trace cleaned up the kitchen as the women went to change. The men grinned at each other as the women's laughter could be heard from overhead.

The men had grabbed their coats that hung by the bottom of the stairs, and waited for the girls. As the four females walked down the stairs together the men's eyes got large and they swallowed. It was always breathtaking when the four women were together. Trace looked at Sam. "That's the woman that's having my baby!"

Sam couldn't keep his eyes off Sarah's long legs in her short skirt and those damn black boots. He was already half hard and he had to make a quick adjustment in his jeans. "Those three beauties came from the most beautiful woman in the world. The woman with the longest legs I've ever seen."

Trace clapped him on the back. "I have to agree with you, Sam. We are lucky sons of bitches. This is going to be a long night of blue balls. Let's go!"

Gemma and Harper had linked arms as they walked ahead. Sarah and Trace had their arms linked in the middle, as Sam and Charlie held hands in the rear. The cool evening smelled like the beginning of winter. It felt a little quieter, like the world was waiting for something. Sam noticed the lull in the air, and knew for certain what he waited for. He was full of anticipation. Anticipation for the next few hours, and anticipation for the rest of his life.

They had only walked a few blocks when Gemma turned to her family behind her. "This is it!"

There were several groups of people that stood outside on the sidewalk. They held their pint glasses as they smoked. A few people recognized Sam as they walked to the front door, and politely, if not boisterously, said hello. A few of the girls also recognized Sarah, which surprised her. No one asked for an autograph. They all just wanted to say hello. The Londoners loved their local boy, and felt like they all knew him.

Harper opened the pub door letting the sounds of conversation and music out onto the sidewalk. Sam and Sarah were the last to enter, as they continued to talk to a few of the kids outside. Sam took her arm and led her inside.

The first thing she noticed was the smell of cigar smoke and beer. The second thing she noticed was Luca. He stood in front of her with a twinkle in his eyes and his arms outstretched.

"Tia amo! Happy Birthday!"

"Luca!" Sarah screamed as she ran to the Italian. She was wrapped in his burly arms as she continued to kiss his cheeks and he kissed her hair.

Trace crossed his arms and looked at Sam. "I saw the way he looked at her when we were in New York. Do I need to take him out?"

Sam laughed. "Not yet, but if you hear about any plane tickets to South America, let me know."

They continued their evening with the things they did best. There was drinking, singing, and dancing with the rest of the pub patrons. Sam was positive Sarah had danced with every single person in the pub. He leaned back in his chair when Luca came and sat down next to him.

The Italian clapped him on the shoulder. "Sam, my man, I see that you still can't take your eyes off our Sarah."

Sam growled softly as he turned to look at Luca. "She is not our Sarah. She is mine."

Luca chuckled as he leaned back in his own chair and watched Sarah dance with two girls who had not relinquished their beers. "So, after nine months, the luster has not waned?"

Sam raised his eyebrows as he turned to look at Luca with a look of incredulity. "Uh, excuse me?" He waved at Sarah who now had several people lined up to teach them a line dance. She laughed as she suddenly looked across the room at Sam. "She is a diamond, Luca. Every facet is perfection."

"That she is, Sam. That she is. You two together make everyone around you a little dull. Everyone around you can see it, and feel it, and almost taste it. I've never seen anything like it, and I'm a little sad for the rest of us. But, I am so thankful that we all get to experience it."

Sam's eyes never wavered from the woman on the dance floor. "Sometimes I feel like I'm going to explode. It's almost too much. But I will never stop wanting her. I will never stop watching her. I will never stop craving her, or loving her."

~~~

The house was quiet as Sam and Sarah crawled between the sheets. Sarah reached for Sam as they slid under the covers. The Egyptian cotton was softness against the hardness of Sam's chest. "Thank you, Sam for the best birthday ever." Sarah lightly kissed his chest over his heart. "Luca was the best present ever. Though, I am a little surprised that he wasn't standing there naked with a big bow wrapped around his hairy chest."

Sam laughed as he reached into the drawer of the bedside table. He handed her a white envelope. "I know that you love the simple pleasures, Sarah. You don't need jewelry, or clothes, well, maybe shoes. I love that the things that are most precious to you were with you tonight. Your friends and family. But that also makes it difficult for gifts. Happy birthday, Amazing Sarah."

Sarah had sat up and slowly opened the envelope. As she read what Sam had written, a smile and a tear appeared. She looked at him intently before she wrapped her arms around his neck. "This is amazing, Sam. A scholarship? For an Arts degree? Oh, God, that means singers, or dancers -"

Sam kissed her gently on the corner of her mouth. "Or photography."

"For talented kids in a rural community, this could be their chance of a lifetime Sam. I love it. I also love the sound of "The Ramsay/Reid Scholarship of Excellence."

"I wanted my name on it, because your photography brought you to me. This scholarship could be something even greater than a degree. It could be two people's destiny." He took the papers from her hands, and set them aside, before wrapping her tightly against his chest. He stayed quiet as he listened to her fall asleep.

December

Chapter 50:

Winter had come to Missouri. When Sam and Sarah walked out of the airport, the cold wind made her clutch her coat more tightly across her chest. Sam wrapped an arm around her as he opened the door of the rental car.

Sarah grinned at Sam as he opened his door and hurriedly got in the car. He blew on his hands, and rubbed them together. "Damn! It gets cold here."

Sarah eyed the overcast sky. It looked and felt like snow. For some inexplicable reason, she relaxed as she laid her head against the seat. She knew it was her body getting ready to nest.

"I think we should stop at the supermarket and stock up on food. It looks like we might get snowed in, and we don't have anything at home. We don't want to starve and have to make the horrendous decision on which one of us will have to die to feed the other." She burst out with laughter as Sam shook his head.

"You are very strange. Is it strange that I suddenly feel more relaxed? My imagination can think of many, many things to keep us busy if we get snowed in." Sam wiggled his eyebrows.

"I can, too. We'll need to cut a tree and greenery. I need to decorate and put the lights on the house. Then I need to make the cookie dough and fudge and peanut brittle –" She stopped as she noticed his expression of disappointment. "Oh, for fuck's sake! I'll make sure I pleasure my husband-to-be in between all the chaos.

You won't be left out."

"It's nice to know you can fit me into your schedule." Sam said sarcastically.

Sarah leaned over as far as her seatbelt would allow, before she said low and raspy, "If you weren't driving on the wrong side of the road, and I wasn't in a hurry to get to the store and home before the weather gets nasty, I would unzip your pants and let my mouth show you just how well I can fit you in."

Sam closed his eyes briefly before he let out a long, deep audible breath. "That will be our new code word."

"Code word?"

He smiled broadly as he laid his hand on her upper thigh. He could feel the goose bumps under her leggings. "Yeah, when I get the urge to see you on your knees in front of me, I'll very politely ask you if you can fit me in your schedule."

They quickly swapped the rental car for Sarah's truck, filled the tank and loaded the back seat with groceries. Sarah found a radio station that played Christmas music. They were both comfortably quiet as they got closer to home. It had steadily gotten colder and heavier. The first snowflakes started as they pulled into Sarah's garage.

They unloaded the groceries first. As Sarah turned to walk to the back door, she saw it. She stopped and set her bags down and stood there in silence. The pool was completed. It had only been a hole in the ground when she left for London, but it was definitely not what she had ordered.

It stood beyond the gazebo. It was completely enclosed with

glass. Stepping stones worked their way from the back door to the glass enclosure. Rope lights lit the way and she could see enormous green plants inside it. The entire walkway was covered with an arbor and grapevines. Twinkling lights were wound among the gnarly, twisted vines.

She slowly turned and walked to Sam. "What did you do?"

Sam sat his own bags down before he pulled her to him. "Please don't be angry with me. My favorite thing in life is seeing you wet."

She looked up into his eyes that were filled with worry. "Sam, you always get me wet. I don't need a pool for that."

As he grinned he pulled her tighter. "And I get hard just thinking about that, but, I didn't change the pool size or anything, your plans were perfect, but I added a few things... Let's get the truck unloaded, and then maybe we can christen the pool? I've always wanted to float in the water and watch it snow."

As they walked out the back door they saw that the snow was thick. Sarah stopped to take a deep breath of the wet, heavy air. She loved the quietness of snowfall. "Listen. You can hear it as it touches the ground. There's nothing more beautiful."

Sam watched her as she closed her eyes, smiled, and inhaled the cold air. Snowflakes fell heavily in her hair and on her nose and eyelashes. "You are more beautiful, Sarah."

He followed her as she walked down the stepping stones. She stopped and almost did a double take. She looked at the snow-covered grass, and then back to the clean stones, before she did it again.

"They're heated. I remember that you told me that you loved snow, unless you had to clean off the truck. You won't have to clean off the stones."

"I can't believe you remembered that. It's seems so long ago, but, on the other hand, it seems like yesterday. I'll bet this tour is going to be full of surprises, isn't it?" She gripped her food tray more tightly as she continued to walk.

Sam watched her look at everything. It was dark, and the rope lighting outlined their path perfectly. As they entered the arbor, he saw her look up at the twinkle light. "Now you'll have lightning bugs year-round."

He shouldn't have been surprised that she knew that's what he wanted. She knew everything about him, sometimes before he even knew himself. As he did a million times a day, he said a silent thank you for his life with the woman in front of him.

As they approached the glass enclosure, Sam reached out with the arm that didn't carry their tray of food, and opened the French doors. He was strangely nervous. He had ambushed her pool plans, but he hoped that all his choices would have been the choices she would have made. Every choice he had made he had made with her in mind.

Sarah was silent as she walked in. The pool was exactly what she had wanted, but that was it. It was surrounded by stamped, stained concrete. It was warm inside the enclosure, and she realized that it had its own heating and air conditioning.

She set the food down on a beautiful glass topped table and

continued to slowly and silently walk around. The pool enclosure was huge. In one corner, a comfortable looking sectional set in front of a large screen television. The television set on an antique glass fronted store display cabinet. Photographs of her children, Sam, and Jack and the girls were interspersed with beautiful rocks and books. A small canvas was propped up in front of a stack. Sarah knew the author of the messy penmanship. It simply said: Together, we are epic.

Sarah was so overwhelmed that she couldn't breathe. Everywhere she looked was pure perfection. The perfection had been achieved because of Sam. It was as if he had looked into her brain and her heart, and then put those thoughts and feelings into the perfection that surrounded her. She burst into tears as she ran to him.

"The pool would have been wonderful, but, because of you, it is beyond wonderful. It's pure perfection, Sam, and all I've seen is this corner. This alone is perfect."

As he wrapped her in his arms, she whispered, "Thank you."

After she had cried herself into hiccups, Sam pointed out that the concrete was to prevent slipping and was also heated. He then pointed out the double hammock in another corner, and the dining table and chairs that she had set the food on had been placed closer to the pool. A hot tub sat in front of an electric fireplace in the other corner, with her Paris bistro table and chairs next to it. Old tin wash tubs were filled with towels and robes and pool toys. Everywhere were huge plants and trees. Sam showed her how the walls were actually doors that slid into each other. They could dine or swim alfresco anytime they wanted.

"The glass blocks that run the length on the other side house the pool equipment and a bedroom and bath, and the cabinet by the hammock has a complete small kitchen." Sam grinned at Sarah as she continued to hiccup. He reached for a remote. He pressed a button, and Annie Lennox started singing "I Put a Spell on You." "This remote does everything. The fireplace, the lights, the jets in the hot tub, the heating and air conditioning –"

Sarah stopped his talking with her mouth. She kissed him with intensity and desperation. Sam could feel her tremble as she continued to devour his mouth while she grabbed his shirt. He thought that the only polite thing to do was to reciprocate. He grabbed her neck and angled her head to kiss her even deeper. He heard her moan as he moved his mouth down her cheek onto her neck, before he whispered against her ear. "You make me want to rip your clothes off, carry you to that pool, lick you senseless, and impale you on my dick, Sarah."

She leaned back and looked up at his dark eyes. "Then do it Sam."

~~~

They lounged in the hot tub until their fingers and toes looked like raisins. They ate as they watched the snow continue to fall in fat, wet flakes. The pool house was dark except for the lights from the pool and hot tub, but the snow covered landscape lit up everything around them. Sam had never heard the farm so quiet. It was as if everything had gone to sleep except the snow. There were no stars, no moon, no calls from the owls, or whistles from the deer. It was as if they were the only two people left in a white landscape of infinity.

Sarah laid her head on Sam's shoulder and watched the snowy cotton balls fall from the night sky. "How did you do this? How did you get all of this done? We were in London, and I definitely would have remembered if you'd taken a quick trip to the states."

He slowly sipped his whiskey. "I knew what I wanted, and Liz was more than happy to assist me. She handled the contractors and took my money. I'm sure the rest of the girls were in on it, too. Everything was delivered, except for the mementos under the telly. Those were in a box in the garage. I just told her where I wanted everything." He looked around, before he kissed her quickly. "She exceeded my expectations."

He stood up and grabbed the white fluffy robes. "It's time we got out before we shrivel up. Let's go to bed."

Sarah stuck an arm through the sleeve that Sam held for her. "Can we sleep out here? I want to watch the snow for a little longer."

"I can never say no to you, Sarah. You know that."

Chapter 51:

The falling snow greeted them when they woke up in the pool house the next morning. The sky was still heavy and gray as they made their way down the warm, snow-free stepping stones.

Sarah turned to Sam with mischief in her eyes and snowflakes in her hair. "Looks like we won't be cutting a tree today. Too much snow. Whatever will we do with ourselves?"

Sam reached to brush the snow from her hair, and softly ran his finger down her cheek. The cold had made them pink. He continued to look at her face that was makeup free and her bed head hair. It looked as if she had stuck her fingers in an electrical socket. He thought she had never looked more beautiful. He knew that his hair looked the same, as she had tugged it all night. "I could really like this snow bound thing, because I can think of *lots* of things to keep us occupied."

"You are insatiable!" Sarah laughed as she continued to make her way to the back door.

~~~

They sat on the sofa with cups of spiked cocoa and looked at their days work. Sam had cut greenery from the cedars and hollies in the front yard. While the branches dripped with melting snow on the front porch, he had carried box after box marked Christmas from the garage. He carried and Sarah opened.

The mantle was laden with the green of the cedar, and the red of the holly berries, along with shiny silver ornaments and candles hidden among all the branches. A fire blazed in the fireplace and

Christmas music played softly in the background. The décor covered the doorways and the tops of the windows. Sarah had filled giant urns and Sam had placed them on each side of the front door with white lights. Bowls were placed everywhere with more greenery and cinnamon sticks. The whole house smelled like Christmas. They had done everything except the tree. The snow had finally stopped, so it would go up in a couple of days.

Sam sighed as he sipped the cup of the warm chocolately goodness. "Please tell me we're done."

Sarah laughed as she got up to tweak a stray sprig of cedar. "The heavy lifting is done, but I'm prone to keep finding things to add until Christmas Eve."

"I can't believe you've always done this by yourself. This was work, and I'm tired."

"I couldn't have gotten all of this done without you. It usually takes me about a week." Sarah walked to him before she bent for a soft, sweet kiss. "You make everything in my life easier."

They discussed the Christmas menu. Sarah had put the kibosh on fruit cake. "Oh, hell no! None of that candied crap that makes a piece of cake weigh fourteen pounds!"

Sam had never had more than a couple of days off for Christmas, so he had never participated in any of the pre-season festivities. He simply showed up at Alex and Danni's or his mum and dad's with gifts. Sarah planned to change that. She filled him in on the Christmas parade and festivities in town, cookie baking, candy making, shopping, and gift wrapping. She would make sure that he experienced it all.

"I usually have the girls over a lot for the cookies and candy making, but I want you to myself this year. It's your first Christmas at the farm and I don't want to share you."

Sam sat up suddenly with a wicked smile on his face. "Do you think we could have a sleepover? Just us, the girls, and Jack?"

Sarah raised an eyebrow. "I don't know what you have planned, but I'm sure everyone would be ready for a break from the madness. Why?"

Sam filled her in on what he had planned. After Sarah stopped laughing, she assured him they could take care of everything in town.

Their yawns became more frequent and their eyes had trouble staying open. A shower and bed was the perfect way to end their day.

~~~

After a quick lesson from Sarah, Sam proceeded to clean off the truck before he attacked the long driveway with the snow plow. He thought that he could actually be a farmhand, especially if he got to play with all of the fun toys, including Sarah.

They had put the tree up in front of the windows at the front of the house. Sam didn't think he had ever seen a more beautiful Christmas tree. It was probably because Sarah had a story for every single ornament and trinket she put on it. She had all of the macaroni and paper ornaments that her daughters had made in primary school, the ornaments she and David had bought the first year they were married, ornaments that had been given to her by neighbors and friends and family. The tree was a living scrapbook page.

Sam watched Sarah walk out of the bedroom with a box. She sat down on the floor with it and started to open it. "Sit with me Sam. I want *our* memories on the tree, too."

Sam sat and helped her remove the top layer of tissue paper. The box was full of individually wrapped items. "Go ahead. Open it." Sarah looked at him with a soft smile.

Sam gently unwrapped a miniature silver Eiffel Tower. He grinned as he stood and placed it on the tree. He then proceeded to unwrap each ornament as Sarah handed them to him. There was a miniature Big Ben and a set of tiny stilettos. There were miniature frames with tiny pictures of Sam's home in London, and another of them on the bridge in Venice. Sarah had even found a red dress and a tuxedo. He unwrapped an airplane and a gondola. A small framed picture of them on the back porch of the farmhouse and another of fireflies made Sam chuckle. Sarah gently gave him the last two as she kissed his cheek. He unwrapped a beautiful Murano glass heart that swirled with color. Sam noticed the small silver tag that magically floated on the inside of the heart. He looked closely and saw that a small metal tag was etched with: "I love you more than lightning bugs."

Before he could say anything, Sarah wrapped his hand around the last piece of tissue. He opened it to be met with a set of wedding rings tied together with a thin silver chain. He looked up quickly to find her smiling through tears. "I love you, Sam Ramsay."

"Ah, Sweet Sarah, I love you more than lightning bugs."

Sam leaned against the island and watched Sarah as she assembled the lasagna at the counter. She swayed her hips and hummed with the Christmas song that played. He walked quietly up behind her before he grabbed her hips and quickly turned her around. She squeaked before Sam grabbed her face and crushed his mouth against hers. She suddenly became pliant as she wrapped her arms around his waist and kissed him back just as vigorously. That turned into heat, want and need. As Sarah drew back to take a breath, Sam bit her earlobe. "What are your plans tonight? Am I included?"

Sarah panted. "I thought we'd watch "White Christmas" and "A Christmas Carol" while we ate, and then we can do whatever you want."

"Hmmmm," Sam growled as he continued to bite her ear. "Anything?"

Sarah gently bit the top of his shoulder. "Anything, unless it involves depravity with farm animals. I do have my limits."

"No animals, except me. But there may be some depravity."

~~~

A fire flickered on the back porch. It covered everything in glowing glimpses of orange and gold. The smell of the burning embers smelled like winter. The warmth of the fire with the warmth of the wine they had with dinner added to the warmth of their bodies that were entangled with each other on the couch. The empty plates sat on the floor, and the first movie of the evening, had been paused. The couple was all quiet caresses, and light kisses.

"One more week until Christmas, Amazing Sarah. Are you ready for the army of people?"

Sarah kissed Sam's strong jaw. "I love a house full of people. I think all of the beds and transportation is taken care of. I'm ready, how about you?"

Sam nipped her earlobe. "I can hardly wait. It's going to be the best Christmas ever."

"Bev and Liz' children are going to the in-laws this year, so I'm happy they'll be able to join us. It wouldn't be the same without them, especially Liz."

Sam leaned into Sarah with a scorching kiss. "Do you trust me, Sarah?"

She stared deep into Sam's eyes. "I trust you with my life."

"Then get up and come with me." He stood and held his hand out for her. "Tonight is not gonna be soft or sweet."

He led her through the house to the bedroom. Sam growled as he let go of her hand. "Stay right there. Don't move."

Sarah's eyes got big as she watched him light the candles around the room. The air was suddenly full of the smell of sandalwood. She had never experienced the bossy Sam, but she kind of liked it. He pushed the playlist and "Wicked Game" sounded from the blue tooth speaker.

He strode back to her and turned her back to the edge of the bed. He was very quiet, but very firm, as he told her, "Take your clothes off, Sarah. Slowly." He stepped back and crossed his arms across his chest.

Sarah swallowed as she watched the massive shoulder muscles that moved like liquid metal under his T-shirt. She was silent as she began to remove her leggings. She moved softly to the beat of the song. She stood before Sam with her arms at her sides. She looked at him with no awkwardness as she waited to see what he wanted from her.

Without taking his eyes off of her, Sam quietly but firmly ordered her to lay down on the bed. She lay back with her head on the pillow. The sheets were cool and soft against her hot body. She was ready to explode with just his words. She clenched her legs together to help the ache that had already started between them.

Sam still stood with his arms crossed, but his eyes were hooded and dark with desire. Sarah was a feast for his eyes as she laid on the bed looking up at him with trust in her eyes. He wanted to devour the buffet of Sarah. "No, sweet girl. Open those legs. No cheating."

Sarah unclenched her legs and continued to watch and wait. Sam had thought about this moment since Thanksgiving, and he didn't want to rush it. He knew this could be something really special for the both of them and prove how much they trusted each other. He closed his eyes and took a deep, calming breath, before he adjusted the painful tightness in his jeans.

"Touch yourself, Sarah. Touch yourself the way you want me to touch you. Don't close your eyes. I want your eyes on me. Don't stop until I tell you to."

Sarah slowly lost herself in the rhythm of the music. As "Need You Tonight" wound its melody through the bedroom she started to softly caress her arms and shoulders before moving her hands softly across her breasts. Sarah gasped a little as she stared at Sam and saw the intensity in his eyes. She continued to softly brush her nipples as she watched Sam watch her hands. There was power in knowing she could make him want her this bad. No shame. No embarrassment, just the desire to please him.

She moved her hands slowly to her stomach as she watched Sam's tongue lick his bottom lip. Sarah's eyes closed for a moment before she licked her own lips and moaned quietly. She brushed her fingers softly across her waxed smoothness and let out another little moan. She closed her eyes as her back arched, but opened them quickly to watch Sam. He looked almost stern. As she circled her fingers across the ache that was almost painful, she watched Sam walk slowly to the bedside table.

He never took his eyes off hers as he opened the drawer. "Don't stop."

Sarah was too far gone to even think of stopping. As her fingers moved faster, her other hand reached for her breast and her eyes reached for Sam's eyes. He stood above her and watched every stroke, every movement and heard every moan and sigh from her. His eyes grew larger and darker as Sarah came undone and moaned his name.

The Black Keys "Howlin' For You" beat throughout the air. Sam's breath was ragged as he leaned over Sarah and gave her a gentle kiss before he reached for his T-shirt. He pulled it over his head before he let it drop to the floor. Sarah reached for the zipper on his jeans but he stepped back.

"Oh, no, we're not done yet, silly girl." He unzipped his own pants and stepped out of them.

Sarah should have been a little disappointed with the fact that Sam wouldn't be helping to put out the fire that still raged inside her, but as always, when she looked at him standing like a Greek God she was filled with a deep want.

He saw her bite her bottom lip as she stared at his stomach. He grinned. "Do you remember this Sarah? Did you think I'd forgotten?" He leaned over and placed Danni's gift between her breasts.

Sarah reached for the birthday vibrator that Danni had slipped to her at the Thanksgiving dinner.

"Holy hell! It's pink! Danni got me a fucking pink vibrator." Sarah laughed loudly before turning it on. Her eyes got big, again, as she realized how many setting were on it. "This might kill me."

Sam chuckled. "I won't let that happen. I want you to do it again, Sarah. I want to see your hands and fingers, and that ugly pink vibrator on your body. Do it now."

"Yes sir," she whispered.

She pushed her breasts together and watched Sam's eyes get as large as hers were a moment ago. She continued to tease him as she kneaded them together before she released them to touch her stomach. Sarah watched Sam as he watched her. She used her fingers to return to the place that again ached for him. She reached for the pink monstrosity and turned it on. As she touched herself she heard John Hiatt's "Have A Little Faith in Me." She whipped her head to the side to look at Sam.

Sam stood at the edge of the bed. He looked down at her as he pleasured himself along with her. His muscles were rigid and his thighs quivered. Sarah couldn't take her eyes off the man who had made himself as vulnerable as he had made her. Sarah wanted to wait for Sam's release but as she watched Sam's large hand and slender fingers, she felt the explosion start at the base of her spine and she started to moan. It was impossible for her to stay still. She bucked her hips. "I can't wait, Sam. Watching you is – oh!"

Tunnel vision was all Sam had. He started to see white explosions. He felt the weight as it started in his hips. He couldn't wait any longer. He quickly hovered over Sarah in the bed and in one, hard thrust, he was home. "Reign O'er Me" crashed over them as they crashed into each other.

~~~

They were both dead weight as they looked at the bedroom ceiling and listened to "Riviera Paradise." Sarah touched Sam's arm and whispered, "The last time I heard this was in Paris. Do you remember?"

He kissed her cheek. "Why do you think I put it on the playlist?"

"Wow, Sam. Just wow. I've never done that before. You were magnificent. Can we do that again sometime?"

Sam softly chuckled. "I've never done that either." He leaned up on his elbow and gazed at her beautiful face. "I wish that you could feel what I feel when I touch you. I wish that you could taste what I taste when I kiss you. I wish you could feel what I feel when I hold you. I wish that you could see what I see when I look at you. Then you would know how much I love you."

"Oh, Sam." Sarah softly brushed his cheek. "I don't know where I stop and you begin anymore. I'm not whole without you."

Sam embraced her tightly. "Together, we are so much that it scares the holy hell out of me Sarah. But being without you scares me even more."

She whispered. "I know. It's almost painful, but, it's beautiful pain. I'm more than willing to live with that. Without the pain of us, we wouldn't have the pleasure."

Chapter 52:

The sun was bright in the sky, and the reflection off the snow made sunglasses necessary when they left for town. The sun shone but it was still bitter cold. They sang along to Christmas carols as the truck plowed its way through the slushy road.

Sarah maneuvered her way to a parking spot behind Liz' store. It always paid to know the owner. They shook the snow off their boots as they entered the shop. Liz always provided the public hot chocolate and sugar cookies on parade day. She greeted Sam and Sarah with hugs and cups of rich, chocolaty hotness.

"Bloody hell, it's cold out there!" Sam removed his gloves and blew on his hands before he reached for his hug and cup.

Liz laughed as she took their coats to her office. "I'm sure it gets cold in London, Sam. Or are you just spoiled being in the Mediterranean and other sunny locals all the time?"

Sam closed his eyes as he sipped his drink. "Oh, it gets cold, but not this cold. And you may have a point. I don't spend a lot of time in cold locales, so I might have lost my edge. I'll take the cold, if it comes with all this beautiful snow. I love it. I can't wait to get Sarah on the slopes."

"Just what slopes do you have in mind?" Sarah grinned as she blew on her cup.

Sam started to wander around the shop. He picked up a gardening book, before he turned to look at Sarah. 'We can go to any slope you want. I've skied in Austria, Germany, northern Italy, Switzerland. I've heard a lot about Colorado. Maybe we could go next month. I could rent a cabin for as long as you like."

Sarah chuckled as she shook her head. "I always forget that your life is so different than mine. Colorado is beautiful. I think you'd love it. It doesn't matter what slope, Sam. As long as it's with you, I'm good."

She walked over to look at the book that he still held in his hand. "I think your mom would love that. Do you want to shop here for a bit? The parade starts in an hour. I found some stuff here a while back that I think Danni would like."

It didn't take long to find all the stocking stuffers for Sam's family, and a few bigger items for his mom and sister. They left their bags in the office, as they bundled up again to find a spot on the sidewalk. The high school band led the parade down the main street. The majorette and flag girls wore gloves. Sam felt bad for the horn players, whose hands had to play their instruments. A tractor with a trailer behind it came next. It was full of the high schools Winter Games court. The girls pretty dresses were hidden by bulky coats and scarves, but all the kids waved and grinned. Their cheeks were red and their breath came out in little white bursts of air.

A local riding club was next. The two front riders held a banner between them with the name of their club emblazed in silk letters. The horses were beautiful as they snorted hot bursts from their noses. Their hooves struck the pavement with sharp staccato strikes. A couple of the riders waved at Sarah as they saw her in the crowd. She grinned as she waved back.

She wasconstantly interrupted by people who stopped and said hello to her, or gave her a hug. She introduced Sam to all of them as her fiancé, which made his heart squeeze with pride. Everyone knew her, and, as usual, everyone loved her. He watched her as she bent down to talk to a little boy with ear muffs on. Her coat was large and bulky, and she had two scarves wrapped around her neck. She wore a stocking cap on her head that looked like a bear. It even had ears. He couldn't keep the grin off his face. He thought she was the cutest thing in town.

"She's just too fucking cute, isn't she?" Liz grinned at him. She noticed that nothing had changed with him. He couldn't keep his eyes off Sarah. "The sweetest thing about her is that she doesn't even realize it. If I didn't love her so much, I'd hate her."

Sam laughed loudly as he wrapped Liz in a big hug. "She's cute, beautiful, sexy, kind, talented, and fucking funny all rolled up into one woman. She has a fucking bear on her head! I've never known anyone like her. How could I not stare at her? Could you keep hugging me? I need the warmth!"

Sam and Liz continued to laugh as the end of the parade appeared. Santa and a horde of elves strode up the street throwing candy. The sound of the children's laughter and shrieks as they reached for the candy made him smile at their antics. He noticed Sarah as she did her own staring. Her arms were wrapped across her chest as she beamed at him. It always made him lose his breath.

She walked to him and wrapped her arms around him. "Thank you."

As Sam hugged her tightly, he knew exactly what she meant. "Thank you, too, Amazing Sarah. Thank you, too."

Sam and Sarah worked in the kitchen. "Cookie dough? Check. Icing? Check. Hot cider? Check. Veggies chopped? Check. Cheese sliced? Check. Red velvet cake? Check, it's in the oven." Sarah stood back to go over the checklist in her head one more time.

Sam grinned before continuing to stir the spaghetti sauce he had made. "You could slice the mushrooms for the sauce."

Sarah kissed him quickly before she grabbed a knife and the mushrooms. They worked together quietly. Sarah grated fresh asiago while Sam minced the garlic bulbs for the sauce and bread. They mixed the salad, covered it and put it in the fridge. Sarah hummed as she made her famous dressing. As she wiped off the counter she felt Sam's arms reach around her waist before he nuzzled her neck.

Sarah sighed, "We're good together."

"I can show you just how good we are." Sam growled before putting his hands on the waistband of Sarah's leggings. She felt the heat of his hands on the skin of her stomach. She shuddered and closed her eyes. Sam kissed the back of her neck as he pulled her leggings down. She stepped out of them before she pulled her T-shirt off and unhooked her bra.

Sam turned around and walked her back to the island. As his mouth trailed fiery kisses down her neck, Sarah unzipped his jeans and pushed them down with her feet. He, too, stepped out of them before he took off his shirt.

He picked her up and set her down on the edge of the island. He lifted her legs and placed them over his shoulders. As Sarah felt the first soft pass of his tongue, she moaned, "Oh, God! We are *so* good together. Be good some more."

~~~

Sarah instructed everyone that the sleep over would be a pajama party. She also reminded the girls that Jack and Sam would be in attendance, so they needed to dress accordingly.

Ashley was the first one to arrive. Sam enjoyed the fact that she was in blue thermals. Long johns seemed to suit her.

Jack and Karen arrived in matching pajama sets. Gray with black trim.

Bev was once again in silk pajamas with matching mules, and Liz wore a flannel gown.

Julie was the last to arrive. Sarah was almost nervous as Julie unbuttoned her coat. Liz caught her eye, and Sarah knew that she felt the same. Ashley looked at Julie with an arched eyebrow. It seemed as if everyone held their breath.

As Julie noticed them, she stopped for a moment and looked at all of them. "What?"

As she took off her coat, they were all met with the sight of Julie in a union suit. It was a pink union suit with brown sloths all over it.

Liz snorted, as the entire room exhaled in thankfulness and nervous laughter. "Hey! They're comfortable!" Julie hugged Sarah before she looked at the rest. "I like sloths, okay?"

Sarah shook her head as she looked at Sam. She was in blue leggings with snowflakes, and a white T-shirt. As Sam never slept in anything, he had purchased soft gray lounge pants. Sarah had insisted he wear a T-shirt.

They made their way to the kitchen where the smell of tomatoes and garlic filled the air. Sam and Sarah had already covered the top of the island with cheese, olives, salami and crackers. As Sam sat plates next to the appetizers, he smirked and remembered what had been on the island a few hours earlier. He felt Sarah look at him and as he caught her eye, he saw her grin, too. It took him immediately back to his kitchen table and the breakfast they had served Danni the morning after the gala. He had to close his eyes for a moment as the vision of Sarah in that red dress caused his pulse to race.

As the group chattered and ate, Sarah cleared the empty plates and glasses. She floured the island top, and retrieved the cookie dough from the refrigerator. She set out the cookie cutters and rolling pins as Sam got the cocktail glasses and whiskey.

"First cookies, then Sam's spaghetti, then we eat cake!" Sarah announced.

Sam put the water on for the pasta as everyone else grabbed a rolling pin. Laughter and mess ensued as the cookies were cut and put in the oven. The pasta and garlic bread finished cooking just as the cookies were put on the cooling rack. More whiskey was poured as plates were filled. The house was filled with the smell of garlic and sugar and the sounds of laughter.

The dishwasher was filled and the island cleaned as Sarah set the pans of cookies and colored icing in front of everyone. They all tried to be serious about decorating the cookies, but as more whiskey was poured more icing ended up on noses and cheeks. When the men started painting boobs on the cookies, Sarah knew that the cookie experience was complete. She laughed as she removed the pans of pornography and replaced them with the red velvet cake.

Liz moaned as she licked cream cheese frosting off her fork. "No one makes red velvet cake like you, Sarah."

Ashley tilted her head back and closed her eyes as she took her last bite. "Promise me you'll make one of these for Christmas. It's such a festive looking cake. It feels like Santa left a gift on my tongue."

"Oooh! That's just gross, Ashley." Julie's voice was muffled with cake. "Santa only comes once a year, and that's down the chimney."

The girls cleaned the remaining cake and chatted about Christmas. Sam had taken Jack to the bedroom to show him something he had noticed with one of the shower heads. Bev picked up the whiskey and a tray of glasses. Sarah followed her into the living room with a coffee carafe and Bailey's. The girls had gotten comfortable, and Sarah added more logs to the fire.

As she got comfortable on the floor she saw Jack emerge from the bedroom. She covered her mouth to try and muffle her laughter but Karen noticed her and turned around to look. "Holy fuck, Jack! What the hell did you do?"

Jack stood in a sheer silk pink robe. He wore tight black bike shorts underneath and fuzzy pink socks. He sucked his cheeks in and strutted in front of the women.

Sarah grinned at them. "Remember when we had our last pajama party? You all modeled for Sam? He thought it was the men's turn."

Jack slowly turned his back before he untied the belt from around his waist. He caught the robe as it fell, and turned his head and looked at them over his shoulder.

"Oh fuck!" Bev snorted before she collapsed against the couch in laughter.

Jack turned around and shimmied the robe off. He slung it over one shoulder and cocked his hip.

"Fucking hell, Jack! You're cut! You could bounce a quarter off that ass." Ashley stared at Jack's abs that were on proud display.

Julie gawked at him. "Who knew that hotness lived under all of those polo shirts? Holy shit Karen! You get to tap that anytime you want? I'm bitter."

"I'm proud of you, baby. You didn't break character once." Karen walked to her husband and rubbed his belly before she gave him a long kiss. She turned and looked at Julie, who was completely at a loss for words. "Yes. I tap that anytime I want."

Liz clapped her hands. "Okay! It's Sam's turn! I cannot wait! This is going to be so good." They all turned in expectation and waited for Sam's entrance.

Sam walked out and stood in all of his six-foot-four-inch glory. All of his height was covered in a red satin floor length robe. White fur covered the collar and the hem. A peek of tanned chest peeked out from the front, and his long feet were bare. Sarah gulped. Even his fucking feet were beautiful. Who knew that foot porn was a thing?

Sam put his hands in the pockets of the robe and strutted like the model he was. He strutted past Jack and the girls, before he turned around and strutted back to the bedroom doorway. He turned and stared at Sarah over his shoulder. She snorted a little as she waited for the surprise.

Sam slowly untied the belt. His massive shoulders appeared as he continued to stare at Sarah.

"Fuck," whispered Ashley. She had definitely said that out loud.

Liz looked at Sarah with panic in her eyes. "I'm so sorry, but I don't think I can stand it! My panties just burned up and all I've seen are his shoulders. God help my sinner soul, but right now I'm breaking one of the Ten Commandments. Thou shalt not fucking covet. Because God forgive me, I covet some of that."

Sarah was in hysterics. "I might need to get the fire extinguisher, because I think even Jack's bike shorts have melted!"

Sam turned to look at all of them as he continued to let the robe slide slowly down his arms. Sarah licked her lips as she saw his pecs clench. His biceps jumped as the robe made its gradual descent down his body. The room was deadly quiet.

The further the robe slid, the more of Sam's skin was exposed. You could see the sharp outline of his obliques. Julie whimpered a little. There was no sign of any other clothing under the robe.

Bev turned to Sarah and hoarsely muttered, "Please tell me there's something else under that robe! If Sam shows us his package I might be arrested for assault when I jump him. I would hate for our friendship to end like that."

Sarah cried with laughter. "Oh, he's gonna show you his package!"

Sam again turned his back to them to show them more. The musculature of his back was beauty personified. The next movement of the robe showed the beginning of the roundness of his ass. As the robe fell to the floor, they saw that Sam's ass was barely covered with white fur. He shook it a little, and all the women whimpered.

Sam slowly turned to face them, and all they could see was his perfect body and his crotch that was covered with his hands. Small tufts of white fur peeked out from the sides. Sam grinned that sexy grin and Sarah heard Liz hiss.

Sam suddenly lifted his arms straight out and did a little bump and grind. All of them were met with the face of Rudolph. His red nose blinked and Sam roared with laughter.

"Can I squeeze his nose? Would that be okay, Sarah?" Julie was mesmerized by the flashing of Rudolph's nose.

Before Sarah could answer, Sam said sternly. "This is for your viewing pleasure. No touching. The only person who gets to squeeze Rudolph's nose is Sarah. And my physician."

Sarah walked to Sam. She hugged him and gave Rudolph's nose a little squeeze. "You guys go put your pajamas back on, and we'll go see the pool house."

Sam chuckled into Sarah's ear. "That was fun, Sarah. I know Julie's your friend, but she scares me a little."

Sarah laughed before she stopped suddenly. "I know. She scares us, too, sometimes."

Chapter 53:

"Are you sure you don't want a caterer? I'm sure I could find someone in the city to do it on short notice, especially if I paid them enough." Sam and Sarah still lounged in bed. The sun had risen a few hours before, but they had chopped morning wood and hadn't wanted to leave the warmth of the bed or each other.

Sarah rubbed her cheek against Sam's chest. "You're too good to me. I'm sure you could find someone to cater, but, I do this every Christmas Sam. Gemma and Harper will be here in three days, and they always help. Trace and Charlie are usually here, too, but they're staying in St. Louis to drive everyone. That was a brilliant idea, by the way."

"I do have brilliant ideas sometimes. Trace offered to drive, so it was just a matter of renting the van. I figured that we could use it to shuttle everyone around, too." He absently rubbed her hip. "Where's everyone staying? You've told me, but I don't remember."

"I thought your mom and dad could have the master suite. Trace and Charlie are upstairs, along with Harper and Gemma, who will share a room. Luca can stay up there, too. Mark and Marta can have the other room."

"Who's going in the pool house?" Sam grinned at her.

"Us, of course. I thought Danni and Alex and the kids could stay downstairs. We have the king bed down there and a bathroom. I've got a couple of roll away beds in the garage, so all we have to do is move your exercise equipment against the wall. Anyone else that drinks too much can have the craft room or the floor. I already got the extra pillows and blankets out."

Sam kissed Sarah's forehead. "You always have everything organized. I never doubt you for one minute. Thanks for putting my mum and dad in here. His knees are a little arthritic, so he won't have to maneuver the stairs."

Sarah sighed as she snuggled closer to Sam's warmth. "It's going to be so great having a house full of people for Christmas. Especially the kids. Oh! The kids are going to be so much fun!. Christmas is always better with children."

Sam gripped Sarah's cheeks before he kissed her gently. "Just think. Next Christmas there will be a little Trace or Charlotte crawling around the house."

The smile lit up her face and lit up his heart.

~~~

freezers in the house were full. Clean sheets were on all the beds and Thomas and Violet's had been made up with Disney characters. Even the pool house had been filled with food and drink. Sam and Sarah thought it would serve quite nicely for quiet conversation and overflow. Sarah had Sam cut more greenery and holly berries to decorate it.

The heaters had been set up on the dock and the gazebo and Sarah had decorated them as well. There was finally nothing left for them to do but relax and wait for the beautiful chaos. Sam loved to watch Sarah in her element. She loved to share her heart and her home with people. It showed in everything she did. No detail was forgotten. She had even placed special creams for arthritis on the bedside table for Sam's dad. She had placed a bowl of chocolates and cider for Trace and Charlie, along with some foot cream in their room. She did it all with no stress or anxiety. She amazed him.

Sarah had gone upstairs to finish some last- minute gifts while Sam updated his Facebook page and answered emails. He and Luca had texted for an hour before Sam finally told him that he would see him in two days so their conversation could continue then. The sun had set and it smelled and felt like snow. Sam grinned as he got up and walked to the foot of the stairs.

"Sarah?" he called up the stairs.

"Sam?" Sarah replied as she walked out onto the landing.

Sam leaned against the newel post and looked up at the woman who had stolen his heart. He smiled his lethal smile. "Why don't you slide on down this banister and warm up my dinner?"

She was silent for a second until she realized what he had asked. She grinned back. "I'm sorry, sir, but the greenery draping the banister could be painful on my lady bits."

Sarah looked down at him and her heart, as usual, stopped for just a minute. His white T-shirt hugged every muscle and his jeans hung low on his hips. His feet were bare and his smile made her clench her thighs together.

Sam looked up at the longest damn legs he had ever seen clad in black leggings. Sarah wore a beautiful aqua sweater that matched her eyes and her feet were bare. He knew that she would forever make him weak in the knees and his heart pound.

He was instantly aware when the mood changed. He could feel it on his skin, the air was suddenly charged. He followed Sarah's movements as she slowly pulled her sweater over her head. She took a few steps down the stairs before she stopped to slide her leggings down one leg then the other. She stood and looked fixedly into his eyes that had turned dark with want. She stepped down a few more stairs before she stopped and unclasped her bra and pulled her panties off. As she reached the bottom of the stairs she whispered, "Do you want to eat now or later?"

Sam captured her lips with a hunger that was almost painful. He laid her down on the stairs as he clutched her hips almost punishingly. He bit her bottom lip and growled in her ear. "I want both. I want to eat now and later."

~~~

Sarah stood at the Aga stirring a pot of homemade chicken noodle soup. Bread was in the oven and salad in the fridge. Sam sat on the island swinging his long legs as he watched her.

"What time will they get here?" he asked anxiously.

Sarah sat the spoon on the counter as she laughed. "They should be here anytime. Are you nervous or something?"

"I'm just excited to get this show on the road. Thanksgiving was so much fun I can't wait for everyone to be together again."

She walked between his legs and placed her hands on top of his thighs. "It was fun, wasn't it? I've realized that I've known you for more than just my lifetime. I've known you were out there for eons, but I think I was waiting for your family, too." She kissed him softly. "I love your mom and dad, and Danni... well, Danni is the sister I always wanted. Alex and the kids are yummy. Our families are so much alike it's weird."

Sam set his head on top of Sarah's and wrapped his arms around her. "I would say it's almost Freudian, or a Shakespearean tragedy, but I know we've both been searching for each other over many lifetimes."

They both raised their heads at the sound of a car on the gravel. Sarah beamed, kissed him quickly, and walked rapidly to the front door. Sam followed quickly behind her.

He leaned against the door and watched Sarah become engulfed in her daughter's arms. He loved their relationship. He thought it was probably a rare thing that a good parent could turn into a best friend, but that's what Sarah and her daughters were. They were devoted to her.

He watched as Gemma and Harper rushed up the steps yelling his name. "Sam! Sam! Merry Christmas you big, handsome hunk of a man!" He, too, was surrounded by Sarah's beautiful smiling daughters.

Gemma had immediately gone into organizational mode. She was so much like her mother that it made Sam chuckle. She had already gone over the contents of the refrigerators and freezers and figured out when to start thawing and cooking. When she found a bowl of sugar cookie dough in the fridge, she squealed with delight. "Yes! I was hoping we could decorate cookies tonight!"

Sarah glared at Sam. "Well, the cookies would have been done, if the men hadn't started to decorate them with pornography."

Harper grinned at Sam. "I'm not even going to ask, but it sounds like you had a good time."

He chuckled. "You have no idea."

The girls didn't know about the pool, so Sam took Gemma's arm, and Sarah took Harper's. As they stepped out of the back door, both girls noticed the arbor. They looked at each other as they walked underneath it. As they passed through, the girls got their first glimpse of the pool house.

Harper looked at her mother. "This isn't just a pool, is it?"

Sarah shook her head and glanced back at Sam. "No, it isn't. This is all Sam."

~~~

Sam and Gemma played pool while Sarah and Harper cut out the cookies. Their quiet laughter caught Sam's attention.

"You still can't keep your eyes off her, can you?" Gemma asked as she sank a blue ball. "That's good. She can't keep her eyes off you either."

Sam still watched the two women in the kitchen. "Look at her."

Gemma walked over and wrapped her arm around his waist. "You two set a very high bar for the rest of us."

Sam kissed her forehead. "Be patient and leave yourself open to ideas that you never knew you had. Everyone has someone out there made just for them. If you're lucky like Sarah and me, you'll find it sweet girl."

Gemma sighed. "Luck, uh?"

"Yes. And destiny."

~~~

Sam and Sarah sat in the kitchen drinking their second cup of coffee. Sarah giggled as Sam whispered dirty things in her ear. Harper slowly walked in yawning and rubbing the sleep from her eyes. She wore Christmas unicorn pajamas. Sarah was immediately taken back to Harper as a five-year-old. It seemed like yesterday. "Morning, you two. Coffee?" Harper's voice was still raspy with sleep.

Sam grinned and pointed at the coffee maker. Harper shuffled her way to the counter and poured a cup before she shuffled her way to a bar stool. Sam and Sarah grinned at each. "Harper is not a morning person." Sarah sipped her coffee.

"Good morning y'all!" Gemma walked in with wet hair. She was already dressed in jeans and a sweater. "Hell yeah! Coffee! Are those biscuits I smell?"

Sarah arched an eyebrow at Sam. "Gemma on the other hand, is up all the time."

~~~

Gemma had talked Sarah into serving buffet style. "It's fucking cold outside, mom! You are not going to make Sam bring in all those tables from the garage! Everyone eats all over the house anyway. Leave everything where it's at, and let's just make the farmhouse table the buffet.

You've got enough linens to make it pretty, and we can put the deserts on the island. It means less work, more conversation, and easier cleanup."

The women spent the afternoon decorating the table and the island and Sam pulled down all the Christmas china and serving pieces. He never knew how much work was involved in Christmas Day. It made him appreciate all the work his mum and Danni went to.

They all ate sandwiches around the fireplace later that evening. Sam told them how much he appreciated all the hard work that women went to for Christmas. They all discussed having Christmas in London next year. Sarah thought it was a wonderful idea. "This trip will be tiring for your parents, and Danni and Alex, trying to keep those two kids corralled. Going there would be easier on them."

Sam reminded her that Trace and Charlie might disagree, as next Christmas there would be a new face in the family. He suggested that they put plans on hold. "Let's enjoy this Christmas before we start worrying about the next one."

There was light snow as they all made their way to the pool house. The lights were twinkling in the arbor and the ground was crunchy under their feet. It smelled clean and fresh. Gemma and Harper were fish in the water just like their mom. Sam realized that Harper was probably a good mix of her mother and her father, while Gemma was a clone of her mom. Charlie was Sarah, but quieter. They all had Sarah's heart, and they all had Sarah's mouth. The three of them had Sarah's eyes and her beauty. As Sam watched them play in the pool and listened to their filthy mouths, he gave a silent thank you to David.

The house had settled down into sleep, but the pool house heard whispered words of love. The snow still fell, and the silence was only interrupted by the soft moans from Sarah, and raspy groans and whispers from Sam. It was as if they were the only two people left on earth, and in that moment, they were.

Chapter 54:

Sam and Sarah woke to a blanket of snow. The roads were still clear, so travel wouldn't be a problem. When they walked in the house they were greeted by the smell of fresh coffee, bacon and French toast. Gemma had Christmas carols playing as she danced her way across the kitchen. There was no sign of Harper. "I think she's in the shower, but don't hold me to it." Gemma hugged them both. "Merry Christmas Eve, you two lovebirds! Grab some French toast and bacon and a cup of coffee. I just cooked the last batch."

"I love you, Gemma." Sam immediately grabbed two plates for him and Sarah. "I'm famished."

The three of them had eaten and drunk another cup of coffee before Harper made her way down the stairs. Before anyone could say anything, she glared at them and held up her hand as she made her way to the coffee pot.

"I swear she does this on purpose to get out of cooking breakfast or making the coffee." Gemma groused.

Sarah shook her head. "No, she's always been this way. You lived with her, so you know it's true."

Harper sat down with her hands clasped around her cup, and took a cautious sip while closing her eyes. "Merry Christmas Eve, now shut up until I get this first cup in me. What the hell time is it, anyway?"

~~~

Trace had texted Sam to let him know that everyone's flight had landed without incident. They had just left St. Louis and would be there in a couple of hours. As he closed his phone he heard Sarah chattering away on hers. He knew his sister had counted down the hours until she could call Sarah. Those two were trouble.

They had chopped veggies and sliced pepperoni, salami and sausages. Sarah had made a couple of different kinds of dip and had made fruit kabobs for the kids. Harper had made hummus and toasted some pita chips. Sam made some sort of chicken rollup with Sarah's help. They could knosh all day. Gemma had defrosted the lasagna that Sam had made earlier in the week. It would go in the oven for dinner. Tonight was about family, friendship, food and drink.

The tree was surrounded by packages dressed in big bows and bags that spilled red and green tissue paper. The house smelled of cinnamon and coffee, and a fire blazed in both fireplaces. Christmas music played softly in the background, and the suns reflection off the snow outside sent beautiful prisms of light through the stained-glass windows. Sam held Sarah tightly in his arms as he danced slowly in the kitchen. "Merry Christmas Eve, Sarah Reid."

"Merry Christmas, Eve Sam Ramsay. This is the best one ever."

~~~

The van had arrived. Sarah, Gemma and Harper waited on the front porch, as Sam went to help his mom. "Aunt Sarah! Aunt Sarah!" Violet's little head bounced up and down as Danni tried to get her seatbelt unbuckled. She jumped out as soon as she was free, to run as fast as her little legs would carry her straight to Sarah. Sarah twirled her around as she rained kisses on her cheeks.

Thomas walked slowly up the front walk trying to be more grown up than he was, but Sarah could tell that he was excited to be there. She bent down with Violet still clinging to her. "Merry Christmas, Thomas! I am so happy you're here. Could I hug you?"

"Yes, please." Thomas whispered before he threw his arms around her neck.

Soon everyone was surrounded by laughter and hugs. Alex picked up a shrieking Sarah and carried her into the house. He spun her around and squeezed her tight. "Merry Christmas, Sarah! I want you for my gift this year."

~~~

Sarah gave everyone a tour of her home and showed everyone their rooms before they settled in the kitchen. Danni asked about all of Sarah's treasures placed throughout her home. Danni noticed everything. Sam knew that Danni would fall in love with Sarah's style. Gemma discussed recipes with his mum; Trace and his dad talked about cradles versus cribs; and Alex, Charlie, and Harper tried to top each other with dirty jokes. Thomas tried to fill his entire mouth with pepperoni. Sam stood with Violet on his hip and observed the most important people in his life. No more empty house. No more months in hotel rooms. No more loneliness.

Sarah watched him as he scanned the room before his eyes landed on hers. He patted his heart and spread his hand across the room before he mouthed, "Thank you." Sarah made her way to him. She rubbed the stubble on his cheek. "I love you, Sam Ramsay. Look what you have given me."

Sam's voice was raspy as he kissed her. "You have given me so much more."

~~~

Gemma and Harper took everyone who wanted to swim to the pool house. Danni and Sarah agreed that it would help wear out the kids. Hopefully between the jet lag and swimming the kids would sack out for the night.

The house was quiet; Sam and Sarah sat with Beth and Ollie drinking a cup of coffee in front of the fireplace. Both men had their legs stretched out, and Sarah snuggled next to Sam. He smelled like wood smoke. Sarah took a deep breath of one of her favorite aromas before she sipped her coffee.

"I love your home, Sarah." Beth smiled as she looked around. "It's full of you, and it makes my heart smile to see that it's full of Sam, too."

Beth's eyes shot up as Sam gazed at Sarah and quietly said, " Ubi amo, ibi patria."

Beth clutched Ollie's arm. "Where I love, there is my home."

Sam and Sarah stared at her, before Sam asked his mum, "How do you know that?"

His mom actually blushed. "My guilty pleasure is adult romance. I've read it a time or two. I always thought that quote would make a beautiful tattoo."

"Son, don't ever discount the results of reading romance. It can lead to some friskiness." Ollie patted Beth on her thigh.

Sarah snorted as Sam covered his ears and yelled, "Bloody hell! That's too much information!"

Sarah just looked at his mom and chuckled. "Romance and tattoos, huh? We'll talk. Later."

After dinner, everyone boarded the van to go look at the small town that Sarah called home and to see the Christmas lights. Thomas and Violet lasted all of thirty minutes. Danni grinned at Sarah. "Great idea."

Sam and Alex carried the sleeping children downstairs to their beds. Sarah made another pot of coffee and loaded the counter with alcohol and soda. "Help yourself to whatever you want. I put my homemade apple cider on the stove. It's really good with the cinnamon liquor."

Sarah watched Ollie, Sam, Alex, and Trace play pool as her girls laughed with Beth and Danni. She was warm in heart and in spirit. Sam caught her eye and mouthed, "I love you." She mouthed it back. After the last few years of quiet Christmases, she was so content to have a house full of people. It's the reason she and David had built the house. They had built it for future son-in-laws and grandchildren. For the last five years she had felt a little melancholy c during the holidays because David wasn't there to share it with her. For some reason she had felt him today. She had felt her mom and dad, too. They embraced her and Sam and the girls, and now Sam's family. Sarah stood in her home with her family and felt completely surrounded by love. She touched her heart and closed her eyes as she looked toward the heavens. She whispered, "Merry Christmas."

Danni wrapped her arms around Sarah. "I love you, Sarah Reid. I will love you even more when you're Sarah Ramsay."

Sam and Sarah made their way to the pool house. Everyone else had turned in early. They were all tired, and everyone was sure that the kids would be up early. Sarah wanted to make sure that the breakfast casseroles were in the oven before everyone got up, so she would be an early riser.

The only light came from the pool and hot tub. They shed their clothes and sighed as they sank into the silky water of the pool. They rested against the wall and watched their legs float in front of them. They enjoyed the silence for a few minutes before Sam put his arm across Sarah's shoulder.

"This has been a great day." Sam rubbed the nape of Sarah's neck.

"Yes, it has. Tomorrow will be even better, especially with the children here." Sarah leaned back into Sam's hand.

"Do you want a whiskey before we call it a night?"

Sarah closed her eyes and floated. "Yes, please. Just one. Morning will get here quickly."

Sam lifted himself out of the water and walked to the bar. Sarah's eyes followed the rivulets of water that ran down the muscles of his back and his thighs. Sometimes she forgot how massive his back was. It tapered nicely into narrow hips and a firm ass. He was magnificent. "God, I love your back. I love your front, too."

Sam turned with the glasses in his hands. "Ditto, Sarah Reid."

They sipped their whiskey as the warmth of the pool water relaxed their bodies. Sam took her glass and sat in on the edge of the pool before he reached for Sarah, and easily lifted her to straddle him in the water. "You do realize that tomorrow is Christmas, don't you, Ms. Reid?"

"Yes I do, Mr. Ramsay. A special day surrounded by everyone we love. That makes it monumental."

He kissed her gently before he pulled back and cupped her cheeks. "The two of us together is monumental. Together we are epic." His gentle kiss turned hotter and harder. He picked her up and carried her to the bedroom.

Chapter 55:

The house was still quiet when Sam and Sarah put the casseroles in the oven. Sam made coffee and Sarah cut fruit. Gemma rubbed a hand through her hair as she walked in. "Merry Christmas, you two. I was going to put the casseroles in, but you already beat me to the punch."

Sarah hugged her daughter. "Merry Christmas."

Sam walked to Gemma with a cup of coffee. He hugged her as she took the cup with a grateful sigh. "Merry Christmas, Gemma."

The three were drinking their coffee when Danni walked in. "Good morning, you guys. Merry Christmas." She poured a cup for herself and sat down beside Sarah.

"The kids are still asleep?" Sarah questioned Danni.

"The little shits never sleep this late at home. Maybe I need to get a pool."

"Ask your brother. He's good at pools." Sarah grinned at Sam.

One by one the sleepy inhabitants of the house arose on Christmas morning to the smell of breakfast casseroles and the sound of laughter. Thomas was on Ollie's lap, and Violet was on Sarah's hip as she and Sam sat the food on the table.

Violet had a mouthful of strawberries when she asked Sarah, "Are we gonna open presents soon?"

Sarah smiled as she kissed her forehead. "As soon as we eat we'll open presents."

"Promise?" Violet reached for a piece of melon.

"I promise. And when I make a promise, I keep it."

The children were patient as the adults leisurely finished their breakfast and drank their coffee. But the children only lasted so long before they kept asking their mom and Sarah about presents. Danni started to clean up the breakfast dishes before Sarah grabbed her wrist. "It will wait. I want to open presents, too. Thomas and Violet, and me, have waited long enough."

The trash cans overflowed with tissue paper, ribbons, and bows. The children sat in front of the fireplace with Sam playing a board game. Ollie was stretched out in the chair with his eyes closed. Beth and Gemma went to find some of Sarah's old cookbooks. Trace and Charlie took Alex to the pool house. Danni and Sarah loaded the dishwasher then sat and discussed the coming new year.

"Sam and I have already discussed spending Christmas in London next year. This trip has to be tiring for your parents." Sarah got up for another cup of coffee.

"Pour me a cup, too, please. Don't start thinking mum and dad are old and can't take the trip. They are loving this! Plus, your house is the biggest. Look around, there's more than enough room for everyone. And, you're going to have a new grandbaby this time next year. Can we make this a tradition forever? Please? I'll let you know if it gets too much for mum and dad." Danni looked at Sarah with puppy dog eyes.

Sarah laughed and shook her head. "Okay! Okay! I'll tell you the same thing Sam told me last night. Let's get this Christmas over with before we start worrying about next year."

"So what time do the shenanigans start tonight? Do we need to start prepping? I can't wait to see your friends again. That Julie's my kind of weird." Danni wiggled her eyebrows.

Sarah guffawed. "Sam said the same thing. She scares him a little. Let's just say that Julie has no filter. That sounds a little nicer. Luca, Mark and Marta should be here by four. They got into St. Louis last night, and the service will deliver them straight to the door. It's just so wonderful that everyone was able to be here on Christmas."

"Yeah, it is. How did you manage that?" Danni got up to pour them both another cup of coffee and grab a cookie.

Sarah thought for a minute. "Yeah, it's funny how that turned out, isn't it? It's kind of like the Gods smiled on us. Liz and Bev's kids are with the in-laws this year, so they celebrated Christmas a few nights ago. Ashley and Julie weren't able to go to their families because of work schedules and Karen and Jacks parents went on a cruise. Luca was on a shoot with Marta in Chicago, so they were already in the states. Mark just met up with them in St. Louis."

"Wow. That sounds like it was pre-destined or some shit like that."

Sarah smiled distractedly. "All of our favorite people are able to gather together on Christmas. It has to be destiny. You are so right. Anyway, the doors open at four and I plan on eating around six."

"Well then, I think we better get this show on the road." Danni got up just as Gemma and Beth walked into the kitchen. The group from the pool house arrived shortly thereafter. The men had been instructed to keep the children entertained while the women started on the evening's dinner.

~~~

Sarah stood in the kitchen going over the checklist in her head when she felt thick arms encircle her waist. She closed her eyes with a smile and leaned back into the broad chest behind her. She grasped the arms and sighed. "Luca."

"Ah, sweet girl. You are my heart." He kissed her head as she turned around to hug him properly.

"I didn't even hear you guys come in!" She heard a squeal and looked over Luca's shoulder to see Marta running toward her with Mark close behind.

Sarah kissed Luca's cheek quickly and ran toward Marta. Everyone watched the two women hug as they jumped up and down like children.

"Merry Christmas Marta! You have no idea how excited Sam and I are that you guys could make it! Come here you hunk of a husband and give me a hug. Not a little pat on the back, but a real big, tight, sexy hug." She reached toward Mark and got exactly what she had asked for. "Merry Christmas Mark!"

Everyone had met at Sarah's gallery opening, but Sarah reintroduced each other and with Gemma's help made sure that everyone had snacks and drinks. Ashley, Julie, Liz and Bev showed up shortly thereafter, followed by Jack and Karen. Sam stood with his arm around Sarah's waist as they watched the people they loved.

Sarah looked up into his eyes. "This day could not be any more perfect."

"Yes, it could." Sam grabbed her tight and kissed her with heat. He didn't care that everyone watched them.

Sarah tried to catch her breath. "How could this day possibly be better than it is right now?"

Sam growled as he kissed her again. "It could be later tonight."

She beamed her smile as she grabbed his ass. Catcalls and whistles from their friends and family came loudly as they continued to kiss each other. Somewhere in the background they heard Thomas shout "Yuck!" They both laughed against each other's mouths.

Sarah whispered in Gemma's ear. "The buffet line was a great idea. Thank you."

Gemma smiled as she hugged her mother. "That's why I'm here. To give you all my great ideas."

They both looked at all their friends and family as they ate and conversed. Laughter was the background music to the evening. "I love you Gemma."

"I love you more mom."

Sarah mingled and collected empty plates. Sam got beverages for empty glasses. Bellies were full and hearts were even more so. Sam watched as Sarah sat down next to his mother. They hugged each other as they conversed quietly. Beth never stopped touching Sarah's hand or her cheek. Everyone was engaged with someone else. He caught Liz's eye as he went into the master suite and shut the door quietly.

Sarah bent over Danni's shoulder. "I have to run upstairs and get some last-minute surprises. Could you keep an eye on everyone's plates and drinks? "

Danni nodded yes as she watched Sarah quietly go up the stairs.

Liz had asked Luca to get his camera for some pictures of the festivities. He grinned at her as he found his camera case on the back of the kitchen counter. "Of course, my sexy vixen. Anything you ask of me." Liz giggled as he smiled devilishly and took his place at the side of the room and started to snap pictures.

Liz took a deep breath as she took her place in front of the fireplace. She cleared her throat and began. "Excuse me, everyone! Could I say a few words?" Everyone quieted as they all looked at her expectantly.

Liz swallowed and said a quiet prayer to herself. "Merry Christmas! It is absolutely wonderful that we are all spending this special night together. Christmas is the season of giving. The giving of gifts, and love, and hope. Tonight, Sam and Sarah would like to share with you their biggest gift. Their gift of love and hope."

Sam walked out of the bedroom in his blue velvet tuxedo. As he took his place at Liz's side, he hoped that Sarah would approve. He knew that she liked simple, but every time he saw the blue velvet in his closet, he thought of the stairs at the gala in London. That night would forever be etched into his memory. It's the night that he became addicted to the drug named Sarah.

Everyone got quiet as they wondered what was going on. Sam caught his mum's eye. She had tears in her eyes and a big smile on her face. Sam knew that she got it. He watched her grip his father's arm and it made him swallow. He knew that he wanted what they had. He knew that he and Sarah had that. She had been worth the wait.

They all heard Sarah start to sing softly from the top of the stairs. The first few verses of "Fly Me to the Moon" made Sam look up quickly. The song continued to play over the speakers as she appeared from the landing. An audible gasp was heard in the air. Sam heard Danni gasp "Fuck!" Or, it might have been him. He didn't know what he was doing, or where he was, or who was around him. All he saw was Sarah in the red dress. As she slowly made her way down the stairs it was everything he could do to stop himself from grabbing her and running to the pool house. Her eyes were bright with tears, her golden skin was luminescent. She literally shone like a star. He swallowed and devoured her with his eyes. He took her hand with his trembling one when she took her place beside him.

Sarah's pulse raced as she looked at her man in his blue tuxedo. It made his eyes look indigo. This beautiful man with his kind heart, quiet manner, and beautiful body was hers. This man loved her. She adored him. She gripped his hand and whispered. "We did it again." She looked at his tux and then at her dress, as Sam leaned his head back and laughed out loud.

Liz looked at the people in front of her. "I have always heard about love at first sight. I have always heard about soul mates. I have always heard about destiny. I never really believed it until I watched Sarah look at her first naked picture of Sam." The laughter was loud. "Well, to tell you the truth, we *all* looked at naked Sam. Hasn't everyone?" Beth bowed her head and shook her head. Sam grinned at Liz and shrugged his shoulders.

"Seriously, from the first moment she saw his picture, she was drawn to him. She saw something in him that only she understood. She saw beyond his beauty. She saw his pain and felt his loneliness. Only someone who has experienced it themselves would have seen it. Sarah has experienced that." Liz stopped for a moment as she cleared her throat. "That they actually met is destiny in itself. That Sam fell in love with Sarah is not a surprise. We all love her. But... Sarah in a T-shirt and panties would make anyone fall in love with her. But, that's her story to tell." They all heard Alex groan. Sam whirled around and glared at him. Again, there was laughter.

Liz continued. "When Sarah came home from London it was pretty bleak in this house. The pain was palpable. But for some reason I knew it would be good. You can't have that kind of pain and heartbreak without love." Sam clenched Sarah's hand tighter.

Liz chuckled. "As usual, I was right. Actually, I was right about that, and I was right about the panties. You can thank me later Sam. But that is *their* story to tell. I am honored to have witnessed Sam and Sarah's relationship develop from the beginning. From the first glimpse of a black and white photo, to the heartbreak of London, to the multitude of texts. I have loved Sarah from the moment I met her in photography class many years ago. I have loved Sam since our first meeting via Skype. That's when he saw Sarah's pictures for the first time, and I knew immediately that he loved her. These two people have earned each other. They deserve every happiness that comes their way. It gives me hope and fills my heart." Liz stopped to wipe a tear. Sarah smiled softly at her as she patted her heart.

"We are gathered here tonight, on this special Christmas, to witness and celebrate the marriage of Sam Aaron Ramsay and Sarah Anne Reid. Love knows no age, as love is ageless. Love knows no boundaries, as an ocean couldn't keep them apart. Love knows no doubt, as they both have proved the doubters wrong. Love knows no confined spaces, as their love for each other is limitless."

Sarah cried quiet tears as Liz looked at them both. She felt Sam's hand tremble again as he gripped hers harder. He looked at Liz with that weapon of a smile. Liz hissed. "Sam Ramsay, I don't care if this is your wedding. You *cannot* do that!" Sam chuckled and Sarah grinned.

"Sam and Sarah have a few words they would like to share. Or maybe it's a lot of words. I have no idea as they haven't shared them with me, but it's their night. They can say whatever they want. Sam, would like to begin?" Liz nodded at him.

Sam turned to Sarah and took her other hand. He smiled so sweetly, and with so much vulnerability in his eyes that Sarah immediately started to weep.

"I haven't even said anything yet, Amazing Sarah." Sarah gazed into his eyes with so much love that Sam couldn't help it. He bent down and kissed her softly.

He heard someone start crying before Liz said, "Hey! It's not time for that yet, Sam!"

Sam cleared his throat and turned to all of their friends and family. He saw tears in the eyes of all three of Sarah's daughters. Trace held Charlie close with a big grin on his face. He was shocked to see and hear Danni sobbing loudly. "This woman loves me. Can you believe it? Oh, and if any of you are wondering, I already have a green card."

He turned back to the woman who stood quietly crying and softly brushed a tear with the pad of his thumb. "Grace. The definition of grace is elegance or beauty of form, manner, motion or action. You, sweet Sarah are the epitome of all of those. You are my saving grace. I will never stop falling in love with you. You make me better. You make me whole. Life is not a certainty, but I am certain of my love for you."

He stopped and held her face. "When I look at you, I see the rest of my life right there in your eyes. You make me drunk and you make my knees shake. I am raw with the wild need I have for you. You are my lust, my hunger and my sustenance. You are my home. Semper tua. I am forever yours. Tesoro mio. You are my treasure. Vita mia. You are my life. Ti amo. I love you. Ubi amo, ibi patria. Where I love, there is my home." He slipped the plain plantinum band on her ring finger.

"You told me almost a year ago that you could almost see my face completed, and that you could almost cry with the anticipation. Sarah, look at me." Sarah looked up at him with a small smile. "My face is completed. My only regret in my life is that we didn't find each other sooner so that I could love you longer."

 Sarah wept so hard that her shoulders shook, but she never took her eyes off Sam. He continued to hold her wet face. "I don't want pages in the scrapbook of our lives anymore, Sarah. I want volumes."

Sarah laid her head against the steady beat of Sam's heart. It beat for her as hers beat for him.

Liz sniffed and wiped her eyes with a Kleenex. "Sarah? Your words?"

Sarah closed her eyes and took a deep breath. She could do this. She wanted her daughters to know what could be possible, and she wanted Sam to feel her words as strongly as she had felt his.

Sarah reached for Sam's beautiful hands. She looked down at the long graceful fingers that played her body like an instrument. The hands that painted her like a canvas and the hands that held her heart in them.

"I believe in love at first sight. I believe in destiny. I believe in epic loves and first and second chances. I believe in painless happily ever afters. I believe in these, because we are experiencing it right at this very moment. I believe that our souls connected in some other lifetime. It has taken a long time for our bodies to find their way to each other, but it's why we knew each other immediately."

Sam openly wept. He could never be embarrassed about his love for the woman who held his life in her hands.

Sarah raised his hand and kissed his pulse point. "I am the lucky one who has gotten a second chance. David loved me as a child, and he loved me as a woman." Sarah heard Charlie cry loudly and she had to swallow to collect her thoughts.

"I loved him. I have grown into the woman I am because of that love. I have three amazing daughters from that love. But I feel as if I've spent my life waiting for you. I think that if two souls are meant to be together, no matter how long it takes, or how far they have to go, destiny will bring them together. You are my destiny Sam." Sarah slipped the plain platinum band on his ring finger. Sarah beamed and Sam sniffed loudly as he looked at the ring on his finger.

"We will be naughty with each other. We will have adventures.

We will drink our whiskey, and we will love our family and friends hard. We will show our daughters that epic loves are possible, and to never settle. You take my breath away. You make me laugh. You make me moan. You make me feel loved. You steal my heartbeats. I watched you sleep last night and I knew that I needed nothing else. You are my everything." Sarah smiled through her tears. "Together, we are epic."

The quiet in the room was thick with tears and an overwhelming sense of love and hope. Sam and Sarah turned to their friends. Sam smiled at his mom and dad. "Sarah and I want to add a few more thoughts. I want to thank David Reid first. I feel as if he is here with us tonight. I want to thank him for helping Sarah become such a loving person. Her heart has the capacity for more love than anyone I know. I especially want to thank Charlie, Gemma and Harper for wanting nothing but happiness for their mother. Their hearts are as big as hers, and they have wrapped me in their love. I have fallen in love with them. Trace, thank God for you. I need all the testosterone I can get. The Reid women are forces of nature." The room erupted in laughter.

"My final thanks go to my mum and dad and my sister. My parents instilled my work ethic and my manners. It has served me well in my life. They also set the example that I've been searching for. That there is such a thing as a deep, soul crushing love. A love with lust, laughter and a deep abiding respect for each other. Danni, you are the bane of my existence, but I love you. I love Alex and I adore your children. You have always been there for me. Without fail. You have always been brutally honest with me, and as much as you drive me crazy, I respect your wit and your intelligence and your great love for Sarah."

Sarah held Sam's hand. "I have felt my mother and father around me this week. And David has been driving me crazy. Their love has surrounded this entire house. Thank you, David Reid. Thank you, mom and dad."

Sarah visibly swallowed as she looked at her daughters. "I don't know what I have done to deserve the three women that sit in front of me. They were all wonderful children who have grown into strong, independent, intelligent women who are my best friends. I have only ever wanted them to be happy and fulfilled. I believe that Trace and Charlie are experiencing that once in a lifetime love that almost makes me burst with happiness."

As she looked at her crying daughters, she continued. "It is humbling to know that all they want is my happiness. They have had no doubts about Sam. I think they love him almost as much as me. I love all four of you so much. And to Danni..."

Sarah looked at Danni who still wept. "Our souls are connected from another lifetime, too. I could not have found a better sister. I love you. Beth and Ollie you have taken me into your family with nothing but open arms and open hearts. You have filled a hole that was in my heart. There aren't a lot of people here tonight. Look around at our little group and know that you all are the most precious people in our lives. Sam and I would post bail for any of you." Everyone grinned and chuckled.

Sam turned to Luca. "You all know about the love that Luca and Sarah have for each other. I really am worried about them running off to South America with each other."

Luca shouted, "You should worry!"

Liz smiled as she looked at Sam. He stepped to her and hugged her hard. "You are my Luca, Liz. I don't know what I would have done without you. Sarah is lucky to have a friend like you and the rest of the girls. I hope I'm now in that circle."

Liz laughed as she clapped her hands. "Hey everybody! I now pronounce Sam and Sarah man and wife. Kiss that bride, you big handsome hunk of a man!"

The room erupted in whistles and applause as everyone rushed the couple for hugs, kisses and proclamations of lust and love.

Sam and Sarah were surrounded by her daughters and Trace. They all shared a moment and spoke quiet words.

Sam gave a loud wolf whistle as Sarah shouted, "As the Queen of France said so many years ago! Let them eat cake!"

Ashley loudly asked, "Is Santa gonna leave another present on my tongue?"

Sarah laughed as she brought the Red Velvet cake to the table.

Julie pushed Ashley with her shoulder. "Stop! That's just gross!"

Luca found Sam in the kitchen. He hugged the boy that had virtually made his career, as he had made Sam's. "I know I tease you about Sarah, and I really would run away with her, but my face hurts from smiling so hard. My heart hurts because it is so full of happiness for you both. You are a good man, Sam. You think you don't deserve her, but I want you to know, that you do. You both deserve each other. I love the talent that you both have, but I love the two people with that talent more." Luca again hugged Sam tightly and kissed his cheek. "Ti amo caro ragazzo."

The house was quiet as friends had left and the house guests had finally gone to bed. Sam, Sarah, Ollie and Beth were the last men standing. Beth had taken Sarah's arm before she went to bed. "Sweet Sarah, our hearts are so full. I look at my son and don't see the loneliness anymore. You have done that for him, and we love you for giving us that gift."

Sarah's eyes filled with unshed tears. "Oh, Beth, I think we both gave each other the things that we didn't even know we needed. We're now a completed puzzle."

Sam carried Sarah through the doors of the pool house and continued into the bedroom. He slowly stripped the crush of red velvet off her body before he placed it on the chair. He knelt to remove her shoes and kissed each foot softly. He stepped back to remove his shirt and pants before he took her hand and moved her to the bed. He kissed her softly. He kissed her reverently. He inhaled the scent of sandalwood.

Sam ran his hands down Sarah's rib cage and watched the goose bumps appear. "Elysian. It means heaven, paradise, celestial and divine. My life with you is a paradise. Your love for me is heaven. Your heart is celestial and your body as it merges with mine is divine. Let me show you that divinity, Ms. Sarah Reid Ramsay."

~~~

The house was empty, and the silence felt strange after being so noisy for the last few days. Trace had driven the van full of Sam's family back to the airport that morning. The sky was gray and felt heavy. Snow had started again, and it looked as if it wouldn't stop anytime soon. You could smell the moisture in the cold air. Sam and Sarah had been lazy. They had soaked in the hot tub and had napped. They sat in front of the fireplace with their whiskey as they watched the golden flames flicker. The crackle and pop of tree sap was the only noise.

Their legs entwined as they stretched them out to rest on the trunk in front of the sofa. Sam pulled Sarah tight into his side and kissed her temple. "Life is full of beginnings and ends. It's the close of some chapters but sometimes the first page of a new book."

Sarah grasped his hand and kissed his knuckles. She sighed as she laid her head against the back of the sofa. "You are my most beautiful chapter, Sam. At the end of my life, I know that the chapters we will write will be my favorite chapters of my favorite book."

"I love you more than lightning bugs."

The End

ABOUT THE AUTHOR

G.M. McGeorge lives in the middle of America with her husband and two Australian Shepherds. She draws, paints and pretends to be a dancer. She loves all kinds of music, but especially the Blues, and thinks that Stevie Ray Vaughan wasn't really human. She loves Irish Whiskey. 2 fingers. Neat. She loves tattoos, and at her advanced age has started on a full sleeve. She enjoys going barefoot, and loves a pair of well-worn jeans, but is addicted to wearing sexy lingerie under them.

With encouragement from her daughters, she finally bit the bullet and put pen to paper. Or more accurately, fingers to the keyboard. VOLUMES is her debut novel, but is definitely not her last. She has a million stories to share, and if people enjoy reading them, she might have two million. She feels that there is a strong need for steamy, sexy stories about older women.

Her great loves, besides the Blues and her whiskey, is her husband and her children. She believes in Happily Ever After. She believes in soul mates. She believes that women after the age of thirty-five are more sexy, more fierce, more knowledgeable and more confident. She strongly believes that life begins at fifty.

For more information, or to contact her, please visit Mac's Meanderings on Facebook, or visit her author page on Amazon and Goodreads.

And, PLEASE, leave a review.

Made in the USA
Monee, IL
02 November 2020

46578025R00411